DEAD OFFERINGS

THE COLLECTED WORK OF
ANTHONY GIANGREGORIO

NOW AVAILABLE AND COMING SOON FROM OPEN CASKET PRESS

RATS
HORROR CARNIVAL
ZOMBIE BUFFET
BIGFOOT TALES
DECAY: A ZOMBIE STORY
CREATURE FEATURE
DEAD CHRISTMAS
HORROR TALES AND TERRIFYING STORIES
2012 ZOMBIE WALL CALENDAR
HOLLOW POINT: A ZOMBIE NOVEL
WARRIORS OF THE APOCALYPSE: BOOK 1

DEAD OFFERINGS

ISBN Softcover ISBN 13: 978-1-61199-039-3
ISBN 10: 1-611990-39-4

Open Casket Press is an imprint of Living Dead Press.
ww.livingdeadpress.com

For more info on obtaining additional copies of this book, contact:
www.opencasketpress.com
Cover art by Jason Bailey

Table of Contents

A BOY AND HIS FATHER 1
A DAY AT THE MORGUE 12
A HARD LESSON 23
ALONE 30
ANGELS OF DEATH 35
BEST MEAT EVER 46
BITTER FRUIT 59
CANNIBAL CAMPING TRIP 73
CHRISTMAS POEMS 93
CLOSE CALL 96
DARK NIGHT 104
DELUGE 110
EMAIL OFFERINGS 122
EVEN ZOMBIES LOVE CHRISTMAS 140
FISH FUCKER 152
FISHECSTASY 158
GOING UP? 164
HEROES OF THE DEAD 170
HIGHWAY OF THE DEAD 184
HOPELESS LOVE 203
HUMP OF THE DEAD 215
IT WAS JUST A DREAM 228
IT'LL ONLY HURT A LITTLE 234
JURY DUTY 250
JUST BECAUSE 258
KRAMER'S FOLLY 268
LAND OF ZOMBIES 282
LOST IN THE WOODS 292
MAN'S BEST FRIEND 311
MISTAKES 320
MOMMA'S BOY 326
MONSTER DETECTIVES 338
MORGUE OF THE DEAD 353
NO MORE CHRISTMAS 367
NURSING HOME OF THE DEAD 382
ONE LAST CHANCE 394

PARADE OF THE DEAD 431
POST OFFICE OF THE DEAD 439
REBIRTH 453
REVENGE 462
SURVIVAL OF THE FITTEST 468
THE AIR ITSELF 479
THE BITCH GETS IT IN THE END 491
THE DAY'S END 499
THE END OF CHRISTMAS 523
THE HOLE 538
THE ILLUSION OF BIGFOOT 545
THE LAST CHRISTMAS 557
THE LAST ONE 567
THE LAST SUPERHERO 573
THE LAST WAR 591
THE LIGHT OF THE FULL MOON 605
THE OTHER FOOT 611
THE SANCTUARY 618
TIME TO MOVE ON 640
UNCLE JOE 650
UNDEAD DELIVERY 654
VALENTINE'S DAY CANDY 662
WHAT COMES AROUND. 673
WHAT DWELLS BENEATH 698
YES, VIRGINIA, THERE REALLY IS A ZOMBIE SANTA CLAUS 710
YOU ARE WHAT YOU EAT 716
YOU ALWAYS EAT THE ONES YOU LOVE 729
WAKE THE DEAD 735

A BOY AND HIS FATHER

Little Timmy Miller was almost six and a half, and though death wasn't something he really understood, he knew enough to know he might not ever see his seventh birthday.

The reason for this was simple.

Sooner or later, the zombies were going to get into the house and kill and eat him and his entire family.

His dad told him not to worry, that he would protect them, and Timmy idolized his father like no other person on Earth. Timmy's dad was tall, strong and courageous, and so far he'd managed to keep the walking dead from getting him and his mom. But though young, even Timmy knew it was a bad time for him and his parents.

Timmy was playing in his bedroom, the matchbox cars spread out before him. He was pretending he was the mayor of a city and the cars were lined up for a parade. It was a parade for his dad, because he was a hero. Because he was a great man who protected his wife and son from the monsters that wanted to eat them.

While Timmy played, he ignored the sounds of hammering coming from the first floor as his dad reinforced the house's windows and doors. He barely heard the sounds of the dead as they moaned and banged on the outside of the house. To Timmy, the zombies were just another part of life. He was a child, he adapted. And if his dad said it would be all right, that they were safe from the monsters, then that was good enough for him.

"Timmy, can you come here, son!" his father called up to his bedroom.

Timmy didn't hesitate, he knew not to. He dropped the toy police car in his hand and dashed out of his room. He took the stairs two at a time, and seconds later, was in the living room with his mom and dad.

His parents were by the far window that faced the street. His mom was holding a large piece of plywood in place with his father. Timmy saw the arm flailing around the plywood, then his dad used his shoulder and pushed in the wood and the arm retreated. Glass littered the floor near his feet where the zombies had broken it.

When Timmy entered the room, his dad pointed to a can of nails and a hammer on the small coffee table a few feet from him.

"Ah, Timmy, thanks for coming so fast. Can you hand me that can of nails and the hammer, please? We put this up and then I realized I didn't have them near me."

"Sure, Daddy," Timmy said and ran to the table. He scooped them up into his arms and then rushed across the room. When he was halfway there, he tripped on his own feet and began to fall, the nails and hammer going flying. The nails landed and the can tipped over, different sizes of nails spreading across the hardwood floor. The hammer fell heavily, left a dent in the floor, and fell over.

"Oh no, are you okay, honey?" his mom asked. Her face was filled with worry at seeing her son fall.

"I'm fine, Mom, sorry, Daddy, I tripped."

"It's fine, son. As long as you're not hurt. Here, give me the hammer and a handful of nails."

Timmy nodded, surprised he wasn't getting yelled at. Normally, his father would have been at least a little mad at his clumsiness, but now, his dad didn't seem to care.

And then something banged on the plywood his mom and dad were holding against the window and his mom let out a small squeak of fear.

"Hurry up, son, I need that stuff now, please," his dad said, his voice seeming to be forcing calm. Timmy looked up at his dad and saw beads of sweat on his forehead. His dad was scared about something, Timmy just didn't know what.

His father began hammering more nails into the plywood, his banging overriding the noise of the monsters outside that were also pounding on the wood.

When his dad finished hammering on his mom's side, Timmy saw his father sigh with relief. "Okay, Helen, you can let go now," he told her.

She nodded and did as he said, then turned and went to Timmy, hugging him tightly.

"Are you okay, Mom?" Timmy asked. She squeezed him tightly. He could smell her hair, the shampoo she used. It smelled like apricots. He loved that smell, to him it meant 'safe' and 'love.'

"Yes, dear, I'm fine, you were very brave just now," she said.

His dad was breathing hard from the exertion of pounding in the nails. "There, that should hold those bastards...for a while anyway."

"Are you sure, John?" his mom asked. "But if they got in once, they'll get in again, won't they?"

"No they won't, not this time. I sank enough nails into the window frame to stop anything," his dad said.

"But they just…" his mom began.

She was cut off when his dad said, "I said it's fine, Helen. Now stop it before you scare the boy." He glared at her and she lowered her gaze, still hugging Timmy.

"Good, now that that's settled, come and help me with the kitchen door, I want to add some more wood to it." Without waiting for her to answer, he grabbed a handful of nails scattered on the floor and headed off.

Timmy's mom hugged him for another few seconds and then let go. "Okay, dear, now you pick up the nails for Daddy and then go back to your room and play. We're fine now, we're safe. You're father will protect us from those nasty monsters."

If Timmy was older, he might have seen through his mother's lies, he might have seen the way her eyes looked away from him, as if she knew the lies she spun were doing more harm than good; but he didn't. He was only six and he trusted his mom implicitly. After all, she was his mother, she was there to protect him, to keep him from harm and make sure nothing bad ever happened to him.

So like any boy who loves his mother would do, he simply nodded and gave her a kiss on the cheek. "Okay, Mommy, I'll do that for Daddy."

"Helen, let's go, I need your help in here!" his dad called from the kitchen.

"I'm coming, John." She stood up, patted and brushed Timmy's hair so it wasn't in his eyes, then walked off, her head low, as if she were crying.

Timmy didn't see this as he had already turned around and was picking up the nails. He hummed a song as he worked, his world really not that different from before the dead began to walk. All Timmy knew that was different in his world was that he couldn't go to kindergarten for some reason or the park. He knew about the monsters but it didn't really sink in to his young mind. And why should it? His dad had said they would all be fine and that was good enough for Timmy.

He finished picking up the nails and placed the can on an end table. He was about to leave and go back to his bedroom when the plywood began to shake, something pounding on it from the other side.

Timmy knew it was the monsters.

Though he was scared, he wanted to see what was going on outside, so he walked carefully over to the boarded-up window and bent over where there was a knot hole at the bottom of the plywood. He looked through the small, dime-sized hole and when he did, he gasped in fear and amazement.

The entire street and front yard was filled with zombies. There had to be two hundred of them easy. Timmy tried to count them, but the shifting heads made it all but impossible. He liked to count and had learned his multiplication tables fast but this was something he never thought he would use them for.

A dark cloud of flies hovered over the heads of the crowd, bobbing and weaving as they fed on the spilled blood covering the animated corpses. Huge horseflies, bloated to the point of bursting, jumped from matted head to matted head as they struggled to stay in flight.

Timmy gasped again when he saw how many were missing eyes, limbs or other body parts. He saw a zombie with a gaping chest cavity, every single organ torn out. The monster looked like a fish that his dad gutted one time when they went camping together. As he looked to the far left and right, he saw that the six foot picket fence surrounding his backyard on both sides of the house was stopping the monsters from getting into it.

Others were eating something Timmy couldn't describe. He saw it was red and runny and glistened in the sun, but other than that he didn't know. He guessed it was meat, but *what kind* of meat wasn't much of an issue to his six-year-old brain.

It should have been.

Large rats ran between the feet of the undead crowd, taking bits and pieces of exposed flesh, and a few dogs darted between the legs, barking and growling. Timmy saw that the zombies didn't seem to care about the dogs, and if he was older he would have understood that the monsters only wanted *human* meat.

"Timmy, get away from that window!" his mom yelled as she ran into the living room and pulled him away from the plywood.

"Mommy, why are there so many monsters out there?" he asked.

She scooped him into her arms, grunting slightly; he was heavier now than when he was younger. "Don't worry about it, honey. Just keep away from the windows, please." She set him down and patted his head, then rubbed his cheek with her hand, caressing his face. "Why don't you go to your room like I asked, dear?"

She reached over and picked up the can of nails—the reason she came back into the room—and cradled it in her arms as if it was a newborn baby.

"But what about all the monst..." he began but she cut him off.

"Timmy, please just do as I ask." She was ready to begin crying and was doing her best not to. She wanted to be strong for her son.

Timmy let out a huff and sighed. "Fine," he said and trudged away from her, dragging his feet on the carpet. Normally, she would have yelled at him for this, but this time she didn't. She was quickly learning that when death was imminent and could come in a dozen different ways, either from being torn apart or eaten, little things like her son dragging his feet on the carpet seemed absolutely trivial.

Timmy was upstairs playing in his room and had been for hours, when his mom and dad began to yell and scream and the sound of crashing wood came to his ears.

Jumping up, Timmy kicked his matchbox cars and action figures with his feet as he ran out of the room. He practically flew down the stairs, following his parents' voices, and charged into the kitchen to see his mom and dad at the back door, the monsters trying to get inside again.

The back door was open about a foot and his dad was pushing on it with his right shoulder. In the doorway was a monster and behind it were many more, all trying to force their way into the kitchen.

The boards that had been on the door were now splintered and broken, scattered by his dad's feet.

"Helen! Get me the hammer! The hammer, damn it!" his dad yelled as he struggled to keep the zombies from gaining entry. The moaning was loud and Timmy stared in shock. Flies had entered the house, too, filling the kitchen like small black storm clouds. They crawled on every surface.

His mom picked up the hammer from where it had fallen on the floor and quickly handed it to his father, who then began pounding the tip into the forehead of the monster in the doorway. Black ichor sprayed across the room, spraying his mom in the face. It went in her mouth and she gagged, spitting it out before vomiting violently.

The monster's head began to crack and cave in with each blow of the hammer, and as gray brains splattered onto the floor, the body slumped in the doorway, now blocking it from being closed. Another was right behind it and his dad did the same to this one, but each one down was one more in the doorway, making a barricade that made closing and locking the door all but impossible.

"Timmy, get your mom and get her out of here!" his dad yelled. "Get her upstairs to my bedroom."

"Are you coming, too?" he asked, feeling scared at the violence before him.

"Yes, but I need to give you two a head start. Go, son, get her out of here before they get in!"

Timmy went to his mom, his legs feeling weak from fear. His mom was finishing her bout of vomiting and Timmy wrinkled his nose, the remnants of her last meal smelly and sticky; it made him want to throw up, too.

He helped her to a kneeling position and then to her feet. With her hunched over and leaning on him, Timmy struggled to get his mom out of the kitchen.

As he left the room, he heard his dad yell out and swing the hammer again. Timmy helped his mom upstairs and into his parents' bedroom. She immediately fell on the bed, pulling him with her. She cried large tears as she hugged him for all she was worth. Timmy had tears in his eyes now, too, his mother's terror contagious.

He heard stomping coming up the stairs and moans filled the house. A second later, his father burst into the bedroom and slammed the door closed behind him. He quickly pushed the large credenza to the right of the door in front of it, blocking it.

"Timmy, how's your mom?" his dad asked as he began pushing a small end table across the room. When he was near the door, he picked it up and placed it on the credenza. Just as he finished, the door rattled in its frame as something on the other side tried to get in. The pounding was loud, and it filled the room and made it hard to hear anyone speak.

"I don't know, Daddy, she's crying," Timmy said through sniffles of his own. "But I don't think she's hurt." That was when he saw his dad's right arm and the blood dripping down it. "Daddy, you're bleeding."

His dad looked down at his arm and waved it off as unimportant. "It's nothing, a scratch. One of them bit me, but I yanked my arm away before it could get a good hold on me." He pointed to the master bathroom off the bedroom. "Could you go get me a towel, son?"

"Sure, Dad, I can do that," Timmy said, glad to have something to do. He returned a few moments later and handed it to his father. His dad patted the wound and winced in pain. "Ouch, that sucker got me better than I thought," he said as he wrapped his arm in the towel. He pointed to Timmy. "Go sit with your mother, will you, Timmy? We're safe for now." He tossed him the towel he'd used to wipe his arm. "And here, use this to wipe the blood from your mom's face."

"Are those the monsters outside in the hallway, Daddy?"

His dad nodded. "Yes, son, I'm afraid they are. Just go sit with your mom. I'll keep you both safe."

"You promise?"

"You betcha, sport. I promise."

The hours passed, and despite the pounding, exhaustion set in and all three of them became tired to the point they couldn't stay awake. Timmy's Mom and Dad were stretched out on the queen size bed and Timmy slept between them, but after a while he couldn't stand them pressing in on him and he climbed out and went to the small daybed in the corner.

The pounding had stopped sometime in the night, but the incessant moaning and groaning still continued. It was haunting and sad at the same time.

At first Timmy hid under his blanket, but slowly, as time passed, he relaxed some more. It was easy to be brave when his mom and dad were right there in the room with him, only a few feet away. Besides, his dad said he would protect them and that was good enough for Timmy, who trusted his dad whole-heartedly.

With the moans of the monsters lulling him, Timmy drifted off to sleep.

Timmy woke up to screaming.

It was dark in the room and at first he didn't know if he was awake or dreaming, but then something hit the shade on the window and pale moonlight flooded the room as the shade fell to the floor.

Timmy blinked sleep from his eyes to see his dad was on top of his mom. She was beating at his arms and chest, but he acted like he didn't feel it.

Timmy saw his dad's arm where he was bitten and saw it was now a massive, weeping wound of pus and dark ichor. Timmy had no way of understanding that the zombies were infectious and his dad had died sometime in the night to wake up hungry.

He could only watch in horror when his father sank his teeth into his mom's throat, tearing out a large chunk of meat. As he chewed merrily and his mom shrieked in agony and terror, blood shot out of her neck to bathe the closest wall red. In the gloom of the room, it resembled a Rorschach painting, only this one was done in blood.

With her last breath, his mom reached out a bloody hand to Timmy and yelled, "Run, Timmy, run! Get away!" Then she lost consciousness from blood loss. His dad continued feeding on her, tearing off her ears with his teeth, then going in for more. His teeth clacked around her upper lip and pulled at it like a feral animal feeding on its kill. His mom's lips stretched like elastics, then snapped off, hanging from his dad's teeth like Gummy worms. Then Timmy couldn't take anymore analogies and he jumped off the daybed and prepared to run.

His dad caught the movement and snapped his head to face him. Timmy was paralyzed with fear. This was his dad, but at the same time it wasn't. The man before him was more like a wild animal than a human being.

His dad growled and crawled off the bed, and Timmy wet himself in fright. He was frozen by his father's dead eyes as the man crept closer to him.

Something inside Timmy told him that if his dad caught him, the man would be doing the same thing to Timmy that he did to his mom.

At the last possible second, Timmy snapped out of it, and with a yell to rival any before, he dashed to the master bathroom, slamming the door as he entered. As he fell near the tub, his dad began pounding on the door, his fists heavy and powerful. The door wasn't made for security and was in fact quite thin and cheap. Already cracks were showing in the painted veneer and Timmy huddled in the corner, too scared to move. It had taken all his courage just to run into the bathroom.

As he huddled in the corner, his eyes were glued to the bathroom door. With each blow from his father, more wood splintered to fall to the ceramic tiles.

"Stop it, Daddy, leave me alone!" Timmy yelled, but his father ignored his pleas. Timmy could barely see, the tears running fast and thick from his eyes. He was sobbing uncontrollably and he felt like he had to go to the bathroom, but he knew he couldn't even if he tried.

The door shattered near the top and a head-sized hole appeared. His dad shoved his head into the hole and shook it back and forth. His face was slathered in blood—his mother's blood—and it fell to the floor in small red droplets, a stark contrast to the white of the tiles.

Timmy screamed again at his father to stop and go away, but his dad only renewed his machinations, his hands tearing at the wood and making the hole bigger. Soon, his father's entire chest could be seen.

Then a bloody hand reached into the hole and began to pull the door apart. Timmy whimpered, trying not to think what would happen when his dad broke down the door.

Timmy began to look around the bathroom desperately, hoping to find some form of escape, and his eyes settled on the small window over the tub. It was more than large enough for him to shimmy through.

Over his dad's growling and moaning, he heard the door collapse and fall apart, and he knew it was now or never.

Jumping up, he turned and reached up for the window. It was unlocked and he pushed it open.

The screen was down and it took precious seconds for him to open it, and by the time he did, his father was entering the bathroom.

Timmy jumped up and began to crawl through the window, and was halfway through when he felt his dad's hands on his legs. Then he was being pulled back into the bathroom.

Timmy yelled in absolute terror and reached out with his hands to the sides of the window, halting his backwards momentum, but an instant later and he was tugged back yet again.

He began to kick with his feet, not knowing why but his fear taking over.

With his dad covered from head to toe in his mother's blood, he slipped in the tub because of it, his feet slick. At the same time, Timmy's right leg kicked out to connect with his father's nose.

The nose caved in and it was flattened by Timmy's foot, and Timmy found he was free of his father's grasp.

Using the kick to push off and through the window, Timmy found himself falling to the grass below from twenty feet up. The lawn in the backyard was overgrown and the added softness saved Timmy from being seriously harmed, and it didn't hurt that he was small and didn't weigh much.

Still, he had the wind knocked out of him when he landed on his back after spinning in the air.

Trying to suck in a breath of air, he stared up at the night sky, dazed.

And then he heard the loud voices, all of them moaning and groaning. He turned his head to the left to see the tall fence bordering the yard now had monsters behind it. He turned to the right and saw that the undead crowd had gathered there as well.

Timmy didn't understand that his yelling had called attention to him and that the zombies out front had moved around to the sides of the house in search of prey.

Hands and arms slapped the tall fence, the posts already groaning under the combined weight of the zombies.

Timmy looked up at the bathroom window to see his father was halfway through it. He squirmed like a worm, and with one mighty heave, popped out to fall to the grass below.

Timmy rolled out of the way and his dad landed right where he'd been. Timmy heard the loud crack of his dad's right leg as it snapped in half.

When he looked at his dad's face, he saw his father made no sign that he felt the pain.

His dad began to crawl across the lawn, his dead eyes focused on Timmy, his mouth hanging open as bloody saliva poured out the sides. Timmy could see a bit of flesh stuck in his father's front teeth and he knew that meat came from his mom.

His dad couldn't move that fast thanks to his broken leg, which he dragged behind him, the limb limp and crooked, some white of bone protruding through the material of his pants.

Timmy spotted movement above and he looked back up to the bathroom window and there, gazing down at him, was his mother. But she wasn't really her anymore. Now she was one of them…a monster.

The sound of breaking wood came to Timmy's ears and he looked over his shoulder to see that the fence was giving way under the onslaught of walking corpses. It would only be a matter of minutes before the fence collapsed and the dead swarmed into the backyard.

His dad let out a hungry moan, pulling Timmy's attention back to his father.

"Please, Daddy, don't kill me, please," he begged, crying again. "I'll be a good boy, I promise. I'm scared. Daddy, I'm really scared. The monsters are gonna get in the yard! You said you'd protect me and Mommy, you promised!" Tears slid down his cheeks to splatter in the high grass and choking sobs filled Timmy with dread. Though he was only six, something deep down inside him told him his life was over. That not all young boys lived forever, and that sometimes, they died…horribly.

Timmy crawled into the corner of the yard, and with his back to the eight foot stone wall bordering the neighbor's house behind his, he waited for his father to reach him.

Two things happened simultaneously. The first was that Timmy's dad reached him and the man loomed up and over Timmy like a wild animal about to pounce on the trapped prey.

The second thing was that the fence gave way on the right side of the yard, falling over and letting dozens of zombies tumble in to fall onto one another. But while the ones on the bottom were trapped, the ones behind them climbed over their fallen brethren and made their way to Timmy, hands reaching in preparation of tearing his small body to pieces.

Timmy closed his eyes, waiting for the end. "I love you, Daddy. Go 'head if you're gonna do it." He held out his arms to hug his father.

Timmy hoped that at least when it was over, he could still be with his father after he died. And maybe his mom would join him and his dad and they could still be a family, albeit a walking dead one.

As his father leaned over and prepared to sink his teeth into his son's exposed throat, Timmy actually smiled as he hugged his father tightly.

At least once he was dead he wouldn't feel pain anymore, or worry, or anger. At least he would be free.

And best of all, he would still be with his dad.

A DAY AT THE MORGUE

"Got another one for you, Doug," the orderly said as he wheeled yet another body into the morgue of the Belham Hospital.

Doug turned around and frowned deeply. "Oh, come on, Roger, really? I've got them stacked two to a table as it is."

"Not my problem," Roger replied as he handed Doug a clipboard so he could sign off on the body.

Doug took the clipboard and scrawled his name at the bottom.

"I just don't know what the city expects me to do around here. It's only me and Bob now thanks to cutbacks and layoffs."

Roger shrugged. "Hey, man, it's tough all over." With a casual wave that said he wasn't interested in Doug's problems, he left leaving Doug standing with yet another body.

Doug sighed as he stared down at the corpse in the black body bag.

"Now where the hell am I supposed to put you?"

As he looked around the large room, he really didn't have an answer to his question.

There were more than thirty bodies in the morgue at the moment, more than half of them thanks to a bus crash out on Interstate 95. No survivors, he'd been told. A drunk driver had cut off the bus and it had gone through the guardrail and into a twenty foot ravine. Many of the corpses were in pieces while others had nothing but bruises, their deaths due to internal bleeding. It had been a horror show.

At least there had been no children involved, Doug figured, as it was a bus heading off to the gambling casino in the next state.

He had a stack of autopsies to do and now he had another to add to the list.

He looked up as Bob walked in, holding a sandwich. He was still wearing his apron, a splash of mustard in the middle of his chest.

"Hey, what's up? Another one?" he asked around a mouthful of pastrami on rye with extra mustard.

"Yeah, another one. I swear, the city's gonna kill me. Give it another week and I'm gonna be on a slab next to the rest of these poor bastards."

Bob said nothing, merely continued chomping on his sandwich.

Doug wasn't please with this. "Tell me, Bob, how would you feel about cutting me open if I was dead and in here?"

Bob shrugged. "A stiff is a stiff to me, Doug, you know that. If you ever ended up on my table, I'd do the same to you as the rest. Hey, it's my job."

Doug couldn't refute the reasoning. "Yeah, I guess you're right." He sighed. "Okay, where are we gonna put this one?"

Bob let out a burp and wiped his mouth with the back of his sleeve. His eyes scanned the room and the available space, which there was none. The best course of action would be to move a body and make that one next for an autopsy, then they could put the new arrival in its place. But Bob hated doing more work than was necessary, and he had an idea.

"Hey, Doug, why don't we just get this stiff done now and then we don't have to play musical cadavers."

Doug considered it and nodded. "You know what? That's not a bad idea. For once your laziness is coming in handy."

Bob gave Doug a mustard-covered middle finger in reply.

"Yeah, I am number one," Doug snapped back, a grin on his face. "Now finish that damn sandwich and give me a hand. I swear, sometimes I have to wonder if you're the boss of me instead of the other way around, the way you act."

"Ah, Doug, relax. I know you're in charge, I'm just messin' with you."

Doug waited by the corpse for Bob to gobble down the rest of his sandwich. When he was finished, he walked over to the rolling gurney.

"Ah, Bob, you got a little mustard on your face," Doug said and pointed to the very large splatter of mustard. It made Bob look like he had a yellow mustache. Bob never was one for food etiquette and Doug was usually glad when his friend at least *chewed* his food.

Bob wiped his mouth with the back of his sleeve and belched again. Doug waved the air with his hand, trying to blow away the odor of regurgitated pastrami.

"Damn, man, it tastes as good comin' back up as it did goin' down," Bob grinned, enjoying the fact that his supervisor was uncomfortable.

"Just give me a hand here, will you please?"

Bob did as he was asked and grabbed the feet of the corpse and Doug did the same to the head. He grabbed the body bag and then heaved it off the rolling gurney and onto a stainless steel table placed in the middle of the room.

There was a microphone connected to a steel pole which was connected to the ceiling. Doug reached up and pressed the bottom on the side of the mic, and as he began to talk, he slid on a pair of new latex white gloves.

"Okay, so we have yet another customer for my table." He unzipped the body bag and barely acknowledged the stench of death. As a coroner for over ten years, there wasn't much that could surprise him.

"Bob, give me a hand sliding him out of the body bag, will you?" Doug asked.

Bob helped roll the cadaver over, and as he held the body on its side, Doug slid the bag off like a night nurse changing the soiled sheets of an infirm patient.

"Wow, this guy is really messed up," Bob said as he gazed down at the face of the cadaver. I wonder what happened to him."

Doug picked up the small booklet that was attached to the body bag. It was a preliminary of what the paramedics had found upon discovering the body.

"Says here," Doug began, "that the body was found in a ditch about ten miles outside the city under mysterious circumstances with no ID." He flipped through some of the pages. "Says here there was no foliage around the body. It was like the entire area had been blasted clean from fire, like scorched earth."

"Cool, maybe this guy was probed and left behind by aliens."

"What?"

"You know," Bob said, "like crop circles and shit."

Doug frowned. "Don't be an idiot."

"What? I'm just sayin'. Hear me out. Guy in a ditch, dead, no living matter around him, looks like it was all burnt. I'm tellin' you, it's an alien dumpsite."

"Like I said before, you're an idiot," Doug frowned.

Bob gave Doug the one finger salute in reply and reached into his pocket and took out his cell phone. As he checked his messages, Doug continued. "Caucasian male, bald with no discernable markings—scars or tattoos—appears to be late fifties or early sixties." He began undressing the man. "Appears to have bruising to right clavicle, but I'll know more when I perform the autopsy." He removed the body's shirt and said, "Oh, wait, revise what I said. Male has distinctive tattoo of what looks like a military insignia. My recommendations for the detective assigned to the case, is to check for military service if a fingerprint hit doesn't come up." He looked at Bob. "Put that damn thing away and take off his shoes, socks and pants, will you?"

Bob slid his phone into a pocket as dexterous as a magician. Then he got to work.

Moments later, the corpse was naked and pale in the harsh light of the room. Doug used a spotlight and aimed it at the torso of the corpse.

"Hmm, this is odd," he said and Bob leaned forward to see better.

"What's odd?"

"This." Doug pointed a latex-covered finger at the cadaver's belly button. "It looks like there's dried blood here, as if something had crawled into him through his belly button. He pulled down a large magnifying glass attached to another bendable pole that hung from the ceiling. Angling it just so, he and Bob studied the odd wound.

"Maybe he got stabbed and it's a coincidence he got it in the belly button," Bob suggested. Doug turned his head and Bob's face was only inches from his. He smelled pastrami and sweat and neither was appetizing.

"I highly doubt you're right but once more, guessing is irrelevant. We'll have all our answers when we open him up." Doug gestured to a tray of instruments on a small rolling table. "Bring that over here and I'll make the first incision."

Bob pushed the small table over so Doug could reach the tray easily. Doug picked up a small, two inch scalpel, and without hesitation, sliced into the chest cavity of the cadaver from neck to groin. When he finished the incision, he put on a small face shield, picked up a bone saw, and began cutting at the ribcage.

Thirty seconds later and he was holding the rib spreader as he cracked the chest cavity and exposed the organs to the harsh, unnatural light of the morgue.

As he set the rib spreader down, he heard Bob utter a small noise, like a squeak. Not looking down at the corpse, he instead turned to Bob to ask him what was wrong. Bob was staring down at the vivisected corpse, his mouth hanging open in what appeared to be shock, surprise, horror, or both.

Slowly, Doug turned away from Bob to look back down at the cadaver. When his eyes connected with the exposed torso, his mouth fell open and he stopped breathing, his pulse pounding in his temple.

In the middle of the exposed chest cavity, covered in gore and slime, was what looked like an electric eel, only this one was thick as a grown man's forearm with two small arms, and a mouth filled with razor sharp teeth. Two yellow eyes blinked clear of the slime covering the head, and as Doug stared in shock, the mouth opened wide and hissed, a small tongue forking out, similar to a snake's only dark black.

"What the fuck is that?" Bob squeaked as he fought the urge to scream.

"How the hell should I know?" Doug gasped in reply.

"What do we do?"

"I don't know, kill it, capture it, make it a pet and bring it home…shit, Bob, this is a little new to me. I don't know about you, but this is the first time I've cut into a corpse and had a friggin' snake pop out of it."

"That ain't no snake."

The eel hissed again, its small head moving back and forth, as if it wanted to look at each of the men at the same time but couldn't. The tongue continued to lick the air, and Doug wondered if it could somehow *taste* them, sense them in the same way a snake did.

"Try and capture it," Bob said. "That's like no snake I've ever seen before. We could make a fortune showing the news it. Hell, maybe it's some kind of weird new species."

Doug looked at Bob and then at the eel. "Fine, I'll try to catch it." He slowly sucked in a breath of air and then cautiously moved closer to the eel and the corpse beneath it, the body for all purposes looking like a gut-filled nest.

When he was less than a foot away, the eel hissed and lunged for his face.

"Look out!" Bob yelled as Doug snapped his head back, the eel whistling by his face by less than an inch. As it passed his face, the tail slapped his nose and left a bit of slime there. He felt the patch of skin begin to burn. He quickly wiped it off and the burning ceased.

"Get it! Get it!" Bob yelled as the eel landed on the floor and slid as if it was on ice.

"You fucking get it!" Doug yelled back.

Now that it was free of the corpse, the two men could now see the bottom of the eel. It had legs as well as arms. Rolling to its tiny feet, it began to run away from them.

"It's getting away!" Bob yelled.

"No shit, go catch it!"

Bob spun and picked up a specimen pan, the four inch deep, one foot round bowl something good to use as a cage in a pinch. With bowl in hand, he turned and dashed after the eel. At the same time it ran under one of the other gurneys with a corpse on it. Bob was so focused on the eel that he crashed into the corpse and knocked it and the gurney over.

The body crashed to the floor with a dull thump, the table making much more noise as steel collided with cement. Bob had fallen, too, and was now lying on the corpse. The body, having Bob on it and becoming condensed such as when you squeeze a balloon, began to release trapped gas. The sound of farts of all kinds, long ones, short ones and trumpeting ones, all exploded out of the corpse's anus, filling the room with a miasma that had both men gagging.

Bob rolled off the corpse and the farting ceased, and for a moment he lost sight of the eel. Then he turned around and looked behind him and saw it staring at him.

"What the hell is it doing…" he began and then the eel began to run at him. When it was three feet away, it jumped into the air, flying directly at Bob's face. Acting fast, he used the bowl as a shield, and with a metallic *clang*, the eel bounced off it and rolled onto the floor. But it was up in a second and it ran around Bob and right at the corpse.

Bob tried to use the bowl to capture it but missed, and the eel skated out of his grasp. Then it turned and dashed for the fallen corpse again.

Bob could only watch in amazement as it ran at the cadaver, and then like it was covered in Vaseline, the head went into the corpse's mouth and the rest soon followed.

Like sucking in spaghetti, the eel had slithered into the head of the corpse and only a slime trail around the lips showed it had ever been there.

"What the fuck?" Bob gasped as Doug came over to him, his eyes looking left and right for the eel.

"Where did it go?" Doug asked.

Bob pointed to the head of the corpse. "In there."

"In where?" Doug was wondering if his friend had cracked under the pressure.

"In there, in the fucking body, the thing just slithered into its mouth and disappeared."

"Bullshit," Doug snapped. "That's impossible."

"No it's not, Doug. Are you calling me a fucking liar?"

"No I... I mean to say I..." He took a deep breath to calm himself. "Okay, let's not fight, that won't accomplish anything." He leaned down and grabbed the arms of the corpse. "Get the legs and let's get this cadaver back on the slab."

Bob stood up and righted the gurney, then he picked up the legs. They both lifted and the body was soon on the slab once more. The cadaver was a woman, looking as if she had died in her late sixties or early seventies. The scar of a pacemaker showed she'd had a bad heart and was the reason for her internment in the morgue.

Doug went to the head of the dead woman and began to examine her mouth, touching his finger to the slime. He raised it to his nose and sniffed, then winced and quickly wiped it off on his apron. "God, that smells horrible, and believe me, I've smelled some terrible stuff in my career."

"So what do we do now? It's in the body. Are we gonna leave it there?" Bob asked.

Doug shook his head. "No, no way. This is Mrs. Wilson. She's got a date with the grave tomorrow at the funeral home and her family is very wealthy. I don't want them suing me for negligence or whatever when I ship her over to the funeral parlor. No, we need to get it out of her. I can fix her up with some glue when we're done if I have to and the mortician is a friend of mine. If I ask for a favor, he'll help me out. One hand washes the other and all that. Besides, she's having a closed casket anyway. Hell, we could bury a couple of bags of cement and no one would probably ever know."

"Then why don't we do that instead?"

"What did I just say? If we tried it and the family found out, they'd sue me into bankruptcy. You know the city wouldn't defend me, not with the budget crisis. I'd be living in a cardboard box by the end of the year."

As Doug talked, neither man was looking down at Mrs. Wilson, so they didn't see the fingers on her left hand begin to twitch.

"So get cuttin', man, get it out of there," Bob said and was about to say more when he glanced down at the body to see the hand squeeze into a fist.

"Oh my God, no fucking way," he whispered and took a step back.

"What? What now? Bob, you need to keep it together if we're gonna do what needs to be done here."

Bob didn't reply, but instead pointed down at the body. Doug slowly followed where Bob was gesturing and his mouth fell open when he saw Mrs. Wilson's hand in a fist, then her other hand rising up.

"But…this is impossible. She's been embalmed," he said in utter disbelief. "She can't be moving. It's physically impossible."

"Well, shit, Doug, maybe someone didn't bother to tell her that," Bob said as he stumbled into a gurney behind him. The body on the gurney began to shift, as if it wasn't sure if it was going to fall, then the gurney tilted that extra inch and toppled. It hit the gurney next to it, and like dominoes, ten bodies and gurneys all dropped on the floor in a splaying of arms, legs and crashing tables, all the corpses as naked as the day they were born.

Bob dropped into the pile between three of the bodies, and as arms fell on him, he began to yell, totally freaked out.

Then he felt hands on him and yelled yet again, knowing it had to be one of the corpses, that the body had revived and was trying to kill him. But it was only Doug, who had run to him to help him up.

"Oh shit, it's only you," Bob gasped as he was helped to his feet. Then he looked over Doug's shoulder to see Mrs. Wilson was now sitting up and her dead eyes were glaring right at him.

"Holy shit," Bob whispered. "She's fucking alive."

Also naked, as she hadn't been dressed for her funeral yet, her pale skin seemed to absorb the yellow light of the overhead fluorescent lights. As she slowly slid off the gurney, her skin undulated, as if a hundred worms were beneath her skin.

"No, Bob, I don't think she's actually alive. I think whatever that snake thing is, it's inside her and somehow controlling her."

"So she's a fucking zombie?"

"No, I wouldn't say that, but it's a fair description for now."

Mrs. Wilson was staring at the two men, and ever so slowly, she reached out to the small table with the instruments on it. Ever so carefully, her fingers touched a scalpel, and she gripped it tightly, a sinister smile crossing her pale lips.

Then she opened her mouth and hissed, one very similar to the eel when it had burst forth from the cadaver.

Both men were frozen in shock, the unbelievable too much for them to handle. The eel was one thing, that at least was something they could relate to as it looked similar to a large snake, but this, an embalmed woman now standing, grasping a scalpel and actually smiling was over the top.

The entire time she grasped the tool, her skin flexed and rippled, like an endless ocean was just under her withered flesh.

"What the hell do we do?" Bob whispered to Doug, who only shook his head.

"I have no idea," he replied.

Before either man could act, the old woman was upon them, moving way too fast for a corpse. The scalpel in her hand was like a living thing, rising and falling as the two men tried to fend her off.

But skin and bone was no match for steel, and razor-sharp surgical steel at that. As hands were raised to block the blows, fingers were slashed off and wrists were sliced to let arteries flow freely.

Mrs. Wilson's left arm was broken in two places when Doug tried to attack her, but a slice to his throat stopped him cold. As he fell to the floor, his life's blood draining out of his severed carotid artery to pool around him, she continued to rain blows down on Bob.

As Doug bled out on the floor, Bob valiantly tried to save his own life. His arms were slashed a dozen times and his clothes were slick with blood from the multiple slashes.

He knew he needed to escape or he would join Doug on the floor, covered in blood.

Taking a chance, he kicked out with his right leg, and though he received a slash to his knee, he managed to kick Mrs. Wilson in her left knee. The shattering of the frail knee cap filled the room and Mrs. Wilson toppled over to break a hip. She had fallen and she couldn't get up.

Bob ran to the left, where shelves of chemicals were stored. One of the chemicals was hydrochloric acid. Breathing heavily, the plastic jar slippery from his blood, he barely managed to open it as Mrs. Wilson began to crawl toward him, her teeth flashing in the light of the room, her dead eyes looking as if cataracts had completely enveloped them. How she could see, Bob had no idea.

When she was within a few feet of him, she tried to slash his legs and he jumped back, uttering a small scream. Behind her, he could see Doug was still, his dead eyes gazing up at the ceiling.

Bob shook his head, trying to stay sane, even if for just a little longer. He wondered if perhaps this was all a dream and he would wake up in his bed covered in sweat but safe.

Hissing snapped him from his wish as Mrs. Wilson came closer. With acid in hand, he stepped forward and then to the side when she slashed at him.

He dumped the acid on her head and back, then jumped away fast. A few drops got on him and he felt the sting as the acid ate through his clothing and into his skin. But they were small and only the top two layers of skin were eaten before the acid stopped working.

Mrs. Wilson was spasming and twitching, a hideous scream leaving her pale lips. The acid ate away her hair, skin and the meat on her bones, the bubbling soup spreading out around her.

Soon, her face was nothing but a grinning skull, and as Bob watched, the tongue boiled and disintegrated, the foul liquid splashing in the goop that was her body, her eyes soon following as they literally dissolved and dripped out of her eye sockets.

The arm with the scalpel tried to reach for him but with half her body eaten away, there was no way she could accomplish her goal. Then the acid ate enough that whatever the eel was using to control her ceased and the corpse slumped to the floor, splashing gore in all directions.

Steam and bubbles rose from the body as the acid continued to dissolve her.

Bob breathed a sigh of relief, and without checking on Doug—or Mrs. Wilson—he turned, and after giving the bubbling body a wide berth, he ran for the exit and freedom. As he ran down the hall, he screamed for help; about alien snakes, walking corpses and murder.

As the door slammed closed and the sound of Bob's yelling and footsteps pounding down the hallway ceased, the morgue grew silent.

Then, a scraping sound could be heard, and under Mrs. Wilson's right leg, the eel popped free of a new hole it had made in the corpse's thigh. It had burrowed into the leg when the acid began to work and had survived unscathed.

Popping free, it ran across the floor and right to Doug. After sniffing at the blood with its tongue, it scampered into the crimson pool and onto Doug's chest. The tongue licked out once more and then the eel slid up to the jagged slash in Doug's neck.

In the blink of an eye, it crawled into the gaping wound and into his body. Like he was swallowing something really large, Doug's throat undulated, then went still once more.

For a few seconds nothing happened and all was quiet in the morgue, with the exception of the bubbling corpse of Mrs. Wilson as the acid continued to eat away at her flesh and bones.

Doug's blank eyes were open and staring at nothing and then they blinked.

His mouth moved as did his hands, and a minute later he was sitting up. He moved his head from side to side, blood seeping from the wound, and when he had composed himself, so to speak, he slowly picked himself up to a standing position.

He swayed back and forth for a few seconds as he regained his balance, then walked over to a small supply closet. Inside was the clothing of the deceased that came through the morgue. Jackets, shirts, pants, socks and sometimes underwear; but not too often.

The latter was usually cut away and disposed of, given the predilection for the diseased to defecate upon death. This was where it was all stored until being taken away monthly.

Doug slowly stripped off his bloody clothes, and as he did, his wounds began to stop bleeding.

With no beating heart there was nothing to pump the blood and most of it was now on the floor anyway.

He carefully wiped himself down, especially his arms, legs and face, then he took a scarf and tied it around his neck to cover his wound.

After putting on a new pair of shoes, he shrugged into a Red Sox jacket and put on a Yankees ball cap, having no idea the two together were a taboo.

After flexing his arms and legs and bending his head back and forth one more time to make sure everything worked the way it was supposed to, he walked out of the morgue.

When he exited, he went in the opposite direction that Bob had taken.

The morgue fell quiet once more, only the bubbling of Mrs. Wilson to break the silence.

A HARD LESSON

"Oh, boy, it's finally time to go trick-or-treating!" James yelled as he galloped up the stairs to put on his Batman costume. He had owned it since September and now, finally, it was time to wear it.

It took him less than two minutes to don the gray and black costume over his clothing, then with his utility belt firmly secured around his waist, including his trusty Swiss Army knife, he ran down the stairs, taking the last three steps in one leap. He flew through the air, his black cape blowing behind him, and landed loudly on the floor.

"James! What did I tell you about jumping down the stairs?" his father yelled from the living room.

"Not to do it," James called back.

"That's right. So get your butt upstairs and walk down those stairs the right way, or you can forget about trick-or-treating this year."

James opened his mouth to protest but quickly closed it. He didn't want to get his father mad at him, not tonight of all nights. He glanced at the clock on the wall to see it was ten minutes to six. Richard and Kyle would be ringing his doorbell any second so they could all head out together. Turning, he crept up the stairs as fast as he could, then slowly, ever so slowly, walked down them.

"Good, see? That wasn't so hard, was it?" his father asked.

"No, Dad."

James turned and walked into the kitchen, where his mom was waiting with her arms crossed over her chest and a big smile on her face.

"Your father caught you again, huh?"

"Yeah, he did," James replied.

"Well, just be glad he's in a good mood and he didn't want to punish you."

"Tell me about it, Mom. It's Halloween night for Pete's sake. I've got stuff to do!"

She looked down at her eleven year old son and shook her head. She handed him a cell phone and a pillow case.

"Here you go, just as ordered. I made sure to reinforce the seam, so it won't break if you fill it with candy," she said, gesturing to the pillowcase. "And you keep that phone on at all times. That's the only reason I'm letting you go out there all alone without an adult present."

"Aw, Mom, I won't be alone. The guys will be with me."

She ruffled his hair. "Maybe so, but if I'm not there with you, then to me you're alone. Just humor me, I'm your mother, it's my job to worry."

The doorbell rang and James ran for the front door. "It's the guys! They're here early!" He threw the door open and laughed when he saw his two best friends, each wearing their Halloween costumes.

Richard was a mummy, wrapped with cut rags from an old sheet. Splashes of black and brown paint were added to the rags to make him look really old. Kyle wore a Dracula outfit, complete with plastic teeth, white face, black cape and a large silver cross on his chest.

"Guys, what's up? You look awesome!" James yelled as he waved to his mom who was standing in the hallway. "Hey, Richard, what's up with the cross?"

Richard shrugged. "Nothin', I just thought it looked cool."

"But vampires don't like crosses," he replied.

"So, I'm a special vampire. Crosses don't hurt me."

"Whatever."

"Remember, no talking to strangers!" his mother called as the door slammed closed.

"What did your mom say?" Kyle asked.

"Nothing," James said, waving the question away. "She said to have a good time."

"So where do we want to go first?" Richard asked. The rags covering his face kept falling into his eyes and he had to push them up. It reminded James of a man wearing a hat that was too large for his head.

"Let's go to Third Street. They always give out the best candy there," Kyle suggested as the three boys walked down the sidewalk.

"Great idea," James said. "Third Street it is."

As they walked down the street, they admired all the other kids out trick-or-treating as well. All wore colorful costumes. They saw little girls in princess attire, three more Batmans, a Frankenstein, a zombie, a Superman and a hobo to name a few. It was a clear night and the temperature was in the high sixties. And with the full moon, it was the perfect Halloween night.

Third Street was four blocks over. It was a large street with houses that were huge, with large, manicured front yards and stone walkways. It took longer to get to each house, but the reward was always worth it. Financially a better neighborhood, the home owners always gave out large candy bars and other assorted goodies.

It was as the three boys were walking that a brown beat-up van pulled along beside them. Behind the steering wheel was a man dressed as a werewolf. He had gone all out with long fangs, coarse hair glued to his face, arms and hands, and even under his shirt collar. The passenger side window was open and the werewolf called out to the three boys.

"Hey, boys, you goin' to the party on Park Street?"

"What party?" Kyle asked, intrigued. He was the wildest of the three boys, always getting into trouble.

"Oh, man," the werewolf said, "you didn't hear about the Halloween party? It's gonna be awesome with prizes, food and so much candy you're stomach will explode by the time you leave."

Richard's eyes lit up. "Oh, wow, that sounds cool! Way better than running from house to house to get candy." He looked at Kyle and James and said, "Come on guys, we gotta go there instead!"

"I don't know," James said, not liking where this was going. "Besides, Park Street is almost a mile from here, that's a long walk."

"Tell you what," the werewolf said. "I'm going there now. Hop in and I'll give you a lift."

"That would be great!" Kyle yelled as he walked to the van's cargo door and slid it open. "Come on, guys, let's go!"

James hesitated. "I don't know, Kyle, this seems funny to me. Maybe we should just go to Third Street."

Richard took a step toward the van as he looked back at James. "What could happen, James? There's three of us and only one of him."

James considered that. There were three of them, not the usual child kidnapping his mom always made him worry about. And he had his cell phone if there was a problem. He looked at the werewolf, who smiled with his pointed fangs. *Man, they really look real,* James thought.

Finally, he said, "I'll go, too." He climbed into the van next to Richard as the door closed behind him.

"Great, glad to have you onboard," the werewolf said. With a howl that made James wonder just how good of an actor the man really was, the van pulled onto the street, leaving the bustling trick-or treaters still ambling about on the sidewalk behind.

A few minutes later, James looked out the small window in the door and realized they weren't going to Park Street. The werewolf driver was going in the wrong direction.

"Uh, guys, I'm getting a bad feeling about this," James said. "We're not going anywhere near Park Street." He reached into his pocket and took out his cell phone, but when he looked at the small screen, it told him he had no reception.

"That won't work in here, boy," the werewolf said. James looked up and saw the werewolf's eyes in the rearview mirror. They were now creased and didn't look at all friendly. He pointed at the roof and walls of the van. "They're shielded."

"Hey, what's going on here?" Richard asked, realizing the werewolf wasn't being as friendly as before. "I thought we were going to a party?"

The werewolf laughed lightly, a low chuckle that seemed to come from deep in his chest. He raised his right hand so all three boys could see, and as each of them watched, talons popped out much like when a cat is scared.

"Oh, you're going to a party, all right, only it isn't the one you thought."

Kyle was the first to say it, though all three boys were thinking the same thing. "Oh my God, he's a real werewolf."

The werewolf nodded. "Sure am. My kind love Halloween. It's one of the few times we can hunt for our prey in plain sight. No one gives it a second thought to see a man in a werewolf costume walking down the street…or driving a van."

"W…what are you gonna do with us?" Richard stammered.

"Oh, let's just say you won't like it much. Hey, have you ever wanted your picture on a milk carton before?" he laughed again, long and loud as he turned the van onto another dark street. James could see through the windshield that they were heading out of town. He knew he needed to act fast to save himself and his friends. After all, he was Batman, it was his duty to be clever, brave and save the day.

Richard looked like he was about to burst into tears, he was so scared, and Kyle didn't look much better. James felt that way, too, but he rallied his courage and pulled his two friends close to him.

"Okay, guys, we need to work together if we're gonna get out of here." He reached into his utility belt and pulled out his trusty Swiss Army knife. He looked at it, but knew it wouldn't be enough. Then, James eyes went right to the silver cross hanging on Kyle's chest.

"Kyle, give me your cross," James told his friend. Kyle did as he was told, pulling it off and handing it to James. Then James looked at Richard, and the rags used for bandages. "Richard," he said, "give me some of those bandages."

Richard nodded, sniffling back a sob as he did so. In the driver's seat, the werewolf was humming a song as he drove onto a dirt road devoid of streetlights.

A minute later, James had all the items he hoped would set them free.

"Okay, you guys get ready, and when I tell you to, run to the back of the van." Both boys nodded.

James crawled up to the back of the werewolf, and as he raised his right hand with the cross in it—the silver cross—the werewolf's eyes went to the rearview mirror and went wide when he saw James.

"Why you little…" the werewolf began, but no sooner did he speak then James jumped forward and stabbed the werewolf in the shoulder with the silver cross. The cross was like acid to the werewolf and the beast howled as James pushed the cross in as far as he could. But no sooner did he do this then he used two of the rags to wrap around the werewolf's closest arm. As fast as he could, he pulled back and tied the rags to the back of the driver's seat. Having to drive, the werewolf couldn't untie his arm and he fought to control the van as it swerved across the road.

"Okay, follow me!" James yelled as he crawled to the back of the van. When he tried to open the door, it was locked because there was no handle, but he used the housing part of his knife to whack the window. It didn't break on the first hit but he tried again and this time it cracked. He kicked it with his foot and it exploded outward, raining safety glass onto the road.

The werewolf lost control of the van and it careened into a ditch lining the road. As this happened, James reached his arm through the broken window and pressed the latch to open the door.

The door popped open as the van tilted to the side, coming to a stop. All three boys rolled across the floor and the werewolf managed to grab on to Kyle's cape.

"He's got me! The werewolf's got me!" Kyle yelled, the terror in his voice apparent. "Help me, guys!"

James crawled over to Kyle and used his Swiss Army knife to cut the cape a few inches from the werewolf's hand. Falling free, Kyle scrambled to the open van door.

"Come here, ya little brats!" the werewolf yelled as he tried to untie himself so he could chase the boys. All three boys jumped out of the van and began running for their lives down the dark road.

They didn't stop until they were more than a quarter mile from the van, each of them breathing hard and gasping for air.

"What do we do now?" Kyle asked, his voice barely a whisper. James was about to reply when headlights lit up the night and all three boys screamed in fear.

"He's back! The werewolf found us!" Richard yelled as he shielded his eyes from the glare of the headlights.

"What are you boys doing out here all alone?" a voice called to them. James knew instantly it wasn't the werewolf.

As the owner of the voice began to walk out of the headlights, and James could see the person better, he saw the reflection of a policeman's badge. And when he squinted some more, he saw the vehicle wasn't a van but a squad car.

They were saved!

The policeman looked up as another vehicle approached them. All three boys turned to look and saw it was the beat-up van, the werewolf behind the wheel. When the werewolf saw the policeman, he continued past them, only slowing enough to glare at James.

The policeman chuckled when he saw the driver of the van. "Huh, Halloween, gotta love it, huh, boys? He must be going to a party."

None of the boys said anything until the policeman looked at them once more. "So, I'll ask again, what are you kids doing all the way out here?"

James shrugged, and with as calm a voice as he could muster, he said, "Nothing much. We were walking and got lost is all. Can you give us a ride to Third Street, sir?"

The officer scratched his forehead and sighed. "I'm not a cab service, son, but yes, this one time I will. It's not safe out here in the dark and I don't want you boys getting into trouble. Hop in," he said and ushered the boys into the squad car.

Once they were all inside and on their way, James looked at Kyle and Richard. The policeman was in front of them in the driver's seat, and with the plastic barrier separating him from them, he couldn't hear what James was saying.

"We make a promise right here and now that we never talk about what happened tonight, all right?" James said in a hushed tone.

"Who would believe us anyway? Hell, I was there and I still don't believe it." Richard said.

"You made me lose my cross," Kyle said. "My mom's gonna kill me."

"Better a hypothetical one than a real one, Kyle," James huffed.

The boys remained silent for the rest of the ride. When the squad car pulled over at the top of Third Street, and the officer climbed out and opened the back door for the kids to leave, he waggled a finger at them and said, "Now, you boys stay out of trouble, ya hear?"

"Believe me, sir, we will," James said as they began to walk down the street. "Thank you for the ride."

The officer was soon distracted when a few new trick-or-treaters walked by him and he chatted with the parents of the children.

James led the way to the first house, and just before he reached the door, his cell phone rang. Opening it, he said, "Hello?"

"James? It's Mom, I just wanted to check on you. Are you okay?"

"I'm fine, Mom, I'm on Third Street. I should be home in a half hour."

"Okay, just stay safe. And remember, no talking to people you don't know."

He chuckled then. "What about werewolves? Can I talk to them?"

"What? Are you trying to be funny?"

"Yes, Mom, that's exactly what I'm trying to do. Don't worry, I'll be fine."

"Okay, talk to you when you get home." She hung up and James put the phone away.

Richard and Kyle returned from the front door of the house and Kyle handed James a big candy bar. "Here, I got you one, too."

"Thanks," James said. "So, are we gonna finish getting candy or what?"

"You bet," Richard said, feeling better now that they were safe and everything was back to normal. He turned and began walking down the path, leaving Kyle and James alone for a second. As they stood side by side, other children walked by them, going to get candy from the home owner.

James turned to look at his friend, who did the same to him.

"So werewolves really exist, who knew?" Kyle asked.

"Yeah, who knew," James repeated as the two boys began walking, quickly catching up with Richard who was already at the next house.

None of the three boys ever spoke of the events of that night, especially when the next day, four children were reported missing, all of them vanishing without a trace while trick-or-treating.

James wanted to tell the police what he and his friends knew, but he was positive that no one would believe him.

But James knew that next Halloween, when the moon was full, he was going to be on the lookout for a battered old van with a werewolf in the driver's seat. And if he found it, well, Batman was a superhero after all, and the werewolf was a villain.

The rest would work itself out.

ALONE

The battery-powered alarm clock began shrieking, seeming like a bomb about to explode if it wasn't given the attention it was asking for.

Brian Williams slammed his hand down on the top buttons, silencing the infernal shriek forever or until the next morning.

Immediately silence descended like a thunderclap and he let out a low moan, similar to what a zombie would make from the horror movies he used to watch when he was a kid.

He laid perfectly still, staring up at the ceiling of his home, wondering if today would be any different than the dozens before it.

At first, groggy from sleep, nothing really settled in, but then it all came back and he felt the loneliness overwhelm him.

He was so alone, damn it.

No one called him and no one sent him mail.

Sometimes he wondered if it was his fault, maybe he should just try and get out there more, you know, to meet new people, but then he would brush the idea away as foolish.

After all, he was a nice guy, why did he have to go out and seek their friendship? Why couldn't they come to him?

He lay in bed for more than ten minutes and then rolled out of bed with another groan and stood up, stretching heartily as his muscles and bones snapped and cracked.

Walking to the end of the bed, he began his regiment of exercises, knowing it would be the only thing to wake him up. He began with thirty pushups then went into crunches, then did a few curls to work on his abdomen. After that he did fifty jumping jacks, smiling the entire time. They always reminded him of high school gym as he jumped up and down, causing a few odds and ends on the nearby shelves to shake slightly.

Finished with his calisthenics, he padded to the small bathroom and took a shower. The water pressure sputtered once or twice and he cursed the damn plumbing in his house, but then it began to flow and soon the bathroom was filled with a wet, warm mist.

Climbing in the shower, he lathered up with soap, then used the small, circular mirror in front of him to shave. As he did so, he stared at the dark green eyes glaring back at him and he wondered if he would ever get to gaze into another's eyes again. But love had never been his forte and he could only hope the future would bring someone into his life.

Stepping out of the shower, now clean and shaved, he toweled off and then headed back to his bedroom. Not one for doing laundry, he dug through a pile of clothing until he found a shirt and pants that weren't too far over the edge of good taste.

Besides, it's not like anyone would be smelling him today, but then he could always hope.

Whenever he left the house, he always hoped he would meet someone nice, strike up a friendship and then he wouldn't be so alone, but so far no one had popped up.

With a small sigh after dressing, he headed to his kitchen and made himself some coffee and toast, the bread coming from the freezer.

As the coffee was percolating, he went to the answering machine and frowned when all it said was zero.

No one had called as he slept and why would they? It was like he was a pariah, no one wanted his company.

When the toast and coffee were ready he ate silently at the table, glancing through an old newspaper more than two months old. He didn't mind, it was something to pass the time and he could have cared less that the news was out dated.

Finally finished with breakfast, he walked into his den and stared at the pictures on the walls. His parents' faces smiled back at him and he missed them terribly, knowing both had died a few months ago. Another picture grinned back next to his parents' photo. It was of his brother, but he didn't know where his brother was. The man had never called, so as far as Brian was concerned the man was as good as dead to him.

There was a small trophy on the shelf to his right and he walked to it, picking it up with an awful sigh of longing. He had won this at the company picnic a year ago. He remembered getting close to Tricia that day. She was one of the many drones in accounting, but she was pretty and smart and acted like she liked him. But now, more than three months after he'd left his job, she had never called once. He knew he shouldn't feel rejected by her as they had never made any kind of commitment, but he'd just felt like they had made that connection, the one that says two people might have a chance together.

Oh, well, all water under the bridge now, he figured.

There were many other fish in the sea, his father used to say, the question was, did he have the right bait to catch one?

Leaving the den, he walked back into the kitchen. There was a pile of bills sitting on the counter, one for the mortgage from more than four months ago. He wasn't worried about paying it, he knew the banks had enough trouble right now and they could come take his home if they had a problem with him. Besides, all it would take would be one phone call and he would gladly pay the bill, hell, he would do cartwheels if they called him.

But know one called him anymore and he knew they might never.

He didn't know what was wrong with him, but everyone had turned their backs on him. He sometimes wondered who he had offended but nothing came to mind.

God, maybe, maybe he'd offended God and this was his punishment.

Deciding he shouldn't think like that, as it wasn't productive, he went to the front hallway and prepared to go out for another day on the town. As he got ready, he wondered if today would be the day he would meet someone new.

He kicked the junk mail to the side where it had sat for months, not interested in it. There were a few he recognized such as the weight loss one and the one where if he took just one small pill a day he would end up with a massive penis to please the ladies.

He ignored them all; he didn't feel like picking them up.

Let the maid do it, he thought with a chuckle.

Going to the hall closet, he opened it slowly, reached inside, and took out his coat. It was a heavy leather jacket with pieces of thin metal sewn into the lining to reinforce it. It was long, to his ankles, and dark black with many pockets. Sliding his arms through the sleeves, he relished the feeling of the heavy material on his shoulders; the smell of the worn leather.

Then he reached into the closet and began taking out the things most people would probably use before going out into his new world.

The first item was a pump action shotgun, the butt worn from use, the barrel splattered with dried blood. The second item was a police issue Glock, taken from a cop who didn't need it anymore. The seventeen round clip was full, thanks to the boxes of ammunition stacked in the top shelf of the closet, and he ejected the clip and checked it, then popped it back in. It never hurt to double check.

One bullet could mean the difference between life and death.

The next item was a long, eighteen inch machete with a wooden grip that had been wrapped with electrical tape to help when his palm got sweaty. The blade was razor sharp and looked like it had already gotten a fair bit of use.

This he hung from his belt, the rope looped through a hole in the handle. It had no sheath and hung free.

The last thing he pulled from the closet was a riot helmet, the top scuffed and scratched from use. Strapping it on, he began running his hands over his body, making sure everything was in place and easy to reach. The Glock was on his right hip, the shotgun he would carry, and the machete was on his left side, swinging gently as he moved about the hallway.

He took a few boxes of shotgun shells out of the closet and dropped them into his voluminous pockets, then checked the shotgun itself to make sure it was loaded.

Ejecting the first shell, he then popped it back in, feeling confident he was ready for anything.

He turned and glanced back through the hallway to the kitchen table, and spotted his breakfast plate and coffee mug still there. He'd forgotten to place them in the sink.

Oh, well, they'd be there when he retuned this evening, he knew that for a fact.

Reaching into his left pocket, he pulled out a pair of heavy leather gloves, then slid them on with practiced ease. The knuckles of the gloves were reinforced with small ball bearings and did havoc to a human face if used properly.

So armed and ready, the heavy leather of his jacket like a lightweight Kevlar covering his body,.he opened his front door and gazed out into the sun-drenched street of his neighborhood.

Though his grass was high and his bushes were wild, he wasn't worried about his neighbors complaining.

Stepping out onto the cement landing, he closed the front door behind him and prepared to start his day.

With a casual gait, he walked down his pathway and in seconds was in the street.

Maybe today I'll find someone, he hoped as he turned and let out a low whistle. Immediately, ten shambling forms at the end of the street turned at his call and began to stumble towards him.

Pumping the shotgun, he stood in the middle of the street, his leather jacket billowing in the gentle breeze.

He planned on working his way to the south side of town today, and then double-back before night fall.

God, I'm so alone, he thought for the hundredth time. *Surely there has to be someone else alive out here in this giant, undead world.*

As the zombies stumbled closer, the gaping wounds and pale, desiccated frames reaching for him, he got to work.

It had been a lonely existence for the past few months since the dead began to walk and swallowed the world whole, but he wasn't about to give up.

Like he'd been doing for months, each day he would head out in search of survivors. And when he found them he knew life would be just a little bit better.

He shot the first two zombies in their faces, sending skull and brain matter across the pavement to twinkle in the sun, and he quickly followed that with three more shots, taking out the rest.

Then he swung the shotgun over his shoulder and pulled out the machete, wanting to conserve ammo when possible. He'd gotten most of them quickly and now the numbers weren't so bad. They were slow and he was fast and he could take them down easily.

Then he would head out for the hundredth time to search for survivors like himself.

As he took down the last zombie in line, slicing its head in half and kicking the corpse to the road, he set off without a backwards glance to the fetid cadavers now sprawled on the road like road kill.

The crows came out of the sky almost immediately to begin feeding on the rotting meat, but Brian never noticed.

All he knew was what was in his mind, his heart, and what had picked at him for what seemed like forever.

And that was how truly alone he was.

ANGELS OF DEATH

The dark alley in the deepest part of Dorchester, just a mile from Boston, seemed to embrace the shadows of the night like a blanket.

Filled with the detritus of a fallen society, rats scurried amongst the trash, searching for another morsel of rotting food. At the far end of the alley, another shadow stood, blending into the blackness as if part of it.

And in truth the shadow was.

Moonlight crested over the dilapidated rooftops and a spear of illumination cut through the dark to expose the visage of the shadow. At first the male face looked human, but as the man who owned that face smiled, the distinct shape of two fangs could be seen.

The man turned after checking his back trail, then he sprinted to a hidden doorway at the far end of the alley. He knocked three times and waited. He hummed a tune from his youth, the song from the early 1800s. He had never gotten into the newer forms of music, having a sense of nostalgia.

But though in many ways he disliked the twentieth century, he had to admit there were a few perks that had never existed back when he had first been *turned.*

A small metal plate in the door about head height slid open and a pair of black eyes glared at him.

"What the fuck do you want?" a gravelly voice demanded.

"Vlad sent me," the man said, his tone filled with sarcasm. There was no Vlad and there probably never was, but even a vampire could have a sense of humor. He did make sure to flash a smile so his fangs could be seen.

A clacking of deadbolts came to his ears, and a second later the door was opening inward.

No sooner did the door open, then the steady drone of a bass could be heard.

The man strolled inside, flashing his most sincere grin to the doorman. As for the doorman, he merely grunted, his bald pate reflecting what little light was in the small hallway.

The man slid the doorman a twenty and nodded as the door slammed close behind him, for all purposes sounding like a steel grating in a dungeon.

He walked down the hallway, the steady beat of the bass growing. There was another door and another doorman, this one with a slight bulge under his dark sports coat. He nodded to this new bouncer, knowing what that bulge was. Though technically undead, a bullet to the head could kill and one to the body sure as hell didn't tickle.

Most of the myths humans knew of vampires were just that–myths. Vampires were still human in many ways and most just wanted to live their long lives in peace. Take sunlight for instance. In reality, a vampire in the sun would just end up with a great tan. Of course they fed on human blood, but then humans fed on the flesh of animals. How is that any different?

The second doorman looked him up and down, waved a wand over his person to see if any hidden weapons were on him, then nodded, seeing he was clean. Turning, he opened the door he was guarding.

As the door opened, bright light and a blast of music hit the man like a wave and he stepped into ***The Underground***, a place where vampires could relax and be themselves.

No sooner did he enter then a shrill voice cried out from a corner. "Adrian, it's about damn time you got here!"

Adrian turned, knowing that voice in an instant. He shook his head as another man jogged over to him, having to weave in and out of the dancing crowd. Adrian had hoped he might get at least a few minutes to get a drink before Carl found him.

As Carl ran up to him, Adrian reached into his mouth and popped the plastic fangs from his teeth.

"You did it again, huh?" Carl asked as he reached Adrian, seeing the plastic vampire teeth in his hand.

Adrian nodded. All around the two men people danced and gyrated, but it was on the edges of the room where the true fun was. Speaking up to be heard over the music, Adrian said, "Yeah, I just love the way Boris looks at me when I smile at him."

Boris was the first bouncer with the dark eyes that Adrian had passed to enter the underground den.

"He says he doesn't like you," Carl added.

Adrian shrugged. "He just doesn't know me, that's all. Is it my fault he doesn't have a sense of humor?"

Carl shook his head and downed the last of his drink. "You thirsty?"

"Yeah, but not for what's in your glass."

Carl grinned, knowing what Adrian meant. "Then go to booth five, there's a chalice with your name on it."

"Sounds good, I'll catch up to you after I've had a bite to eat."

Carl was going to say more, but Adrian didn't let him. He spun and slid into the crowd, moving through the sea of people. A few familiar faces smiled at him and he did the same, a few women receiving a peck on their cheek in greeting. The entire club was filled with vampires, each having a fun night on the town.

Adrian reached the edge of the dance floor and counted booths that lined the wall until he came to booth five. Sure enough, it was empty, with the exception of the exquisite beauty lying naked on the table. She wore a small gold pendant of a cross on her neck and Adrian chuckled at that. She was a defiant one, then. Though crosses were nothing to vampires, just another harmless myth, every vampire knew what it represented and none enjoyed having the one thing they couldn't have thrust in their face; for to be one of the undead meant Heaven was forever out of reach.

Just before Adrian went to her, his mouth already watering, he caught a snippet of conversation from behind him. Two men were conversing and both sounded troubled.

"So did you hear what happened over on Cambridge Street in Boston?" one asked the other.

"No, spill it," the other replied.

"One of them suicide angels found a flat with us and tore the shit out of some poor bastard. They said when she was through, only dental records were gonna identify the guy."

"Shit, I didn't know they were so close. I heard of something going down in Philly a few weeks ago, but here, too?"

"Think we got to worry?"

"About what? If one of them bitches ever tries for me, I'll cut her fucking angel heart out. They don't scare me a bit."

"Not me, man, I don't wanna deal with them, they're relentless. I hear if they get your scent, they're like bloodhounds."

"Bah, more bullshit. It's all hype. So one of us gets whacked, it happens. These angels are becoming bigger than they are."

"Yeah, hey, I'm empty, wanna get another beer?"

"Sure, then let's get something to eat, too, I'm famished."

The two men moved off and Adrian glanced over his shoulder as they moved across the large room of the nightclub. So there had been another angel attack.

They were becoming more frequent lately.

Though no vampire wanted to admit it, as every one of them felt they were the dominant species on the planet, something new had been added to the equation.

They were being hunted by what had been dubbed suicide Angels.

These *angels* were relentless killing machines who never spoke and wanted nothing more than to kill every vampire they could find.

Whether the vampire race wanted to admit it or not, they were being hunted, and so far no one had escaped alive, and it was only thanks to brief glimpses that any Intel on the angels was known at all.

His stomach rumbled and he could feel the hunger calling, so deciding what had happened in Boston was none of his affair, he crawled into the booth. With a nod to the chalice, he began to feed, the woman writhing below him, slowly coming to an orgasm as a small amount of her life's blood fed him.

Not enough to kill her, in fact, it was more like donating blood to a local hospital.

Chalices were volunteers who wanted nothing more than to become a vampire. True, there were some who simply got off on being with a mythic creature, and some were so into Goth that the vampire scene was the only way to reach *true* fulfillment, but some simply just got off on getting *fanged*, as the saying went.

Of course, fangs were a myth and in reality two small cuts of the flesh on the neck were all that was needed to get the blood out of the chalice without causing serious harm. Adrian had even heard of a few vampires who had taken to getting dentures with fangs in them so they could go the whole Bela Lugosi route.

Hey, one man's disgust is another's fetish and all that.

A small metal poker, looking a lot like a skewer for shish-kabobs, sat next to the woman's head, the tip coated in a thin sheen of her blood from when Adrian had poked her. He leaned back and smiled, relishing the aftertaste on his tongue, as he wiped his mouth with a napkin. Always the gentleman was Adrian, and proper etiquette was a must.

"Damn that's good, aged to perfection. How old are you, darlin'? Twenty? Twenty-one?"

"Twenty," she purred as she rubbed her hands between her legs. Feeding and sex were intertwined to the point the lines had blurred for her. If Adrian was correct, he bet the chalice couldn't orgasm unless she was being fed upon. And like drug addiction, each time she would need to go a little farther to get the same rush. It was possible one day she would be sucked dry. It had happened before, though no one wanted to talk about it; bad for business and all that.

A chalice wouldn't be so excited about volunteering if they knew they might end up being sucked dry till they resembled a withered grape in the sun.

Carl popped up with a beer in each hand and sat down across from Adrian so he had to look over the woman's breasts to see him. The chalice's nipples were rock hard and her eyes were closed as she moaned in pleasure, savoring the last of her orgasm.

"One of those for me?" Adrian asked.

Carl looked at him blankly, then nodded. "Huh? Oh, yeah, here ya go. Thought you might be thirsty."

"Yeah, I am," Adrian said as he took the beer. A few droplets of condensation from the bottle dripped onto the woman's chest. The drops slid into the valley between her breasts and then rolled down her stomach, where she used her hands to rub the water over her warm skin.

Adrian watched her and debated if he should take her home and screw her. All he had to do was ask and she would jump at the chance. But he didn't, maybe for that exact reason. When there was no hunt involved, no pursuit, it sometimes became dull, lackluster.

He turned and gazed into the gloom-filled room, his eyes studying the other patrons. About twenty dancers were on the dance floor at the moment and the hard bass of the juke box blasted from the speakers mounted in every corner. There was an empty stage in the far right corner. On Fridays and Saturday nights a live band would play. They were called the *Bloodsuckers* if you believed it, an inside joke if there ever was one. All four band members were of course, vampires.

But the stage was empty tonight with the exception of a young couple sitting on the corner of it, talking together, their heads pressed forehead to forehead so they could be heard over the music. Adrian let his gaze slide to the booths on either side of him. Chalices were on each table, their naked bodies glistening under the soft lights overhead. Smoke filled the large room like it was a giant fireplace with the flue closed, and the cacophony of music mixed with people yelling and talking was an uproar of horrendous proportions.

In other words, just another night at *The Underground.*

Adrian finished his beer and felt his bladder pushing on his belt. Though technically undead, with a heart that didn't beat anymore, what went in still had to leave sooner or later, so he decided it might as well be sooner.

"I gotta use the head," he said to Carl who was playing with the chalice. He was sucking her right nipple and gently nuzzling the breast with his chin. By the look of it, Carl would be bringing the chalice home tonight. "I'll be right back."

Carl looked up and barely acknowledged Adrian as he moved off to the bathrooms at the rear of the dance floor. When he reached the small hallway leading to the bathrooms, he had to slide between two women who were sniffing cocaine off the back of a man's hand. Adrian knew immediately the man was a vampire, thanks to a sixth sense he and other vampires had for recognizing their own kind. The women were human, and were probably the man's escorts, or perhaps even mates.

Entering the bathroom, he heard the soft sounds of a woman grunting in pleasure. Walking to the stalls, he saw a pair of feet, male by the shoes, and behind those he saw the feminine feet of a woman, both of her feet spread apart so her toes were pointing at right angles. By the sound of it, she was certainly enjoying herself.

Adrian went to the urinal and did his business. He wasn't there for more than five seconds when the woman cried out and there was a scuffle in the stall. The door slammed open and Adrian saw an attractive redhead with dark eyes storm out while adjusting her skirt.

"I said not in the back, I told you that already," she snapped as she left the bathroom. A man came out right behind her, saw Adrian and flashed him a knowing grin. As he did, he was zipping up his fly then chasing after the woman. "Oh, come on, baby, let's talk about this," he pleaded as he chased her back into the nightclub.

Adrian smirked to himself and finished his business.

Flushing, he went to the sink and washed his hands, always the dutiful vampire. He remembered what his mother used to say about cleanliness and doing it for yourself, not for others.

He stared at his face in the mirror, seeing a few dark circles under his eyes. He wasn't getting as much sleep as he should and he made a mental note to correct that. Though immortal, he still needed to take care of himself. It was his choice if he wanted to go through life as an overweight vampire, a rundown one, or a healthy, vibrant one.

Wetting his hands, he ran them through his hair, using his fingers as a comb. Wiping them with a brown, paper towel from the pile on the sink, he turned to head back and join Carl.

It was as he was reaching for the door handle to the bathroom that he froze at the massive sound of something being smashed coming from the dance floor. Immediately, the jukebox cut off and he could hear screams and yells mixed with gunshots.

His hand hovered over the door handle as he listened to what sounded basically like a war was being fought in the nightclub.

His hesitation was no more than a second, but to him it felt like a lifetime.

Then his hand became unfrozen and he reached for the knob, throwing open the door, and charging into the nightclub. As he ran down the small hallway, he could see brief glimpses of chaos as the gloom-filled club was ravaged by something so powerful it was a blur.

Adrian reached the end of the small hallway and his mouth fell open as he stared at the carnage before him.

Every vampire in the room was fighting for their lives as a blur with dark black hair weaved in and out, always avoiding grasping hands, but at the same time dealing death with each blow made.

He watched as the blur grabbed a man by the arms and tore them off like the man was no more than a doll stuffed with straw. The blur spun and began using the arms like bludgeons, smashing people to the floor until the arms were nothing but bits of bone and flesh.

And even then the blur found a use for the arms. Down to the nubs, the blur spun the arms around and used each one as a dagger, plunging the tips into the eyes of two screaming patrons.

A chalice ran screaming past the blur and Adrian could only watch in abject horror as the chalice had her head torn off and tossed aside.

Then Adrian saw Carl, moving up on the blur, a ruthless Bowie knife in his right hand. Adrian remembered the knife well, the two having been hanging out together on Kneeland Street at the Army/Navy store when Carl bought it.

With a throaty yell, Carl leaped at the blur, but as he hung in the air, mouth and eyes wide in attack mode, knife gleaming in the gloom, the blur spun, ripped the knife from his hand and then gutted him with it, all in the blink of an eye.

Carl's insides splashed onto the floor amid a hot sticky puddle of blood and viscera as his body continued its motion to roll and come up against another vampire.

"No!" Adrian screamed but stayed rooted to his spot, not knowing what to do. Meanwhile, the blur wasn't idle, whipping amongst the other vampires and ripping heads off and severing limbs in a cyclone of blows and impacts that seemed to shake the very foundation of the nightclub.

Adrian glanced to his right to see the two bouncers, both bodies now missing their heads and one having no arms. Something came up against his feet and Adrian looked down to see it was the bouncer with the dark eyes, the orbs now glazed over in death. Blood still spurted from the gaping neck where the head had been separated from the torso, a few inches of spine twitching like a dying worm.

Adrian kicked it away with a grunt of disgust and weighed his options.

He could try and fight whatever was destroying his friends. Or he could try to reach the exit and escape. To his right the shattered doorway beckoned, the cool air from the night seeping in.

The blur took off another head and tore the legs from a screaming chalice, the legs becoming large clubs to beat down all that stood in its way.

Adrian tried to get a better look at the blur, to see what it could be that was decimating his fellow vampires, but all he saw was the obsidian hair and a blur of bare shoulders. As the blur paused for a fraction of a second, his eyes picked up the ornate tattoos on the blur's shoulder, both in the shape of stars. But then the blur was in motion again and a spray of blood was left in its wake as it weaved through the dancers of the club like a scythe through wheat.

Adrian had been standing at the edge of the dance floor for no more than a few seconds, and in that time, the blur had killed every single person in the nightclub.

Then, as if in slow motion, the blur paused and finished off the last vampire. This one was a man, tall, with large shoulders and bulging muscles that could have crushed a normal assailant with ease.

The man managed to grab the blur, and for the first time since entering the club and seeing the carnage, Adrian saw what was killing his people.

It was one of them—a suicide angel.

The angel's hair was so black it seemed to absorb any light in the club touching it, sapping it into itself like a sponge to water. The angel was a woman, or more precise, a girl, a waif of one to be exact. Her limbs were thin and seemed like they could be snapped in two easily. The angel wore tight-black leather pants and a halter top, also black, the white skin of her shoulders exposed to the air. The two star tattoos seemed to gleam in the wan light, as if they had a mind of their own.

All in all, the angel looked frail, thin and harmless.

But looks could be deceiving as the larger vampire was about to find out.

Adrian watched in amazement as the angel reached out and grabbed his head, placing her thumbs over his eyes. As the man tried to break the angel's arms, the girl pressed her thumbs deep into his eyes sockets, crushing his orbs to mush and then continuing until her thumbs were so deep in his skull they disappeared. She flashed perfect teeth and her eyes went wide as she squeezed the head in her hands. Like a rotten melon, the man's head seemed to give out, such as a deflated balloon would do when gently released of its air. The skull cracked and brains slid out to spill onto the floor, splashing at the man's feet.

When the angel released her grip, the head was nothing but a mangled mess of bone and brain matter. The hands holding her arms released their grip and she was dropped to the floor where she landed effortlessly, her grace that of a gymnast. The dead vampire swayed on legs that were devoid of control and the body toppled to the floor, crashing like a tree in the forest after a lightning strike.

The angel wiped her bloody hands on her halter top and then spun to face Adrian. Her porcelain skin was streaked with crimson, bloody rivulets dripping off her chin to splatter onto her boots–black of course.

Adrian was still motionless, as only seconds had passed since the large man had grabbed the angel and was killed, and Adrian quickly came to the realization that his time had run out.

As he looked around the club, past the angel, he realized he was the only one still standing.

Everyone else was dead.

In every direction there was nothing but torn and ripped body parts, a charnel house where blood was the currency. Offal and copper filled his senses and he breathed out as he gagged on the stench. Yes, blood he craved, but not like this. Vampires were a civilized race, and wanton carnage was not in their makeup, though myth would say otherwise.

He was about to take a step back, run to the bathroom and bar the door, maybe try and escape through the bathroom window, and pray the angel might not follow–leave him alive–when she crossed the dance floor in a blur that was too fast to see.

One second she was standing over the body of the dead vampire, then she was standing in front of Adrian, her head no higher than his chest. Up close, she looked like she was a teenager, a Goth one at that, with the dark hair, clothes and tattoos, but as those eyes bore into him, he knew what stood before him was not innocent, and was in fact the deadliest creature he had ever had the misfortune to come across.

Remembering the rumors about the suicide angels–for he knew that was what she was–and seeing first hand what she could do, he knew to attempt to battle the angel would be useless after witnessing her power, so Adrian tried one last ditch effort to save himself. He said, "Why? Why are you doing this to us?"

If he expected a reply, he received none, the angel mute to the point of frustration.

As Adrian looked down at her, at her wide orbs, he would have believed if he'd had a chance to think about it, that he would have seen his coming death swirling in her cold eyes. But he didn't.

Faster than his eyes could track, both of the angel's hands snapped out and grabbed his head. He had time for one quick yell of, "No!" before the suicide angel twisted and tore his head clean off his shoulders.

Dark blood shot through the jagged stump of his neck to hit the ceiling and the overhead fluorescent lighting– the ones still intact.

With his severed head in her hands, Adrian looked out through eyes that didn't believe what he was seeing. In the seconds his brain remained active, he saw his decapitated body drop to the floor and lay still, blood still spurting from the neck stump; then he was spinning as his eyes took in the destruction around him for the last time.

But the oxygen in his brain was fleeting, and as he looked out on death in its truest form, his vision began to dim, similar to the battery in a camcorder slowly fading as the power ran out. Then his vision shut down and everything went dark.

A second later, his severed head was tossed into a booth to fall between the legs of the same chalice he'd fed upon only minutes ago. The chalice was very dead, her throat torn out by razor-sharp fingernails, her blood pooling out to drip onto the floor in a steady pattern.

The angel scanned the nightclub, admiring her handiwork, her face impassive; her eyes hard and void of emotion.

Nothing moved with the exception of the shifting of the bodies as they still sputtered blood, as gravity helped them to settle into the pile of corpses now in the center of the dance floor.

A mangled body slid off a table in another booth, and the sounds of splashing– something wet landing in something wetter. Overhead, the light fixtures, the ones still intact, swayed back and forth, casting shadows where none once were as they swung back and forth. One light fixture in the far corner, hanging only by wires, finally broke free and crashed to the floor in a halo of sparks, as electricity hissed and sparked in the ceiling; the smell of ozone joining the redolence of death.

On the left corner wall, even with a picture of the Boston skyline, a security camera was mounted, its dull red light still blinking, recording the entire tableau of death.

Behind the wall the camera was mounted to, was an office, and in this office was a small monitor sitting on a table to the right of a desk for the nightclub manager.

The manager wouldn't be returning to the office, for his quartered body was laying on the dance floor under a dozen others.

In crystal clear, glorious black and white the monitor showed the destroyed night club, and the single figure standing in the midst of the destroyed bodies, a small VCR to the left of it.

On the monitor, the suicide angel stood covered in blood, the lack of color on the monitor taking away from the horror of what had happened this night.

The angel looked around, her eyes seeming to study each corner of the nightclub, and then she paused as she stared directly at the camera.

The suicide angel flashed into motion and was gone, only to pop up directly in front of the camera lens, her face covered in gore–but without the color of the blood, her face was still beautiful, almost heavenly.

Black hair, deep eyes that seemed to shift in intensity, the angel glared at the camera, her head tilting to the side in curiosity; until she figured out she was being filmed.

In a move too fast for the camera to record, her hand snapped out, and her blood-red palm–seeming gray on the screen thanks to the lack of color–was exposed for a brief second before she grabbed the camera and tore it from the wall.

The monitor went dark.

BEST MEAT EVER

"I'm telling you, this place has the best steaks in town," Tim said to his girlfriend as they walked along the avenue.

"I've heard that before, Tim," Alice replied cynically. Tim was a connoisseur of meat. He would take her out almost every Saturday night to some new steak or rib joint, and it wasn't unheard of for Tim to drive two and three hours to reach the newest restaurant he'd found on the internet.

"No, Alice, I'm serious this time. I heard some great stuff about his place. They've got steaks as thick as your fist and for next to nothing."

"That doesn't sound too profitable." She crossed her arms as they stopped at the corner, the light was red and the cars were buzzing past. She pressed the button on the pole so it would change and they could cross safely.

"You'd think so," he said. "But the owner must buy in bulk or something." He laughed as he clapped his hands together, rubbing them greedily. "Hell, I don't care why he does it. I'm just glad he does!"

The light changed, halting traffic, and they crossed, surrounded by other pedestrians off to who knows where.

"If this place is so great," she said, "then how come you never heard about it before today? I mean, you go to every single one you can find and this one's right in your backyard, so to speak?"

"Yeah, I know, weird, huh? It seems this one just popped up a few weeks ago. No advertisement, nothin'. It wasn't there and then it was."

"So we're going there now?" she asked.

He nodded. "Yes, but like I said, I promised dinner *and* a movie so we'll go see a movie first and then have a late dinner."

"Okay, I want to see *Impossible Chances*?"

He rolled his eyes. "That new movie with the guy who is kind of a geek but the really hot chick falls for him anyway, right?"

She nodded.

"I don't blame you, it's so original."

"I don't care, I like those movies and you said I could pick," she said.

"Fine," he sighed. "It's your choice, but then we get to go eat."

"Deal," she replied and the two continued on.

Two and a half hours later, the movie now over, the young couple were back on the street making their way to the restaurant.

"God, I can't believe how long that movie was," he said.

"It was for character development."

"Character development? More like developing an ulcer. God, the lines were so clichéd, who wrote that thing, a fifteen year old girl?"

"Are you sure you know where this place is?" Alice asked, changing the subject. She had liked the movie and didn't want to hear him trash it. They'd been walking for almost a half hour and she didn't like the neighborhood they were in. The word 'seedy' came to mind.

"Yeah, I got the directions off the internet; it's only a few more blocks away."

"But you said that three blocks ago, my feet are killing me," she complained.

He frowned. "Hey, it's not my fault. I told you not to wear heels," he said and pointed to her black pumps. "I said *sensible shoes.*"

She frowned. "These are sensible shoes…for me, anyway."

He rolled his eyes as he wrapped an arm around her waist. "Hey, baby, I'm so excited to eat at this place I'll carry you if I have to. Even that terrible movie hasn't ruined my appetite."

She smiled then, her mood lightening. "I just may take you up on that offer to carry me if we don't get there soon." She shifted to the side, her short blouse riding up on her waist, and Tim's eyes went right to the exposed skin, his manhood stirring slightly.

"What're you looking at?" she asked coyly. Not wanting to come off as a horndog, Tim pointed to her tattoo. It was of a red butterfly with a carnation in its mouth. He had never seen one like it before and loved to look at it, as it was on her back, and he would stare at it as he made love to her from behind. He was on a first name basis with that tattoo, so to speak.

"Nothing, baby, just admiring your tattoo."

"Uh-huh," she replied but she leaned over and kissed him. "This place better be as good as you say it is."

"Oh, it will be, it will be." The two walked on, weaving in and out of the pedestrian traffic as Tim's mouth watered in expectation of the steak he would be eating in less than an hour.

Chef Vito Arturo stared at the almost empty shelves of the meat locker, shaking his head in disgust.

He was out of inventory…again.

Reaching into his pocket, he pulled out his cell phone and pressed the first number on speed dial. Seconds later, the phone beeped and another voice picked up.

"What?" the small voice said through the speaker.

"We're almost out, I need more product," Chef Vito said.

"I'm workin' on it," the voice said. "It's getting' scarce out here. The bums are gettin' wise to me."

"That's not my problem, that's yours," Vito said firmly. "I pay you to keep my supply coming and that's what I want you to do."

"Yeah, well, the supply is gettin' thin. It might be time to pick up and move on to the next city."

Vito ground his teeth, frustrated. "Is it really that bad out there?"

There was a pause, then the voice said, "Yeah, it's that bad. The bums know their fellow buddies are gone, there's almost no one on the streets anymore, they all go to homeless shelters now. Pickings are slim out here, Vito."

Vito sighed heavily, accepting what he knew was inevitable. "Fine, just try to get me one more specimen and then we'll call it a day here. I want to get in one more crowd for dinner tonight and maybe tomorrow, too, then we'll pack it up."

"Sounds good, and I'm sure I can rustle up at least one more," the voice said. "I gotta go, I see a potential target now. Man, he looks down on his luck."

The phone went dead and Vito ended his side of the call, slid the phone back into his pocket, and stepped deeper into the meat locker to study what was left of his supply.

The right side of the cold room was empty, but the left side still had a few items here and there. Vito was already going through the menu in his mind, thinking where he could use what piece of meat for in a recipe.

He went to the shelf and picked up the first cut of meat. It was a human leg, as were all the meat cuts in his cold room. The leg had been from a large male and he stared at it as he pressed the meat with his thumb, testing elasticity.

"Hmm, I could make a nice roast with this one," he said to himself as he set the leg down and went to the next piece of meat.

Four human arms lay stacked like cordwood, each wrapped in plastic. He studied them and decided he could make a nice stew after carving the meat from the bones. The fingers could be used as a substitute for Buffalo wings. He always found it amazing how after he slathered them with sauce and kept the lighting in the dining room low, how the customers never noticed it wasn't chicken they were eating.

He picked up a severed head–one of five– and held it in his hands. The brains could be used in a red gravy. When cooked, the brains resembled tripe and the eyes of each head could be added to a soup; of course he would tell the customers the eyes belonged to lambs.

Setting the head down, he went to the remaining three torsos. The insides had been gutted and were now nothing but hollow cavities. Two of the torsos had been woman and the breasts had been removed to be used in a stir fry. He planned on smoking the torsos, then slicing the ribs and marinating them in barbeque sauce. When they were finished, they tasted better than beef.

Of course, it looked like he might not get that chance now that supplies were growing thin.

The homeless population took a while to catch on, but when they did, they began staying off the streets. Once that happened, Vito had to move on to the next city. He only took the homeless, as anyone else would be missed and investigations conducted. But no one cared about the homeless and the meat was free, so he had an astronomical profit margin.

It wasn't hard to rent a building that had the necessary kitchen, add a few tables and paint the walls, keep the lighting low to hide any defects, and he was open for business.

He went to a bucket containing livers, hearts, and kidneys of the slaughtered bodies.

The livers would be sautéed with mushroom and onions, the kidneys sliced and made into a pâté. As for the hearts, well, he still hadn't figured out what to do with them. As the major organ in the human body, the heart was all muscle, so it was very tough and chewy. He'd tried steaming, frying, boiling, and roasting it, but no matter what he attempted, the heart always reminded him of eating rubber.

Vito had begun eating human flesh back in Vietnam. He was a POW for more than five years and in that time, when he and the other prisoners were starving, they had no choice but to do things so extreme the average American would have preferred to die than do them.

At first it had been foul, and he had fought to keep the meat down, but as time went by, he found the taste had grown on him.

The people he and the other prisoners ate were of their own group, ones that died from sickness or other ailments. But for each one that died, the rest of the group thrived, and by the time he was rescued, he actually had some meat on his bones, and didn't look like an emaciated POW should look. Of course, the meat on his bones, so to speak, wasn't actually his, but he was alive and that was all that mattered.

When he returned to the states, he found he still craved human meat, and no substitute would suffice. Always the entrepreneur, he figured out a way to feed his habit and make a living at the same time.

The voice on the cell phone was Matt, another POW who had acquired the taste for human flesh. Together, they were a team. Matt found them and Vito cooked them up, and the two maintained their hunger. Vito reached out and took the bucket of organs, then carried it out of the meat locker and to the stainless steel table in the center of the kitchen. It was time to begin preparing the house special for the dinner rush that would be arriving in only a few short hours.

He pulled out the livers, set them on a cutting board, and began chopping them into pieces, his stomach already rumbling with hunger from the odor of fresh human meat.

But there was no time to eat right now. He needed to get the torsos into the oven, trim the meat from the leg, fry up the kidneys for the pâté, and chop the fingers for the mock Buffalo wings.

He smiled to himself as he worked, thinking how truly stupid the customers were. Slap some ground meat on a bun and tell them it was beef and no one ever questioned it, they just dug in, for all purposes nothing but ravenous dogs in a feeding frenzy.

He chuckled at the thought. The customers were just so damn gullible.

Tim and Alice arrived at Vito's well after the dinner rush. Stepping inside into the small foyer, the restaurant was empty, no other diners present. It looked as if the place was closed for the night.

"Are you sure this is the place?" Alice asked. "No one's in here."

Tim made an aggravated face. "Well, of course not. We took so long getting here we're just lucky it's still open. Guess we're the last customers of the night."

"Oh, so you're blaming me that the movie was filled up and we had to wait till the next showing, is that it?"

"Yes, Alice, I am. We could have gone to see that new action flick; we didn't have to wait for an hour and a half to see that stupid movie. And for your information, it was terrible."

"Well, I'm so sorry you didn't like it as you've so plainly stated, but we did something I wanted for once," she argued while crossing her arms over her chest. "You know, I didn't even want to come to this stupid restaurant, I did it for you, to make you happy. I don't even eat meat that much, you know that." She looked hurt and Tim felt bad.

"I'm sorry, baby, I guess I have been a little bit of a jerk. Look, we're here now. Hopefully, I can get them to make me something, even if it's to go. I didn't come all this way for nothing."

He looked up to see a man in a dirty apron walking from the back of the restaurant. He had dark hair and his Italian descent was obvious to a blind man.

"Can I help you folks?" the man asked. "I'm Vito, I own this place."

"Uh, hi, yeah, uhm, I heard a lot of great stuff about your meat and I was hoping we could get a table." Tim wrapped an arm around Alice's waist.

Vito scratched his head. "Geez, pal, I'd like to help you, but I'm cleaned out. I get limited amount of stock and it's all gone."

Tim wasn't about to give up that easily. "Oh, come on, sir, surely you must have something lying around. Look, like I said, I came a long way to get here. I just found out you even existed and I was really hoping I could get a steak or a burger or something. I've just got to try out your food."

Vito shook his head. "Sorry, like I said, I'm all out."

"But you don't understand," Tim protested, "I've been dying to come here, you can't send me home, not without at least trying some of your meat."

Vito had a feeling this guy wasn't going to take no for an answer so decided he might as well just give the man what he wanted and send him on his way. He scratched his head and smiled at Alice politely. "Well, I'm supposed to get a short order delivered tonight but I don't know exactly when that might be. The order could show up in five minutes or forty-five."

"I don't care, we'll wait!" Tim yelled happily, excited that he wasn't going to be turned away.

Vito mulled it over for a few seconds as he let his eyes play over Alice. She was an attractive woman and he was a red-blooded man.

Finally, Vito sighed. "Fine, have a seat, you two, and I'll get you some drinks. My waitress has gone home for the night so I'll be serving you."

"That's fine, that's fine, really, we're not fussy," Tim said as Vito led them to a table near the kitchen doors.

"What do you want to drink while you wait?"

"A couple of beers would be great," Tim said.

"Okay, two beers comin' right up. You care what kind?"

Tim shook his head. "A beer's a beer, right, Alice?"

She shrugged. "Whatever." She wasn't pleased at all.

Vito nodded and left to get the beers and returned a minute later. After setting them down, he grinned once more. "You two get comfortable. When the order arrives I'll whip you up somethin' tasty. All right?"

"Yes, yes, thank you again, you've been great. I'll be sure to tell my friends about this place."

Vito nodded at that, knowing by the time this guy's friends arrived, he would be long gone and setting up in another city.

"I'll be in the kitchen. I have some more work to do. If you need anything, just yell. We're informal around here. But don't come into the kitchen." His face grew hard. "We don't allow the customers into the kitchen."

"Okay, thanks," Tim replied, barely noticing Vito's change in demeanor as he walked away, pushing through the swinging door to the kitchen to disappear. A few seconds later, pots and pans could be heard rattling as he worked.

Tim opened his beer and sighed happily. "Well, we're here and we're gonna eat. All's right with the world."

"Is that what you think?" Alice asked. "Look at this place, it's a dump," she waved her hand around her, signifying the restaurant. Tim looked at the other tables, the floors, and the walls. There was new paint on the walls, but even in the dim light, he could tell it was tossed on haphazardly. Some of the tables had broken legs hastily fixed with duct tape and the table he sat at was wobbly and had chips on its top. Some of the chairs didn't match and the floor was dirty, but Tim shrugged it all off. "It's ambience," he said. "Any good restaurant doesn't need a lot of fancy shit, the food speaks for itself."

"That's your answer?" she asked.

"Yes, it is, now drink your beer and try to relax, I want to enjoy this and so far your being a drag."

She sighed and took a sip of her beer. "I know I am, but…well, Christ, this place is a dump."

"Maybe, but it's got the best meat this side of the city so be nice. I went to your movie so let me have this, please?" He batted his eyes like he was trying to romance her.

She grinned slightly, and a small chuckle escaped her lips. "You know I hate it when you do that, you look so goofy."

"I thought you loved it when I was goofy?"

"I do," she said.

He reached for her hand and took it gently into his.

"We good?" he asked.

"For now."

The couple sat quietly in the empty restaurant and drank their beers while in the kitchen, the clatter of pans filtered out like New Wave music.

An hour later and Tim was growing impatient. Vito still didn't have his meal ready and it was going on midnight. And Alice was angry, and for the past twenty minutes had been demanding to leave.

"No, it can't be that much longer," Tim said.

"I don't care, I want to leave. I'm hungry and I'm tired of waiting."

"Look, we've been here this long, what's a little longer?" he asked.

On the table in front of them were three more beers each. Vito had apologized twice and said the delivery should be arriving soon, but the delivery man wasn't answering his phone.

Alice stood up, crossing her arms over her chest. "No, that's it, I've had it. I've been asking to leave for almost a half hour and it's clear you have some sort of obsession over this place, well fine, I'm going to the bathroom and then I'm leaving."

"Oh, come on, Alice, don't be that way," he said, reaching for her arm.

She pulled it away and took a step backward. "No, forget it, it's too late now. I'm leaving and there's nothing you can say to talk me out of it."

His face grew dark. "Fine, go then, I'll eat by myself, thanks for nothing," he said and waved her away.

She made an aggravated noise from deep in her throat and headed off to the bathroom, leaving Tim to mull over her actions. As far as she was concerned, she was already gone, and was now forgotten as he stewed in his frustration.

Alice went to the rear of the restaurant, assuming that was where the bathrooms were. She wanted to go before she left. It was so gloomy, the lights on so low she could barely see, let alone read anything, and she found herself stumbling around. She found a small hallway and she took it, now her bladder letting her know it needed to be emptied. Those beers had caught up to her and she hurried down the hall, searching for the door marked **Women's Room**.

She could hear the clatter of pans again, and before she realized it, she reached the end of the hall, pushed through a small door, and found herself in the kitchen, to the far right of the swinging door Vito used after talking to them.

As she moved into the kitchen to ask Vito where the bathrooms were, she saw the man was standing at a table in the center of the room. He was cutting something.

A shelf of pans was in her way and she slowly moved closer, hesitant about bothering the chef. Would he be mad that she was in his kitchen? Perhaps, she had known some cooks to get very upset if you entered their domain and he had said they weren't allowed in his kitchen. But she was a woman and an attractive one, too. Usually she would just show some skin and bat her eyes and most men would melt and do anything for her.

When she reached the shelf, she peered through the stacked pans to see Vito more clearly, and when her eyes went down to what he was cutting up, her eyes went wide with shock.

It was a human head, the skull cracked open like a pineapple. The brains were on a butcher block cutting board and Vito was chopping them into small pieces where he then placed them in a steaming kettle.

Alice's eyes went to the head, seeing the empty eye sockets, the eyes now gone. The mouth was hanging open and the tongue was missing, the visage locked in a silent scream for all eternity.

Her mouth fell open, mimicking the severed head, and she felt her breath lodge in her throat. What she was seeing was a mistake, a gag, it had to be. But as she watched in horror, Vito picked up the head, scooped out the remaining brains and set the empty head to the side, to then take out another, fresher head. She watched in absolute terror as he used the cleaver and chopped at the skull, the process reminding her of how someone opens a coconut.

She felt her mind swirling as he cracked the skull and once more scooped out the brains. She saw the head was female, a ragged, aged face, like a cocaine user or someone withered by sickness. She had no idea she was looking at one more street person, the visage corrupted by living on the streets.

She knew she needed to leave now, to get Tim and run for the front door; they needed to tell the police what was happening in this house of horrors. But as she went to turn around, a handle of a pot was extended on the shelf and she bumped it with her shoulder.

The pan rattled and Vito looked up immediately, his eyes seeing her instantly as she looked back at him in petrified shock, for all purposes resembling a little girl caught taking a cookie from the cookie jar before dinner, her hand in the jar upon discovery.

Like a striking panther, Vito was moving, and before she knew what was happening, he reached her, locking her right wrist in his hand like a vise.

He shook his head as he glared at her and she saw genuine regret in his face. "I'm sorry you saw that, honey. Now you leave me no choice."

She opened her mouth to scream, to call out to Tim to come save her, but before she could utter a signal screech, Vito's fist came around and sent her into the dark oblivion of unconsciousness.

As she fell into oblivion, she realized she'd found a place to go to the bathroom, as warmth slid down her leg.

Tim looked up when Vito exited the kitchen.

"Good news, my delivery finally came, I'll have your meal ready in about ten to fifteen minutes."

"Well, it's about time. My girlfriend already left and I have to tell you, I was about to leave, too."

"Then my guy came just in time. So let me get you another beer and in a few minutes you'll be eating the best meat this side of the city." He left then, returning a moment late with another beer, flashed Tim a smile, and went into the kitchen.

Tim pulled out his cell phone, dialing Alice's number. She only left a few minutes ago and maybe she was still close by and would return if asked nicely. He frowned when it went right to voice mail and he left her a brief message, apologizing, asking her to come back, and that he loved her. He set the cell phone on the table and took a sip of his beer. Well, at least it would be worth it in the end as Vito was making his meal.

Twenty minutes later and Tim was growing impatient once more. He was about to get up and go to the kitchen and tell Vito he was tired of waiting and was finally leaving, when the man pushed through the swinging door with a plate of steaming food.

"Ah, at last, I was about to leave," Tim said as Vito set the food down in front of him. Tim breathed in, the savory aroma of the meat causing his taste buds to water.

"I'm glad you didn't. This is a very special cut. Tender to the point it'll melt in your mouth." He raised his hands in front of him like he was pushing an imaginary person. "Eat, go, enjoy, there's steak sauce on the table but I doubt if you'll want any. The spices I season with are usually enough for even the fussiest palate."

"Well, it sure smells good, what is this beef or pork?"

Vito ignored the question. "Okay, so if you need anything just yell, I have to clean up in the back. It's to close for the night." He went to the front door and turned the sign around so it now read **CLOSED**.

Tim nodded, distracted by the heady aroma of the food. There was also a baked potato as well as a side of buttered corn, though he pushed both onto a small side plate used for bread. He'd come here to eat meat, not potatoes and vegetables.

The meat on his plate was quite pale, though it resembled a rump roast. It was a healthy cut and covered in peppercorn and Tim decided he had waited long enough. Cutting with his knife, he stabbed the piece he'd carved and placed it in his mouth.

It was tangy, the flavor something he'd never had before. He tried to put his finger on it. Rabbit? Venison? Ostrich? No, it wasn't one of them. He wondered if it was some endangered species, perhaps even horse or bear. Hell, it could be dog for all he knew; but as he took another bite, he decided he didn't care. It was fantastic.

As grease slid down his chin, and juice slipped out of the corners of his mouth, he devoured the meat like it was his last meal.

When he had finished on one side, he found a bone went down the middle so he turned the meat over and began working on the bottom. The juice had seeped out of the meat and the crust wasn't as hard as it should be here, the peppercorn coating falling off in some spots.

This shouldn't have happened but sometimes not every recipe goes as planned.

Tim could have cared less and he dug in, slicing thick chunks off and shoving them into his mouth. It was heavenly, the best roast he'd ever eaten in his life. He knew he would be coming back here every week from now on, as he was already hooked on the flavorful meat.

It was as he was carving the end of the roast that he paused for a second, his eyes seeing something under the coating. The peppercorn had fallen off in this section, exposing the fatty tissue of the meat, and as he looked closer, Tim's mouth fell open, his eyes went wide and he began to taste bile, the entire contents of his stomach threatening to explode out of his esophagus.

There, on the corner of the roast, as plain as day, was the unmistakable tattoo of a red butterfly with a carnation in its mouth.

His mind tried to tell him he was wrong, mistaken, that this was some kind of sick joke, but he knew this wasn't the case, for he had stared at that tattoo countless times as he made love to Alice.

While he had thrust deeply into her, his eyes had studied every nuance, every dot of ink on the tattoo on her back, and there was no doubt he was looking at the same one now.

Even the pedals on the carnation were exact, right down to the right pedal being slightly off, as if the artist's hand had slipped at the last second.

He dropped his knife to clatter off the plate and leaned back in his seat, feeling dizzy and nauseous at the same time. His world was spinning as he tried to wrap his head around what he was experiencing. The most flavorful meat he'd ever eaten, the most juiciest cut of flesh, was in fact, his *girlfriend*!

The dining room seemed to go dark as he tried to fight off the wave of dizziness filling him and he stood up, staggering across the dining room, knowing he needed to leave, to tell someone what had happened, and as soon as possible. He felt his stomach heaving yet again and it was all he could do not to vomit over his shoes.

He stumbled to the front door, his mind reeling with the reality that he had *eaten* his girlfriend, and that it was the best thing he'd ever tasted, he found himself blocked by a shadow.

He stopped and looked up to see a man he didn't know standing perfectly still and he opened his mouth to tell him what had happened, that they needed to get the police, when he saw the man held a large knife.

Tim gasped in fear and tried to take a step backward, but as he did, he backed up into another body standing there, and before he could react, an arm came up and hovered in front of his face.

He saw the arm's hand held a large knife as well, and before he could so much as scream, the knife came close and slid across his throat, slicing his carotid artery and jugular in one smooth motion.

Gagging on blood, he pressed his hands to his bleeding throat but there was no staunching the flow. With each beat of his heart, he died a little more. He slipped to the floor to lie prone, now staring up at the ceiling with eyes that wouldn't see.

Vito looked down on Tim with a shaking of his head and he gestured to the new man in the dining room.

"It's about time you got here, Matt. I thought I was gonna have to take care of this guy on my own. His girlfriend saw too much and I had to kill her, then I had to stall this guy until you got back."

"How'd you do it? Keep 'im here?" Matt asked.

"I carved up his girlfriend and served her with a peppercorn coating, that's how. Now come on, help me get him into the back. From what he said, no one knows either of them came here tonight.

Once they're cut up into steaks and filets, no one will ever know they were here. Get his arms, I got the feet," Vito ordered him.

Tim was falling into a darkness he would never awaken from as the two men picked him up and carried him into the kitchen. As they set him on the large stainless steel table in the middle of the kitchen, Tim's head fell to the side and when it did, he found himself staring into Alice's dead eyes, her severed head glaring at him, as if in accusation.

Next to her head were her arms, now dissected and laying carelessly like large chicken drumsticks. Her legs were off to the side, just at the edge of his peripheral vision, and he saw her torso had been sliced in twain and gutted, the lower half missing—which was what he'd eaten.

He wanted to tell her he was sorry for getting her into this, and that he was sorry for her death, but before he could so much as gurgle one syllable, darkness began to fall and his heart beat for the last time.

As he let out his final breath, he could hear Vito talking to Matt.

"I want to get this guy cut up before I go home tonight. There's a dinner party for twenty coming in tomorrow and this guy'll be the perfect special. After that, we'll pack up and head to 'Frisco."

Tim's last thought as a connoisseur of meat was that he hoped he would be served in a peppercorn crust, because though it had been Alice he was eating, he had to admit, it was still the best meat ever.

BITTER FRUIT

Martin cut into the plump steak on his plate, watching as the juices pooled around it. It was medium rare, just the way he liked it. The outside was charred and the inside was warm and pink.

He liked his meat the way he liked his women.

With the cut piece of meat on his fork, he slowly raised it to his lips and placed it in his mouth.

Ever so slowly, he pulled the meat off the fork with his teeth and let it roll around on his tongue. The juices began to coat his taste buds and he rolled his eyes in ecstasy.

God, this is better than sex, he thought.

When he bit into the succulent morsel and a burst of juices filled his mouth, he actually moaned in pleasure. Chewing ever so slowly, he swallowed, relishing the feeling as it slid down his esophagus and into his stomach.

He paused, letting the taste remain on his tongue, and then cut himself a new piece. He repeated the process yet again, until finally coming to the last piece.

It was with a heavy heart that he stabbed the morsel and ate it.

But he took joy in knowing there was more where that came from, and though he knew he should stop, he decided to have himself another steak.

What the hell, he thought. I deserve it. *I've been working very hard lately and this treat is mine.*

Placing his fork and knife on the table, he stood up and crossed the kitchen.

But he didn't go to the refrigerator to get another steak. Instead, he went to the basement door to the left of the fridge.

The door was padlocked with a combination lock and he quickly dialed in the combination, then opened the door.

A cool breeze wafted over him and he detected the smell of dampness.

But he detected something else in the odor, something that made his loins quiver with excitement. He took another dish from the nearby counter and descended the stairs leading into the dark basement.

A single light bulb hung from the ceiling. It was old, with a pull chain. When he pulled the chain, the naked bulb illuminated a twelve-by-fourteen foot room. Cinder blocks made up the walls and a thick rug covered the stone floor to help soak up noise. The cinder blocks were thick enough that sound couldn't penetrate to the outside world.

If he wanted to, he could scream his head off in his basement and his neighbors would never hear him.

There were no windows, the three having been bricked up years ago, and no light filtered in from outside.

In every respect the basement was a tomb, or worse, a torture chamber.

There was a butcher block table in the middle of the room and plastic sheeting was underneath it to protect the carpet from blood spray. Along the outer wall was a peg board, and on this were an assortment of tools.

Handsaws, hammers and screwdrivers were a few of the tools available. On a workbench below the peg board were more tools, these larger in size. A skill saw, jigsaw and an electric drill were the main ones, but an electric sander and nail gun were also there, both looking as if they hadn't been used in years, both covered in dust.

The saws however looked like they were used a lot, and there were small red dots on them, looking as if paint had splattered. It looked like paint, but it wasn't.

It was something far worse.

Martin walked over to the workbench, barely glancing at the table and what lay on its surface, tied down by all four limbs, the ropes wrapped underneath the table to hold it in place.

He ignored the whimpering and muffled cries for mercy behind the gag in the woman's mouth, but instead concentrated on the assortment of knives on the workbench.

Taking a large carving knife, he raised it to his face, seeing his reflection in its shiny surface. He smiled slightly at his visage and then turned to face the strapped and hogtied figure on the card table.

He stared at the naked and gagged woman, her eyes glaring back at him, both of her dark-blue eyes as wide as dinner plates. Tears ran down the sides of her face and pooled near her head, while her legs and arms spasmed as she tried to free herself.

On her left leg, at her thigh, a large piece of meat had been sliced off, leaving a running, bloody wound. Blood had collected and congealed on the table and some had dripped off to land on the plastic. There, catching in an impression in the plastic and the rug beneath, it made a small pool.

Martin said nothing to her as he crossed the short distance separating them. There was no need to speak. After all, when a man goes to the supermarket, he doesn't talk to the steak he buys, does he? Or at least he didn't.

No, it would be foolish to talk to his supper.

She began to kick harder as he reached her, the knife in his hand already coming down to her untouched right leg. Without hesitation, he began cutting and slicing into the meat of her thigh and then curving it up as he finished the cut.

When he finished, the woman now screaming in agony behind her gag, he had himself a six inch piece of human steak.

He carried the steak to a plate on the workbench, and after placing the tender flesh on it, he began wiping his hands clean on a towel. There was a bucket of water with a spoonful of bleach at the end of the workbench and he dropped the knife in it. He would clean it later with the others in the bucket, but for now he wanted to eat his prize.

More blood dripped off the table and he wondered if he had accidentally cut an important artery or vein in the woman's leg. Truth be told, he wasn't very good with medical stuff and could have easily zigged with the knife when he should have zagged.

With a slight shrug, he figured if she bled out then he would simply dispose of her sooner rather than later.

He gave her one last glance as he held his plate of raw meat. He eyed her naked form, not even the slightest hint of sexual arousal crossing his mind. Though her breasts were perfectly formed and the junction between her thighs shaven to a V, her stomach flat, her buttocks well-rounded, he didn't see her in that way. To him, she was merely a meal, a cow laid out for the slaughter.

As the woman cried behind her gag and shook her head in pain and fear, he left the basement, turning off the single light bulb on his way to the kitchen. When he closed the basement door, the muffled sobs ceased…at least to his ears.

With the smell of cooking meat—reminiscent of pork—filling the kitchen, Martin daydreamed as he seasoned his meal. His stomach was content, but there was still room for more, and he knew he would really slow down and enjoy this second piece of heaven.

As he drifted off in reverie, he thought back to how he'd captured the woman now trapped in his basement. It had been so easy, really. He had wrapped his left arm in a sling and pretended it was broken, then had gone to the supermarket and waited until a half hour till closing. At that time of night, there was almost no one around and the lot was practically deserted.

He had then used his props of filled paper bags containing what looked like groceries, but were in fact empty cans and hollow packages of cookies and egg boxes.

He waited until a woman that caught his eye came out of the market, then he went to the rear of his van and made sure to drop the grocery bags sitting on the rear bumper onto the ground, spilling them everywhere.

With his arm in a sling and his small stature, no woman ever felt threatened by him and this woman was no different. As he dropped the groceries, she saw him, and as he bent down to try and pick them up one-handed, she came to his aid to help.

After she knelt down to help, he made a quick look around to make sure it was still clear, then he simply cracked her over the head with a small club he carried and rolled her into the rear of the van.

All this took less than a minute. Seconds later, he was driving out of the parking lot before the first can of soup had stopped rolling across the asphalt.

He always made sure to pick different supermarkets all across the state and sometimes he went further, driving to neighboring states. So far, the police had never put the multiple abductions together, and he always made sure to never leave a trace of the body when he was through with them. It was easy to get rid of the evidence when you ate most of it.

He flipped the meat in the pan over, the sizzle it made music to his ears. He sprinkled some fresh ground pepper and basil on it, then poured a tablespoon of olive oil over the top, the aroma heaven to his olfactory senses.

When it was cooked to his liking, he turned off the stove and slid the meat onto a fresh plate. He hated reusing dishes.

Sitting back down at the kitchen table, he poured himself a glass of red wine and began to eat, relishing the taste as only a true connoisseur of meat could.

He hadn't always been a cannibal, but after years of eating every meat known to man, he had become bored and had wanted something new. But there was nothing new to eat.

After eating everything from tiger from Africa to monkey brains from Nepal, he was craving something new.

That was when he heard about an underground club that served the juiciest meat of all…human.

It had taken a lot of money and favors to finally be invited to the exclusive club, but when he finally got in and sampled the ultimate cuisine, he found he was hooked for life.

Unfortunately, the club only met once a month. You see, it was extremely dangerous to take someone from the city and make them a meal. Homeless people were out because of their disease-ridden bodies, so someone had to be taken from the middle class. The owners of the club usually tried to take single people, most often with no close family, but if an opportunity arose they would take anyone.

Martin didn't like this once a month thing. He found human meat was something he wanted more than anything to be a weekly if not daily basis, and to wait an entire month to savor the sweet juices was too much for him to take.

So he went off on his own and found it worked well for him. And best of all, he didn't have to share with others.

Finishing the last bite of his steak, he leaned back and sighed. He found human meat reminded him of pork butt, but with an aftertaste he'd never known before. It was gamey with a hint of sweetness.

Retiring for the night, he placed his dish in the sink. After checking to make sure the house was secure, he went to bed, already planning on dreaming about frying up the woman's breasts with bell peppers and onions the next afternoon.

His plans for a lavish lunch were destroyed when he walked down the basement stairs and pulled the cord to the light.

The woman was dead, having bled out hours ago. It seemed he had indeed severed an artery or vein and she had bled to death sometime in the night. As he walked over, he was careful not to step in the congealing blood pools. Bending over, he touched the tip of his finger to a wide puddle and tasted it. It was cold, she had been dead for many hours.

For just a moment, he wondered if he could eat her anyway, but no sooner did the idea cross his mind then he brushed it away.

No, he wouldn't eat meat from a dead body, it had to be alive. He wasn't a ghoul, after all. And besides, that was what made it so savory, knowing that minutes before cooking, the meat had been on a living, breathing body.

With a heavy sigh, he went to the workbench and began donning his gear. First was a white, Mylar jumpsuit similar to a hazmat suit. Next he put on a clear faceplate, similar to what coroners use when performing an autopsy, so when they saw into the body, blood spray doesn't hit them in the face.

He picked up the jigsaw, plugged it in, and played out the extension cord. After testing it to make sure it was in working order, he walked over to the corpse and began working.

He had to dismember the arms and legs, sever the neck from the shoulders, then slice the torso into four parts. When he was done, he would drive out to the desert and bury the parts in four different places.

As he began dismembering the body, he began to hum.

He lasted almost a week before he knew he had to go on the hunt again. He was craving human meat worse than a pregnant woman craves pickles and ice cream.

He got into his costume again—the sling on his arm making him look like a wounded baby bird—then headed off to a supermarket three towns over.

The capture went off without a hitch, and soon he was driving back home with an unconscious woman in the back of the van.

As he drove, he glanced in the rearview mirror to study the shapely form of his captive.

She was in her later thirties by the look of it, with large breasts, a thin waist and dark brown hair. She had on a little too much makeup, as if she was trying to hide her complexion, but Martin barely gave it any thought. Makeup could be washed off after all and soon he would have her naked and strapped to his table.

He licked his lips at the thought, deciding he would start with this one's breasts first, thus making up for the loss of the last woman.

Pulling off the highway and onto the back roads, he made his way home, his stomach already growling in anticipation.

Hours later found him in his basement again, with a new body on his table. The woman was naked and strapped down, the same gag in her mouth as the previous woman. Martin didn't see any reason to change it.

He studied her curvaceous form and heaving breasts, his mouth salivating like a dog called to eat after missing a few meals. He couldn't wait to taste her.

He had been playing with the idea of drinking blood, wanting to savor it like a fine wine, and he decided this woman would be his first.

He used an ice pick and carefully slid the sharp tip into her left wrist, directly above the vein. As he slid out the ice pick, the blood began to flow, and he was waiting with a small basin. He let more than two glasses of plasma fill the basin before using a rag to tie off her wound. He didn't want her bleeding out…at least not yet.

The woman had yet to plead, beg or cry. All she did was stare at him, seeming as calm as if she was in her own bed. Martin decided it was shock and didn't pay it much mind.

He left her then, turning off the bulb and climbing the stairs.

Sitting by the fireplace, he sipped her blood from a crystal glass, smacking his lips at the coppery taste.

He decided he liked it and would now make it a habit each time he had a meal on his table. He also planned on using her blood as the base for a hearty sauce, figuring peppercorn would go with it nicely after he made a roast from a chunk of her well-formed thigh.

He loved the thigh and for good reason. It was one of the best places to take meat from a human being and he assumed all cannibals did it.

He watched some television, the news mostly, and he felt a nervous tingle when they began to cover an abduction from a local supermarket a few towns over. At this time there were no leads…just the way Martin liked it.

Two hours later and he was ready for the main course, a lovely sautéed piece of meat from the woman.

Rising from his chair, he went down into the basement and walked directly to the workbench. The knives were there, now cleaned, and he took a flensing knife. He crossed the room and hovered over the woman, who looked up at him with cold eyes.

She still didn't beg, didn't plead. It was as if she had resigned herself to death. They never did that. They always had hope that they would either be set free or escape. None had ever accepted they would die…at least until the very end.

Without pause, he carved a beautiful piece of flesh from her thigh and he saw she didn't cringe in pain. A single tear slid from her right eye, but otherwise she was stoic.

Not wanting to have to come back down for more later, he also carved off one of her breasts, thinking he could slice it into thick chunks and fry it up with vegetables.

He was about to leave when he went for a delicacy. With only two per captive, they had to be eaten and appreciated...savored like caviar.

Taking a soup spoon, he went to the top of the table and leaned over her face. With the skill of a surgeon or someone who had done this many times before, he slid the spoon into her right eye socket and carefully plucked the eyeball out. Done correctly, it barely caused the victim pain, though there was a lot of discomfort.

He planned on boiling it, and with some salt and pepper, it tasted a hundred times better than any hard-boiled egg he'd ever had. Three minutes would do nicely.

After placing his prizes on a small platter, he winked at her and left, the light going out as he pulled the cord to leave her in darkness.

He did hesitate halfway up the stairs for a few seconds, listening to her breathing hard through her nose. He expected to hear her crying now that she thought she was alone, but still there was nothing. He shook his head, not understanding.

Why was this woman so fearless when others were terrified?

Why didn't this woman beg and cower behind her gag, saying muffled prayers to God to save her?

And then he heard something that made no sense to him.

She began to laugh.

It was muffled, but it was definitely laughter.

He stood silently and listened for almost two full minutes before ascending the remaining stairs. He decided she must be mad with pain and fear, and instead of sobbing, was laughing instead.

That must be it. After all, what else could it be?

Closing the basement door when he reached the top, he shut out her laughing and carried his plate full of goodies to the kitchen to have himself a feast.

The next evening, after returning home from work, he felt his stomach rumbling and went down into the basement to carve himself a fresh piece of meat.

Reaching the bottom of the stairs, he turned on the naked bulb to see her looking right at him with her remaining eye. Even behind her gag, Martin could see she was grinning from ear to ear.

As he moved closer to her, she began to laugh again. It was crazed laughter, but it was definitely directed at him. He found himself growing angry.

His food wasn't supposed to laugh at him! It was supposed to grovel and beg for its life, not mock him. He was so angry he knew this would be the last meal he took from her before killing her.

He went to the workbench, chose a large carving knife, and went back to her. With a clean platter on the table beside her leg, he began carving off her remaining breast. He then sliced off more meat from her thighs and some from her upper arm. He didn't care for this part much, finding it tough, but had found with vinegar peppers and a lot of garlic, it made a nice stir fry.

When he finished taking what he wanted from her, Martin leered down at her still body. She had only stopped laughing to grimace at the pain she had suffered as he skillfully sliced her up like a Thanksgiving turkey.

It was a high point when she finally passed out from the pain. Her laughter was grating on him. It was as if she knew something he didn't and he felt terribly left out.

He took the knife and placed the edge to her neck. Though it wasn't really the best knife for the job, he knew it would do the trick. With one smooth motion, he slid it across her throat. Blood spurted forth to cover her chest and drop onto the table and then to the plastic covering the carpet. This was a new sheet of plastic, since replaced after the last 'meal' was disposed of.

As she bled out, he picked up his platter and left, already forgetting about the woman and looking forward to his meal.

He would take care of her tomorrow, what with cutting her up to destroy the corpse. It was Saturday and he would have plenty of time. He didn't work on Saturdays. As he turned off the light and ascended the stairs, closing the door when he reached the top, in the darkness, only the soft sound of dripping blood could be heard.

When Martin returned to the basement the next morning after a restful night's sleep, he was surprised to see the woman wasn't dead, though she was close.

By the amount of blood congealing on the plastic, it was clear she wasn't long for this world, but the simple fact she was still alive defied logic.

Crossing the distance and avoiding the pooling blood, he stopped so he was standing behind her head. As he looked down on her, he found she was staring up at him with her remaining eye.

And then she began to laugh again.

It wasn't strong, as she was too weak to really get into it, but there was no doubt in Martin's mind that, yes, she was laughing at him again.

As he looked down to her neck, he saw where the blood had slowed and realized he must not have done a very good job at severing her carotid artery. So yes, she had bled out, but much slower than normal, the incision allowing less blood to pump through the wound each time her heart beat.

She began to choke behind her gag and Martin reached down and pulled it off. No sooner did he do this then she spit blood, coughing and hacking. Spasms wracked her body and Martin thought she would die right then, but she didn't.

Her eye had closed as she coughed some more, but now it opened again. There was no fear in the single orb, only hatred and something else…something he couldn't put his finger on.

Her blood-covered lips curved up into a wan smile and she began to chuckle, blood bubbling forth each time she breathed.

She was very close to death.

Martin could take no more, and though he had never spoken to one of his 'meals' before, this time he did.

"Just what the hell is so funny to you? Hmm? I've eaten half of you and taken one of your eyes, and now you're about to die. I promise you, no one will ever find your body. Soon, you will be one of thousands of women who disappear every year without a trace. So I ask you, no, I demand that you tell me…just what in God's name do you find so damn amusing?"

She laughed again but stopped when it turned into a coughing fit. Spitting blood across the basement, she said in a voice that was more of a hoarse cackle than a whisper, "I'm laughing, you bastard, because you don't know what I know. But you will." She began to spasm and her single eye rolled up into the back of her head, her neck wound leaking more profusely as it was torn open, the congealing blood broken free to allow fresh plasma to seep forth.

She was about to die.

No, she can't die, not yet! Martin screamed in his mind. *She knows something I need to know! I can feel it!*

As she began to fade out, he grabbed her head on each side and held it in his hands.

"Don't die yet, you bitch! Tell me what you know! *Tell me!*"

He began shaking her head back and forth, the neck wound squishing as blood seeped from it. The flow had slowed to next to nothing, there was no more blood inside her.

Suddenly, her eye snapped back to the center of the socket and it focused on Martin one last time. With her last breath, she spit into his face, the blood striking him on the right cheek. He ignored it as he looked down at her now placid face.

She was dead.

And whatever she knew was gone with her.

His rage was so great he began to twist her head, turning it round and round like a corkscrew. With the neck already sliced open, it was easy for the head to slowly become separated from the torso, until with a dry *snap*, the spine cracked and split and he found himself holding her decapitated head in his hands.

Still filled with rage, he threw it against the wall. It slapped messily, leaving a semi-round red spot, the head rolling on the floor to stop with its left cheek facing down, droplets of blood dripping from the jagged neck.

Martin screamed to the ceiling, feeling cheated.

Eventually he calmed down, and when he was in full control, he began to chop up the headless corpse. He was so mad he didn't bother to don his gear. And soon, as blood splattered his face and he licked his lips clean, he found he was in a much better mood.

Four months later, and with many more bodies eaten, Martin found he wasn't feeling very well.

It had happened gradually over the past few months and now he was sluggish and barely had any energy to get out of bed in the morning. The worst part was his appetite had waned to next to nothing. Concerned there was something truly wrong with him, he went to his doctor to be examined.

The doctor had been rather quiet and had told Martin he would need to have him get some blood work done before he could say with any certainty what was wrong with him.

Once that was accomplished, the doctor would have a better insight into Martin's ailment.

The next week went by slow for Martin as he waited for his blood work results to come in. On the eighth day, he received a call from his doctor asking him to come to his office.

Martin had wanted to know right then what was wrong with him, but the doctor had been adamant about Martin coming in to see him face to face. With nothing else to do, Martin did as he was asked.

"I don't know how to tell you this, Martin, so I'm just going to come right out and say it," the doctor said from behind his desk a week later.

Martin, in one of the two chairs in the office, shifted uncomfortably as he waited for the news which he now knew wasn't good.

With a heavy sigh the doctor said, "I'm afraid you have a mutated form of AIDS. Not HIV either. It's progressed to a new strain of full-blown AIDS. Your white cell count is dreadfully low which explains your lack of appetite and low energy. Unfortunately this new strain hasn't been susceptive to the drugs AIDS patients have been taking. And so far it has a one hundred percent mortality rate." He shook his head slowly. "I'm so sorry."

Martin didn't know what to say. His mouth had fallen open and his eyes were wide. He felt like someone had punched him in the stomach with an anvil. He was floored. It was all too much for him to take.

He had just been handed a death sentence.

A painful death sentence.

"But how could this happen?" Martin gasped.

The doctor sat up straighter in his chair. "Well, surely you know the ways to acquire the disease. Have you had unprotected sex? A blood transfusion perhaps?"

Martin shook his head. "No, of course not. I haven't been with a woman for more than six months." His mind went back to the hooker he had paid to have sex with him. "And I haven't been to a hospital in years...well, until I went to get blood drawn last week."

The doctor nodded slowly. "I see. Well, what about sharing needles? Have you done drugs and shared a needle with another person?"

Martin was offended. "How dare you even suggest such a thing? I *do not* do drugs, Doctor," he snapped.

The doctor raised his hands in surrender. "I'm not judging, Martin, but I need to ask these questions if we're to figure out how this terrible thing happened."

Martin calmed down slightly. "Of course. Sorry for getting angry but it's just..."

"No apology needed," the doctor said. "I understand completely." The intercom buzzed and the doctor answered. "Susan, I told you not to disturb me, I'm in a meeting with a patient."

"I'm sorry, Doctor," the secretary's voice came over the intercom. "But Mrs. Carmichael is on the phone and she's in a panic over her blood pressure medicine. She really sounds upset."

The doctor sighed. "Fine, I'll be right out." He looked at Martin. "I'm very sorry about this, Martin. Mrs. Carmichael is eighty-three and she panics easily. Just let me calm her and we can get right back to discussing what will happen next for you." He stood up to go out to the secretary's desk to take the call there. "I'll leave you here to take all of this in. Maybe while I'm gone you can retrace your steps over the past year and try to come up with how you contracted the disease."

"Fine, fine, go," Martin said. "I could use a few minutes to myself anyway."

The doctor nodded and left the room, closing the door softly. A few seconds later and Martin could hear his distorted voice through the door as the man talked on the phone.

As he sat there, Martin began to wrack his brain for how this could have happened. He went over his movements for the past year and nothing came to mind. He worked and went home and other than eating the women he captured, he did nothing else that would...

Wait a minute, he ate other people. If one of them had been sick with the disease and he had eaten them, drank their blood, or had gotten it in his eyes, then that could only mean...

His mind raced back to months ago when he had that woman who always seemed amused. She had laughed at him, as if she knew something he didn't, as if though he was killing her, she somehow knew she would get her revenge, even from beyond the grave.

The doctor returned and sat down, mumbling more apologies. Martin heard none of it as the realization of what was happening hit him full force.

"Doctor, I have a question for you. Hypothetical of course."

"Please, what is it?" the doctor asked.

Martin chose his words carefully. "Well, if a person ate someone infected with this mutant AIDS virus, or say, drank their blood, could they contract the disease that way?"

The doctor laughed despite the morbid moment, thinking it was a joke. "Well, I suppose so, unbelievable as that sounds, but yes, if you ingested the blood or flesh of a terminally ill patient you would become infected yourself. But surely you're joking. Why, that would be insane, and the person ingesting the meat would be committing suicide by all counts."

Martin chuckled slightly, forcing a slight smile to crease his lips. "Of course, I was joking, and it's a bad joke at that."

He talked to the doctor some more, finding out what would happen next. From the progression of the illness, he had about four weeks if he was lucky, probably less, by the way the virus was eating into his body and had been for months.

Then he would be too weak to take care of himself and would have to check into a hospice. Other than painkillers to make his death tolerable, there was nothing that could be done to help him.

Martin left the doctor, finding it ironic that he shook the doctor's hand, as if he was grateful to find out he was dying and would soon be dead. Or worse yet, would be suffering terribly.

The doctor had let slip that it was a very painful way to die and many patients simply killed themselves before it became too much to bear, thus saving themselves and their families further suffering.

As he left the office building the doctor's office was in, and stepped out onto the sidewalk, he thought back to the laughing woman and how amused she'd been.

She'd been dying, too, and though he had tortured her when he sliced meat from her body, in the end he had put her out of her misery by killing her. The pain she'd felt was nothing compared to what was to come when dying from the disease.

Martin finally understood what she'd been laughing about.

She'd been fearless because she had nothing to lose; she was already dying and had felt relief in knowing he was saving her from suffering further. And to top it all off, she knew she would get her revenge by infecting the man who was eating her flesh and would eventually kill her.

Unfortunately, there would be no one to do that for him.

CANNIBAL CAMPING TRIP

The Land Rover pulled into the parking lot for the camp ground in upstate New York at half past two on Saturday afternoon.

No sooner did the vehicle come to a stop, then the doors were opening and the Johnson family stepped out, stretching and yawning after the long drive from New York City.

Doug Johnson turned to look at his family with pride and admiration.

His wife, Tina had just stepped out of the passenger seat and was smiling at him as she wiggled her right leg, which had fallen asleep. Behind her, his oldest daughter, Alicia, was standing and holding her cell phone up to the sky, as if it would magically work because she raised it two more feet over her head.

"Dad," Alicia said, stretching out the word. "There's no signal up here, how am I supposed to survive for two whole days with no phone service?"

Doug chuckled at her, thinking of that saying about how a cell phone can only be separated from a teenage girl's hand when it's taken from her dead body.

"Well, I guess you're just going to have to rough it, honey," he said with a grin, Tina showing him one of her own.

"Alicia wants to talk to Jamie, that's why she's mad there's no signal," Doug's youngest daughter, Amy, said with a contemptuous smile. "They're in love. They're gonna go all the way next week at the Prom."

"Shut up, you little twit!" Alicia snapped as she spun on her sister, who danced away laughing.

"Girls, girls," Doug said and looked at Amy. "Stop trying to get your sister into trouble. She and her mom talked about next week and I have total faith in her judgment."

"Thanks, Dad," Alicia said and stuck her tongue out at Amy.

Doug laughed, always finding it amusing how Alicia would act so much younger around her sister.

Tina walked around the Land Rover and gave Doug a hug. "Where is everyone, honey? This place is empty," she said.

Doug took a real look around for the first time since pulling into the parking lot. "Hey, you're right, it is empty. Wow, that's weird." He shrugged it off as soon as he spoke. "Hey, more woods for us, I guess. Maybe the campers skipped this week and we got lucky and will have the forest to ourselves."

"Great," Alicia said as she raised her hands up and then down in frustration. "On top of everything else, there's no one else to talk to but you guys."

"We love you, too, dear," Tina said as she pulled out a pack of cigarettes, took one out, and lit it. Doug frowned, took the lighter from her hand and put it in his pocket, but said nothing to her. She had agreed to not smoke in the house or the car so he had to leave her alone. It was her choice, he kept telling himself. She eyed him angrily but then her mood shifted and she turned away, taking another drag as she did so.

Doug clapped his hands together to get his family's attention. "Okay, so enough chit-chat. Let's get the packs and tents and get hiking. It's a good two hour walk to the glade where we'll be setting up for the night."

"Why do we have to go so far in?" Alicia asked. "Why can't we just go over there and set up?" She pointed to a copse of trees just off the gravel parking lot.

Doug sighed. "Because it's not real camping if the car is a stone's throw away, honey. We need to be deep in the forest, away from man and civilization. We need to have to rely on our wits."

"And what we brought with us, like food, water and magazines," Amy said with a sly grin. She was a wise-guy and Doug loved her for it, but sometimes it did get annoying.

"Yes, dear, and what we bring with us."

Doug went to the back of the vehicle, popped the rear hatch, and began taking out the camping gear. Fifteen minutes later, he pressed the button on his key ring, locked the Land Rover, and led his family into the wilderness.

"Are we there yet?" Alicia whined for the hundredth time.

"I think so. It should be just around that bend at the top of the path," Doug said as he led his family ever onward. Tina was quiet, too tired to speak, and Amy had run out of energy to talk almost an hour ago. Only Alicia seemed to have the energy to complain and she did so at five minute intervals.

Ten minutes later, they crested the bend in the path and each of them let out a gasp of amazement at the vista before them.

There was a wide glade, and to the left of it, was the edge of a cliff, overlooking a massive amount of forest and surrounding mountains. It was truly breathtaking.

"Wow, Doug, you said it was beautiful, but I didn't believe just *how* much when you told me," Tina said as she dropped her pack and walked to the edge. It was a very steep facade and if a person was to fall, there would be no surviving the drop.

"I know, huh? Mac in accounting told me about this place. Said he found it by accident. We're so deep into the mountains that no one else knows about it."

Alicia picked up a candy wrapper and shoved it under Doug's nose. "No one, huh? Looks to me like people have been here."

"Well, what I meant to say is, not many people know about it. It's way off the hiking trails and unless you want to take a chance and go free-hiking, the odds of finding this place is pretty slim."

"So then, Dad, what's with the path?" Amy asked. "If there's a path then people must come up here."

"Good point, honey. But that's not a people path we were on, that was an animal path. See, animals are a lot like people and they pick the easiest path to use. Then others follow, and before you know it, there's a discernable path in the woods. Usually you see them by streams and lakes where animals go to get water."

"Oh, okay, makes sense I guess," Amy said as she went to join her mother.

"Don't get too close, Amy!" Doug called. "Tina, keep an eye on her," he said.

"I will, I got her!" Tina called back.

Alicia dropped to the ground, not very interested in the view. Doug didn't mind. He had seen her eyes go wide when they first crested the bend and knew she was impressed.

"So, Dad, do we make camp here?" Alicia asked.

"No, honey, we have to walk a little bit more. It wouldn't be safe to make camp here for obvious reasons."

"Great, more walking."

He chuckled, knowing his daughter's mood swings. "It's not far. I promise; no more than ten minutes. Mac told me there's this wide circle devoid of foliage and there's logs set up around it. At one time someone set up a camp there but it was years ago, maybe longer."

"Fancy words there Dad, *devoid*. Why not just say no trees and junk?"

"Because I'm trying not to talk down to you now that you're older, that's why. It's a compliment; you should take it as such."

"Whatever. God, Dad, you're such a goofball."

Amy came running back and hugged her father. "Wow, Daddy, it's beautiful. It makes you think you could just jump off and fly away."

"Well, I suppose so, but you know you can't, right?"

"Of course, Daddy, I'm not a kid anymore," she said and trotted off to join her sister, who snapped at her impatiently as siblings will to one another.

Tina returned and wrapped her arms around Doug, kissing him on the cheek. "Oh, Doug, what a gorgeous view. It was certainly worth the hike to see it. I'm glad you decided to take us on this trip. I think it's just what our family needs."

"I couldn't agree more, honey. So what do you say? Do you want to stay here a little longer, or do you want to keep going to the place Mac told me about and set up for the night?"

"Sure, let's go. Once we're unpacked we can make some s'mores," Tina said.

Doug picked up his pack and looked over at Alicia who was fiddling with her cell phone. "If it didn't work down by the Land Rover, honey, it's sure not gonna work way up here. Just put it away, will you please? Would it kill you to be a part of this family for just a few days?"

"Yes, Dad, it would. God, I should be with Kathy at the mall today. She said Jamie is going to be there and I wanted to see him."

"She likes Jamie a lot, Daddy. They want to kiss and stuff," Amy said and pretended she was kissing her hand.

"Knock it off, ya little runt."

"Alicia, watch your mouth!" Tina snapped.

"What, Mom, I said *runt.* God, everything I do I get in trouble."

Doug began walking. "Come on, let's forget it ever happened and keep moving. You'll feel better once we have a fire going and your tent is set up."

"Doubt it," Alicia said and began walking. Tina and Amy took up the rear as the Johnson family continued their hike.

A short time later, Doug and family reached the circular area empty of plant life and set up their tents. One tent for Doug and Tina and one for Amy and Alicia. Doug managed to get a fire going after more than fifteen minutes of work, and when he finally did, Tina clapped and cheered him, boosting his failing spirits.

They sat around the fire, talking and laughing and even Alicia was getting into it. Doug saw the little girl who used to run to him when he arrived home from work every night. The short-tempered teenager had melted away, and he relished her change in personality, knowing once they returned home and her cell phone worked, and she was bombarded with the massive machine that was corporate America, filled with sex, sex and more sex, she would revert back to the annoyed teenager she had been for the past two years. So for now, he laughed with her, listened to her talk, and tried to imagine that this was reality and what was left behind was all a dream.

As night fell, and the fire began to die, the family of four each went to their tents to get a good night sleep. Doug was amazed when Alicia went to him and gave him a goodnight hug, something she hadn't done in years.

Amy was right behind Alicia, and she hugged her dad and then went to her mom and hugged her, too, and with a round of "Goodnights," everyone turned in.

As Doug stretched out on his sleeping bag, Tina curled up beside him, he closed his eyes and listened to the sounds of the forest. He could hear crickets chirping softly, and the wind blowing through the trees, and though he was used to the sounds of traffic buzzing by his bedroom window as he slept each night, he found the sounds of nature lulling him into a deep sleep, the long hike up to the camping spot also helping to knock him out almost as soon as his head touched his small pillow.

Doug awoke to the screams of his wife and daughters, and for a moment, he didn't know where he was.

For almost a full ten seconds he was lost, his mind trying to figure out where he was, what was happening, and if he was dreaming.

As his mind cleared, he saw the flap to the tent was open as well as a long tear in the material of Tina's side of the tent. It was as if a knife had sliced into the material.

As his mind focused, he saw Tina's legs, kicking frantically, as she was dragged out of the gash in the tent. She was screaming for help and Doug didn't know what to do. He was in shock, not understanding what was happening. In the background of his panic, he could hear Amy and Alicia yelling for Mommy and Daddy.

The tent flap was open, and it wasn't empty. In front of the tent, stooped over, was a human figure, the face lost in the shadows of the night, but Doug's nostrils were assaulted by feces and the odor of an unwashed body.

With his brain frantically trying to make him snap out of it, the dark figure reached inside the tent and grabbed his stocking feet, then yanked, dragging Doug out of the tent like he was nothing but a stuffed doll.

He slid across his sleeping bag to find himself staring up at a half-moon, the night sky clear of clouds, a few stars winking down at him as if they were watching his drama with amusement.

He heard Tina cry out to his left and his head turned to look for her. He saw her pulled to her feet by two shapes hidden in the night. Tina was a fighter and never stopped struggling, and she got lucky and her right hand snapped out and struck one of the figures in the nose. Even over the cries of his children, Doug heard the distinctive snap of a breaking nose and one of the figures fell back, sputtering blood from the same nose.

But Tina's victory was short-lived as the other figure pulled a knife, and in less than a second, slid it across her throat, almost severing her head from her shoulders, the blade cut so deep.

Doug could only lay still, his eyes wide in utter horror, as he saw a gout of blood shoot out of his wife's open throat to splatter the ground like warm rain. Her body twitched and spasmed and the figure holding her stepped away from her, Tina's body falling to the cold ground to writhe in its death throes.

"Tina!" Doug yelled, but only managed the one word before he was smothered by the figure that had dragged him from the tent. Something hairy covered his face and he sucked in the funk of old meat and sweat.

Acting on instinct, he fought and kicked to try to extricate himself but the figure was larger than him and he was overpowered.

Rolling on the ground, he got lucky and managed to squirm free of his captor. No sooner did he do this then the figure was grabbing him again. He kicked out with his right foot and felt the satisfying squish of testicles under his heel. The figure moaned in pain and fell to the ground and Doug rolled to his knees. A few feet away, he saw Alicia and Amy being dragged into the woods by more shadows shaped like humans. His girls were screaming for him, yelling for their mother, but no help was coming.

Doug jumped to his feet, preparing to run and save his girls, to take them back from whoever had them, but before he took two steps, another shape came at him from behind and brought a large wooden club down onto the back of his head.

Doug saw stars then, small pinpricks of light flashing before his eyes. As he fell to the ground, slipping into unconsciousness, two things followed him into the abyss; the dead eyes of his wife as she lay on the ground in a pool of blood, and the haunting cries of his two daughters.

Then the lights went out.

Doug returned to the land of the living somewhat slowly. Once more he didn't know where he was and it took the constant scraping on his back to pull him back to the real world.

When the next pain struck him, he became fully awake.

The pain came from the countless rocks and branches littering the forest floor, which were cutting into the skin on his back.

He looked up to the see it was still dark, and as his body flowed over a thick patch of twigs, he realized he was being dragged across the forest floor. He looked down at his feet to see two men pulling him, each one holding a foot. His shirt was now nothing but rags, and with each yard they dragged him, more of the skin on his back was ripped away.

Wincing, he held his tongue, not wanting to alert his captors he was awake.

By the way he was being dragged, he had a feeling his captors assumed he was dead, and for the moment he had no reason not to want to perpetuate that assumption.

Moving his head to the right, he spotted another man walking. This man carried a burden, but in the darkness it was hard to see what it was. He could see the burden was draped over his shoulder like it was the carcass of a slain deer. The part Doug could see swinging loosely, like a ball on a tether, swayed with the cadence of the figure's gait.

Then the figure passed under an opening in the canopy of trees and the thinnest bit of moonlight cast a pale glow on the figure. Doug controlled his reaction to scream when he saw that the part of the man's burden that was swinging, was actually Tina's head, hanging by a thin bit of flesh, constantly moving back and forth like a macabre pendulum.

He heard a screech of pain and his head snapped to the left to see three more figures, each carrying a burden.

In the gloom of the forest night, he immediately knew it was his daughters, both awake but gagged by the sounds of their muffled cries.

His entire body welled up with panic for his daughters, then the loss of Tina filled him with grief and he fought the choking urge to yell, to kick at his two captors and fight to save his little girls' lives.

But though filled with fear and rage, he remained calm, knowing he was outnumbered and acting irrationally would only get him killed…like Tina.

His eyes went to her swinging head once more and he felt choking sobs rising up in his throat. His wife of over twenty years was now dead, and he had been there to see her die. He hadn't protected her and now she was gone.

But his daughters were still alive. If he could save them, escape the woods, they could still be a family. They could mourn Tina's loss but continue. They had to, for the memory of his wife. He knew she would want him to do everything in his power to save her little girls, her babies. The only question was how? How could he hope to prevail over the greater numbers of his attackers?

One of the figures spoke to another one and Doug didn't recognize the words. They seemed like English but were garbled, like they were being spoken by a retarded person, the syllables low and guttural, dragged out when they should be short.

His head felt woozy and he almost fainted, only his force of will keeping him awake.

Looking back up at the night sky, he saw the moon wasn't where it had been before. He didn't know what time it was, but he could tell he'd been out for a while. Where he was being taken, along with his family, was far from his original campsite.

As he scanned the surrounding woods, all he saw was isolation. Nothing looked familiar, no paths, nothing.

Wherever he was, he was far from civilization. He knew the woods went on for miles upon miles and it wasn't far-fetched to believe that these people, whoever they were, could somehow live in the mountains somewhere, never found in the endless miles of forest by man.

Of course, as he thought about this, he realized how ridiculous it sounded. That was the stuff of horror books, where the inbred family lived in the woods and would attack unwary travelers to kill and take their valuables.

Somehow he didn't think they wanted his wrist watch or his Land Rover. If they did, then why carry Tina's corpse through the woods? Wouldn't it have been easier to dump her body off the path or perhaps bury it? His head hurt, and the more he tried to rationalize the actions of his attackers, the more it didn't make any sense.

Thirty more minutes of being dragged like a sack of laundry and the trees began to open up. He saw ramshackle buildings, no more than shacks, each resembling small tool sheds. They were built in a rough circle, the interior of the circle made up of mud, rocks and a large fire pit in the center.

As the two men dragging him reached the edge of the circle, each one let go of his feet. His right heel struck a sharp rock when it fell and it was all he could do not to cry out. The man on the right turned around to look at him and Doug closed his eyes and feigned death. The man grunted, satisfied that his prey was harmless, then looked back to the other man.

Opening his left eye a small amount, Doug saw his daughters and Tina's corpse being carried into the circle. Tina's body was dropped to the ground without respect, her arms flapping over her side to lay still. It broke Doug's heart see his wife handled this way but he forced his anger down, knowing he was vastly outnumbered and he needed to bide his time; for what he didn't know yet.

His daughters were carried to the edge of the circle where wooden posts were embedded in the ground. Each girl was tied to a post with their hands behind their backs. Their clothes were quickly cut away until they were stark naked, tears running down their cheeks as they sobbed in terror.

The two men who had been dragging Doug took a step away from him, one peeing on a tree while the other called out to another figure lost in the darkness.

And that was when Doug saw his best chance to escape.

Jumping to his feet, he picked up a fist-sized rock as he stood. Before the man who was urinating knew what was happening, Doug smashed the rock into the back of his head, the man's knees giving out as he fell into his own urine pool.

The other man heard Doug's attack and turned to see the supposedly dead prey very active. He yelled out and Doug dropped the rock, then he began to run, the shouts and alarm of the others in the camp sounding out behind him.

"I'll come back for you, Alicia, stay strong!" he yelled and hurdled a fallen tree to dash into the underbrush.

Behind him, he heard the footfalls of a half dozen figures and knew he needed to run for all he was worth. He knew if they caught him, they would make sure he was dead this time. There would be no second chances.

The low-hanging tree branches slapped his face and arms as he charged through the forest. In the darkness, trees seemed to jump into his path, and he deftly avoided them, more than once striking one with his shoulder. The pain was excruciating, but he shrugged it off, knowing to pause was death.

Behind him, his pursuers grew closer, their footfalls growing louder.

For more than fifteen minutes, Doug ran at full speed until his lungs began to labor and spots danced in his vision. A shooting pain had sprung up on his left side and he knew he was at the end of his rope.

Behind him, the whooping calls of his pursuers grew ever closer.

It was when he was about done for and he knew only a few more yards and he would collapse, that the ground fell out from beneath him and he found himself falling down a steep incline. Though he tried to control his descent, he was soon falling upside down, then right side up, then sideways. Branches and brush slowed his descent, and more than once a sharp branch jabbed his flesh mercilessly. His head struck a rock and he began to lose consciousness.

He yelled out once or twice but he had no time for such frivolity. And then he reached the bottom and splashed into a deep stream, the cold water snapping him back to full alertness. The current wasn't strong, more than enough to pull him along, and as he swam to the surface, sputtering and coughing, he caught the briefest glimpse of his pursuers on the ridge slightly behind him. As he floated downstream, they began to follow him, running along the ridge.

Doug knew he was still far from free.

Sucking in a deep breath, his heart pounding like a steel drum in his head, he dove underwater and went to the bottom. His hands found a mud slick rock bigger than his body, and he held onto it, then closed his eyes and counted in his head. His plan was that his followers would continue running downstream, assuming he was still moving with the current, and when he finally resurfaced, they would have no idea where he was.

He stayed under water for nearly two minutes, and as his head broke the surface and he swam to shore, he could barely focus, he was so oxygen deprived.

A small copse of branches and leaves had built up along the shore and he moved into it, his head now hidden from view. With the darkness all but complete, he knew there was no way he could be seen and he waited, never moving, only half his head exposed, his mouth hidden in the water as his nose touched the surface.

Once or twice, he heard yells and shouts, but soon it was lost amongst the steady gurgle of the stream.

He waited for over an hour, and with his body shaking from the cold temperature, he climbed out onto the shore and slowly made his ascent to the top of the ridge.

He sat there, his eyes darting back and forth as his blue lips trembled from the cold, but there was no sign of his pursuers.

Ten minutes later, his heart beat slowing, he knew he had lost them. But he couldn't leave, not yet. His daughters were still in the camp. And though he wanted to run back to civilization as fast as he could, he knew he couldn't leave his daughters. After what those monsters had done to Tina, he knew his girls were in grave danger.

So, shaking off the cold, and only in his stocking feet, he slowly got his bearings, crossed his fingers he was going in the right direction, and began to make his way back to the camp to save what was left of his family.

It took more than an hour for Doug to find the ramshackle camp again. Over the course of that hour, he panicked more than once, thinking he wasn't going to be able to locate it.

It was pure luck that allowed him to discover it once more.

As he was creeping around in the dark brush, trying to retrace his steps, he accidentally blundered into one of the members of the camp.

The woman was as shocked to see him as he was to see her, but Doug was the first to go into action. She had been squatting to pee, and it appeared these people picked any old place to leave their waste, and before she could yell out and sound the alarm, Doug's hands reached out and wrapped around her dirty neck. She fought back like a wildcat, kicking and scratching, one of her knees going into his crotch, but he never let up and eventually she began to sag in his hands as she lost consciousness.

By the time she collapsed at his feet, her face was a dark blue; when Doug got a better look at her, he saw she was filthy, in her early twenties, and look like she had Down Syndrome.

The first thing he saw was the necklace she wore, and on closer inspection, he was horrified to see it was made of human ears, more than one with the earrings still attached. The second thing he saw was the knife hanging from her belt, a man's belt if he was correct.

Because it was dark, it was hard to see clearly, but he'd already seen enough.

Taking the knife from her, he looked down on the unconscious woman and knew right there he needed to decide what to do next.

His moral compass began a battle in his head of what he should do with her. If he left the woman be, she would wake and alert the camp he was near, but if he killed her to silence her, then he became a killer, a murderer that was no better than the attackers who had taken his family…and killed Tina.

But then, they had kidnapped his daughters, slaughtered his wife without mercy, and tried to kill him. He hadn't asked for this; they had been the aggressors. His mind raced with right and wrong and he may have spent another hour wrestling with the decision if the woman didn't make it for him.

As he sat over her, trying to decide what to do, her eyes snapped open and she let out a guttural growl. Without thinking about it, moving purely on instinct, for survival, Doug slashed at her throat with the knife, slicing her jugular and causing her beginning yells to become low gurgles.

Blood shot from her neck to coat her small breasts and more than two pints splattered on him before he fell away in disgust, now covered in the sticky plasma.

He stared at her as she twitched on the forest floor to then lay still, her eyes glazing over to then stare up at the night sky. He looked at the bloody knife in his right hand, the arm beginning to shake as he realized what he'd done, but as time passed, his hand grew strong and his jaw taut as resolve filled him.

He had killed this woman and he was fine. He was still Doug, no better or worse. It was as he gazed down on the still form that he truly realized to kill wasn't such a bad thing. It was easy actually, no harder than crossing a street or cutting the lawn. It was a chore that he needed to do to save his daughters. The taboo of 'Thou Shalt Not Kill' had been shattered and he felt free, more alive than he had in his entire life, and he knew it was time to save his family and get revenge for the death of Tina.

Thinking this way, he knew he could now kill others of the camp if he had to, and he was fairly confident that would be the only way to rescue his girls.

Standing tall, blood sluicing down his shirt and pants, he turned and trotted off into the forest, heading for the camp which by luck or fate, hadn't heard the woman's cries. He knew before the night was over, either he would be dead or his new knife would taste more blood.

It was still more than two hours before dawn when Doug reached the perimeter of the camp and crouched low behind a thick patch of blackberries. Through the thin branches, he was able to see the fire in the center clearly.

But whatever courage he'd felt before reaching the camp quickly vanished as he stared at the macabre tableaux before him.

At the fire, ten people sat, each eating like they were starving animals.

The meat was raw, and at first he didn't know what they were eating, but when a body shifted to the left, he saw the corpse of his beloved wife, Tina, sprawled in the dirt.

Her head was now fully severed from her corpse and it sat on a rock like a bizarre trophy. Her torso had been gutted, the organs extracted, and as Doug watched mystified, two men picked up the torso and rammed a pole through it, then placed the torso on a spit over the fire. A woman with a malformed face began sprinkling what had to be spices on the meat while the others continued chopping up the arms and legs like it was a carcass after a hunt.

Not able to withstand the horror, Doug knelt over and puked, his eyes squeezed tight as vomit left his mouth to spray his feet, tears sliding down his cheeks.

He didn't know how long he sat there in the brush, crying, but in time he was pulled from his grief by the screams of his little girls.

Scanning the camp, he watched them appear from out of the darkness, dragged by their hair by two more men. Doug saw that the brows of both men protruded heavily; giving them a Cro-Magnon look. After seeing the features of the woman he'd killed, he was starting to get an idea who these people were, though it seemed so far fetched as to be unbelievable. Still, the reality was before him.

His naked daughters were in tears, their faces covered in streaks of dirt and grime and Doug wracked his brain for a way to save them. But there was nothing feasible he could do. If he charged into the camp, he would be quickly overwhelmed and brought down.

Alicia was first as she was dragged close to the fire, only a few feet from where Tina's corpse was gutted. Doug squeezed the knife hilt so tightly his knuckles turned bone white, but there was nothing he could do.

Alicia was tossed to the ground, and without so much as a hesitation, the man dropped down over her and slit her throat. As blood shot out of her torn carotid, he began to gut her, dragging the knife from her neck to her groin, cutting off extra skin when feasible.

Doug stared in utter shock, his mouth opening and closing as he slipped into a state of absolute terror. From where he hid, he had a perfect view of his daughter's death, and as he watched, the man reached into her gaping chest cavity, cracked the ribs, and pulled out her still beating heart. With a throaty yell, he sank his teeth into it, tearing and chewing at the engorged muscle. When he was half done, he tossed it to a woman who yelped merrily and began feeding. The man then pulled out organ after organ, handing them to the greedy camp dwellers, each ripping and tearing at the organs with their teeth, blood sluicing down their chins to cover their naked chests.

Doug was frozen in place, his entire world crumbling beneath him. He felt nothing. He was alone in a void where there was no light, no sensation.

Alicia was cleaned, gutted, her limbs severed, and her torso placed on a spit next to Tina's. As the torso was lifted onto the spit, Doug spotted a tattoo of a dolphin at the crease of her back, right where her butt would begin. His daughter had always loved dolphins and he hadn't known she even had a tattoo.

For some reason, seeing that tattoo caused him to fall to the ground, crying harder, his shaking shoulders scraping the dirt. He may have stayed like that forever if not for the screams of his younger daughter, Amy.

Peering through the brush, he could only watch helplessly as she was also killed. For some reason, the man who dealt with Amy was more merciful. He took her small head in his hands, then twisted sharply, snapping her neck and ceasing her cries.

But Doug found out this wasn't so merciful when the man picked up Amy, hung her by her feet, then slit her throat to let the blood seep out into a cracked ceramic bowl beneath her. His little angel, his sweet daughter, was being drained of her blood like she was common cattle. It happened so fast that Doug barely had time to register it. One second she was screaming, then she was hanging while her blood dripped into a bowl.

His mind raced with everything he'd seen, and as he watched the cannibals eating his family, their malformed faces flickering in the firelight, he found himself about to pass out from the pressure.

With the visions of his family being slaughtered fresh in his head, he gladly welcomed death, in fact, he prayed it would come soon, as he slid into unconsciousness once more.

But he did awaken, and as he slowly sat up, he moved a few branches aside to see the camp was quiet.

He saw a few bodies lying prone around the waning fire and by the subtle twitches of their limbs he could tell they were asleep.

Looking up at the sky, he saw he had less than an hour before dawn would arrive.

Looking back at the camp, he could see the remains of his family, their bones set in a pile near the fire. Their heads were used as trophies, the flesh peeled away so only red, grinning skulls remained. He tried not to think about what those skulls truly were; his lost family.

The time he was unconscious had helped him. Though only fading wisps of smoke, he faintly remembered terrible dreams as his mind tried to process the carnage he'd witnessed, the absolute grief no man should have to experience in one lifetime.

But whatever his mind had rationalized, whatever it had decided while he was unconscious, he now felt only one emotion fill him from head to toe.

Revenge.

Pure...unadulterated...revenge.

Coming to his knees, he crawled into the camp, careful to stay away from the flickering firelight.

It took him more than ten minutes to reach the first sleeping figure. It was a man. The lips were twisted and the nose was crooked, but as the sleeping man shifted and blew out a snort, Doug knew his assumption was correct.

For some unknown reason, these people were all mentally retarded. The distorted features of their faces sealed the deal along with their jilted speech patterns. How these people ended up in the middle of the mountains, miles upon miles from civilization, was a mystery; one he wasn't in the mood to figure out.

Where normally he would want to help these unfortunate people, after what they had done to his family, all he wanted to do was kill them.

Creeping over the sleeping figure, he raised the knife, then in a fluid motion, placed his free hand over the deformed mouth and slid the knife across the exposed neck.

The eyes went wide on the retarded man's face but with Doug's hand clamped over the mouth, nothing but a few muffled grunts slipped free. It took less than fifteen seconds for the flailing arms to grow weak, to then fall back to the ground.

Doug was splashed with hot blood but he ignored it; in fact he relished it. The warm spray was a baptism of murder, one he would continue until every evil being in the camp was destroyed.

When he was sure the man was dead, he crawled over the corpse to the next sleeping figure.

It was a woman and her small, pint-sized body showed the stunted growth of a dwarf. The protruding jaw and large forehead added to what he'd already come to accept as fact. These were what the civilized world called *special people*, but now they were only killers and murderers, and worse, cannibals, feeding on the flesh of their fellow humans.

He fell on top of her, plunging the knife into her chest, right over her heart. He felt the blade slide in and the subtle resistance as it passed through her ribcage, then the pressure lessening as the tip of the knife cleaved her heart in two.

The woman's eyes snapped open and she elicited a gasp, but nothing more escaped her lips. Her head rose a few inches as she spasmed, and other than releasing her bowels, she gently lowered her head to the ground to lay still.

Doug grunted at his handiwork, amazed at how truly easy it was to kill another human being.

Guilt filled him for a fraction of a second, but when he glanced at the skulls and pile of bones that was his family, he brushed it off and renewed his vow of slaughter.

After killing each of the sleeping figures around the dying fire, he then began entering each of the ramshackle huts. One at a time, he crept in like a thief in the night to steal their lives one at a time.

By the time he was finished and every occupant of the camp was dead, he was bathed in blood from top to bottom, the sticky plasma becoming a new skin.

If for even a moment he regretted his actions, when he came upon the last hut he knew his action were righteous, and not for his own personal vengeance.

For inside the last hut were shelves upon shelves of bones and grinning skulls. To the left of the doorway were piles upon piles of wallets, wrist watches and shoes. All kinds were prevalent, from high heels to hiking boots, the menagerie of footwear told a gruesome tail of murder and carnage.

He took a pair of hiking boots that fit him and exited the hut.

He had killed close to twenty men and women this night and he felt nothing but sorrow. One, two, ten, twenty, what did it matter?

His family was dead and gone and he was alone.

Fresh tears spilled from his eyes and he fell to the ground, weeping softly.

Time passed, the sun rose and still he lay immobile, too weak to move. When he finally pulled himself up, he wondered if he should just torch the place, burn it all to the ground. But though lost in grief, he still was a part of civilization and when he returned with his incredible story, he would need proof of what happened.

With one last glance at the camp, he turned and began walking, knowing he would have to try and pay attention to the direction he went in so as to bring back the authorities. As for the slaughter of the camp's residents, he would keep that a secret for himself.

It was as he reached the edge of the camp, traversing a section he hadn't passed before, that his foot came down on a small pile of leaves in the center of the path.

Suddenly, there was a metallic sound and his leg felt like it was on fire. He yelled out in pain, and in the nearby trees, birds took flight, disturbed by his outcry.

Doug fell over, landing hard and yelling out once more as his ankle was twisted and his leg felt like it had been dipped in acid. His knife was gone, tossed away when he felt the bite of pain, and it was now lost somewhere in the leaves carpeting the forest floor. It could be anywhere and would take far too long to even attempt to search for it.

The knife could be a few feet or ten feet, he had no way to know for sure, let alone what direction to begin his search.

Looking down, he saw he had stepped into a bear trap, the metal mouth with its sharp teeth now clamped tightly over his ankle, trapping him. He reached down and tried to open it, but the second he touched it, blinding pain filled his vision and he lost consciousness.

When he came to, the sun hadn't moved very far and he figured he'd been out for a short time. Breathing heavily as fresh tears of pain leaked down his cheeks, he tried again to free himself.

Once more he failed miserably and slumped to the ground exhausted.

When he had the energy to try again, he decided to see if he could just drag the bear trap with him. As he dug around the trap, he found it was attached to a long metal chain, and when he pulled it, he saw it had quite a lot of play.

Maybe something in the camp could help him get free.

He began crawling back to the camp, one inch at a time. Each time he dragged his body, blinding white light filled his vision, but after the first ten feet or so the pain began to dull, though it was still agonizing. He figured it was his pain receptors on overload.

One excruciating yard at a time he crawled back into the camp, and when he was only a few inches from the first body, the chain finally went taut, causing him to cry out yet again.

But he managed to reach the body and pull it to him. He yelled out in glee to find a knife on the corpse. It wasn't big enough to pry open the trap with, but it was something.

Through his pain-addled mind, he wondered what the bear trap was for and why there was such a long chain on it, but then such matters were forgotten.

There was nothing close to him that he could use to pry the trap open and he slumped to the ground in defeat, soon fading into a fever-induced sleep that had him waking and passing out again and again over the next day.

On the second day, he awoke to darkness, and other than insects arriving to feed on the corpses, all was silent in the camp. No predators had arrived yet, though a few birds hopped about. He threw rocks at them and they flew away.

He was so thirsty it hurt and his leg throbbed with a steady rhythm, like a motor on a ship. With nothing else to do, he slept, sobbed over his lost family, then slept some more.

Days passed and he began to grow weak from hunger. He knew a man can only go for a few days without food and water and he knew he was close to his breaking point.

But he didn't want to die, not yet anyway.

His stomach was already bloated from hunger and his throat was raspy as he barked out laughter. Looking down at his foot, even in the darkness, he could see it had swollen in mass. Soon gangrene would set in if he didn't attend to it.

He knew there was only one thing he could do.

Sitting up, he took off his blood-soaked, dirt-covered shirt and tied it around his leg just a few inches above the teeth of the bear trap, the makeshift tourniquet cutting off blood flow to the foot. Then, with gritted teeth and a scream on his lips, he began to cut at his leg, sawing back and forth as pain filled him.

He passed out.

When he came to, he went back to work, cutting and hacking at his leg to severe his foot from the bear trap. He passed out three more times, and each time he woke up, he went back to work. The bone was the hardest, as he had to chip away at it with the tip of the blade. Each time the tip struck bone, his vision dimmed and he shuddered in agony.

He lost count how many times he passed out, and if time still mattered, he would have guessed it took him a full day to severe his foot from his leg.

But finally, with one last hack of the knife to bone and flesh, he pulled his leg free.

But he knew he was far from done yet and he crawled to the fire pit, pulled out Tina's cigarette lighter still in his pocket, and lit some kindling.

He was sweating profusely and had the shakes by the time he was finished, but a small fire was now burning in the center of the pit.

Without pausing, he sat up, spun around, and stuck his leg into the flames, searing his open wound and cauterizing it. He passed out yet again and it was only luck that his leg fell out of the fire as he collapsed to the ground.

Smoking, the redolence of charred flesh filling the area, Doug slid into oblivion once more.

When he woke up, he knew even with his leg cauterized, he would still die of hunger. He remembered when he had crawled through the camp to kill its occupants; he'd found no other food source other than human flesh.

At first he balked at the idea, but as the hours passed and he felt the constant gnawing of hunger and grew ever weaker, he knew he had no choice.

Damn it, he wasn't going to die here. Not after everything that had happened.

If for nothing else then to let the world know what had happened to him and his family. He needed to survive, to escape this charnel house of death.

He let his eyes play over the corpses, now bloated from days in the sun, and his stomach roiled inside him. No, he wouldn't be eating them; he would die due to eating the rancid meat if nothing else.

Then his eyes spotted his severed foot, still lying in the middle of the bear trap.

Crawling across the ground, he picked up his foot. He stared at it, studying it like a connoisseur would a particular cut of meat. The foot was fresh, it had been on him only hours ago.

He brushed the dirt off the top where he had sliced it off, took off the boot and sock, and stared at it. He saw his toenails needed to be clipped and that made him laugh. Hell, he could bite them shorter with his teeth now.

Another tinge of hunger pain ripped through him and he grunted, then, his resolve firm that he would survive, he bit into the heel of the foot, his teeth sinking into the soft flesh.

Pulling his head back, he began to chew.

He didn't know what he was supposed to expect, but he knew it probably wasn't what he tasted.

As he took another bite and the raw meat slid down his throat to fill him with energy, he didn't gag, and instead took yet another bite.

The more he ate, the more he grew accustomed to his decision. By the time he was almost done, his eyes were closed and he was savoring the taste.

He thought of that old saying about how it would taste like chicken.

He laughed to himself, feeling better with each bite.

It didn't taste like chicken at all, in fact, it taste just like…

CHRISTMAS POEMS

CHRISTMAS IS DEAD

Twas the night before Christmas, when all through the morgue,
Not a creature was stirring, not even a corpse.
Its internal organs, were weighed on a scale with depth,
In hopes the mortician, would find cause of death.

The rest of the bodies, were snug in their deathbeds,
While visions of Heaven and Hell, danced in their heads.
The cadavers were wrapped, nice and tight in their body bags,
As the mortician settled down, with the day's bloody rags.

When out back in the cemetery, there came a loud sound,
The mortician investigated, as there was no one around.
Away to the back door, he flew like a wraith,
And tore open the portal, there was no time to waste.

The moon reigned down, over the new-fallen snow,
As the mortician searched, both high and then low.
When what to his searching eyes did he find,
But a corpse in a Santa suit was walking, the first of its kind.

The ghoul was stumbling, not too fast or too quick,
He knew in a flash, it was a living dead man named St. Nick.
His face was pale, his cheeks far from red,
And when he exhaled, it was foul, the legend surely dead.
Zombie Santa turned, and waved his claw-like hand,
And eight zombie reindeer, stumbled across the land.
"Kill them, Dasher Dancer, Prancer and Vixen!
Eat their brains, Comet, Cupid, Donner and Blitzen!"

He shambled to his sleigh, and moaned to his deer,
Who joined him then, and snarled with a leer.

As zombie Santa and deer, flew off into the night,
The apocalypse had begun, the world over by first light.

The mortician heard Santa, call out to the night,
"Christmas is dead! It's no use to fight!
For the dead will walk, and eat your brains,
The world has ended, with blood and with pain!"

So hug your kids, your pets and your mice,
Because the dead now live, their teeth like a vice.
And run for the hills, for your death is in sight,
Christmas is dead, you can't stop the night.

DEAD CHRISTMAS

Twas the night before Dead Christmas, and all through the land,
Not a living creature was stirring, except a few severed hands.

The last family left alive, was barricaded inside,
While visions of death and carnage, danced in their minds.
The undead were hungry, as they searched for food,
And the humans knew their time was short, all of them in dire moods.

But then in the backyard, of this particular house,
There came a loud noise, and it wasn't a mouse.
Away to the back door, the family ran with haste,
For the dead were breaking in, there was no time to waste.

Moonlight bathed the new fallen snow,
As the family searched both high and then low.
But then did their searching eyes finally find,
It was a dead man in a Santa suit, and behind him more of his kind.

Though hard to believe, he was not false but the real deal,
And as he stumbled from his sleigh, eight undead reindeer snorted
with zeal.

His eyes were glazed, his flesh pale and white,
And as he let out a low moan, anyone within earshot was chilled with fright.

Zombie Santa waved the undead horde onward,
And hundreds of animated corpses began to stumble forward.
As the ghouls began to break into the home,
The family cried out, their screams swallowed by undead moans.

The living dead began to feed, and the carnage was great,
As Zombie Santa looked on, the last human family suffering a terrible fate.
When all were killed and only bloody shards were left,
Santa climbed back into his sleigh, carrying a single severed head with some heft.

He held it aloft for all the zombies to see,
And reached inside to pull out the brains, and handed them to two ghouls, not three.

"The last humans are dead and we rule the land!
We are the true creatures God wants on hand.
Humans were weak, and we are strong,
And this night, our reach is long!"

"The dead walk the Earth, and so the world will burn,
Humans are gone, never to return.
So the next time you hug your loved ones, don't take them for granted,
Remember, how fast they can be supplanted."

CLOSE CALL

Francesca Jones walked down the lonely hallway of the second floor of the office complex. She was alone and she was happy about it.

Being cooped up with two men in a small office space could become very irritating and she needed some time to be alone, to organize her thoughts about her life and her future.

As if sensing her inner turmoil, the baby in her belly kicked, causing her to wince and smile at the same time. The young life was growing and three more months would be all it would take to bring the new baby into the world.

An undead world.

For more than four months the dead walked the Earth and man was an endangered species.

No one knew why this was happening, though suppositions and ideas ruled the airwaves. But the one thing that was true was that the dead walked and they were not going away anytime soon.

So she, Paul and Shaun, had resigned to live for as long as they could inside the massive office complex while the world crumbled outside the brick and mortar walls. Thinking of the two men made her think of Richard, but she pushed the memories aside. He had been dead for months now and it was still as bitter a pill to swallow as the day they buried him in the small garden by the small pond in the center of the office complex.

Shaun had teared up, but Paul had stayed stoic as always, his dark complexion never so much as cracking.

Francesca sighed wearily as she strolled from store to store, staring at the best of 1978's fashions. All the metal grates were up and she had the entire building to herself.

She had left Shaun and Paul playing cards back in their makeshift apartment, the two gambling with thousands of dollars taken from the nearby bank on the next block. Of course, the money was worthless now, with the exception of being used as toilet paper or kindling for a fire.

As she walked, she tried to remember what the office complex would have looked like when it had been crowded. Children with their mothers, complaining they had to get clothes or shoes as they visited their husbands and fathers, old men and women out for a walk on the street in front of the building, fascinated by this massive building devoted to capitalism, to the almighty dollar of import/export.

But now they were all dead or walking around as one of the living dead.

A chill went down her spine and she found herself cradling her belly, wanting to protect the young life inside her from the dangers of the world. Of course those dangers were now so much more than what they once were.

She slowed when she reached a small jewelry store, admiring the beautiful necklaces and pendants in the window. Inside the store proper, racks of earrings, gold and sterling silver the most predominate, glittered under the fluorescent lights.

Glancing over her shoulder and feeling like she was somehow doing something wrong, she stepped into the store to see what she could take.

The smell of wetness on cardboard tickled her nose and she looked for the source. Moving deeper into the store, she searched the floor and ceiling, and sure enough, at the corner of the ceiling, right over the door that would lead to the backroom, she saw a small water spot about six inches in diameter.

She smiled to herself as she brushed her blonde hair off her face. Even this, a brand new building, had problems such as leaks.

Deciding she wasn't going to worry about it and would tell the men later, she began browsing, seeing what might catch her eye. The entire time she looked, Shaun was in the back of her mind as she wondered what he would like to see her wearing. Another smile creased her thin but shapely lips as she thought of Shaun. He had actually asked her to marry him a while back, but she had turned him down.

Without a ceremony, without a priest, it all seemed so hollow.

A set of solid gold, 14k earrings caught her eyes and she placed them to her ears, admiring them in the small mirror on the counter. She felt rich as she admired herself but finally set them down, realizing whether the earrings were made of gold or simple iron, they were worth nothing now.

Monetary wealth was a thing of the past, and she knew she was one of the richest people still alive.

Why?

Because she had safety, shelter and food. And lots of it, and in a world where the dead were looking for their next meal, that was all anyone could ask for.

She leaned against the glass counter, thinking about how her back hurt. Looking for a chair, she found one near the end of the counter. It was more of a stool, but it would do the job of letting her get off her feet just fine.

Sitting down, she sighed, feeling the baby shift inside her. Even now, months later, it still fascinated her how an actual life could be growing inside of her.

She leaned her head on the glass counter with her arms for a pillow and closed her eyes, thinking she would just rest for a bit. Then she would go back to the men and start supper.

Though she had once told them she wouldn't be their surrogate mother, that was exactly what she had become, and though Paul would cook sometimes, usually it was just her.

She didn't mind, it gave her something to do.

Closing her eyes, she sighed one more time, and though she wasn't planning on it, she drifted off into a light nap.

A tapping sound filtered into her dream of Shaun and her running on a beach, the surf gently cascading over the rocks lining the shore. At first she didn't know what the tapping was, the noise flowing into her dream, but then she opened an eye, realizing the tapping was external.

Yawning and wiping the corner of her mouth where spittle had collected, she blinked up at the fluorescent lights, their soft humming at first the only sound detected.

But then she heard the tapping again and knew it was real.

Standing up, she felt a wave of dizziness and waited a moment for it to pass. Her weaning strength was due to the baby, she knew this, and though Shaun hounded her to get some more rest, she usually didn't sleep much.

That was when the nightmares came and she thanked whatever god was up in the heavens for giving her a slight repast when she had slept on the stool.

Then she heard it again, the tapping sound, almost like Morse code. Not that she knew Morse code, but she had watched old Navy movies with Shaun and it sounded close enough.

Her ears tried to focus and she soon found herself looking at the door leading to the back room. She bit her lip nervously as she decided what to do.

She should go get the boys; they would deal with whatever was back there.

But as the light tapping continued, she felt her nervousness abating. It couldn't be a zombie for one of them wouldn't be tapping like that. No, they were clumsy, hideous things that would never have the dexterity for something as gentle as tapping.

With a glance to the hallway outside the jewelry store, she decided she wanted to check on her own. Sure she was pregnant, but she wasn't helpless. She could still fight and shoot and do what had to be done. She knew the boys didn't think that, but it was the truth.

Besides, it was probably something simple. After all, the boys had cleared the office complex of zombies months ago and if there had been one still around, it would have been found by now.

For the ghouls didn't lie in wait, they weren't that smart. They would have come out of hiding long ago in search of fresh meat.

So Francesca took a step towards the backroom door, and with an intake of breath to strengthen her resolve, she entered the dark back room.

It was dark and even mustier in the back room, and she reached out to the wall near the door to see if she could find a light switch.

Her hand slid across the smooth painted wall until she found the switch she was searching for.

Flicking it up, the room was quickly bathed in a white light, one that cast no shadows due to its glare. With a fluorescent light every four feet on the ceiling, there was no place for a shadow to hide.

With the hum of the lights now on, she waited to hear the tapping again. When more than two minutes came and went and still no tapping, she began to wonder if she imagined it.

It was when she was ready to leave, to just forget the entire thing, that she heard it again. It was coming from her left, and with her curiosity peaked, she began to walk in the direction of the noise, her heart beating fast in her chest.

As she walked, her feet stirred up small dust bunnies and a thick layer of dust was brushed aside. This told her immediately that neither Paul nor Shaun had been back here for a long time, if ever.

She could see that though it was the backroom to the jewelry store, it was also part of another store, one that must sell houseware items according to the boxes she passed. Many held Tupperware and silverware to name a few items.

Passing by piles of boxes stacked head high, she had a feeling of dread that maybe she should go back, that if the men hadn't cleared this room she could be setting herself up for trouble.

The office complex had become her home and this comforting feeling had dulled her sense of danger. The place was huge and it was possible a zombie could still be hiding within its walls, whether in the basement or in a back room somewhere; perhaps trapped by its own stupidity.

It was just as she was making up her mind that it was time to leave that she rounded a corner and stopped cold, her mouth falling open in a silent gasp of fear.

Standing in front of her was a zombie, wearing what looked like a security guard's uniform.

It wasn't hard for her to figure out the dead man must have worked for the office complex and it was all to clear what he was doing back here and what the tapping she had heard was from.

The undead security guard was handcuffed to a steel water pipe and every time he pulled on it, the handcuff would tap and scrape the pipe. How he had become handcuffed was unknown but a hundred reasons came to mind, one being one of his fellow workers had done it when he had turned.

At first Francesca wasn't worried and felt her heart slow at the sight of the handcuffed ghoul. For if the zombie was attached to the water pipe, it was harmless and it would be simple to just go get Paul and have him destroy it.

But it was either a coincidence or simply that the sight of fresh meat got the dead man to pull harder, but the security guard yanked so hard that his arm popped out of the socket and the rotting meat stretched like aged elastic until it tore in twain.

All Francesca heard was the ripping of what sounded like dry paper and then she saw that where the arm had stuck out of the blue, shirtsleeve, there was now a missing limb.

And that the ghoul was now free!

Before Francesca could turn and run, the security guard was upon her, knocking both of them into a pile of boxes. Francesca yelped in terror as she was buried under the boxes, the zombie still on top of her.

Using her hands, she jammed them under its chin and felt the coldness of the dead skin. As she watched, her hands slid into the flesh, becoming buried in it, and she gagged on bile at the feeling.

The zombie was only half a threat thanks to only one arm and Francesca so far was managing well, but she knew with her baby inside her she wouldn't be able to fend it off for long.

Quickly her eyes began searching for a weapon, any weapon in which to protect herself and destroy the foul ghoul trying to kill her and her baby.

Though she was terrified, she still wouldn't scream. Never would she scream, but she would growl. Removing one hand from the zombie, her arm began to flail about, her fingers touching anything that was around her.

Her throat vibrated with her growls and the zombie moaned and wailed. Teeth clacked only inches from her face, her nose seeming to be the preferred choice on the menu today. Turning her face away, she felt cold saliva drip onto her skin, causing her to want to vomit. Only her force of will kept her lunch inside her.

The zombie wasn't letting up. It had been trapped for months and the sight of Francesca was too much for it. Its entire world was only her and it wanted her badly, only Francesca's desperation keeping the dead man at bay.

And then Francesca felt something long and hard under her flailing hand as she grasped it, not knowing what it was.

Pulling it to her, and then up and at the zombie's head, she was shocked to see it was an electric carving knife.

Glancing to the floor where she had found it, she saw dozens of them spread out, their boxes open, the plastic they were in sagging.

Never hesitating and thanking whatever good fortune was shining down on her today, she brought the immobile twin blades up and under the zombies chin.

Shifting her hand still on the ghoul lower so it was now pressed against its clavicle, she began to saw back and forth at the security guard's neck.

As she did this, cold, coagulated blood poured out of the jagged wound, mixed with browns and blacks of what had to be blood, too.

The entire viscous contents splattered down onto Francesca's lower face and chest and she closed her mouth tight as well as her eyes.

She didn't need her sight to finish what she had started. Sawing back and forth, she felt the blades pause and she had no idea she had hit the zombie's spine. Still sawing, her body lathered in gore, she moved her arm with all her might, knowing she was fast tiring.

And then the blade was pushed free and there was no longer tension on it. She felt something fall onto her forehead and bounce off to roll away.

At first she did nothing, merely laid there breathing heavily from her exertion, ready for the zombie to try and attack again. But when the corpse remained immobile, she set the electric knife down and used her sleeve to wipe her eyes clean of gore.

When she was confident she had cleaned herself enough to open her eyes, she gazed up at the headless security guard, a small amount of brown blood still seeping out of the jagged neck stump.

Pushing the corpse off of her, she sat up and wiped her face some more, spitting as much as she could, and fearing the unknown. As far as any of them knew, a bite killed but what would happen if you got some tainted blood in your mouth? Was it saliva or something else? No one knew and she didn't want to find out the hard way.

Rolling to her side, she then spotted the severed head on the floor a few feet away. It was lying on its left ear and she saw the head was still very much alive.

Standing slowly, as it was hard to get to her feet without help, she reached down and grabbed a towel draped over a box across the aisle.

She wiped her face and neck as much as she could and knew she would be heading directly for a shower when she was through here.

But there was still one last thing to do before she left and told the boys she had found a zombie, that they had missed one.

Bending over, which was never easy when you were pregnant, she picked up the electric knife and walked over to the severed head. The eyes rolled in their sockets and the mouth opened and closed, but without a larynx, there were no sounds.

With her right foot, she tipped the head over, using her foot to keep the pale features looking straight up at her. Then, using the electric knife like a dagger, she jammed it into the head's right eye socket.

The eye exploded and the socket began to ooze clear ocular fluid as the other eye began to bounce back and forth. It was hard to see this as a thick film of cataract had grown over the eye, but if you stared at it long enough, the dilated pupil could still be seen floating within a sea of white.

She twisted the knife in the socket, metal scraping on the sides, bone shavings joining the mix, but the blade did its job, slicing the brain to pieces and killing the head for good.

Standing up, she dropped the knife to the floor, ignoring it when the casing cracked and pieces flew off. It didn't matter; it wasn't like she would ever use it to cut a ham or roast taken from one of the voluminous freezers or walk-ins.

Gazing down at her handiwork, she didn't move for a few seconds, just glad to be alive. Her adrenalin was till pumping and the fight or flight was still there, only she had chosen to fight. Or was that because she didn't have a choice?

Her baby kicked inside her and she reached down and cradled her belly. Touching her extended abdomen, she was relieved to discover everything was fine. She hadn't been hurt in the assault nor was the baby.

And she knew this was true without a doubt.

A mother knows these things, she thought and then began to chuckle. Just imagining herself as a mother was still hard to contemplate.

With one last look at the decapitated security guard, she turned and walked away.

As she entered the front of the jewelry store again and passed by the glass counter where she had set the gold earrings down, she paused and then picked them up again.

Looking at them now, they took on an entirely new light for her.

"I earned these," she said to herself, knowing the earrings would always be a reminder to what had happened here today. And best of all, it would remind her how she had triumphed, by herself, with only her wits to get her by.

Squeezing the earrings in her palm, she grinned from ear to ear, then she headed out into the hallway to then go down to the main floor.

There was a shower with her name on it and, that too, she had earned.

DARK NIGHT

The ship broke in half like a giant egg, throwing men into the sea, where they sputtered and drowned. Debris covered the surface of the ocean, larger pieces smacking into men's flailing heads, knocking them unconscious and sending them into the briny deep. Only a few men survived; those lucky enough to grab the floating debris.

"Smith? Smith, where are you? Are you there? I can't see anything. It's too fucking dark." Smith was the XO. He was last seen falling into the water; he didn't resurface.

There was no moonlight, the night sky shrouded in clouds. Other voices called out in the darkness, each one filled with fear, more than one with terror.

"I don't know where I am!" a voice cried out. "What happened? Are we even alive?"

"Hollister, is that you?"

"Captain?"

"Yes, Hollister it's me. Who else is out there? Everyone, sound off!" He pulled himself higher on the debris he floated on, trying to get a better look at any survivors. He still could see nothing.

"I'm here."

"Who said that? State your name," the captain said.

"It's me, Mitchell, sir."

Mitchell was one of the engineers. A good man. The captain knew him well, though they'd had their problems with one another.

"Who else is out there? Come on, sound off. The only way we're going to survive this is if we pull together," the captain said.

"I'm here, sir. Capt. Rogers, sir."

Rogers strained to recognize the voice but it didn't come. "Say your blasted name, sailor. Speak up, that's a bloody order."

"It's Peregrine, sir."

Rogers nodded. Peregrine was one of the deck hands. "Good, good. Glad to know you survived, Peregrine. Anyone else?"

"I'm here, sir. It's Johansson."

Rogers hated to admit it but he had no idea who Johansson was, so he said, "Good to know you're alive, Johansson. Stay strong. We'll get through this."

"How, Captain?" Mitchell asked. "No one knows where we are. I know for a fact we didn't get a radio transmission out before the ship cracked up. No one knows we're out here. We're as good as dead."

"Stow that kind of talk, sailor. We'll get through this. We have to have faith."

"Faith? Sorry, sir, can't say I agree with you on that," Hollister said. "I'm afraid I have to be with Mitchell, though by doing so I suppose I'm signing my own death warrant."

More than five minutes passed in silence, no one speaking. Only the sounds of the waves slapping against the debris filled their ears.

Rogers used that time to try to come up with a plan. Surely there was a way for them to survive this terrible predicament. He mentally did a count of who had survived. There was himself, Mitchell, Peregrine, Johansson and Hollister. Out of a crew of fifty, only himself and four crewmen had managed not to go down with the ship.

"Well, Captain, you really fucked up, didn't you?" Mitchell said. "It looks like you killed us all."

"What are you talking about, Mitchell?" Rogers asked.

"The ship going down, sir. We shouldn't have been out here in the first place and now we're all going to die because of you."

"Fuck you, Mitchell. You knew the risk when you signed on to my crew." Rogers felt something on his leg. He tried not to give it much thought, hoping it was stray debris.

Peregrine spoke up. "Shut up, Mitchell. The captain's right. We knew what we signed on for when we went on this tour."

"No, you shut up, Peregrine," Mitchell snapped. "Fucking kiss ass." Was it Roger's imagination or did Mitchell's voice sound farther away.

"You know, Rogers," Mitchell kept going. "You wanted to get on top, you wanted to be rich and that's why you dragged us out to the middle of nowhere. I was warned about you and I didn't listen and now look at me now; look at all of us!"

Though Rogers wanted to defend himself, he knew Mitchell was right. He had taken on a salvage operation, hoping he would strike it rich. From the darkness surrounding him, he looked back on his life. There was one main regret. That regret was that he wished to go on living. That he wouldn't die out here in the middle of the ocean.

He could hear the men talking, calling to one another, and yes, their voices were becoming fainter. The current was taking each of them in a different direction, separating them from one another.

"We're drifting apart. We need to get back together. It's the only way to survive."

"Where are you? I can't see you. I don't even know which way to swim." The voice was Hollister's.

"This Way, Hollister. Over here, this way!" Rogers called out.

"I'm coming. Hang on, keep talking!" Hollister cried out but as he continued paddling his voice became fainter.

"No, Hollister, wrong way, come this way!"

"You know, I never liked you Rogers," Mitchell said. "From my first day on the ship I could see you were an asshole. But I swallowed my annoyance of you in the hope you might actually make me some money."

"So sorry to disappoint you, Mitchell. You make it sound like I planned this. We're all in the same boat here, so to speak."

"Well, at least I led a good life up till now." It was Hollister. "I had a good wife and mistress on the side and a few bucks in the bank. I drank and partied hard. Can every man say they've done the same?"

"Hollister, shut the hell up," Mitchell yelled. There was anger in his voice and Rogers wondered if it wasn't just from the stress of the situation. Perhaps Mitchell was jealous, too.

Suddenly, there was a tugging at Rogers' left leg, then he felt an odd sensation, something he had never felt before. He was pulled down, but no sooner did he almost go under than he bobbed back up, only his tight grip on the floating debris preventing him from going under for good.

The water was cold, frigid, he could feel his lips chattering. That was probably why, whatever had struck, was barely felt by him. His limbs were already stiffening. He slowly reached his left hand down into the cold water, and touched his leg where he had felt the tugging. As his fingers slid down his pants to where his knee would have been, his mouth dropped open in shock and horror. There was nothing there below the knee, it was gone. He could feel blood seeping out of his leg, warming his fingertips, and he already could feel slightly dizzy as the blood seeped into the ocean, draining his body of life.

Acting fast and knowing he had only a minute before he would bleed out, he tore off the shirtsleeve of his right arm and quickly applied a tourniquet. Pulling it as tight as he could, not worrying about restricting blood supply to the rest of the leg, he hoped the stump had stopped bleeding.

Somewhere in the distance, one of the other men cried out and Rogers wondered if that man was also being visited by an undersea predator. He thought the voice had belonged to Johansson.

These waters were shark invested and he was mildly surprised they had been in the water for as long as they had before the first one arrived to feed.

Rogers had lost his limb, and had applied the tourniquet in silence. He didn't want to worry the other men, they were his responsibility and he would do his best to keep them calm. God he was so cold and tired.

The darkness surrounded him like a shroud, a cloak of death he knew there would be no escape from.

He knew then that there was no surviving this ordeal.

Not if the sharks had already arrived to feed.

I'm dead. This is it, this is the end of my life. No more chapters, no sequel. No part two.

From across the dark void, Peregrine began to scream. Some of the other men called out to him, trying to get his attention, but there was no reply. The screams were quick, and far too brief, and then all was silent, only the other men calling out.

Rogers knew Peregrine had succumbed to the sharks.

"Are you happy, Rogers? Peregrine's dead. It was sharks, wasn't it? Had to be. My only hope is that you die before I do, you bastard!" Mitchell was screaming now and Rogers imagined the man's face must be beet red, despite the frigid waters.

"Go to hell, Mitchell," Roger spat.

Hollister cried out next. "Shit, something just bumped me. Oh God I'm next. I don't want to die! Please, God, I don't want to die!"

"Hang tough, Hollister. You can get through this," Rogers said, trying to be strong for his crewman.

"Hang tough? You surely can't be that stupid, Rogers!" Mitchell was yelling again. In a strange way, it seemed that Mitchell was enjoying himself, as if all of them dying was somehow justifying Mitchell's opinion of Rogers.

And then Hollister screamed again. It was high-pitched and filled with terror. The screams went on far longer than Rogers would have preferred. Soon they were mixed with gurgling sounds, as Hollister was pulled under the waves to then bob back up, desperately trying to suck in one more ounce of precious air, to live for one more brief second before the oblivion of his death consumed him forever.

And then it all became silent, only the slapping waves once more filling the night, the cacophony a gentle background to each horrible death.

"It looks like it's just you and me now, Rogers," Mitchell called as he began to laugh manically. Rogers could tell the man was losing his mind, not that he could blame him though. They had been out here for less than an hour, though it seemed like days. With no light and no way to measure time, it felt as if death had already swallowed them whole.

"You know, Mitchell, despite everything you said, I still can't hate you. If anything, I hope you'll accept my apology. I failed you. I failed myself, and I failed the crew."

Mitchell began laughing even harder, sometimes choking on bile as hypothermia set in.

If the sharks didn't get him, the freezing water would.

Rogers felt something bump his other leg, or should he say, 'remaining' leg. Whatever it was—as if there was any doubt— it was leaving him alone for the moment, although he had no doubt it would be back soon enough to finish the job.

Rogers looked up at the dark night sky, devoid of light. He thought how this would be the last sky he would ever see, and that soon he knew he would be gone from this world. But the sky would remain, as would the stars and the moon.

As he gazed up at the darkness above him, he truly felt significant, just another microorganism in the giant body that was the universe.

He felt something bump him again, and knew it wouldn't be long now. From somewhere in the distance, how far he had no idea, he could hear Mitchell laughing and cursing his name. It seemed Mitchell was dealing with his death by hating Rogers to the point it consumed the man, leaving nothing else—no fear, no terror, only anger.

Rogers had never felt so alone in his life than at that exact moment. Mitchell's voice was nothing but an echo now.

What can I do? Rogers wondered. What can I do to make up for the mistakes I've made in life? It's too late to repent now. Heaven or Hell, his fate was sealed, and his maker was now simply waiting for him to arrive.

He felt another tugging on his good leg and this time there was more of the pulling. Despite his numb limb, he did feel a subtle pang of pain. He didn't want to reach down, knowing what he would find, but he did so. He was correct, the leg was gone from just below the thigh. Whatever shark had taken a bite this time was greedier than the first one, and he could feel his blood pumping out with each beat of his chilled heart.

He didn't bother trying to staunch the blood flow, knowing to do so would only delay the inevitable.

There was a rushing in his ears and at first he thought it was the waves, but then realized it was his own beating pulse throbbing within his head.

He knew he was dying, that he had perhaps a minute left. With the last of his strength, he called out, "Well, Mitchell, it looks like this it for me! One thing I can be grateful for, unlike the others, I don't seem to be in much pain."

He heard Mitchell reply, but the words were garbled. And then whatever the man was trying to say was lost as he began screaming, shrieking in pain. Rogers knew the sharks had found Mitchell as well.

Rogers didn't know how long Mitchell lived, for with the man's screams fading in his ears, Rogers began to grow faint, as his remaining blood seeped into the ocean deep.

A small inner voice told him he was truly lucky, for unlike the others, he wasn't suffering as bad, but then he felt a tugging on his thigh, and he was yanked below the surface of the water.

As adrenaline filled his system, he struggled to climb back aboard his floating debris, and only managed to get his mouth and nose clear of the water. Then something sank its massive teeth into his torso and he felt every single tooth pierce his flesh.

He managed one final scream before he was pulled down, the darkness swallowing him whole.

DELUGE

"Daddy, why is there so much water now?"

Jason Patrick looked down at his five-year-old son and frowned, not having an answer for him.

After all, how do you explain to a young child that the world he had known, the one he'd lived in for the past five years since he was born, was now gone forever, swallowed under billions of gallons of seawater.

"I...I don't know, son, it just is," he said, knowing he was taking the coward's way out by not giving his son a true answer.

"But, Daddy, there's so much water, where are all the houses?"

Jason actually chuckled then, his son's naive face so innocent, so trusting. Jason peered over the side of the small rowboat he and his son were in, and as he gazed into the water's surface, he could just barely see the top of the fifty story skyscraper they were floating over. Off in the distance, a few radio and cable antennas sprouted out of the water like thin reeds in a swamp.

But it was what he saw more than five miles away, a lone silhouette jutting out of the water by only twenty or thirty feet. It was hard to gauge size from such a distance.

Off in the distance there was an object that looked out of place in the middle of an ocean of emptiness.

It was the a Statue of Liberty, her torch held high, but below that torch there was nothing, the rest of the statue swallowed whole like the rest of the world.

Jason turned around, searching for something in the emptiness, but there were no boats other than his small rowboat.

"Daddy, aren't you gonna answer me?"

Jason sighed heavily. "No, son, I suppose not. Look, Ricky, why don't you see how much food and water we have left. Can you do that for me?"

Ricky nodded, wanting to help his father.

"Good, then go to it while I figure out where we're supposed to go next."

"Okay," he said and went to the aft end of the boat to search through the beat up red Igloo resting there.

"Daddy?"

"Yes, son?" Jason asked, but he wasn't really paying attention to him.

"I miss Mommy."

And as Ricky said those words, the last one was like a punch to the gut and Jason couldn't help but remember everything that happened in the past few months, and as the thoughts flooded his mind, he nodded to his young son. "Yes, Ricky, I miss her, too."

It was ten months ago and Jason was watching the news.

"And for some unknown reason," the meteorologist was saying, *"the Polar icecaps have begun to melt at an alarming rate. Scientific teams have been dispatched to the Antarctic but at this time the great minds in their fields are stumped. Predictions have been made and if they are true, the water level of the Earth will begin rising more than a foot a day with no end in sight. Populations below the waterline have been urged to…"*

Jason turned off the TV, not wanting to hear anymore.

He turned at the sound of his wife, Karen, walking into the den.

"Everything all right, honey?"

Jason shook his head, pointing at the blank television screen.

"I doubt it. According to the eggheads who get to tell us what to do, the world is about to become one big swimming pool."

She chucked at that. "Oh, dear, I'm sure they're just making it worse than it sounds, like they always do. Give it a few days and it'll all blow over."

He snorted lightly. "Hmmph, I hope your right 'cause if you're not then we're all gonna have to grow gills real soon."

A month later things were worse than Jason could have ever imagined, as he gazed out from the roof of his house at the other rooftops of his neighborhood. That was all that was left, the rest now under water. He watched a Buick Pontiac float by upside down, the undercarriage covered in seaweed and bits of ocean refuse. When the car was even with him, a limp hand slipped out of the window when the car bobbed for a moment. The arm was missing flesh in a dozen places, thanks to the marine life in the water.

The surface of the water was filled with the floating detritus of a dead civilization.

Beer cans, clothing, trash barrels, couches, all were mixed in with larger, uprooted trees and shrubs. It was all mixed together in a massive soup that swirled around in the current. The waterline was now to the gutters of the house and Jason knew in another day; those too, would be hidden under the muddy and tainted water.

The water would either kill or make every human ill who tried to drink it, as it was full of contaminates from oil, to gas, to chemicals from factories; not to mention raw sewage.

But none of that was as bad as when a human body floated by, the abdomen always bloated with decomposing gases, which allowed the corpse to float for a time. Jason had to admit it was the eyes that always got to him the most. The wide, dead eyes that stared at nothing. The mouths were usually open, too, sagging and filled with putrid water. Usually, some form of creature was using it as a floating haven. Rats had taken to hiding in the bodies, floating with the corpses as they had nowhere else to go. It was a gruesome sight and whenever a body floated by, Jason made sure to distract Ricky so the boy wouldn't see.

Karen walked up to Jason from the other side of the roof. It was steep, but not so steep it couldn't be traversed with care. She had gone to the other side to pee, not wanting to do it in front of her family.

Ricky was sitting on the roof near Jason's feet, playing with a small model of a cruise ship. There was the logo of *Walt Disney World* on the side of it, a souvenir from their vacation on their *Disney* cruise. He wondered where that ship was now. Was it floating around out there somewhere?

She spoke low so Ricky wouldn't hear her. "What're we going to do, Jason?"

He looked at her and thought it was a valid question that he didn't have an answer for. He could feel the rage welling up inside him because of it. He wanted to yell at her, tell her to stop asking stupid questions.

For more than two weeks they had been on the roof, waiting for a rescue that would never come. At least he was coming to this realization.

"We wait," he said softly, the anger in his voice hidden, yet still there. Karen nodded, seeing his face and knowing the turmoil he was feeling. Hell, she felt it, too. She went and sat down next to Ricky and the two played as she hugged him to her.

Jason gazed down at them for more than a minute before looking back up. He let his eyes scan the rooftops once more, seeing no one else looking back at him. It was like they were the only people left alive in the world.

He knew now he should have evacuated with the rest of the neighborhood, but he'd worked hard for his home and he was dammed if he was going to just walk away from it. Of course now the house was ruined, and he was trapped without a future.

"Daddy, I'm thirsty," Ricky said.

Jason heard his son and nodded, and as if he was on autopilot he went to the chimney. There, tied with phone line, was a red Igloo full of bottled water, juice, and food, whatever they could salvage. He pulled up the line and the Igloo bounced off the insides of the chimney. Then he was pulling it out. He opened it, grabbed a juice box and returned the Igloo to the inside of the chimney.

It was hidden for the simple reason there had been a time when it was possible others might have wanted the food and water, so Jason had figured out how to hide it. And he didn't think he would need his phone line anytime soon.

Jason and Karen both looked up at the same time at the sound of an engine.

Jason, moved back down the roof so he was standing with Karen, looking out over the rooftops at the approaching powerboat. It was a sleek craft, built for speed, with lightning bolts down the side. As it drew nearer, the roar of its powerful engine echoed off the water and through the rooftops.

"Is it help?" Karen asked hopefully.

"I sure as hell hope so," Jason said.

There was nothing to do but wait, and slowly the motorboat grew closer until it began to power down, coming up to the edge of the roof like it was a dock.

As the boat pulled up, Jason had his first real look at the craft's occupants and his blood ran cold at the sight of the three men glaring back at him.

They all had hard eyes, unshaved faces and disheveled hair. But that wasn't what had Jason fearing for himself and his family.

It was the weapons each man carried. One man carried a shotgun, the metal faded and worn, while the other two carried what looked like assault rifles. Jason wasn't an expert on guns, but like most Americans he had seen enough movies to know a gun was a gun and any one of them could kill you if it was pointed at you and the trigger squeezed.

"I'm scared," Karen said softly as she moved closer to Jason. He had to agree with her. The three coldhearts didn't look like they were here to rescue them.

The man with the shotgun hopped onto the roof as the other men leveled their weapons at Jason and family.

"Good day to you folks," the man with the shotgun said. He was looking into Jason's eyes as he spoke. "We were just passing by and we noticed what an attractive woman you had in your midst. We were wondering if perhaps she might like to accompany us back to our home."

Jason was caught off guard. That was the last thing he expected to hear. With no gun of his own he was basically helpless, but he'd be damned if he was going to give up Karen without a fight.

"I'm sorry, but my wife would like to stay with me," Jason said, his voice level but utterly terror-stricken inside. The muzzle of the shotgun looked awfully big.

"Daddy, what do the men want?" Ricky asked.

"Quiet, Ricky, grown-ups are talking," Jason snapped.

"Hmm, cute kid," Shotgun said. He turned and looked over his shoulder at one of the other men. "Hey, Bert, can we use a kid?"

"Nah, the damn rugrats just get in the way. Leave him."

Shotgun nodded and turned back to face Jason. "Well, you're in luck, pal, we'll just take the woman and be on our way."

"Like hell you will," Jason said and took a step forward in anger, but no sooner did he do so then three weapons were cocked, muzzles leveled at him.

Shotgun actually chuckled, knowing he held all the cards.

"Shit, either you're the bravest or the stupidest asshole I've met in a while. Listen, here's how it's gonna go. We can either shoot you and the kid and take the woman, or we can shoot you, take the woman and leave the kid alone on this roof, or you can just give us the woman and we'll go." He smiled, showing off yellow teeth. "You found me in a good mood today and I don't feel like wasting bullets if I don't have to."

Jason opened his mouth to tell the man no when Karen raised her hand and touched Jason's arm.

"No, Jason, don't. Let me go with them. You need to think about Ricky."

"But I can't just let…"

"Yes, you can. You have no choice."

"But Karen..." Jason began but Shotgun cut him off.

"Look, enough with the Oprah moment, you, bitch, get in the fucking boat, now," Shotgun growled.

"Okay, okay," she said. "But can I say goodbye to my son?"

Shotgun rolled his eyes and sighed as he glanced at his two men who shrugged.

"Fine, just hurry the fuck up. Christ, I'm too good to people."

Karen turned and knelt down so she was next to her son. Ricky was crying now, having heard enough to understand his mommy was leaving.

"But I don't want you to go, Mommy. I want you to stay with me and Daddy."

"I know that honey, but I need you to be brave for me, okay? I'll be back soon, but for now you need to take care of Daddy for me. Can you do that?" Tears welled up in the corners of her eyes but she fought them off, wanting to be strong for her son.

Ricky nodded.

"Good, that's real good." She leaned over and kissed him on the forehead, then each cheek, and then a peck on his trembling lips. "Remember to do what Daddy says, all right? And always know that I love you."

Ricky nodded, crying some more, sniffles filling the air. Karen pushed off her knees and stood up. She turned to see Jason who was staring at her, his hands curled into fists.

She knew him well, and though it would be certain death, all she had to do was nod and he would rush the man with the shotgun and try to save her. But she didn't nod, instead she smiled.

"I love you, Jason, you take care of Ricky." She looked at Ricky. "You both take care of each other."

"Aww for cryin' out loud, enough with the bullshit. It's like a fuckin Hallmark movie goin' on here!" Shotgun yelled. "You, get the fuck in the boat, last warning."

Karen hugged Jason briefly, sharing one tender kiss, then Shotgun was yanking her out of Jason's arms and shoving her toward the boat. The two men grabbed her and pushed her to the deck where one of them pulled out some zip ties and secured her hands. Shotgun took a step back to the boat as he grinned at Jason.

"Nice doin' business with ya, pal. Now you have a nice day."

"Fuck you," Jason spat.

The man looked like he might change his mind and just shoot Jason and his son, especially after hearing Jason's epitaph, but instead he only grinned wider.

He turned and climbed into the boat and it started up. A second later it was roaring off and Jason could only catch the silhouette of Karen receding with the boat.

Then it banked around a rooftop a block away and was gone.

Soon the roar of the engine faded away as well and only the lapping of the water against the house remained.

With tears in his eyes, Jason hugged his son.

"Daddy, I'm hungry," Ricky said from the aft end of the rowboat. Jason heard his son but he didn't reply. Instead, his head sagged in sadness.

The two had been floating for days and were out of food, their water supply dangerously low. Jason's stomach was tied up in knots. One of those knots was his hunger and thirst as he was giving his son almost all of their rations, and he had only drunk enough to be able to still function.

The boat had drifted out to sea now and the torch from the Statue of Liberty was behind them, only a distant shape on the horizon. As he stared down into the boats innards, he remembered how lucky they had been to even find it. It was pure luck that had given them the chance to escape the rooftop of his home.

It had been days after Karen was taken and it was pitch black outside, no power anywhere for as far as the eye could see. Once in a while an airplane or helicopter would fly overhead, high up in the night sky, but where it came from or went to was a mystery. Jason had to wonder what was left of dry land. Surely the highest mountains were still above the new sea level.

And then he heard a soft thump in the darkness.

At first he wondered if the raiders had returned for him or Ricky, but when there were no new sounds of trouble, he figured it must have been a log or something similar that had struck one of the nearby rooftops.

But the next morning he awoke to see an actual rowboat caught between the eaves of his neighbor's house. Ricky was still sleeping so Jason jumped into the cold water and swam for the boat. There were no oars but still, it was better than nothing.

There was a rope attached to an eyehole and he used this to pull the craft back to his roof, swimming like a drowning man on his last legs. The boat was heavy and swimming and towing a boat was harder than he thought it would be.

But huffing and puffing, he reached his roof and climbed back onto it. Ricky, disturbed by the noise, woke to see Jason grinning happily, though now soaking wet.

"Daddy?"

"Ricky, it's time we got out of here. Come on, son, let's get what we have and see if we can go find Mommy."

Ricky snapped fully awake then, moving off the roof to gather their few belongings.

Jason knew to give his son false hope was wrong. The odds of finding Karen were slim to none, but at the moment, false hope was all he could offer.

The rowboat rocked back and forth with each gentle wave as father and son sat lifelessly in the bottom. The torch for the Statue of Liberty was now more than ten miles behind them, the current pulling them along deeper into the ocean.

Both were tired and exhausted, the bright sun baking the tops of their heads and cooking their exposed flesh.

Jason was drifting in and out of sleep when he felt the rowboat buck beneath him.

One second he was dreaming about dry land, the next the boat was flipping over and tossing him, Ricky and all their possessions into the water.

"Daddy!" Ricky screamed as he went flying into the air to splash like a rocket into the choppy surface.

"No! Ricky, No!" Jason screamed as he went under water, sucking in a mouthful of seawater. As he went under, he spotted the reason for their crash in the middle of an ocean. They weren't as far into the ocean as he imagined and the rowboat had caught on a radio tower of some kind. The current had been so strong the boat had capsized, spilling him and Ricky into the water.

Jason swam to the surface, his only thoughts for his son. When he popped up and into the air he sucked in a lungful of the best tasting oxygen in his life. He spotted his son to his right. The boy was holding onto the red Igloo, using it as a flotation device. Already Ricky was floating away from Jason, the current pulling them apart.

"Daddy, help me!" Ricky screamed, scared out of his mind.

"Hold on, son, I'm coming!" Jason replied, and began to swim towards his son's bobbing body.

It was when he was halfway there that his blood turned to ice and he felt his stomach drop out of his body. The reason for his terror was the white fin that broke the surface of the water, slicing through the waves like a dagger.

No sooner did one appear then another rose to slice the surf, the menacing triangle a figment of death to anyone who saw it.

Jason wasn't scared of the sharks though, his worry for his son overrode all else. Gritting his jaw, he began to swim faster, needing to reach his son before the sharks attempted to attack him.

Ricky was crying now, only his dunkings under the surface slowing his sobs.

"Hold on, Ricky, I'm coming!" Jason screamed as he powered onward. But he wasn't in shape and he could already feel his arms tiring as he forced himself to continue.

The sharks were circling Ricky now, like wolves would if they had trapped wounded prey. Jason used all his remaining energy to push himself to reach Ricky. When he finally was within a few feet of his son, he used his fist to punch a shark as it swam by.

"Fuck off, you bastards, get outta here!" Jason screamed.

"Daddy, I'm scared!" Ricky yelled.

"I know, son, just hold on to that cooler and be brave! I won't let anything happen to you!

If only Jason could have kept that promise, he gladly would have given his own life in return.

As he punched and kicked at the sharks as they swam by, in truth he knew it was like a rabbit pummeling an elephant.

It was as he was staring at Ricky, his son's eyes wide in terror that one of the sharks decided it was through playing with its food.

It came up from below, Ricky's twitching legs a beacon to it, its mouth open wide, a double layer of teeth gleaming in the reflecting surface of the water.

Jason was fighting with the other shark and he glanced to his son to see him staring at him. Father and son locked gazes and Ricky said, "Daddy?"

Then, like the flash of a picture bulb, it happened so fast, Ricky was yanked under the surface. The Igloo was still tightly gripped in his small hands and it went under with him.

"Noooo! Ricky! Noooo!" Jason screamed when his son was pulled from view.

Seconds later, a growing circle of blood rose to the surface and the red Igloo popped up like an air balloon, bouncing on the ocean surface like a stray float at a pool party.

"Noooo!" Jason screamed, slapping the water with his fists. The other shark was gone now, diving under water to feast on the remains of its catch.

Jason treaded water and tears washed away as fast as he could make them, his heart broken to the point it would never heal. As he wept, a piece of Ricky's shirt floated to the surface and Jason swam to it, grabbing it with his right hand and touching it to his lips.

"Oh my God, no. How could this happen? How can any God let this happen?"

Of course there was no reply, only the sounds of the ocean and a few seagulls flying way up in the sky, the birds too high to hear his pleas for answers.

And then he felt a bump on his left foot and he knew the sharks were back. His son was the appetizer and he was going to be the main course. Though the anger and loss he felt for his son was absolute, Jason still wasn't ready to die, so he turned and began to swim to the overturned boat. As his instinct for self preservation pushed him, the tears still cascaded down his cheeks to be washed into the ocean.

Another brush of something large struck his kicking legs and he cried out. As he swam now, he knew at any moment he would feel the bite of teeth that would take his leg off and send him to a watery grave.

A half thought caressed the front of his mind. Would that be so bad? Would it be so bad to just die? Sure there would be pain, but not forever. He imagined it wouldn't last that long at all. Then he would be oblivious, life's torture finally ended. What was there to live for anyway? His son was dead, devoured by the monsters of the ocean and his wife was captured by bandits, probably dead as well.

But then he felt another bump and he knew he wanted to live. God help him, despite everything, he still wanted to live.

He began swimming for the overturned boat, and when he reached it, he grabbed the rough side and pulled himself up. It was hard, his arms weak from swimming. When he was halfway out of the water a fin appeared, circling around him. He screamed in fright as he struggled to pull himself higher. It was just as his feet left the water that a massive shark appeared, its teeth clamping down on his left foot.

But the shark's aim was off and all it got for its trouble was Jason's shoe. Pulled from his foot, Jason slid down the side of the upside down boat, but he managed to hold on. The shark disappeared and Jason pulled himself higher.

Climbing to the top, which should be the bottom, more fins appeared and they circled for another half hour, but eventually they disappeared, deciding whatever food there was to be had was gone.

Jason balanced on the upside down boat and cried tears of loss, of pity and of sorrow. He cried until there were no tears left, and then he simply dry-sobbed.

He couldn't get the last look of Ricky's face out of his mind. The way his son had looked at him, knowing his father would save him. But he hadn't. He'd only let his son die.

He turned his head to the left and right, seeing nothing but ocean in all directions. Any possessions in the boat had floated away to be lost from sight. The place where Ricky had been killed was lost, any blood now dispersed into the water. His son was one with the ocean now and Jason knew sooner or later so would he.

With nothing to do but lay still, as the boat was far too large to flip over on his own, especially when he was in the water, he lay on his side and closed his eyes, wanting to live and at the same time wanting to die.

The row boat floated onward, deeper into the ocean. Not that it mattered for the entire world was one big ocean and he was lost in it.

Three days later, Jason could barely lift his head.

He was dying, he knew that without a doubt. Any tears for his lost son and wife had dried up more than a day ago and now only hoarse sobs escaped his dry, cracked lips.

In every direction there was nothing but water, the sun above slowly cooking him like a roast in the oven.

Where his flesh was exposed it was now a dark red, blisters appearing to pop and ooze.

Jason's vision was blurring and a few times he imagined he saw land, but no sooner would his heart beat faster, then the mirage would fade away to be lost in the infinite ocean.

The vastness of the water was hard to imagine. New York was gone, as was the rest of the eastern seaboard. He assumed a few mountain peaks may have survived the flooding, but they were far, far away from his position.

One time, as he raised his head, he saw Ricky looking back at him. His son was floating in the water, no more than six feet from the overturned boat, both his hands held out to Jason, pleadingly.

Jason raised a hand to his son, begging for him to come closer, but then the boy was raised out of the water, the bottom half of his body stuck in a shark's mouth. Jason saw the boy's entrails as they spilled out of the cavernous mouth, and saw the shark bite down, chewing merrily. Then the image was gone to be replaced by the endless waves.

By the fourth day, Jason was all but lifeless. He managed to move his head to the left and right side just once, praying to spot a ship or anything on the horizon that could bode a rescue.

But there was nothing there.

No help would come and save him on his eleventh hour, no ship would ride out of the sunset to take him on board.

No, this was real life. And in real life sometimes people died and the good guys didn't win.

He knew this was one of those times.

Though he had tried his best to save his family, he had lost miserably.

As he craned his head to the side of the boat, he knew there was only one thing left to do.

With hopelessness filling him, one so great he barely thought about what he was doing, he used the last of his strength to shift his weight and tumble into the cold water.

He was so weak from hunger and thirst that he barely moved as his body plummeted below the surface.

He didn't fight it, there was no reason to.

He was a man who knew what he was doing. He was going to die, the only question was whether he wanted to bake like a poached egg on the boat or let the cool water consume him.

As he sucked in the water and it filled his lungs, he had yet another vision of Ricky.

This time his son was whole, and he reached out with his small hands and embraced Jason, taking him onward to whatever came next after death.

As Jason began to choke, the ice cold water slowly killing him as he drowned in an ocean world, he actually smiled.

Though Ricky was obviously a mirage, it was all he could ask for as a begging man had to take what he could get.

With the sun looking down on the empty rowboat, Jason closed his eyes and became one with his new world.

EMAIL OFFERINGS

Date: 7 July 2010 08:12
From: John <JohnM@medent.com>
To: Max <warvet101@gmail.com>
Subject: I need your help!

Dear Grandpa,

Mommy and Daddy are dead.

I'm in the attic now, hiding.

The monsters have gotten into the house and I'm so scared. I know I should be brave, after all, I'm almost seven but I can't help it.

When Mommy and Daddy made me come up here, Daddy gave me his laptop. He told me to hold onto it for him.

It was as I climbed into the attic that the monsters came up the stairs.

Mommy screamed and Daddy turned to fight them. He told me to be brave, to not come down no matter what.

Daddy tried to get Mommy to climb the small, fold-down stairs to the attic but she wouldn't leave him.

That was when one of the monsters got by daddy and grabbed Mommy.

I…I try not to think what Mommy looked like as the monster sank its teeth into her neck. I saw Mommy's eyes go wide with pain. But there was something else there, too. Something I don't really understand. It was sadness, I think, the sorrow of knowing she wouldn't get to see me again.

Pretty smart, huh, Grandpa? Mommy says I'm smarter than I should be for my age.

Mommy pushed the ladder closed and told me to stay quiet. That was all I could do, I was so scared. I still am.

Just before the ladder closed and locked me in the attic, I saw Mommy and Daddy surrounded by those monsters, and then the monsters were eating them.

I sat in silence for the next two hours, not moving, not breathing. I could hear the monsters down below, walking around, banging against the walls. The sounds of them feeding made me sick and I almost threw up once, but I remember what Mommy said and I stayed quiet.

When I thought it was safe to move, I crawled to the fold-down ladder. There was a really thin line separating it from the floor. By looking through the line with one eye closed, I could see down below.

I saw Mommy and Daddy but they didn't look like I remembered them.

Mommy had no face, half her scalp was now missing, and Daddy only had one arm, his other in the mouth of another monster. His stomach had been torn open and his insides were hanging out, swinging back and forth as he stumbled around the hallway. I stared at them for almost five minutes and finally I couldn't look anymore.

I cried then, I cried for Mommy and Daddy, and I cried for me, too. I was an orphan now, what was I supposed to do?

I sat there, silent, alone in the attic darkness for almost a half day when I realized the laptop was right there. I used it all the time so couldn't believe I had ignored it. I bet Daddy would have said it was shock I was feeling.

And that's what I'm doing now, Grandpa, I'm emailing you to tell you that I don't know what to do. You told me before that you were in the war. So I need you to come kill the bad monsters—Mommy and Daddy too now—and save me.

I'm hungry now, too, Grandpa, and I have to go to the bathroom. There are no windows up here so I can't see outside, but I can hear the screams of people and the crashes of cars and stuff.

Please come save me,

Your grandson,

Timmy

Date: 7 July 2010 09:11
From: Max <warvet101@gmail.com>
To: John <JohnM@medent.com>
Subject: Be Brave

Dear Timmy,

My heart goes out to you, my daughter-in-law and my son, Timmy. If I wasn't seeing the 'monsters' for myself, I would think you were playing some kind of game with me.

From what you told me, I have to believe my son—your father —is dead and has become one of them. Your father was a good man, Timmy, you should know that, and from what you told me, it looks like he died trying to save your mom, too.

I have some bad news to tell you, son. I'm afraid your grandma is dead. It happened a few hours ago. We were in the kitchen, the house boarded up tight, when one of what you call a monster broke through the barricade on the back door. Grandma tried to stop it from getting in but she was bitten on the back of the hand as she did. She did manage to kill the monster. Your grandma is a tough old woman, and she used a broom to do the job. She spun it around and jabbed the top of it right into the monster's eye, shattering its milky orb and plunging the handle into its brain. It was as she was pulling the broom handle out that the zombie—that's what they're really called— had a little life in it yet and bit her on the back of her hand before dying for good.

We didn't know at the time what would happen, as the news had mentioned it. But I found out soon enough.

First she grew sick, her skin paling to the color of tapioca. Her eyes became sunken in and her lips were pulled back off her gums, making her look like she was grinning. Only this grin was morbid, a sick rictus of a smile that would make any man sick with revulsion.

We had enough time to say our goodbyes, and though she didn't want to die, you should know Timmy, she was okay with it. See, son, me and her have both lived full, long lives and if the good Lord calls us now, we're ready to go.

But not you, Timmy, it's far too early for you to go meet the Lord.

When she came back at first I didn't realize it. I was sitting in that old armchair in the bedroom as she slept. The sheets were pulled up to her face and I thought it was so she could shield her eyes from the sunlight seeping behind the curtains. But now I think she just wanted some privacy in her last moments alive on this earth.

The low moan was the first sign that she wasn't right. I shifted in my chair and watched as she slowly began to sit up, the sheet slipping off her face and chest. At first I was elated, thinking she was better, but as soon as I saw her face…well, I don't need to tell you all the details. But the pronounced veins spider webbing under her skin, and the way her eyes were glassed over and now a milky white, told me my wife wasn't my wife anymore.

I used the baseball bat I kept in the hall closet—the one you and me used a few times in that field a block from my house—and I killed her with it. I guess I killed her again with it if she was technically dead already.

As I write this to you, Timmy, I'm in the living room; the zombies are still outside and banging on the boarded up windows.

Grandma is upstairs, still in the bed we slept in for over forty years. I covered her up and left her there. It was hard to ignore the blood as it seeped into the sheets and blankets but I closed the door and I don't think I'll be going back in there anytime soon. The place we laid down for sleep, loved and spent so much time together is now her makeshift mausoleum. I wish I could do better for her but it's all I can offer her at this moment in time.

I probably shouldn't be telling you about all this, son, but I feel you need to know the truth. It's the only way you're going to survive the next few days.

You need to stay brave, Timmy, for you won't be alone for long. As soon as I finish this email and hit SEND, I'm going to the basement, getting my double barrel shotgun and my .45, and I'm coming to get you.

You're my only remaining family, Timmy, and I won't let those dead bastards get you, too. They won't take my whole family, I won't let them.

So stay quiet in that attic and wait for me. I don't know how long it will take but I will email you along the way to keep you up to date.

I love you, grandson,

See you soon,

Grandpa

Date: 7 July 2010 09:45
From: John <JohnM@medent.com>
To: Max <warvet101@gmail.com
Subject: Okay, I'll wait.

Grandpa,

I just opened Dad's laptop and saw your email. I'm so glad you got the one I sent.

I will wait for you, Grandpa but I don't know how long that will be. See, the zombies as you told me to call them are getting angry, or it seems like that to me.

They know I'm up here hiding in the attic and I saw Dad trying to get at the string that pulls the fold-down ladder down. It's funny. He doesn't seem like my dad anymore, but somehow he still remembered how to open the ladder, or sort of.

Mom doesn't do much anymore. Since she died, she just walks back and forth in the hallway.

One of the other zombies brought up something bloody and gross. It was eating the stuff and when the zombie reached the rest in the hallway, they all began to fight over it. It looked a lot like raw steak but with bits of tendrils and gross stuff hanging from it. I didn't look too hard as it made me sick. I keep peeking into the small line between the ladder and the floor so I have a good view of them walking around below me. I know a few of them, they're my neighbors. I saw the Stewarts there, both of them. Marge looks pretty bad but Phil only has a small hole in his neck. I liked them because they always let me call them by their first names. They walk around the hallway and act like they don't know my parents, which is weird. They've known each other for years.

I have to go the bathroom now but I'm holding it in. If I can't hold it anymore, I guess I'll have to go on the insulation in the corner. I know my dad would kill me for doing it but seems he's one of the zombies now, I don't think he'll care.

Please hurry, Grandpa. I'm trying to be brave and I want to cry but so far I'm keeping it in. You taught me to be strong, so did Dad, and that's what I'm trying to do. But it's hard, especially with Mom and Dad below me and the way they look.

They look dead but they're still walking around.

Please hurry,

Your grandson,

Timmy

Date: 7 July 2010 13:04
From: Max <warvet101@gmail.com>
To: John <JohnM@medent.com>
Subject: I'm on my way

Dear Timmy,

I'm in my car, parked outside of a Starbucks, using their internet connection so I can email you and let you know what's happening. I hope you're still okay. I pray you are.

It was tough for me to get this far, I'll tell you that. The roads are choked with zombies and stalled cars, fires are everywhere and explosions are common as underground gas lines keep erupting.

It's like a war zone out here.

If I had to guess how long it would take me to reach you, I would have to say I should be there by sunset. So far, I've managed to keep moving in my car. If I have to leave it, well…I don't want to think about that far ahead. I don't like my chances on foot, I know that.

It was tough leaving my house though. Once I had my shotgun and .45, I went to the back door and pulled off the boards. As soon as I did this, five of the dead bastards came for me. I shot two in the head and the others I shot in the chest.

I saw the two that got hit in the head stayed down, but the other three were trying to get up pretty quick. I sidestepped them and ran to the garage, and was in my car and leaving before the dead bastards were on their feet again. That's when I learned it's the head that takes them down for good. Makes sense. No brain, no way to control the body.

But when I got into my car I couldn't believe my bad luck. There was almost no gas. It seemed my now late wife, God rest her soul, hadn't bothered to fill it up. So the first thing I had to do was go to the gas station.

This proved more difficult with zombies everywhere. I pulled in to the pumps and no one was around. There were a few zombies across the street and I quickly began filling up—thank the Lord for pay-at-the-pump—as they started heading toward me.

It was when the tank was a little more than half full that a zombie came out from behind another parked car at the pumps and sank its teeth into my left arm. Well, Timmy, let me tell you, I was plum scared out of my britches.

The damn thing was gnawing on my arm like it was a turkey leg, and as it kept chewing and spitting out the material of my shirt, I pulled my .45 and shot it in the head. Then I checked my arm.

The damn plastic was all scraped up by the zombie's teeth. I tell ya, Timmy, do you have any idea how much a prosthetic arm goes for these days? My veteran's disabilities insurance only goes so far.

As more of the zombies came for me, I topped off the gas tank and jumped back in. I was gone a few seconds later as I watched the stumbling corpses try to follow me in my rearview mirror.

There are a few around my car now as I type this but with just their fists, they can't hurt me. As soon as I'm done with this email, I'll send it to you and get on my way.

Stay safe, Timmy, I'm comin' for ya.

Love Grandpa.

Date: 7 July 2010 13:50
From: John <JohnM@medent.com>
To: Max <warvet101@gmail.com>
Subject: It's getting bad here

Dear Grandpa

I don't know how much longer I'll be safe up here. I'm so scared and I'm crying all the time. It's so hot up here in the attic and I'm so thirsty. I finally went pee in the corner. I had no choice. Now it smells bad up here.

But that's not the worst thing I want to tell you about.

About a half hour ago, the zombies almost got me.

It was Dad. He managed to get the ladder down. As soon as it dropped down, the zombies tried to get up the folding stairs. Luckily for me, they can't seem to really climb that well and the ladder was a tricky obstacle for them. (I learned the word 'obstacle' in school). The zombies still kept trying to climb and finally they just crawled over one another to reach me.

It was my mom that was the first into the attic opening. She didn't look too good, Grandpa. Her skin was so white and her mouth and chin were covered in blood from when she was eating some of that gross stuff that other zombie had brought in earlier. I swear to God, Grandpa, when she looked at me, I almost peed my pants. Her eyes were so dead but yet they were alive, too. There was something in them now, too, something hungry.

Okay, so when Mom began coming into the attic, I knew I couldn't let her, or the ones behind her, so I grabbed the first thing near me—a plastic Santa Claus. I hit Mom over the head with it and it bounced off her like it was…well, plastic.

With nothing else on hand, I hit her again as she tried to reach out and bite me, and after the second hit, she lost her balance and fell. She struck the zombies behind her and they all fell down to the floor. But Dad wasn't in the group and he began climbing over the bodies to get at me.

I used the rest of the Christmas decorations and pushed them into the opening. They fell down and landed on Dad, covering him with garland and tinsel.

I would have laughed if I wasn't so scared. There was other stuff in the attic so I began pushing it into the hole. Down went the old record player you gave Dad a few years ago, and down went my old box of toys I asked Mom to save for me.

I managed to shove enough stuff into the opening that it's now clogged.

I'm fine now, but there's one thing I should tell you about, Grandpa. I have a cut on my wrist and I don't know how I got it. I think Mom might have bitten me before she fell. Does that mean I'm going to turn into one of them, like Grandma? I don't want to Grandpa, please don't let me turn into one of them. It's not fair if that happens. That's all, it's just not fair.

I'm going to go now. The battery on my dad's laptop is getting low. I'll check Dad's email account a little later to see if you're almost here to save me.

I love you Grandpa,

Timmy.

Date: 7 July 2010 17:44
From: Max <warvet101@gmail.com>
To: John <JohnM@medent.com>
Subject: I'm outside!

Timmy

I made it Grandson, I'm outside your house!

It was a hard ride here, I'll tell you that. The zombies are everywhere, and the front of my car looks like I drove it through a slaughterhouse. The engine is coated with blood and is smoking something awful. The smell of charred flesh is filling the air around me, making me want to gag as it blows into the vents. But I need the air as it's hot out and I have to keep the windows closed or risk getting attacked.

I'm looking at your house now and I don't like what I see, son. There are zombies everywhere. Your front door is open and they're walking in and out like it's a summer house party. Oh God, I just saw your mother. She walked outside and stumbled away. Wait, there's your father!

Oh my God, my only son…he's dead. The tears are coming despite my resolve to be strong. I want to go over and hug him but I know that would be a mistake. Wow, I can't believe it, they're all dead.

Only you remain, Timmy, and as soon as I figure out the best way to get inside your house and kill all the zombies, I'll be right there.

I hope you've been safe since your last email, and I hope you've…..

Oh sweet Jesus, oh no, I don't believe it, not you, too.

Date: 7 July 2010 18:52
From: Max <warvet101@gmail.com>
To: John <JohnM@medent.com>
Subject: Goodbye

To my grandson, Timmy,

I'm sending you this email even though I can see you on your front lawn. I'm so sorry, Timmy, I tried to get here as fast as I could. I tried to save you.

Oh, you see me, good, that will make it easier for me to do what I must as your mother and father are also close by.

I'll finish this email in a minute.

Okay, it's done. You, your mother, and your father are now dead with bullets to the head. I can't believe I had the courage to shoot all three of you, especially you, my grandson. But it's for the best. I don't want to think about you wandering around as zombies. And now that you're at rest, we can all meet up in Heaven as I'm sure your grandma is waiting for us.

So this email isn't for you, as you're dead and will never read it. This is for me, so I can leave my last thoughts somewhere. I need to as there's no one else to tell.

See, there's no reason to continue.

No, I'm not a coward and taking suicide isn't an easy way out…not to me anyway On the contrary, I actually find suicide an almost heroic act. To override one's survival instinct and commit the ultimate act is one of strength, courage and resolve.

And I will admit right now, it's easy to be this way when there's nothing left to live for.

I've lived a long life, my grandson. I've served my country but that country is gone, replaced by a land of the dead. My entire family is gone and as far as I know, I'm one of the last few in this state left alive.

Sure, I could try to find other survivors, but for me, at my age, what would be the point? The future is for the young and I'm of the past.

So as soon as I finish this email, I'll send it, and maybe one day someone will read it.

And as my left index finger hits send, my right finger will be wrapped around the trigger of my .45, the barrel in my mouth and angled up so it will penetrate my brain. I try to see the screen as the tears flow freely but it's getting difficult.

Whoever is left alive to read this, I wish you luck in your undead world and know that Max Carlson was a man who loved and was loved, and that in the end, he took the only real option left to him.

SEND

Date: July 2010 13:14
From: Will <Willtrent@hotmail.com>
To: Tim <Tim7theman@juno.com>
Subject: Dinner Party

Hey Tim,

What's up? Listen, I don't think I'll be able to make it to your dinner party tonight. I'm afraid something's come up, something beyond my control. See, I'm trapped in my car and there are zombies swarming the highway. There's at least ten of them banging on my car right now and I don't know how long the windows will be able to handle their pounding.

The zombies are something else, all covered in rotting flesh and pus. They're ruining the paint job on my car. Hell, I just got it washed yesterday. Why is it always like that? You wash your car, spend the ten bucks, and bam, a zombie outbreak arrives.

So anyway, I had heard from Greg in accounting that Cheryl was going to be at your dinner party. I heard she was hot, and man, I wanted to meet her. But I guess you'll just have to say hi for me in my place.

I would have called but I left my cell phone at the office and luckily I had my laptop with me in the car.

Man, they are really pounding on the windows, slobbering over the glass. They remind me of Pavlov's dogs and I guess I'm the dinner bell.

Funny, whenever I thought about how I was gonna die; it was never as the Blue Plate Special for a horde of zombies.

But, hey, win some, lose some, I guess.

Oh, wow, looks like the guy in the car next to me just lost a bet. He actually opened his door and tried to make a run for it. He didn't get far. He made it like ten feet before he was brought down by an old bag with half her face missing. Oh sweet Jesus, they're tearing into him like he was a cooked chicken at a homeless Christmas dinner. He's screaming something fierce but there's no one to help him. Not me, anyway. I'll stay here in my car till either the traffic moves again or the zombies get to me.

So anyway, about Cheryl. I hear she's easy, is that really true, Tim? I can't say I'd want to marry a woman like that but I would sure have some fun with her for a while. I'd treat her like a car I'd leased once. I'd ride her hard, put a shitload of miles on her, never change her oil, then trade her in for a new model. Ha, am I a cold SOB or what?

Oh, shit, they just got another traveler, a woman in her mid-twenties. She was in a Volvo but its safety features didn't seem to save her from an assload of zombies. They broke her rear window and then crawled into the car as she screamed and cried out for help. There are so many bodies in the car I can't even see her anymore.

LOL, it's fucking hilarious the way they're all in that one car; like clowns at the circus. Yeah, I know, Tim, you're thinking I'm taking this all in stride, that I don't seem to be too afraid of dying in the most agonizing way possible—by being fed on. Well, you know what? That's horseshit man. I'm fucking terrified, but hell, crying about it isn't gonna change it. Either I'm gonna live or I'm gonna die, I can't change it, so why bother?

Oh crap, a zombie picked up a brick from the side of the road and is coming right for me. Damn it, the dead bastard is using it as a bludgeon to break my driver's side window! Here he goes, he's using it! What the fuck, I thought zombies were supposed to be stupid?

Now there's small marks on the surface where the corner of the brick connected with the glass the first time he hit it, and he's pulling his arm back again! This time is gonna do it, and it looks like I'm gonna have to wrap up this email.

So listen, Tim, it's been great knowing you and if there's enough left of me to reanimate, I'll still try to get to that dinner party. Hell, maybe I'll take that bite out of Cheryl yet! LOL, a little zombie humor for you.

Oh, shit, the window just shattered and the zombies are reaching in for me. Well, I'm gonna sign off, Ow, fuck, one just bit my shoulder. And more are climbing into the car as I type this.

Fuck, get off me you damn pusbag! Shit, sorry, Tim, I didn't know I was typing still, as I am in searing pain as they feast on me flesh. Oh, Christ, one just ripped into my stomach and blood is shooting everywhere. I can't see the damn screen anymore. Well, this is me, signing off, saying see you in the afterlife, or whatever the hell is waiting for us............

Date: 8 July 2010 12:20
From: Eugene <Zombiephreak88@hotmail.com>
To: Mom <Sweetums543@yahoo.com>
Subject: I miss you Mom

Dear Mom,

I'm getting worried as you haven't returned home from the store yet and I know you didn't bring your cell phone. I saw your lap top was missing from upstairs so I decided to email you.

I'm scared, Mom, I don't like being alone. I know I'm twenty-one and I should be more mature but I can't help it. And of course it doesn't help that my acne is so bad the kids in the neighborhood call me Pizza Face and that I've never been able to get a girlfriend.

I know that you know I'm a virgin because I told you a few months ago when we sat up late and had one of our 'special talks'. And even if I met a girl, once I tell her I live in my parents' basement, she'll pretty much lose interest.

The zombies are still outside which makes me worried for your safety.

They can't get in the house, though, I'm safe.

The internet is still up and I'm keeping busy on it. I just got through leaving this really mean and scathing review for this writer I found on the internet. I found some stuff that anonymous people said about him and though I have no idea what's true or made up, I believe it anyway as we both know my IQ was never the highest.

Yes, Mom, I know, you would call me a sheep, someone who believes anything I read on the internet. But isn't that the truth? After all, if it wasn't true, it wouldn't be posted there.

But as I am writing this, I might as well be honest. Truthfully, I have no idea what the writer I left the review for is like. For all I know, he's the nicest guy in the world, or the biggest asshole. See, I'm too scared to email him personally, so I troll the internet and say mean things about him.

Yes, I know what you'd tell me, Mom, but what can I say? I'm a petty man and have no life.

As I look out the basement windows and see the zombies out there, I know I'm gonna die a virgin. My dick has only known the sweet touch of my right hand, and that on one too many occasions.

Maybe it's your fault, Mom. Maybe if you had raised me better and Dad hadn't left us one night. Maybe if you had taught me right from wrong and how to treat other people with respect. I blame the internet, the cesspool of corruption where every asshole gets his say, no matter whether it's relevant or not.

'Open mic night', someone said of the internet; say what you want, say the first thing to come to your mind, but don't worry about how factual it is. If it's in print, then it must be true.

I can't help but think about that writer I slandered and harassed, though. See, he wrote zombie books and now look what's happening outside? I wonder if he's doing well, after all, you write enough about zombies, doesn't that mean you can survive an outbreak of the walking dead?

Maybe I should have befriended the guy instead of attacking him for no good reason. For all I know, he lives on the next block, and if he had been my friend, he could have helped me.

Oh, well, water under the bridge.

So, Mom, when are you getting home? My underwear needs to be washed and I need you to cook me dinner.

Pathetic? Me? Yeah, I guess so, but hey, what do you want from me? I mean, I spend my free time harassing people on the internet. But I have to admit, as I'm such a loser, at least if they talk to me I can somehow feed off their fame and get attention for being an ass. It's better than being ignored, I suppose.

Oh shit, I heard a crash from upstairs. I'm gonna go check it out and I'll be right back to finish this email.

Oh, Christ, Mom, they got into the house! I ran down here, and I know I shouldn't be typing anymore, but I need to finish this. I have a feeling this might be the end for me.

When those zombies broke in, they really looked at me like I was an actual pizza. I ran from them but as you know I'm overweight and I couldn't move that fast. I heaved my bulk through the doorway as the man boobs on my chest bounced like Bo Derek's perfect breasts in the movie 10.

You remember that movie, Mom? I do, I jerk off to it all the time. I do a lot of that as I have never had a woman. Oh sorry, I already said that. You'll have to forgive me, but I have to say it's a touchy point with me.

Oh God, they're coming down the stairs! There's no place for me to hide in here either. As you know, it's just my bed, bureau, desk with my computer—my only way of feeling like I'm part of the world—and the washer and dryer. I thought about hiding in the dryer but it seemed pointless as I'm way too fat.

Oh Jesus, there's Janey from next door! She's sixteen and oh so hot. Remember that time she caught me jerking off to her in the bushes as she sunbathed in her backyard? That was embarrassing.

Actually, she doesn't look that bad right now. Her throat is torn out and the blood has coated her shirt. But that's good news 'cause now I can see her nipples pressing up against the material. And they look so perfect.

There are three other zombies with her and I need to take care of them.

BRB.

Okay, I'm exhausted, but I killed the three zombies that were with Janey. I used my old baseball bat—the one I never used for playing the actual game—and I cracked their skulls open.

Janey I didn't kill, after all, she may be dead, but she's still looking good. And best of all, if she's technically dead, then she's not underage anymore.

So to sign off Mom, be safe out there in the zombie world and do me a favor if you do make it home?

Knock once on the basement door before entering, because in a few moment's I'm gonna be busy.

I guess I won't die a virgin after all.

You know what? Maybe this whole 'the dead walking thing' will be good for my social life; after all, I'm not that picky.

Your son,

Eugene

Date: 19 July 2010 12:52

From: George <Toomraider@gmail.com>

To: Chris <ChrisDellmont_gg@yahoo.com>

Subject: Wanted to tell you something

Dear Chris,

I know you won't ever read this email, because as I look out my window, I can see you on your front walkway getting eaten by zombies.

Still, I can't help but want to send this last email to you for the hell of it. Hey, I have nothing do, as I'm trapped in my house.

See, I wanted to tell you what an asshole you are and that I fucked your wife.

Yup, did her for almost two months every day when you went to work.

It wasn't an emotional thing, purely sexual. She said you didn't please her and I guess she was looking for something on the side. And that's where I came in.

You remember that time I let you borrow my lawn mower and you gave it back with no gas and a broken front wheel? Well, I do. And how 'bout the time I let you use my hedge clippers and you gave then back all rusty after leaving them in your backyard in the rain? They're still pitted to this day, you jerk.

So when your wife started coming on to me, I couldn't say no, hell, I loved it. She's quite a hot piece of ass, Cindy is, or she was until that pack of zombies ripped her face off a few minutes ago.

I don't know why you didn't board up your doors and windows like they said to on TV. You made it so easy for those dead bastards to get at you.

Oh, well, live and learn, I always say.

After I send this email to you, I'm gonna get my shotgun, stick it out my second floor bedroom window, and wait for you to come back from the dead. I just peeked out the window and it looks like the zombies are gonna leave more than enough for that to happen, too. I only see one arm missing and though your insides have been torn out, we both know you won't need them anymore anyway.

Your wife didn't fare as well, I'm afraid. It looks like she won't be coming back. They tore off her damn head! Wow, that's cold. Her mouth is still moving up and down and her tongue is hanging out, or it was until a pale hand tore it from her jaw. Damn, those things are strong. They were fighting over her insides like she was a piñata. A couple were playing tug of war with her intestines, well, they were till it snapped, sending both falling on their undead asses!

Okay, it looks like I'm ready to finish this email as I just saw you begin to stir.

I've been looking forward to this for a longtime, and now that you're a zombie, it's all nice and legal.

See you in Hell, Chris my boy, dress light, I hear it's warm down there!

Your ex-neighbor,

George

Date: 11 July 2010 12:44
From: Bob <BCcaster87@yahoo.com>
To: Mary <MarRobbin2@comcast.net>
Subject: One last thought

Dear Mary,

I don't know how much time I have but I had to email you this one time while I still can.

I... I don't even know how to begin. After all, from the first time I saw you I knew I loved you. Remember at the cafeteria when you dropped your purse? That was me who swooped in and picked it up for you.

I can only hope this email gets to you and doesn't end up in your spam file because this will be the last email I will ever send.

See, the living dead are about to break into my house and I know it won't be pleasant.

So I just wanted to tell you what I never had the courage to say to you in person.

Wait...I hear something coming from the back of the house. It's louder than the usual pounding of the dead I've heard before. I'll be right back.

Okay, so it was nothing. One of the zombies managed to knock a board off a window. I quickly nailed it back on and for the moment I'm safe. But not for long, I know. As more of them arrive, eventually there will be too many for me to stop them all together.

I'm sorry, I got off track, I do that sometimes. It's funny, I just keep typing my thoughts, not even realizing I'm doing it.

To get back on track...

I've wanted to talk to you ever since that first day but each time I tried, I would chicken out at the last second. No matter how many times I tried to get the courage up, something inside me would always stop me. I know, silly, isn't it? I mean, I will talk to hundreds of people by email every day, even flirt with a few of the women, and when it came down to actually talking to someone in person, I folded like a proverbial deck of cards.

And believe me, I wanted to so badly.

I think it was your hair I noticed first. Its auburn brown color, long, the way it caressed your shoulders. Then I followed down the curve of your shoulders to the small of your back. I admired the way your dress hugged you like a second skin. I have to admit though the love was already there, there was more than a little lust as well.

Huh, funny, I could never have said that to you in person. I don't know what it is about email, I find it so freeing.

Oh shit, there's another loud crash, I'll be right back...

Okay, three more tried to get in and this time one actually did. As the first one crawled through the kitchen window, a protruding nail caught its side, and hard as this is to believe, the nail began pulling on its skin like the ghoul was wearing a loose jumpsuit. As I watched in horror, the nail held fast and the skin began to stretch, to separate from the body until it finally tore free.

Underneath were the black and red muscles and tendons, making the zombie look like an anatomy experiment.

I had a rolling pin prepared for just such an occurrence, and though my eyes were closed, I used it on the ghoul's head like a bludgeon. I will never forget the meaty *thwack* as wood met skull but I do know the zombie went down.

I left the broken body where it lay, its brains seeping out of the large gash I made in its head. I tried to ignore the congealed blood spread across my kitchen floor, but I swear, I almost began to clean it up.

The other two weren't as persistent and I was able to push them back outside and board the windows up yet again.

So, where was I?

Oh yeah, I was trying to tell you something...something I've never had the courage to tell you until now.

So Mary, I know you basically don't even know me, I know that other than a few polite smiles in the hallway on the way to the copy machine, you've never so much as looked at me, but I just wanted to say that I lo....

Oh damn, they're in!

Oh my God, there's so many of them. They're coming through the windows, oh shit! They just knocked down the front door! They're coming in, swarming into my home. I know I shouldn't be typing still but there's no way I can fight them off and even if I did, what's the point?

The world is overrun by them. For all I know, you're not even alive any longer. For all I know, this email will go into your inbox and never be read, lost in the quagmire of the internet forever.

Uh, one of them has me....I...punched it.

I can't keep this up, Mary...

Ow, the bastard bit me!

I'm typing with one hand now, the other is bleeding so bad I think the damn zombie got an artery.

Ah, another has my leg. I…Mary, this is it, I'm sorry I never talked to you, I wish I had now.

Now that's it's over, I can't help but think of all the lost chances, all the times I could have done something, said something, but instead I hesitated, and my God I wish I could do it all over again.

Mary, if your still alive, be safe, and know that out there in the world, there is someone who loves you more than life itself.

Ow, damn it it, that one took off a piece of my thigh! Jesus all the blood!

Oh God, my neck, that one tore out my neck! Christ it's bleeding really bad, its spurting through my fingers. It's so warm and sticky, I never really knew just how warm blood can be…

I can't…see straight…getting woozy. Huh, it's funny, I don't even feel them eating me anymore…

If I become one of them, if you are one already, I promise that this time, if I see you in the new world—the dead world—somehow, someway, I will remember who I am, who you are, and…

This time…I will talk to you…

EVEN ZOMBIES LOVE CHRISTMAS

Santa leaned back in his stuffed red leather chair as he read over the wish list of children all across the globe.

"One white male arm, one black left hand, one Asian right foot, a kidney from a Mexican, a spleen from an albino." He paused. "An albino? Who the hell do these kids think I am?"

Herman the elf stopped writing and waited patiently for Santa to continue.

Santa kept mumbling to himself and then stopped, scratched his beard, and looked down at Herman.

"Ready when you are, Santa."

"I lost my train of thought. Where were we?"

"An albino spleen."

"Oh yes, A spleen. I tell you, Herman, things were so much easier back when there were living people and the dead didn't rule the Earth."

Herman shrugged. "Well, we did learn to adapt, right, Santa?"

Santa sighed. "I suppose, but you have to admit, things are a lot bloodier than they were before. So, how are the human pens coming?"

"Hang, on, I'll call Sherman and check." He reached into his pocket and pulled out his cell phone. Hitting the number one for speed dial, he paused a few seconds, humming a Christmas tune as he waited.

A voice came on the other end. "Go for Sherman."

"Cut it out, answer the phone right, you idiot," Herman snapped. "Listen, I'm here with Santa, and he wants to know how the human pens are doing."

"All good, fed and watered. We're ready to start chopping them up as soon as Santa gives us the list."

Herman covered the phone with his hand and said, "Just waiting on the list, Santa."

Santa nodded. "Then let's finish this up so I can go see Melvin."

Herman spoke into the phone quickly, telling Sherman what was going on, then snapped it closed and pocketed it. Santa nodded and continued reading off the list of items, and Herman kept writing them down.

An hour later, Santa was at Melvin's cottage at the end of Santa's Village. At one time Melvin had been the tailor, but due to the change in world events, the elf was now the armorer for the village.

As Santa entered the cottage, a small bell rang over his head.

Melvin looked up from the desk he was sitting behind, a strong white light illuminating the small red orb in his hand.

"Ah, Santa, just in time. Here, let me show you what I've been working on. Follow me outside, please."

Santa followed Melvin outside and around to the back of the cottage, where the snow was churned from what looked like explosions.

The two stopped by a four foot wall of ice and snow.

Melvin held up the orb so Santa could see it. "My new invention, an Ornament grenade." He handed it to Santa, who studied it.

"Well, I can see why you call it an Ornament. It looks just like the ones hung off of Christmas trees."

Melvin gestured to the top of the grenade, where there was the typical loop for where a hook would go for hanging. "Exactly. Now slide your finger in the loop and pull."

Santa did as he was told. "And?"

Melvin's eyes went wide. "And throw it, Santa! Throw it!"

"Whoops," Santa said and tossed the ornament downrange, where it landed and erupted a second later, sending a shower of ice and snow in all directions.

Melvin and Santa closed their eyes as the wave subsided, hiding behind the ice wall.

"Not bad, Melvin, not bad, but you know, you didn't need to make it look like an ornament. A simple grenade would have been fine."

Melvin shrugged. "Traditions die hard with me, Santa. I know things have changed for the worse, but we can still try to hold on to the old ways."

"If only that were true, Melvin," Santa agreed as the elf led him back inside, talking the entire time.

"I have a whole new arsenal for you to take with you this year, Santa," Melvin said as they entered the cottage and closed the door. Melvin waddled over to a bench stacked with what looked like harmless items. "Here, come take a look."

Santa shuffled over and examined the array of items. He spotted a few sugar cookies and he reached down and picked one up. It was in the shape of a star, and as he opened his mouth to take a bite, Melvin grabbed his arm and shouted, "No, don't eat that!"

"Why not? Melvin, I'm Santa, I love cookies."

"Yes, Santa, but that's not a real cookie. Here, give it to me, let me show you."

Santa handed him the sugar cookie and Melvin held it in his hand and turned to face the far wall, where Melvin then pointed. Santa let his eyes go to the wall and saw there were numerous indents in the plaster, like something sharp had been thrown into it; like a knife.

Melvin pulled back his arm and threw the cookie like it was a baseball. The cookie sliced through the air and ended up sticking in the wall by one of its points.

Melvin smiled. "See? It's modeled after a Ninja star. Perfectly balanced. You can throw it any which way and it always soars true and finds its target."

Santa frowned. "So you're saying there aren't any cookies to eat?"

Melvin looked at Santa like he was an idiot. "No, there aren't any cookies."

"Okay then, I'll have some of this cocoa," Santa said and reached for the open plastic thermos next to the sugar cookies/throwing stars. He picked the thermos up, and was about to take a sip when Melvin yelled, "No, wait, stop!"

Santa had the thermos half tipped back and all he had to do was move his arm a little bit more to pour out the chocolately goodness. He held his arm in place and looked at Melvin. "What now?"

"Santa, please, carefully hand me that hot cocoa and I'll show you. But be very careful you don't spill any on yourself."

"Why the hell not?"

"Santa, please just trust me, all right?"

Santa sighed and did as he was told, and a second later Melvin was holding the thermos of hot cocoa.

"There, good, wow, that was a close one. Here, let me show you what this really is." He walked over to a small statue of a snowman and poured some of the hot cocoa onto the top of its head. When the dark liquid hit the statue, the snowman began to hiss and melt.

Santa swallowed hard, imagining the liquid going down his throat. "What is that?"

"Hydrochloric acid that smells and looks like hot cocoa."

"Acid? Now why in all that's holy would you go and make it smell like…" Santa stopped and composed himself, realizing who he was dealing with. "You know what? Never mind, it doesn't matter."

Melvin smiled and walked over and put the cap on the acid, then handed Santa a large candy cane about the size of a walking stick.

"What's this, a throwing spear?" Santa asked sarcastically.

Melvin smiled. "You're getting the hang of it but no, it's not a spear." He gestured to the top where the cane curved. "Turn that and pull."

Santa did as he was told and a second later was holding a long sword the length of the cane.

"Now this I like," Santa said with a smile and waved it around.

"Toledo steel from Spain," Melvin bragged. "Will take a head off like...well, like a hot blade through butter."

Santa slid the sword back into the sheath and smiled. "What else do you have for me?"

Melvin showed Santa a few more clever items, such as smaller candy canes that worked as nun-chucks when they were attached or individually as daggers, the points sharp enough to pierce the skull of a human. He also had the standard firearms, such as pistols and revolvers, shotguns and machine guns and a few Uzis. Everything a Santa on the go would need as he made his rounds in an undead world.

"Good, good, it all looks wonderful. Melvin, my boy, you've outdone yourself this year."

"Thanks, Santa. I have to admit, this is a lot more fun than making your red and white suits."

"Well, it shows, it certainly does. Have all this stuff sent to the sleigh and I'll be ready come tomorrow night for Christmas Eve."

"Will do, Santa, you can count on me."

Santa left the elf armorer and headed across the village. Mrs. Claus was working on his suit and he was looking forward to what she'd done to it.

Mrs. Claus was busy working when Santa entered their home on the north side of the village. As he entered, she looked up, a wide smile on her face.

"There you are, and just in time, I'm about done with your new suit."

"And how's it coming?" he asked, joining her and giving her a kiss on the cheek.

"Very well, the leather was a bit tough to sew but I managed."

"Leather? On my suit? Really?"

"Of course, dear," she said. "Remember what happened last year? You were nearly bitten and it was sheer luck that old man had no teeth in his mouth. If he'd died with his dentures in, why, you wouldn't be here today!"

He had to admit she was right. He'd been in a nursing home delivering presents when an old man had come out of the shadows. The old zombie must have been in his eighties when he'd died and returned, and before Santa could react, the old man sank his teeth into his arm—or tried to. But the zombie was tooth-less, and other than leaving behind a trail of bloody spittle, Santa had been unharmed. He'd caved in the zombie's skull and got out of there before any others had seen him.

"That was a close one, wasn't it," he mused.

"It sure was. So I made sure something like that can never happen again. Here, have a look at what I've done to your suit."

He stepped closer to see his red and white suit was on a mannequin. He grunted a little in annoyance when he saw how fat the mannequin was. It made him uncomfortable. Though he'd always been rotund, he'd also always been sensitive about his weight. He played his eyes over the suit, admiring his wife's handiwork. She was an excellent seamstress and her skill showed in the fine stitching.

The suit was still red and white, only now it had touches of black leather as well. The arms and legs were completely encased in thick leather, as were the shoulders. A lightweight wire mesh surrounded the main torso and the belt was made of copper with a small, two inch knife hidden within the emblem of Santa on his sleigh. As he studied the suit, it reminded him of what gladiators in Greece wore when entering the arena in battle.

"Go on, dear, try it on for size. I just finished before you arrived."

"Okay, will you give me a hand?"

She nodded and helped him slide the suit off the mannequin, then helped him dress. Moments later he was wearing his new suit and he had to say it fit pretty well. It was heavier of course, but the leather was supple. As he walked around the room, he squeaked a little, the leather being broken in.

She frowned at the squeaking. "I'll see what I can do about it but I may not be able to stop it."

"I'll deal with it," was all he said as he waddled across the living room, bending and stretching to limber the leather.

"Did you see Melvin?" she asked.

"Yes, he has a full arsenal for me."

"Good, I want to know you can defend yourself if you have to," she said.

He walked over to her and kissed her again. "No worries there. One thing's for sure. Tomorrow night when I make my rounds, the living dead will find me a hard nut to crack."

The sun was just beginning to set as Santa Claus left the village behind and began his trek to the real world—or what was left of it.

Behind him, in his magic bag, were all the items from the wish list. The bottom of the bag was soaked with congealed blood and flies could be heard buzzing within it. Santa was just glad he was in the open air and the stench of body parts was lost in the wind.

For the thousandth time he wondered if what he was doing was right. Of course he knew it was wrong to kill the humans in the pens at the village, but he really had no choice. He was Santa Claus after all. His job was to fulfill the wish lists of children all over the world. Only now, the undead children didn't want bicycles, ponies or choo-choo trains. They wanted arms, legs and internal organs to feed on.

It was a new world and he either adapted to it or would die out. He may have been around for centuries but that was only because he was needed by the children. If they stopped needing him…why, for all he knew he would simply grow old and die. Or worse, fade away into nothingness. He'd really never thought about it much, and who would? Why contemplate your own existence and lack thereof?

No, better to do his job, no matter how macabre it might be now.

But that didn't mean he would let them use him as a human buffet. Oh no, he may have to deliver them body parts once a year but he'd be damned if he'd let them eat him too.

So where once he would simply drop down chimneys and leave presents under trees—the only danger that of being seen by some insomniac child—now he had to worry about being attacked by the undead homeowners, who were looking for a midnight snack.

Time passed and soon he arrived at his first home in the United States. He wanted to get the US over with first before going on to other countries. Out of all the places on Earth, the US was hit the worst when the dead began to rise. As far as Santa knew, there were no other human beings left alive in the world, with the exception of the ones at his village, and they were kept for only one very gruesome thing.

Luckily, if you took a man's leg or a woman's arm, it didn't mean they were dead, but could go on for years with the missing limb as long as they were cared for and the severed limb was taken correctly. For the limbs and organs had to be fresh or the dead wouldn't eat them.

Pulling on the reins of the reindeer, Santa steered for the first rooftop he came to. It was a ranch-style house with a three-car garage and a large swimming pool in the backyard. Of course, the pool now looked more like a swamp, with a few rotting bodies floating in the muck that was once clean water, and half the garage had been burned in a long-ago fire, and the grass of the front and rear lawn was more than three feet tall and had fallen over onto itself.

It had been years since the dead began to walk and the world collapsed, and in all that time, Santa had stayed at the North Pole, only coming out once a year like always. When he thought about the first year he'd gone out and found nothing but death...well, he tried not to think about it too much. It was too hard to bear.

As the sleigh settled on the roof, he climbed out and stretched. Then he checked his list for what this house had asked for. One white right arm and a black penis, complete with testicles. He blinked and took another look to make sure he'd read it right. Then with a shrug, opened the bag of parts and began digging.

Moments later he found what he needed and prepared to enter the home.

This was one of the tricks Santa used magic for, one of the few. There was only so much magic to go around so he had to use it sparingly. He used it for mainly three things. To go down and then up the chimney, and the third was too keep his gift bag bottomless. How else could he carry all the presents in one trip?

His nose wrinkled from the smell of rotting meat as he appeared in the living room. Though he was used to the odor enough that he didn't gag, it was still hard to accept fully.

There was a Christmas tree in the corner, a fresh pine by the looks of it, but instead of tinsel and ornaments made of glass or plastic, the tree was decorated with intestines and fingers, as well as a few eyeballs. On the top of the tree, instead of a star or an angel, a severed head looked out, only the eye sockets were empty, gaping black holes.

On the table near the chimney was a plate and a glass, but where once cookies and milk would be waiting for him, now the plate held a kidney and pieces of intestines; what the owners of the home thought Santa would like to eat.

Oh, how wrong they were.

Wanting to finish up and move on to the next house, he quickly laid the body parts under the tree and was about to leave when he heard footsteps come from behind him. He looked up to see two zombie children standing in the doorway.

With a hiss and a groan they were on him, small mouths biting and snapping as they tried to feed on Santa. Lucky for him, their teeth couldn't penetrate his new suit and it was simple to toss each child off him where they landed on the couch across the room.

"Merry Christmas," he said quickly and was gone before the children could attack again, back up the chimney in a flash. Once on the roof, he listened at the opening to the chimney as the two zombie kids gnashed and moaned from below. Santa shook his head at the thought of only a few million more homes to go before he could call it a night.

Climbing onto his sleigh, he flew off into the darkness, his destination the next house on his list.

Hours later he was still going strong. He'd had a few close calls but nothing he couldn't handle. He was in the Midwest, in some town he would forget the second he left it. Landing on the roof, he slipped down the chimney, his mind already thinking of the next delivery.

As he appeared in the living room, he found he was surrounded by seven zombies, all with different rates of decay. One was so rotted it was nothing but skin and bones, the organs within its torso desiccated to the point they were useless.

The second Santa appeared, they lunged for him, teeth gnashing and fingers clawing at him, the tap sprung. One got a good grip on his long beard and only a punch to the face could get the ghoul off him.

Acting fast, Santa reached behind his back and pulled out a set of candy canes, each with a sharpened point. With one in each hand, he jabbed them into the eyes of two zombies, the points slicing into their brains and killing them instantly.

With a gap in the advancing line of zombies, he dashed through it and came up short at the opposite end of the room. Turning, he pulled out two ninja sugar cookie stars and threw them at another zombie. One cookie struck its face right below the left eye, but the second one hit paydirt, slicing through the skull and into the brain. The ghoul dropped to the blood-soaked carpet, dead.

Not having the patience for any more combat, Santa reached into his pocket and pulled out an Ornament grenade. Pulling the pin, he tossed it at the zombies with a, "Merry Christmas, assholes!"

The zombie in the center caught the grenade like it was a ball and looked at it with curiosity. It could see its reflection in the shiny red coating of the grenade and was fascinated.

Meanwhile, Santa dived behind a ratty couch and the entire home shook on its foundation. Bloody parts and gore flew in every direction, the walls becoming an original Jackson Pollock.

Poking his head up over the couch, he saw more than half the zombies were down. Taking his chance, he dashed to the chimney opening, and as the ghouls began climbing to their feet to renew the attack, Santa let out a laugh and yelled, "Sorry, fellas, but I'm not on the menu tonight. See you next year!" Then he was up the chimney and on the roof once more.

Later, with the United States finished, he landed on his first roof in London. It was an orphanage.

There was no chimney so he had to use the front door. It was locked but a little Christmas magic soon had him inside.

As he walked through the foyer and down a short hallway, he soon found himself in a wide open room similar to a hospital ward. Bunk-beds lined each side of the room, a thin walkway down the middle. At the end of the path was the Christmas tree. This one was old, the pine needles having fallen off years ago. The air was rank with death, but Santa swallowed the bad taste in his mouth and began walking to the tree.

When he was halfway there, he heard movement to his left, then his right, then from behind. Pulling a flashlight from his pocket, he shined it on the cause of the noise, and when he did, his heart lodged in his throat.

Undead children, more than two dozen, were coming out from under the beds and the shadows.

This had happened to him before, unfortunately, and so far he'd always managed to escape in one piece. Some zombies wouldn't settle for what he delivered them, but instead wanted to feast on his fat ass.

"Now, now, kids, let's not do this. I have some presents for you," he said and reached into his bag and tossed a few kids some bloody body parts. They grabbed them off the floor and began to feed on them, but the rest still kept coming for him.

He began to back away, but already his retreat was cut off by more undead cherubs. He was trapped.

With a low hiss, a little blonde girl with sunken-in features charged at him and he kicked her in the chest, sending her sprawling away. Then more jumped into action, charging at him, their small hands curved into claws, their mouths open in anticipation of the kill.

A small boy tried to jump on his back. Santa pulled the thermos of hot cocoa from his pocket, and with lightning speed, whipped off the top. He splashed the hot cocoa smelling acid on the boy's face, who hissed in anger. The small zombie fell to the floor, his eyes melting, his face sloughing off, the flesh turning into a puddle of goo, the tongue dissolving, the teeth sliding out. The boy kept twitching until the acid finally ate into his brain and killed him.

Acting fast, Santa reached over his back and retrieved the Uzi he'd had hung there for just such an occurrence.

"Merry Christmas, you little dead bastards!" he screamed and squeezed the trigger, sending steel-jacketed rounds into the small bodies again and again. Heads exploded, limbs were chewed off, and legs were crippled, blood and gore flying in all directions. The main line of children was quickly chewed up and it made a clear hole for Santa to use. Jumping over the first body, he ran for the door, shooting as he ran. More zombie kids were taken down as he fired.

His clip ran dry and there was no time to reload, so he let the Uzi fall from his hands to hang on its strap, then pulled a Glock from inside his suit. As a small boy came at him, he shot the kid at point blank range, blowing out the back of the boy's head in a spray of brown and yellow brain matter.

When he reached the door, Santa stopped and turned around. The children were crawling and limping towards him, some too wounded to move.

"There's a reason you little bastards didn't have parents before you died!" he yelled, angry at himself for even saying it but getting tired of always being the blue plate special. In reply, the zombie kids hissed and growled at him. Santa pushed through the door and locked it behind him, then made his way back to the roof. Despite this and other setbacks, he still had a long night ahead of him.

That was okay; he also had a full load of ammunition as well.

By the time he was finished for the night and had returned to the North Pole, he was exhausted. He'd had countless battles with the dead as the night had progressed but his wits and weapons had seen him through unscathed. His new suit had a lot to do with it as well. There were many places where teeth marks could be seen on the leather and actual teeth were lodged in the metal mesh over his chest and back, but not one got through and touched his soft flesh beneath.

After making sure the elves in the stable were taking care of his reindeer, he made his way back home and his waiting wife.

When he entered, her eyes lit up with relief and Santa saw that she wasn't alone. Herman and Melvin were with her, no doubt keeping her company till he returned.

"I'm home," he said as he entered the house and she ran into his arms for a kiss. "Now, now, not too close or you'll get blood on you," he told her, his suit covered in zombie gore.

"I don't care, I'm just glad you're home and safe for another year."

He patted her shoulder and then extricated himself from her loving embrace. "I need to get out of this thing, it's killing me," he said and began to shrug out of the suit. "You two, give me a hand, will you please?"

Herman and Melvin did as requested and a few minutes later, Santa was standing in the middle of the living room in nothing but his red long-johns.

"How did the new suit work out?" Mrs. Claus asked.

"I have to tell you, the suit worked marvelously," he told his wife. "I can't imagine ever having done tonight without it."

"I'm so glad to hear it," she said. "In fact, I have a few more ideas for next year. How about a helmet and gauntlets and oh, what about a shield and…"

"Later, you can tell me later," he cut her off. "For now I just want to sit down and have something warm to drink."

"Here are your slippers, Santa," Herman said and slid the slippers on his feet as Santa dropped down in his favorite chair by the fire. To the right of him a beautiful pine Christmas tree brought back from the real world blinked with colorful lights. But only the standard red, blue and green ornaments on this one—no body parts at all.

Melvin went off to the kitchen and came back a minute later with a steaming mug. "Here, Santa, I made this just for you."

Santa took the mug and sniffed. It was hot cocoa. He gave Melvin a stern look and Melvin nodded and said, "Yes, Santa, it's real cocoa."

He hesitantly sipped it, and after he swallowed the first mouthful and his throat wasn't being eaten out from the inside, he began drinking it with gusto.

"How did my weapons work out, Santa?" Melvin asked eagerly.

Santa let out a hearty laugh and patted the small elf armorer on the shoulder. "They were excellent. Couldn't have been better. Thank you again, Melvin, you probably saved my life more than once because of your inventions." He winked. "And the guns didn't hurt either."

"That's so great to hear," Melvin said. "Because while you were gone, I was still working and I came up with even more great ideas. How about fig pudding that's really Semtex or tinsel that can be used as a garrote, or a stuffed animal that can be used as containers for nerve gas; just pull off the head and toss it. And…"

"Okay, okay, enough, please, not now. There's plenty of time for all that tomorrow." Santa finished his cocoa and handed the empty cup to his wife, who took it with a warm smile. "One thing I've learned since the dead began to walk is that we have all the time in the world."

"Amen to that, dear," Mrs. Claus said. "And Merry Christmas to you."

Santa smiled, his cheeks puffing up as he let out a hearty, "Ho-Ho-Ho. Thank you, dear. It's nice to have someone say it to me for once!"

Herman began to chuckle and Melvin joined in, and soon they were all laughing.

The dead may rule the Earth and death and decay were everywhere, but here, at the North Pole, life still flourished…and so did Christmas.

FISH FUCKER

In the small village of Squire's Junction, lived a man with a peculiar fetish. He loved to fuck fish.

Johnson Mahoney knew it was wrong, that it was unnatural, but he couldn't help himself. There was just something about a fish. From the sleek scales, the slickness, the lipless mouth devoid of teeth, that got him hard every time.

The palms of his hands were cut up from grasping the scales as the fish would try to escape him, but he accepted it as part of the fun.

Others in town knew of his predilection to fish and they would comment to one another as he passed them on the street.

"There he goes, the damn fishfucker," they would say.

"He's sick, is what he is," others would say. "What kind of a man fucks a fish?"

"Oh, I don't know," one man said to another one time at the local pub. "Maybe it feels good, you know, all slick and wet."

The man was looked at with astonishment by the other men in the pub and he quickly changed his tone. "I was only joking, fellas. Ha, got you, you thought I was serious."

A few more looks were tossed the man's way but then something of interest was brought up and the man's outburst was forgotten. Johnson didn't care what any of them said. He loved fish and that's all that mattered.

Every Sunday morning he would go out to the shore at the edge of town and he would row out to sea more than half a mile. There he would drop his fishing line and patiently wait for a fish to take the bait on his hook. As he waited, he rubbed himself gently, his mind already on the pleasure to come, wondering what sort of fish would be his lover this day.

A Grouper would be nice as the mouth was nice and tight, or perhaps an eel. A Trigger fish would be exciting or better yet, if he was really lucky, he might catch a Sweetlips. He had almost tried a Bluefish once, attracted to the small scales and the bluish green coloring, but the teeth had been too scary and he had let the fish go, not wanting to take a chance he would hurt himself.

Still, the Bluefish had been so sexy. The one he caught had weighed a little more than three pounds, with a sexy mouth and dainty scales. And the way it had looked at him, as if it had been begging him to do it. But in the end, the teeth were too risky and he had let it go free.

He sighed, thinking of the last time he was out here. Last week he had caught a flounder. The Fluke had been almost two pounds and its small, tight mouth had done the job well. He wasn't that big himself, a little over five inches, and he wasn't that thick, which made fish fucking all the more easy for him.

He closed his eyes and remembered the sensation as he held onto the fish and it sucked on him, filling with an ecstasy he had never been able to find in a normal woman.

He sometimes wondered why he was attracted to fish, and why he could only seek pleasure in his aquatic brethren, but he would usually not think on it too hard.

He was who he was and had learned if he wanted to live with himself, it was easier just to accept it.

Besides, he wasn't hurting any of them. After he had his way with them, he would set them free, though a few had their mouths stretched a little bit more. But if he hurt them he never gave it much thought, always thinking of himself.

Sometimes he wondered if another fisherman had caught one of the fish he fucked. Did they take it home, clean it and fry it up, eating his love juice as they dined on the meat?

He didn't know how he felt about that and tried not to give it much thought.

The line began to move and he sat up, excited he had his first bite of the day. His pants were tighter now in expectation of what would soon be happening. Breathing hard and fast, he began to reel the line in. At first it was easy, but soon the line grew taut. He found himself struggling to stay in the boat and the fish tugged and pulled harder.

The sun beat down on his head, causing him to sweat profusely, and he battled the fish for all he was worth. He would let the line play out, then take it in, only to do the same again and again. Slowly, ever so slowly, he drew the line in.

He still didn't know what fish he'd caught but his imagination was running rampant with imagery. He even imagined a mermaid and wondered how that would be. But he quickly pushed the thought down. First they weren't real and second, if a woman was attached to the fish body in any way, it wouldn't be the same. It had to be all fish, that's what made him feel whole…like a man.

The battle continued for hours and though he tried to reel it in, the fish more often than not got the better of him. There were times when he had to let loose the reel, the line playing out once more.

But he never gave up, for this would be the fuck of his life. He didn't know what he'd caught, but a fish this size would be incredible. Hell, maybe he could screw it from behind, like a person. That was something he had never done as the fish were never that big. With the idea of an entirely new position in his future, he redoubled his efforts to pull in his catch.

The hours crawled by with still no luck and he began to grow tired. Johnson waited for a chance when the fish wasn't fighting him and he reached down for the canteen of water he had taken with him. Slurping it down, he let some overflow his mouth and wet his chest.

Closing his eyes, he sucked in a breath of cool sea air. The fish was a fighter, there was no doubt about it, and though he was tired, he knew it would be worth it when he finally had the fish in the boat.

The tug of war continued, with neither winning until, an hour later, he finally had the upper hand. He assumed the fish was tiring and took the advantage, quickly reeling the line in. And then, finally, Johnson peered over the side of the boat to see a glorious catch, one that would have him remembering the experience for years to come. This would be his greatest exploit, the one that would have him laying in bed and touching himself, imagining the large form beneath him. Though it was so big he didn't think he could get it into the boat.

It was as he was leaning over the side, his mind lost in fascination, that his catch jerked back, catching him totally off guard. Before he knew what was happening, he was falling into the water, the air in his lungs replaced by the frigid liquid that caused him to cough and choke.

Spinning around under water, he swam back to the surface. Reaching up, he grabbed the edge of the boat and hung on, spitting sea water out of his mouth.

He needed to catch his breath, and when he did, he would pull himself back into the boat.

His catch was forgotten now as he thought only for his life. He was alone in the ocean, no one around for miles, and if he died, no one would know it until they found his derelict boat when it drifted back to shore.

It was as he was gathering the strength to climb into the boat that he realized there was something behind him.

Turning around, he saw his catch floating there, the same one that had been on his line. His heart stopped in his chest as he stared at the massive teeth, the beady eyes, and he knew he was about to die. But his catch didn't attack, instead it looked at him, the eyes seeming to say, "Hi, what brings you out here on a Sunday morning? Are you single?"

For some reason it hadn't left and it wasn't attacking, and though he thanked his savior for this, he still wondered why it was still here...with him. And then he found out why.

Murray was a great white shark.

Though the lower forms of sea life feared him as a predator, around others of his kind he was teased and sometimes shunned.

The other sharks would talk about him behind his back, saying things like, "There goes that human fucker."

"There's the shark that likes two legs, the sick mammal."

Murray tried to ignore their comments but still it hurt.

He didn't know why he was different. He didn't know why he liked to fuck humans. All he knew was their pink skin and warm orifices turned him on like no other shark ever could.

Murray was twenty years old and if he played his cards right, he would have another ten years of life. He was almost fifteen feet long and weighed more than three thousand pounds. He was a handsome specimen for a shark and he was proud of it.

He would swim in shallow water and close to shore, waiting for some ignorant fisherman to drop his lines, then he would take the bait, only instead of being pulled into the boat, he would pull the fisherman into the water. From there he would screw the human till he was exhausted.

Usually the human would survive and swim away, but there had been a few times when they had died.

He felt bad when that happened, but not bad enough to stop. After all, they had been trying to catch him to eat him.

So when he saw the line of yet another fisherman in the water about a half mile from shore, both his penises began to twitch in expectation of what was to come next.

He had taken the bait and the fisherman had tried to pull him in, but Murray had stayed well below the waterline and the man had no idea what he had caught. The tug of war went on for hours as Murray slowly chipped away at the strength of the fisherman.

Then, when the time was right, he showed himself, pulling on the line at just the right time and toppling the man into the water.

As the man struggled to climb back into the boat, Murray went into action.

He rolled against the man, causing the man's pants to be pulled off, then he spun around, pulled the man deeper into the water, and mounted him.

Like many shark breeds, Murray had dual penises, both side by side, similar to how two fingers looked pressed together. Called claspers, these two members would unite inside the mate during copulation, forming a channel for sperm.

As the fisherman slid beneath the waves, Murray went to work, sliding both members inside the man, using his bulk to keep him in place.

If a shark could smile, Murray would have done so.

Johnson's eyes went wide as he slid beneath the waves and found himself penetrated by a great white shark. He opened his mouth to scream but nothing came out but gurgles.

His head filled with spots of light as the pressure grew inside him. He felt like his insides were about to explode and he realized he was getting a taste of what it must have been like for the fish he'd molested over the years.

His lungs filled with water and he knew he was going to drown, when as fast as it began, the pressure on his rear was released and the shark let him go. As he turned his head, in the wan light under the surface, he watched the rear fin swinging back and forth as the shark swam away.

With his oxygen fading fast, he made a last ditch effort to swim to the surface. It was as everything was going black that his head broke the surface, and as he coughed and spit sea water, he sucked in the best tasting air of his life.

He kicked off his pants that were around his ankles and swam back to his boat, which was a hundred feet away. Apparently, while he was underwater, the current had taken him.

As he reached the boat, he had to rest before climbing inside. But then he thought he saw a shadow beneath him, and he suddenly had the energy to climb over the side and tumble into the boat.

Lying on the deck with no pants, his ass pointed up at the sky and breathing heavily, he felt like he would never walk right again. He was sore at the waist level, and when he rolled over, he moaned loudly.

Though hard to believe it, he knew he had been raped by a shark!

The question was; what to do about it?

He couldn't tell anyone. No one would believe him, and even if they listened, after what they knew of him they would only say it was a just dessert for the sick things he did with fish.

Shaking terribly, he went back to shore, never wanting to go to the sea again.

He already planned on selling his boat to the first person who wanted it and he knew the trauma he'd suffered would haunt him for the rest of his life.

Just remembering what it felt like to be under the water, a massive shark behind him as it pumped in and out, in and out. Ugh, he felt like he was going to be sick.

When he arrived at the dock, he tied up his boat and went home, taking the next three days to recuperate. He was lucky and though in pain, by day three he was doing fine and his backside was okay. Evidently, the shark had been gentler than he had ever been with all the fish he'd taken as lovers over the years.

Just thinking of fish made him cringe and he knew he was finished fucking them forever.

But then, how to satisfy his sexual urges?

Going outside to get some air, he walked into town, ignoring the jibes and comments of the townspeople. He watched the women as they walked past him, but try as hard as he might, they still didn't turn him on.

Giving up after a few hours, he walked back home, taking the scenic route through the countryside.

It was as he passed a herd of sheep that he paused and admired the animals.

He watched them graze and stand around, doing nothing of any particular interest. He was about to leave when he spotted a stunning female at the far end of the herd, with a glowing white pelt and deep eyes that seemed to call to him.

"Well, hello there, beautiful," he said with a smile.

FISHECSTASY

It was Friday night and the college dorms were hopping as usual.

Keggers were going full blast with many students already unconscious from over indulgence. On the second floor, room 15, three college pals were taking shots and trading stories.

"So, what's the strangest sexual experience you guys have ever had?" Mark asked his two buddies, Chris and Jeff.

Chris took a moment to think. He swayed back and forth as he tried to stay conscious. Alcohol poisoning wasn't far from the truth. "I did it with a piece of liver once."

"You what? How?" Mark asked as he sipped his beer. He was the sober one of the bunch. He had learned more than a year ago that if he stayed sober, or less drunk than everyone else, he could find out all sorts of interesting things about his friends; information he could later use against them.

Chris belched as he formulated his response. "It's not hard really. You take a piece of raw liver, and put it in some saran wrap. Then you heat it in the microwave. Not too much, just enough to get it warm. Then you slide your dick in it. It's just like a nice warm, moist pussy."

"Oh, God, that's so fucking gross!" Mark yelled as he laughed.

Chris belched again, drank half a beer and shrugged. "Did it with a loaf of fresh baked bread once, too. Almost burned my dick that time, as I rushed it and didn't let the loaf cool enough."

"Oh my fucking God, no way, that is incredible!" Mark yelled, loving all this great stuff. He couldn't wait till he needed something from Chris and had this info to use later to make him cooperate.

Jeff gulped half his beer and said, "I did it with a dog once."

Both Mark and Chris turned and stared at their friend.

"You did what?" Mark asked, not believing what he just heard.

"Yup, right in the pooper. I was horny as fuck and the family dog was right there. Hey, a hole is a hole. I even think the bitch enjoyed it," Jeff said, his words slurring from all the alcohol he'd consumed.

"No fucking way. You're bullshitting us," Mark said.

Jeff shrugged again, finished his beer, and went for another one from the cooler beside him.

"Nope, did it three times after that too when I was too horny to just jerk off."

"So why'd you stop?" Mark asked.

Jeff smiled. "That's when I got me a girlfriend and got to fuck the real thing."

Chris let out a burp so loud and smelly the entire dorm room smelled like old, regurgitated beer. As Mark waved his hand before his face to clear the air, Chris said, "Oh, come on, Mark. You never gave it a thought at the aquarium?"

"What do you mean?" he asked.

"The fish, Mark, the fish!" Chris yelled. "You never were there one night, all alone, horny as hell and the idea never crossed your mind?"

Mark stared at Chris, not fully understanding his question.

Chris seemed more lucid after his burp and he waved his hands in the air as his eyes went wide. "The fucking fish, Mark! You never thought about fucking any of the fish?"

"That's sick, of course not," he replied, making a disgusted face.

"But what about the dolphins, Mark?" Jeff interjected, liking where Chris was taking the conversation. "Technically, they aren't fish, they're mammals. Bet they got a nice warm pussy, too. And to do it in the cold water, only your dick nice and cozy. Shit, I think I'd try it if I had the chance."

Mark stood up, realizing he was now the center of the topic. "I gotta go guys, thanks for the beer."

As he turned to leave, Chris called after him. "Just think about it, Mark! All alone in the aquarium, those nice soft and warm fish pussies just waiting for you to fuck them!"

"You two are sick fucks, screw you," Mark said, opened the door, stepped through it, and slammed it behind him.

The two friends stared at one another, neither having anything to say.

Finally, Chris spoke up. "So you really fucked a dog?" he asked Jeff, wanting to get the conversation going again.

"Shut the fuck up and give me another beer," Jeff said in reply, the two going back to drinking. Ten minutes later, the conversation about screwing this and that was a distant memory, and neither would remember in the morning.

But Mark did remember as he wasn't drunk, and though he didn't want to admit it, Chris had planted an idea in his head that no matter how hard he tried to forget, he just couldn't shake it.

That night he went on the internet, trying to see what he could find about men fucking fish. There wasn't much there, some women with eels and the like. Other than the typical barnyard porn, the aquatic stuff was missing.

He went to bed that night thinking about work, how easy it would be to do exactly what Chris said.

Finally, as the college dorm partied long into the night, Mark fell asleep.

Tomorrow was another day. A day he would be working...at the aquarium.

Mark showed up for work at six p.m. sharp. He worked the night shift, after the customers had gone home. His job was to feed the fish, clean the tanks and make sure the filters had been flushed and cleaned. He worked until two in the morning and he enjoyed it. With his headphones on, he listened to music and had the place to himself. He did his job well and his supervisor liked him.

The customers left at nine, and by ten the place was all his. The last fellow worker was gone by ten thirty, leaving Mark to do his thing.

He worked diligently, moving from tank to tank, dropping in food where it was needed. It wasn't a large aquarium, as it was a small town, but it was one of the only attractions in the area and so had enough business to keep afloat financially.

Mark finished with the shark tank and moved to the dolphin tank.

It was set into the ground with a four foot glass wall surrounding it. There were two adult dolphins in the water, Matty and Mary.

Matty had been rescued from the ocean after becoming hurt by a boat propeller. Mary had come from another aquarium when it had closed due to lack of funds.

"Hi, guys, how are you tonight?" Mark asked as he carried a bucket full of raw fish to feed them.

Matty swam up and let out a few squeaks, then back flipped into the pool. Mary swam up to him and floated, watching Mark as he walked around the pool.

When he was near the small diving board set up for the announcer during shows, he dropped down on it and began scooping out the fish, letting it fall into the water. Matty and Mary quickly ate, enjoying the last meal for the day.

As Mark fed them, Chris' words came back to him. *"Come on, Mark, you never thought about it? Even once?"*

He shook his head to clear it, trying to concentrate on his job, but the more he watched Mary play in the water and eat, the more he began to get aroused.

By the time the two dolphins were done feeding, his pants were tight in the crotch area.

He hadn't had sex for more than three months and as he was nineteen, his hormones were raging and he would have killed to have a female right then and there to screw.

But there was no female there…well, not a human female anyway.

The more he watched Mary, the more he realized how horny he was and Chris' words still rang in his head, prodding him on.

He had to admit, Chris had a point. Dolphins were mammals and so were warm blooded. He knew he was crazy but his drive to have sex was too much for him, and despite his better judgment, he decided to go for it.

Quickly stripping off his clothes, he stood on the edge of the diving board with his boner protruding ahead of him like a stubby flag pole.

With a tingling in his belly in expectation of what was to come, he dove into the pool.

Swimming to the surface, he slapped the water and Mary and Matty swam to him. He pushed Matty away, wanting only Mary, and Matty rolled in the water, not happy at being snubbed. Mark sucked in a great big breath of air and went under the water as he held onto Mary's dorsal fin.

His first try failed miserably, but the second time he adjusted his position, and with him hugging Mary and his belly pressed to hers, he positioned himself and penetrated her.

As he slid inside the dolphin, his cock was surrounded by warmness and he had to fight to keep from groaning in pleasure, not wanting to suck in water.

Mary never stopped swimming and as Mark held onto her, she slowly moved around the pool. Mark was in heaven as he slowly slid in and out of her. Each time he pulled back, his dick would be surrounded by the cool pool water. Then he would push in and the warmness of the dolphin would surround him. As if she knew he had to breathe, she even moved to the surface so he could suck in a breath of air.

He stroked in and out, back and forth, until he had an orgasm that shook him to his core. As he let her go, he floated in the water, realizing Chris had been right.

Fucking that dolphin had been incredible!

As Mark treaded water, his face wearing a look of contentment, he never saw Matty swim up behind him. Dolphins were well adept at mimicking their human masters and Matty was no different.

Before Mark could so much as cry out in surprise, Matty plowed into him and wrapped his fins around Mark, holding him in place.

Mark screamed to be let free, sucking in water, and a moment later felt blinding pain in his ass as Matty began mating with him, just like Mark had done with Mary.

Mark began to scream as his backside exploded with fire, the larger dolphin trapping him like a child would a kitten.

Mark fought the best he could but he was no match for the dolphin, and as he sucked in a lungful of water and began to choke, he realized he was dying!

He imagined what would happen the next day, when his naked corpse would be found floating in the pool. What would people say? What rumors would be spread? After all, how does an employee of the aquarium end up naked and dead in the dolphin pool? And when the autopsy was performed and they found out he'd been raped by a dolphin, what then?

He imagined the look on his father's face at hearing the news, or his mom's!

And he would have died right then and there if not for Mary bumping into Matty playfully, causing Mark to become dislodged. There was another blinding pain as Matty withdrew from his ass and then he was sinking to the bottom.

With his last seconds of air, Mark kicked up to the surface and sucked in the best tasting air he had ever had the pleasure to breathe.

Coughing and spitting, he swam to the ladder and pulled himself up and onto the edge of the pool. As he lay there naked, he saw diluted red pooling under his ass and realized he had gotten the pounding of his life.

When he looked back into the pool, he saw Matty and Mary were now mating, going at it like two lovesick teenagers.

Coughing and vomiting water, Mark pulled himself together and got dressed, feeling humiliated and sore.

He was shaking so badly he could barely get dressed, and when he had his clothes on, he limped away from the pool.

Matty sent a few squeaks his way but Mark didn't look back. He didn't want to think what those squeaks might have meant.

Hey, Mark, thanks for a good time…call me!

His sexual escapade had turned into a disaster. For the rest of his life, he would have to live with the knowledge that he was raped by a dolphin.

He finished his shift on auto pilot that night and went home early, leaving his keys on the supervisor's desk along with his resignation.

He didn't want to work around fish any longer.

The following week, the college dorm was hopping once more.

Keggers were once again in full swing and Mark was with his friends, drinking again. He was pretty quiet, though, and had been like that since the previous week.

As the three friends drank and laughed, Chris slapped Mark on the arm. "So, Mark, did you ever do it with one of the fish like I suggested?"

Jeff laughed hard but Mark said nothing. Mark turned and looked at Chris, frowned deeply, and then punched Chris right in the face.

"Fuck you, asshole," Mark snapped as he got up and walked out of the room.

Neither Jeff nor Chris noticed that Mark was walking funny, and had been for a week.

Chris was knocked onto his ass and he rubbed his jaw where Mark punched him. He looked at Jeff with an odd expression and said, "What the fuck did I say?"

Jeff shrugged. "Who the hell cares, just give me another beer."

The two friends continued to drink without Mark, and as time went by, Chris looked at Jeff and asked, "So, what's the strangest sexual experience you ever had?"

GOING UP?

Paul Francis paused as he walked through the massive foyer while on his way to the bank of elevators in the high-rise building in the middle of Manhattan.

All around him were the signs of life as people moved about on their daily errands. The high-rise was filled with the offices of lawyers, doctors and a hundred other occupations, all wrapped up in sixty floors of steel and stone.

And it was all his.

Paul Francis was one of the richest men in New York.

He had made his first million by the age of twenty two and had cleared a net of five million plus by the time he was twenty five.

Of course, that was more than twenty years ago.

Now Paul was in his early forties and he planned on living another fifty if he had his way.

Though not an evil man, Paul had done his share of distasteful things in his life and had been so focused on making money he had become somewhat of a hermit.

While not an angel, as no one who had managed to amass the fortune he had could be, and he had broken the rules now and then, he still considered himself to be a good man.

The only thing that plagued him was how alone he was in this world he had created for himself. Though a wealthy man, he had no one to share it with. His parents had died many years ago, both victims of a variety of ailments.

So, though Paul had more money than he knew what to do with, in truth, he wasn't necessarily a happy man. The spark he once had, that thrill of life, had long ago left him, like smoke caught in a gentle updraft. He'd tried many things to jump start his will to live, but none had taken affect on him.

With a weary sigh, he began walking again, his destination his private elevator which would take him to the top floor of the high-rise. From there he could gaze out on the majestic beauty of New York and imagine how it would all be his some day.

Upon reaching the elevators, he frowned deeply when he saw his private elevator was open, a man in an engineer's uniform crouched inside. The man's tools were spread out around him and a small yellow sign hung near the bottom, warning others the elevator was out of service, which was silly.

After all, the elevator was only for him, and no one else could use the lift to his office and private sanctuary.

Stepping closer, Paul leaned over the man's shoulder while the engineer played with the control panel in the elevator.

"Ah, excuse me, are you almost done? I wanted to get up to my office," Paul said with a slight grin. He may be rich, but he still knew of the common courtesy all humans deserved. He hadn't fallen so far into stagnation that he wasn't a polite soul.

The engineer turned around, setting his screwdriver down so he could look up into Paul's face. He was a plain man with a balding pate and small eyes. Laugh lines as well as a few wrinkles were scattered about the pleasant visage.

"I'll be finished in a sec', Mr. Francis. Sorry to keep you waiting," the engineer said in a subservient tone.

Paul checked his watch, his impatience getting the better of him. The thing was, he really wasn't in a rush. Once he reached his office, he merely planned on twirling his thumbs while his corporation rolled onward. He had created such a massive machine; he truly believed it would go on forever, long after he was dead and gone from this mortal coil. But of course that wouldn't be for a long, long time.

"Fine, fine, I have a few calls to make. I'll just wait over here," Paul told the engineer as he pulled out his cell phone.

The engineer nodded, picked up his screwdriver and got back to work. As for Paul, he did make a call or two but they were really not that important. He let others handle the complexities of running his business now and found he had more idle time to waste his life with nowadays.

The public elevators opened and closed, children, adults, and parents looking harried, all coming and going to their private destinations. Ten minutes later, the engineer waved to Paul, getting his attention.

"All set, Mr. Francis, but I think I should ride up with you just to make sure everything's working properly."

"Fine, fine, whatever, just as long as you're done," Paul said with a touch of impatience in his voice.

The engineer took a step back, gathered his tools, and Paul entered the elevator, the engineer following with a smile.

Paul used his key card and slid it into the slot, this allowing him access to the top floor. The polished stainless steel doors closed and the elevator began its ascent.

Paul looked down at his shoes, checking to see if they had received any smudges on his walk through the building. He had recently had them shined and took great pride in the thousand dollar loafers.

When you were rich, money was plentiful, so it meant nothing, merely a means to an end.

It was when he looked back up and caught the engineer's reflection in the elevator doors that his heart seemed to stop in his chest and his blood began to run cold. His breath lodged in his throat, his mouth opening slightly, no words escaping.

Instead of seeing the reflection of the plain man in an engineer's uniform, Paul stared at the visage of Death incarnate.

The figure was now seven feet tall, the top if its head scraping the ceiling of the elevator. A dark black cloak shrouded the figure in darkness, and when the form shifted, Paul could see just the hint of white, like a skull, from where the visage of a human face should be. Two red dots glowed where eyes would have been on a face, and Paul felt his bowels wanting to let go, only his willpower stopping him from soiling himself.

The figure's hands were the most unsettling.

Skeletal, bleached-white fingers held onto the elevator railing, the figure leaning back as any casual rider would, as the elevator shot upwards to what could feel like Heaven, the tall building like a spire in the sky.

Paul said nothing, the figure watching the control panel, eyeing the electrics to make sure everything was working properly.

Paul blinked his eyes, squeezing them closed; telling himself what he was seeing was impossible. It had to be, because the reality would be far too much to contemplate.

After all, why would Death himself be standing behind him if he wasn't about to die?

The chilling figure had come to harvest his soul, and Paul felt utterly helpless as he gazed into those glowing red eyes.

His forehead began to sweat and he could feel dampness under his arms. His heart had begun beating again, but now it was like he had his own personal drum solo in his chest.

The entire time, Death never moved, never wavered, only stood behind him, staring at the elevator panel.

As the elevator shot upwards to the top of the building, Paul reflected on his life, how he had lost his way.

Sure, he had money, but what had he done with it to truly help others? He could easily spend half of what he'd earned on others and he would have never, ever felt the loss financially.

One time, his father had told him how greedy man was and how he would always want more, even when he had his fill. How man was a glutton, and could have enough food and money to last three lifetimes and yet the greed inside would still want more, even if that meant others would suffer.

Paul reflected on all that now as he stared at the grim visage of Death and waited for that bone-white finger to come down on his shoulder, taking his soul to whatever world came next.

And what would come next?

He had been a devout Catholic his entire life, but now? When death was literally at his door, so to speak, he couldn't help but wonder if all he had been taught, all he had believed, was nothing but crap.

But then, if that was so, how could this entity exist at all?

The numbers flashed by on the elevator panel, and Paul sensed that when the elevator reached the top floor, so too would the end of his life.

He found himself full of regrets; of wishing he had done things differently.

He realized if he had only had a second chance, he would do things so very, very differently. He could start a few charity organizations, and other human related charities that could help with the betterment of mankind.

And most of all, he would find someone to love him, as he would her. They could start a family and he could remember what is was like to be alive, not so wrapped up in work and greed that he forgot about the simpler things in life; the things that connect us all and make us one.

Paul realized at that moment in time he would do things so very differently if he had the chance.

But it was now too late.

The elevator was slowing, the numbers ticking by as it approached the top floor. Behind him, Death shifted his weight, and Paul knew the hand would be coming down on his shoulder and he would feel…what? A blackness? A void? What would happen?

He didn't want to know, he knew that with all his heart.

He felt faint now, his shirt filled with perspiration and making his flesh sticky under his tailor made jacket. His legs felt weak and he just wanted to sit down, right on the floor of the elevator.

He could feel tears welling up in his eyes and he tried to fight them back, wanting to at least go out like a man, with a modicum of pride and courage.

The elevator stopped with a gentle nudge, so soft it would be ignored by all but the most perceptive of people. But Paul was perceptive and he found at this moment in his life, when he was about to die, his nerve endings and impulses were filled with fire for wanting to live!

Why now, when he was about to die, did he realize how much he wanted to live? Why had he squandered so much of the precious gift of life when it was with him and only now that he was losing it did he realize what he'd had?

The doors opened with a soft chime and the engineer grinned, nodding to himself.

Paul waited, knowing what was coming and helpless to stop it.

"Well, Mr. Francis, aren't you going to leave?" the engineer asked.

Paul said nothing for almost ten seconds, only his beating heart filling the void of silence, then he managed to utter a few words, the tone sounding like a five-year-old's.

"Aren't... aren't you going to take me? Isn't it my time?"

The figure leaned forward slightly and Paul was now able to see into that void where a face should be. The dark red eyes were floating in what seemed the air, a glimpse of a skull flashing like a strobe light, and below them nothing but darkness.

Deep, ebony darkness that seemed to go on forever.

"Do you want it to be your time, Mr. Francis?"

Paul managed to shake his head back and forth, not fully understanding what he was being asked, but knowing the answer was no.

"Fair enough, then," Death replied.

Death moved past him, and out into the hallway, then turned and gazed back at Paul with those crimson eyes.

"It looks like your elevator is all set, Mr. Francis. It was just a short in the control panel. It's all fixed now."

Paul's mouth slid open and he looked like a bug catcher.

"But what about...?"

"What about what? What about taking you with me?"

Paul nodded, his mouth still open.

The engineer waved his hand in front of him idly, like someone does when they don't believe what you are telling them is true.

"I'm not here for you, Mr. Francis. I'm just working my day job. Even Death has to eat, you know. You shouldn't have been able to see through my guise. You're quite a perceptive man, Mr. Francis, more so than most people I interact with." There was a blurring and then the visage of Death was gone and only the engineer remained.

The engineer shrugged. "Well, take care and make sure that elevator gets scheduled maintenance."

Paul nodded again as he watched Death stroll away across the hallway. The figure transformed back into Death for a brief moment and then back to the engineer again, and Paul stared as the man with the bag of tools headed for the opposite bank of elevators from him.

The engineer pressed the call button and tapped his shoe while he waited, Paul watching the entire time, dumbstruck.

The chime signaled the car's arrival, the doors opened and the engineer stepped inside, a subtle wave to Paul as he entered.

"Be seeing you," the engineer said with a knowing grin that spoke volumes and nothing at the same time.

Then the doors hissed closed and the figure was gone.

Paul stood perfectly still, staring out through the elevator doors and into the carpeted hallway with its thousand dollar light fixtures and paintings adorning the walls. He didn't move for the next ten minutes.

But slowly, in time, his heart slowed, his mouth closed, and his perspiring stopped. Blinking his eyes clear, he finally made himself move, stepping into the hallway. The doors slid closed behind him and he stared off to his office door at the end.

He still didn't understand what had just happened to him, but he felt like he had just been pardoned by God Himself.

For some reason he was still here and he realized what a truly wonderful gift he'd just received.

He was now able to make good on all those regrets he'd made only minutes ago.

With a bounce to his step, he headed off to his office. He had a lot of calls to make and knew he would be very busy for the next few months, but that was okay, as he knew he would be enjoying every second of it.

Something had changed inside him and he now felt alive, more alive than he had in years.

It was good to be alive, and if he could help it, he would stay that way for a long time to come, and he would do it by appreciating every moment he had on God's green Earth.

HEROES OF THE DEAD

The city was in ruins, most of the population having either evacuated, died or they had become part of the undead army of walkers.

No one knew how the dead began to walk, though before the news channels cut out, there were accusations of global bio-warfare. The word terrorism was used a lot, as it always was nowadays when something bad happened.

Only the superheroes were left to hold back the living dead from sweeping across the entire city, the rest of the country already consumed.

Near the north side, where the buildings had high stones walls and ornate steel gates, the last of a dying city holed up, only the few remaining superhuman protectors between them and a fate worse than death.

Most of the superhumans had been taken down by the virus, most through bites that had turned infectious.

Only five heroes remained.

The first was the Cowl. Dressed all in black, with a flowing dark cape and a utility belt with more gadgets than James Bond; he was a ferocious fighter. The most amazing thing about him was that he didn't have any special powers. He wasn't superhuman; he was only a man, albeit a man who had trained nearly his entire adult life for only one goal. And that goal was to fight crime.

After losing his parents at a young age to a carjacking, it was a way to channel his grief. His father owned a fortune five hundred company, so the Cowl was never in need of money. Now, that money was put to good use as the man bought weapon after weapon to fight crime.

The second superhero was Red Dragon. Also an ordinary man, but one with a power ring that allowed him to conjure anything his mind could think of. The object would manifest itself in bright red, glowing with the energy from the ring.

The third hero battling the dead was called Night Rider. Female, she was barely out of her teenage years, but she was blessed with the gift of invisibility.

The fourth was named Screamer. A woman in her thirties with flowing blonde hair and an athletic form, she had the gift of using her voice much like a cannon. Through sound waves, if she screamed, she could knock an army to its knees, her very voice taking apart the army by its very molecules.

The last hero to round out the remaining five was the most powerful of all.

He went by the name Captain Heroism, not his choice, but the name the city bestowed on him years ago.

With the power of super strength, heat vision and super breath, as well as the ability to fly, and his skin harder than titanium, he was the one the other heroes relied on the most.

Being invulnerable, he could swoop into a crowd of walking dead and begin systematically killing them, without fear of being bitten.

Time and again, he saved the citizens of the city as well as his four remaining teammates.

But alas, even Captain Heroism's might was no match for the awesome indefatigable resolve of the undead. Many heroes had been taken down, many also becoming infected. The super powered ones had been the most dangerous and it was Captain Heroism that had taken them down, being the only one able to withstand their force.

It had been hard killing his friends, but he knew once they died and returned, they were no longer his friends…they were one of *them*, the living dead.

This day, all five heroes were battling a horde of over two thousand walkers.

The Cowl was in his jet plane as he soared above the city, dropping acid bombs on the crowd below. Flesh melted, skin peeled and bones turned to mush as he dropped bomb after bomb into the moaning dead.

Red Dragon added his might as well, coming up with ingenious contraptions to destroy the zombies. From out of his ring a bright red bulldozer appeared, and as Red Dragon flew overhead—a red tendril connecting the energy machine to his ring—the bulldozer chugged along, its treads crushing body after body to mush as the front loader ran over the zombies, beheading them before running them down.

Night Rider used a katana, the lightweight weapon perfect for her to wield. She waded through the horde of walkers, slicing back and forth. To the ghouls, they understood nothing as to why a sword was floating in the air. They smelled her but could not see her, and thus she was able to take out each one that scented her before it could even try to find her.

Screamer hung from a telephone pole after being left their by Captain Heroism. Each time she screamed, she took out twenty feet of zombies, her sonic attack destabilized their bodies, causing the zombies to literally fall apart, much like a doll with loose limbs would. As she shifted direction, in her wake was a sea of body parts, all wiggling and jiggling as they slowly stopped moving.

Gore covered the streets by more than a foot, the zombies sloshing through it as if it didn't exist. Massive clouds of blowflies hovered over all, feeding on the undead masses, their small bodies bloated to the point some could barely fly.

Then there was Captain Heroism. At first he used his heat vision, swooping over the crowd and slicing bodies into halves, the upper parts sliding off torsos to splash in the viscera coating the pavement. Later, he changed it up and began using his frozen breath. Freezing hundreds at a time, he would then fly through them, shattering the crowd into thousands of crystal pieces, which would thaw out to become more gore.

When that became boring, he would pick up cars or trucks left abandoned on the roadside and fly above the crowd, then drop his payload. The three to five ton vehicles would squash bodies to paste, red and brown slurry seeping from under the crushed machines.

Each hero had a radio mic in their right ear so they could communicate with one another, though with the undead moaning and groaning, the team was hard-pressed to hear each other…that is except for Captain Heroism who had super hearing.

"There's so many of them," Screamer said between bouts of killer decibels. "How will we ever win over these kinds of numbers?"

Red Dragon cut in next. "We don't have a choice, Screamer. We're the last hope for the remaining citizens of our city. If we can't stop this horde, they're all doomed."

"Did you really just say the word *doomed*?" Night Rider asked. "You sound like a bad comic book character. Just because we wear costumes doesn't mean we have to be a cliché."

"Speak for yourself, Rider," Screamer said, "I like running around in spandex and beating up the bad guys like a character from a B movie."

"Will you people be serious," Cowl growled. "This isn't a game, millions are dead and more will be soon if we can't stop this latest horde."

A horde was a work of nature itself. No one understood how hundreds of zombies could somehow gather together, then more would arrive until there were thousands. They would wander the streets like a giant wave, devouring everything in their path.

Yes, a zombie horde was a force of nature.

Captain Heroism listened to his teammates banter, mildly amused by it. He wasn't one for talk, but kept his mind focused on the task at hand.

Swooping down, he landed in a thick clump of bodies and began pummeling them one at a time. Arms were ripped off torsos and heads were pulled from necks as if they were made of paper.

It was as he destroyed hundreds at a time that something happened that had never occurred before.

Whether by bad luck or simple misfortune, as Captain Heroism squeezed a head together, the skull cracking like a rotten egg, some of the brain fluids squirted into the air to land in his mouth.

He immediately began gagging, the taste so foul he wanted to vomit, but he held it down.

That may have been a vital mistake.

He had gotten bodily fluids of the infected in his mouth before, as only a bite was infectious, but unknown to him, this time it was actual brain fluid, where the virus was most potent in walkers.

With his quick metabolism, the virus suffused his system, changing his cells, necrotizing them, until in a matter of seconds, Captain Heroism was gone, another animated corpse replacing the once mighty hero.

The second he became one of the walking dead, the other zombies stopped attacking him. Captain Heroism stood in the center of the crowd, looking back and forth as he tried to decide what to do. His mind was unfocused, confused, and he may very well have stayed there all day if not for a red blur that caught his attention in the sky.

Red Dragon had shifted his energy ring into a giant anvil, which he was bringing up and down like a sledgehammer, smashing zombies to pulp. Each time the anvil was raised, body parts and dark slurry dripped from its surface, before being slammed down yet again.

Captain Heroism's superior sense of smell went into overdrive when he spotted Red Dragon, and in the same way a zombie knows it can still walk upon its return from death, so too, did Captain Heroism know he could fly.

He shot into the air, a ten foot hole left in his wake from the kinetic energy of his takeoff. Zombies were pushed into the hole where they began to pile up, the crowd pushing dozens of them in until the hole was full of wiggling bodies.

Red Dragon was about to open his mouth and make a quip about flattening the zombies when he was hit from behind. The force of the blow snapped his spine and he was instantly paralyzed from the neck down.

Captain Heroism flew to a nearby roof, where he dropped the limp Red Dragon and landed beside him, his mouth already dripping in expectation of the feeding to come.

"*Huuuu, ggghhh,*" Red Dragon gasped, unable to speak. He was dazed, confused and in massive pain, but as his eyes locked onto Captain Heroism, they went wide in fear and terror.

Captain Heroism had been the picture of a handsome man. With a square jaw, dark brown hair, piercing blue eyes, he was every woman's fantasy, and every male's inspiration for what they wanted to be. With broad shoulders, a muscled abdomen and thighs just as powerful, Captain Heroism had looked all but perfect.

That wasn't what the Red Dagon gazed at now.

Captain Heroism looked as if he had been dead for a week and had just crawled from the grave. His skin was sagging, pale with dark blotches, his hair was thin, small clumps ready to fall out. His forehead was more pronounced, the eyes recessed. The eyes…that was what made Red Dragon cringe internally.

The eyes that were once vibrant and strong, were now vacant, void of humanity, only a raw hunger floating within, a hunger that needed to be quenched.

Red Dragon may have been paralyzed, but he still had his mind and that was all he needed to control his ring. Conjuring up a giant chainsaw, he sent it floating across the space separating the two heroes, the red blade connecting with Captain Heroism as it began to whirr.

Captain Heroism did nothing to ward off the saw, there was no need. It was like a fly to a horse, it was so pointless.

He strode forward as the saw morphed into a flamethrower, white hot searing flame scorching Captain Heroism. This too, did nothing. Though undead, Captain Heroism was still invulnerable and only incredible bad luck had caused him to become a zombie.

Shape after shape morphed before Captain Heroism as Red Dragon tried to stop his undead foe, but nothing worked. The roof was beginning to collapse under the barrage of power deflected from Captain Heroism, and Red Dragon tried to speak once more, his indomitable will the only thing keeping him conscious.

Captain Heroism reached the supine Red Dragon and his teeth flashed in the sun as he prepared to sink them into his helpless victim.

Red Dragon's eyes were wide in fear, and panic was setting in. Just as Captain Heroism leaned down to sink his teeth into Red Dragon's neck, the fallen hero had an idea to at least warn his teammates as to what had happened.

Using his ring, he formed his voice box within his throat, making what was paralyzed work again.

The words were robotic, but they only needed to be understood once.

"*Heroism...zombie...enemy...run...*"

That's all he was able to manage before teeth as strong as diamonds tore into his flesh, severing his carotid artery and tearing out half his throat in one bite. Blood shot into the air to spin and swirl in the wind before pattering back down to earth. After uttering his last words, Red Dragon sent up a signal flare with his last ounce of life, the red flare as large as a sky-scraper.

The flare exploded into a massive array of reds, all shades allowed by the ring, and then, as if a light switch had been flicked, the flare was gone, for when the owner of the ring died, so too did any conjurations.

On the rooftop, Captain Heroism began to devour Red Dragon, tearing the body apart as a hungry man rips open a roasted chicken. In seconds the rooftop was stained red and bits of internal organs were scattered about. Captain Heroism's bright blue uniform with an American flag emblazoned on the chest, was soon awash with another color.

The color of death.

The Cowl looked up as he dropped another acid bomb on the undead crowd below, to see the giant flare fill his windscreen. At the same moment he heard Red Dragon's dying declaration and the Cowl's heart skipped a beat as he deciphered the man's last words.

"What was that?" Screamer asked. "Did you guys hear that? That sounded like Red Dragon."

"He sounded hurt. And what was that flare about?" Night Rider asked as she waded through the zombies on the ground. She had already beheaded hundreds of ghouls and knew before the day was through she would have to kill hundreds more. Though blessed with the power of invisibility, she was still human, and her strength was that of a normal person. Her arms were aching now and she wondered how much more she could take.

"I'm doing a search for Red Dragon now," Cowl said. "I can triangulate the signal he sent." As he waited for the computer to search the city, he dropped two more acid bombs. The bombs exploded on impact with the zombies, the spheres popping open to spray a liquefied gas into the air. The gas was formulated so it would only remain airborne for seconds before falling onto the animated corpses. He was always aware of his teammates' positions so he didn't accidentally drop a bomb on them by mistake. A beeping alerted him that the computer had found Red Dragon.

Shifting position in his seat, he banked his aircraft west and headed for the small blip on the screen.

Just before he reached the location, the blip faded away. Cowl knew that couldn't be good. The signal he'd honed in on was one all the teammates used. A small micro-transceiver was embedded in their bodies; it monitored heart rate, respiratory, and stress levels as well as other vital signs. It could even tell if blood pressure was high.

Captain Heroism had to swallow his as his skin was impervious to needles. Every week he had to swallow another one, as his stomach acid would eat each transceiver and make it cease to operate.

The Cowl waited until he was over the exact spot of the signal before it faded, then he ejected from his plane. His cape was designed to be used as a parachute and he used it now to steer him to the rooftop below.

Coming down harder than he wanted, he rolled across the roof and came up next to an air conditioning unit.

He remained hidden, sensing something wasn't right. He could see the rooftop was riddled with cracks and in many places there were large holes in the surface. He began moving from the a/c unit to another, then to a collection of ductwork. The roof was no different than the city itself, with many objects to use for cover. The Cowl hid in the shadows of each structure as he made his way across the rooftop. He knew the signal—before it faded—had been on the far side.

It only took him a few minutes, and soon he was at the precise location. His eyes took in the blood-stained gravel and he frowned, knowing something terrible had gone down here.

The area was wide open so he stood up and walked the remaining feet. His eyes took in the pools of blood, small bits of viscera, and stray pieces of red material that once belonged to a uniform.

Then he saw it, reflecting the sunlight a few feet away.

He didn't hesitate as he sprinted across the rooftop to the small object. He prayed deep down he would be wrong, that what he was going to find was nothing more than a piece of glass, or perhaps a candy wrapper, the foil glinting in the light.

But he wasn't so lucky.

As he reached the small artifact, he reached down and picked it up, holding it between his thumb and index finger.

It was Red Dragon's power ring.

As the Cowl studied the ring, his eyes saw small indentations on the ring. On closer examination, he could have sworn the indentations were teeth marks.

Odd, and impossible.

He was about to call in to the others when the entire building began to shake. Before he could act, the rooftop exploded upward as something incredibly powerful broke free of the top floor of the building. The Cowl used his cape to protect himself from falling debris, as he rolled across the roof to avoid falling rubble.

When he came up in a crouch, he found himself looking at Captain Heroism.

The once mighty hero for justice landed on the roof, no more than a few feet from the Cowl. The Cowl's mouth dropped open and his eyes went wide behind his mask as he took in Captain Heroism's condition.

The Cowl's mind took in the information before it and in less than two seconds he'd accepted what had happened and began to deal with it.

Lightning fast, he reached behind his back and pulled two Cowlarangs from his utility belt. Each one had three ounces of C-4 inside it. Faster than the human eye could see, the 'rangs were sent across the space separating the two heroes. On contact, the C-4 exploded, the sensors within going off. The rooftop was immediately destroyed in a firestorm of awesome power. More dust and grit rained down as the Cowl rolled away to avoid the shockwave of the blast.

When he came up again twenty feet away, hidden behind an a/c unit, he waited a few seconds before preparing to see the damage to Captain Heroism.

But before he could move, the a/c unit began to vibrate, then it was pulled from the roof, the clamps connecting it to the rooftop torn asunder. The Cowl found himself standing still, looking up thirty feet into the air as the a/c unit rose ever higher.

Then it was falling back to earth, right where he was standing, dumbfounded.

Before the a/c unit struck the roof, the Cowl snapped out of his shock and rolled away, coming up in a crouch as the unit crashed into the roof. Two more 'rangs were in his hand as he searched for a target.

He never got the chance to use them.

From out of the smoke cloud of the destroyed a/c unit, two twin laser beams of heat sliced into the Cowl, severing him at the waist. His face never changing, his eyes not so much as blinking, his upper half began to slide off the lower half until it splattered onto the rooftop.

The laser beam had been so hot it cauterized the wound instantly, and the Cowl found himself in great pain, but still alive, only with no lower half.

Rolling onto his back, he screamed loudly as Captain Heroism landed over him.

The Cowl tried to punch him but his blows were harmless and Captain Heroism barely acknowledged them.

"Night Rider, Screamer, come in," the Cowl groaned into his microphone. He was in and out of consciousness and it was hard to stay focused.

"Go, Cowl, did you find Red Dragon?" Screamer asked.

"Yes, I did. He's dead. But that's not the worst of it. Captain… Heroism…he's one of them. Don't know how but he's a walker now…"

Captain Heroism reached down and pulled off the Cowl's right arm, causing the mysterious man in black to shriek in agony. Blood shot out of the wound and he could already feel himself growing faint from blood loss, each beat of his heart bringing him closer to death.

"Screamer…be careful…he may be dead but he's just as powerful. I…tried…I…I really did… I have one more thing to try…" he gasped into his mic.

The Cowl reached down and pressed a small device on the side of his utility belt. It was something he thought he would never use, something he would fall back on as a last resort, when all hope was lost and there was no winning.

He knew this was one of those times.

Captain Heroism reached down and tore off the Cowl's other arm and began to feed on it, chewing chunks of meat off with his blood-red teeth.

The Cowl didn't care, he had pressed the button.

As he began to slip into unconscious from blood loss and the death that would follow, he could hear the high whine of the unit cycling down to zero.

It was three seconds before the unit hit zero, and in that time, Captain Heroism used both hands to crack Cowl's ribcage open to get at the juicy organs within.

The Cowl spit blood as he looked up at his undead friend, and he actually smiled. "I win, Captain…" he coughed.

The unit cycled to zero and there was a blinding flash, one that lit up the sky as if a sun had fallen to earth. The unit the Cowl had activated was a micro nuke and it now blasted the top ten floors of the building and took out a city block's worth of structures in all directions.

Six blocks away, Screamer and Night Rider stopped their battle with the dead and each looked up as the world went white.

Though they didn't know what the explosion meant, they had heard the Cowl's last words and it wasn't hard to piece together.

The origin of the blast may have been unknown to them, but one thing wasn't. Another hero had fallen.

"Night Rider, meet me on the north side of the city. There's nothing more we can do here. We need to fall back and protect the remaining living citizens," Screamer said into her mic.

"Gotcha," Night Rider replied as she began to retreat. She still took off heads with her katana as she did, but now she was moving in a different direction.

As Night Rider made her way through the undead crowd, she tried not to think about her two lost friends, three if she counted Captain Heroism. And there was no reason not to. He was one of the walkers now, he was gone. The man she knew was no more.

She had made it three blocks and was about to cross over to the next street, when a shadow blocked out the sun. At first she didn't understand what was going on, but when she looked up, her mouth fell open in horror.

There was a massive fuel tank from the gas yard on the outskirts of the city. One side was incredibly dented, the weight of the fuel inside pulling the tank downward. Only the multiple layers of steel prevented the tank from simply rupturing on the spot.

"Screamer, there's something going on here…" she began and then felt her heart stop beating as the tank began to fall to the earth.

There was nowhere to go, nowhere she could get to fast enough to escape the giant gas bomb falling from the sky.

She knew she was dead.

In her terror she lost concentration and her invisibility shield faded. In the middle of the undead horde she became visible.

The horde cared not for the falling gas tank, all they knew was that the human smell that had been in their midst for so long was finally before them.

Night Rider didn't understand why every zombie face around her suddenly turned and stared right at her. It was only when she glanced down at her hand, the one holding the katana, that she saw she was visible.

She tried to blink back into invisibility but it didn't matter, the zombies knew she was there. Together, they lunged for her, raking at her with claw-like hands as they tore into her flesh, shredding her uniform of colorful spandex and tearing at the skin beneath.

She only had to suffer for a few seconds, though, as the fuel tank was still falling towards her.

It was a shame those seconds were in unbearable agony, as her body was torn apart as if by wild animals, the zombies tearing and feeding on her even as the tank struck the ground, pulverizing everything beneath it as one spark ignited the fuel.

A rolling fireball washed through the streets, incinerating everything—living or dead—in a one mile radius of the initial blast.

Night Rider wasn't so much as dead but it was like she never existed, not so much as her ashes now remained in the intense heat of the conflagration.

From a nearby rooftop, Screamer watched the flames roil into the sky, the black smoke filling the horizon until it was as if night had fallen.

She knew Night Rider was in that part of the city, and she knew though she might call her, Night Rider wouldn't answer the hail.

Another hero had fallen.

Screamer turned and made her way back to the remaining citizens, knowing if—or more likely when—Captain Heroism came for them, it would be her last stand.

"What's wrong? Where are the other heroes?" a man asked when Screamer arrived at the main gate.

"They're all gone," she said sadly. "The walkers got them."

"What about Captain H? Surely he's okay," another man said as more gathered around Screamer.

She didn't want to tell them. She knew when she did, what little hope they had would flutter away like smoke in the wind. But she had no choice.

"He's one of them now. Somehow he was infected."

"What? How?" a voice asked.

"That can't be, he's invulnerable," another said.

"If he's gone, then what hope do the rest of us have?" another said.

Murmurs filled the crowd surrounding Screamer, voices yelling out for her to explain what happened. Of course, she had no answer.

Finally, she stood up on a wreck of a car with no tires, and raised her hands to silence them.

No one would listen to her, they just continued to yell and ask questions.

Finally, she opened her mouth and with her scream set on low, she let loose. The shriek she sent out wasn't enough to kill, but it stopped everyone in their tracks. A silence went over the crowd, she raised her voice to be heard.

"Look, I know you don't want to hear this. Frankly, I don't know what to tell you. Red Dragon, Cowl and Night Rider are gone and I know for a fact it was Captain Heroism who killed Cowl. As for the others, I can only assume it was the same thing." She made eye contact with most of the crowd. "Now, listen to me, please. Captain Heroism is still out there and with this being the only remaining community of living people in the city, it's only a matter of time until he arrives here."

"What can we do?" a woman asked.

"We fight, there's nothing else we can do," Screamer said.

"But he's too powerful, we're no match for him," another said.

"Maybe so," Screamer replied, "but we have no choice. Go get ready, gather all the ammunition you have, all the weapons. Because I can tell you this much, when he comes, he won't be the man you knew. Now he's one of them, a killing machine."

"What if we can't stop him?" another asked.

"Then God have mercy on our souls," Screamer said softly.

They came at dawn.

The undead horde swarmed through the streets until they were at the very walls of the enclave.

Men and women alike gathered on the walls, shooting into the zombie masses, but no matter how many they took down, there were hundreds more to take their place.

Screamer stood on the wall as well, using her sonic scream to take out dozens of zombies at a time. As the scream flowed around the undead, their bodies began to shake, then disperse into gel, puddles of gore collecting at their feet, which didn't melt, the feet being too low to the ground and not hit by the sonic wave.

Hours passed and still the undead attacked, the community doing its best to repel the assault.

Screamer was exhausted, but she knew there would be no rest until the horde was destroyed. As she wiped her brow of sweat and looked up into the sky, her blood ran cold as to what she saw.

Floating above the tallest building was Captain Heroism.

From this far away, Screamer thought he looked normal, and she would have stayed with that opinion until Captain Heroism used his heat beams to slice a dozen guards in half, slicing them in twain from groin to head. As the bodies toppled into the undead crowd milling at the base of the wall, the feeding frenzy began.

Immediately, all weapons' fire was directed at the undead hero.

Screamer waited and watched. She knew Captain Heroism was too far away for her sonic scream to hurt him, if at all, and though she dreaded him coming closer, she had no choice but to wait.

Bullets bounced off the mighty man's chest as if they were nothing but rain and he laughed at the feeble defense of the humans.

Then he swerved right and came out of the sky, a crimson and blue rocket. He was heading right for Screamer. She planted her feet firmly and prepared to send her most powerful sonic blast at the undead hero.

When he was no more than fifty feet away, she let out a blast so powerful that every person on the wall had to cover their ears or risk going deaf.

Captain Heroism took the full brunt of the sonic wave, and as everyone watched, it was as if his very body began to shift, the molecules changing.

But still he held together, his pale face hard, his dead eyes impassive.

Screamer kept at it for as long as she could, but eventually she had to rest.

When she stopped, silence seemed to blanket the area, even the zombie horde remaining quite.

Captain Heroism actually smiled slightly, and Screamer knew that not only was he truly infected, but he had somehow retained some of his intelligence.

Though exhausted, she prepared to send yet another sonic blast at him, when he dipped his body and swooped in, coming at her like a rocket.

Screamer barely had enough time to register the human missile that was coming for her before Captain Heroism's right fist connected with her chin.

The blow was so precise and powerful that Screamer's head was sheered from her shoulders, the head flying off to land in the courtyard within the walls. The headless body stayed immobile, standing tall, and as blood geysered out of the neck stump, it swayed and toppled into the zombie horde below.

They immediately began to feed, their moans rising in pitch with each passing second.

The guards on the wall realized their last hope for salvation was dead, but still they fought on, for to give up was death for themselves and their loved ones hiding in the buildings within the enclave.

As more gunfire erupted, Captain Heroism landed on the wall and looked around, the bullets not even a nuisance. To him, the barrage didn't exist.

A man ran up with a LAW and fired it at almost point blank range. The blast blew out a portion of the wall and sent more than three dozen people flying into the waiting horde below.

When the smoke cleared, Captain Heroism was unharmed, floating above where the wall once was.

His eyes glowed red and his heat beams shot out, the beams slicing man and woman alike until there was nothing left of the defense force but twitching bodies and parts of bodies. A few were still alive but they wouldn't be for long.

Captain Heroism flew off and landed on the wall nearest the gate, and with one stomp of his foot, he fractured and then sent the wall crashing down.

Almost immediately, the horde swarmed in, the moaning and groaning filling the air.

As he flew into the first building where the sick, the old, the women and children were hiding, Captain Heroism smiled one more time, his blood coated yellow teeth glinting in the haze of the day.

Soon, the dying screams of the survivors echoed through the streets surrounding the enclave, rivaling the moans of the dead.

HIGHWAY OF THE DEAD

The 405 was clogged with cars, bumper to bumper for the next five miles.

Inside the car, Brad M. Quincy shifted impatiently in his seat, his knuckles white around the steering wheel.

"Damn it, come on," he said for the hundredth time as the lane to his right began moving. All he could do was watch the cars moving by him as he sat idling behind a minivan. Inside the van, a six-year-old boy stared at him from the rear window. Every time Brad looked forward, the kid would stick out his tongue and make funny faces at him.

At first it was amusing, but now it was just damn annoying.

"Damn kid," he muttered. "Should be in a car seat not jumping around like an idiot."

Checking his watch yet again, he muttered a few choice imprecations. He was going to be late for dinner. And this wasn't just any dinner. It was with his in-laws. Now, normally that wouldn't be so bad, but his in-laws didn't like him very much.

They had a good reason, too. He and his wife had been having marital trouble, the reason obvious to him, but to no one else.

In a nutshell, his wife was a bitch. Yes, that's what he was thinking. His wife was a Grade-A bitch.

You see, whatever he did wasn't good enough for her. Sure, things had been fine when they had first met, but a year later, after the honeymoon was over, she began changing. Everything he did was wrong. He could never please her. And to top it off, she would constantly shit on his dreams of being a writer.

Brad had written three books, but so far they had never left his office at home. She had read them for him, as a good wife should, but to her they were never good enough to put out there in the real world.

Now Brad didn't agree with her. He knew many writers who had put out their own books, all by themselves. It was a new world with new opportunities. Sure, he would be taking a chance his work was good enough, but ask anyone who is a success and they will tell you the same thing. They had to go for it and take that chance. If you don't, then nothing good will ever happen.

Of course, she didn't agree with him and shot him down at every chance she got.

His wife, an English teacher at the local college, was always quick to criticize. Because in her opinion, his books were never good enough, she would constantly belittle him again and again about it.

His plot wasn't well thought or his prose weren't real enough. No matter what he did and what he wrote, she would always knock him back down.

To say she was a negative influence on him was an understatement.

So now, four years after they had tied the knot in a beautiful wedding at the neighborhood church, they were in talks of divorce.

Which was what the dinner was about. Susan's parents were hoping to get it all worked out. They had never liked him anyway and this was their chance to finally get rid of him.

See, his father-in-law was a lawyer and the second he found out about the troubled marriage he'd stuck his nose in their business.

Like father like daughter, huh?

So now he was stuck in traffic and would be late for the dinner. When he got home he knew he was going to hear about it. How he didn't care enough and was selfish, which was why he hadn't come home for dinner on time.

Checking his cell phone for the thousandth time, he saw he was still in a dead zone.

Though cell towers were everywhere, there were still parts of California that didn't have them yet. Especially closer to the outlying mountains which was where he was now.

He shifted lanes, cutting off a grandmother in a blue Toyota, hoping the lane that was moving would now help him.

Glancing in his rearview mirror, he saw the grandmother flipping him off. Her dentures gleamed in the fading sun as her finger saluted him, announcing he was *number 1*. He shrugged and waved, apologizing, but she just shook her head, annoyed.

No sooner did he straighten out in his new lane, his car now moving past the minivan so he was now side by side with them, then the kid in the van shifted windows, now dragging his mouth over the glass like a blowfish.

Brad ignored this, pretending he was focusing on the car in front of him, and as he silently urged the car in front to move, it then stopped and he watched the minivan begin to crawl forward, soon three cars up and still moving as he sat idle.

"Oh, come on, that ain't right," he snapped as he wiped his brow.

It was warm out, despite the fading sun, and his air conditioning had cut out a week ago and he hadn't wanted to let go of the car to get it fixed. Now he was paying for it as he sat in the warm car roasting like a turkey in an oven set at 475.

Deciding he needed a distraction, he turned on the radio, the station set to the news.

"...and at this time the reports are inconclusive. To reiterate, scenes of mass hysteria are coming in from across the country. No one seems to understand what is happening and reports have been fuzzy as authorities try to make sense of what's happening, but it appears the d..."

"Forget this shit," Brad growled under his breath. It was just more ways the mass media would try to make everyone scared over nothing. He bet a few political radicals were bitching about the Iraq war again. All the tree huggers wanted it to be over. But, hey, they didn't mind having oil heat their homes did they? They needed gas for their VW vans and Volvos. It's easy to take the high horse when it's not your ass about to get shot off in some Godforsaken desert country.

Idiots, all of them. They all needed to get a life.

He sat in traffic for another two hours, his body probably sweating out at least a quart of water, but finally he reached the end of the clog and the road opened up once more.

As he passed the reason for the hold up, he wanted to scream with rage and annoyance. Two cars were on the side of the shoulder of the highway and it looked like one had tapped the other by accident. There was no damage to either car, perhaps a scratched bumper if anything, but they had to pull over and change papers for insurance. And the best part was the first car hadn't pulled over enough, so now traffic in that lane had to merge into the middle one. All this shit, all this time wasted, simply because one asshole was too selfish to park correctly in the break down lane.

He honked at them as he passed by, flipping them off. The guy in the second car yelled at Brad and waved his fist but then Brad was gone, shooting down the road and gaining speed with each passing second.

Brad had to wonder what they were waiting for. Were they really waiting for hours for a police car to arrive? Well, that would take a while as the cop was probably stuck in traffic, too. He had seen more than one car on the shoulder in the break down lane, which would mean the squad car wouldn't be able to get by.

It was as he glanced in his mirror at the receding accident that he saw a police car finally arrive. Too late to speed him up, of course, he thought. Figures.

His foot was heavy on the gas as he tried to make up the time he'd lost.

He wasn't the only one. All the cars around him had floored their gas pedals, finally free of the traffic jam. It was like a race track at the start of the race as each car shot forward like a rocket, every single vehicle late for something, no doubt.

Finally, he was making good time as he and the other commuters shot down the highway like rats deserting a sinking ship.

But no sooner did he get a few minutes of freedom, then suddenly every car and truck in front of him seemed to hit the brakes, more than one swerving to the left and right as others began rear ending one another.

Like the classic domino effect, each vehicle crashed into the one in front of it. And when something larger, like a tow truck, or one of those massive SUV's that could be used as tanks in Third World countries, crashed into smaller cars, they crushed them instantly into twisted metal; it was beyond horrible.

Inside those twisted metal vehicles were people, but now they quickly became exploding bags of meat as the bodies were pummeled and battered by the force of the accidents.

One car, a Honda Civic, was struck from behind by a Lincoln Navigator. But the Navigator didn't just rear end the Honda. Instead, with its higher wheel base, it simply ran over the Honda, flattening the roof of the small car and pulverizing the three people inside it. As the Navigator bounced over the car and then rolled onto its side amid a shattering of glass and groaning metal, the Honda began to leak something dark and red out of the bottom of doors, and it most definitely wasn't oil.

Even if the passengers had worn seat beats it wouldn't have mattered, for when a giant hand seems to come out of the sky and swat your car flat like a bug, there's no chance for survival.

Another car rear ended the one in front of it, and the impact was so abrupt that the driver was catapulted through the windshield, the bloody body flying ten feet into the air before landing heavily on the road. But no sooner did the body land and come to a stop, then another car drove directly over the body, the left tires driving straight through the still form and bifurcating it as easily as if the tires had been blades. The man, now in two parts, was somehow still conscious and he screamed in agony as his intestines slid out of his severed half as he tried to use his one working arm to scoop them back in. His other arm was useless, the ulna bone poking out at an odd angle.

Similar acts of carnage were happening all across the highway as car after car, truck after truck, crashed into one another in what would later be called the largest multiple vehicle pile-up in the past ten years.

Brad felt his car slide as he applied the brakes, and before he knew what was happening, he was upside down and sliding across the pavement, the roof of his car flashing sparks in all directions. As his car spun like a top, he gripped the steering wheel, trying to get the car to do something he wanted it to. Of course being upside down, there was nothing he could do, and if someone had watched him, it would have been amusing to see a car sliding upside down along the highway while the driver tried to steer it, the front tires turning back and forth like a radio controlled car that had been flipped over.

He screamed as the sound of grinding metal filled his ears and then the car spun forward and he saw he was heading right for the pile-up. He only had time for one brief gasp and then his car joined the rest, the airbag deploying and slamming him in the face.

The impact was like a giant had punched him, and before he knew what was happening, he lost consciousness as behind him, more cars and trucks crashed into him, crushing his car into a junkyard mess of steel and fiberglass.

Brad was dreaming.

In his dream, he was at a book signing for his first release, a best seller too. In his dream he had taken a chance and had put out his book by himself, ignoring his wife's complaining, and had been discovered in less than a month.

People loved his book, many wanting to own multiple copies. The book's plot was so original, so ambitious, that all ages, male and female alike, could relate to it.

In less than a month after publishing his book, he was a household name. Fans screamed to see him, wanting his autograph, and of course his book was soon to be made into a major motion picture.

As he sat behind the table signing autographs, the fans lined up out the door and around the block, all wanting to get a glimpse of him, or maybe better, to actually get to talk to him.

Oh, yes, all was right with the world as fans screamed for him, some fighting with others to be next in line. But then the fans grew ugly, battling one another to be next. Soon there was utter chaos and a riot broke out, and before Brad knew it, he was being swallowed by a score of hands and feet as they tried to grab him, wanting a piece of his clothing or a clipping of his hair. But it didn't stop there. Soon they were pulling at his actual body, more than one fan wanting to take the ultimate prize. As he yelled in pain, his arms and legs, his eyelids, ears and nose were ripped away from him as glorious crimson and scarlet fluid sprayed into the fan's faces. But instead of being horrified, they lapped up the blood, wanting to taste his essence, and a few became so aroused they then set in with teeth and fingernails, digging into his chest as more ripped at his throat.

As he gurgled his last shriek of pain, the fans, the ones who were supposed to love him, began to eat him, slowly devouring him alive. It was then that he realized there was a two-edged sword to being discovered, and perhaps it wasn't so bad not publishing his books and remaining anonymous. It might have been better to remain unknown by the public and the opinionated, off balance fans that waited to step on his work and crush his dreams before they could begin.

Brad slowly opened his eyes, not understanding where he was, and for one brief moment he thought he was back in his dream. It sure seemed that way, after all, he could hear people screaming and yelling, sounds of people in agony. In the air was the scent of spilled blood, coppery and sweet, and mixed with it he could detect the scent of gasoline and engine oil, burnt or burning by the smell of it.

Mentally, he did a quick inspection of himself, and as he wiggled his toes and fingers and tried to move his legs, he didn't feel anything was damaged and he didn't cry out in pain. His seatbelt and airbag had saved his life.

Reaching up, as he was upside down, he undid the seatbelt and dropped to the roof of his car, which was now the floor.

Being careful not to cut himself on the safety glass littering the headliner, he began to climb out of the car, wiggling like a worm leaving an apple. When he was halfway out, he wrapped his hand around the window frame and pulled himself the rest of the way. With his legs still inside the car, he rested for a second. Though muffled, he could hear the cries of people calling for help, but he ignored them. He needed to worry about himself right now.

With his upper body protruding out of the car, he began to feel rain on his neck. But then he realized rain wasn't usually this warm.

Reaching down, he touched the dark liquid on his skin, and when he pulled his hand back to see it, there was blood on his fingers.

Thinking it was his and beginning to panic more than he already was, he glanced above him to see a headless torso draped over the undercarriage of his car, the drip, drip, drip, of the blood coming from the jagged open neck wound where the head should have been.

Crying out in revulsion at the sight of a headless corpse, he scurried the rest of the way out of the window frame and rolled to the side, wanting to distance himself from the sight of the corpse. Then he rested his head and closed his eyes as he thanked God he was still alive. But he didn't stay there for long, the smell of burning vehicles coming to his nose as the sky filled with smoke.

Taking it slow, he went to his knees, a wave of dizziness suffusing him, but then it dissipated, leaving as fast as it had arrived now that blood was pumping throughout his body. Looking around, he still couldn't see anything. The other vehicles around him blocked his view of the rest of the highway and pile-up. But then he spotted one familiar vehicle.

There was a minivan to his left, and as he looked into the shattered rear window, he saw the same child who had been teasing him only minutes before. The boy was now upside down, his arms and legs limp, his eyes staring at nothing. There was a piece of metal in the boy's head, looking like a shark fin. It was embedded in his forehead and Brad had to look away, feeling guilty about what he'd thought about the boy when they had been stuck in traffic.

Stumbling to his feet, he gasped at the overwhelming sight that greeted him.

For hundreds of yards in both directions there was nothing but a sea of twisted metal and steel. Bodies were everywhere, draped over hoods and bumpers and lying on trunks of cars and trucks like they were sunning themselves at the park. An eighteen wheeler was near the back of the pile-up and it had rolled, flattening ten vehicles before it came to a stop. Blood seeped out of the crushed frames, the people inside not just dead but entirely destroyed.

Brad took a few faltering steps, not knowing where to go, and he came upon a station wagon. A family of five was inside, but they were all dead now. The driver, the father, had a four inch round electrical pipe through the middle of his face. The reason for this was the pickup truck he'd rear-ended was carrying the other pipes and electrical supplies now spread out across the pavement.

The children all had broken necks and the wife was hanging out of the fractured windshield, her head almost completely turned around. Her wedding ring flashed in the setting sun and her eyes seeped blood, as if in her last moments on Earth she wept for her lost family.

A man came towards Brad, shambling slowly; hands out in front of him like one of those Frankenstein movies. The eyes were glassy and there was a large wound on his scalp. Slowly, the man shuffled towards Brad, who still hadn't noticed him, too caught up in the visceral carnage of death before him.

Horns blared, small fires popped and crackled, and in the back of the pile-up a vehicle exploded, spraying fire and burning fuel in all directions. If this wasn't Hell on Earth it was a damn good facsimile.

Brad turned when he noticed the shadow of the figure coming up behind him and he spun at the last second to stare into the glossy eyes of the bloody man.

"Please help me, my family, they're trapped in my car back there, please," the bloody man gasped as he reached out for Brad, wrapping his fingers in Brad's shirt.

"Fuck off, buddy, I've got my own problems," Brad said and tore the man's hands away from him, then shoved him away.

The man barely acknowledged the snub, too dazed from the accident to fully understand what was happening. He stumbled away to seek help elsewhere.

Brad stumbled along himself, staring at scenes of death in every direction.

To his left was a jeep and under the front left tire was a baby. The infant couldn't have been more than a month old tops, but now the little one would never see another sunset. The head was nothing but a deflated balloon, the tire having pulverized the small body. One hand was sticking out of the mass of meat, the tiny fingers still holding a rattle with splotches of blood on it.

This was too much for Brad and he leaned over and let his stomach empty its contents across the highway, the hotdog and salad he'd eaten for lunch splashing and then rolling with the slant of the road.

When he could function again, he averted his eyes to prevent another bout and moved on, searching for help, he supposed.

Everywhere he looked there was nothing but suffering. Human arms and legs were strewn about, more than one lone, decapitated head lying on the pavement like a lost soccer ball. The eyes in the heads were always open, the mouths hanging slack in shock or surprise. He couldn't help but wonder what was the last thing they saw before their heads were separated from their shoulders.

He heard another child crying and turned to see a small girl, maybe five. She was covered in blood from head to toe and was calling out for her mommy. Then she turned and wandered in the opposite direction to be lost from sight behind the wreck of a Saab.

"You, there! Hey, you!" a voice called out to his right and Brad at first didn't turn to it. He was so lost in his own world of misery and despair he thought he had stumbled into one of his own worst nightmares. But then the voice called out again, the strong authoritive tone snapping him out of his fugue state.

"I said you, hey, wake the hell up, man! I need some help over here!"

Brad followed the sound of the voice to see a man in between two cars with locked bumpers. The man was hovering over a woman who was sprawled on the road like she'd decided to take a nap.

The man looked up when Brad reached him and he pointed a blood-covered finger at Brad.

"Yes, you! Get your ass over here. I need help if I'm going to be able to save this woman."

Brad did as he was told, moving more on autopilot than an actual want of helping. It was just a thing he did when he didn't know what to do in a situation. If someone else acted like they knew what they were doing, Brad would follow them without question.

Brad was what you would call a *follower*.

When Brad had shuffled a few feet closer to the man, the blood-covered finger pointed down at the woman.

"Come on, get over here! Hurry up, damn you!" he snapped and Brad did as he was told.

"Uh, what do you want?" Brad mumbled.

"Lean down here, I need your hand," the man said. "I'm a doctor and I need to work fast or this woman will die."

Brad knelt down, and when he moved to the side of the doctor, he could now see the woman's upper body.

"She looks pretty dead now. What's the point?"

"Just do as I say, and don't argue with me," the doctor snapped.

Brad did as he was told, though he felt it was a waste of time. To say the woman was a mess would be an understatement. A seven inch long and three inch diameter pipe was sticking out of her chest; right between what Brad would have normally called a great rack. He knew this because her shirt was draped to the side so her entire upper body was exposed. But any sexual excitement was lost when he stared at the pipe jutting out of her chest like a flagpole in a front yard.

Blood seeped from the wound as the doctor tried to save the woman's life.

"The pipe is cutting off her airway. She's got a punctured lung and at least two ribs are completely shattered. I need to remove the pipe so I can reinflate the lung. And I need your help."

"My help? What the hell can I do? I'm not a doctor or a nurse. I'm an accountant for Christ's sake!" Brad snapped back, a little more of himself returning. All around them people were yelling, screaming, wailing, running around, some calling out for loved ones, begging and pleading for someone to help them. A few sirens could be heard as fire and emergency services tried to get to people who could use them, but there were so many it would be hours, maybe days before everyone was helped and found under all the wreckage.

"It doesn't matter what you are, I just need your hands," the doctor said gruffly.

"Fine, what do you want me to do?" Brad asked.

The doctor reached down and grasped the pipe with both hands.

"I'm going to pull this out. When I do I need you to place your hands over the wound or she'll bleed out. I'd let you take the pipe out but it has to be done a certain way, not just yanked out. We clear?" He looked at Brad who was staring down at the woman.

"I said, are we clear?"

"Yes, we're clear, I heard you, shit, I'm not deaf," Brad snapped back.

The doctor nodded and without waiting a second longer, he pulled on the pipe at an angle, sliding it out of the woman's torso.

The woman, who had been unconscious, suddenly woke up from the pain, her mouth opening wide in a guttural cry. Blood shot from her mouth to spray Brad's face and he sputtered as he wiped it away.

"Your hand, get your hand on her wound, damn it!" the doctor screamed as he set the pipe down.

But Brad hesitated, too overcome with shock as the woman stared at him with terror-filled eyes, her pupils as large as quarters. As for where the pipe had been, a geyser of scarlet shot out of the ghastly opening; a small Old Faithful shooting the blood straight up. The doctor, disgusted at Brad, dove in and placed a hand over her wound, but no sooner did he do this than the woman began to choke, convulsing as she died, her eyes rolling back into her head and then her lids closing forever.

It wasn't drawn out. One second she was alive, then she was dead, the blood slowing as her heart stopped pumping.

The doctor worked on her frantically, but after a two full minutes he leaned back and sighed, his hands so covered in congealing blood it looked like he was wearing crimson gloves

"Damn it, she's dead." He turned to glare at Brad. "What the fuck is wrong with you, man? I told you to do a simple thing. She bled out in seconds. She'd already lost a lot of blood. She couldn't afford to lose a tablespoon more." He frowned heavily. "Thanks to you she's dead."

Brad's eyes went wide at the man's words. "Whoa, now just back the fucking truck up there, Doctor! Don't try to blame this shit on me. I didn't cause this fucking pile-up. I didn't kill her! Hell, I didn't even want to help in the first place. So you can take your accusing tone and shove it right up your ass!"

"Well, I've never…" the doctor gasped.

"I couldn't give a goddamn what you did or didn't do. Don't make me your scapegoat. The bitch was dead the second that pipe went into her. Anyone with half a brain could see that!"

"My Lord, man, how can you be so heartless? She was a human being for God's sake!"

"Yeah, well, she's nothing but dead meat now, so fuck off and leave me alone!"

Brad got up and turned to walk away and the doctor, still leaning next to the dead woman, looked up to stare at Brad's back.

"It's people like you that make the world what it is!" he called after Brad who ignored him.

It was as the doctor looked back down at the woman, wanting to cover her chest again and give her some dignity in death that the woman's eyes suddenly opened.

The doctor didn't see this, concentrating on buttoning her blood-soaked shirt, but when her head tilted to the side and her mouth opened and closed slightly, he gasped in amazement.

"Good God, she's still alive!" he cried and reached down to check her pulse to see how strong it was. It was as he reached his hand to her throat that she suddenly turned her head and raised it, her left arm coming up, her hand grasping the doctor's wrist.

"What are you…?" was all the doctor got out before the previously dead woman sank her teeth into his wrist, tearing out a two inch chunk of his flesh.

The doctor screamed and pushed her away, punching her in the head with his free hand. It was instinct, something he would never have done in normal circumstances, but as her teeth came away with a chunk of his arm and his blood shot out to bathe her face like syrup, he found himself not worrying about etiquette and only worrying about himself.

Brad had walked a ways a bit and he now turned around to glance over his shoulder to see what the doctor was yelling about. Brad was about to tell the guy to fuck off once and for all, but when his eyes locked onto the man and the prone woman, things didn't look the same as when he'd left them a few moments ago.

It looked like the woman was moving, as impossible as that seemed, and the doctor seemed to be bent over her.

Mildly curious as to what was going on, he spun about and jogged back to them, and when he reached the doctor and peered over his shoulder, his mouth fell open at the sight before him.

The dead woman had managed to get her teeth into the doctor's throat and now was chewing like a dog on a meat bone. The doctor was helpless, locked in her grip, as both of the woman's hands held his head firmly between them.

"Jesus Christ! What the fuck is going on here!" Brad yelled, astonished at this graphic scene that made absolutely no sense. It was amazing that the woman was alive, but more than a little odd that the first thing she would want to do is eat the man who had saved her.

The doctor's throat was shooting blood and he managed to pull his head free of her grasp and stand up. As he did this, blood geysered out of his torn jugular to splash Brad with warm gore.

"What the hell? Holy shit!" Brad screamed, having no idea what to do. His legs were frozen as he watched the doctor stumble away to then fall onto the road, his arms and legs twitching as blood spilled out onto the pavement.

Brad's mouth was hanging open and he could taste the doctor's blood on his tongue. He didn't know what to do. In the back of his mind he began hearing more screams and yells, but they sounded different now, more terror added to the tones.

And then his eyes went back to the prone woman who was even now sitting up, her face and upper chest covered in the doctor's warm blood, the plasma mixing with her own congealed blood covering her breasts. Her mounds of glory swayed back and forth and Brad found his eyes going to them, but then his eyes went higher and he saw her chewing on the doctor's skin. She swallowed the flesh and then hissed at him, Brad taking a step back, not understanding what he should do.

Should he run? Should he try to help her? He'd seen what the doctor did when he tried to help her and he didn't want to end up like that.

The woman crawled on her knees and then stood up, using a nearby car for support. When she was standing, there was that circular hole in her chest which allowed light to seep through like a peep hole. She began stepping toward Brad.

Brad's mouth dropped so low it seemed to scrape the road as he stared at this woman who should definitely be dead. The hole in her torso was perfectly round and as he watched, he saw people running around behind her. He was using the hole like a telescope!

And then she lunged at him, her hands grabbing his arms as her teeth clacked an inch from his face.

"Get away from me, you crazy bitch!" Brad snapped as he shoved her away. She was smaller than him and she was pushed back, but then she was at it again.

Brad, out of patience, realizing whatever was happening was so off the charts of reality it couldn't be rational, waited for her to come at him again, and this time he punched her squarely in the chin. The woman's head rocked back and her jaw dislocated, the lower half hanging like an old swing; still she came for him again.

"I'm warning you, lady, try it again and I will clean your clock." He looked around to see if anyone was around who could help him but there was no one. Everyone else was dealing with their own worlds of misery and death.

The dead woman didn't listen and came for him again and this time Brad decided that was it.

As she charged him, albeit slowly, he dodged away from her and scooped up the pipe lying on the ground. The same one she had been impaled with.

Spinning, she hissed again, her lower jaw now resembling an old necktie, her tongue mimicking the jaw. Brad waited for her to come forward again.

"Okay, I warned you," he said firmly, and when she stumbled forward at him, he raised the pipe and whacked her on the side of the head.

Once more her head rocked to the side, and this time when she turned it back to Brad, he saw a large gash on her cheek. Bone could be seen peeking through and the sides of her molars were now visible, but if the woman cared she didn't show it.

"Son-of-a-bitch," Brad gasped as he stepped away from her.

Gargling her anger, the woman came for him again, but Brad had had enough and he decided there were two choices. Run or kill her.

Running was easier and wouldn't land him in jail for killing her, so he turned and was about to run when he found himself face to face with the doctor. The same doctor who had died moments ago from blood loss.

But the doctor's eyes weren't as clear as before, now they were vacant, dead of emotion and personality.

As Brad stopped cold, the doctor wrapped his arms around him in a bear hug and tried to sink his teeth into his throat.

Screaming, Brad tried to break free and then felt the woman come up against him from behind. Her breasts pushed against his back and even in his terror he felt their softness. But when her face went to his and she tried to bite his ear off, he screamed yet again.

She couldn't do it; however, her lower jaw useless and she seemed to kind of rub her tongue and upper teeth on his face. Blood and saliva was left behind and Brad felt his stomach heaving as he fought for his life.

The doctor turned to bite him again, teeth coming so close they might have taken a chunk out of him, and Brad managed to elude his advance. Then he got his right arm free, the one still holding the pipe.

When the doctor tried again to taste his flesh, Brad brought up the pipe and jammed it into the doctor's left eye. He would never have done this normally, but in his panic he just acted, and as the pipe slid into the socket, scraping bone, he could already feel the revulsion for what he'd done.

The pipe slid almost five inches deep before hanging up on the socket, the doctor falling away from him, releasing Brad. The body hit the pavement hard and the doctor's head whacked with such force it cracked. As brains seeped out of the fracture and also out of the tip of the pipe like ground hamburger, Brad threw up, coating his shoes with bile and whatever remained in his stomach from his last bout of sickness.

He shoved the dead woman away as he was vomiting and fell backwards to trip over her legs, falling to the road like a drunk. Brad, not wanting to deal with anymore of this shit, picked himself up and stumbled away, wiping his mouth as he went.

If things had been bad at the pileup before, then they were downright hellish now. Everywhere he looked the people he'd seen that had been dead, the kid in the minivan, the family in the station wagon, the man with the pipe in him, all of them were now moving about.

As impossible as it seemed, these people, who had most definitely been dead, were now up and about and seemed to be searching for the survivors.

Wherever Brad looked, the people who had managed to live through the crash and had been helping others, were now set upon by the victims who had been dead only moments ago.

Brad saw a man pulled down by three children covered with what were obviously mortal wounds, one child having half its chest torn out when it had gone through the windshield of a car. Intestines hung like garland from the boy's abdomen to slap the ground as he moved. Screams filled the air, a symphony of death no man should ever want to hear and Brad stood in the middle of it, watching with dumbstruck eyes.

His throat stung a little, and when he reached up to touch it he felt warm blood. But it wasn't old blood, this was fresh. Feeling with his fingers, he found a wound there, a small bite. But it wasn't life threatening so he ignored it.

Three more dead people popped up behind a squished Volvo and Brad backed away as the undead crawled over the hood of the car.

He knew whatever was happening was so very wrong and he also knew he needed to go…now!

Turning, he ran to the shoulder of the road and began running down the highway, sometimes having to climb over cars that blocked his way. To his right was the guardrail and to his left was the massive pile-up of twisted wreckage and human bodies.

As he ran, he glanced to his left to see people now attacking people. One living dead guy with an arm missing, the other hanging by a few tendons and flesh, was snapping at an old woman like his head was a chicken's. But instead of coming back with bird seed in his beak, his mouth would pop up with a piece of the old woman's face.

Carnage was everywhere and as Brad ran, the sun began to disappear on the horizon, casting the entire scene in a pallid, otherworldly gloom that just made it seem all the more preposterous.

He felt himself growing tired and when he raised his hand to his throat to inspect his wound again, he felt the blood still flowing.

It looked like the doctor had gotten a piece of him after all.

Eventually he made it to the top of the wreck, where the first car had sideswiped another vehicle, causing the cascade of death and destruction, and as he slowed, he saw there were a few cars at the point that weren't in the wreck. These cars were from people who had seen what was happening in their rearview mirrors and had stopped to then drive back to assist in saving lives.

That was fine with Brad, for now one of these cars was going to save his life.

He found an old, beat up Chevy, the engine still running, and he hopped in. He didn't know where the owner was and didn't care, all he knew was he wanted away from this place.

Slamming the transmission into drive, he took off like a rocket, his eyes going to the rearview mirror.

Behind him, what was visible was the walking dead chomping on the living, a feast of meat and internal organs that would rival any horror movie. He heard the sounds of rotors beating the night sky and glanced up into the night sky to see three helicopters approaching the massive accident, the spotlights already lighting up the night.

He didn't care about them, about any of it. None of it was his problem anymore.

Stepping on the gas pedal harder, he drove off into the night. Though he felt woozy, not understanding that he was losing blood at an alarming rate and would die of blood loss if he didn't get medial assistance fast, he headed home for the dinner date with his wife and in-laws,

By the time Brad reached the street his house was on, he was as white as a ghost and could barely see the road in front of him. Thinking it was foggy, he put the high beams on, but it did little to help his situation.

His mind was fuzzy, his reactions were slow, and he sideswiped more than one parked car on his way home. But there were no police out this night, as every available officer was back at the massive pile-up on the highway.

It was as he approached his home, only a few doors down, that his vision finally began to fade.

His will was so strong that he forced himself awake and managed to swing the Chevy into his driveway, but no sooner did the front tires touch the asphalt, then his head slumped forward, he closed his eyes, and passed out, seconds later descending into death.

The front bumper of the Chevy ended up hitting the garage door, but with Brad's foot now releasing the gas pedal, the car only tapped it, barely scratching the paint on the roll up door and pushing the door in less than an inch.

The Chevy sat idling, the garage door preventing it from wanting to move, and Brad's still body remained that way for another ten minutes.

The man was clinically dead, his clothing saturated with blood, a few pints adding to the grime of the filthy seat of the Chevy.

Nothing stirred in the neighborhood except for a few barking dogs in nearby yards who wanted to be let inside, but then, inside the Chevy, one of Brad's fingers began to twitch.

Soon, the rest of the fingers were moving, and then Brad opened his eyes and sat up, his head coming up solely, like he was underwater.

His hands reached out, flailing, and his thumb hit the ON button for the radio, turning it on. An announcer was droning on about the massive pile-up out on the 405 and how the scene of a tragic and terrible series of accidents had transformed the crash site into a riot, with the people who had suffered injuries now attacking the rescue workers and anyone close to them. The state police had been called to the scene in force and were even now rounding up the attackers. It was also added that the National Guard had been called in to make sure things didn't get out of control.

Reports were still sketchy, but the news station had been hearing reports of people being shot and killed who wouldn't stand down. More information would be told when it came in.

Brad never heard any of it, his ears now feeling like they were stuffed with cotton.

His dead mind remembered one thing, however.

He had a date, a dinner date to attend.

A hand that felt like mush managed to open the driver's door after a few trial and errors and Brad stepped out into the driveway, swaying back and forth like he was drunk. In the darkness of the street, his clothing didn't look so bad, the crimson stains blending in with the original color of his shirt.

His eyes shifted in his head and then rested on his front door a few feet away.

Stumbling like a drunkard, he made his way to the front stoop and reached out for the door handle.

There was no elation, no pleasing thoughts as he squeezed the handle and opened the door. It had been unlocked hours ago by his wife in anticipation of him returning home.

As he stepped into the foyer, the lights were off, but the living and dining room lights were on high, thus casting the foyer into even darker shadows than by those standing in the brighter part of the house.

As the door closed behind Brad, voices could be heard, dishes and silverware clinking and clanking as everyone seated at the table got up at once and moved into the foyer.

Brad stood by the door, the shadows of the foyer hiding his pale complexion and blood-stained clothes.

As one, his wife and her parents appeared at the opposite end of the house and stared at him standing there quietly.

"Well, Brad, aren't you going to come in and say hello to my folks?" his wife asked arrogantly.

She had always been the power in the relationship and he had always kowtowed to her, never being a man and standing up for himself.

His father-in-law took a few a steps forward into the foyer. He didn't have his glasses on so Brad appeared to be nothing but a blur.

"Well, son, aren't you going to say hello? You know what? Forget it; let's not waste time with pleasantries. You know why I'm here so there's no reason to dance around it. Because you didn't bother to show me any respect by being on time for dinner I'll just lay it out for you. I want an answer to the question you've already been asked. Which is, are you going to give my daughter a divorce?"

"Uhm, Daddy, I don't think Brad's all right. I think there's something wrong with him," she said as she tried to see into the dark foyer.

"Nonsense, he's perfectly fine. He's just stalling," her father said and then turned back to Brad. "So, son, what's your answer? Are you going to give her what she wants or what?"

That's when Brad lunged forward, sinking his teeth into his father-in-law's throat, tearing out the man's carotid artery as he sucked in the warm plasma. It felt fantastic and it filled him with strength as the warm fluid slid down his throat.

As he chewed merrily, he gazed over the man's twitching shoulder to see his wife and mother-in-law standing there in utter shock.

Brad let go of his father-in-law, the man slumping to the floor dead. But that was all right, he would be up soon enough.

As he took one faltering step towards his wife, he actually managed a slight grin, his dull brain thinking about what his father-in-law had just said about giving it to his wife.

Oh, yes, he was going to give it to her, but not a divorce. Instead he was going to give her everlasting life…as one of the undead.

Lunging forward, he grabbed her by the hair and sank his teeth into her cheek, tearing her skin from her face like it was the skin of a roasted chicken.

No sooner did he do this then he went for her throat, the thin, swan like neck that had so aroused him when they had been dating now torn to shreds.

And as his teeth sank into her ivory flesh, she screamed, and he relished it. For once he was in charge and would stay that way for all eternity.

When he was through with her he would then take care of his mother-in-law, but for now he was savoring his victory over his shrew of a wife.

Their screams filled the house and floated into the street, but no one heard them as the other homes on the street had their own screams as the walking dead slowly swarmed into the neighborhood to attack the living.

As he fed on his wife's spasming body and she succumbed to death, she let out one ear-piercing scream before the same screams were swallowed by gargling noises as she drowned in blood.

To Brad, it was music to his undead ears.

HOPELESS LOVE

The ride to the cabin was fraught with peril, and Bob Garrison had to dig deep down within himself to stay sane every time he thought about what was happening back in the city, hell, the entire world.

Beside him, in the passenger seat of his beat-up Ford pickup, his wife lay sleeping, her right arm cradled in her left, thanks to the large bite wound there.

He had bandaged it quickly using what rags and rope he could find in the rear bed of the pickup, and he knew the second they reached the cabin he would have to clean it.

The road was a quagmire of ruts, valleys and rocks, thanks to the rainstorm last week. The road was dirt and after the rain, had become a giant mud pit. After it dried, the mud became speed bumps, some as large as two feet high, thanks to the rushing water that shaped it.

He hit a rather big mud bump and Angela moaned beside him.

"Easy, baby, we're almost there," he said as he winced at the sight of her. Her skin was clammy and she was sweating, her once perfect complexion now pale. She didn't look well at all and he couldn't imagine why. Other than the bite, she was healthy, or had been. He had to wonder if the bite from one of those *things* had somehow infected her with some virus.

Not much was known about the walking dead and most people still refused to believe it. Bob believed, having seen an old woman torn apart with his own eyes on his way home from work the previous day. That was enough to make him a believer, so he gathered up as many necessities that could be tossed into the rear bed of the pickup, and dragged Angela out of their two bedroom condo in Framingham, Mass and headed for the New Hampshire White Mountains.

He was confident they had escaped the chaos of the city. It was a long drive to the mountains and he had no choice but to stop for gas. The gas station/convenience store on the highway had looked deserted when he'd pulled into the first bay, but he found out quick enough that it wasn't.

Angela had wanted to go inside and get some snacks for the trip, and for when they arrived at the cabin. Bob had only packed canned and dried goods, and items such as potato chips and pretzels had never crossed his mind, despite knowing Angela loved her junk food.

When she told him she was going inside the store, he had barely heard her. He was busy trying to get his credit card to work in the gas pump reader. The last thing to cross his mind was that she would be in danger. After all, they were twenty miles outside of Boston, and he was confident they were safe from the walking dead.

But the dead knew nothing of distance, and unknown to Bob, the clerk had died hours ago after being attacked. He was even now slumped behind the counter, too stupid to know what to do after reviving. When Angela walked into the store, the clerk had popped up, and just as Angela reached over the counter for a bag of chips, the dead clerk grabbed her arm, sinking his already yellow teeth—from too much smoking—into her arm, tearing off a bite-sized chunk.

When Angela screamed, Bob forgot about his credit card. He snatched up a tire iron from the rear bed of the pickup and charged into the store. He gasped at the sight before him. Angela was cradling her arm, blood spurting between her fingers as the dead clerk chewed on the piece of meat. His head slowly turned as Bob entered, but Bob snapped out of his shock, and with a roar of anger and fear, ran at the clerk and swung the tire iron as hard as he could.

The blow connected with the middle of the clerk's head, caving in the skull and smashing the newly revived zombie's brain to mush.

The chunk of arm meat popped out of his mouth like he'd been given the Heimlich maneuver, and the body dropped behind the counter to remain still.

Bob rushed to Angela who was slowly going into shock. Just as she was about to faint, he caught her in his arms and rushed her back to the pickup.

After getting her inside the cab, he ran around to the pump, and though shaking in terror, he somehow managed to get his credit card in the reader and for the pump to register the sale. He threw the tire iron into the rear bed once more.

"Hang on, baby, we'll be out of here in a minute," he said, trying to reassure her though it may have been more for his own morale. If he could have, he would have left then, and to hell with the gas, but the gas gauge on the dashboard was on E and he knew they wouldn't get far without refueling.

The next three minutes were the longest of his life, as he held the nozzle and filled his tank. It was all so surreal. To an observer, he must have looked like any traveler getting gas, as he stood there by the pump, but how Bob felt inside was so far from normal to make him want to go insane.

Just as the pump turned off, telling him the tank was full, he heard footsteps behind him. Pulling the nozzle out of the pickup, he spun to see another zombie stumbling towards him. It was a woman.

He could tell because of the dress she wore. Her face was nothing but muscle and tendons, her skin having been peeled off her like she was a giant orange. Her permanent rictus of a smile gleamed at Bob and her bottom jaw dropped open, allowing her bloated tongue to slide out and wiggle, as if tasting the air.

She was only a few feet away before Bob snapped out of his stupor at the grotesque form before him.

The woman let out a low moan that seemed filled with death and pain, and Bob felt his bladder prepare to let go, right there in the pump bay.

It was as the woman stepped closer, and the wind shifted, allowing her foul stench of shit and blood to waft over him, that Bob used the only weapon at his disposal at the moment.

The gas nozzle.

Squeezing the trigger like it was a gun, he sprayed the undead woman with gas. The caustic fluid covered her from head to tow, the liquid eating at her eyes and sliding down her throat, pooling at her feet. She began flailing her arms as she went blind, but by dumb luck, she began heading directly at Bob.

More by luck than any form of courage, Bob pushed her away and threw the gas nozzle at her.

The nozzle hit the ground a few inches from the woman and the metal tip made a spark, which ignited the fumes of the spilled gas.

The zombie was consumed immediately, the flames washing over her as if the fire was a living entity, an orange and yellow wave that absorbed the spasming body.

Bob stood in horror as the woman's skin began to crack and blister, charred flakes falling off her to catch in the wind and float away.

It was as he watched that he gazed down to see a small trickle of gas seep past his shoe and meander toward the pickup truck.

"Oh shit," he gasped, realizing what was about to happen.

Turning, he dashed for the cab of the pickup, lunged into the open driver's door and started the engine, stepping on the gas with the door still open.

As the pickup shot out of the pump bay, the puddle of fuel on the ground ignited and like a fuse, the trickle burned, missing the rear tires of the vehicle by only a few inches.

Bob swerved onto the highway as, behind him, the pumps erupted in yellow, orange and red flames, a massive explosion soaring skyward, the very highway shaking with tremors, making Bob think the entire road was about to collapse under him.

The pickup careened down the highway as the first of the debris began to rain down. Burning tires from the garage bay next to the gas station, car parts, and flame-coated tools landed all around the pickup, causing Bob to scream in panic, especially when a socket wrench hit the roof of the pickup and left a two inch dent after it rattled off to fall onto the road.

Then Bob was clear of the blast radius and he let up on the gas pedal. Beside him, Angela had her eyes closed, tears running down her cheeks as she held her arm close, looking like a bird with a bad wing.

As he pointed the pickup north into the mountains, he couldn't help but let his eyes drift to his rearview mirror, where all he could see was dark black smoke and fire.

Bob slowed to a stop in front of the cabin. As he turned off the engine, he studied the one-story structure.

All the curtains were drawn and there was no disturbance leading up to the front door. The ground looked untouched, pine needles and leaves strewn about, the same as the day they had fallen from the trees surrounding the cabin.

He slid out of the cab and went around to the passenger door to help Angela out. She could barely walk and he half carried her to the front door. For a moment he panicked when he couldn't find the door key, but then his finger's touched it at the bottom of his coat pocket.

Unlocking the door, he entered the shadow-filled cabin.

The only odor to touch his nose was one of un-use, and he quickly helped Angela to the only bedroom. After changing the dust-covered top sheet, he laid her down and treated her wound. He found an old bottle of aspirin in the medicine chest and had her down four of them—instead of the recommended two—hoping an extra dose would make up for the expiration date.

He let her sleep, then, pausing at the door to watch her rest for almost a full minute, he went into the main room to see what kind of supplies were already there.

"Bob? Bob. Are you out there?" Angela called from the bedroom.

He put down the dishes he was washing and went to the bedroom, almost running.

"Thank God you're awake, I was getting worried," he said as he rushed into the room and sat down beside her. "You've been sleeping for almost a full day."

"What happened?" she asked and then looked down at her arm. A twinge of pain shot up her body when she tried to move it.

"One of those things bit you. I managed to get you away and then brought us up here like we planned. Oh, baby I was so worried about you."

She slowly sat up. "Well, I'm fine, Bob, really. I mean, my arm hurts obviously, but to tell you the truth, I feel pretty good."

He nodded. "Must have been all that sleep, your body had a chance to heal itself."

She nodded in agreement. "I'm starving, is there anything to eat?"

"Sure, you want some canned soup or something?"

She shook her head. "Ugh, no, gross, I want something meaty, the bloodier the better."

"Really? You want something so heavy?"

"Yup, and please be fast, I'm absolutely ravenous."

"Uh, okay, I think there's a few steaks in the freezer, but I have to warn you, they've been in there for more than six months, from last season when we were last up here, I think."

"I don't care, just nuke one and put it on a plate." She slid off the bed. "I'm gonna take a shower while you make it for me."

Bob watched her rise and cross the bedroom. She glided into the bathroom and began taking off her clothes. Bob watched her and immediately felt a rise in his pants. They had been married for more than a year and the lust for one another was still going strong.

He let his eyes roam over the curve of her back, the small dimples on each side of her buttocks, the flat stomach and gentle flaring of her hips. As she turned to grab shampoo before getting into the shower, he felt himself growing harder as he gazed at her erect nipples, the small juncture of her thighs, where just the hint of her vagina could be seen amidst the neatly trimmed hair. She was well groomed and he loved to go down on her every chance he got. The only item to mar the perfect beauty of his wife was the bandage on her arm.

Feeling ashamed at being horny at a time like this, he stood up and left the room, as Angela turned on the shower and stepped in.

As he walked into the kitchen and opened the freezer, he could hear her singing.

He let out a sigh of relief, unaware he'd even been holding it in.

It looked like things were going to be fine. They were together, alone in the cabin in the middle of the woods, and whatever happened to the world was out of their control. At least they had each other.

Angela polished off the last of the steak, licking her lips with a loud smacking noise.

"Wow," Bob said, "I can't believe how much you ate."

She nodded and wiped her mouth with a napkin. "Tell me about it, I don't know what's gotten into me. It's like this is the first time I've ever eaten meat before…and I love it!" She closed her eyes and opened them slightly, her lip curling up in a sensual pose. "And I'm still hungry, but this time I want a different kind of meat."

He smiled slyly. "Why you dirty girl, I guess you are feeling better."

She stood up and took his hand, leading him into the bedroom. He followed like a lovesick puppy.

All she was wearing was the bathrobe she'd donned after her shower, and she now let it drop to the floor, her nakedness an immediate arousal for him.

"Fuck me, Bob, fuck me like you've never done before," she breathed as she sat on the edge of the bed and spread her legs wide, exposing her inner warmth.

"Yes, ma'am," Bob said and dropped to his knees before her. No sooner did he do this, then she grabbed his head and shoved it between her thighs, forcing his face so deep into her he could barely breathe. He tried to lick her but there was too much pressure to even get his tongue out of his mouth.

Meanwhile, she was grinding her pelvis into his face like he was a bronco and she the rider. He began to see stars from lack of oxygen, and as he tried to pull back, her grip only tightened on his head.

Finally, he used his legs and arms together to kick off the bed, breaking her grip so suddenly he fell sprawling on his back.

As he lay on the floor, gazing up at the ceiling, he sucked in air. His mouth and chin glistened with her wetness and he let out a loud outtake of breath. "Damn, Angela, what the hell has gotten into you? You nearly suffocated me to death."

She acted as if she didn't hear him, and as he got up on his elbows, she jumped on top of him, dropping her pelvis onto him like he was an inflatable male sex doll. Before he could protest, her pussy enveloped him and he gasped at the heat now enveloping his dick. As he sucked in a fresh lungful of air, Angela began bouncing on him, her animalistic urges seeming untamable.

She leaned over and began sucking his shoulder, his nose pressing against her neck. Though his dick was in heaven, his nose picked up a faint odor of decay, as if somehow Angela's neck had been exposed to rotting meat. The odor was faint, but there was no doubt it was coming off her. He also detected the apricot shampoo scent from her hair, but deep down under it, was the scent of rot.

Then she ground her hips and he felt his dick respond.

Closing his eyes, he laid back and enjoyed his wife's wild attentions, the faint scent forgotten, and two minutes later when he orgasmed, it was so powerful he could barely remember his name afterward, let alone anything else. She curled up beside him, and after pulling a sheet off the bed, they both napped right there on the floor, wrapped in each other's arms.

Bob slowly opened his eyes, as he woke up. Glancing to the window, he saw the sun was just beginning to rise.

Beside him, Angela was also stirring, and as he touched her shoulder, she turned over to look at him, her eyes creased as she struggled to wake up.

"Hey," he said. "How are you feeling this morning?"

She smacked her lips together, her eyes going inward as she assessed herself.

"My stomach hurts," she whispered. "I've got cramps."

"You look paler, too," he said as he studied her face. It was true. Her complexion had turned a pasty white, her skin looking as if it would slide off her if she smiled too hard. She winced and he asked, "You okay?"

She nodded slightly. "Yeah, like I said…cramps."

He was about to get up, wanting to use the bathroom, when she reached out and grabbed his dick, stroking the 'morning wood' hard member.

"But I know what'll make me feel better," she breathed heavily.

"You do?"

"Uh-huh. I want you to fuck me again, Bob. Fuck me hard."

"I…uh, wow, okay, sure, but just let me go to the…" Before he could finish, she was pulling the blanket away and climbing on him.

"No, right now, Bob. I need you inside me *now*."

Though taken off guard, he loved his wife and wanted to make her happy, and hesitation went away when she slid onto his hard member, her body wrapping around him. What was odd was the fact that normally when her pussy covered his dick, he would gasp from the warm sensation, but this time was different, much different from the previous night.

As she began to grind her hips up and down on his dick, he found her pussy didn't seem that hot at all, and in fact, it was similar to room temperature.

Discarding the sensation as an anomaly, he reached up and cupped her breasts. As he touched her, he realized she felt cold. And now, when he thought back to a few moments ago when he woke beside her, he realized he hadn't been warm from her body heat, that he had actually been a little cold, like he'd been sleeping without a blanket.

She leaned forward and nuzzled his neck, their bodies pressed close. She felt so cold, her breasts like ice against his chest.

He breathed in her scent as he often did when in coitus with her, but the once fragrant aroma was absent, to be replaced by an odd odor that reminded him of spoiled meat.

Angela wasn't in a thinking mood at the moment. Her head was thrown back and she was gasping, her nipples hard as she jumped up and down on his dick.

She was wild, her gyrations like he'd never seen before, and when she finally began to shake as she orgasmed, he realized he was feeling more relieved than turned on.

She slid off him, sighing as she stretched out. "That was wonderful," she breathed heavily. "I feel better now."

"I'm glad," was all he could think to say.

She jumped up, naked, and padded to the kitchen. "I'm starving. I want something meaty."

He watched her go, and as she walked away, he saw that her back, thighs and buttocks—the parts of her that had been touching the floor as she lay on her back—were now a dark brown-bluish color, as if all the blood had left her body and pooled there. A word came to mind. One a coroner would use…lividity. But that couldn't be what was happening here, could it?

If gravity had done its work, and all the blood had settled to the bottom of her body, then that could only mean one thing

She was…dead. She was like one of the *things* that had bitten her.

But somehow she wasn't a ravenous monster like the others they had seen when they'd fled the city. Somehow, Angela was still Angela.

But she was dead. Only *she* didn't know it yet.

Angela walked back into the room, a partially thawed steak in her hands. She was chewing on it like a ravenous dog, the juices dripping between her breasts, to then make their way to the juncture of her thighs. She hadn't noticed this, as she was busy merrily chomping.

Bob sat up. "I can't believe I'm saying this, Angela, but I think you're dead. I think you died last night after we fell asleep."

She made a dismissive noise as she chewed and waved his words away. "What? That's crazy. Why would you say such a thing? Especially in light of everything that's happened."

He began to explain how she was acting and about the blood pooling on her back and thighs. He told her of how cold she was.

"Well, of course I'm cold. I'm naked, silly." She finished off the steak, her front now covered in dark juices. She looked like a murder victim without the wounds, the red juices like blood, now covering her like she'd been sprayed with a hose. Her pale skin only added to the image. "I'm going to take a shower and get cleaned up." Without waiting for Bob to reply, she spun on her heels and trotted to the bathroom.

Bob watched her go, his eyes instinctively going to her ass. The perfect apple sashayed back and forth, and despite himself, he found a stirring down below. He pushed it away, feeling ashamed. This was most definitely not the time to be thinking about sex. He guessed it was true what they said about men, about them always thinking about sex, even at the most inopportune time, and even after just having it!

He stood up and began dressing, trying to figure out just what exactly he was supposed to do with Angela now. Even if he was wrong, if all the symptoms were false, she was definitely acting strangely, and with her bite wound, it couldn't mean anything good would come of it.

As he slid into his shirt, he tried to rationalize everything he'd seen, but no matter how much he attempted to lie to himself, the facts always reared their ugly head. Angela was dead…she was a zombie.

They talked some more after her shower, but Angela refused to accept what he said, even when he checked her pulse and it wasn't there and put a mirror to her mouth and there was no fogging of the glass.

Eventually, after enough tests were done, Angela had no choice but to accept her fate. She was dead, a zombie, but for some reason she could still think. Her soul was intact.

But one thing she did have was a hunger for flesh. She hadn't known it at first, but it didn't take long for her to come to the realization she had cravings.

So far, two things had worked to stop her from wanting to kill and eat Bob, though at the time she hadn't known about either of them.

The first was a meat substitute.

As they discussed what had happened to her and how she'd changed, together they figured out that alone, the substitute wouldn't have worked, but combined with sex, it appeared to be enough to quell her hunger.

Once they both understood what needed to be done, sex became a daily ritual, five and sometimes six times a day, if not more.

Bob sometimes had trouble getting hard, but Angela knew how to blow him like no one he had ever known, and though he hated to admit it, knowing she was technically dead was a big turn on for him. It was so....*taboo.*

And of course, now he didn't have to worry about getting her pregnant.

It was two weeks from the day he realized she was a zombie that things took a turn for the worse.

He was on top of her, fucking her like a teenager, while she wiggled beneath him, that he found out that their situation wasn't fool proof.

They had overcome the whole lubrication thing by simply squirting Canola oil in her pussy. Though room temperature, her vaginal hole was slippery and welcoming, and he was banging away with abandon when he leaned over and began to nibble on her ear.

She smelled worse now, and even the perfume was working overtime to cover it up.

Bob didn't care; he slammed his dick deep into her dead pussy and sucked on her earlobe.

Then he felt himself ready to orgasm and he slammed into her hard, pushing her body a few inches higher on the bed. As he felt himself shoot within her, his teeth tugged a little harder on her ear. Normally, back when she was alive, this would have been no big thing, but with her decaying daily, he found out something he hadn't known or considered.

Body parts fall off as the body rots.

As he shot his load deep within her, his teeth clamped down on her ear, and before he knew it, he had torn it right off her head and was swallowing it whole.

But it was too big for his throat and he began to choke.

Angela, unaware of any of this, assumed as he spasmed and choked, that he was simply becoming creative in their lovemaking.

As Bob suffocated on top of her, she raised her hips some more so he would slide in deeper.

Bob was turning blue, but with Angela's eyes closed, she saw none of this.

Bob let out one final last gasp and collapsed on top of her, a second ejaculation following the first as he came one last time in death.

Angela lay with him on her, not feeling his weight now that she was dead, and she waited for a full minute before tapping him on the shoulder.

"Wow, Bob, that was great, but you can get off now."

No answer from him.

"Uh, Bob, what's wrong? Don't tell me you fell asleep. Talk about a male stereotype," she joked as she began to rock him, slapping his back harder to wake him.

Then she felt something wet between her legs, and when she reached down and touched it, her fingers came back with something brown on them.

Her sense of smell hadn't left her, and when she moved her hand close to her nose, she saw it was shit.

Bob had shit himself? That made no sense.

Panicking, she pushed him off her, the body rolling right off the bed and onto the floor.

She sat up. "Bob? Oh my God!" she yelled and jumped off the bed and went to him, reaching down to roll her husband over.

Bob's face was slack, his face blue from choking. Acting fast, she tried CPR but to no avail, and when she finally stopped ten minutes later, she began to weep. Only with her tear ducts dried up in death, nothing came but her gurgling attempts at sobbing.

"No, Bob, don't leave me. I can't be alone," she wailed as she touched his face.

She wept for more than half a day, or tried, and only the hunger within her pulled her from her vigil over her husband's body.

Leaving him, she went to the kitchen and sliced a piece of the venison sitting in the sink. Bob had taken to hunting to keep her fully stocked with meat.

She began to eat, but this time something was missing when she tried to quell the hunger, she just didn't want to accept it.

Two days later, the venison was gone and Angela was on the kitchen floor, bent over, hugging her stomach as cramps seized her. She needed meat badly, the agony filling her unbearable.

She suffered for hours until finally, she did the only thing available to her, as she wasn't fast or fit enough to hunt on her own.

Walking into the bedroom, she kneeled down beside Bob, who had begun to bloat in death. If she could have cried, there would have been tears in her eyes, but like before, there was nothing.

The hunger was too much, she couldn't fight it, and though he might be dead, Bob could still help her, at least for now.

"One last blowjob," she whispered.

Slowly, ever so slowly, she leaned over his crotch, his naked form still and unmoving, and wrapped her lips around his dick.

She began to blow him, taking his limp dick deep into her mouth, her tongue licking the tip, caressing the head the way he used to enjoy it, the action driving him wild with passion.

She began to rub his balls in her right hand as she stroked the soft member with left, her lips making sucking, gurgling sounds.

When she was good and horny, her eyes closed as she imagined Bob was still alive, relishing the pleasure she was giving him, she bit down hard with her teeth, then snapped her head back.

She began to chew, chomping away on Bob's flaccid cock, as coagulated blood seeped from the corner of her lips.

After all, meat was meat.

And she was hungry.

HUMP OF THE DEAD

"Well, son, it's your eighteenth birthday and I have a surprise for you tonight," Jim Burns grinned. He was sitting on his front porch, his son by his side.

Mark looked up at his father as he sat on the front steps, his father on the swing, and his eyes went wide with expectation.

"If I ask will you tell me?" Mark said.

Jim shrugged. "I might, but what would be the fun in that? No, Mark, you need to wait till tonight. After dinner we're gonna take a ride someplace… special."

Mark wanted to try and get the secret out of his father, but as he opened his mouth to speak, Jim shook his head, his eyes saying he wasn't going to be spilling the beans anytime soon.

The two chatted for ten more minutes and went their separate ways for the day. It was a little after six as they leaned back in their chairs at the kitchen table that Jim raised the surprise again.

"Ah, Helen, that was wonderful," Jim told his wife. "Look, I have something special planned for Mark tonight so I'm taking him out."

Helen frowned, knowing exactly what Jim was speaking of. "You're taking him to a strip club, aren't you?" she asked. "You men and your rights of passage." She turned and walked over to the sink with dishes in her hands as she began clearing the table.

"You're taking me to a strip club?" Mark asked his father, whispering so his mother didn't hear.

Jim seemed to hesitate, then nodded slowly. "Yes, but we'll talk more later," Jim whispered in reply.

Mark was going to ask more but Helen returned to get more dirty glasses and dishes. Jim winked at his son and they went silent, the two men smiling politely at Helen.

She looked from one to the other and was about to say something when she stopped and said instead, "I don't know what you two were talking about and I don't want to know. Jim, you just make sure our son stays out of trouble."

Jim grinned. "Hey, it's me, Helen. I'll take care of him."

"Harrumph, that's what I'm afraid off," she quipped. "Mark, you take care of your father, you hear? Don't let him do anything I wouldn't like."

Mark nodded. "You can count on me, Mom. I'll watch him for you."

She turned and walked back to the sink and father and son shared a knowing smile. Then Jim looked to the back door, his gaze saying it was time to leave. Together the two men stood up, Jim kissed Helen goodbye, they grabbed their coats, and left, Jim leading the way. He was driving, as he knew where the big surprise was located.

The strip club was on the outskirts of town, in a wide open area where nothing but sparse trees and scrub was. The austere landscape was like a white piece of paper, the strip club a dark black stain in the center. A neon light flashed the figure of a woman as she bent over and wiggled her behind. To the left of her were the words, **The Pink Pussy**.

Back when the strip club first set up shop, the town charter had tried to ban the club name for being lewd, but in the end they had lost miserably. The club being a mile outside of town meant the town charter had no say in what the club did or didn't do.

As Jim pulled into the parking lot, Mark let his eyes roam over the other vehicles parked there. A few pickup trucks of varied conditions, an old Honda, a brand new Escalade and a Navigator, and one Prius, was the staple of vehicles. A few others were spread out as well, and a Harley Davidson was parked near the front door.

Jim turned off the engine and shifted in his seat to look at his son. "Well, we're here, what do you think?"

"About what?" Mark asked.

"About what? Son, we both know you haven't been with a woman yet and it's high time you were, so I've decided to get you laid for your birthday."

Mark only nodded, not sure what to say.

Jim sighed slightly. "Look, Mark, this is a right of passage for you. My father did the same thing for me and years later, when I met your mother, well, I was glad he did. Instead of being a bumbling fool with your mother, I had the experience to show her what a man can do."

"Eww, Dad, please, too much information," Mark said and cringed.

"What? Why? Believe it or not, son, parents of children like to fuck, too. How the hell do think you got here? In fact, once upon a time your mother was a hot piece of ass."

"Dad, please, if we're gonna do this, you need to stop sharing with me."

Jim didn't hear him, lost in his thoughts. "But not now, though. Now she's a prude in bed, says she's lost all her passion when the menopausal thing hit her. I'm lucky if I can get a blowjob once a month."

"I'm going inside," Mark said, "I can't hear anymore of this."

Jim looked up at the sound of the car door opening. "Huh? What? Oh shit, I was rambling. Wait, Mark, I'm coming." He got out of the car and followed his son. "Listen, what I said in the car, forget it, okay? I love your mom, no matter what I said or problems we might be having in the bedroom."

"Whatever, Dad, whatever, come on, let's go inside and have some fun."

Jim nodded and followed his son into the club. The bouncer at the door asked for ten bucks each and Jim paid the man, then they found a table near the stage and took a seat.

After ordering drinks—a beer for Jim and a coke for Mark—the two relaxed and admired the women who strutted on stage.

Three more drinks each later and Jim decided it was time for Mark to do the deed. He called over a stripper who was standing near the bar and whispered into her ear.

After he told her what he wanted, she studied him for a moment, as if assessing if he was a cop or just a customer. Finally, after glancing at Mark for the third time and the way his eyes were bulging wide as he stared at the girls on stage, she decided he was legit and nodded.

"Two hundred bucks for normal play for half an hour. Anything more will cost ya extra," she said into Jim's ear.

"That's fine. Look, he's my son and this is his first time, so be gentle with him, all right?"

The stripper smiled knowingly. "Oooh, a virgin, I like 'em innocent. Don't worry, honey, I'll take good care of your boy." She walked around the table and wrapped her arm around Mark's neck, then whispered into his ear. Mark's head snapped to the left to look at Jim and his father nodded, waving him to go with the woman. Mark was hesitant, but the stripper coaxed him up and led him away.

Jim watched them go, inwardly wishing it was he who was going to get laid. The stripper had been spectacular, with full breasts, dark red lips and big brown eyes to go with her auburn hair.

A body made for fucking, was the saying that came to him.

Figuring he had a half hour to kill, he leaned back, ordered another drink, and tried to ignore the pressure in his crotch as he admired the sexy women on stage.

Ten minutes into his vigil, he began letting his gaze drift around the club. He studied the different men also in attendance and the different types of women strutting their stuff.

From a quick count, there were more than a dozen strippers scattered about the floor, trying to make the clientele buy them drinks and perhaps even more.

It was as he was watching a stripper and a customer walk to the back of the club that he saw them disappear through a different door than the one Mark had used—each of them knocking, answering a reply when a small, four inch window slid open in the door, then allowed to enter.

Curious for some odd reason, he found himself watching the door, and over the next five minutes, he saw more than six male customers come and go, each knocking, waiting for the window to open, then being allowed in after speaking to whoever was on the opposite side of the door.

He didn't know what made him get up instead of waiting for Mark, but he did stand, and before he knew what he was doing, he was crossing the club to stand before the door.

Deciding he had nothing left to lose, he knocked three times, like he'd seen the men do. No sooner had he wrapped the third time, then the window slid open.

"Password."

"Huh?" he said, now nervous.

"No password, no entry. Fuck off." The window slid shut abruptly.

Jim stepped back, feeling dejected.

No sooner had he done so than another man walked up to the door and knocked three times. The window slid open and the new man said, "Pil-lato."

The window slammed closed and the door opened, the man slipping in through the opening.

Jim waited another full minute and went to the door again, knocking three times. The window slid open and the man asked, "Password?"

Jim expected the hidden man to recognize him but apparently, one customer looked like another, and he gave no inclination he'd just given Jim the boot only minutes before.

"Pillato," Jim said in as confident a voice possible.

The window slammed closed and Jim figured he'd been found out, but a second later, the door popped open. Jim stepped inside, the door closing behind him.

As soon as the door closed, the music from the strip club ceased, only the slightest sound of muffled bass filtering through the heavy door.

"Sixth door on the left," a voice said, the same one who had spoken to Jim through the door window.

Jim began walking, his eyes trying to get used to the gloom.

He was in a hallway, and though the club had been dim, the hallway was down right dark. Only a few small, naked, red light bulbs on the ceiling illuminated the corridor and he carefully made his way, passing doors on each side of him.

As he walked, he heard sounds of either pleasure or pain coming from behind the doors, each with a number painted on its surface.

He counted as he walked until coming to the sixth door. It was painted bright red with scrapes in the facade, as if someone had scratched it with fingernails, and there was the number six in black paint in the center about head height.

To the right of the door, mounted to the wall, was a red button with the words, Emergency Call on it in white paint.

A cry of pleasure or pain erupted from the door across from him and he spun, his back now against the door that was for him. He swallowed deeply, his jaw taut with tension.

This felt like something out of a horror movie, where he would soon find himself facing down against a man in a leather apron and a machete...or a chainsaw.

He was already deciding his curiosity had gotten him far enough, and was about to leave, when the door behind him clicked open, now an inch ajar of the doorframe.

Before he could move, the door opened wider and a hand shot out, grabbing him by the arm, and yanking him into the room. Jim let out a startled squeak, but quickly regained his composure when he realized one of the stripper's had grabbed him.

At least, that's what he thought the first moment he looked at her. But as his eyes took in the shapely feminine form before him, he realized though she was indeed a woman, she was not like the ones he was used to.

And the reason was simple…she was dead.

Or undead, as the case may be.

"Holy shit," he gasped, staring at the zombie before him, unsure what to do. The dead woman did nothing, merely stood there, her glassed-over eyes looking at him. She was like a robot that wasn't turned on yet. She was wearing a black lace bra and panties, the nipples of the bra visible thanks to the clear material.

They were a dark brown and perky, the breasts full and round, each the size of large oranges.

Jim's eyes roved down to her stomach, to see the zombie had abs a gymnast would kill for, and a small tuft of blonde hair at her crotch. The hair on her head was blonde as well, and though frightened out of his mind, in the back of his head he thought it was sexy that the 'carpet matched the drapes.'

A small, twelve inch monitor flicked on to his right and his eyes went to it. On the screen, was a well dressed woman with a low cut blouse and lips any man would want to kiss. She looked like the sexiest secretary ever made.

"Hello, and welcome to the Pink Pussy's exclusive 'Necro Club' where all your fantasies will come true. Here at the Necro Club, we offer the finest in undead entertainment. Anything goes, and you may feel free to experiment with your consort as you see fit. Nothing is out of bounds, no matter how kinky or experimental. If you look to the wall, you will see an assortment of sex toys for you to play with."

Jim cast his glance to the wall to the right side of the full-sized bed to see it was filled with dildos—strap-ons and battery powered—lubes, whips, handcuffs, butt-hole beads, and another two dozen items he'd never seen and wouldn't know what they were used for if his life depended on it.

"Your *date* is completely docile. She will bow to your every whim and feels no pain so don't worry about hurting her. Here, in this room, you may do whatever you want to her. Here, you may be master or slave, king or peasant, all can be yours. There is only one rule. There is a collar around your date's neck. On it is a green light. If for any reason the light was to turn red, please exit the room immediately and press the emergency call button located in the hallway next to your room door. Before you can begin, please go to the desk in the corner and take care of the invoice there. The card reader takes all credit cards and debit cards. Sorry, no checks. If we do not receive payment within five minutes after the end of this video, we will escort you out of the club. And once more, on behalf of the Pink Pussy, we hope your stay with us is one you will remember for a lifetime."

The screen flicked off and Jim stood motionless. Then, as if on auto-pilot, he went to the corner and picked up the invoice.

It was for two thousand dollars, and it said clearly that his credit card would be billed with the name, Milltown's Lumber and Supply as a way for the charge to be discreet. He could have left then, exited the room and never looked back, but when he turned around and stared at the stripper, he felt something stir in his groin that far surpassed what he'd felt while watching the living women stripping on the stage.

Reaching into his pocket, he pulled out his wallet, took out his Visa, and slid it through the card reader. A few seconds later a receipt was printed out and he pocketed it with his wallet.

Turning around, he gazed at the zombie standing before him. His eyes looked past her to see there was a small sign on the wall with a few important facts about his 'date.' The only one he cared about was the second one, which stated that his date's name was Tiffany.

"Uhm, hi, Tiffany," he said, his voice cracking a little.

She cocked her head slightly like a dog hearing its name, but did nothing else. Not knowing what to do, as he was still so nervous, he walked over to her and stood before her, his heart beating a mile a minute. He couldn't believe he was doing this and for a brief second he thought of Helen.

Then a voice filled his head. It's not cheating if the woman is already dead.

"That's true," he said out loud. When he looked at Tiffany, she was still immobile. He decided to try something. "Get on the bed," he told her and she did just that, not so much as hesitating for an instant.

Jim felt the tingle in his groin grow at the thought of what he was about to do. He'd heard about underground clubs like this one but had no idea where they were—not that he would have gone to one anyway.

Ten years ago there had been a small zombie uprising in the Midwest. For more than a week there had been chaos until the local authorities got a handle on things and put the uprising down. But though the dead had been destroyed, many had been either taken away for study or had wandered off.

The rumor went that a few enterprising souls had taken these dead roamers and were using them to make more zombies for such trades as picking fruits in California to sex slaves in New York clubs. U.S. law stated that any zombie found had to be killed on sight and there was a ten year jail sentence attached to anyone caught with a zombie, no matter what excuse they gave. But like in every vice in the world, from drugs to hookers, the undead still thrived if there was an outlet for it, and undead hookers were at the top of the list.

To have a woman that you could do absolutely anything to and not feel guilty was a dream come true to many men and the underground sex shop became a reality.

Jim only knew what he saw on the news about clubs that were raided, but the few times he'd seen the zombies on TV before they were destroyed, always fascinated him.

So here he was, in a room with a beautiful woman…even if she was dead, and a wife at home that was as frigid as a cube of ice, who acted dead.

He quickly stripped off his clothes and crawled into the bed. Tiffany laid there, her chest still, no breath leaving her bright red lips.

Ever so carefully, Jim reached over and touched her left breast. He didn't know what he was expecting but it felt exactly like a breast should.

It was soft and malleable and the nipple pointy. He felt himself growing hard as he pinched the nipple between his thumb and finger.

"Take off you bra and panties," he told her, breathing heavily and feeling more confident. After all, he was in control here. He had paid for a zombie slut and could do what he wanted.

Tiffany did as asked, having to sit up to undo her bra. When she was done and her panties were on the floor, he told her to lie back down, only this time on her stomach.

After she did as ordered, Jim reached for the KY Jelly on the end table beside the bed and lathered some on his dick, then he climbed on top of Tiffany and placed the head of his dick so it was just touching her asshole.

Closing his eyes, he said, "Okay, Helen, take it like the bitch you are," and he pushed his hips forward, sliding into Tiffany's ass. It was tight, tighter than he would have imagined, and no sooner did he thrust for the second time, then he came hard, imagining it was Helen's ass he was sodomizing. For Helen had told him flat out years ago that he would never, ever get to put his cock in her ass, and though he had told her it was okay, secretly he had always hated her for it.

His body shuddered as the orgasm filled him from head to toe and he sagged on top of Tiffany, who had barely moved. She was like a sex doll, totally compliant in every way.

He slid off her and lay there for a few minutes, then he said, "Suck me off, bitch."

Tiffany rolled onto her side, leaned over him and took him into her mouth. She began blowing him, slowly sliding her lips up and down his soft dick.

In less than a minute he was growing hard again.

He grabbed the back of her head and began forcing it down on his dick, but where he expected to hear her gagging, he heard nothing, only the soft sounds of her slurping. Of course she wouldn't gag, he realized, she was dead, she didn't need to breathe. He began bucking his hips as he forced her head down as each time the head of his cock touched the back of her throat, he felt waves of pleasure fill him. It didn't take long for him to cum again, shooting his load into the back of her throat as waves of pleasure filled him.

"Holy shit, that was incredible, Tiffany. Tell me, can you teach my wife to take it like that?"

Of course she said nothing, merely waited for him to order him.

This time he needed a few more minutes to recover. He passed the time by playing with Tiffany's pussy.

It was soft and moist and though not warm, only room temperature, it was still inviting. He was fascinated with her. He touched and prodded her, seeing how her skin was malleable, and as he began sucking on her perfect nipples, he soon found himself growing hard for the third time.

This time he decided to take her in the good old missionary position. This was also the only way Helen liked it and Jim liked the idea that he was now banging Tiffany.

"You know, Tiffany, it's funny, you or my wife, if I close my eyes, I probably won't know the difference as neither one of you is going to move while I fuck you."

Tiffany said nothing, just stared up at the ceiling.

Jim climbed on top of her, his dick hovering above her pussy. His cock was still wet with his cum and Tiffany's mouth juices—whatever they were—and with no warning, he slid into her, slamming his dick in so hard he thought he would hurt her. She did nothing, just moved slightly so her head touched the headboard each time Jim slammed his cock home.

He closed his eyes and began to get into the groove of it. Even with his eyes closed, he realized he knew he wasn't fucking Helen.

His wife's pussy was looser and he now found out that it curved a little to the left, while Tiffany's veered slightly to the right and was much tighter. Each time he slid in, it felt like a vacuum cleaner had a hold of his dick and was trying to pull it off his body.

The friction was incredible, and he soon found himself ready to reach orgasm for the third time.

After a while his arms grew tired and he let his weight fall onto Tiffany, her soft breasts crushed beneath his chest. He could feel her nipples pressing on his skin and it drove him wild. As he pumped away, he found she smelled like apricots and wondered what sort of bath her handlers gave her to smell like that.

He began to grunt as he reached climax and he was so wrapped up in his own world of pleasure, that he didn't hear Tiffany begin to grunt as well.

If he had opened his eyes, he would have seen that Tiffany's eyes weren't glazed anymore, that they were now filled with a hunger...for something that was right on top of her.

Jim was breathing hard and fast, and as his dick began to throb, a second from exploding, this time the climax so strong he thought his dick was going to blow off him, Tiffany let out a loud snarl and opened her mouth wide, her perfect teeth reflecting the wan light from the one lamp in the corner of the room.

"Oh God, here I go, this is gonna be my best one ever," Jim panted as he felt the tip of his dick fill with pressure and then release, a mini volcano exploding out of his groin.

At the exact moment he shot his load into Tiffany, she bent forward and sank her teeth into his throat, taking out a two inch chunk that severed his jugular in one smooth motion.

Jim gasped in pain and horror and jumped off the bed, his hand reaching up to his wound as blood spurted from between his fingers.

His mouth opened and closed as he stared at Tiffany, who was even now sliding off the bed, one hand holding the chunk of bloody meat to her mouth as she chewed. Jim's eyes flashed to Tiffany's collar, the light on it now a bright red. Through his pain-induced fugue state and blood loss, he turned and stumbled to the door. Somehow, he managed to open it and his hand reached out to slap the wall.

Bloody prints were left behind as he hit the wall three times before his flapping limb found the emergency call button. As his palm hit it, he began to black out, his blood pooling around him as it splattered the walls and floor.

He slipped into death so quickly that he didn't even get to have a last thought, but as he fell to the floor, his cock continued to spurt the last of its cum, and if Jim could have formed one more idea, he would have admitted that, yes, it truly had been the best orgasm of his life.

Two men charged out of a side door in the hallway and ran up to Jim.

"Oh shit, not again, I thought those damn collars were fixed," the first man said.

"Guess not," the other said.

"So, what do we do this guy?" the first one asked.

"Call Beth, she'll know what to do. For now let's get him back inside the room."

They dragged Jim into the room, and after dropping him on the floor like a sack of potatoes, they wrangled Tiffany, gagging and tying her. She snarled in the corner, her blood-covered breasts shaking as she tried to free herself and get at the two men.

One of the men pulled out a cell phone and made the call, and minutes later, the secretary from the video joined the others. She let her eyes play over the scene before her. Her arms were crossed, her left Manolo Blahnik tapping impatiently as she thought about what to do.

"I have an idea," she finally said. She kicked Jim's corpse for emphasis. "Make sure he came here alone and if he didn't, then make up some story to get rid of his friends." She settled her gaze on Tiffany. "And you, young lady, have been very bad. What have I told you about eating the clientele?"

Tiffany didn't reply, merely snarled and groaned. Beth rolled her eyes at the zombie. "Get tech support in here to fix her collar, then get this room cleaned up. I want her fucking her next date in an hour."

Both men nodded and got to work, while Jim's corpse cooled on the floor.

One week later.

"And in local news," the voice on the radio said, "the search for a missing man from Fairview County has halted until more information can be learned about his disappearance. Jim Burns was last seen at the strip club the Pink Pussy and authorities are not ruling out foul play. Burn's car wasn't at the club which leads authorities to think he may have just up and left, but Mark Burns, the son of the missing man, says that is the farthest thing from the truth, and says his father would never leave his family…On the international front, Saudi Arabia has just…"

Susan O'Brien turned off the radio as she pulled into the parking lot of the male strip club. She'd been looking forward to this day for almost a year, ever since she found out about the underground club on a website a friend had referred her to.

Exiting her car, she paid to enter the club, the neon sign over the door proudly proclaiming it as the **JOCK STRAP**, and entered the gloom-filled building.

She barely looked at the sexy, oiled men gyrating on stage, for she had no interest in them. She hadn't been turned on by a living man in many years and had a feeling she never would. It was when she first saw a male zombie on television years ago, that she felt a tingling in her crotch, a sensation that had never been there before. After doing more research she found out that she had a condition known as necrophilia. She loved to have sex with corpses, and a zombie fit the bill perfectly.

At the back of the club was a door with a small window in it. Susan knocked three times and the window slid open.

"Password," a man said from behind the door.

"Jellybean," Susan said, trying not to snicker at the word. The password changed daily and she had a feeling the creators had run out of serious ideas and now just pulled a word out of the dictionary or their minds.

The window slid closed, the door opened, and Susan slipped inside a dark hallway only lit by naked red light bulbs.

"Third door on your right," the man said as he sat back down on a stool and picked up the Penthouse he'd been reading.

"Thank you," Susan said and walked down the hallway. She glanced at the red button to the side of the door with the word, Emergency Call. She turned the doorknob and entered the room, her breath already coming heavy in expectation of having an undead dick in her pussy.

Her date stood before her in the middle of the room, the light on the collar of his neck blinking green.

She smiled as she looked at her *date*. "My, you're a handsome one," she said heavily. "We're gonna have some fun tonight." She began to unbutton her blouse. "Now get on the bed and lay on your back so I can ride you like the stallion you are."

The zombie said nothing, only did as ordered.

The welcome video had been playing and Susan barely listened to it, though she did here the part about *no pay, no sex*, so she went to the corner of the room and paid with her credit card. The rest of the video's information, such as about the collar, she ignored, too wound up in preparation to fuck.

When she was naked, she slid a finger into her pussy, amazed even to herself how wet she was.

God this is going to be incredible, she thought.

She straddled the zombie and slid its cock into her warm pussy, relishing the feeling as she began to pump up and down.

With her eyes closed, she never noticed that her date's throat had been repaired with cosmetics or that the dead man's eyes were dull and vacant as she grinded against his pelvis.

As she neared her first orgasm and began to shudder, she never saw that the blinking light on the collar had changed from green to red, nor did she see the sign on the wall.

It said her date's name was Jim.

IT WAS JUST A DREAM

Tom's eyes snapped open and he rolled over on the couch, his face now sinking into the plush material.

Turning his head so he could breathe, he stared up at the ceiling.

His heart was beating in his chest and he could feel perspiration crawling down his back and saturating his clothing.

Wow, he thought, *that was some dream.*

He was still wearing the jeans and polo shirt from the day before, the mustard stain from the hotdog he'd had at lunch still prevalent on his chest. The Nike sneakers he'd bought at Footlocker a week ago for $79.99 were on his feet, too, the laces still tied.

The room was dark, all the shades drawn, and he held up his right arm to check his wrist watch. The luminous dial told him it was three a.m.

He barely registered the fact there was no sound coming from outside his windows. Usually, there would be the constant cacophony of traffic, horns beeping and motors racing, but in his fugue-like state, he didn't notice there was only silence.

He felt a kink in his back, so he stretched, trying to push the images of the dream from his mind.

And what a dream it was.

In his dream, the dead had begun to walk, as ridiculous as it sounded. And the dream had been so vivid. He clearly remembered his fright and shock at watching the first shambling corpses stroll down Main St., the first one with a toe tag on her arm and a large V on her torso from her autopsy.

Tom recalled she was strikingly beautiful, with long, golden tresses and a trim figure, though a little pasty for his taste. Perhaps she could go to the tanning salon? Just because she was dead didn't mean she still couldn't look good. He remembered how her face had sagged to the right and the left eye was curved upward, though the face was still attractive.

Then in his dream, he'd been distracted by the next ghoul he had seen. A few feet behind the blonde zombie, a headless man walked along like he was going for a Sunday stroll.

His head was still with him, however, only now it was in a paper bag in his left hand. While the dead man walked, the bag swung back and forth to the rhythm of his stride, a few spots of blood dripping onto the street from the bottom of the bag. There was a toe tag on this animated corpse, too.

And a brief description of an automobile accident and a decapitation on the tag, scrawled out in the coroner's messy, stilted handwriting.

The next ghoul in line was small—it was a little girl. She had red and blue marks on her neck from where she had been strangled, after being ruthlessly raped and murdered. In her right arm she hugged the dolly that had been her safety blanket for most of her young life.

Unfortunately, the dolly hadn't protected her from the monster of a neighbor who had lived next door to her and had secretly watched her while she played in the backyard with her dolls. Then one night, only two days ago, he'd acted on his impulses and had taken a young life not meant for the realm of death just yet.

Tom could only stand in the street, mouth agape, as the young ghoul shambled down the sidewalk, her plodding footsteps making her look like she was sleepwalking. It was only when Tom saw the milky white dead eyes that he realized she wasn't alive, but truly dead.

Arriving after getting a call about a naked woman and a headless man, a policeman pulled his squad car over, jumping out with nightstick in hand. He had gone over to the ghouls, wanting to stop the naked corpse from strolling down Main Street.

Not understanding the full extent of what was happening, he could only assume it was some sort of prank, or perhaps a college initiation gone too far. He chose the naked ghoul first as there was a public nudity law in effect and she would need to get some clothes on or risk going to jail.

When the cop moved closer and saw the dead eyes and autopsy scar on her chest, his mouth dropped open and he began to stutter. Reaching for his two-way radio, he called in to the station about the odd looking woman, and when he saw the headless corpse behind her, he dropped the radio and took a step backwards. On instinct, he drew his service revolver, aiming it at the headless corpse.

In the decapitated body's hand, the paper bag had ripped open, the still moving dead eyes of the severed head glaring back at the officer.

Shouting a warning, and frankly not having a clue what he should do, the policeman opened fire on the headless corpse, round after round striking the center of the ghoul's chest.

The heavy .38's ripped into the ghoul, shattering organs and fracturing ribs. The front of the headless corpse didn't look that bad, only a few holes to show where the rounds had entered the torso, but it was on the rear of the ghoul where the true damage was obvious. Large, fist-sized holes had appeared as if by magic, the bullets exploding outward, shredding the body like it had been dropped into a blender.

Gobbets of flesh and gore bathed the street, splattering the road with crimson. The blood was slow, syrupy, the plasma slowly congealing since the owner of the viscous fluid was dead.

Behind the headless ghoul, the little girl was splashed with red, small crimson dots appearing on her gaunt face like tiny freckles. Her dolly received an ample dose of gore, as well; chunks of viscera landing on the dolly to slide off and fall to the pavement with wet splashy sounds.

But the cop had been concentrating too much on the headless ghoul and had let his guard down on the naked woman. Before he realized it, she was on him, her teeth sinking into his forearm, ripping his uniform sleeve and a large chunk of his flesh with it.

He screamed, dropped his revolver and panicked, then pushed the woman off him. Reaching down, he pulled his nightstick off his belt. The nightstick cracked over the naked ghoul's head, leaving a large indent in her forehead.

Her head turned with the blow, but as the cop watched, her head slowly turned back to face him, her mouth and chin now coated a dark scarlet from his blood. It dripped off her chin and between her breasts almost seductively.

The vermillion ribbons sluiced down her chest, sliding between the once shapely breasts, now deformed thanks to the autopsy scar, then continued on to the dark hair between her groin; she seemed to lick her lips in ecstasy.

Despite his terror, the officer noticed the carpet did not match the drapes, but then he was backing away from her, his wounded arm out, his other arm swinging the nightstick for all he was worth.

The naked ghoul hissed, blood shooting from her mouth like she was spitting, then she lunged for him. He swatted her with the nightstick, the tip striking the woman's left eye socket, puncturing the white orb within, but the ghoul never slowed.

Tom stared at the tableaux at the end of the street, watching helplessly as the naked woman fell on top of the officer and began sinking her teeth into the side of his neck.

Even from his distance away, Tom saw the blood fountain arch upward, then fall back to the ground like rain, as the ghoul severed the man's jugular with her teeth. Then the small girl was with the naked ghoul and they both began feeding on the hapless policeman.

In less than two minutes, the cop's kicking legs faltered and he stopped moving, while the two ghouls continued to feed. The headless corpse shambled up and the body leaned over, allowing the severed head to try and take a bite of the cop's body. Chewing bits of bloody meat, the pulped flesh slid out the bottom of the neck, to splatter onto the sidewalk.

The head didn't care, of course, and went in for more.

Tom continued to stare, mouth hanging slack, blinking continually as he watched the visceral scene of death only a few dozen feet away.

Then, coming around the far corner, he saw more people, more shambling forms slowly moving towards him. At first his legs wouldn't work, and no matter how hard he tried, he couldn't run away.

In his dream, he screamed to himself to run, to get away before he joined the cop in a dismembered death.

A moaning sound filled his ears, a despairing, wailing tone that filled his soul with hopelessness and loss, and of pain and suffering. Tom realized the sound was coming from the slow-moving people coming towards him.

Then he snapped out of his stupor and his legs were free!

Like they had been incased in ice and then the block shattered, his legs were able to run. And so he did, all the way back home.

Slamming his front door, he'd sat down on his couch in a daze, unable to believe what he'd been witness to, the dream flowing like a movie on a giant screen in his head.

His mind refused to accept the utter unbelievably of what he'd seen, and he shook his head again and again, as if that gesture alone could change the facts.

Ten minutes later, the first sounds of a city falling apart came to his ears. It was an explosion across town, the pillars of smoke drifting into the sky to blend with the clouds, tainting the once blue horizon gray.

Then the sounds of crunching metal could be heard; two cars fornicating as they struck each other head on, bodies going head first through windshields to fall in a tangle of bloody limbs on the warm asphalt of the road.

Gunshots filtered into his head, some of the citizens fighting back, but soon, they too, would evaporate, becoming less and less noticeable as the day wore on.

Tom wondered where his roommate was. William should be home by now, and surely with everything that was happening, he would have left work, wanting to reach the safety of his home.

In his dream, Tom felt weary and laid his head down, falling asleep from stress and exhaustion.

And now he stood up after waking. The room was still very dark and he realized the shades were drawn on every window. The house was silent. He went to the bathroom and splashed water on his face as he tried to wash the images of death and destruction from his mind. The bathroom light didn't work which was odd, but there was just enough light from the moon outside to filter through the drawn shade.

Finishing up, he went back into the living room and stood quietly with his hands on his hips as he stared at the darkened room.

It was then that William stepped out of the kitchen to see Tom was awake. He carried a candle in his hand, the pale glow giving his face a pallid look. The man looked haggard, as if he'd been worried about something.

His clothes were torn in a few places and there were a few stains of red on his shirt. Tom assumed the man had spilled ketchup on himself, as William was notoriously sloppy when he was eating.

William stepped into the living room and put the candle down on a small end table, then dropped onto the couch. "Good, you're up," he said. "When I came home earlier, I thought I'd just leave you alone. It's good to see you made it, too. How're you feeling? It's some crazy shit going on, huh?"

Tom didn't know what William was talking about, but he nodded. "Yeah, guess so. I tell you, I had the craziest dream. You wouldn't believe me if I told you."

William only bent his head to the right, gesturing for Tom to go on. "Try me, after the past day I think I'd believe anything."

Tom was about to open his mouth, to share with William the crazy dream he had of dead people walking and a world fallen into chaos, when there was a pounding on the front door, the staccato beat like a bass drum.

"Good God, who the hell is beating on our door like that?" Tom asked angrily, turning and walking to the door in one smooth motion, his hand already reaching out to unlock it and give the person on the other side a piece of his mind.

William's eyes went wide with shock as he watched Tom reach out for the doorknob. "Wait, Tom, what the hell are you doing! Don't open that door! You'll kill us both!"

But Tom wasn't listening, too wrapped up in what he was going to say to the jerk pounding on his door.

Opening the door, with William's words echoing in his ears, Tom prepared his retort to the intruder opposite him, the epitaph already lodged in his throat. Before he could do or say anything, however, multiple bloody, claw-like hands reached out and grabbed him, yanking him through the doorway and away from the safety of his home.

He screamed when his hair was pulled from his scalp and a dozen hands ripped at his clothing. Snarling faces looked down on his, and he felt himself forced to the ground.

Then, just before the first set of blood-red teeth descended over his face, blocking out his surroundings, he let out one blood-curdling exclamation, his words intertwined into the scream like a mantra.

"No! No! It was just a dream! It was just a *dream*!"

Before he could scream again, mind-numbing pain filled his mind and he was lost in a sea of anguish and agony, while outside on the street, the city burned, the flames engulfing everything.

While Tom was having his insides torn from his body, devoured by the hungry masses of the undead, shadowy, shambling forms swarmed through the metropolis, consuming everything in their path.

For perhaps it is *life* that is the dream and *death* is the true reality.

IT'LL ONLY HURT A LITTLE

The grunting grew louder as Clyde prepared to climax for the second time that night.

His hips grew tense and his face took on the look one gets when a particularly difficult shit is wracking one's body.

"Oh, God! Oh, yeah, here I come, baby!" he screamed as he felt himself release and shoot his load into the cold cavity of the dead girl's pussy.

"Oh, yeah," he breathed as he rolled to the edge of the crypt in the center of the mausoleum, sighing happily.

Next to him was the two month old corpse of a sixteen-year-old girl.

The girl's name had been Stephanie.

She had been hitchhiking one night when she'd gotten into the wrong car. The driver had sodomized her, beat her and just plain treated her like a pile of shit.

Stephanie hadn't survived that night, and the massive black and blue bruises covering her broken neck proved this. Even the mortician's makeup couldn't completely hide the marks.

Now, two months later, she was being abused again, this time by Clyde.

Clyde Milton worked in the Rosemont Cemetery, home of over thirty thousand graves. Loved ones from all walks of life were interred here, each mostly forgotten by the living.

Sure, people would drop by on weekends and religious holidays, but for the most part Clyde had seen that once you died, people forgot about you. Not that he blamed them. You had to move forward or you'd be miserable all the time.

But Clyde didn't forget all those dead and buried people—especially the women.

A few weeks ago, a mother of forty had died of a coronary. Clyde had waited for the funeral to end, and when he knew everyone was gone, he had opened the coffin and snuck the body to his old and beat-up van. The same one he carried the flowers and yard implements to keep the cemetery landscaped.

The Rosemont sign was painted on the side, too, of course.

He'd brought the dead woman back to his small shack at the back of the cemetery and had ridden her for a week straight. Even when the smell had begun to get overwhelming, still he had ridden that fine, dead ass.

It was when he had the woman on her knees, holding her arms up so she wouldn't fall over that he knew it was time to put her back into the ground.

As he pumped her from behind, her right arm had begun to separate at the upper socket. First the flesh began to tear and finally with a dull *pop*, the arm detached. Clyde had been about to cum and he'd been thrown off balance as both he and the woman tumbled to the dirt-covered wooden floor.

She'd ended up on top of him, and as he shot his load into the air, her face had come down on his, like she was kissing him, perhaps thanking him for such a lovely evening.

Clyde had screamed, pushing her off him, thinking she had somehow come back to life and was now trying to get him for what he'd done to her. But as he tossed her away from him, the body merely flopped down, then lay still.

His penis had deflated like a shrunken balloon and he laid on the floor panting, his heart feeling like it was going to burst from his chest.

After that little experience he didn't touch another corpse for three weeks, but soon the urge overcame him and he knew he couldn't resist.

Which worked out well, because that was when Stephanie arrived. She had looked so sweet in the open casket, as the wake had been held in the main funeral house.

Clyde had managed to sneak in, and he had grabbed a peek of the body.

The instant he saw those small pert cheeks, the budding bosom, the small nose, he knew he had to have her. As he left the house, his pants were pitching a tent something fierce and he had to do his best to hide it.

It had been a long day and a half, and then he had to wait for the wake to end, then the next day the funeral, too, but finally it came and went. He watched from the edge of the treeline as the family mourned poor Stephanie and said their goodbyes.

Eventually the funeral ended, everyone left, and Clyde knew it was his cue to drop the casket into the hole with the winches and fill it, but as he stared down at the coffin, he knew he had other plans for the sweet thing within. He didn't even wait to get her back to his shack, but instead brought her to the nearest crypt.

Clyde had always been an odd bird.

When he was twelve and first found out about sex, he'd gotten the idea to see what it would feel like to fuck the neighbor's dog. As he had tried to wrestle the animal to the ground, his pants down around his ankles, he ended up snapping the dog's neck.

As he stared at the dead animal, his mind racing for what to do next, he came to the conclusion that what just happened might not be such a bad thing.

After all, the dog was still warm and now it couldn't fight him.

But later, when the dog had grown cold and he'd fucked it again, he found his orgasm was even better than the first time.

After that experience, Clyde found he had a natural attraction to dead things.

Having sex with a live woman was out of the question, what with their moving eyes, breathing, and making noises.

Oh, no, he liked them quiet, not noisy as he pumped and pumped till he exploded.

Back in the present, Clyde rolled over and stared at Stephanie's dead face. The makeup from the mortician had sloughed a little, or maybe that was her skin. Her hair was still in great shape and her body was still soft. It would be weeks before she would begin to decay to the point he would have to get rid of her.

His right hand reached out and began to stroke her left breast. It was still soft, the nipple forever firm and perky. He could already feel his loins stirring and he leaned over and gently kissed the nipple, then wanting more, he began to suck it, caressing it with his tongue.

In no time he was hard again and he climbed on top of her, sliding himself into her cold cavern again. He liked it cold and wondered how any man could get off sticking his dick into a warm pussy.

As he stroked and pumped, he closed his eyes and imagined all the past fucks over the years. His breathing grew heavy, and before he could stop, wanting to enjoy every second, he felt himself exploding yet again.

Grunting in pleasure, he fell on top of the young, dead girl and sighed happily. Breathing in, her hair smelled like chemicals and to him it was the sweetest perfume. There was just the subtle hint of decay coming off her, and it reminded him of cherished ambrosia.

Climbing off her, he pulled up his pants, ignoring the small bits of decayed meat still on the tip of his member. He'd clean it off later if he felt like it. Picking her up in his arms, he left the crypt, tossed her in the back of his van, and went home, happy as a pig in shit that he'd just gotten laid twice in one night.

The distance to his shack from the crypt wasn't far, and before he knew it, he was pulling into the small, one car driveway.

Climbing out of the van, he skipped once in happiness at the thought of fucking young Stephanie later that night. He wanted to do her again now, but he wasn't as young as he once was and needed time to recover.

Cracking open the rear doors of the van, the moonlight seeped into the interior, casting Stephanie's face in a pallid glow.

For just a second it looked like she was staring at him, as if she was going to get up, and like a zombie from a horror movie, come at him, all gnashing teeth and clawing hands.

But then the shadows receded and he saw she was truly dead, just the way she was supposed to be.

Chuckling to himself at his silliness, he picked her up and tossed her over his shoulder like a slab of meat, her head and hands hanging down his back. She was naked and he couldn't resist squeezing her ass cheeks with his free hand, enjoying the way the flesh felt under his palm.

The door to the shack was unlocked as there was nothing inside worth taking.

Stepping through the doorway, Clyde's eyes rested on the heavy wooden table he used to eat on, and sometimes fuck corpses on.

Off to the left of the table, in the small room, was a sink, refrigerator and oven, and to the right was one door which led to a very small bedroom. Across the room was one last door which led to the bathroom, a two-by-four of a room with a sink, shower and toilet. Clyde always had to be careful when he sat on the throne or else he'd whack his head on the edge of the sink, it was that tight in there.

Clyde carried the dead girl to the table and laid her down, her head smacking the table.

"Oops! Sorry, doll, guess it didn't hurt too much anyway, huh?" he chuckled as he went to the refrigerator to grab a beer, cracked it, and took a pull, burping loudly.

That was when he realized he wasn't alone in his small shack and he spun around to see a tall black man wearing a crisp black suit with a white carnation on the lapel.

Clyde knew the man instantly. It was Mr. Rosemont, the head mortician, as well as the owner of the cemetery and mortuary.

Both had been in Mr. Rosemont's family for years and it was rumored the man, as did his father and grandfather, had a hand in the voodoo arts that went all the way back to his heritage from the dark pits of Africa.

Clyde thought it was all a load of shit, but the man paid his salary so he didn't give a fuck if the man knew God himself.

"Oh, shit, Mr. Rosemont, sir, ya scared me half ta death," Clyde said as he moved forward to shake Rosemont's hand. He was so used to having dead corpses around him that he didn't even think to be concerned that he'd just been caught with one in his shack.

Mr. Rosemont stared at the filthy hand like it was a snapping dog, and would be an idiot to consider shaking it.

The man held an aura of power, his hair cut close to his scalp, his nails neatly manicured. This was a man whose family had crawled up from the gutter and he remembered where he came from.

Ignoring Clyde's proffered hand, he pointed at the dead girl on the table.

"You sick bastard, Clyde. I've been hearing rumors about what you've been doing to the bodies of the recently deceased but I couldn't believe it, so I decided to come here and talk to you about it. Out of respect for your years of loyal service to this cemetery I was hoping to get it all squared away. I told myself that no one could be so disturbed as to be fornicating with corpses, even you."

Clyde blinked at the man's words, realizing he was caught red handed. His mind racing, he knew what he needed to do immediately. He began to inch over to the small kitchen counter next to the oven while Mr. Rosemont followed, all the while talking.

"You'll go to jail for this, Clyde, you know that don't you? Do you know what they'll do to a pervert like you? Well, I don't want to even think about it. So you like to rape dead corpses, do you? Well, I have a feeling when you get to prison, the shoe will be on the other foot."

Clyde reached the counter and his left hand crept around his back to grasp the handle of a cleaver resting on its surface. His other hand still held the beer, and he took another pull, finishing half the can off in a few gulps.

"Now, Mr. Rosemont, be reasonable. I ain't hurtin' anyone. Shit, they're already dead. It's not like they know what I'm doin' to 'em."

Mr. Rosemont's eyes went wide as he took a step closer to Clyde.

"They don't know? But I do, damn it. People come here to put their loved ones to rest, not to have them desecrated by the likes of you. I'll see you pay for this with the maximum sentence allowable, Clyde. I have influence in this town. You're through, you hear me? Through!"

Clyde chuckled as his grip became so tight on the handle of the cleaver his knuckles turned white.

"Yeah, I hear ya, but it's you that's through." He brought the cleaver around and it sank into the side of Mr. Rosemont's neck, blood shooting out of the wound as soon as metal kissed flesh.

Mr. Rosemont stumbled away, his hand going to the cleaver embedded in his throat, and with shock filling in his eyes, he pulled the cleaver free.

More blood shot out, his carotid artery sliced in twain. The man stumbled and went to his knees, his breath coming in gasps. "You…made a big mistake here, Clyde…" he gasped, his final moments on Earth drawing to a close. "Do you know who I am? What I can do?" He went to all fours as he grew weak from blood loss.

Clyde stepped closer to him and looked down, shaking his head.

"You mean that voodoo stuff? Shit, that's a load of bullshit and you know it, sir. You just let everyone believe that so you can keep people fearin' ya. Well, not me, I'm not afraid of no one."

"You will be," Rosemont gasped. He slumped forward, his dark face now covered in blood. Clyde leaned over so he could watch the light leave his eyes. He was fascinated with death and he was already rubbing his crotch from the excitement of the kill.

Mr. Rosemont found the white carnation on his suit with a shaking hand and plucked it from his lapel. With his last gesture, he shoved the flower into his mouth without Clyde seeing, and mumbled something so low Clyde could barley hear it.

"I will be avenged. My death at your hands is only the beginning. You will pay…" he said around the carnation in his mouth. If he had more to say, it was lost when his eyes fluttered, then closed, his head sagging forward into the pool of blood.

Clyde snickered as he stared down at Rosemont.

"Gonna make me pay, huh? Seems to me you're the one that paid, you nosy bastard. Shoulda just left me alone. Shit, I wasn't hurtin' no one, the bitches are dead for Chrissakes."

Clyde stood up and walked to the door. He opened it and stepped outside. He went to the van, opened the driver's door, and got behind the steering wheel, then backed up the vehicle until the rear doors were facing his shack's front door.

He didn't feel like carrying the body any further than he had to.

Walking back inside, he splashed through the blood and picked up Mr. Rosemont's body, carrying it to the van where he tossed it inside without care. The body rolled over, the limbs flopping around, the once immaculate suit now a mess. Mr. Rosemont's mouth opened and the carnation could be seen within, but where it was once white with a few spots of blood on it, the flower was now ebony black, as black as the darkest night or the deepest forest in Africa.

Clyde never noticed, and he slammed the van doors closed, the matter of murder already forgotten.

With a smile on his lips, he went back inside to have some more fun with Stephanie, as he was now worked up after killing Mr. Rosemont. As he walked, he was already unbuckling his trousers.

He was so horny he thought he would burst, especially knowing that the young dead girl was waiting patiently for him to return to her.

As far as Mr. Rosemont was concerned, he could bury the man later.

And buried he shall be, for after all, Clyde lived in a cemetery, there were a hundred and one places he could bury the body where no one would ever find it. But first a little fun.

An hour later, a few plot rows away from Clyde's shack, a fresh grave was being filled again. Clyde was sweating something fierce after digging the hole, but he wanted to get it done now before the next morning arrived.

There was a full moon high in the sky, but despite this, the cemetery seemed as dark as the darkest night. It was as if the moon and stars didn't exist or that somehow their feeble glow wasn't reaching the cemetery below.

It was eerie, as if something not of this world was about this night.

Clyde ignored the ominous feeling and patted the top of the grave, the loose dirt sliding off the mound.

Mr. Rosemont was four feet in the ground now, he would never tell a soul what he'd discovered about Clyde. His dirty secret was still his alone.

As for Clyde, he tossed his shovels back into his van and headed back to the shack where the cool body of Stephanie still waited on the kitchen table.

As he drove through the cemetery, the moon waxing on the dull tombstones, he could already feel himself growing hard again in anticipation of what he was going to do to the girl's corpse.

Hours later, the moon now beginning its slow descent from the night sky, as it prepared to vacate the horizon for another day, the darkness was complete.

The leaves in the trees of the cemetery fluttered as if of their own accord, the lack of a breeze disquieting. Nothing living was about this night, and no crickets could be heard, no night birds called to one another. It was like the graveyard was truly dead, devoid of all life, mimicking the residents interred within its rod-iron gates.

On the fresh grave of Mr. Rosemont, the dirt began to shift, as if a rather large earthworm was working its way to the surface. This went on for almost an hour, but eventually the dirt parted and a black hand appeared, dark as night and blending into the surrounding gloom.

Eventually the hand became an arm, followed by another hand, then a head. To someone watching, if a living being had been in the cemetery this night, it would have seemed to be the stuff of nightmares, or low rated Z horror movies.

The earth shifted once more and Mr. Rosemont pulled himself free of his shallow grave, flopping onto the soil like a man pulling himself from the surf after almost drowning. His black, curly hair was filled with dirt, and when he moved slightly, the soil cascaded off his shoulders and hair to fall back onto the soft mound beneath him.

Dead eyes that somehow still could see gazed about the cemetery, his cemetery, and for a few moments his face was a blank slate. Then his right hand reached up and plucked the black carnation from inside his mouth, and with a moan, he set it back onto his lapel, the magical emblem filling his dead body with life.

Oh, yes, Mr. Rosemont had learned a lot from his daddy, and grandfather, to the point he never went anywhere without some sort of talisman.

Though he was dead, he would still get to exact his revenge on the person who killed him before being released into the oblivion of final death.

Standing on shaky legs, stiff with rigor mortis, his head slanted to one side, the bloody gash in his neck now filled with dirt, he raised his arms into the air and began to chant. The syllables were unknown to a civilized being, the words of the lost language handed down for so many years their true origin was lost in the folds of time.

The words were powerful, containing mystic spells to bring the dead back to life. They breathed into the desiccated corpses buried around him a semblance of life, one that had evaporated from their bodies upon their death, like a puddle of water on a hot summer's day.

Where the man in black stood, slowly the graves around him and beyond began to tremble, as each corpse within the distance of his spell slowly stirred in their dark coffins. Soon, hundreds of graves were shaking as the bodies within fought their way back to the surface...to freedom.

Of course it would take time for them to reach the surface and many would never be free. Those who were placed in solid oak or metal coffins could never hope to break free of their cocoon-like prisons. But many were homeless people, indigents, who had been buried in simple pine boxes, others in body bags if the mortician thought he could get away with it, thereby saving a few more dollars off the already meager stipend the city gave him to inter bums and John Does.

These were the graves that began to vibrate as the bodies slowly crawled to the surface and freedom. The older the corpse, the older the wood of their prison, thus allowing them to tear through and into the wet soil above. Not needing to breathe, the dirt that might have suffocated them was ignored, and in time the first pale, skeletal hand began to push the moist earth to the side as the body slowly crawled into the cool air of a night of wonders, or a night of nightmares.

Hours later, more than a thousand zombies stood on rotting legs or crawled across the moist sod towards Mr. Rosemont. What was odd was that they were all once men. No female corpses filled this army of the dead.

The mortician waited until all were close and then raised his arms high once more, moaning to the heavens. In turn, each ghoul with the ability to make speech in some form returned the gesture, and a thousand undead voices cracked with decay and filled with dirt, all wailed into the night sky.

The sea of shifting heads seemed to undulate and sway as the massive crowd of dead folk waited patiently for their marching orders.

Satisfied, the zombie master smiled, the crease on his face looking like another gash similar to the one on his neck. Turning, he began moving towards the shack where he'd been murdered, to the shack where he would have his revenge. And the man waiting within who would feel his vengeance in full.

Clyde was screwing the corpse of Stephanie again, his eyes creased in pleasure as he slid in and out of her cold hole. A jar of Vaseline was to his left, one he used quite often. The dead weren't slick down there, so unless he wanted to chafe, he had no choice but to add a little lubricant to the party.

His brow was sweaty and he grunted with each thrust, the dead girl below him shifting slightly. She was on her back, her eyes open, staring at the ceiling, and her mouth hung slack. She was like a mannequin made into flesh as Clyde abused her with each thrust of his body.

Then Clyde felt the moment coming, and with a yell of pleasure, he filled her with himself and collapsed on top of her. His nose sucked in the scent of decay wafting off her and he could already feel himself growing hard yet again.

Only his next bout of unnatural love was interrupted when the door to his shack began to shake in its frame.

"Now what the hell?" he mumbled as he crawled off the dead girl. "I don't know who's bangin' on my door this late at night, but they're gonna get an ass whuppin'," he muttered as he climbed off Stephanie and began to dress. His penis was covered in Vaseline and a few bits of flesh, but he could have cared less.

Zipping up his pants, he picked up the cleaver, the same one he'd used on Mr. Rosemont, and went to the door to chase away the damn fool banging on his door.

Behind him, Stephanie lay still in death, her head now lolling to the side like a rag doll. He reached the door, and with the cleaver held high to scare whoever was there, he opened it.

And promptly screamed with fear and shock.

Standing in the doorway was a rotting man, complete with maggots squirming in his eye sockets. How the dead thing could see was anyone's guess, but as the door opened wide and Clyde yelled, the zombie lurched forward to wrap its arms around his neck.

Clyde hadn't cried out because of one lone zombie, he'd screamed because of the hundreds waiting behind the first one, all in a similar state of decay.

But Clyde had been around dead people his entire adult life, hell, he had sex with them almost every day, and it didn't take him long to snap out of his fear induced stupor and deal with the zombie coming for him.

As the ghoul stepped into the shack, Clyde pushed it away from him and kicked the door closed, thus blocking the other ghouls from entry. Immediately, the door began to shake and the two windows of his shack imploded as undead hands reached inside for him.

With the cleaver held high, he swiped it at the ghoul's neck, the dry muscle parting like old parchment. The head bounced away to roll into a corner of the room, the mouth still opening and closing. The body was still active, too, and whatever had let it see without eyes still controlled it.

The zombie stepped towards Clyde, who with a snarl, slashed both hands off at the wrists. The hands dropped to the floor where the fingers still grasped air, then the severed hands flipped over and scampered away like large, white spiders.

Clyde saw this but only out of the corner of his eye, as the zombie was still coming for him.

"Die, you dead bastard!" he screamed and hacked at the body again and again, taking it apart piece by piece. Though the pieces still twitched, they were now harmless, and he ignored them as he went to the windows and began slicing off hands at the wrists, then arms at the elbows. The limbs dropped to the floor like wilted roses off a bush after a big storm, where the hands then scampered away to be lost in the shadows of the shack.

As for Clyde, he was yelling and cutting, taking off each hand foolish enough to invade his domain.

Eventually, he realized there were far too many to stop on his own so he went to the corner of the shack and grabbed the old pieces of plywood, planks, nails and a hammer. With a snarl on his face, he ran back to the windows, and using the hammer to beat the hands away, he began to nail the wood over the window frames and then one across the door, just to be sure it was solid.

As he was hammering, he felt an itch on his leg, like a mouse was crawling up his pants. When he glanced down, he saw one of the hands trying to climb up his leg and he whacked it with the hammer. But just as the hammer was about to connect, the hand dropped away and Clyde howled in pain as the hammer whacked his knee.

Muttering a thousand curses, he began to limp as he searched for the damn hand so he could destroy it. There were more hands about, leftovers of his cutting rampage, and they were lying in wait in the shadows of the shack.

Then the lights went out, one of the zombies outside pulling the electrical wires from the box out back of the shack, and the entire room was thrown into darkness.

Clyde stood perfectly still, only the banging of the dead now piercing the inky blackness. He moved to the small kitchen and found what he wanted, a small camping lantern he used when he needed to search for fresh bodies to fuck late at night.

The room was blasted with light as the lantern was lit and Clyde gasped when he saw more than two dozen hands surrounding him on the floor. If they had eyes it would have been like a herd of rats.

"You little bastards, I'll get ya for this!" he screamed and began running around the shack, stepping on the hands and smashing metacarpals to bits. When his foot left a pulverized hand behind, the fingers still twitched ineffectually, but they were done for.

He ran back and forth, knocking things over and grabbing the hands like he was an exterminator on the biggest job of his career. One hand got under his pant leg and he had to strip to get if off. When he was holding said hand, the fingers snapping back and forth like stubby snakes, he brought the hand to the kitchen sink, shoving it into the garbage disposal. It was an old model, found in the trash and installed by Clyde, and it sounded like a locomotive was driving by, which was why Clyde rarely used it.

The disposal ground to life and Clyde smiled as he forced the hand into the circular opening. The hand seemed to scream in protest as it was slowly devoured into pulp, the bones finally jamming the disposal.

But the purpose was served and the hand was finished.

"Ha, I got another one of you bastards. I'll get you all and then I'll be safe. Your brethren can't get in here, these walls may look old, but they're strong as hell!"

The hands scurried about, Clyde chasing them back and forth. One time, when he tried to get one that had scurried under the sink, he inadvertently knocked Stephanie off the table. The corpse of the girl tumbled to the floor where she landed on her side. Clyde ignored her and chased the hands, and as he went to one that slid behind the refrigerator, he was so preoccupied he didn't hear Stephanie as her body slowly began to twitch, then rose up and began to crawl towards him.

Clyde was pushing the refrigerator away from the wall and using a broom handle to get the hand to leave the safety of its hiding place, so was oblivious to Stephanie closing on him.

With the moans of the dead and banging of fists on the shacks walls, the inside of the shack sounded like the crowd of a rock concert without the music. He never knew he was under attack until Stephanie used the hammer Clyde had put down, and cracked him over the back of the head.

He went down like a steer with a bolt in its head to lay sprawled on the dirty wooden floor. As soon as he dropped, the hands scurried out of their hiding places and hopped onto his body, some seeming to be sniffing the air with the tips of their fingers. On the verge of unconsciousness, he stared at the hands on him and gazed up at the dead face of Stephanie—even in death she was beautiful—and saw her smile. As his bladder let go in terror at that grin, he fell into a darkness he assumed he would never awaken from.

There were worst things than death and Clyde was about to find out one of them for himself. As he lay unconscious on the floor, Stephanie went to the door with the hammer and pried off the wood to open it to the hundreds of waiting zombies.

As the door opened inward, Mr. Rosemont was waiting, a tight grin on his face at the sight of Stephanie.

"Well done, my dear, soon you will have your revenge and your final rest," he said, his voice harsh now that half his neck was sliced. Turning, he gestured for a dozen zombies to enter the shack, which they did, one at a time or in trios. Three tried to enter the door at the same time and their shoulders became wedged, much like an old Three Stooges movies. The three decrepit ghouls were stuck, and though each pushed, their bodies were wedged in good. Mr. Rosemont sighed wearily and stepped up and grabbed two of the ghouls by the hair.

Yanking to free them, all he managed to do was pull the dry tufts free, scalp and all. With another weary sigh, he grabbed the middle one by the shoulders and yanked again, popping it free of its two buddies.

Now that the doorway was clear again, the ghouls swarmed inside. Mr. Rosemont directed a few to pick up Clyde and bring him to the table. The same one Stephanie had been abused on only minutes ago.

As the zombies did as they were told, Mr. Rosemont smiled malevolently. Soon Clyde would wake up and then the fun would begin, while outside the shack, a thousand zombies waited patiently for their orders.

At first Clyde didn't know where he was and assumed he was in his small, filthy bed, but then he felt a hardness under his chest and stomach and realized he was lying face down on something, either metal or wood.

On further inspection, he could feel his legs dangling off the edge, as if there was no weight on them, the hardness only pressing up to his groin.

His head was at such an odd angle that, it too, seemed to be almost dangling off whatever he was on.

So he couldn't be on a floor, he reasoned.

Slowly he cracked his eyelids and no sooner did they open, then they snapped apart like small, spring traps.

He was still in his shack but he was now spread-eagled on his kitchen table.

And he was naked!

And it got worse. There was a room full of what were obviously zombies, as their state of decomposition would leave no denial. When he tried to turn his head and get up, he found he couldn't.

Shifting his head as far as it would go, he saw he was being held down by five zombies. The severed hands he'd been trying to capture earlier were now sitting on his back, their cold fingers pressing on his flesh, causing him to shiver.

The zombies weren't moving, they only stood silently around him, a few moaning softly. Then another shape came closer and Clyde was looking down at the dirt-covered shoes of Mr. Rosemont.

"What the hell are you doing here? I killed and buried you, you're dead! This has to be some kind of a dream."

"No, Clyde, it's no dream," Mr. Rosemont croaked. "You did kill me, but I was prepared for something like this to happen. You know of voodoo, black magic? Well, it's real and so am I." He looked at the closest zombies. "As are my friends."

"Let me go, you bastard, or so help me…"

"So help you what? What are you going to do exactly? Go to the police and explain that you killed your supervisor and then he came back from the dead. Or better yet, that you've been raping dead bodies for years and got caught? No, Clyde, even if you somehow escaped, which is unlikely, you won't be saying a word about this night. About any night, ever again."

Clyde tried to pull his arms free, but the zombies held him fast.

"So then, what are you gonna do with me?"

Mr. Rosemont moved closer and leaned to the side so his face was less than an inch from Clyde's nose.

Clyde winced at the smell, not used to fresh rot. The man was already decaying and Clyde realized the stench of pure rot was very different from when he got the bodies after they were embalmed. He didn't show he was uncomfortable. He used to fuck dead dogs, he could handle the redolence of his former boss.

"When I get outta here I'll kill you again, damn it, and this time I'll make sure you can't get outta your hole."

"No, Clyde that won't be happening, for you see, I came back for a reason and that is to make you pay. For what you did to me and what you've been doing to the dead."

"Fuck you!" Clyde snapped.

"Oh, no, Clyde, not fuck me, it's fuck *you*," Mr. Rosemont said and nodded to the first zombie who was standing behind Clyde.

The ghoul moved up between Clyde's spread legs and positioned himself just so. Clyde's eyes went wide when he felt something moist and cold between his butt cheeks.

He felt terribly vulnerable being naked, and for the first time since waking up, he began to think he may have a problem here.

"What's going on back there, hey, cut the shit!" Clyde yelped to no avail.

Mr. Rosemont began to laugh as the zombie moved closer, positioned its stiff penis just right, then slammed it in, Clyde screaming as he was penetrated like a virgin on her wedding night.

"What the fuck? Get off me, you asshole, goddamn it!" he screamed as he felt himself being violated. No sooner did he scream then another zombie was instructed to step up to his face, which was perfectly positioned at waist height. As he shrieked in pain at being violated from behind, the next zombie dropped trousers and shoved its shriveled, yet hard dick, into Clyde's mouth.

Clyde shook his head to escape, and before he knew it, he tore the penis off the ghoul. Stuck in his mouth, he used his tongue to force it out of his teeth, where he then spit it out.

"You bastard, I'll see you die again, I'll get you!" Clyde yelled.

Mr. Rosemont shook his head as he motioned another zombie to move up to Clyde's face and then shove his stiff, yet desiccated penis into Clyde's mouth.

Meanwhile from behind, the zombie had stepped back to allow another to take its place. This one had been a big black man in life and his member was huge, over ten inches long, and before Clyde knew it, he was being impaled like a spear had been shoved up his ass.

The zombie began to pump as Clyde's muffled screams came out from around the zombie's dick pumping his mouth.

After a minute, Mr. Rosemont waved the large black zombie away and let the next one in, who was soon slamming its dick home like it was no one's business. Clyde's anus was torn and stretched, the man bleeding internally, but still the next zombie came and began to pummel him like a fresh fish in prison.

"How does it feel, Clyde, hmmm? How does it feel to be violated the way you have done to so many of the dead? Like poor Stephanie here who had to lay there and take it. Now you can see how it feels."

Another penis broke off in Clyde's mouth and he began to gag, but then he retched and the seven inch cock slid out of his mouth to bounce on the floor. One of the severed hands scooped it up and ran off, perhaps wanting a hand job.

Clyde sucked in a breath of agony as the next zombie slid between his legs and began to pump. Another zombie came to the front and shoved its maggot encrusted penis into his mouth, the steady rhythm as it pumped causing Clyde to taste bile.

As the zombies continued to fuck Clyde to death, Mr. Rosemont glanced out the shack's doorway, at the long line of a thousand ghouls, which meandered through the cemetery, each waiting their turn to fuck Clyde in the ass and mouth.

With a slight chuckle, the mortician grinned, his white teeth a sharp contrast to his dark face, and he leaned down close to Clyde's ear.

"I told you I'd make you pay for what you did to me, but don't you worry, Clyde, just try to enjoy it, just like Stephanie and the ones before her. There are only a thousand or so zombies to go. In fact, if you close your eyes and try to relax, I bet it'll only hurt a little."

JURY DUTY

James Wilson stepped off the elevator and into the large foyer with marble walls and floors. He was in the Superior Court house in Boston, Mass.

He had been picked for jury duty, and though he was dreading it, he still boarded a train and came to Boston, doing his civic duty.

The foyer for the second floor was decorated in contemporary modern, with polished stone floors and white, imported marble walls. On each side of the foyer were two banks of elevators, the doors shiny, like stainless steel.

There was a line, fifty people strong and still growing, as jurors stepped off the elevators and lined up one after the other. In their hands, they carried white pieces of paper that had arrived in the mail. As James studied the faces of his fellow jurors, he saw the same grim countenances on each of them. All had lives to get to and jury duty was a nuisance none of them had chosen. Still, more than a hundred of them had arrived.

Getting in line, James couldn't help but people watch, especially the women. In his early thirties, it was in his blood to admire the pretty ladies.

All walks of life were here today, a real melting pot of America. There were Spanish, Asian, Haitian, black, white, brown, young, old and middle-aged. There was nowhere else James could imagine where such a diverse assortment of people were gathered together.

"Some line, huh?" a man asked.

James glanced over his shoulder to see a middle-age man with a balding pate, pale skin, and a beer belly he carried proudly, wearing a white shirt, blue slacks and loafers. James was in a similar outfit, only with a tan shirt and black slacks.

"Yeah, it's always like this when I come here."

"Oh?" the man inquired. "You've been here before?"

"Yeah, a few years ago," James replied.

"You get picked?" the man asked.

"Nah, I sat around for a few hours and then went home."

"That's good," the man said. "I'm Steve by the way." He smiled, offering his hand to shake.

"James. Nice to meet you."

"Likewise," Steve replied as they shook hands.

The line continued to move, albeit slowly, but twenty minutes later, James reached the door to the jury pool room. Stepping through the doorway, he was ushered to a desk where he was signed in and given a number.

As he went to find a chair, he read his number. "113? Is that good or bad?"

Steve moved up next to him and James realized he had made a friend whether he liked it or not.

"Depends if you're superstitious," Steve replied.

Moving past the desk, James studied the room. It was large, with at least a hundred chairs in it. They were blue, and all of them were lined up in rows of twelve. Almost all of them were occupied now, a few bored faces glaring back at him, though most had their noses buried in books or newspapers. A few had laptops perched on their laps as they tried to get some work done, despite being trapped at jury duty for the day.

James picked a seat between a heavy set man—who filled his chair without leaving an inch to spare—on his left, and a young Asian man on his right. One seat over was an older black woman. She had her head down and was snoring softly. James couldn't help but smile at this because she had the look of a cleaning lady, or someone who worked hard for a living. He assumed she worked nights, and instead of going home and getting to bed, she had to come here.

From somewhere up at the front of the room, someone was coughing loudly. In fact, it was so loud that James wondered if the person was coughing up a lung.

"Hey, James, how you doing?" Steve asked from behind him.

James turned in his chair to see Steve's grinning face.

"I got a seat right behind you; lucky, huh?"

James forced a smile. "Yeah, lucky me." He tried to give his most apologetic smile. "Look, Steve, I have a lot of work to do, so…"

Steve looked at him for a full ten seconds before he finally understood.

"Oh, shit, sorry. I won't bother you anymore."

"I hope you understand. I don't want to be rude," James said ruefully. Now he felt guilty at coming off as antisocial.

"No, James, it's okay. I totally understand. I have a book with me. Go 'head and do what you have to do."

"Okay, thanks for understanding," James replied.

Steve patted James arm and then leaned back in his chair. James was relieved; it seemed Steve did understand and Steve seemed nice enough that he didn't want to offend the man; after all, the man did try to befriend him.

James leaned over and opened his briefcase, planning to get some work done before the court officer got started with the introductions.

As he began working, the infernal coughing at the front of the large room continued, sounding like a habitual smoker was getting his payback.

The next three hours went by in a boring daze for James. After the introduction by the court officer and the prerequisite video about the civic duty of all Americans to serve on a jury, everyone grew comfortable and tried to pass the time.

James concentrated on his work, but with each passing hour, it grew harder and harder to focus. The reason for this was because of the infernal coughing coming from the front of the room.

It was at the point now where the man—James had found it was a man earlier—acted like he had pneumonia. The coughs were deep hacks that wracked the man's body like he was being pummeled by invisible fists. A few times, the court officers—a man and a woman—had asked the man if he needed help.

James thought they should have excused him for being sick, but as most people know, it takes a lot more than a bad cough to get a person excused from jury duty. So the man had taken the glass of water offered to him and was left alone.

By 1 p.m., the man was pretty much alone in his corner of the front of the room. The coughing was so annoying that anyone sitting near him had moved away.

It was twenty past one when the man did more than just cough.

He was having a really bad bout when he suddenly began to gasp, then, like he was slapped from behind, he toppled out of his chair to fall face down on the low-weave carpet, a bit of blood dripping out of the corner of his mouth.

Cries of shock and surprise filled the room as jurors called out for help. A woman in her forties dropped to the man's side, trying to see what she could do. Checking his air passage, she wiped away the blood and began to perform CPR on him, but no matter how hard she tried, he remained immobile.

James was still in the back of the room, and from his vantage point, he couldn't see a thing. Heads and shoulders crowded around the hapless man, all eager to see what was happening.

A court officer—James saw it was the woman—forced her way through the throng of people to see what was happening. The room was in chaos, everyone on their feet, wanting to know what was going on.

"He's dead," the forty-year-old woman said blandly as she stopped performing CPR on the still man. She touched his neck again and shook her head, not finding a pulse.

The room filled with "Oh my God's!" and "No shit's?" as the crowd crammed forward for a better look.

The female court officer knelt down beside the other woman, both looking down at the dead man. The man's eyes were still open, and the woman who had performed CPR on him reached out and closed them with her fingertips. "It's so sad, someone needs to call someone," she said softly.

"We already called, an ambulance is on the way," the court officer said.

The woman who had performed CPR leaned both hands to either side of the dead man as she prepared to push up on her arms and legs so she could stand, when the dead man's eyes snapped open like they were spring-loaded.

Before anyone knew the man was alive again, he turned his head sharply to the right, and with his mouth wide open, he moved his head in and sank his teeth into the woman's right wrist.

Everything seemed to happen in slow motion.

The woman with a dead man eating her wrist, screamed in pain, not understanding what was going on while the female court officer jumped back in shock, as blood squirted from the wound, and onto her face and white shirt, staining it red.

She pulled her revolver and aimed it at the man, yelling. "Stop that, get away from the woman now or so help me, I'll fucking shoot!"

The dead man ignored her threat, still feeding.

Deciding she had done a textbook warning, she shot the man twice in the chest. The bullets impacted and shook the man, blowing fist-sized holes out his back, but the man seemed not to care. After recovering from the rounds, he went back to his meal.

Meanwhile, the crowd of onlookers began to yell and scream, as three male onlookers who were watching everything play out, lunged at the dead man and tried to pry his teeth off the beleaguered woman's wrist.

The teeth were in there like a bear trap, and as the arm was yanked away from the bloody mouth, tendons and muscle tore as fragile veins were severed.

The woman fell backward and landed on her butt, all the while waving her arm around, the blood shooting from her wrist wound splashing those around her.

As each droplet landed on another juror, all hell broke loose and the people tried to get away, as if the blood was acid and could somehow kill them.

At the same moment, the dead man was rolling onto his side, seeming to still have more than a little life in him. He growled loudly and shook his head like an animal, while blood dripped from his mouth and off his chin to splatter the carpet with small circles of crimson.

The three men who had tried to help the woman were still holding on to the man, and one of them got a rude shock when he felt a sudden pain in his forearm and he saw the dead man was now eating him!

Another man punched the dead man in the face, the teeth knocking out on impact. With eyes wide with hunger and rage, the dead man turned on the next available target, a small man with a toupee who had been the last to help.

Before the Good Samaritan could so much as utter a warning, the dead man jumped him, both falling to the carpeted floor. The small man hit his head on a chair on his way down and he saw stars for a few seconds, now dazed and confused.

He came back to his senses when the dead man sank his teeth into his throat, tearing out a large chunk of flesh before diving back in to slurp at the flowing blood.

Trapped under the dead man, the supine man kicked his arms and legs as he screamed to the rafters in agony. But no one came to help him, for chaos now ensued in the jury-pool room.

The male court officer, acting fast and wanting to contain the violence, followed protocol and locked down the room, closing all the doors and locking them. For all that officer knew, a biological outbreak was occurring, which wasn't far from the truth.

The small man with his toupee now knocked off his bald head and a torn-out throat, stopped kicking as the last of his blood pumped out of him and spread across the carpet in a growing halo. The original dead man climbed off him, his face now lathered in scarlet, his eyes darting back and forth, as he searched for another target. He found it in the form of a young blonde woman huddling in the far corner, crying tears of terror.

Like a wild animal, the dead man jumped onto a chair, leaped to another one, then seemed to fly across the room with his leap. The young blonde woman managed one scream before she was attacked, then her cries became muffled as the dead man fed on her, his face buried in the crook of her neck.

The now bald Good Samaritan's eyes snapped opened and he rolled to his feet, growling and moaning like he was in pain. His eyes darted back and forth, and as a shrieking woman ran past him, he reached out his hand and grabbed her by the hair. Yanking back, he pulled her to him, then forced her to the floor where he sank his teeth into her cheek. She screamed so loud for a moment her voice topped all others, then her screams turned to sobs as the man feasted on her again and again.

The young blonde woman was dead on the floor, her eyes staring at nothing. But no sooner did she die, then her limbs began to twitch and her pupils began to move again.

Swiveling her head slightly, she found she couldn't move too well thanks to half of the flesh and muscle torn away from her throat. Coming to her knees, she crawled across the floor, slid under a chair, and sank her teeth into a juicy ankle.

The old woman looked down to see a bloody face feasting on her leg and she cried out for help. But there was no one to help her, and she was pulled from her chair where she was climbed on and promptly torn apart, the Good Samaritan joining in the fun, the dead man and woman like a gore-covered tag-team.

They feasted on the old woman like she was a gazelle and they were lions, after taking down their kill in the wild. Red-tinged hands dug deep into wrinkled skin, tearing off the offending clothing to get at the soft flesh and entrails within.

The old woman was alive for most of her death, her mouth stuck in an 'O' shape as her eyes popped out of her head like a character in a Tex Avery cartoon.

That ended quickly when another raging, undead killer reached down with two fingers and plucked one, then two eyeballs out of their sockets.

Like they were quail eggs, the killer popped one and then the other eye into his mouth, chewing happily as eye juice squirted between his lips like he had eaten a grape tomato.

When he was finished, he turned and went after another hapless soul.

James and Steve were standing in the far corner of the room, along with another man who was still holding his laptop. All three were staring in wide-eyed horror at the carnage before them.

"We're trapped!" Steve yelled. "The fuckers locked all the doors!"

"It's procedure in a situation like this," the third man said.

Steve looked at the man as if he had sprouted horns. "And what fucking situation is this exactly?"

"Fuck if I know," the man shrugged. "But acts of violence, like a riot, are locked down until it can be contained."

"This isn't a riot," James said as he watched a man get taken down by three blood-soaked people with mortal wounds to their bodies.

As he stared at the gore-fest, his mind tried to take it all in. He watched one blood-covered, animalistic person at a time attack a normal person, taking them down and killing them in the most horrific way imaginable.

Then, after less than a minute after death, the victim woke up and began attacking others, now joining the killers who murdered them.

One of the raging killers broke through the pack and came at the three men. James held his fists up, ready to fight to the last, but the undead killer went right for the third man, as if he was a missile homing in on its target.

The third man yelped in terror and used his laptop as a weapon, swinging it sideways and connecting with the attacker's face.

Teeth and pieces of the inset keyboard went flying in all directions as the dead killer went falling backwards.

The third man had broken the dead man's jaw, and it now hung like a trap door on loose hinges.

But the man wasn't down yet, and with a growl and a roar, he lunged for the third man again. Both went down in a tangle of arms and legs as James jumped back, not wanting to get involved.

But when a young woman with a curvaceous form and a hunger for human meat came at him, James had no choice but to punch her in the face. The woman took a step backward as her head snapped back from the blow.

No sooner did she do this then she righted herself and came at him again.

She never got close though, because Steve used a chair to whack her on the back, right at her shoulders, sending her to the floor with a broken neck.

She twitched and writhed on the floor as her nerve endings shut down, then went limp, her eyes still open and glazing over in death.

The room was slowly shifting from screaming, suffering normal people to walking dead killers with a taste for human flesh.

Steve and James backed into the furthest corner, both standing back to back as close to one hundred jurors slowly stopped feeding on their victims and turned their attentions to the last remaining normals in the room.

James looked around, at the barred windows, the locked doors, and the blood-covered faces dripping gore from chins and mouths, and he realized he was absolutely and totally screwed.

Just before the undead horde came for him, he couldn't help but roll his eyes and say, "Civic duty my ass. I should have said I was a racist on the return flyer."

JUST BECAUSE

The pliers were cold and slippery as they slid into Seth's mouth; he could taste the metal.

The rough metal teeth on the tool scraped against his rear left molar, the operator of the pliers lazy, not worrying about whether or not he was pinching the tongue. The upper and lower ends of the pliers locked down on the tooth and Seth squeezed his eyes shut, knowing what was coming.

There was a slight pause as the owner of the tool braced himself, then there was a blinding white pain and the tooth was ripped from its mooring of twenty-six years.

Blood exploded outward from the gaping hole in his lower gum and Seth let loose a blood-soaked scream that would have shattered glass.

The scream was long and loud, filled with pain and suffering. In time, the screaming abated and Seth grew quiet once more. His lower jaw throbbed with each pulse of his heart and he felt like he was going to throw up. Bile crept to the top of his throat and he knew any second he would vomit.

His vision swam with white light as the agony that was his mouth subsided to a dull roar. When he was finally able to open his eyes, he found himself looking up at his torturer.

The man was tall, well over six feet, with muscles that strained his tight shirt. His simple pair of blue jeans and the tight shirt was now covered in blood splatter. Seth knew that it was his blood splatter he saw.

"Please, no more, don't do this to me," Seth whimpered, but just like before when he'd begged the torturer for mercy, his pleas were ignored. "Why? Why are you doing this to me?" he whispered, wanting to know the answer, but as always the tall man who was causing him so much pain said nothing.

Seth looked up once more at the mask-covered face, wishing he could at least make eye contact, but the mesh over the eyes hid everything, and all he could see was the hint of the orbs hiding within.

The man picked up a four inch long, thin stick, reminding Seth of a shish kabob skewer. Without preamble, the man placed the skewer at the tip of Seth's left index finger, the pointed tip touching just under his fingernail.

As the tip touched the tender flesh under his nail, Seth yelped, knowing what was coming and ill prepared to handle it.

"Please, God, no, don't do it. For the love of all that's holy, don't do it," he begged, tears running down his cheeks in a steady stream.

The man still acted like Seth wasn't there, as if the hand didn't belong to another human being, and with a flexing of his arm, he slid the skewer under the fingernail, causing Seth to shriek in agony. There was no way to truly describe the intense pain he felt and he thought he was going to black out, praying he would, but there was no mercy for him, no relief as he stayed conscious.

His entire hand and his lower arm felt like it was dipped in acid, the skewer sliding in with little difficulty, slicing through the meat of his finger. It felt like the skewer had been shoved in more than a foot, though in reality one small inch was all, and as the white light of pain danced across his vision, Seth prayed for death once more.

But he knew it wouldn't come, for if his torturer wanted him dead, he would have killed him a thousand times over already.

As Seth's mind swam with fog at the pain he felt, he tried once more to remember how he ended up in the chair of a torturer.

He remembered going to the night club, drinking, having a good time. He stayed till closing, and as the few other patrons and himself left to find their cars, he remembered reaching into his coat pocket and retrieving his keys.

It was as he was about to slide the key into the door lock that he caught the hint of a reflection in the side window, then he felt hot pain in his neck as his body began to convulse before he passed out. He now knew it was a taser that was used on him.

When he awoke, he was secured to the chair, his arms tied to each side of the arm rests, and his ankles were tied to the two front legs of the chair.

He was in the same room he was in now; bleak, no windows with peeling paint, dirt on the floor, and one naked bulb hanging from the ceiling on an old extension cord. It reminded him of a small room in a warehouse, a stockroom perhaps, but each time he screamed and no one came to help him, he knew that wherever he was, no one was around to hear him beg for mercy.

He was absolutely and totally at the mercy of his captor, a man who hid his face from view.

He cried out again as the car battery sent waves of voltage into his genitals. The torturer had placed the positive and negative ends to his scrotum, the two inch alligator clips biting into his flesh enough to illicit screams of agony by themselves. But then the man flicked the switch and let the electrical current flow to his groin and the rest of his body, the clips then becoming a mild nuisance in comparison.

His body spasmed and jerked in the chair and his hair stood on end. He wet himself and was glad his pants were now lying in the corner of the room. Even as he twitched from being electrocuted, he found it ironic he would so much as give a passing thought to his pants. After all, at the moment, urine on his pants was the least of his problems.

The torturer flicked the switch and the current stopped. Seth let his head sink onto his chest as he shook his head to clear it, saliva dripping out of the corner of his mouth to spill onto his chest. Electrocution was an agony there was no actual description for either. The closest thing was when a person got zapped messing with an electrical outlet but for some reason couldn't let go. If the current continued feeding into the body, as teeth chattered and limbs locked up, that was as close to a description as was possible. The switch was flicked once more and Seth began to jump in the chair, his arms and legs straining at their bonds. He began to smell an odd odor, sweet, as if someone was cooking meat on a barbeque grill, and when he realized he smelled himself cooking, he threw up, splashing warm vomit between his legs.

The torturer jumped back so as not to be splashed and he backhanded Seth with a blow that had his teeth rattling in his mouth. The switch was flicked and a second later the current ceased.

Finished with this part of the torture, the large man simply yanked at the two electrical cords attached to Seth's scrotum. The metal alligator clips refused to let go of the flesh between their teeth and that skin went with them as they were pulled away. Seth yelled out once more and looked down at a pool of blood in his crotch. His balls were bleeding now and he let out long wail, as any man would do in the same circumstance.

Defiance filled him and he hissed at his torturer, spitting bloody vomit across the distance separating them from one another.

"Bastard, so help me if I get out of this fucking chair, then we'll see how tough you are!"

The torturer's shoulders shook and Seth believed the man was laughing.

"Don't fucking laugh at me! Why are you doing this to me! Tell me, you bastard!"

The large man didn't reply but instead walked over to a small steel table which had on its smooth surface an assortment of knifes and other implements used in torturing a human being. He hovered over the scalpels, knives and needles, and Seth watched with wide eyes, knowing what the large hand landed on would spell more suffering for him.

So when the hand landed on a simple metal spoon, such as one used with tea and biscuits on a sunny afternoon, to say Seth was relieved was an understatement.

"Hah, a fucking spoon? What the hell are you gonna do with that? Make me eat a bowl of soup?"

No answer was forthcoming but Seth still felt a surge of renewed energy. Perhaps his captor had run out of ideas and the torture was finally over.

The man crossed the distance separating them and he hovered over Seth, gazing down on him from behind his mask. Seth watched the man's chest go in and out as he breathed.

The man reached out with his left hand and it locked onto Seth's forehead, pushing it back to the point his neck might very well snap. Seth struggled to break free, but with his limbs firmly secured, he had no leverage. Desperate, he spit a glob of coagulated blood onto the man's shirt, then clacked his teeth to no avail.

He still didn't know what was going to happen and he had to admit that after everything he'd been through, to have his neck snapped now seemed silly, anti-climatic, but he waited for what was to come next.

He didn't wait long.

As the man held Seth's head in place, the right hand holding the spoon slowly came up and hovered in front of Seth's eyes. It waved like a snake in a trance, moving back and forth.

Then, like a striking snake, the spoon dove downwards and the tip slid into the side of Seth's right eye. The metal was cold as it dug in deep, the spoon separating membranes and ganglia as it went in deep enough that the man pulled on the handle and popped out the eye like a melon baller to a piece of cantaloupe.

On the right side of Seth's vision, it was like someone had flicked a light switch, the world going dark as blinding pain filled his skull. He screamed as the spoon scooped out his eye, leaving a bloody, gaping socket behind. As he screamed, the open socket touched the air and Seth could feel the cool air caressing the inside of the raw socket. He blinked with his remaining eye but the right side of his vision remained dark.

No sooner did he slow his screaming, the pain finally subsiding to a dull throb, then the torturer brought back the spoon once more. The tip was now bloody, dripping with a clear fluid, and Seth, even in his madness, wondered where his eye had gone to. Where was it now? Did the man toss it into the trash? Or was it in a jar with chemicals to preserve it?

He never received an answer before the spoon was going in once more and the last image he saw was the mask of his captor, then the spoon went in deep and his other eye popped out to plunge his world into darkness.

Seth sat in the chair, sobbing, his world now nothing but darkness. He could feel the blood and ooze sliding down his cheeks from his gaping eye sockets, his eyes now torn from his skull.

He didn't know how long he was left to wallow in misery but finally he heard footsteps and someone breathing. His head popped up and he muffled his cries, his ears now straining to pick up any telltale noise. With no sight, his nose also picked up the slack and he detected a musky smell that hadn't been there before.

It was his captor, his torturer, returning from whence he came; back to do more evil unto him no doubt.

"Why?" Why are you doing this to me? What did I do to deserve this?" Seth cried as his head fell back to his chest.

Once more there was no answer, but his head was grabbed by the hair and snapped back so his neck was exposed.

Though eyeless, he squeezed his eyelids closed, waiting for the final end, and truth be told, he welcomed it now. He was in so much pain he could barely breathe and death seemed like a welcome release.

Something metallic was being picked up, he could hear the rattle on the nearby table and then he tasted metal again.

"Oh, God no, no more!" he screamed around the end of the pliers but the captor ignored his pleas and went to work once more. Like a dentist from a B horror movie, the man was cruel beyond words. Not settling for one simple molar, this time he began tearing out tooth after tooth, Seth screaming as each one was ripped from his mouth in a bloody spray.

Bloody drool slid from his mouth to coat his chest in crimson and he howled in utter agony, the unbelievable pain causing him to pass out more than once.

But smelling salt aroused him each time and the torturer went right back to work. Seth wondered if when he passed out the man would go grab a smoke, maybe a cup of coffee. Like a man in an office building, he would pause and run to the smoking area, suck on a cancer stick to then run back to his cubicle and resume working.

When all but two of his front teeth were removed, leaving his gums a wrecked amalgam of raw meat, he left Seth alone again. He couldn't see but nevertheless, white light flashed before his mind's eye as his mouth throbbed with the electricity of exposed nerves. It felt like he was gargling lava, the nerves flaring each time he breathed. He passed out more than once but sooner or later would awake once more.

Time lost all meaning in his prison of darkness and agony. Days, weeks, or perhaps minutes, it all was one large entity to him now.

His captor returned when he was awake one time and the torture began anew.

Seth heard him pause and then the sound of a glass jar being opened. Even in his agony, he was amazed how sharp his hearing had become in such a short time. He had heard when a person loses their sight, their other senses grow stronger, but he had never truly believed it until now.

There was a lull in the torture as the man did something with the jar. Seth continued to move his head to the left and right, trying to pick up a telltale sound.

And then something touched his leg, something cold.

No sooner did the liquid touch him then the cold turned into searing heat that filled him from his toes to his head. He shrieked loudly, spitting blood and phlegm from his mouth. As he shrieked in pain, his nose detected the scent of burning meat and he quickly realized it was *his* meat he smelled.

Acid! It was acid!

Another few drops touched his other leg and he roared in agony as the acid ate into his leg, his flesh and muscle dissolving into a sticky red goo.

He kicked his legs as if he could shrug off the acid but it did nothing to slow its descent into his limbs, and soon he couldn't even do that. The acid had eaten into his legs to the point the nerves to control the legs had been severed.

He passed out again, but was quickly revived, and as he swooned in delirium, he heard something that had his stomach falling out from within him.

He heard his legs drop off and fall to the floor from where they had been severed from his thighs, thanks to the acid eating away at the flesh and bone.

With the wounds cauterized, he wasn't going to bleed out, and though his legs were now long gone, he swore he could still feel them.

As if it was a game, his captor picked up the legs and slapped him with them a few times, his own feet striking him in the cheeks to leave welts and bruises. Just before he passed out, and heard the sound of his legs being tossed into a corner of the room. Then he welcomed the oblivion once more.

Smelling salts revived him and though technically awake, he was so out of it from the pain he could barely think straight.

Suddenly he felt something cold slice across his left bicep and he let out a small yell. A second later, another cold slice went across his lower arm, then another and another all over his body. At first he didn't understand. Though it stung, it was certainly not as painful as the other tortures he'd received at the hands of his captor but then, as the air slowly touched the paper thin cuts, he realized what his captor had planned.

Similar to a Chinese torture, he was being cut, sliced if you will, dozens upon dozens of times. The thin cuts stung with an intensity that a simple slice from a knife could never accomplish, the razor thin slices were similar to paper cuts and each one stung a little more with each passing second until it felt like his entire body was on fire.

He didn't know how many shallow wounds he received, but he knew when his captor was through he was going mad with the stings as each one throbbed and pulsed with a life of its own. It was like an itch he couldn't scratch and he yelled and jumped in his chair, but he was trapped and would never be free.

"Oh God, fucking kill me and get it over with, you son-of-a-bitch!" he growled, the words slurring without all but two of his teeth. And he did want to die. Sightless, no legs, pretty much no teeth, death would be a welcome release from the hell his life now was. And yet he still didn't know why this was happening to him.

He detected the torturer near him and he shifted his head, trying to hear where the man was.

He quickly found out when yet another skewer was placed under the fingernail of his left thumb, the wood jammed deep, causing him to shriek loudly. Red spittle flew from his mouth and phlegm dripped from his nostrils as he cried and shook with agony.

His world was now nothing but blinding pain wrapped in a sea of darkness and he cried and screamed, switching out which one depending on the torture.

And then, through his sobs, he heard the unmistakable sound of a blade being honed on a sharpening stone. By the breadth of the scraping blade, Seth knew it was long, and visions of pangas and machetes flitted through his mind.

He wondered if this was finally it. If this was the time when he would finally be released from the prison that was his mangled body. He felt something being tied around his right wrist—rope by the feel of it—and when it was pulled taut, he yelped but controlled his voice. He knew if he was yelling then he couldn't hear what his captor was doing to him.

No sooner did the rope grow tight then his hand began to hurt as all blood was prevented from flowing into it. The man walked away and the honing of the blade continued.

As Seth's hand began to throb, reminding him of how it felt when as a boy he had wrapped a rubber band around his index finger and watched the tip grow purple from lack of blood, the sharpening stopped. Then he heard footsteps and he muffled his sobs as he listened to the large man step ever closer.

He didn't hear the blade rise into the air nor hear it fall, but he did feel it when the blade chopped off his hand, a bolt of lightning-quick pain filling his mind and causing him to pass out as soon as it suffused his body.

When he awoke, his hand throbbed, but when he tried to move it he could feel nothing. The more he tried to wiggle the hand, the more he could feel nothing, though there seemed to be a phantom ghost of the limb still there.

He could hear heavy breathing near him, and just before another burst of blinding pain filled his insides like liquid fire, he realized his other wrist had been wrapped in rope, then the blade came down and the hand was lopped off to fall to the floor in a splatter of blood.

Once more he slid into unconsciousness, the overwhelming pain too much for his receptors.

He came to again, lost in a world of darkness. He didn't know how long he stayed that way and each time he passed out he hoped it would be his last, but smelling salts would always revive him.

But no matter how much his captor wanted to make him suffer, there was only so long a body could survive the abuse his was receiving and now the only defiance he had was to die, to finally spoil the fun his torturer was having.

But what could he do to kill himself? He was tied to a chair, no legs and no hands, sightless, what felt like a hundred stinging yet shallow wounds covering his body. Even if he lived, if right now he was saved, what kind of a life would he have?

He wracked his pain-befuddled mind to figure out some way to kill himself, but nothing came to mind.

Until one idea, though drastic as it was, finally came to him.

He didn't know if he could do it but he had no choice.

For whatever reason, his captor had left him two teeth, both at the front of his mouth. They weren't properly lined up but he shoved his tongue between them, the slippery muscle slipping out more than once.

He could hear his torturer puttering about, and he heard the sound of metal objects, that noise letting him know more pain was to follow soon.

He clicked his remaining teeth together but each time his tongue slid free. He could hear his captor walking toward him now and he let out a soft whimper and forced his tongue between the two teeth, then clamped down as hard as he could. Pain flared in his head as he began to grind the two teeth together, shredding his tongue into a mangled mess. Even when the two teeth had sliced into the tongue, he opened his mouth, repositioned his tongue, and then slammed the teeth together, more pain filling him until he wondered if he would pass out yet again.

As his teeth shredded his tongue, he tasted blood, a lot of it, as it began to slide down his throat. At first he tried to swallow it out of instinct, but as more and more hot blood gushed out of his mangled tongue and slid down his throat, he found he couldn't keep up.

But that was what he wanted to happen.

He began to drown on blood.

He heard his captor yell, "No!" and the man raced to Seth, trying to pry open his mouth. But with a resolve of a dead man Seth refused to open, though fingers probed around his lips and force their way into his mouth.

Unable to keep his jaw shut, the fingers pried his lips apart but the blood continued to flow, slipping out onto his chest as well as down his throat.

"No, no, you bastard, you can't die, not yet! I'm not done with you!" his captor yelled in frustration.

Seth began to laugh as his lungs filled with blood. He was dying, and best of all, he was cheating his torturer of killing Seth himself.

He began to cough, his breathing becoming difficult, and as the torturer cut his bonds and threw him to the floor to work on him, trying to save him with CPR, Seth knew the man was too late.

His mind was growing fuzzy and he knew this time he would not awake, and he managed one last word to his captor, though he didn't expect an answer. "*Why?*"

He was sliding into the dark void of death, but this time his torturer replied, knowing his victim was done for.

"No reason, really, just because."

In his last second on Earth, after hearing that statement, Seth knew if he'd had just one more second, he would have laughed at the irony of it all.

But that second was denied him.

KRAMER'S FOLLY

Kramer slapped the bugs away from his face as he made his way through the dense underbrush of the African coast and back to his hired ship. Sweat beaded on his skin, making his entire body feel like a slick eel. His thighs chafed and he had more bug bites on his skin than he could count.

For the hundredth time since setting sail from Charleston, he was regretting his decision to come to Africa.

But then he thought about the money he was saving by finding and capturing his own slaves and his pains went away.

The slave trade was one of many mouths, all wanting to be fed. By the time a slave was captured in Africa and transported back home, it had exchanged so many hands that the price was quadrupled, if not worse.

So Kramer, being the thrifty soul he was, had decided to hire a ship and set sail for Africa himself, planning on taking his own slaves to bring back to Charleston to work on his cotton plantation. And he knew in the economy of 1854, every penny saved was a penny earned.

And though he was miserable beyond miserable, his plan had worked flawlessly.

Behind him, led by two Spaniards helpers, he led an even score of slaves, each manacled to the last so that if one tried to escape, the other nineteen would stop the escapee fast.

Kramer had swooped into their village just before sunrise, and after killing five of the village men who tried to attack and stop him, the rest had fallen in line, fearing for their lives. There had been so many before they had escaped into the surrounding forest and it killed him to let them go, but he had filled his quota nicely.

Kramer smiled as he eyed the ten dark men and ten women, admiring the exposed breasts of the women. Well, all except one that is. Nine of the women were young and healthy, but the Spaniard hadn't followed his orders to the letter and had taken an old woman for the tenth. She was weak and could barely keep up the pace he set.

As Kramer turned to look at the old crone, she fell yet again, her fellow slaves picking her up again.

Kramer motioned to one of the Spaniards as he gestured to the old, woman.

"Why in blazes did you pick her, José, she can barely walk as it is. She'll never make it back to the ship."

José nodded respectfully and moved closer to Kramer.

"I am sorry, señor Kramer. When I took the other women the old woman insisted on coming, too." His accent was heavy but Kramer could understand him. The other Spaniard didn't speak a lick of English, but that was fine as long as one of his helpers could.

"Are you serious? That is madness. When they see slavers coming, the black bastards run for the hills, they don't demand to be thrown into irons."

"Si, si, señor, but she did. I had no choice. It was either that or kill her."

"Hmmph, should have killed the old maid." He pulled his revolver and prepared to do just that when the Spaniard stepped in front of him.

"No, wait, señor. I know a little of the language and the old woman is holy to them. If you kill her the others will be trouble."

"So what? I will just kill one or two to keep the rest in line."

"Si, si, but won't that cut into your profit, señor. *Our* profit?"

Kramer halted then, realizing the Spaniard was correct. He had promised to pay a cut of the sales of the slaves to José in payment, and if he went ahead and began killing them, then his gross earnings would suffer. That would be foolish. No, he would only kill a slave if he had no choice.

"Very well, José, I have to agree with you. But the old woman better not slow us down. We need to get to the ship by nightfall so we can sail out with the morning tide."

"Si, si, we will, señor." He turned and barked a few words in the native tongue of the slaves and they seemed to stand taller, though the hatred in their eyes never waned. The old woman was helped to her feet and they set off again, all the while Kramer thinking of the money he would make once he returned to Charleston. For he only needed fifteen slaves to work his plantation, the rest he would sell on the open market. Those would pay for the entire trip, leaving him with what basically came down to slaves taken for nothing, and a profit to boot. He only wished he could have taken more than twenty, but they were enough of a handful with only himself and his two helpers to keep in line. As he trudged through the underbrush, he was already making plans to return with a larger crew next month. And then he would take back triple the number!

Why, it was like minting coins himself, this doing it yourself. Cut out the middle man. He was just glad more people didn't think of it.

Less than a mile from where the ship was moored, the old woman faltered once more, stopping the other slaves in their tracks. As Kramer turned to investigate, the slaves surrounded the old woman, wanting to protect her.

Kramer shoved the barrel of his pistol under a tall, male black's chin, his eyes cold as he stared at the slave.

"Best you move out of my way, blackie, or I'll make an example out of ya."

José moved to Kramer's side, touching his shoulder slightly. "No, señor, wait, please. Let me see if I can get them moving again."

"Fair enough, but my temper wanes with the night," he told his helper as he lowered the pistol. José called to the other Spaniard in his native language and the two moved into the crowd of slaves. Kramer stood a few feet away, wary of any of the slaves trying anything. Kramer knew it would be foolhardy on their account to try, but he had heard stories from other traders when at the market for purchasing new help.

They told tales of how faced with a life of servitude under the white man, slaves were known to do desperate acts, even if it meant losing their lives.

Kramer could hear José talking to some of the slaves, the banter going back and forth for almost two minutes before he called José to him.

"Well?" Kramer demanded.

José shook his head sadly. "The old woman, she is dead, señor. The slaves want to bury her, at least that way she will be one with Mother Earth."

"Out of the question. There is no time and even if there was I won't waste time on a slave, especially a dead one. No, unshackle the corpse and toss it into the brush. The scavengers will have a feast this night."

"I don't think they will like that, señor Kramer," José said as he looked at his feet.

"I don't give a damn what they like! They are my property now and they will do as told or I will see them suffer! And that goes for the people that work for me. Do I make myself clear?"

"Si, si, señor, perfectly," José said as he turned to his fellow helper and they began unshackling the corpse of the old woman. No sooner did they begin then three of the slaves tried to stop the two Spaniards, pushing them away from the corpse.

José punched one away and the slave struck back. It was possible an uprising may have taken place right then and there if not for Kramer firing a shot into the air. Birds in nearby trees took flight and the night went silent as the report echoed throughout the forest.

"Enough! The next black bastard who so much as looks at one of my men cross-eyed will get a bullet in the head!"

He could see the slaves didn't understand him, but they understood the pistol in his hand. They knew it could kill without Kramer so much as blinking his eyes.

The slaves fell back, their desire to live overriding even their protection of the old woman.

Kramer pointed to the corpse. "All right, José, dispose of that now so we can keep moving."

José motioned to the other Spaniard and the two men quickly unlocked the manacles on the corpse. Once finished, they gathered the withered dark body and walked to the side of the beaten path, then carelessly tossed it into the shrubs. When the body landed roughly, it became impaled on a fallen tree, the broken branches like spears. The neck cracked and the head was nearly turned around, the eyes open and staring at the ground in death.

As one, the slaves howled in loss and grief of their holy mother and José and the other helper moved closer to Kramer, fearing the slaves as they moaned and wailed.

As Kramer watched, they began to chant, a steady rhythm that conjured up the depths of the African continent. It was as if jungle drums could be heard, steadily pounding to the rhythm of a beating heart.

"What are they doing?" Kramer asked José as he began to sweat nervously.

"They are mourning their lost mother, señor. And…"

"And what?" Kramer demanded. "Out with it, what are they saying?"

"They are singing: 'Death to Kramer, Death to Kramer.' "

Kramer's eyes went cold and José nodded as he studied his worn shoes once more. "I am sorry, señor, but that is what they are saying."

Kramer listened for another few seconds, glaring at the dark sweating bodies, at the nineteen slaves he had left, and then he shrugged. "No matter, they can sing for my death all they want. As long as they march I am a happy man. Now, José, get them moving, we have a timetable to keep."

"Si, señor," José said and he moved to the rear of the slaves. He had a whip for times such as these and he used it now, whipping the closest bodies. The song went up in pitch as the slaves cried out in pain, but eventually they began to walk once more.

Kramer walked along side them, listening to the chanting the entire time. *Let them sing! Let them sing all the way back to Charleston, for all the good it would do them*, he thought as he began to count his money in his head.

With dawn only hours away, Kramer finally led the slaves to his waiting ship.

Far from any coastal town, the ship was anchored just off the shore. After piling the slaves into the boat and making them row, Kramer soon found himself on the sturdy deck of the ship, the slaver-captain, McBride, standing next to him as he supervised the storing of the slaves in the ship's hold.

"We're ready to leave as soon as the tide rolls in, sir," McBride told Kramer. "And there is plenty of room in the hold for that lot you brought. A fine looking group, too, if I may say so, sir. I'll have my men take off those irons once they're situated."

"No, Captain, do nothing of the kind. Leave those manacles where they are," Kramer ordered.

"But, sir, slaves don't do well in shackles. They won't eat and they get sick, dampens their spirits, you see. Some may even die on the trip back to Charleston."

Kramer turned to stare the captain in the eye.

"I pay you for your expertise as a captain, my good sir. I thank you not to give me advice on how to treat my property."

"Aye, 'tis true, and I shall honor your wishes, sir." The captain cocked his head as if listening. "Sir, do you know what they are saying down there? They seem to be chanting it over and over."

Kramer waved it off. "Ignore it, Captain. One of their number, an old crone, died in the trek back to the ship. They are mourning her."

The captain nodded but then he cocked his head again. "But, sir, it sounds like they are saying your name as well. Is that true?"

Kramer knew it was but was not in the mood for idle chatter.

"Whether it is or not is none of your concern, Captain. Please make your ship ready to sail. It's a long journey back home and I wish to take my leave of this ghastly continent."

"Aye, sir, I'll do just that." The captain turned and began hollering orders as his crew began to work. Kramer eyed the removable floorboards that led to the hold, now replaced and refastened. He could hear the chanting easily through the decking, and though he refused to admit it, it made him shudder.

The following day, a few hours before nightfall, a white sail was spotted on the horizon.

Captain McBride stood at the aft deck with a telescope as he studied the distant ship. Still on the horizon, the ship would disappear with each wave it crested, only to reappear. But it was easy to see the ship was making good time in their direction.

"Damn it," McBride cursed, " 'tis a British ship of war, sir. And she's seen us."

"So?" Kramer spit.

"No, sir, you do not understand. The British have sworn to stamp out slavery. If they catch us with what is in the hold, they'll scuttle the ship and take us all into irons. It will be over for us one and all."

"Then I suggest we lose them, Captain," Kramer said as he eyed the bouncing dot on the horizon.

McBride nodded and began yelling once more. His crew went into action, raising the sails and trying to squeeze as much speed out of the northerly wind. Kramer watched the activity with a nod, then paused as he heard the chanting once more. The black bastards were still at it, it seemed. Well, they could sing till they were hoarse, for all the good it would serve.

Captain McBride's crew did their best to coax more speed from the wind but in time, as night was about to fall, the British ship was much closer.

McBride stood at the aft deck once more, and when he lowered his telescope, he shook his head.

"It's no use, sir," he said to Kramer. "They'll be on us soon." He pointed to a flash of light on the British ship. "See that? That is the signal to lay to and wait for them to board us." He shook his head. "It's over. We'll spend the rest of our lives in the Queen's jail."

"No we won't, sir!" Kramer yelled. "Keep going, just till nightfall."

"But sir, they will catch us. They are sailing four feet for our every two. We have no chance of escape."

"Nay, good Captain, escape isn't my plan; just keep us out of their reach before nightfall and I promise you we will be safe."

Desperate and with little option, Captain McBride nodded. "Aye, sir, that I can do, but not by much." Then he went back to making his crew work harder. Kramer called José to him who was always within earshot.

"Si, señor?"

"José, get the slaves ready and have them on deck when I give the word."

"Señor?" José asked, not understanding.

"Just do it, José, no backtalk. Unless you would like to spend the rest of your life hanging in a cell in London?"

"No, señor, no I would not. It shall be done."

Captain McBride was true to his word and he managed to keep the British ship in their wake, and as night fell and the British ship wasn't able to discern what was happening on the deck of the slaver ship, Kramer called José to him.

"It's time. Get the slaves on deck, and hurry man, there is no time to waste!"

"Si, si," José said as he had his fellow Spaniard and a few of the ship's crew to help him.

In five minutes time, all nineteen slaves were on deck, each glaring hatefully at Kramer. None looked broken, each still holding the spirit of free men in their hearts.

Kramer chuckled as he walked to the first slave in line and picked up the hanging manacle from which the old woman had been affixed.

The slaves were amidships and only a few feet away was the ship's anchor. With a malevolent look on his face, his eyes gleaming in the wan light as dusk fell across the ocean, he clamped the open manacle to the chain of the anchor.

As he worked, the chanting began once more, Kramer now recognizing his name in the rhythm.

"Keep going, you black bastards, you won't be singing much longer. There is more of you in Africa, and when I return, I will recoup my losses from this voyage and still come out ahead." He stood up from the chain with a wide grin on his face. "Here, have a drink on me!" Without waiting for a reply, he kicked the anchor off the opening on the deck rail and watched it splash into the murky water. The coiled chain began to play out and at first no one understood what was happening. That is until the chain went taut and the first slave in line was tugged off his feet to slide across the decking, following the same path as the anchor.

As the slave began to slide, the rest of the chained slaves were pulled as well, a tug of war they could not possibly win.

One at a time, they were pulled from their feet, to slide across the decking, screaming and scrabbling for purchase. Fingernails broke and bloody trails were streaked across the decking as wails of torment and doom filled the night.

One after another, the manacled slaves were pulled into the ocean depths, each one into the water adding to the weight so that the rest could never so much as attempt to halt their progress.

By the time the last of the nineteen were sliding down the deck, the look in their eyes was absolutely chilling. The dread and fear was palpable, as each man in the ship's crew stood in utter shock at what Kramer had wrought, at the merciless murder of nineteen souls—no matter what color their skin.

As the last one went screaming into the ocean, Kramer turned, and his grin faltered when he saw the faces of the crew. "What! Stop looking at me like that. I did what had to be done. If they were found on this ship, we'd all be in irons with them? I saved you all. I'm a goddamn hero!" He pointed at McBride. "You told me the British would show no mercy. I saved your ship, Captain."

"Aye, sir, I guess you did, but at what price to our very souls?"

"Bah, rubbish, all of it. They were nothing but slaves. Now stay out of the British's reach until daybreak so they don't know anything is afoot."

Captain McBride nodded and did as he was ordered, staying just out of reach of the British warship.

As the dawn touched the horizon, the chase was over and the British ship fired a warning shot across the slaver's bow, and they were hailed and ordered to drop sails and be boarded.

McBride did as ordered and minutes later a small boat with four solders and an officer pulled away from the British ship and crossed the small distance between the two vessels.

Boarding, the British officer signaled the four soldiers to lower weapons as the man studied the deck of the ship and the crew men on display.

"We are here to search this vessel. Do you deny me permission?" the officer asked, though everyone knew the result if the answer was no.

McBride, standing next to Kramer, nodded respectfully. "My ship is your ship, go where you please, sir."

The Englishman grunted and sent his soldiers to begin their search. He didn't need protection, for the British ship of war had its cannons trained on the slaver. One act of defiance and the slaver would be sent to the ocean floor.

Time passed and eventually the soldiers returned. One stepped up to the Englishman and whispered into his ear. When the report was made, the man looked at both McBride and Kramer. "It appears no slaves were found but the odor of men packed in your hold like cattle still exists."

Kramer weaved the accusation away as if he were at a tea party. "Nonsense, there are no slaves here. If there were, where are they now, my good sir? I think you should watch yourself before accusing good citizens of wrong doing."

McBride said nothing, though he was sweating profusely.

"Indeed," the Englishman said, scowling. "But we both know they were here, murderer, and where they went, and if I could prove it without a doubt what you have done, I would see you join me back in England to spend the rest of your natural life in a jail cell."

"Ah yes, sir, but you can't, because there were never any slaves on this ship. In fact, my good sir, I believe you should apologize and take your leave of us. We are on a tight schedule and don't have the time to lay about all morning in the middle of the ocean."

The officer pointed to where the ship's anchor should have been. "And how do you explain that? All ships have an anchor. Why is yours missing?" His tone of voice told Kramer he knew exactly where the missing anchor was and what it had been used for.

"It was..." Captain McBride interjected but Kramer cut him off.

"A simple mishap, sir, that is all. It will be replaced at the next port we moor at," Kramer grinned.

The Englishman looked dejected at having no case. "We will meet again, sir, I promise you that. And next time it is I who will be the victor. Your type of butchery *will* be punished. If not by me then by some other."

"That sounds like a threat, sir, I think you have overstayed your welcome. I now say good day to you," Kramer said indignantly.

The officer and his men disembarked the ship and sailed back to the waiting British ship of war.

Kramer, looking smug, patted the captain on the shoulder. "Ah, well, Captain. Profit and Loss, profit and loss. Take me home, sir, I have had enough adventure for a while."

As the British ship veered off and headed south, Captain McBride got his ship underway.

Two weeks and a day later found Kramer at his home. His plantation was only a mile from the sea and on this night he found himself tossing and turning in his bed.

As he lay sleeping, he began to hear a familiar chanting. At first he remained asleep, lost in the nightmare, but something caused him to snap awake.

Looking around his bedroom, at first he thought himself back on the slave ship, after leaving Africa. And then he realized why.

The chanting.

It was the same one the slaves had voiced and had continued to voice after he had disposed of the old woman's corpse.

Sitting up in bed, he looked left and right, as if he expected to see the slaves in his bedroom, but though the chanting continued, there was no one in the room with him.

Sliding his feet into his slippers, he stood up and went to the window overlooking the northern side of his property. Over the trees, a mile away, he could just see the glint of the moon off the ocean and the footpath at the edge of his property that would take him there.

The chanting seemed louder now, as if it was coming directly from below his window. Opening it, he looked out into the darkness, but there was no one to be found.

Thinking it was some sort of trick, some prank by someone from the ship—a crew member perhaps who hadn't been able to live with what Kramer had done, he went to his mantle and opened the top drawer. Here he took out two pistols.

They were well crafted, with polished grips and hair triggers. He had practiced many a day in the fields behind his home and could shoot the wings off a fly at twenty paces. Many a man had also suffered the guns first hand when he was challenged to a duel. Five so far and he had not so much as suffered a scratch, while the men he'd gone up against were now six feet under the cold earth.

With dexterity made from constant practice, he poured in glazed powder from a small container, dropped in two leaded balls, then set percussion caps on the touchholes.

Now armed and feeling more confident, he turned up the light of the lantern on his bedside table and slowly crept down the steps leading from the second to the first floor of his home.

Passing the doors to the servants' quarters, he paused for a moment, wondering if one of them could be the originator of this ruse, but then decided it was impossible. No servant would dare play a prank on him, not if they didn't want to suffer twenty lashes in the courtyard when he found out.

No, it must be from an outside source.

Reaching the front door, he slowly opened it, feeling the coolness of the night touch his exposed flesh. In nothing but his nightclothes, he felt exposed and regretted not dressing before coming down. He considered returning to do just that when the chanting began anew, pulling him from his musings and deeper into the night.

The moonlight waxed down on the land and he turned off the lantern and set it on the footpath, thus freeing his other hand to carry a pistol more easily. With both hands now firmly holding a weapon, he thrust his chest out and prepared to send some fool or fools to their doom.

He wasn't worried about killing whoever it might be. They were trespassing on his land and so he had the right to use lethal force if necessary. And that was what he planned to do when he found the blasted fools.

Following the path leading from the house deeper into the forest, the chanting seemed to always float just out of reach. If he had time to consider his actions, he would have realized how foolhardy it was to enter the forest alone, but he was angry, and his emotions had ruled him since he was old enough to walk.

He made his way down the winding path until finally coming out onto a small beach leading to the ocean. Looking back, he hadn't realized he had come so far and now it seemed as if he had been in a daze the entire time. It reminded him of the story of the sirens, who called men to their deaths by making them crash their sailing vessels on the rocks before them.

Shaking himself to free his mind from whatever spell he'd fallen under, he was about to turn and return home, feeling quite silly for his midnight walk for no apparent reason, when he paused as he stared out onto the dark water.

Slowly, as if the figure was still walking underwater, a head appeared, breaking the surface of the water.

From where he stood, Kramer couldn't make out the features of the figure, but he gripped his pistols tighter as he watched in fascination. There was no thought to turn and run, no idea of perhaps leaving as fast as his legs would carry him. It was as if he was rooted to the spot.

With treacle-like slowness, another head broke the surface behind it, followed by another and another. In all, nineteen heads appeared, soon followed by their bloated, pale bodies.

In the darkness, the figures were all but invisible, only their outlines silhouetted by the wan moonlight of the crescent moon hovering in the sky, ignorant of what was occurring on the beach.

Kramer, still planted to the earth, could only watch in horror as the figures slowly took shape, and when the first one was close enough to see clearly, he realized who—or what—these figures were.

Snapping from his fugue state, he raised his revolvers and shot the first figure in the face. But if he expected the figure to go down, he was sorely mistaken.

A clear hole appeared in the forehead of the creature, and the head snapped back from the force of the lead ball, but other than that there was no sign of distress.

Slowly, the head righted itself and the figure continued to stumble forward.

By now the last figure had left the water, and Kramer saw each one was attached to the other by manacles. Together, all nineteen shambled up the beach, moving directly toward Kramer.

Filled with a terror he never knew could exist, he fired again at the next figure in line. His bullet struck directly over the figure's heart and a small hole was made in the torso, a larger one out the back by the force of the round as it continued onward to strike yet another figure.

The figure took a step back and seemed to rock on its feet from being shot. But the one behind it pushed it forward and it didn't fall down. Kramer could now see the moonlight filtering through the hole he'd made in its body, the heart still inside the ribcage, only now it was still.

When the first figure was close enough for him to touch, Kramer let out a loud gasp, still unable to believe his eyes.

The slave was a rotting, diseased-filled corpse, the body now pale as the white sand at its feet, the body bloated with sea water to the point of bursting. Pieces of the face were now missing, as if fish and other sea life had been picking at it as the corpse made its way across the ocean floor.

And Kramer realized that was what must have happened. These slaves, the ones he'd sent to a watery grave, had walked across the ocean floor for two weeks straight until finally coming out here on the shore of Charleston.

The chanting was louder now, and Kramer could hear his name in the voices, the voices now warped by disuse and decay. One of the figures stepped forward and its arm fell off, the flesh and sinew rotted to the point it could no longer remain attached. Another opened its mouth and a small crab crawled out with the corpse's tongue in its claws. It dropped to the sand and scuttled away.

Some had no eyes, the orbs, once tender and juicy, eaten by sea life more than a week ago. But they were chained to their undead brethren and so did not need to see, led like dogs on a leash.

Kramer shot twice more, each bullet scoring a hit, but the undead slaves ignored their wounds.

"No, this cannot be! You're dead! Dead!"

But the slaves didn't reply, only shambled forward with their irons clanking amongst them, the chanting never ceasing.

"Kill Kramer, Kill Kramer," they sang in their native tongue.

Kramer finally snapped out of it and turned to run, but as he took his first step, his right foot became tangled in his nightclothes and he tumbled to the beach. Spitting sand, he rolled over to see the slaves bearing down on him.

He threw his right pistol at the closest face glaring at him. The barrel of the weapon struck the slave's cheek, leaving a long tear in the flesh. As the skin opened, no blood seeped out, the blood long dried and congealed.

He threw his other pistol at a figure but it merely went wide, falling to the sand where it was crushed under the decayed feet of more undead slaves.

Crying out in terror, he closed his eyes and prepared to be torn apart, but after a full ten seconds and still no pain, he opened them to see the slaves surrounding him.

"What do you want? Revenge? Then go ahead and kill me. I did what I had to do and I would do it again, by God."

They said nothing, even the chanting halted. Only the sounds of the waves crashing on the rocks now filling the void of the night.

And then the last slave walked through the crowd, and Kramer saw what he was holding in his hands.

It was the empty manacles of where Kramer had attached the slaves to the chain connected to the anchor. The same manacles the old woman had worn before she had died.

He let out a scream then, understanding what they intended, and as cold hands grabbed and held him still, the slave with the manacles locked them to Kramer's wrists and ankles, then stood back.

Kramer stopped screaming, sobbing silently as he looked up at the dead faces of the men and women he'd killed mercilessly.

His chest heaved with anxiety and his vision was filled with spots as adrenalin suffused his body.

And then the slaves turned and began walking back to the sea.

Kramer heaved a sigh, believing he was safe.

One by one they turned and shambled back into the surf, bits and pieces of their rotting bodies left behind in the sand.

Kramer lay there, perfectly still, wondering if it was all a dream when the last slave turned and began to walk away. This slave, the last in line, was connected to Kramer.

He was yanked hard, and before he realized what was happening, Kramer began to be dragged across the sand.

"No, no! You can't do this to me! I'm your master, you hear me? I'm your master!"

But the slaves never slowed, as each one shambled into the water and back out to the waiting sea. Kramer dug his hands into the sand to halt his progress, but nothing could slow his descent to the ocean. No matter how hard he tried, it was like an anchor was on the other end, slowly pulling him into the cold, cold water.

Nineteen water-logged bodies were more than a match for one man, and as Kramer screamed for help, his vocal cords soon raw, he was sucked into the water. Still he screamed, his hands flailing, his legs kicking, and as ice cold water filled his mouth, he screamed some more.

As his lungs were filled to bursting, he waited for death to claim him but for some reason he wouldn't die.

As the muddy ocean floor stirred up around him, he realized he was deep underwater, and though he should be dead, he quickly found out being alive was no blessing.

As the undead slaves continued their journey back into the murky ocean depths, Kramer realized he was spared death for only one reason, so he could suffer for all eternity with the same cursed souls he had sent to their watery graves. For now, he was one of them, a slave.

And they were all slaves of Death itself.

LAND OF ZOMBIES

The Ford Bronco with a white number 8 painted on both front doors slowed to a stop outside the small town of Steubenville, Arkansas. The engine idled softly as the four passengers inside the vehicle stared through the front windshield at what looked like a small town, devoid of life.

"It looks quiet," Idaho said from the passenger seat. He was just shy of his nineteenth birthday, with an innocent face and curly brown hair. He had the look of a scared cat, his eyes constantly darting back and forth, as if he expected the world to explode at any moment.

"Looks can be deceiving," Tennessee said from the driver's seat. He was in his forties with a bald pate and hard eyes. His jaw was square, giving him an angry scowl even if he was happy, but the eyes, where you would expect them to be cold, to match the rest of his gruff exterior, were two dark pools of compassion. Though his exterior was rough, he had a heart of gold.

"Are you two ladies gonna talk about it all day or are we going in?" Georgia asked from the back seat. She was just over twenty with dark black hair and eyes that any man would fall for. She was trim and in shape and the t-shirt she now wore accented her thin waist and ample bust. Since Idaho and Tennessee had saved her and her sister two weeks previous, she and Tennessee had become an item, though things had cooled in the past week.

The sister in question sat quietly next to Georgia. She was twelve going on twenty, with long brown hair and eyes that were wise beyond her years. Like the others, she had picked up a nickname, and now even her sister called her Atlanta.

The four survivors of the zombie apocalypse had become a tight-knit family since meeting so long ago in Texas, and now traveled together across a zombie blasted landscape that was once America. Atlanta wasn't paying attention to the conversation; instead, she was concentrating on the PSP in her hands. She had found it in a store outside of California, and after raiding the store for whatever they could use, she had taken the hand-held game console as well as the five game discs found with it.

"Hell, yeah, we're goin' in," Tennessee said. "I'm out of Twinkies and I bet you dollars to donuts there's a general store in that town with a shelf full of 'em."

Idaho reached over the seat and picked up his double barrel shotgun. "Then lets go, daylight's wasting."

"That's want I wanna hear! Ye-haaaa, let's ride, boys and girls!" He floored the gas pedal and the Bronco surged forward, leaving a trail of rubber on the deserted highway.

The Bronco came to a screeching halt in the middle of town, the setting sun reflecting off the polished chrome like a giant mirror. Only the dried blood spots on the bumper and grille marred its perfect finish. The Bronco had been acquired just outside of California after three tires had been blown on the Cadillac they were using, when Tennessee accidentally drove over a spike strip left by some dead policeman.

With nothing else to do, the quartet had walked for three miles until coming to a car dealership. Tennessee had picked the Bronco, hotwired it, and off they went, no worse for wear with the exception of sore feet.

"You always have to make an entrance, don't you," Idaho said to Tennessee as he scanned the street for zombies.

Tennessee shrugged. "It's my nature, come at 'em hard and fast. You should know that about me by now. Now quit bitchin' like a woman and get ready to fight."

"Looks quiet enough," Georgia said as she looked through the rear window. The rifle in her hands was loaded and ready if needed.

Tennessee cocked the Uzi in his hands and opened the driver's door. "Quiet or not, that store has a Twinkie with my name on it and I'm gonna go get it."

His alligator boots slapped the warm pavement as he exited the vehicle, his white, wide-brimmed cowboy hat shading his eyes from the sun.

Across the street from where he stopped the Bronco was a general store, one that sold everything from milk, to smokes, to Keno every hour. The name on the sign read, **DEGREGIO'S PRODUCE** and below the name was the picture of a dancing tomato and potato.

"Atlanta, you stay here, Georgia come with me, Idaho, you watch our backs," Tennessee said as he crossed the street without waiting for an answer.

Idaho was stepping out of the Bronco as was Georgia. They made eye contact for a brief instant and it spoke volumes. She smiled wanly and he did the same, then they moved across the street behind Tennessee. Just because the town seemed deserted, didn't mean it was, and at any second a horde of zombies could come screaming around a building, hungry for human flesh. It had happened before and would so again, that was a fact of the new world order.

"You okay back there?" Georgia asked her sister who waved a hand in a *leave me alone* gesture. She was concentrating on her game and wasn't interested in their escapades at the moment. "Fine, but lock the doors, will you please?"

"Ugh, fine," Atlanta said as she reached forward, locked the doors, to then fall back into her seat. Like her three traveling companions, she had adapted to her new world quite easily, accepting a world ruled by the ravenous zombies as a matter of fact.

Georgia looked up to see Idaho and Tennessee walking to the front entrance to the store and she jogged after them, her eyes looking all around, waiting to see the first sign of a zombie. But so far, it was quiet.

Tennessee reached the door and opened it casually, as if he was a regular customer on a regular day that needed to do some shopping.

Stepping inside, the cool air wafted over his face. The power was still on, as it was in many cities across the U.S. He assumed it would go out eventually but for now the power plants across the states were still on autopilot, chugging along and kicking out electricity.

His eyes took in the aisles of assorted items. Food of course, but also a section for hardware and magazines. To his left were a few items for those who succumbed to impulse buys and he grinned widely when he spotted an interesting item to use as a weapon.

"Looks clear," Idaho said from his side as he stood still, his shotgun in his hands, his eyes darting back and forth like a thief about to get caught. Georgia came up behind Idaho and stopped.

"Okay, boys and girls, I got a system how I clear these places out, just stand back and watch," Tennessee said with a grin. He picked up a glass jar of mustard and one of ketchup, and with a wink at the others, tossed them into the aisle so they scraped the ceiling.

As the two condiments arced through the air, they quickly soared downward. Upon striking the floor, they shattered, the loud crash filling the store and becoming a dinner bell to any zombies inside.

Idaho was looking sideways at Tennessee, taking the bigger man's lead and waiting, and Georgia was leaning against a rack of magazines. She was confident whatever happened would be taken down easily.

And then the first sounds of footsteps slapping the tiles came to their ears.

"Here we go, I knew there was some in here," Tennessee said as he picked up his improvised weapons, his grin growing wider in anticipation.

A second later, a skinny zombie rounded the end of the aisle, woofed twice like a dog, then charged at the three survivors. Idaho raised his shotgun but Tennessee placed a hand on the barrel and pushed it back down.

"I said I got this, just like before," he said calmly.

He took a step in front of Idaho, the wide smile on his lips never faltering, a gleam in his eye. He loved killing zombies and if he was seeing a psychiatrist, the doctor would have told him it was therapeutic.

The zombie powered forward, an apron on its torso, tan chinos on its legs and a pair of sneakers. It had been a cashier or a bag boy but it was obvious by the name tag—which read Brad—that the zombie had worked in the store. As the zombie powered forward, Tennessee swung his improvised weapon under his arm, and with an underarm heave, like he was bowling, he let loose with the lawn dart in his hand.

The dart soared across the few feet separating him from the zombie, and true to his aim, the dart struck the head in the right eye. The metal tip—the darts taken off the shelves because of the danger—slid into the eye like a hot knife through butter—and the zombie's head snapped back to spin it in the air and fall onto the floor, flopping like a fish.

"Piece of cake," Tennessee said as he took a step forward, another dart in his hand. "What do you think, zombie kill of the week?"

Actually, the zombie kill of the week went to Mrs. Virginia Fulsome of Brentwood, New Jersey.

With the help of her neighbors, Mrs. Fulsome dug an open pit in which she then filled with Pungi spikes. She covered the pit with a large tarp and dusted it with light dirt and leaves.

Whenever a zombie would chase her home after she went out for supplies, she would make sure to avoid the pit by jumping over it to land on her front porch.

On this particular day, a large brute of a zombie with pus dripping from every orifice and teeth as red as a Crayola crayon, was chasing her.

Mrs. Fulsome hurdled the pit, almost slipping at the edge, and as she opened her front door and fell inside, the zombie, unaware of its doom, placed its foot onto the tarp. Plunging head first into the pit, the first Pungi stick entered its left eye, then continued straight into its neck until exiting out the zombie's rectum. Like a roasted chicken on a spit, the zombie flailed about until succumbing to death, more than a half dozen sticks now penetrating its body.

It should also be mentioned that second place went to Mr. Jeremy Higgins of Johnstown, New York, who jury-rigged a leather couch over his front door, and when he was being chased, pulled the lever and dropped the couch onto the zombie just as it began to pound on his door after he'd entered.

Flattened, the zombie's insides were sprayed across the door and ground. Later, Mr. Higgins dragged the corpse away, hosed off the area, reset the couch, and awaited his next target.

No sooner did Tennessee step three feet down the aisle, then another zombie rounded the bend. It was female and she was covered in blood, her mouth a gaping maw of red and black, her once blonde hair painted brown with dried blood. She wore a yellow dress, now torn in the front, and her perfectly curved breasts—implants obviously—swung back and forth like two erotic pendulums.

"Next!" Tennessee said jokingly as the zombie powered forward, a screech on her bloody lips. Tennessee prepared another dart, and as the zombie came for him, he chucked it overhand like he was throwing a spear.

The dart went straight for the right breast, punctured it easily and then into the zombie's heart. Silicon squirted from the breast and oozed down the flat stomach but other than that the zombie kept coming.

He was out of darts but not out of ideas, and Tennessee reached out to both sides of the shelves and grabbed a can of chili and a can of beef stew. As the zombie ran at him, he threw each can like it was a baseball, the metal projectiles soaring at head level until they connected with the zombie's head. The first one hit hard and put a dent in her head and she slowed for a second, but no sooner did the can fall away then the second one was connecting. This one struck her head on the corner and sliced a jagged wound in her head. She fell to the floor, her brains exposed, but still not out of the fight.

Tennessee walked over to her as she tried to get to her feet and he took a restaurant-sized can of chocolate pudding from off a shelf next to him.

Raising it over his head, he brought it down like a bludgeon, the can smashing the head to pulp and breaking open. Chocolate pudding and brains mixed into a gooey sludge as bits of blood spouted out to course through the mess like imitation lava running off a mountain.

Tennessee turned to look at Idaho and Georgia, his smile so wide it looked as if it would crack his face.

"I'd stay away from the pudding if I were you," he said, and was about to turn and search for his Twinkies when he halted in his tracks.

Normally, when he entered small grocery stores, there would be one or two zombies within, the few that were too stupid to figure out how to escape, but this time there was something different, something he couldn't quite put his finger on.

As he waited in the aisle, he began to hear the sound of dozens of slapping feet.

He looked at Idaho who only shrugged, not understanding what was happening. Georgia had dropped the magazine and was now standing with her rifle leveled at her waist, her beautiful face now covered with a mask of concern.

And then the first figure rounded the bend at the end of the far aisle. Directly behind it, more came around, a few taking the turn so fast they slid on the polished floor, their bodies crashing into the aisle and knocking canned goods to the floor. Others stepped on the canned goods and found it was like stepping on large marbles, these bodies then falling to the floor in a heap of arms and legs. But there were still more than a dozen who climbed over their fallen brethren as they charged down the aisle in pursuit of the three survivors.

"Oh, shit, this never happened before," Tennessee said and took a step backwards. It looked like a large crowd of people had sought shelter inside the store, only to become zombies themselves. And now they wanted Tennessee and the others for a snack.

All fooling around aside, Tennessee pulled his gun and shot the first zombie as it charged down the aisle. The bullet hit it in the chest and the body flipped over backward, striking others who pushed it aside and continued onward. Three zombies stepped in the pudding gore on the floor and their feet went out from under them. They fell to the floor in a mock Three Stooges parody.

That gave him an idea and he grabbed more glass jars off the shelves, then began smashing them on the floor as he walked back to Georgia and Idaho who had begun shooting.

Tennessee tossed more than two dozen jars onto the floor, each one smashed and spewing its contents.

As the first zombie reached the slick floor, its legs went out from under it like it had stepped on ice. Horizontal for a moment, gravity took over and the body crashed to the floor, the head striking so hard the skull cracked. Seconds later, there was a massive pile-up of bodies as each zombie fell over the other and slid on the floor.

"I changed my mind, I don't like this place, let's go shopping at another one," Tennessee said casually, though his voice cracked slightly. He was fearless but not stupid and there were way too many to fight off for no reason. Retreat was the best option.

"No argument here," Idaho said as he popped open his shotgun, slid two more shells into the breach, snapped it closed, and fired at a zombie who was only a few feet away.

Spinning about, the three kicked open the door to leave, and before even one foot could be placed outside, the horn on the Bronco began to sound, the blaring an indication of two things. The first was the situation outside was so bad that Atlanta wasn't worried about calling attention to herself, and the second was that she was blaring the horn *and* calling attention to herself.

Georgia was in the lead as they exited the store and slammed the door closed behind them. A sign about free magazines was to the right and Tennessee grabbed it and shoved it into the handle of the door. No sooner did he do this then the first body slammed against it. The door shook on its frame but he could see they had more than enough time to get to their vehicle and vamoose.

Tennessee was grinning once more, proud of his escape, when he turned around to see what was going on out front in the street.

The horn was still blaring and the passenger window was open as a panicked Atlanta hung out of it, shooting her rifle. That, plus what was behind the Bronco, appearing like locusts, told him all he needed to know.

From down the street, swarming between alleyways and from out of buildings, more than a hundred zombies had appeared, and they were all hungry for human flesh.

"Oh, hell no," Tennessee said as he brought up his Uzi.

Idaho swallowed hard as he stared at the approaching horde. "I think we need to go, right now."

"Ya think?" Georgia yelled and jumped off the porch as she ran to the Bronco.

"Hurry up, they're almost here!" Atlanta yelled and shot a zombie in the chest. It was wearing a pair of grease and blood-soaked coveralls, the name **William** stitched in red thread over its chest pocket. The zombie fell back and sprawled on the ground to be crushed by two dozen feet. When it was clear to stand, its arms were broken, the ulna on both limbs jutting through the flesh.

Tennessee could see if they were going to escape alive, the herd would need to be trimmed, so he jumped onto the hood of the Bronco, then onto the roof, and sprayed the horde from left to right. His bullets peppered bodies, taking out fist-sized chunks of meat and flesh, the gore-splattered bodies falling to the pavement to twitch and spasm.

Idaho followed Tennessee's lead and shot two zombies in the face, one after the other. As the heads exploded into crimson gouts of bone and brain matter, he reloaded, trying to keep his shaking hands from dropping the shells.

"Come on!" Georgia yelled as she climbed into the driver's seat and put the Bronco into gear. "Forget them, let's just go!"

"Ye-haaa, look at 'em twitch!" Tennessee shouted and sent an entire clip into the mass of zombies. Bodies were piling up and so far none had managed to reach them.

From the far side of the street, independent of the horde, two zombies came at Idaho. He didn't know they were there until he heard their feet slapping the street and he was still loading his shotgun. Turning, trying to snap the weapon closed, he saw two puss-covered faces charging at him.

Then one, followed by the other, were shot down and he turned to see Atlanta smiling at him, her rifle aimed at where the zombies had been moments ago. He touched his index finger to his forehead and gave her a salute for a thank you. She smiled, her elfin face belaying the hardness she now held inside her. If she wanted to survive, she had no choice and her sister had already taught her how to be strong long before the apocalypse began.

"Whoo-haaa. Come and get it, kids!" Tennessee yelled as he popped in another clip and sprayed the horde. More than three dozen bodies now lay twitching on the ground as he fired relentlessly into the attacking horde. Then he lost his balance as the Bronco shifted into drive, Georgia rolling forward.

"Hey! Cut the shit, I'm up here!" he yelled.

"Well get the hell down, there's too many of 'em!" Georgia yelled back and revved the engine. She pointed to Idaho and waved for him to get inside the Bronco. Turning, Idaho shot a zombie that was too close, only clipping the sprinter as it came at him, then he spun and ran for the Bronco.

"Get in the back!" Georgia yelled, the front seat was full with her and Atlanta. Idaho did as he was told and climbed in while Tennessee continued to shoot and yell in abject glee.

"What the hell is he doing up there?" Georgia yelled and moved the Bronco again, then hit the brakes. Tennessee lost his footing and fell, landing on his back on the hood, hard. He was a big man and the hood had cushioned his fall but his eyes glared at Georgia, the two equal in spirit and will power.

"Hold on!" she yelled out the window at Tennessee who did as he was told, grabbing the edge of the hood right where it touched the windshield. She floored it, sending Tennessee's face into the windshield, his cheek pressing so hard it flattened. She ignored it, only worrying about the zombies coming up behind her. The Bronco's tires spun and it took off just as the first three zombies grabbed the rear bumper. As the vehicle drove away, the three zombies fell, only their tenuous grip on the bumper keeping them attached.

As the Bronco shot down the street, the three bodies bounced and swung back and forth on the rear, boots and sneakers grinding away or falling off completely until bare feet began to grind against the pavement. The Bronco swerved around a corner and Tennessee almost fell off, but he managed to hold on. Behind the Bronco, the three bodies left long, red streaks as feet were ground down and legs became nubs.

Finally, the zombies couldn't hold on any longer and one at a time they let go, their bodies rolling across the ground to remain still. One let go at a bad time and when it fell away, it immediately came up against a Postal mailbox. The blue box turned red as the body exploded on impact, internal organs and intestines shooting out in all directions like a water balloon.

The Bronco continued onward, leaving the zombie-infested town behind.

Outside of town, with nothing around but a few abandoned cars and open fields, Georgia pulled to a stop and an exhausted Tennessee slid off the hood to fall onto the road. The inside of his fingers were cut where he was holding onto the hood and he picked himself up slowly, leaning against the vehicle to steady himself.

Georgia sat behind the wheel, a sly smile on her lips as Tennessee walked around the Bronco and climbed into the back with Idaho.

"That looks like it hurts," Idaho said as he looked at Tennessee's fingers. He handed Tennessee a Kleenex to wipe off the blood.

"*That* is the stupidest statement I ever heard," Tennessee said in a low voice.

Idaho said nothing, knowing Tennessee had mood swings. One second he was amenable, the next he was angry, but deep down Idaho knew they had become friends and that was enough for him.

Georgia and Tennessee made eye contact in the rearview mirror and he opened his mouth to say something but Georgia's gaze was firm. Her eyes seemed to say, *go 'head, say something.*

Tennessee closed his mouth, waved his index finger at her in a threatening gesture, and began wiping the blood from his fingers. He looked at Idaho and said, "Give me another damn tissue."

Georgia looked at Atlanta, took her smaller hand in hers, and gave her sister a loving squeeze, then stepped on the gas pedal, the Bronco surging forward. She looked in the rearview mirror to see Tennessee mumbling to himself. Idaho made eye contact with her and he gave her a salute. She winked at him and then turned her attention to the road ahead.

The highway was filled with the detritus of a fallen society. Abandoned cars, a burnt out hulk of a small, crashed Cessna, a school bus with bloody windows and flat tires, were just a few of the assortment of dead relics.

Accepting this as her new reality, and knowing her fellow survivors did the same, she drove around a stalled car with its hood up and headed for the horizon.

"Maybe the next town will have some Twinkies, Tennessee," she said and he looked up, his eyes alight with happiness, like a puppy glad to see its owner return home.

"I sure do hope so, I surely do."

"Maybe they have snowballs, too," Idaho said as an afterthought. "I could go for some."

Tennessee turned to Idaho, his jaw set tight, and said, "That'll get you one at half strength." He punched Idaho on the shoulder, making the skinny man wince. Georgia laughed and so did Atlanta, and as Tennessee flashed each of them a wide grin, Idaho frowned while rubbing his sore shoulder.

He should be used to it by now; after all, it was just another day in a land of zombies.

LOST IN THE WOODS

"We're lost, aren't we?" Sharon asked from the passenger seat as she stared at the map spread out before her.

"No, we're not," Thomas replied while steering the car around a sharp bend in the road.

Over two hours had passed since the road had changed from asphalt to gravel, and then to dirt. The rains had carved deep grooves into the road, causing the car to jump on its shocks, like Thomas had decided to take them offroading.

"We need to turn around," Sharon said as she tossed the map into the back seat where their camping supplies were. Only the sleeping bags and their tent were in the trunk. "*You* need to turn around," she said again as she stared out through the front windshield at the woods.

Though the sun was high in the sky, the tree tops stopped more than half the light from penetrating. Because of this it seemed almost like twilight, only a few thin rays cutting through the holes in the leafy canopy. Birdcalls could be heard over the sound of the car's engine and sometimes deer could be spotted grazing off in the distance, between the wooded glades they drove past.

"We can't turn around, dear," Thomas said, saying the word *dear* sarcastically. "There's no place I can manage it. The damn trees grow right up to the edge of the road and even if I still tried the shoulder's muddy. This isn't a truck you know, we'll get stuck."

"Oh, is that what you call what we're on, a road?" she added in a sarcastic tone of her own.

He glanced away from the road long enough to stare her down.

"Be nice, this isn't my fault," he said calmly.

She had been prepared to snap at him, expecting him to do the same, but when he ended up talking calmly it threw her off.

"Oh, I…I know that, Thomas, it's just, we're getting deeper into the woods, who knows what's out there. We need to turn back. What if we break down?"

He nodded at her words, taking them in.

"Yeah, I was thinking the same thing." He pointed to his cell phone on the dashboard, the cord to the cigarette lighter keeping it charged. "Check that will you? Do we even have a signal out here?"

She did as he asked and a second later shook her head. "Nope, no signal."

"Shit, that was what I was afraid of." He shrugged slightly. "Look, Sharon, this road has to go somewhere. All we need to do is follow it until I can find someplace safe enough to spin around."

"This was a mistake," she said as she wrapped her arms around herself protectively. "We shouldn't have come out here. We're city people, camping isn't our thing."

"Oh, please," he said. "I used to go camping all the time when I was a kid."

"Yes, you did, but that was with your father when you were eleven. He did everything. You didn't have to do a thing."

"Maybe, but I still remember enough so we can have some fun."

"Not anymore, we must be miles from the campsite by now."

"No, dear, more than that. We've been driving for hours. I'd say twenty miles, easy."

She turned to him, then, her eyes grew wide. "You mean to tell me we're more than twenty miles deep into the woods?"

"So what?" he chuckled as he swung around another dip in the road. "Come on, Sharon, this isn't the movies, there's no man with a leather mask and a chainsaw or inbred hillbillies who want to eat us for lunch out here. That's just the stuff of Hollywood. We're perfectly safe."

She shook her head, her brown tresses caressing her cheeks. "I don't know, Thomas. We haven't seen any signs of civilization for hours. For all we know we're the only ones out here."

"Yeah, maybe," he replied and concentrated on the road.

With the car jumping and bucking like a wild bronco, they drove deeper into the dense forest.

"You know, it's funny..." Thomas said, fighting the wheel as the car bounced over yet another bad dip.

Sharon waited for him to continue, and when he didn't, she frowned.

"What's funny?" she prodded.

He shrugged slightly, something he was wont to do when he was considering something.

"Well, it's just that we're so far in the woods now, you know? I mean, this is the kind of place you'd find Bigfoot skulking around between the trees."

"Bigfoot? Oh, Thomas, don't be silly. Besides, Bigfoot has sightings only in the Northeast, we're in the west."

He looked at her, his left eyebrow coming up in curiosity.

"And how in the world do you even know that?"

She shrugged herself, brushing her hair from her face. "I just do. I read and watch TV too, you know."

He reached out and cupped her chin in his hand, rubbing her cheek with his thumb. It was times like this when he was reminded of just how much he loved the woman sitting next to him. It was when she showed something about herself he didn't know was there. Even after almost twelve years of marriage she could still surprise him.

It was as he was looking at her, his eyes off the road, that the right front tire found a deeper, wider pothole than most of the ones Thomas had been dealing with. Without warning, the car's front tire plummeted into the pothole, the vehicle coming to a halt so hard and fast they were thrown forward. Neither of them had on their seatbelts, deciding that in the middle of nowhere, it wasn't needed. And with the new laws demanding they wear one in the city, they both felt like little rebels by unbuckling them as soon as they'd hit the mountain pass.

But now those lack of seatbelts was a detraction as they were tossed around the car like rag dolls.

Sharon's head struck the windshield and she was lifted a foot off her seat and Thomas cried out as the steering wheel dug deep into his upper chest. He felt sudden pain shoot through his body and his mind told him he'd probably cracked a rib or two.

The car lurched forward like a torpedoed ship, the rear end coming up off the road slightly from the momentum. But then it rocked back to earth as the two passengers were slammed back against their seats. There was a small blood spot on the windshield where Sharon's head had connected with the glass; her body now slumped forward in her seat, unconscious.

Thomas sucked in a breath of air, trying to fight the pain in his chest, but his body went into shock, and before he could stop himself, he felt the world going dark. He reached out and tried to touch Sharon, wanting to see if she was all right, but before he could, his arm dropped to the seat and he slipped into oblivion.

There was a tapping sound filling his dream as Thomas finally came back to wakefulness.

For a brief second he thought he was blind. His eyes were open but he couldn't see a thing. Looking left and right, he heard the tapping growing louder now. It was coming from above him and as he reached out and felt the switch for the window, he pressed the button, the window rolling down.

Immediately he was splashed with water and he realized the noise was rain hitting the roof and hood of his car, so he raised the window.

The car had stalled and he looked to the dash and could see the dim glow of the numbers and letters. Reaching out, he turned on the dome light and was blinded by the glare until his eyes could focus again.

And then he gasped in shock to see Sharon slumped in her seat, her head resting against the passenger window.

"Oh my God, Sharon? Are you all right?" he asked as he leaned over and pulled her to him. She groaned slightly and he thanked God she was alive. He felt her head, and when his hand came away with blood on it, he gasped again. When he inspected her scalp, he found the small cut on the top of her forehead where her head had whacked the windshield.

She groaned again and then her eyes fluttered open.

"Ohhhh, what happened?"

"I don't know, I think we crashed," Thomas said.

"Crashed? We were in the middle of a deserted road. How on God's green Earth did you manage that one?"

"Like I just said, I don't know. Are you hurt? I mean, other than that cut on your head?"

She took stock of herself, groaning as she sat up, but after a minute she felt she was fine, only a splitting headache the result of the crash.

"I'm fine, just a headache. You?"

Thomas nodded in the glow of the dome light. "My chest hurts a little, but I'll live."

She smiled slightly. "Want me to kiss the boo-boo and make it all better?"

"Ha, ha, I really don't think now is the time for that," he joked as he shifted in his seat.

He put the car into park, the engine having stalled, and now he turned it over, the motor starting right up, but as he tried to move the car it wouldn't budge. He could feel the engine wanting to push the car along but the vehicle felt like it was dragging or like it had a flat. He knew there was only one thing to do.

Turning off the engine, but leaving the headlights on, he reached into the backseat for his jacket and a flashlight as Sharon watched silently. She rubbed at her window, the condensation coming away, but she couldn't see a thing. It was pitch black outside on the road and the surrounding woods.

"How long was I out?" she said to herself, but Thomas thought she was speaking to him.

"Don't know, a few hours I guess. I was out, too. We both took a beating. Guess that's what we get for not wearing our seatbelts."

Her reply was a soft grunt. She didn't need a lecture now about auto safety.

He opened his door and was about to get out when she grabbed his arm.

"Wait, where're you going?"

"I have to see what's wrong with the car, Sharon."

"But it's raining out, you'll get soaked."

He grinned at her. "Sharon, it's only rain, I'll be fine. Now you stay here and try to rest, I'll be right back."

"You be careful," she told him and he nodded while pushing the door open and stepping out.

As soon as his foot came down, it was swallowed by a six inch puddle and he felt the cold water seep into his hiking boot. Cursing silently, he ignored it and slammed the door closed to keep the inside of the car dry. Then he turned on the flashlight and shrugged into his jacket, all the while moving to the front of the car. The headlights barely helped push back the night, the rain and fog from the moisture in the air bringing visibility down to nothing. But he managed to make it to the front bumper without falling on his face. Once there, he flashed the light on the tires, and after checking the left side and seeing all was well, he checked the right tire.

But what he'd hoped for, namely a flat, wasn't to be. The entire tire and rim was bent outward from the bottom, and when he got down on one wet knee and inspected it more, his head an inch from the muddy water that had filled the pothole, he saw that something had snapped behind the tire. Without a better inspection he guessed it was a tie rod or a ball joint, but in the end it didn't really matter.

The bottom line was they were screwed with a capital S.

Climbing to his feet and leaning on the hood, he looked out into the penetrating darkness.

And it was then he spotted a small twinkle of light coming from the south. He stared at it for a few seconds, wondering if he'd imagined it, but as he watched longer the light didn't move.

He took a few steps to the side of the road, his eyes never leaving the light, and when it didn't disappear he felt confident he'd found something.

But then the light blinked out like it was never there to begin with.

But Thomas knew what he'd seen. The light hadn't been his imagination. A light had been on and then turned off. But it looked far away, a mile at least. He knew light would travel in the darkness of the woods, and sometimes things that appeared close were miles away.

Must be a ranger station or something this far out in the woods. What else could it be? he thought.

He decided he had two choices. He and Sharon could sit in the car until Hell froze over as the chances of someone else coming down this abandoned road was one in a million. Or they could head out towards where he'd seen the light and hope for the best.

It took him all of a minute of standing in the rain to make his decision. Turning, he moved back to the car and opened the door, then climbed inside. Sharon flinched away from him, not wanting to get wet. He found it ironic she did this as in a minute or two she would be as soaked as him, she just didn't know it yet.

He turned to her and stared into her eyes. Not saying a word. She waited silently, and when he didn't speak, she prompted him with a question.

"Well? Is the car okay?"

"No, Sharon, it's not. It's not going anywhere. But we are."

"What're you talking about?" she asked.

He shook his head. "Don't worry about that now, I'll tell you on the way."

"On the way? To where?"

"I saw a light to the south of here. It has to be a rescue station or ranger station or something."

"And?" she inquired.

"And we're going there. So get your stuff, were going on a hike."

"In this rain? Are you crazy?"

He smiled then, the water running down his cheeks, his matted wet hair making him look like a school boy. "Maybe, but now's as good a time as any, so let's go. I'll go without you if I have to if you don't mind being all alone in the middle of nowhere."

Not waiting for an answer, he opened his door and stepped out, closing the door again. He knew she would never stay alone and by pretending to leave her he would save precious time not arguing.

"Thomas? Don't leave without me, Thomas?" But he wasn't listening as he began trudging to the edge of the road.

"Oh, and don't forget our gear!" he called out with a slight grin, knowing she would be right along behind him.

"Ohhhh, you jerk," she mumbled.

She knew what he was doing. She wouldn't stay alone, he knew she would come, and by leaving the car he stopped her from complaining and trying to talk him out of it. She knew all his tricks, but she also knew this one would work on her.

Feeling outmaneuvered and hating him for it, she reached in back and got her jacket and their backpacks, then opened her door.

As she stood up, slamming the door behind her. Thomas flashed her a smile, the flashlight illuminating his face.

"You ready?"

"As if I have a choice," she pouted.

"Exactly," he said, then turned and moved off, Sharon running around the car to catch up.

As she reached him, he slowed and she handed him his pack.

Then he reached out and took her hand, and though wet and cold from the falling rain, she gripped it tight, the two moving off into the woods in the direction Thomas had seen the light.

"That doesn't look like a ranger's station," Sharon said blandly as they slowed down to rest under a tree. The rain was so heavy even with the thick canopy above, the rain found its way through. Only now the water dripped off leaves, the droplets thicker as they struck the ground and them.

"Yeah, you're right, it's not," Thomas replied as he studied the ramshackle structure fifty feet in front of them.

Through the few trees, he could see the small shack had been built hastily or by someone without much skill as a carpenter. On top of logs that were obviously found scattered about the forest floor, after lightning strikes, there was a mishmash of man made wood mixed in as well. Old pieces of plywood and two by fours made up the framework of the small…well, it had to be called a cabin, but just barely.

"What should we do?" she asked as she wiped her brow with a soggy sleeve.

They were both soaked to the bone, having been walking for over an hour.

"Not much choice really. We go see if anyone's home." He set off then, carefully making his way over the soggy deadfall. "I know I saw a light on earlier, that's why I knew where to go. Someone's got to be inside."

"I doubt they're going to want visitors, Thomas. Especially if they live way out here in the middle of nowhere."

He shrugged, the gesture lost in the darkness.

"It's probably just some hermit or survivalist who's preparing for the end of the world."

"If it is he could have a gun, Thomas," she stated nervously.

"Oh, please, you're letting your imagination run away with you again. We'll be fine."

Crossing the remaining distance, they stopped when they were only a few feet away from the cabin. Now that they were closer, they could see moss growing on the sides and actual tree branches jutting out of the foundation. It looked like it was fifty years old and only the debris mixed in with the walls told it wasn't that old. Thomas stepped up to the door and to the right he saw soda cans and glass bottles mixed with mud lathered on the outer shell of the cabin. When he reached out and touched it, the mud felt hard, though some did come off on his fingertips. He had a feeling whoever lived here must have to constantly keep up on the walls or the rain would end up washing it all away.

With a glance to Sharon, Thomas knocked on the door. He rapped three times and waited, and when no one answered, he knocked harder, and this time the door opened a little.

Only an inch, the door dragged along the floor and Thomas pushed it open some more, stepping inside.

"Wait, Thomas, don't go in there," Sharon whispered.

"Why not?" Thomas called over his shoulder. "I didn't come all this way to leave 'cause no one's home. Come on in and get out of the rain," he called as he disappeared into the darkness of the cabin.

"But why wasn't it locked?"

"There's no one around for miles and miles, what would be the point?" he called from the darkness. "Now come on in and quit being a baby."

Sharon stood at the doorway for all of ten seconds, then she looked behind her at the dark forest, gazed up at the full moon hidden behind the clouds, and entered the cabin, not wanting to be left alone. She closed the door behind her to keep out the rain.

As she entered, her nose scrunched up in disgust at the charnel house smell permeating the cabin.

"Oh my God, what's that smell?" she gasped. "Thomas, where are you?" she called as she stood near the door, not wanting to go in further.

"I'm over here," he said and then the flashlight was on and he was pointing the tight beam at her face.

"Get that damn thing out of my face, please," she growled angrily.

"Huh? Oh, sorry, honey, wasn't thinking." Thomas dropped the light and then played it across the cabin's surfaces, the circular beam roving over the walls and a table in the corner. It was a one room structure with a bed in the corner and a closet at the opposite end. A sink and table was set up in the other corner and a small, homemade couch was in the middle. A smaller table was next to the couch and a few well read books and magazines lay strewn on its surface. Thomas went to these first and picked one up.

"It's over ten years old," he said.

Sharon was still looking around in the gloom of the only flashlight and she spotted something over by the sink and table.

"What's that over there?"

Thomas dropped the *People* magazine and turned, flashing the beam where she wanted.

"I don't know," he said as he moved closer. It was when he was right over it that the light brought it into focus and he gasped in surprise. Then he felt his stomach churning and he leaned over the sink and expelled his earlier lunch of tacos and beer.

"Thomas? What's wrong? Are you all right?"

Thomas wasn't listening as he vomited into the sink. When his stomach was empty, he sighed and wiped his mouth with the back of his soggy jacket.

Sharon began to cross the cabin towards him and he raised his hand to stop her.

"You don't want to see this," he said as he caught his breath.

"Don't tell me what I do and don't want to see, Thomas, I'm not a child," she snapped as she stepped closer and gazed down at what had freaked Thomas out.

"Oh, my God. Is that?"

"Yeah, I think it is," he replied.

But Sharon appeared to be made of sterner stuff and her stomach stayed calm as she leaned over and studied the thing on the table. There was a small stick to the side and she used it to pick up the thing, and as Thomas flashed the light on it, she nodded.

"Good God, Thomas, this is human skin."

"It can't be, that's crazy. You're mistaken," he said even though he thought this too and that's why he'd vomited.

She shook her head and then slowly turned what looked like a dried piece of pale leather so he could see the other side. "Then what do you call this?"

Thomas looked where she pointed and saw a tattoo of a heart with an arrow and the name Cheryl in the middle. The tattoo was faded, the owner probably getting it years ago, and as he stared at it, he felt his stomach building up like Old Faithful and he turned and spewed into the sink again.

Sharon ignored him and set the disgusting thing down. Though gross, this still didn't explain the smell of rancid meat she'd detected upon entering the cabin. Now that she'd been in here for a bit, it wasn't as bad, but she could still detect it.

"Here, tough guy, give me that light," she said.

Thomas handed it to her and she used it to search the corner some more. There was a small cabinet with a single door and she opened it.

As the door opened, the smell of putrid, rotting meat wafted into her face and she jumped back, kicking the door closed. It was as the door slammed shut that she was able to glimpse the shelves were full of meat; maggots and flies crawling along the ridges and valleys of the tissue. After seeing the skin, she didn't want to think about what kind of meat could be in there.

"Thomas, we need to leave here right now," she said.

"No argument from me," he replied and grabbed her by the arm as they headed for the door.

But as Thomas reached out to grab the doorknob, they both heard the sounds of footsteps as someone banged their feet on the side of the cabin to clean off the mud picked up while walking in the rain.

"Oh, shit, someone's here," he squeaked.

"What'll we do?" she asked, her eyes wide.

Thomas turned and looked about the cabin, searching for a way out, but there was none. There was the one window next to the only door, probably the one that light had bled through, but the rest of the cabin was solid walls. But then his eyes landed on the closet in the corner, and without asking, he ran to it, pulling her along with him.

"Quick, the closet, we can hide in there and sneak off whenever they leave again."

"But we don't know when that'll be," she protested.

He stopped at the closet and turned on her. "Do you have a better idea?" he hissed, his face manic with fear. Whoever was out there had human skin on his kitchen table. He didn't want to meet that person if he had a choice.

"No, I..."

"Then come on and shut up," he said, rushing into the closet and closing the door with her next to him, just as the outer door to the cabin opened.

Thomas kept the closet door slightly cracked so he could see into the cabin, and he prayed whoever was coming in didn't need anything or want to hang something up in the closet.

At first he couldn't see a thing. With the flashlight doused, the cabin was pitch black, but the figure of a man moved about without light, knowing his home well.

A second later, an oil lantern flickered to life and cast a pallid glow throughout the small interior. Thomas stared at the man, who was soaked to the bone, wearing a raincoat and rubber boots.

At first he looked like something out of a slasher flick, but then he pushed the hood of the coat off his head and Thomas saw the man was as ordinary as himself.

Thomas whispered to Sharon that it was just a man, and only one at that.

The man shrugged out of his jacket and kicked off his boots, letting them fall anywhere in the cabin.

In his left hand he carried two skinned rabbits, and he went to the kitchen and tossed them next to the human skin. If the man noticed the skin wasn't where he'd left it, he gave no sign.

Thomas cursed Sharon for her sloppiness for when she'd set the skin back down on the table.

The man poured some water into a bowl and began washing the rabbits, for all the world his actions as mundane as could be.

"What's he doing?" Sharon asked from behind Thomas. She couldn't see what was happening.

"Nothing. He's got some rabbits and it looks like he's getting them ready to cook."

"What are we gonna do?" she whispered.

"We stay here," he whispered back. "Sooner or later we can sneak out. Maybe when he falls asleep."

She nodded, and he felt her chin brush his shoulder, then he went back to watching the man prepare his dinner.

As Thomas watched, he couldn't understand what the deal was with the human skin. This man didn't look like a killer, or a psycho, but if not, then why would there be human skin in the cabin?

The man went about his business, cooking the rabbits in oil, eating, then when he was through, he went to the homemade couch and plopped down and picked up a magazine while his left pinky poked at his teeth where a piece of meat had become lodged.

Thomas' stomach was rumbling now, the smell of the cooked rabbit hanging in the air. As he'd watched the man eat, he wanted nothing more than to jump out and introduce himself, then hope he could get some of that rabbit.

Behind him, Sharon had dozed off, and he could hear her breathing softly. The fact she was sleeping while standing up told him how truly exhausted she was.

The man read magazines for more than an hour and a half, and as Thomas' eyes grew heavy and he too wanted to sleep, the man finally stirred. He checked his wrist watch to see the time and then did something Thomas wasn't expecting.

He stripped off his clothes until he was standing in the nude. He was a hairy male specimen, with dark black hairs covering his chest and back.

As the man turned to his side, Thomas' eyes went wide at the sight of the same tattoo on the man's arm as the one on the skin on the table. That didn't make one bit of sense, but Thomas, now awake again, watched the man kick his clothing to the side and stretch out on the couch to go to sleep.

Feeling slightly uncomfortable, like a pervert peeking into his neighbor's windows, Thomas looked away then by pulling his eye away from the crack in the door. He stared at the inside of the door, listening to Sharon's breathing behind him and tried to get comfortable for a long night in the closet.

Fifteen minutes after the man in the cabin had stripped, Thomas could hear him snoring loudly and Thomas knew it was going to be a long night. Checking his own wrist watch, the dials luminous, he saw it was just about midnight and he was surprised at how many hours he and Sharon had already been trapped inside the closet. And then he felt pressure on his bladder and realized he needed to pee.

Oh great, he thought. *If things aren't already bad enough.*

With nothing to do about it now, he leaned against the side of the closet and tried to get some sleep, envious of Sharon, already lost in slumber.

Three hours later a loud screaming filled the cabin, snapping Thomas awake. Sharon, behind him, also came awake and both were paralyzed with fear as they hid in the closet.

"Oh my God, Thomas, what's going on?"

"I don't, know, Sharon, shhhh, he'll hear you," Thomas said as he wiped drool from the side of his mouth and leaned towards the still open door. He'd been sleeping hard, evidently as exhausted as Sharon.

As his right eye lined up with the vertical crack of the door, he peered into the interior of the cabin and his mouth slowly began to fall open in utter disbelief.

"What's happening?" came Sharon's voice. She could hear the screaming and she was scared to death. Her hands were now wrapped around Thomas' forearms and he could feel her shaking. He couldn't blame her. What he was witnessing inside the cabin was the stuff of nightmares, of fairytales.

For just a second, he wondered if he was dreaming and he squeezed his eyes shut and willed himself to wake up, but when this didn't happen and his bladder announced he still needed to pee, he knew he was awake. He'd never had to go pee in a dream before.

More screams filled the cabin and Sharon pushed closer to him so her face was buried in his back. Though they had been inside, out of the rain, for hours, their clothes were still damp and the funky smell of wet wool came to his nose. His skin was cold and clammy and felt itchy in a few places he couldn't scratch at the moment. But then another bellow of pain filled the cabin and he focused on the crack, where the door met the frame.

The naked man who had fallen asleep on the couch wasn't exactly a man any longer. Thomas watched in horror as the man now rolled across the floor, his face twisted into a mask of utter agony.

But that wasn't what was so off-putting. It was what was happening to him.

As the man rolled about on the floor, his skin began to move, undulate, and bones began to shift and stretch. Pieces of skin, not able to stretch with the new shape his body was twisting into, were splitting and falling off to land sloppily on the floor. Where the pink skin once was, red muscle glistened in the light of the oil lantern, and as Thomas watched in abject horror, hair follicles appeared, slowly growing out of the scarlet tendons to coat the body. The hands and lower legs began to stretch, inches added to the length, and fingernails grew more than four inches. The face was the most frightening to Thomas. As he stared in fascination and fear, the cheekbones receded and the jaw extended, teeth inverting and popping out as others came in. Incisors grew to points and hair began to cover the entire face until the man's visage was gone, replaced by some creature of myths.

Like a fetus emerging from the womb, the man curled into a tight ball as he endured this transformation, but eventually he calmed and stretched, like a human waking after a night's sleep to yawn and stretch tired limbs.

With the molting skin of the man strewn across the floor like dirty laundry, the beast came to its knees and then stood. Its ankles were now at right angles, the creature standing on the tips of its toes, looking like it could pounce in an instant, its thigh muscles looking powerful, cords of muscle flexing under the dark, black fur.

Thomas couldn't believe it, but he couldn't doubt his eyes.

He was staring at an honest to God werewolf.

The werewolf raised its head to the ceiling and roared in what Thomas assumed was pleasure. The creature had broken loose of its human shell and was now free to roam the land.

But what Thomas hoped might happen, namely that the werewolf would leave the cabin to dash through the forest, didn't happen.

Instead, the werewolf, with its new heightened sense of smell, slowly began flicking its head back and forth as it looked about the cabin. It took Thomas a second to realize what was happening, and when he did, he felt his bladder let go and urine roll down his pant leg.

The beast was getting the scent of him and Sharon. It knew something was added to the redolence of its home. He knew they were hiding in its lair!

No sooner did he think this then the werewolf spun on its feet, its black eyes staring directly at the closet.

Faster than Thomas could see, the creature lunged for the door and swiped at it, its long, four inch claws slicing through the wooden door like it was paper.

He screamed then, as did Sharon, the darkness of the closet and the cacophony of the werewolf attacking the door sounding like a train had fallen in with them. But then the werewolf locked the door in its paws and ripped it off its hinges, exposing Thomas and Sharon to it.

The door was ripped away like it had been caught in a hurricane and Thomas and Sharon found themselves staring up at the gaping maw of this mythical beast of legend. The creature had over a foot on Thomas, the seven foot stature making it look even more threatening, not that the teeth and claws didn't do the job nicely.

Absolutely locked in panic, Thomas turned into a coward and forgot about Sharon, only wanting to escape this nightmare vision. Dropping to the floor, he crawled between the legs of the werewolf and the creature looked down to see Thomas' butt disappear behind it. But then Sharon screamed and the werewolf's attention became riveted on her.

As Thomas scurried into a corner of the cabin, Sharon shrieked as she was grabbed by paws as large as her head and dragged out of the closet.

Thomas, now in a corner, watched in horror as Sharon was picked up, her feet dangling more than a foot off the floor.

"No, Sharon! No! *Sharooon*!" he screamed, realizing what he'd done. He'd left his wife at the mercy of the beast. True, if he'd stayed he would only have been taken first, but still, she was his wife, he should have died trying to save her.

But it was too late to take back his cowardice now. He could only watch in shock and terror as the werewolf raised its right paw with claws extended, the other holding Sharon by her head like a basketball, and swipe at her abdomen with those razor-sharp claws.

Sharon's screams abruptly stopped as her lower torso became warm, first blood spilling out, then her lower intestines. They poured out of her abdomen like boiled spoiled sausage from an over packed grocery bag cut at the bottom, and when they hit the floor, they splattered blood and gore in every direction.

Sharon's voice was locked in her throat as her mouth opened and closed like a landed fish. Thomas could only stare in shock, his left hand held out to her, but he was too petrified to move.

But the werewolf wasn't done with the invaders to its domain and as Sharon's mouth fluttered up and down, the beast raised its now bloody claw over its head and sliced her from neck to groin, opening her up like a boned fish.

Her ribcage was sliced in twain from the claws and her heart could be seen beating within, the steady beat fueled by her fear. The werewolf reached in, wrapped its claws around the pumping heart, and yanked it free in a bloody geyser that struck the rafters of the ceiling. Sharon's eyes went wide in pain and then her twitching limbs sagged, her body now resembling a rag doll.

The werewolf tossed the heart away and then shook Sharon, not understanding why she wasn't moving. Like a disgruntled child annoyed that its toy wouldn't work, it tossed her away to land in a heap of limbs in a corner. As the fresh corpse landed, the cracked ribcage allowed organs to spill out, a bloody pool of plasma spreading wide as the insides seeped out like soiled porridge.

Thomas squeaked in disbelief. This couldn't be happening! It was all a lie. There was no way in hell his wife had just been gutted by a werewolf and now the beast was turning towards him, licking its claws with a long pink tongue as it breathed in and out like a massive dog panting after a jog with its owner.

The werewolf dropped to all fours then, and began moving in a circle towards Thomas.

Now it was his turn.

If his bladder wasn't empty he knew he would have pissed himself again as he gazed at those dark black eyes with absolutely no mercy in them.

Knowing if he didn't move he was dead, Thomas forced his frozen legs to let him move and he shifted across the floor, sliding very slowly. The werewolf raised its hackles and Thomas could see it was about to attack, similar to when a guard dog is ready to pounce or a cat is about to leap on a play toy, its back legs seeming to wiggle from side to side.

Thomas could see instinctively he had less than a second to do something, anything, to save himself, and as the werewolf leaped, he reached up to the table where the rabbits had been prepared and managed to wrap his left hand around the hilt of the skinning knife lying amidst the offal and flesh of the leftover pieces of rabbit.

As his palm felt the cool hilt, the werewolf leaped, flying through the air and striking Thomas in the chest. Both went flying across the cabin to roll around and Thomas fought for his life to keep those sharp teeth and claws away from him.

But he was only human, battling something *more than* human, and he knew in the end he would loose. He felt claws bite into his hip, then another one slice into his right arm, then he felt teeth sink into his right shoulder.

Turning his head as he screamed, he found himself staring into the right eye of the beast as its jaw clamped down tight on his shoulder blade.

Thomas didn't know how he kept his head then. Maybe the pain he felt brought focus to his dazed mind, but as he turned, screaming as he stared back into the dark orb, he realized he'd found his chance, his one opening, to come out of this battle the victor.

As the pointed teeth sank deeper into his shoulder, he swung the skinning knife up and around and stabbed it into the right eye of the beast. The tip was sharp and it plunged into the eye like the orb was a black egg, continuing deeper into the brain. The full six inches of the blade slid into the socket, until the hilt began to grind on bone.

The werewolf's teeth receded and it railed backwards, its paws going to its damaged eye.

But it was too late to prevent its demise. As the creature howled in agony, its legs grew weak and with a mighty *huff*, it dropped face first onto the floor. Its claws carved long grooves into the wooden floor as it spasmed, but in seconds they ceased and the body tensed, then relaxed.

Thomas brought his left hand to his shoulder wound and pressed his palm to it to staunch the flow, then he sat perfectly still, too frightened to move, too terrified of what might happen if he did.

Eventually morning came, and as the sun touched the treetops and a dull gloom suffused the cabin through its one window, the werewolf slowly changed back to the man it once was.

Thomas watched the transformation with dull eyes, the impossible not as exciting as the night before, back when his wife was alive.

An hour after the beast had reverted back to a man, Thomas finally made himself move.

Crawling to the corpse, he used his boot to push the head, ready to crawl away if the dead man moved. But the man was dead, the hilt of the skinning knife still protruding out of the eye socket.

Still wanting a weapon, not feeling safe without one, Thomas went and with clouded eyes, wrapped a hand around the hilt of the knife and pulled it free. With a sucking sound it popped out and Thomas held it in front of him, ready for what might come next.

But nothing came next and he waited another panic-filled hour. He kept his attention away from Sharon's body, lying only a few feet from him. Every time he glanced at her face, her open eyes accused him of leaving her.

Tears fuelled his eyes and clouded his vision and he let the tears flow, weeping over his lost mate and what he'd suffered. When he had the strength to stand, he did so, even to the point of washing up in a bowl near the sink.

As he did this, he washed the skinning knife clean, too, not wanting to get blood on his hands after washing up, and he read the small words on the side of the blade, near the hilt.

STERLING SILVER was etched in fancy script.

"Well, I'll be, that shit's really true, too," he said, staring down at the corpse.

After bandaging his wounds, all but the bite to his shoulder not serious, he rested and tried to deal with his situation. His shoulder wound was bad, the punctures deep. He would need stitches, but for the moment all he could do was rip a sheet and use it to wrap the wound. It hurt like hell when he moved his right arm, but it couldn't be helped. He did find some aspirin which he popped greedily and then found a bottle of Vodka which he used to swallow the pills and deaden his senses.

The booze helped a lot when it came time to bury the bodies.

Knowing he could never explain any of what happened in the cabin to the authorities, he waited until he was strong enough and then dragged each of the bodies out of the cabin and through the woods a ways until he found a nice glade still within site of the cabin.

Then he buried his wife and the man who had killed her. The man got no marker on his grave, Thomas didn't care about him, but for his wife he cobbled together some stones. Then he made a cross out of branches, using some dried weeds to tie it together. It would do for now, he could do more later if he wanted when he was feeling better.

His morose task finished, he went back to the cabin, and though there was blood everywhere, on the floor and walls, he fell to the makeshift couch and passed out. When he awoke hours later, he drank the rest of the Vodka and fell back into oblivion.

He awoke that night, as the full moon touched the sky, and began screaming in agony, mimicking the previous owner's cries of pain. It felt like his insides were being ripped out with invisible hands.

Falling to the floor, he writhed in pain, and just before he passed out, the agony too much to bear, he saw hair follicles begin to grown on his arms as his nails grew an inch. Then, mercifully, he passed out, the conscious human mind not able to withstand the transformation he was about to succumb to.

The next morning, he opened his eyes to find himself on the ground outside the cabin. He was naked, his feet covered in mud, and his skin felt tingly. As he sat up, he found he had no hangover which was good. Standing up, he realized he hadn't felt this good physically in a long time, though mentally he was in utter anguish over the death of Sharon. It was still so hard to believe and he wondered if it was all some acid-induced dream. Maybe he'd eaten some bad mushrooms found on the forest floor.

As he glanced down at his naked frame, he saw the places where he'd been clawed the previous day were gone now, and as he checked his shoulder wound, he found nothing there but the slightest hint of a scar.

Somehow he had healed over night.

Entering the cabin, he found more skin on the floor, this layer added to the one the man had shed when Tom had watched him change from inside the closet.

As he inspected it with his foot, he saw some of the skin had the same claw marks and slices he'd suffered, and he knew without a doubt this skin had been his.

And like a runaway freight train, it hit him hard and fast, the realization of his fate sending him to his knees.

Though the original owner of the cabin was gone, there was now someone new to replace him.

And what else could he do? If he went home to the city, to his old life, there would be questions about how he went camping and didn't come back with his wife. And what about the curse? If he went home and then changed, he would only infect others upon biting them, and he knew this deep down in his gut, it was what the beast would do if other humans were around. It was its nature.

No, he wasn't an evil man; he wouldn't bring this curse back to the civilized world.

And then he knew why the first man had lived here like a hermit, locked away from the rest of humanity.

He was protecting the world…from him; from what he had become.

Knowing he had no choice, Thomas slowly accepted his new fate, and once he did, he went back inside the cabin to clean it up.

He wasn't like the other man; he wouldn't live like a slob. If he was going to live here in this cabin…alone, he would need to tidy up a bit.

It was as he stepped into the cabin to see what clothes he could find to put on and get to work that he paused and gazed off into the glade where he could see the marker for his wife's grave.

At least he would still have Sharon with him. At least he would still be close to her.

And though many would find their new fate a prison, Thomas nodded and smiled, then he entered the cabin to get to work, the door slowly closing behind him.

MAN'S BEST FRIEND

Barney Roosevelt ran as fast as he could down the dock, but he was too late.

"Damn it!" he yelled as the deep sea fishing tug chugged away. He dropped his fishing rods and bait to the dock and stamped his foot in anger.

"Looks like someone's not having a good day," a voice said from behind him.

Barney turned to see a man in his seventies with a bald pate and wire rimmed glasses. He had the classic beer belly most men his age had and he wore a t-shirt, shorts, and flip-flops.

"Yeah, you could say that," Barney replied, not wanting to be rude, though he still wanted to scream to the heavens in frustration.

Of all days to get a flat tire. By the time he'd changed it and was on the road once more, he had come in too late for the deep sea fishing trip.

"I had a deposit with them, too. It's nonrefundable."

The old man shook his head. "Gee, that's tough. Tell you what. I was going out myself in a few minutes. Got me a small twenty footer. It's nothing big but it gets the job done." He stepped up closer to Barney. "I could use some company if you don't mind listening to an old man talk about his life."

Barney's frown slowly disappeared. "Really, you'd let me go with you? I can't pay; I spent it all on that damn tug." He pointed to the fishing vessel as it rounded the bay and headed off to sea.

The old man waved his hand as if he was swatting a fly away. "Ah, that's not what I meant. I'm inviting you to come along. No charge, just bring your ears and we'll be good." He held out a hand to Barney. "The name's Charlie."

"Barney," he said as he shook the older man's hand.

Charlie smiled widely. "Well then, now that it's settled, get your stuff and follow me. I was about to cast off anyway, just like I said."

Barney did as instructed, and with his hands full, he followed Charlie to the opposite end of the dock, reveling in his good fortune. Barney had begun fishing in his early twenties and now that he was in his forties, he found he was a true fan of the sport. He tried to get out on a deep sea excursion at least once a month.

"*The Second Chance*," Barney read when he saw the writing on the hull of Charlie's boat. "Any significance?"

"Yup, there is. Had me a heart attack three years ago; almost died. Was right there at death's door, and at the last second, the doctors snatched me back from oblivion. After that it took a year to recover and when I did, I retired and bought this boat. Can't take it with you, Barney, so you might as well spend it, fuck it, and play with it while you're alive."

Barney chuckled at Charlie's words. "Amen, Charlie, I couldn't agree with you more."

They boarded the boat and ten minutes later were chugging out to sea.

"I can't thank you enough for this, Charlie," he said as he leaned back and enjoyed the sun on his face.

"Not a problem, son, there's room for two easily," Charlie said. "And I know the best spot to fish. Much better than where those damn fishing trips go to. You'll see; we'll be landing flounder, bass and tuna before you know it."

"You know, Charlie, I'm really glad I met you," he said. Charlie nodded, and with a grin, he opened a beat-up red cooler and tossed Barney a beer.

Catching it, Barney's smile went from ear to ear. "Damn, now I'm really glad to meet you." he two men laughed as the boat headed out to sea.

Four hours later and Barney wished he had never met Charlie.

The old bastard would *not* shut up. All he did was go on and on, and no matter how many times Barney tried to deflect the conversation and make the man be quiet, Charlie would just keep going.

The old man talked about his time in the war, his dead wife, his two good-for-nothing-sons and a hundred other things.

"If we're lucky I can introduce you to my friend," Charlie said between speeches.

"Huh, what?" Barney asked. He was doing his best to tune out the old man's droning voice but the last sentence seemed to penetrate the cloud that was his inattentiveness.

"My friend; if we're lucky he'll show up. Don't know when he'll show but he always does."

"Sure, Charlie, whatever you say," Barney said, not caring at all. This day had turned out terrible. First he missed his fishing trip, then lost his money for the deposit, and now he'd ended up in the middle of the ocean with an old man who wouldn't shut the hell up. And then to add to the list, the old geezer was turning senile, and was talking about an imaginary friend.

What friend? They were in the middle of nowhere. The old guy was losing it.

Barney concentrated on his rod, gripping it tightly in his hands. The knuckles in both his hands were bone white and he was grinding his teeth in frustration.

Charlie walked up and leaned against the railing so he could look Barney in the eyes.

"So, as I was saying, my second son, he's the oldest, well, he goes and gets himself arrested. So he calls me and wants me to bail him out. I, of course told him no, that he should learn a lesson and stay there, but do you think he was all right with that? Hell no. He tells me if I ever want him to come visit me again, I better bail his ass out of jail. I told him not to blackmail me; that I was his father and he should respect me. He said it was my duty as a father to bail him out as he was my son. Can you imagine that? Like it was my fault he was in a bar fight and was arrested in the first place? So anyway, I told him…"

Barney had a headache—no, not a headache, a migraine. One that began behind his eyes and wrapped around his head and into his neck. It felt like a workman was holding a hammer, and with each tick of the clock, the man was hitting him on the head.

As his heart beat, so too did the pounding continue. Barney gripped the fishing rod in his hands so tight that it actually began to bend a little, the rod tough enough to battle a small shark, but unable to take the stress of Barney's aggravation.

"So you know what I did?" Charlie asked, not waiting for a reply. "I went down there and bailed him out. And the ungrateful bastard didn't even say thank you. Instead he borrowed twenty bucks for a cab and left me standing there like a fool. Now I ask you, did I deserve that? How can a son do that to his own father? Well, I tell you, I was so mad I turned around and went…."

Barney screamed as the world went white, then red.

Without realizing what he was doing, his mind shutting down from pure anger and rage, he dropped his fishing rod, picked up a long pole with a hook on it—the pole used to drag in fishing nets—and hit Charlie over the head with it like it was a baseball bat.

The tip of the pole, where the curved hook was, embedded itself into the top of Charlie's skull, severing the brainstem from his cranium in an instant. Charlie's eyes rolled up into the back of his head and his arms began to twitch. He dropped to the deck, a copious amount of blood pumping around the hook and onto the deck as his body spasmed as if it was flooded with electricity.

The end of the pole slid from Barney's hands and clattered onto the wooden deck and Charlie's boots made a staccato of drumbeats until finally slowing and then stopping altogether.

Barney stood perfectly still, blinking as he stared down at Charlie cooling corpse.

"I...I didn't mean to do that," he said to Charlie. "I just wanted you to shut the fuck up. Oh, Jesus, I didn't want you to die. Oh, Christ, what the hell do I do now?" He looked around the boat and then out into the ocean. It was absolutely quiet, with the exception of the water slapping the hull.

No one had seen him kill Charlie; no one knew what he'd done. He thought back to when they had left the dock. No one had been around. That meant no one had seen him leave the dock in Charlie's boat.

If he waited until nightfall and disposed of the corpse, he could sneak back into the harbor, wipe down the boat for fingerprints like he'd seen on that CSI TV show, and he would be in the clear.

He looked down at Charlie again, feeling guilty for what he had done to the old man.

But he couldn't take it back so the only thing to do was cover his ass.

With a sigh, he bent over and dragged Charlie's body closer to the railing. Though he wanted to just toss it into the water, he was smart enough to know it would only float. It had to sink.

Thinking hard on the subject, he came up with only one conclusion.

Like a balloon, Charlie had to be popped.

Pulling his fisherman's knife from its sheath on his belt, he knelt down, placed the tip of the six inch blade at Charlie's throat, and pushed down.

The blade slid in easily, and Barney winced as the flesh gave way. Only a small amount of blood pooled around the blade, as Charlie's heart wasn't pumping anymore.

With a deep frown of disgust, Barney began cutting downward towards Charlie's groin, gutting the old man like a fish. As he cut, clothing and flesh parted.

The rib cage was hard to slice through but Barney persevered, working at his chore with mechanical precision.

Sweat poured off his forehead as he sawed down to the corpse's belly button. Intestines popped out of Charlie's abdomen like they were springs forced into a small tube, then suddenly set free. The rank odor of blood and offal assaulted his nose and he had to fight off the temptation to vomit.

When he finished his task, he wiped his brow of sweat and used Charlie's pant leg to clean the blade of blood and bits of flesh. When it was clean, he put it away. He took a deep breath of clean air by turning his head to the side, then bent over, picked Charlie up under his armpits, and tossed him over the side of the boat like he was a piece of trash.

The body landed without fanfare, sinking into the ocean like a rock.

Barney stared at the spot where the body had sunk for almost a minute, then went into the wheelhouse to begin cleaning up any trace he was on the boat.

While Barney busied himself in the small wheelhouse, at the aft end of the boat, there was a small, steel, mesh, one foot step that was at water level. As if rising from the very depths like a monster from an old movie, the body slowly resurfaced.

It seemed to float on the water, defying the ocean current, until it drifted to the boat and slid onto the mesh step. It lay there, unmoving, still very dead, as the waves caressed the slack face.

Barney finished cleaning up the boat of his presence as best he could, and as the sky grew dark, he went to the aft end of the boat to pull in the anchor.

It was as he did this that he spotted the dark shape on the steel step, and as he moved closer, his jaw dropped when he saw it was Charlie's corpse.

Already the body was beginning to show decay from being in the water. The skin exposed to the air was a pale white and the intestines floated in the water, still attached, waving like red and brown streamers in the wind.

"What the hell?" Barney said to himself as he stared at the corpse.

He looked around the boat, wondering if someone was playing tricks on him. After all, he watched the body sink into the ocean. How the hell did it return?

He decided it was a fluke, somehow air had been trapped in the body and it resurfaced to end up back on the boat—a one in a million oddity.

Using the pole with the still bloody hook, he pushed the corpse back into the water, then poked it a few times to break the skin and allow more water into the body.

Once more the corpse drifted away to sink below the surface.

Satisfied the body was gone for good this time; Barney went to the wheelhouse and started the engine.

It turned over on the first try, and as he pushed the throttle forward, he began moving, deciding his ordeal was finally over.

So when he spotted the dark shape off the starboard bow of the boat, at first he didn't give it much thought. He merely assumed it was some debris, such as a log or perhaps the carcass of a large fish.

As the boat moved closer, he swung the bow to port and let the shape come abroad. There was a spotlight on the boat and he used it to illuminate the shape.

His eyes went wide when he saw it was Charlie's corpse, once more bobbing in the water, like the man had gone for a swim and was resting. The body was face down, the head tilted so that the entire skull was submerged. But there was no mistaking the clothing. Besides, what were the odds Barney would have another, different corpse pop up exactly where he had killed Charlie?

Once more the odds were enormous.

Deciding he needed to take more drastic measures, he used the pole and hauled in the corpse like it was the catch of the day. This time, he wasn't fooling around. Using a long-bladed carving knife taken from Charlie's deck cabinet, Barney began carving the body up like it was a turkey on Thanksgiving.

The blood in the body had congealed and was now a thick paste, and as he hacked and cut, he was having the hardest time slicing through the tendons connecting the bones to one another. By the time he was finished, he was covered in gore, and Charlie was in a dozen pieces.

One at a time, he lobbed the bloody parts into the ocean, satisfied when each one sank below the water line. Last was the head, and as Barney looked into Charlie's glazed eyes, he shook his own head sadly.

"Sorry about this, old timer, I just wished you hadn't talked so fucking much." He tossed the head into the water with a, "So long."

The head seemed to float for a few seconds, then tipped upside down so the jagged stump of the neck was pointed up, then it was lost in the water as it sank like a rock.

Barney quickly washed up, though he didn't do as good a job as he should have. He washed his face and arms, then wiped his clothes as best he could, but they were still soaked with blood. He decided he could explain it off as fish blood if he had to, on the off chance he was stopped by a straggler at the dock when he returned.

Satisfied the murder was covered up for good, he went to the wheelhouse, pushed the throttle all the way forward, and headed back to port, a sly smile creasing his lips.

He had actually gotten away with murder, something he would never have believed was possible, and especially not the act itself.

Humming a tune to himself, he steered the boat for the faint lights of the distant shore, feeling better than he had all day.

With night having fallen hours ago, 'The Second Chance' chugged into the harbor. Barney swung the boat around so the starboard side connected with the old car tires tied to the side of the dock to protect the hulls of the ships.

It was silent and empty on the dock as he tied the mooring lines and disembarked. He was confident he was in the clear when an armed security guard walked up to him from out of the shadows.

"Hey, there, how's it going tonight? Out for a little late night fishing?"

Barney nodded as he hid his face. If he could get out without the guard stopping him, he would be home free. If only he had known the dock had security, he would have come up with another plan.

"Yeah, something like that," Barney said curtly. He wanted the man to leave—now.

"Catch anything?" the security guard asked.

"Nah, no bites today."

"Too bad."

Barney didn't reply. He was about to climb off the boat and walk to the exit, figuring he could ignore the guard if the man called out him again, when there was a splash at the aft end of the boat.

No sooner did the splash echo off the docks then something flew through the air and landed on the deck of the boat. It was round and it rolled across the worn boards until it came up right between Barney's feet.

The security guard heard the splash and had seen the shape in the wan moonlight. As it thumped and rolled, he pulled his flashlight out and aimed it at Barney.

That was when he saw the blood covering Barney from head to toe.

As the beam of light played over Barney, it settled at his feet and the security guard's mouth went wide when he saw the decapitated head of Charlie.

"What the fuck? That's Charlie!" The guard drew his sidearm and aimed it at Barney. "Don't fucking move, mister!" The security guard aimed the flashlight at the aft end of the boat, reading the name of the vessel when it was illuminated. "This is Charlie's boat. I don't know what the fuck is going on here, mister, but you have a lot of explaining to do to the cops."

Barney was so scared he thought he would die right there and then, and he was about to make a break for it when the security guard shouted, "Don't try it! You move and I shoot!"

But Barney was in fight or flight mode and flight was the one he picked. With the dock out of the question, he dove over the side of the boat and into the water, hoping to swim around the boat and lose himself among the other vessels moored to the docks. If he was lucky, he could be long gone before the police arrived. The security guard didn't know who he was, no one did on the dock. All the police would have would be a sketch of his face, and if he stayed in hiding for a while, nothing would come of it. And even if it did, it was all circumstantial.

But no sooner did he hit the water and swim to the surface then he was hit from behind by what felt like a giant fist.

The air was knocked out of him and he let out a scream, sucking in water. Sputtering, he tried to swim away from what was attacking him, but when he tried, he was hit from the front, the air leaving his lungs in a *whoosh.*

He was knocked so hard he saw stars as he flailed in the water. Once more he was struck, this time from the side, and he could barely stay afloat.

As he floundered, knowing he was going to drown, he was struck on the side again, only this time he was pushed until his shoulders struck the tires lining the dock. He was just forward of The Second Chance and the security guard was right there waiting for him.

The man reached down, grabbed Barney by his collar, and hauled him up as Barney used his legs to get some purchase on one of the tires to pull himself up. He fell to the planks of the dock choking and spitting water, and as he laid there, helpless, weak as a baby, he felt his hands pulled around his back to be handcuffed. His clothing, though soaked, was still bloody and he knew, from that same show on the television that DNA or whatever could be taken from the diluted blood.

As he was pulled to his knees, he blinked water from his eyes, and as his vision cleared, he was greeted by his first look at what attacked him.

It was a bottle-nosed dolphin.

"What the hell?" he sputtered through a coughing fit.

"Looks like you met Earl," the security guard said as he called in to dispatch to report a murder and called for the police. His two-way radio crackled with a response seconds after he spoke into it.

"Who the fuck is Earl?" Barney gasped as he sucked in a breath of air. His front and back hurt from where he was struck by the nose of the dolphin.

"Earl was Charlie's best friend. Charlie would feed him fish when he was out in the bay. It got so that Earl was like a dog, always hanging around Charlie's boat. Charlie would toss a ball out to Earl and the dolphin would always bring it back. It's the damndest thing. Charlie used to say he thought Earl might have been in one of those aquariums or zoos, like a trained dolphin. Then they must have set him free."

"So that was the friend he was talking about—a fucking dolphin. But why did it hang around bugging me?" Barney asked.

The guard shrugged. "That's a good question, mister. Maybe it thought you were Charlie seems you were on his boat, or it didn't like what you did to its friend. Where's the rest of Charlie, you sick fuck, huh?" He gestured to Charlie's severed head still on the boat. "Either way, I reckon you're gonna have a long time to figure out why Earl stayed around you."

"What?"

The guard smiled slightly. "I liked Charlie, mister, and you should he glad I don't kill you right now and let the dolphin take your carcass out to sea. But as I knew Charlie well, I know he wasn't a violent man. See, we don't have the death penalty in this state, but I reckon you're going away for life. I'd bet my pension on that one." As he finished his small speech, the sound of a siren could be heard and moments later the red and blue lights of two squad cars approached.

Barney, still on his knees, let his shoulders sag in defeat, and he ignored the pain of his handcuffed wrists.

"Christ, I wish I never took up fishing," he said to himself.

As if in reply, the dolphin jumped up, did a spin, and let out a few choice squeals and clicks, then swam back out to sea.

MISTAKES

It never should have happened.

Actually, looking back to when it all began, it should have been impossible for it to happen.

The dead don't walk; they don't get back up and smile at you.

Dead is dead.

Right?

Well, that's what I thought, too, but I had no idea of the real world, about what I was dealing with in my struggle to find a breakthrough.

Things existed in this world that most would believe only existed in books, in the movies, but I found out a year ago exactly, through my own machinations, that make believe can also be reality.

But maybe I should go back to the beginning, as in the very first moment when things began to go so terribly wrong.

You see, I was a doctor of medicine, but since then I have lost my license to practice. One more thing taken away from me, my entire life stripped away on that one fateful night.

It was my wife you see. It was her fault.

No, wait, that's wrong of me. It wasn't her fault she came back from the dead, any more than it was my fault for hitting that tree and sending her through the front windshield of my Suburban.

You see, we were out for a night on the town. God, how I loved her. She was so full of life, and her beauty, well, it was none surpassed by any other woman I knew of.

We had a wonderful time that night. Dinner, dancing, oh, it was absolutely marvelous. And as we were heading home, she had begun to whisper promises of the passion to come once we returned home.

But that wasn't to be, at least not in the way we planned, for a stray cat appeared before me in the road and I swerved to avoid it. Looking back, I wish I had run the damn thing down, for if I had, my sweet Rose would still be alive to this day.

But alas, instinct took over and I jolted the wheel to the right, trying to swerve around the cursed feline.

But where I missed the animal, I didn't miss one of the large oak trees lining the road and the vehicle plowed into it like a tank onto the beach of Normandy. I had my seatbelt on and that was probably what saved my life, but Rose, well, she hadn't put it on. If she had, perhaps it would have saved her.

Ah, mistakes a plenty that night, now that I look back, but they say hindsight is twenty-twenty.

She was catapulted through the front windshield, her neck snapping on impact. Her body flew onto the hood, slid across it, and crashed into the tree where it slid off to lay unmoving on the ground.

At first I was stunned by the impact, but slowly, I came to my senses and realized my darling Rose wasn't beside me. That was when I climbed out of the vehicle and saw her lying so very motionless; her head at such an odd angle I knew there was no way she was still alive.

Looking around myself, I saw no one about. By luck or God's will, the road was devoid of other residences or people out for a walk in the cool night air.

Even through my grief of seeing my beloved Rose lying there dead, I knew this would ruin me, my career. For I had been drinking, rather heavily actually, and once word got out I had killed my wife while driving drunk, well, my practice would be over.

As I bent over her and cupped her face in my hands, a small idea pricked at the back of my mind. I knew it was fantastic and utterly improbable but in my desperation and grief I wasn't thinking clearly.

Gathering her up into my arms, I placed her back in her seat, then after a few faulting tries, managed to get the Suburban running again. The tree may have been stout, but the Suburban was a tank on wheels. The front grille was pushed in and the bumper was ruined, but the engine was intact, though the fan blade seemed bent.

So, with a squeaking of twisted metal as the fan blade whacked something metallic, I drove on, my eyes flicking to my wife only to pull them away.

You would think with me being a doctor that the sight of blood wouldn't bother me but that would be the farthest thing from the truth. I had always found the sight of blood distasteful, but had learned to overcome my aversion for the greater good.

I drove to my medical practice, a small, refurbished house on the edge of town. It had been one of a dozen cottages at one time, but as time passed, the city had torn them down to put up storefronts filled with everything from copy paper to shampoo outlets, all mercifully closed now. But mine had remained; a little old lady living there until she was ninety-three. When she had died, her grandson sold it to me, for I had been his physician for many years and we had a relationship as acquaintances.

I drove right up to the door, and when I saw the coast was clear, I went around to the passenger's side door and took Rose out. As I cradled her in my arms, she felt so light, so fragile. Her neck was twisted and I was looking at the back of her head instead of her face, but I know I could fix that once I had her inside, in my lab.

What would I be doing with a lab you ask?

Simple. I was a doctor yes, but I was also interested in halting death. I wanted to find the Holy Grail that could reanimate dead tissue.

I worked in secret, knowing if I so much as attempted to tell the scientific community about my work they would have my license revoked and have me run out of town.

So I worked in secret, in the cellar of my practice. As I gave physicals and checked sore throats on the first floor, none of my patients had any idea as to what was below their feet.

It had taken me years, but I managed to acquire a complete working laboratory. The internet is amazing you know. You can buy almost anything there for the right price. And it is all shipped to your door anonymously.

I carried Rose down the steps, and with my elbow managed to turn on the light switch on the wall. The harsh hum of the phosphorescent bulbs banished the darkness as I carried Rose to the steel table set up there for precisely this purpose. As I stared at her glazed-over eyes, my heart broke inside me, and if there had been any chance I may have changed my mind, it left me then. For I loved this woman more than anything in the world, and though I knew I needed to hide this night's events to save my career, love also drove me onward, the pair of reasons more than enough to see my designs reach the coming conclusion.

Before this, I had only attempted my experiment on dead animals. I'd had some small luck with cats and dogs, but each time it had gone awry and the specimens had to be destroyed.

I didn't know if this was because of the decay of the brain or perhaps another reason, such as improper blood flow. That was what I had been working on with the last subject—a dog.

I had gotten a dog at the pound in the next state. I needed to do this because if I went too regularly to the same ones, the handlers would know something was amiss.

I brought the dog home, a Collie if I was right. The breed didn't really matter to me I'm sorry to say, and I wasn't much on dogs and the different breeds. An animal was an animal to me.

I placed a large amount of rat poison in the dog food, making sure to wet it as the instructions on the bag stated. It became a rich stew, and though I was loathe to admit it, the food didn't smell too bad, in fact it was quite attractive to my taste buds. Of course, the rat poison turned away any idea of sampling some out of curiosity.

When I gave the trusting dog the bowl, it devoured the meal in less than a minute, licking its chops and looking at me with woeful eyes. I have to admit that I would always feel a twinge of guilt when the animal's looked at me like that, but I knew the death of one more animal was for the greater good, and though my heart wasn't hardened, it was determined.

I have to confess, I would never watch the animals die. This dog as well, I left to expire alone.

Closing the door to the small room the dog was in, I went about my work and ignored the pitiful cries of the dying animal.

Upon returning an hour later, the dog was very dead, with blood pooling around its muzzle, the legs twisted into unnatural angles.

I picked it up, carried it into the main room, and placed it on the steel table, then took a hypodermic of the liquid I had worked so hard to create—the re-agent. It glowed a pale orange, and to this day I didn't know why this was. Something about the chemical makeup I suppose.

I injected the liquid into the dog's heart—the only place for it to go for the best possible effect—and began to massage the ribcage as I manually pumped the revitalizing re-agent through the dog's system.

From past experiments, I would be lucky if the dog so much as twitched, such as the cats I had worked on previously, but something in the re-agent must have had a different effect, for this time the dog's eyes snapped open and it began to howl as if it was on fire.

I admit, I was shocked, and I fell back against the wall. Meanwhile, on the table, the dog jumped up, and though its legs could barely sustain it, bent at odd angles, the head swiveled towards me as the abhorring yelping continued.

The dog appeared to be in utter agony, and as I watched, it bent its head at an unnatural angle and began to gnaw at its chest, directly where I had injected the re-agent.

Then, to my absolute shock and surprise, the dog began to eat at its chest, to tear its flesh and fur away as its muzzle began to burrow deep into its chest.

I didn't know what to do so I stared silently, my mouth open and my eyes wide. As the dog continued to chew and tear at itself, the yelping never ceased. It was a sound to make a compassionate human being cringe with empathy.

The dog's head was halfway into its torso by now, congealing blood dripping onto the table. As I stared in amazement, the dog ripped out its rib cage and spat the crimson bones aside only to go back in for more.

Then, with the yelping slightly muffled as the head was now deep inside the bloody cavity, the dog found the organ causing it so much pain. Sharp teeth clamped on its heart like a vise, and with a mighty yank, the animal pulled its heart from its body, the organ now pulsing in its mouth as my re-agent worked to revitalize the heart.

The dog was still yelping though the sound had faded in pitch, and as I watched, the dog clamped its teeth down as tightly as possible, slicing the heart in twain, the incisors tearing jagged gouges into the now faltering organ.

As the dog removed its heart, so too did its animation wan and it fell off the table to land stiff, the heart still seeping blood from inside the dog's still mouth.

My greatest success had been a disastrous failure and I can't tell you how long I stayed there, staring at the animal before finally doing the grisly task of cleaning up the mess and destroying the carcass.

So why was I here now with my dead wife on the table, another hypodermic in my hand?

Simple, I had to, I needed to, and if I can be honest, once my initial grief and panic had waned, I realized I would never get another chance like this again. To have a corpse so fresh it was still warm.

And since that day with the dog, I have modified the re-agent. In fact, three weeks ago, I had excellent luck with a squirrel and before that another cat.

I gently brushed the hair from my wife's forehead and fixed her head so it was facing the correct way. There was a protuberance pushing out under the skin on the side of her neck but I ignored it.

With a heavy sigh, and after wiping my eyes clear of tears, I became focused on the task at hand.

With a nod to myself, I plunged the needle into her chest, into her heart, and when the re-agent was inside her, I withdrew the needle and began to pump her chest, allowing the re-agent to course through her system.

Looking back now, I wonder if it was a mistake, if I should never have experimented on human beings, but should have stayed with the four-legged variety.

But the past is the past and what's done is done, as they say.

As I pumped my sweet Rose's chest, I cried for her, but mostly for myself, and as I stopped after three full minutes and still nothing, I fell back against the wall and let out a wail to rival that dog that had torn out its own heart.

It shouldn't have happened, for the time the re-agent should take effect was passed, but as I cried and shook my head with grief, I didn't see that on the table, my wife had opened her eyes.

MOMMA'S BOY

"Harold! Get up here, I need changing again! Harold!"

The shrill voice filled the house, seeming to slice the air like a dagger through flesh. The voice floated from the second floor bedroom, down the hallway, and then down the old worn wooden stairs.

The voice floated through the dark house, all the shades drawn, and finally settled on the young man sitting at the dining room table, with hands clenched into fists.

His knuckles were white with the pressure as the face of the young man cringed at the sound of his name.

"Harold! Did you hear me?"

And then, to add insult to injury, a bell began to chime. A tingling bell that should remind him of Christmas, but instead it drove him crazy. To him, the bell was the sound of death.

He would like to think it would be his mother's death, but the truth was he didn't think the old crone would ever die.

Stricken with a debilitating illness, she had been wasting away for almost seven long years now and every time he thought she finally expired, she would open her eyes and snap at him.

Oh, yes, she would snap at him. Instead of being grateful that her only son had given up his life to take care of her, she constantly belittled him, nagging and poking at him like a crow would at the open wound of a corpse.

She never let up, he never did anything right. If he made her soup it was too hot or too cold. If he made her a sandwich the cut in the bread was off. If he made her pudding there was too much milk in it. He could never please her and though at one time he did love her, as a dutiful son should; now all he wanted was her dead.

But he was too much of a coward to do it.

"Harold!" This followed by that damn bell, the tinkling filling his brain like an ice pick.

With a deep sigh of regret, he relaxed his fists, the skin tone returning to normal, and he stood up from his chair.

"Coming, Mother!" He called as he began walking to the kitchen.

The clock on the wall said it was 6:10 p.m. and he knew she wanted her evening tea. She was very predictable, his mother. She would eat lunch at precisely 12:30, then at 2 p.m. she would have a bowel movement, one Harold would then have to clean. She wouldn't use a bedpan, and Harold had to change her like she was a one-year-old, the large diapers wrapped around her skin and bones like bandages on a mummy.

He thought she did it to belittle him even more than she already did. She could use a bedpan if she preferred, but she liked the idea of her son having to wipe her ass.

Then, at 5:30 p.m. she would have her supper, which usually consisted of something light.

And then, finally, at 6:10 she would have tea with a cookie or something sweet.

As Harold prepared her tea, he had dark thoughts of slipping in something poisonous. He imagined her sipping the tea, telling him how too hot or cold it was, then she would suddenly stop talking, drop the tea to her lap as she began to spasm. She would roll her eyes and reach for her throat as she gasped her one final breath of air. But then a dry rasp would come from her open mouth and she would slump forward, dead at last.

But he knew that wouldn't be happening. He watched enough crime shows to know if he poisoned her they would know it.

No, he just had to wait for nature to take its course, no matter how many more years that would be.

"Harold, damn you, boy, where the hell is my tea?"

Pulled from his reverie, he finished making the tea, added a couple of Graham crackers to the tray and slowly plodded up the stairs.

As he walked through the gloom-filled house, his eyes scanned the pictures on the wall hanging haphazardly, most crooked. They were crooked because he didn't have the energy to fix them. He never left the house, as he was now a full time nurse. His mother had a wealthy bank account, the stipend more than enough to support them both for many years to come.

"Harold, where are you, boy?"

"Coming, Mother, I'm almost there," he called as he began walking up the stairs, the boards creaking with each footstep. There were more pictures here as well, some with his father in them. But the man had left when Harold was just a boy, barely five, the man not able to deal with his shrew of a wife any longer.

And so Harold had become husband, son and best friend to his mother, and sometimes, when she had been younger and more amorous, she'd come into his bedroom late at night when he was asleep and crawled into his bed.

Then, hands would go places they should never go and he had become so much more than just a son for her. And it made him feel dirty every single day of his life until she finally stopped.

He had no friends, as he was home schooled, and truth be told, to him, there wasn't a life outside the dark walls of his house. Though he wished for his mother's death, at the same time it frightened him.

What would he do when she was finally gone?

"Hurry up, Harold, it's almost 6:15," she said from the bedroom.

"Yes, Mother," he replied as he reached the top of the stairs and entered her bedroom.

The odor of death permeated the room, or the odor of death waiting in the wings for its time to arrive. Harold barley noticed this; the redolence of decay had been hanging in the air of the bedroom for so long it was as natural to him as detecting salt on an ocean breeze.

Standing in the doorway, he gazed across the room at his mother.

"Well, it's about time, Harold. What were you doing down there, Mmm? Looking at those dirty magazines I bet, filthy boy,"

"Yes, Mother."

As he crossed the room with the tray, he took in his mother's gaunt appearance. She was so frail she looked like she was dead already, but the fire in her eyes belayed that. Her skin was tight against the skull, the bone protruding in places so that it looked like you might cut yourself if you rubbed her face too hard with your palm. Her hands were like brittle claws, curved and gnarled like old tree branches. Dark warts and liver spots covered her flesh to the point the original, flesh tone was gone forever. As he moved closer, he detected the ammonia of urine.

Great, she's pissed herself again, he thought.

"Give it here, boy, it's almost too late now," she barked as he set the tray on her lap. She was sitting up, one of the few things she could still do without help, but leaving the bed was practically impossible. For bathing, when she would allow one, he would carry her and use the special chair setup in the shower stall.

But no sooner would she be clean and bathed then an hour later she would smell like urine or shit herself again, all that work for nothing.

Her buttocks and back were covered with bed sores, most weeping a yellow pus that never seemed to stop. The sheets were crusted like moldy bread and a pungent odor hovered around her like bees to a flower.

"Here you are mother, just the way you like it," he said as he left the tray and stepped back.

She gazed at the tea, then without preamble picked it up and as she raised it to her lips she looked at Harold.

"I hope it has the right amount of sugar in it."

"Yes, Mother," he replied, knowing there was nothing else to say that would please her.

She sipped the tea, and no sooner had the liquid touched her lips then she spit it out, followed by tossing the steaming liquid at her son, though she still held onto the tea cup.

"Damn it, boy, it's too cold! Get me another one!"

Harold screamed as the scalding tea landed on his lower torso and crotch. At first the tea seared his flesh, but soon it was cooling, but he knew when he undressed that night he would have red welts where the tea had touched his flesh after seeping through his clothes.

"And change your clothes, your all wet," she demanded. "But not until you get me another cup, and this time make sure it's hot!"

Panting from the pain, he stepped to her and took the tray, wincing as he moved his legs.

"Yes…Mother," he gasped.

She shook her head, her stringy, greasy hair shifting slightly.

"Such a weak thing you are, Harold, no wonder your father left you. He was ashamed of having such a pathetic son."

Gritting his teeth, he nodded. "Yes, Mother, I suppose so. I'll be right back with a fresh cup," he said as he walked way.

"And get me some of those biscuits I like, not those damn graham cracker cookies. You like those, not me!" She called after him. "Damn fool of a boy."

He hunched his shoulders as he listened and then continued onward, back down the stairs, passing the family photos and back into the kitchen.

As he began making more tea, wincing each time he moved, he could hear some noise coming from the street in front of the house. It sounded like screams, then a crash of metal on metal, followed by a car horn. The horn was blaring, but then it stopped and he was about to go check, wondering what might be happening, when his mother's voice filled the house.

"Harold! Harold! Make sure you get the sugar right this time, too!"

Thinking of checking what was going outside was forgotten as his mother's voice penetrated his mind. Focusing on the tea, he got to work again and in no time was slowly climbing the stairs once again.

As he did, he thought of his childhood years, and how his mother had treated him. She had never really treated him as her son, no, he was more like her pet, there for whatever she needed him to be. Whether it was a lover, a maid, or a confidant, he was always there for her. Deep down he did love her, he had to, she was his mother after all, but there was something else there, too, something that had been growing for so many years it was a part of him.

Hate, pure unadulterated hate for another living person.

As he reached her room, she was waiting for him. She had the TV on, and she impatiently flicked through the channels. The news was on every channel, people talking about a crisis, about people attacking others. But no sooner did Harold hear a few words, tidbits, then she shut off the television and tossed the remote away from her.

"Ah, all fools, damn country. When I was young, my generation knew how to do things," she looked to Harold. "Not like you and others your age. They're all fools, Harold, running this country to the ground. You should listen to me; I know what I'm talking about."

"Yes, Mother," he said softly, not wanting to get her started. To her, everything in the world was his fault. His *generation* as she called it. He took it all with a stiff upper lip, but deep down it made him want to scream, or cry, or both.

"Ah, good, my tea, now let's see if you got it right this time."

He answered by setting the tray on her lap again, the tray wobbling for a moment.

He stepped back again, but not as far as last time, thinking the tea had to be fine. He had boiled it to the point there was nothing left of the water in the pot, and had then rushed up here as fast as he could once he'd poured it. Water was not able to be made hotter by standard means and he was confident she would be pleased.

So when she took a sip and with a snarl tossed the scalding tea into his face, he lost it, his mind finally cracking from all the abuse and torture he'd suffered under his mother's hands.

With a yell, blinded by the scalding liquid, he reached out and wrapped his hands around her frail neck.

"Harold, what are you doing?" She squawked. "Release me at once!"

But Harold wasn't listening anymore. Now lost in rage, all that was left was an abused man who'd had enough.

"No, Mother, not this time, now it's time to die!" Harold screamed loudly, his mouth curved up in rage as he squeezed the life out of her. She began to gasp, her tongue protruding, then she began to beat her hands at him.

A small part of his mind realized if he strangled her people would know, they could tell, so he let her neck go and then grabbed a pillow, then climbed on top of her, sitting on her lap like she had done to him time and again in the middle of the night.

He pressed down on the pillow, her face now lost under the feathered material and her legs kicked and fluttered behind him and her arms waved, her hands trying to find his face.

Her right hand managed to find his cheek and nails raked his flesh, leaving a deep, bloody gash. But Harold ignored the pain, his face already bright red from the hot tea. His eyes were blurry from either being burned or it was just a killing lust, but still he pressed, putting all of his weight on the single pillow.

At first she fought him, body jerking, but soon she began to tire as her lungs struggled for oxygen. Then, as he prayed it would happen, she finally stopped moving and her arms fell to her sides and she became immobile.

Breathing hard, panting like a dog, he still pressed, not believing she could actually die. She was like a demon from Hell, never fully destroyed, but always returning just when you thought you were free.

He stayed on top of her, pushing the pillow onto her face for almost five minutes, like a statue frozen in time, and then he blinked and sat back, taking the pillow off her face.

And there she was, dead at last.

He mouth was parted, her tongue slightly poking out, her eyes still open but seeing nothing. Her skin was taut and he could detect the odor of yet more offal and urine, the woman evacuating her bowels and bladder in death.

So, she was finally dead. He had done something he never thought he would have the guts for and yet here it was.

He was free, finally free.

"Mother?" He said, expecting her eyes to snap forward and then her words to attack him once more, but nothing happened, her face was stiff from death.

Checking her neck, he was relieved to see there was barely a mark there. No matter how hard he had squeezed, the wattled, off color skin more than hid any telltale marks of strangulation. Besides, he had stopped and switched to the pillow long before he could have done any serious damage…he hoped.

She looked almost like she was sleeping, but with her eyes open, so he reached out and closed them, still expecting her to turn her head and belittle him again. As he closed her eyes, his hand began to shake and he climbed off the bed, feeling the first stages of shock seeping in.

But despite this, he felt like he was the happiest man alive, like he had been given a life sentence in Hell and was suddenly released for no apparent reason.

A chuckle came to his mouth, filling the room and it sounded wrong somehow. Laughter wasn't allowed in this room, now or before. Feeling guilty, he left the room after glancing one last time at his mother.

He thought he should go cover her with a sheet, but decided against it. No, better it looked like she had died in her sleep and he hadn't touched her at all.

It wouldn't be hard to act like he was grieving for her, for there was a small part of him, the child of so many years ago, that was going to miss her.

Though she was a shrew, she was his mother, his only mother in this life, and now she was gone.

Sighing heavily, he went to the bathroom, cleaned up and then went to the phone to call the coroner, the entire time fighting to keep the hint of a smile that kept trying to appear on his face.

He was actually free!

"Oh, Harold, I'm so sorry for your loss," the night nurse said from the hospital at the other end of the phone call. "But we don't have anyone available to get your mother right now. The coroner's up to his eyeballs in bodies tonight."

"What do you mean you can't come get her? She's dead. That's what you do right? When someone dies you're supposed to get them," he said into the phone.

The nurse didn't say anything to him for a moment, as she dealt with something Harold couldn't see. The nurse knew Harold and his mother well from the times he'd brought his mother in for checkups when she wasn't feeling well. Of course later, she was at the point she was bedridden and never went back, but the town was small and the nurse knew Harold well as the dutiful son who looked after his ailing mother.

"I know that, Harold but there's something weird going on tonight. People are acting crazy. Haven't you been watching the news?"

"No," Harold replied. "Mother doesn't like me watching the news. She says it's all lies put there by the mass media."

"Oh, well, I see, look, Harold, I have to go, it's a madhouse here." Then her voice sounded far away as she spoke to someone. "Oh my God, he looks horrible, what happened, did someone bite him? Put him over there, Lisa?" Then she was back on the phone. "Harold, I have to go, I promise we'll get the coroner there as soon as we can, until then, well, once again I'm so sorry for your loss, your mother was a... sweet woman."

Harold almost laughed then remembering how awful his mother was to the hospital staff. Almost as bad as she treated him.

"All right, well, I'll be here waiting, thanks for your..." he stopped because the line was dead, the nurse had hung up.

Setting the phone back in its cradle, he went and made himself a cup of tea, thinking of his mother as he did so. No more tea, no more wiping her ass, no more listening to her belittle him.

It was hard to believe it was truly over.

Despite this weight lifted from his shoulders, another part of him was still saddened. Even though she could be cruel, she was his mother and now she was gone.

Going into the living room, he sat down and sipped his tea. He glanced up at the sound of someone yelling outside, but decided it was none of his business. No one would come to his house for help if there was something happening outside, he knew this with a certainty. And at the moment though, he could have cared less, lost in his inner turmoil of loss and happiness at the exact same time.

Guilt riddled his mind for what he did, but at the same time he felt good about it, like standing up to a bully in the schoolyard and winning, and then becoming the hero of the school.

The entire neighborhood knew to stay away from this particular house. The **No Trespassing** signs scattered around the property were there to make sure of it, too.

When his tea was done and his adrenalin had worn off, he felt himself becoming drowsy, and before he realized it he'd drifted off into a restless slumber.

As he dreamed, visions of his mother came to him. She was young again and she was good to him. This was before the disease had begun withering her body away and changing her personality into something as deformed as her bent figure. Of course, back then he didn't know there was any other way to live. He assumed everyone had a mother like his.

Hours later, he snapped awake and in the darkness of the room staggered to his feet, then flipped on a light.

He could hear the sounds of sirens and yells from somewhere outside, but it didn't sound close like before. A few fireworks, or what sounded like fireworks, could be heard in the distance, or maybe it was a car backfiring.

Or maybe it was gunshots? No, that would be ridiculous.

The lamp in the corner banished the darkness and he saw by the clock on the mantle it was well past midnight and close to morning. As the fugue of sleep left his mind, he realized no one had shown up to take his dead mother away.

Walking up the stairs, he entered her bedroom again. In the shadows, he could see her shape outlined, and it looked like she was sleeping once more. He could almost imagine he heard her breathing as she sucked in one more ounce of air.

Turning on the small lamp by her bedside, he gazed down at her still form. He reached out and touched her throat to make sure she was still dead and breathed a sigh of relief to see there was no pulse.

For some reason he just wanted to make sure she was dead, as if it had all been a dream and she was still alive and well.

But, no, she was dead, her blue complexion and swollen tongue the evidence of that. Turning, he went back downstairs and called the hospital again, wanting to know where the damn coroner was, but this time all he received for his trouble was a busy signal. He hung up and redialed three times, but each time he got the same droning signal.

Disgusted, he hung up the phone and went to the sink for a glass of water, then searched for the bottle of aspirin he kept in a drawer. His head was pounding and he swallowed three at once, hoping it would stop the jackhammer rattling around in his brain.

Not knowing what to do, he dimmed the light and went back to the couch, figuring he would just have to wait until morning and then he could try the coroner again. Surely whatever was happening was isolated and by morning it would all be sorted out.

He considered going to change, but was too exhausted to bother and his clothes had dried partially thanks to his body heat.

Soon, with the aspirin taking affect, he drifted off to sleep again, nightmare visions of his dead mother's face haunting him.

He snapped awake again an hour later, but he didn't know what had awoken him. Looking around the room, it was the same as before, but he knew he'd heard something, as if a person had called his name.

And then he heard it again. And as when did, his testicles slid up into his abdomen and his blood went cold as he gasped in fear and disbelief.

"Harold, where are you? Where's my damn tea?"

The voice was like dead leaves rustling in the trees in late autumn, a hoarse, dry rasp, like crackling paper.

"Mother?" He gasped impossibly. "But it can't be, you're dead," he whispered.

He waited to hear her voice again and when it didn't come he tried to tell himself he must have imagined it. After all, he'd seen her corpse, she was as dead as dead could be. This was just his guilt making him suffer and imagine things.

"Harold! Where the hell are you, boy? Give me my tea! It's time for my tea!"

No, he'd heard it that time, it was real; it wasn't in his head.

Swallowing the knot in his throat, he stood on shaky legs. His bladder was holding on by a shoestring and he forced himself to stay calm. Something inside of him shriveled into a ball, then. It was the freedom he thought he'd won, now snuffed out like a candle in a thunderstorm.

And then the ringing began, the damn ringing of the bell that drove him slowly mad.

The voice now joined the ringing until they seemed to blend into one voice.

"Harold!"

Ring, ring, ring.

"Harold!"

"I…I'm coming, Mother!" He called as he slowly crept towards the stairs.

He began climbing them one at a time, the shadows across the pictures twisting the faces into macabre reflections of what they had been in daylight.

As he reached the top landing, the voice and ringing became louder.

"Harold, damn you, boy, bring me my tea!"

He stepped into her bedroom and let out a gasp of shock.

There she was, sitting up, waving her hand as the bell tinkled back and forth. But she wasn't exactly how she had been before.

Her head was lolling to the side and the handprints of where he had squeezed her neck and crushed her windpipe were now prevalent. It had taken lividity to show the marks post mortem. Her limbs were stiff from rigor, but she worked her way through it, her bones seeming to crack each time she rang the bell.

"Mother? But how…?"

"How the hell should I know, boy, now where's my tea? You damn fool, you came up and didn't bring it? You tried to kill me, don't think you won't pay for that. I'll make your life a living hell from now on!"

"I…I'm sorry, Mother, I lost control. I'm glad you're all right. I'll go get your tea right away," he said as he turned and ran down the stairs while she called him names and cursed his ever being born.

Downstairs in the kitchen, Harold moved about as he prepared her tea, his mind frozen in shock. He was on automatic, his brain unable to register what was happening. He'd seen her, she was dead; there had been no question in his mind about it.

She was dead!

When the tea was prepared, he dropped a tea bag into the hot water and carried the tray up like he'd done so many times before. He barely felt the dampness of his clothing as he climbed the shadow enshrouded stairs. He didn't need more light, having gone up and down the stairs so many times he knew where every piece of wood was and how it would react to his weight on it.

Upon entering the room, the redolence of death was stronger now, more like rotting meat, and he scrunched up his nose at the smell.

Walking over to her, he set the tray down and then stepped back. She wasn't paying attention to him, however, as she had turned on the TV and was watching a news report.

"…and at this time, we have reports, unbelievable as it seems, that the recently dead are returning to life and are able to function in a similar capacity as before they passed away. Reports are coming from all over the world, that this is not an isolated…" she turned off the television and threw the remote to the bed.

"Bah, fools, the dead are coming back to life. What do they take us for, idiots? Damn mass media." She sipped her tea and when it wasn't to her liking, she threw it at Harold who yelped in pain as he felt his skin bubble from where she'd scalded him earlier that night.

"Damn it, boy, can't you do anything right? It's too hot this time, now get me another cup! We can do this all night until you get it right!"

Still thinking about the news report, he nodded in a daze. "Yes, Mother, right away," he said as he picked up the tea cup near his feet and took the tray from her lap to make her a fresh cup.

He went down the stairs slowly, like a man who was being led to a lifetime prison sentence, and in a way he was.

For you see, Harold had always tried to keep that small bit of hope alive inside him, knowing that one day, eventually, his mother would die and then he would be free, but now…

Well, he had just discovered that he chose to kill his mother on the one night, of all nights, when the dead were returning to life.

He'd just resigned himself to a lifetime of taking care of her as she now could *never* die. And if he decided to kill himself to end it all, he would only come back and remain her slave for all eternity.

He was truly trapped even worse than before, though impossible as that was to believe.

And as he began to boil a new pot of water for her tea, and she began calling him again in her hoarse voice, the bell ringing like a bell tower of doom, he began to laugh, a hard, manic laugh that set his chest on fire and made him cough between bouts.

And as his laughter grew louder and louder, he prayed it would somehow drone out the sound of her voice and the infernal bell, because he planned on laughing until his voice grew raw and he finally made his mind snap, for this night, the only salvation for him would be insanity and the only freedom for him was to lose his mind forever.

But even as he slowly tried to lose his mind to madness, his mother's shrill, hoarse voice seeped into his brain, boring into his head like a massive drill, and he knew he would never be free of her and would be her prisoner to the end of time.

"Harold, where's my damn tea?"

Harold slumped to the floor and wept.

MONSTER DETECTIVES

My name is Frank but everyone calls me Frankie.

Frank N. Stein, get it?

I'm the leader of the monster detectives.

My partners are a vampire and a zombie.

Strange you say?

Perhaps, but what most people don't realize, is that deep within our society, under the dark underbelly of humanity, lies a world the average citizen would never believe existed.

Monsters, demons, the supernatural, its all true, and it's up to me and my two partners to ferret it out and destroy it.

The hard part is doing our job while remaining anonymous.

It's not that hard for Vinnie to do. With the exception of disliking garlic and an aversion to wooden stakes and daylight, not to mention his pale complexion, he's basically normal looking. He can work at night with ease and with the exception of his fangs, no one would ever assume he's anything but human.

Even Zack the zombie has an easier time of it than me. Zack may be a rotting pile of meat, but with some dark sunglasses, a hat, and half a dozen cans of Lysol, he at least doesn't smell like week old road kill. He can usually wrap his face in bandages, put on some gloves and a heavy jacket, and get away as a burn victim as well.

And me?

Well, it becomes a little difficult to hide a seven foot tall man with green skin and bolts coming out of the left and right side of his neck. Though I should point out that in a few circles, I actually do blend right in and my bolts are considered a 'fashion statement.'

Together, we're the Monster Detectives, and if you experience something that doesn't make sense, that logic can't explain, then we're your *men,* so to speak.

The only thing we ask beside payment is that you don't ask too may questions.

I was sitting at my desk reading the newspaper when Zack and Vinnie came into the office. We rented half the floor of a rundown building on the south side of town.

"You read today's headline yet?" Vinnie asked me as he sat down in one of the two chairs in front of my desk. He was wearing a dark cloak to protect his pale skin from the sunlight and he threw the hood back to expose his handsome visage.

Zack merely stumbled in and plopped down in the other chair. I could smell him the moment he entered my office, but after all the years of working with him, I was used to it.

"Yeah, I just finished it, why?" I asked.

Vinnie nodded to the paper. "And the headline didn't sound a little, oh I don't know...off?"

"Off how?"

"Well, the cops said that a couple of teenagers were up on Overlook Point necking, right?"

I nodded.

"And that they were attacked by some kind of wild animal, probably a bear?"

"Yes," I said.

Vinnie smiled, showing his fangs. "Well, if that was the case, since when do bears rip off car doors and shred people into lunchmeat?"

I nodded, considering what Vinnie was telling me. "You think it's something that we might want to get involved in?"

"Sounds like a Lycan to me, Frankie," Zack said as he pulled out a plastic Tupperware bowl with a cover and popped off the top. Inside was something bloody, a liver or a pancreas. Without hesitation, he reached in and began shoveling it into his mouth. Zack was what you would call a 'messy eater' and he ignored the blood dripping off his chin and onto his shirt.

"Do you have to do that here?" I asked him.

Zack shrugged. "Sorry, Frankie, I missed breakfast. I may be dead but I'm still a growing boy." He let out a burp filled with the stench of rot and I fanned my hand in front of my face. I was technically dead, too, but the difference was my insides worked. My heart beat and my organs did what they do in any human, the only thing was mine came from different people.

I ignored Zack, or tried to, and looked back to Vinnie. "Is that what you think, too, Vinnie? That this was a Lycan attack?"

"I'd bet my left fang on it." He smiled, showing both fangs. "I say we find the next of kin and see if any of them want us to investigate, to find out what really happened to their loved ones."

I rubbed my chin as I considered it and finally nodded. "All right, I'll call my contact at the police station and see what I can find out."

"Good," Vinnie said and stood up. "You can reach me on my cell. Till then I'm gonna grab some shuteye." He yawned. "It's been a long night and I could use a few hours rest."

Vinnie walked out of my office. He was heading to his own office at the end of the hall. Once inside, he would go to his desk, open the lid to expose the hidden compartment inside that looked like a coffin, and climb in. The desk/coffin was custom made by a family of wood elves and Vinnie had said every penny he'd spent was worth it.

It was lined with purple velvet, had a mirror on the inside of the lid, and a small five inch television with a satellite uplink. That way Vinnie could watch TV before he drifted off to sleep.

I looked at Zack as he finished his breakfast. "Thanks for eating that in here. You got blood all over the floor."

Zack shrugged. "The maid will clean it. It's not like it's the first time she's found blood on the floors of our offices." He stood up, his limbs creaking like an old sailboat too long at sea. "I'll be in my office, too, let me know when you have something." He turned, and without so much as an apology, shambled out the door the way zombies often do.

I leaned back in my chair and sighed, wondering if it was all worth it sometimes. Then I decided I really didn't have much choice in the matter. For better or worse, I was stuck with a vampire and a zombie for partners.

Reaching for the phone, I called the local precinct and my contact to see what dirt I could *dig* up on the young couple's death.

Later that night, a little after the sun had gone down, the three of us stood by the police impound lot, by the south fence, and out of sight of the security monitors. My contact had told me this was where the car of the dead couple was taken when the CSI team was through with it.

Vinnie was dressed in black, and with the sun down, he looked relaxed and confident.

"Okay, Vinnie," I said to him. "This is all you. Neither me or Zack can climb well, so go on in there, check out the car, and get back here before you're spotted."

Vinnie flashed his fangs at me. "Piece of cake." He looked at Zack with a grin. "Sorry you can't come, too, deadhead."

"I'll get over it," Zack said as he munched on a severed hand.

I never asked Zack where he got his body parts for snacking and he never offered.

Vinnie spun around and ran to the fence. As quick as a cat, he was up and over, landing lightly on the ground. He turned and waved to me and Zack through the chain-link fence. Then he was gone, a wraith lost in the falling shadows of the night.

While Zack and I waited, we chatted a little. We didn't have a lot in common and to tell you the truth, Zack wasn't much of a conversationalist. Maybe it was his rotting brain, but he just wasn't one for chit-chat.

Ten minutes later, Vinnie was back, and after scaling the fence, he dropped down between me and Zack and held up a digital camera he'd had on his person.

"Wait till you see what I got on this," he said as he handed me the camera. I took it from him and then pointed to our car parked ten feet away. "Later, once we're away from here."

They both agreed and we headed to the car. It was a black limousine, more than ten years old, and it was one of the only vehicles I can sit in comfortably. Vinnie drove, and Zack and I sat in the back.

I began studying the pictures in the camera.

Most looked like what you'd expect if a car was attacked by a bear. The windshield was smashed, the mirrors broken and hanging by their wires that powered them. The side of the car the 'bear' had attacked was dented and scratched, but as I looked at one picture in particular, my eyes creased in thought.

"Did you find the one I zoomed in on yet?" Vinnie asked from the driver's seat as he wove through the city traffic.

"You mean the one with the claw marks?" I asked.

"That's the one. Notice anything different about it from say…a bear's claws?"

Zack looked over my shoulder and said, "There's five claw marks instead of four."

I looked at Zack, then at the camera, and nodded in agreement. "He's right," I said. "A bear would have probably left four marks, but if it really was a werewolf, there would be five."

"Bingo," he said from the driver's seat as he cut off a cab and laughed when the cabbie honked at him.

"Okay," I said. "So we definitely have a werewolf on our hands and this one is hunting for human prey." I glanced out the window at the full moon.

"Chances are it's gonna be on the prowl tonight as well. We'll need to act fast if we're going to find it."

"But what about the family of the couple? Don't we need to get a client first?"

I shook my head. "There's no time and we can't let this monster keep killing. We made an oath to protect humanity. You remember that, Vinnie?"

"Yeah, yeah, don't go getting all high and mighty with me, Frankie, I remember just fine."

"Good, so get going to Overlook Point. Werewolves stake out their territory like regular wolves do. If it's going to attack again it'll be in the same place."

Vinnie shook his head. "But the cops cordoned off the area with tape and signs; there won't be anyone up there."

I chuckled. "You think so? Vinnie, my boy, you've been undead for far too long if you don't remember what its like to be a teenager. Trust me; there'll be someone parked up there, maybe even more than that."

"Huh, I guess we'll see," he said and turned off the main road to a side street that would take us through the west side of the city to Overlook Point.

Overlook Point was in the middle of nowhere. By chance, a fifty foot section was devoid of trees or shrubbery. If you drove to the edge of the road, you had a grand view of the city below.

The Point had been active with teenagers looking to get hot and horny for more than twenty years and I knew even a bear attack—or an assumed bear attack—wouldn't stop sex-starved teenagers from coming here. The attitude of it always happening to someone else was prevalent in teens, and as we approached the Point, my hunch was correct.

Three cars sat at the edge of the Point, two cars and a pickup truck to be exact. The police tape that had cordoned off the area was on the ground, blowing in the wind, thanks to the first car that had driven through it and snapped it.

As we slowed down and stopped, Vinnie put the limo's transmission into park. I smiled when I saw the shocks of the pickup truck moving up and down slowly.

"So what's the plan?" Vinnie asked me as he turned around in his seat.

"We wait for the werewolf to show up and then do what we do best."

"Are we going to kill it?" Zack asked.

I shrugged. “No, we need information from it, but if the beast leaves us no choice, then yes, we’ll have to kill it.”

Vinnie patted his chest as if he was searching for something. “And I’m fresh out of silver stakes,” he said with a sly grin.

I patted my chest. “Don’t worry about that. If it comes to it, I’ll deal with the killing.”

“So were just going to sit here and wait for it to show up? We’re just going to use those kids over there necking as bait?” Vinnie asked.

I nodded. “Yeah, I’m afraid so. Nothing works better than live bait.”

Zack shifted in his seat beside me and pulled something raw and bloody out of a Ziploc bag he’d had hidden in a pocket. “Well, if we’re gonna wait, I might as well have a little snack.” He began tearing into the bloody object, his pale lips smacking as he sucked in the crimson gruel. Once more I wondered where he got his body parts.

I rolled my eyes at the sight of Zack eating, and Vinnie laughed and turned around. He turned on the radio, put his feet up on the dash, and we all got comfortable for the stake out.

I checked my watch for the tenth time in as many minutes. It was a little past midnight and I was growing impatient.

Out at the Point there were three new cars, each with fogged windows and bouncing shocks.

In the driver’s seat, Vinnie was playing solitaire, and beside me, Zack was sleeping, his grunts and groans reminding me of a zombie from the movies. See, Zack was dead and he was a zombie, but his bite wasn’t infectious and he could think as well as talk. Still, he did love to eat humans, though he didn’t actually kill them for sustenance. Like I said before, I often wondered where he got the body parts he was always snacking on. I made a mental note to ask him when this case was over.

I was so lost in thought that at first I didn’t hear the scream that rent the air, coming from one of the cars, but as the second shriek filled the night, I snapped back to reality.

“Looks like he’s back,” Vinnie said as he sat up straight, the cards he’d been playing with falling to the floorboards.

“Come on, let’s go before he kills someone else,” I said and kicked my door open and heaved my seven foot frame out of the limo. I made sure to slap Zack on the right cheek on my way out, and with a few grunts and groans, he snapped awake.

Zack's white eyes took in the inside of the limo, and when he heard the next scream shatter the night, he realized what was happening.

Vinnie was right beside me as he jumped from the driver's seat and we ran across the gravel to the three cars which weren't shaking anymore.

As we reached the cars, two of them put on their headlights and then backup lights lit the night. With screeching tires, the pair backed up and tore off down the road, leaving the one car behind.

This was the one being attacked, and as the overhead clouds parted and allowed the moonlight to bathe the area, I saw a large, hairy back as the werewolf leaned into the broken side window of the car, trying to get at the frightened couple trapped within.

"You go left and I'll go right," I told Vinnie, who nodded and sprinted around the car to come at the werewolf from behind. I could hear Zack's feet crunching on the gravel as he tried to catch up to us. Zombies don't run very well.

I ran to the driver's side of the car, and when I reached it, I didn't like what I found.

The once fogged windows had been wiped clean thanks to the terrified teenager trying to break free of the werewolf, the boy's hands pounding on the glass in terror. As I studied the scene, I wasn't pleased with what I found.

The werewolf had killed the girl in the passenger seat immediately after reaching inside and her throat was torn out, her blood still sputtering to cover the front seat and dashboard of the car. The teenage boy was still trying to fend off the werewolf, but the same time I reached the car and was grabbing the door handle to open it, the claws of the beast lashed out and basically tore the teenager's face clean off. The teen's arms and legs were waving and kicking as blood shot out to splatter the interior glass.

Meanwhile, the werewolf was gutting the girl, ripping out her organs to feed like the carnivore it was.

That's when Vinnie reached the werewolf, and with superhuman speed and strength, he grabbed the beast by its shoulders and yanked it free of the car.

It rolled across the ground and came up in a fighting crouch amid a cloud of dust.

Zack caught up to Vinnie and the two stood side by side, ready for what the werewolf did next.

As for me, I opened the driver's door to see if I could help the couple.

The door was locked so I used my strength and tore it off the frame. As the door popped off and I tossed it aside, the teenage boy rolled out and landed heavily in a heap of arms and legs. He was dead, there was no question of that, and when I peered into the car, the girl was already cooling, her torso ripped wide open from the claws of the beast.

There was nothing I could do for these two poor souls so I stood up and went to join the fight with my partners.

Just as I stood and turned to see what was going on, the werewolf lunged like a charging bull and ran at Vinnie.

Being a vampire, Vinnie was safe from being killed—unless he was beheaded by the beast—and he ran at the werewolf also, the two meeting in a loud slap of flesh and fur.

The werewolf tried to rake Vinnie's face with its claws and the vampire darted to the left and used his own fingernails to claw the back of the beast. He scored a hit and the werewolf howled in anger and pain.

Vinnie laughed, but in his overconfidence, failed to see the claw that swung around to tear open his throat.

Only his supernatural speed saved him from a beheading, but he still received a nasty cut to his left cheek and lower jaw. He jumped back and rolled away as the werewolf snarled and growled.

Zack had pulled a knife and he slashed at the beast's back while it was busy with Vinnie, the blade sinking in more than two inches before the werewolf spun around, knocking Zack to the ground.

I heard bones crack as Zack fell, but the zombie's face was as placid as ever. When you're dead, you don't feel pain.

The beast would have finished Zack off, or tried to, but Vinnie was back in the fight and jumped onto the werewolf's back, his fingernails trying to gouge out the beast's eyes.

By this time I was only a few feet from the fight and as Vinnie fought not to be thrown off the werewolf like it was a bucking bronco, I ran up and punched the beast in the gut, causing it to let out a *woof* that had all the air from its lungs spewing forth in one mighty gush of an exhale.

I was about to send an uppercut to its hairy chin when it spun around, causing me to sucker punch Vinnie in the side. The vampire yelped in pain, and I heard ribs crack, and he gave me a look filled with acid. I smiled, trying to relay my regret, but then Vinnie was flying through the air as the werewolf finally freed itself from him.

I was about to reach out and grab the beast when it dropped to all fours, spun around and took off into the woods bordering the Point.

It was gone in less than a second, swallowed up by the treeline. I watched the leaves shake from its passing, and was about to let out a curse that we'd lost it when I looked down, and there in the moonlight, I saw the bright crimson drops of blood.

It seemed that Zack had caused a deep enough wound with his knife that the beast was bleeding profusely and the blood was an easy trail to follow.

I went to Vinnie and helped him up. He shook me off as he wiped his clothing free of dirt and dust.

"I got it, Frankie, don't touch me," he snapped as he took a step away from me.

I held out my hands in apology. "Hey, I'm really sorry about that punch. I didn't think it was going to turn like that." I tried to rationalize it. "And besides, you'll heal fine. By tomorrow night you'll be good as new."

"That's beside the point," Vinnie said and winced slightly from his cracked ribs.

"Fine, we can talk about how sorry I am later, but right now we need to follow that werewolf. It's bleeding and there's a blood tail. We can follow it right to its lair and end this tonight."

Vinnie nodded. "Okay, let's do it, but you're right, were not done talking. You owe me, Frankie."

I was about to reply when I realized Zack wasn't where he'd fallen. I looked left and right and was about to call out to him, when I heard slurping sounds coming from near the car. I began to walk back to it, and as I rounded the rear bumper, I saw Zack leaning over the dead teenager, his face deep inside the boy's chest. He was tearing into the corpse's heart, his face and hands covered in blood and viscera. As he chewed and swallowed, the slurping grew louder and though I was a monster, I have to tell you, I tasted a little bile as I watched Zack feed.

"Zack, what in the Creator's name are you doing?" I asked.

Zack looked up, blood dripping off his chin. His mouth was full of meat as he chewed and swallowed. "What? Why let it go to waste? He's dead, right? And I'm hungry."

I sighed. I had to admit that Zack had a point. He needed to eat human meat and the boy was definitely dead. I turned to Vinnie. "Go move the limo so it can't be found, then get back here pronto. The cops are sure to be here soon. One of the cars that left had to have called for help, and with everything that's already happened around here, the police won't be long in coming."

"Got it," Vinnie said and limped away. He flashed me an annoyed look and I knew he was limping for my benefit. Vampires are tough, and though I can punch as hard as a mule's kick, I knew Vinnie could handle it.

Three minutes later and Vinnie was back. He had hidden the limo about a half mile down the road in a small cutoff. No one would find it there, especially not with the cover of darkness.

Together, the three of us headed into the woods.

Vinnie was first. With his heightened vampire senses, he could detect the faint scent of spilled blood. Next came me, trying my best to be stealthy, but my large form seemed to crash through the underbrush like a bull, or so it sounded to my ears.

Last was Zack. He had a coil of slimy intestine in his pocket and was holding a bloody organ in his hand, as he munched on it happily while bringing up the rear. Luckily, the wind was blowing away from him or else his bloody clothes—thanks to his feeding—may have confused Vinnie's olfactory glands. But as it was, the vampire was having no problem following the werewolf's trail.

Vinnie led us deep into the forest, and when we were about a half mile in, I could hear the faint sound of police sirens from behind us. It seemed the police had arrived at Overlook Point to investigate another 'bear' attack.

We walked for almost two miles until Vinnie held up his right hand and made a fist, signaling us to stop. Behind me, Zack was silent. He had finished his meal more than half a mile ago and had done his best to wipe his face clean of blood. He didn't do a very good job and even in the almost complete darkness of the forest—only what little moonlight penetrating the canopy to see by—I could see blood splatter was still on his face.

I waited to see what Vinnie had discovered, and then I began to hear grunts and snarls. Vinnie pointed to a copse of trees ten yards ahead of us and signaled that he was going to investigate. I nodded for him to go, and no sooner did my head bob up and down, then Vinnie was moving, a shadow lost amongst thicker shadows.

Zack and I stood together, looking at one another, me over a foot taller than him, when Vinnie appeared behind us a few minutes later.

I was so startled that I had my right arm raised and my hand curled into a fist, ready to smash whatever had popped up. When I saw it was Vinnie, I pulled my punch, feeling slightly embarrassed at being startled. I mean, I was a seven foot tall monster. What did I have to be afraid of?

"So, what did you find?" I asked Vinnie in a whisper.

He shook his head and said, "It's not good."

"What do you mean it's not good?" I asked. "Did you find the werewolf or not?"

"Oh yeah, I found him, and then some."

I was about to ask what he meant, and to tell him to stop being so cryptic, when he gestured for me and Zack to follow him.

Taking a wide berth of the area directly in front of us, Vinnie led us around in a wide circle. Five minutes later, he told us to stop and pointed to another copse of shrubs in front of us.

Doing my best to be silent, which isn't easy when you're my size, I crept up to the shrubs and reached out a hand to part them.

As I peered through the branches, I saw a glade, and frowned deeply, the sight before me not at all what I expected. The snarls and growls were louder now, too.

"I see what you mean," I said. "This complicates things."

The wind shifted, blowing the scent of myself, Vinnie and worst of all, a blood-covered Zack, into the glade.

In the small clearing beyond the shrubs, were five werewolves. In the middle of the group was the werewolf we had previously fought. The others were administering to his wounds, and when the wind shifted, all five heads perked up at the smell of intruders—namely us.

The pack snarled and spread out, and like someone had fired a starting pistol, they charged me first.

"Oh shit!" I yelled and that was enough to let Vinnie and Zack know we had a problem.

As the first werewolf came at me, I jumped forward to get free of the shrubs and we collided in the air. I was heavier than the beast, but it was solidly built.

We fell to the ground and began to roll around, as Vinnie and Zack fought battles of their own, the other four werewolves attacking en masse.

The werewolf clamped its jaws on my right wrist and I roared in pain. I used my free hand to punch the beast in the side. I felt bones break under my blow and the grip on my wrist weakened.

I took this opportunity and moved to my knees, then using all the strength in my seven foot frame, I threw the beast off me. It landed ten feet away and rolled end over end before coming up in a crouch. Its ears were lowered against its head and I could see blood on its fangs. It was my blood.

Then the moon went behind some clouds and the glade was all but lost in darkness.

I could hear Zack and Vinnie fighting behind me and I wanted to help them, as the odds were against them, but as I turned to assist my partners, the werewolf I was fighting came at me again.

I had no warning in the darkness.

Its dark fur blended into the night and I knew it was upon me when I felt its front paws hit my chest, knocking me onto my back.

Once more I was in a battle for my life. Science had created me but being rent from head to toe would still kill me. Though I didn't age—thanks to the formula of my creation—I could still die from bodily harm, fire being the worst.

As we rolled around on the ground, the werewolf tried to snap at the side of my neck, but each time all the beast got for its trouble was a mouthful of steel bolt. Luckily, the bolts in my neck were protecting me from harm.

Once more I began to pummel the werewolf with my ham-sized fists, and each time I landed a blow, I felt bones crack and snap.

Finally, I got my arms under it enough to push it off and the beast rolled away to come up fighting.

Then, thankfully, the moon broke through the clouds and I could see once more.

The werewolf was five feet away and was already preparing to lunge at me.

Acting fast, I reached into my jacket and pulled out a six shot revolver. The bullets had silver tips, made for just such an occasion. I didn't use it before at the Point because I was hoping to take the werewolf alive.

As the beast lunged into the air, its muzzle aimed at the front of my throat where the bolts couldn't stop its attack, I fired, my aim perfect.

The round caught the beast in the chest, and with a yell and an all-too-human scream, it dropped to the ground and remained still.

I was already turning to aid my partners, while behind me, the werewolf began to transform back to a human man.

Zack and Vinnie had managed to fight their way into the glade so they had some room to move. Vinnie was trapped beneath three of the beasts while the fourth—the original werewolf—had Zack's right arm locked in its maw.

No sooner did it bite Zack then it let go, making a face as it tasted the foul and rancid meat of the zombie. Zack used this moment to punch the werewolf in the face, his undead strength enough to knock a few of its teeth loose.

I raised my gun and was firing the second I had the first beast locked in my sights. The round hit the werewolf in the head, penetrating the left ear and blowing out the right side of its head in a spray of blood and brain matter.

As it fell to the ground, I shot the next one, the round striking it high on its shoulder. It fell away yelping in pain, and Vinnie dispatched the last one attacking him by gutting it from crotch to neck, his fingernails digging in deep and tearing into the fur and flesh as if it was paper.

Blood and organs spilled out, viscera coating Vinnie in a soupy mess as the werewolf slumped on top of him. It began changing back to human form almost immediately.

I turned to shoot the werewolf attacking Zack but found that my undead partner had things well under control.

He had both his hands inside the beast's mouth—one on the upper and one on the lower jaw—and with a low growl, he pulled up and down, prying open the mouth until the jaws snapped. The beast yelped once and went still, collapsing to the ground in a puff of dust. Zack never slowed. He released the dead beast and flipped it over. As the werewolf returned to human form, Zack tore into the deceased man's ribcage, quickly shoving the warm organs into his mouth like a starving dog at dinner time.

I didn't say anything. It was dead anyway. Man or werewolf, it didn't matter. Zack had to feed, it was his nature. If he didn't eat his daily requirement of human flesh, he would wither and rot away.

I vaguely thought how since this case began, Zack had been eating quite well.

Vinnie was on his feet again and trying to wipe the worst of the gore off him. He wasn't succeeding.

"If you had a gun with silver bullets all along, Frankie, why the hell didn't you use it before?" Vinnie asked me.

"Because I wanted to take that first one alive, that's why. But when I saw we were outnumbered, then all bets were off." I walked over and put a hand on Vinnie's shoulder where there was a clean spot devoid of gore. "Just be glad I had the foresight to bring the gun in the first place."

Vinnie had to give me that one. "Fair enough, but still, it would have been nice if me and Zack had known about your little ace in the hole."

I merely grunted in reply. I turned to see Zack gorging himself on human meat. I looked away, not wanting to see anymore. I may be a monster but even I had my limits.

I scanned the glade and the bodies strewn about. Four were male and one was female. They were all very dead.

I knew I couldn't leave the bodies like this, but what to do? Shallow graves were an option but then if these people had been here, it was possible they had clothing or vehicles somewhere nearby. Even graves wouldn't stop cadaver-sniffing dogs. No, I needed a better way to dispose of the evidence.

And then I had it.

I looked to Vinnie and said, "Grab as much dry brush and leaves as you can and put it over the bodies."

"What for?" he asked.

"A funeral pyre," I said. "This area is dry as a bone. We can set it ablaze and when the fire is out and they find the burnt bodies, the authorities will figure they were campers who got trapped in the wildfire."

Vinnie nodded. "Not bad, Frankie, that just might work."

"I hope it does," I said. "If the humans find out about werewolves, then they may look deeper into where they came from. The only reason we can survive in this world is that no one believes we truly exist." I looked over at Zack and said, "Hey, Zack, stop eating for a minute and help Vinnie get kindling."

Zack looked as if he was going to protest but I stomped my right foot, shaking the ground. Zack knew this wasn't the time to argue, and with reluctance, he left the corpse he was feeding on and began helping Vinnie gather brush.

Fifteen minutes later the three of us stood on the edge of the glade as the fire began to spread from body to body, the darkness pushed back by the crackling flames. It was just like I said. One match to a pile of brush, and in no time the blaze was going strong.

Already the flesh on the bodies was bubbling, the fat popping as it sizzled in the fire. The odor of roasting meat began to fill the glade, sweet and sour smelling.

Zack looked disgusted and I realized the redolence of cooking flesh was probably distasteful to him. He liked his meat raw.

We turned and began our two mile trek back to the limo. Vinnie led the way and he constantly had to fan away the flies that were hovering around him, thanks to his gore-covered clothing.

He glanced over his shoulder at me and frowned. "You owe me a new suit, Frankie, this one is ruined."

"Send me a bill," I said with a grin.

Zack caught up to me, let out a loud burp, and said, "You do know we made nothing on this job, right? We didn't have a client."

"Yes, Zack, I know that all too well. Let's just wrap this case up to protecting our secret. Like I said, if the humans find out monsters are real, then we're all in trouble."

Vinnie grunted. "Still, Frankie, it would have been nice to make at least a few bucks."

I shrugged my wide shoulders. "Hey, you win some, you lose some. Maybe our next case will pay better."

For the next twenty minutes no one spoke, we merely concentrated on walking.

Behind us, a glow lit the sky as the fire grew out of control, the smell of smoke tickling my nose.

Finally, Zack was the one to break the silence. "I'm hungry."

I couldn't help it, I chuckled at that.

At least some things never changed.

MORGUE OF THE DEAD

Neil Fredrickson pulled into the parking lot of the Amherst Funeral home in upstate New York.

Fresh out of high school, his father had managed to get him the job by calling in a few favors with the home's owner, who was an old friend.

As Neil stepped out of his car—a beat up old Ford—and walked up to the back door to the funeral home, his mind went back to just a few days ago when his father told him he'd found his son a job.

"But, Dad, I don't want to work in a funeral home," Neil had said.

"Nonsense, no son of mine is going to hang around all summer doing nothing. Mr. Vincent is a good friend, and when I asked him if he could help you out with a job, I was lucky he said yes. Now, as long as you live under my roof, you'll do as I say and I say that if you graduate from high school then you need to work, to pull your weight. So on Monday, at eight in the morning you better be at the rear door of that funeral home. You hear me, son?"

Neil had nodded, mumbled a soft, "Yes, Dad," and had gone to his room to surf the internet and listen to some heavy metal.

So here he was, Monday morning and ready to go to work as a mortician's associate. He'd never seen a real dead body before, though he had seen enough on television to last a lifetime. Still, it creeped him out to think that the person that would be lying dead on a slab in the morgue was once alive.

There was a sign on the rear door. **PRESS BELL FOR ENTRY**. Deciding that was what he should do, he pressed the bell and waited.

When nothing happened, he pressed it again and a second later a low buzz filled the air. Pushing on the doorknob, Neil opened the door and stepped inside.

The hallway was dim, and no sooner did he close the door, then his senses were assaulted with the smell of formaldehyde. The cloying odor seemed to stick to the back of his mouth and it made him want to gag.

The hallway was thin, three feet at most, with only a small light bulb in the ceiling for illumination. Once the door was closed, all outside light vanished.

Figuring he should walk to the end of the hall, he did just that and a few seconds later he was at another door. This door was made of metal, and when he turned the doorknob, it opened easily, sliding inward on greased hinges.

As the door opened, white light bathed him and Neil had to blink while his eyes adjusted to the brightness.

When his vision was clear, he took in the main floor of the funeral home and the massive room where the bodies were embalmed and prepared for viewing. As he let his eyes play over the machines and wall of stainless steel doors, he heard footsteps coming from his right. He turned his head to see a man in a rubber, black apron, with thin hair, beady eyes, and a weasel's nose, coming toward him. He knew from his father's description that this was Mr. Vincent.

"Hello, there, my boy, can I help you?" Mr. Vincent asked. His voice was low and sounded like a fog horn, the tone entirely belaying the outer look of the man.

"I-ah, yeah, uhm, my dad told me to be here this morning. I'm Neil."

Mr. Vincent's eyes lit up at the name and he nodded, clapping his hands with apparent glee. "Ah, George's boy, of course, of course, come on in and let me show you around."

Swallowing the lump in his throat, Neil entered the room.

"So, my boy, you want to work in the field of death, hmmm?"

Neil's first thought was to say, *Hell no,* but his father's voice in the back of his mind told him not to say that. So instead he only nodded and said, "Yes sir, for the summer anyway."

"Ah, of course, of course. Ah, how I miss my days of youth. Fresh out of school, with the summer ahead, swimming holes, ice cream, and pretty girls. Ah, the years, they pass so fast and before you know it you're old like me."

"Uh, yes, sir. I guess so."

Mr. Vincent patted Neil's arm "Oh, you don't have to patronize me, son. I know what you're thinking and you're probably right. It takes a special kind of person to do the job I do. I just hope you're up to it."

"Me too, sir," Neil said.

"Well, enough chit-chat, are you ready for the grand tour?"

"Sure," Neil shrugged slightly.

"Oh, good, then follow me and we'll start from the beginning."

Mr. Vincent led Neil across the room to a strange looking machine that he thought might belong in a hospital. It looked a lot like a blender with a large clear glass container on top and the bottom was the controls with a, on/off switch and two knobs to regulate pressure and flow of the fluid.

"This is the Porti-boy embalming machine manufactured by the Turner Company, my boy. This is how we prepare a body for burial and viewing." He pointed to a four inch metal hollow tube that was connected to the machine by a rubber hose. "This goes into the deceased's neck. I stick it in a vein there to be used for the drainage of blood. Meanwhile, I use another tube, the arterial canula, to pump in the embalming fluid. When the fluid is injected into the corpse, the blood is forced out of the drainage tube until all the blood is evacuated." He looked at Neil, his eyes creasing slightly. "Do you understand so far?"

"Yes, sir, I got it. Sounds easy."

"Ah, it is, actually. The machine does all the work." He turned and walked to the wall of doors. Each was square, two feet by two feet with hinges on one side. "This is where we keep some of the deceased before they are prepared." He pointed to a walk-in refrigerator in the far corner. "And that is also where we keep the ones that are next in line to be embalmed. Now, Neil, did your father tell you what I need you to do for me here."

"No, not really, sir."

"Ah, well, your job will be to prepare the bodies so I can embalm them. I will need you to undress them and to wash the bodies. Then, after I'm finished embalming them, I need you to dress them. After that, I have someone come in and do their makeup and style their hair. Can you handle that, my boy?"

Neil swallowed deeply, realizing he had to touch the dead bodies.

"I uh, I don't really know if I can do that."

"Ah, a truthful answer. One can only ask for the truth. So, I tell you what, why don't you try it for a day and if at the end you don't think this job is right for you, you can leave and I'll tell your father something that will let him know it wasn't your fault, hmm?"

"Okay, I can do that," Neil said, already knowing what he would say at the end of the day.

"Ah, good, good, so, why don't you go get an apron from that closet over there and we can get to work. I'm a bit backed up right now, that's why you're here. My helper quit rather abruptly two days ago and I've been shorthanded."

Neil did as he was told and soon was standing beside Mr. Vincent with a black apron on, just like his boss'.

Mr. Vincent nodded approvingly and went to the walk-in, opened it, and wheeled out a very large body under a very big sheet.

"Neil, I would like you to meet Aunt Bertha. Or her legal name, Bertha Matheson. She was a regular at the burger joint at the end of the street and it finally caught up to her."

"Huh?" Neil asked.

"Heart attack, my boy, she had a heart attack. All the kids called her Aunt Bertha and after a while the name sort of stuck." He wheeled the gurney to the embalming machine and then pulled the sheet off. There on the table, was Neil's first dead body.

Bertha had been fat in life and she still was in death. Her ponderous breasts draped over both sides of her naked body like sagging water balloons. The folds of her flesh were layered and Neil wondered how the woman was able to reach around herself to wipe her ass. Then he thought he was being disrespectful of the dead and stopped thinking about such things. She had three chins, each one larger than the last and her eyes were two small impressions in a face made of flab. She was truly an enormous woman. As Neil studied the corpse, a loud fart escaped from beneath the folds of flesh and Neil found himself bent over and gagging. Mr. Vincent chuckled and patted Neil on the shoulder.

"Sorry about that, my boy. I should have warned you about it. Bodies decay and they pass gas like a lumberjack. It's a natural thing."

"There's nothing natural about that smell, sir," Neil gasped as he sucked in a breath of air through the sleeve of his shirt.

Mr. Vincent chuckled as he got the gurney in the proper position and prepared to turn on the embalming machine. "Now this isn't your job but you should see how it's done," he said as he took both steel tubes, and slid each one into the left and right side of Bertha's neck. It took him a little longer to find a proper vein, but Neil didn't know that.

"There, she's all set to go. Now I'll just flick this switch, and we're off to the races."

The machine began to hum and the fluid began pumping into the cadaver. Neil found his stomach roiling as he watched the flesh of Bertha undulate as fluid seeped through her now dead veins and arteries, filling her extremities with embalming fluid.

"Okay, while she's draining, I'm going to take out the next few deceased I have to do. These you can begin undressing and preparing for the embalming process."

"Okay, I guess," Neil said, not relishing the idea at all.

"Excellent. You'll see, Neil, once you get used to doing it a few times it's really no big deal. We all die eventually, my boy, and what we leave behind is just meat; nothing more and nothing less."

Mr. Vincent went to the walk-in and wheeled out three more cadavers, then went to the stainless steel doors and took out two more. In all there were now five cadavers on gurneys surrounding Neil, not counting Bertha, and he got the shivers just thinking about it.

When Mr. Vincent was done, he wiped his hands on a rag and went to Neil. "Okay, I need to use the bathroom, and I want to get a cup of coffee from upstairs. Can I get you anything, my boy?"

"No, I'm good," Neil replied as he stared at the corpses.

"Okay, then while I'm gone, you can begin taking off the clothing of the three in the corner there. The clothing will be laundered and then donated to Goodwill so just toss it in that laundry sack against the far wall. There's a good lad."

Without waiting for a reply, Mr. Vincent went to a door on the right side of the room, opened it, and was gone. Neil could hear the man's footsteps as he ascended the stairs.

He looked at the cadavers and swallowed hard. Glancing at Aunt Bertha to see she was doing fine, though he cringed at the sight of the dark blood that was being sucked out of her as the yellowish fluid was pumped in, he got to work. Walking to the first body, he began to undress it.

He was halfway done with the third body, a woman in her late forties who had died of an aneurism, when the fingers on her right hand began to twitch.

Neil didn't notice this as he was busy shifting the body to remove the cadaver's clothing. He did notice the woman's firm breasts, and though very dead, her flat stomach and perfectly shaped and trimmed crotch hair was causing him to get aroused.

He knew it was wrong, but at eighteen the sight of a naked woman, even a dead one, was all it took to give him a woody, though he felt dirty for thinking such thoughts about a corpse. But each time his hand brushed the dead woman's breasts, the boobs still soft and supple, he found his pants growing tighter.

Deciding he needed a break, he stopped undressing the cadaver and walked to the far end of the room, where a water dispenser was located.

Taking a cup and filling it with water, he quickly drank it, then poured himself another.

Behind him, the embalming machine chugged away happily, draining and filling Aunt Bertha, basically giving her an oil change. In fact, the machine made so much noise that Neil never heard the woman cadaver shift on her gurney as she slowly sat up.

Unknown to Neil, he'd picked the worst possible day to work at a funeral home, and worse, to work in the morgue of the home. For today, the dead were rising, an unknown force reviving the recently deceased to walk amongst the living once more. The origins of this phenomenon would forever remain unknown, but to the survivors of the aftermath, such things would be trivial.

Neil leaned against the water cooler, drinking cup after cup of water, and he didn't know anything was wrong until he heard something crash behind him. Spinning around, he dropped his half-full cup to the floor as he stared open-mouthed at the tableaux before him.

All five bodies were now moving on their gurneys, the dead woman sitting up, her head swiveling towards him. Neil saw her nipples were erect but he highly doubted it was from stimulation, especially when her complexion was so pale, as if she'd had flour dusted over her entire body. And though her eyes were open, Neil could see, even from a distance, there was no life existing within those milky white orbs.

Falling off the gurney, the woman struck the floor hard, her right knee cracking loudly. Neil winced as he watched in shock as she slowly pulled herself to a standing position. The other four bodies were now twitching spastically on their gurneys, like they were being electrocuted. Neil glanced at Aunt Bertha to see that she, at least, was still doing her job at playing dead.

The dead woman opened her mouth wide and where words once issued, now only a gurgle-like moan slid out. The moan was void of emotion, more of a sound made from instinct, and Neil felt his bladder let go as the woman took her first stumbling steps toward him.

It was at this precise moment that the far door that led upstairs opened and Mr. Vincent stepped out, a cup of coffee in his right hand. When he saw the naked woman on her feet—the one he knew had been very dead when he left to get his beverage—he dropped his coffee, letting the mug shatter between his feet. Ignoring the hot coffee that splashed his shoes and pants, he stared with mild surprise.

"My word, how can this be?" Mr. Vincent asked as he stared at the aberration of nature.

"How the hell should I know?" Neil gasped. "Shit, this is my first day? Christ, Mr. Vincent, you never said anything about the bodies getting up and going for a walk."

"My dear boy, I assure you this has never happened before. I…I don't know what to say."

"Then how 'bout getting her away from me!" Neil yelled as the woman moved closer and Neil backed away from her.

"Just stay calm, I'll handle this," Mr. Vincent said and calmly walked over to the woman, his plan to take her upstairs where he would call for an ambulance. Obviously, her diagnosis was incorrect and she had merely been unconscious. Perhaps a snake bite? Yes, he'd heard stories of where people were bitten by snakes, pronounced dead to amazingly wake up on the autopsy table. He knew the woman hadn't had an autopsy performed. She was Jewish and the family wouldn't allow it.

"Mrs. Greenburg," Mr. Vincent said, placing a hand on the naked woman's shoulder. "It's so good to see you up and about. Please accept my sincerest apologies for any mental trauma you may have suffered from…" That was all he got out before his words were transformed into an earth-shattering scream.

Neil could only stare, horrified, as Mrs. Greenberg, freshly returned from the dead, turned about and sank her strong white teeth into the left side of Mr. Vincent's face. She didn't so much as bite his face, however, as she seemed to swallow it whole. Her mouth was quite large and now it was more than adequate for this new chore in her career as one of the walking dead.

Teeth bit deep into flesh, scraping skull bone as top and bottom layers of teeth connected once more. When she snapped her head back, the entire left side of Mr. Vincent's face was nothing more than a bloody, gaping wound, the eye on that side now looking alone, a dab of white in an otherwise scarlet sea.

Mrs. Greenberg began to chew, using her hands to tear at the flesh as if it was beef jerky, and Mr. Vincent screamed louder, which then had Neil screaming.

Mr. Vincent stumbled away, half blind with pain, and he tripped over another moving cadaver that had just fallen off its gurney.

All the cadavers were now on the floor, writhing as new life flooded dead tissue.

No sooner did the mortician fall into the embrace of a middle-aged man who had died of cancer, then the dead man was taking a bite out of Mr. Vincent's throat, tearing the carotid artery and spraying half the room in blood and gore.

Neil was standing still, his eyes wide, the scream he'd just passed still vibrating on his lips, when Mrs. Greenburg turned her sights on him again.

Her breasts were covered in crimson, the nipples jutting out at attention, the hair between her legs now matted with blood. She was just finishing up chewing on Mr. Vincent's face, and by the look of her dead eyes, she was still hungry.

Neil, snapping out of it as the dead woman approached, began to stumble backwards, no idea where he was going.

Mrs. Greenburg was only a few feet away when Neil's back came up against the far wall. His hands slapped the wall and began reaching up and down, sliding across the wall as he desperately tried to find something to use as a weapon. His pants were now wet from when he'd lost control of his bladder and his legs felt so weak he was waiting for them to collapse in upon themselves. He imagined in a flash what would happen if he did collapse. The dead woman would fall on him, her teeth gnashing and chewing, tearing at his face and neck, the same thing happening to him as to Mr. Vincent.

His eyes darted past Mrs. Greenburg to see Mr. Vincent lying sprawled on the floor, one of the dead people on top of him. His former boss' abdomen was now torn open and his intestines were spread out around him like Christmas garland carelessly strewn from a storage box. Mr. Vincent's eyes were wide, a silent scream on his lips. It looked like he'd died very painfully.

And then Neil's left hand rested on something about two inches wide and three inches thick. Grabbing it quickly, he pulled it up in front of him to see it was a simple piece of wood. It was a misshapen two-by-four. He glanced down to see a few more pieces of wood on the floor, the pile looking like a handyman had been on a job, had set the wood in the corner to go home for the day, only to return at a later date.

Neil, using the wood like a club, waved it in front of him. "Stay back, I'm warning you, I'll hit you!" he screamed. Mrs. Greenburg ignored his threat and took the few remaining steps to reach him.

Closing his eyes, Neil swung the wooden club as hard as he could. There were two bent nails sticking out of the end of the wood and both of them tore into the dead woman's head, followed by the full weight of the club.

Mrs. Greenburg's head didn't so much as exploded, but collapse in on itself as the skull gave way under the force of the blow. She staggered to the right, her breasts swaying like heavy pendulums, let out one muffled moan, and then dropped to the floor, her pulped brains leaking out of the top of her head, now exposed to the air.

Neil, seeing what he'd done, promptly bent over and vomited up his breakfast of hash browns, eggs and bacon. After emptying his stomach, he was pulled back to his dire reality at the sound of more moaning. Looking up, bile dripping from his chin, his eyes went wide to see the other bodies now standing erect and each of them looking directly at him.

Four dead people were now shuffling towards him, and as Neil stared in horror, he saw Mr. Vincent stir behind the walking figures. Slowly, like he was under water, Mr. Vincent came to his knees, then with the help of leaning on a gurney, he raised himself to a standing position. His intestines hung between his legs like spent phalluses and his grinning skull glared at Neil, the lips now gone and the gums exposed, a macabre Halloween mask of living flesh. He slowly joined the ranks of the other four, and with hands outstretched like a Universal monster, he began moving toward Neil.

As for Neil, his eyes darted to the exit of the morgue but it was too far and there were bodies in his way. If he tried to run, they would be on him before he was halfway to freedom.

With a muffled whine in his throat, he raised the now bloody wooden club with bits of meat still attached to the nails, and prepared for the battle of his life, for if he lost, he had no doubt he would end up like Mr. Vincent, wandering around as one of the dead people, and eating others while half his insides hung out.

Neil went in swinging, the club connecting with the first ghoul's face. Skin tore and bone shattered as the body toppled to the floor. No sooner did he knock that one away then another was reaching for him.

The corpse was that of an old man, the white hair over the autopsy scar shaved clean, the stitches already straining as the old man moved about. Neil, jumping to the right, used the club and whacked the old man on the shoulders, sending the body falling to the floor to break both its wrists. There were more of them than him but they were slow and he was quick.

But there were others coming for him, along with Mr. Vincent.

Remembering how Mrs. Greenburg had gone down with her head cracked open, Neil now focused on the hitting the corpses' heads. The club went up and came down again and again; cracking skulls and sending putrefied brains across the stone floor.

The ghoul he had knocked down a moment ago was up, but no sooner did it regain its footing, then the club mashed its head into a flattened pile of brains and gore. The body swayed for a moment, then plopped onto the floor, brain matter splattering out to spray the floor with pink and grays.

Breathing heavily, huffing and puffing, Neil made a resolve to quit smoking as he looked Mr. Vincent right in his dead eyes. The man was definitely dead; a big chunk of his throat was torn out as well as half his face was missing. He moaned loudly and reached for Neil, who raised the club once more. He brought it down, the blow resembling a lumberjack chopping wood.

Mr. Vincent's head imploded from the weight of the club and he teetered for a few seconds, only the club jammed in his skull holding him up. Then he fell over, taking the club with him. Neil felt himself falling and he let go of the club, then took a step back to see the carnage he'd wrought.

All five cadavers as well as Mr. Vincent were sprawled on the floor, their insides and brains now spread out in small piles of blood, flesh and meat.

His stomach heaved again and he threw up, only spittle and stringy strands of saliva escaping his mouth. As spasms rocked his body, he coughed and spit, his mind reeling with the last few minutes, somehow trying to rationalize what had happened.

How would he explain the day's events to the police? How could he ever justify his actions?

He was pulled back to the world of walking dead people when the embalming machine stopped whirring, and he looked up to see Aunt Bertha still prone on the table.

It was as he watched the large body that he saw one of the fingers on the obese dead woman's right hand began to twitch, then another, and then, ever so slowly, her head began to move back and forth, for all purposes looking like she was waking up from a nap.

Neil stood still, staring as Aunt Bertha slowly began to sit up, the tubes in her neck becoming dislodged as she twisted on the gurney. Her legs slowly, ponderously, slid off until they were over the edge, her feet swinging back and fourth slightly like a child sitting on a swing. And then, like a behemoth raised from the murky depths, she slid off the gurney to land on the floor.

Was it Neil's imagination or did the floor tremble slightly when she landed?

Aunt Bertha had undergone an autopsy before coming to the funeral home and the V-shaped scar stood out sharply against her pale skin. Her large, fatty breasts swung back and forth as she began to walk, and Neil saw these were a far cry from the perfect orbs of Mrs. Greenburg. These were nothing but fatty tissue, with dark brown nipples at the ends, making him think of cow utters.

Aunt Bertha slowly opened her mouth to speak but all that slipped from those dry, bloated lips was a low moan, the sound sending chills down his spine. Aunt Bertha was nearly six feet tall—in life she would have been an imposing woman, and would have loomed over the other cadavers now strewn about the floor like dolls after playtime at daycare.

She took another step forward and Neil reached down and picked up the wooden club, tearing it from Mr. Vincent's head with a wet squish. He raised the club, knowing instantly it was woefully insufficient to protect him, but still, it was all he had.

Suddenly, Aunt Bertha moved like a linebacker, not running, but a fast walk that had her on Neil before he realized what was happening. At the last possible second, he swung the club, the tip of nails landing squarely on her right breast. Like a large marshmallow, the club sank into the folds of flesh and Neil found it was stuck. As he backpedaled, he tugged and tugged but it was firmly entrenched, as if a massive pile of cement had trapped it. Letting it go, he turned to run, but instead slid on a pile of gore. His legs went out from under him and he fell onto his back, seeing stars as Aunt Bertha came for him

But, she too, slipped on the gore and Neil looked up to see a towering mound of dead flesh falling towards him. He imagined someone yelling, "Timber!" but it was a fleeting thought amongst the horror filling his mind. When she landed on him, she would kill him by suffocation alone; if not crack his ribs and puncture his heart.

As she fell to the floor, he rolled to the left, her mounds of flesh missing him by a fraction of an inch. When she landed, the folds of fat swayed and undulated like a massive wave machine. Neil, shaking off his dizziness from the fall, scurried backwards. But he went the wrong way and found himself in the far corner, Aunt Bertha now blocking the only exit as she rolled to her feet, belaying her massive girth. Neil looked to the side and wondered if he could reach the door Mr. Vincent had used to go upstairs, but as he took a step forward and Bertha shifted with him, he knew he would never get there in time.

To his right sat the embalming machine and the gurney Aunt Bertha had been lying prone on. With nowhere else to go, he began to shuffle to the side as Aunt Bertha moved closer. Her mouth hung slack, her eyes lost in her puffy face, and he saw her autopsy sutures had snapped, her chest cavity now partly exposed. To his horror, he saw her ribcage was cracked, and inside the organs were missing, removed at the time of the autopsy. But if she had no organs, how in God's name could she still be walking around?

He continued sliding across the wall as Aunt Bertha positioned herself for the kill. It was when he reached the embalming machine that he ran out of room to escape. The corner of the room was only a few feet away and if he tried to run, she could move at an angle and cut him off. Swallowing the scream in his throat, he stared at his oncoming death.

She lunged for him and he yelped as he jumped to his right, his body hitting the embalming machine. The vat of formaldehyde gurgled in the machine as it swayed precariously on its stand. Aunt Bertha growled low in her throat as she swung her heaving bulk around to attack again, and Neil's hands went to his sides, reaching for something, anything to use as a weapon.

His right hand landed on the tube that had been in Aunt Bertha's neck artery. He turned his head slightly to look at the on/off switch on the machine, then the knobs to the left of it. He had remembered what Mr. Vincent had said to him before turning it on to let the machine flush out the blood and replace it with embalming fluid.

Aunt Bertha was coming for him, and with his heart in his throat, he flicked the switch back to on and turned the knobs for the flow and injection pressure to their maximum settings.

When Aunt Bertha lunged for him, he jumped to the side and jabbed the tube into her right shoulder blade. He lost his balance, tripped over his own feet, and fell to the floor, whacking his head hard enough to see stars.

Aunt Bertha landed chest down on the gurney as the embalming machine began to chug away, forcing fluid into her once more. Only this time there was no evacuation point, and as the machine pumped pint after pint into her already bloated body, her internal pressure began to build, the skin stretching as veins and arteries began to fill up with fluid.

Neil rolled to his knees and crawled away on all fours, while behind him, Aunt Bertha moaned with what appeared to be pain, though he had to admit all her moans seemed to sound the same.

Turning to see if she was following him, he saw she was on her feet again, and as she walked towards him, she began to drag the embalming machine behind her, the table it was on having wheels.

The machine was pumping extra gallons of fluid into her dead body, the skin growing and growing until she resembled a giant balloon; her face distorted and twisted, the membranes of her flesh stretching like faded pink elastic. And then, as it had to happen, her flesh finally couldn't take the pressure, and every artery, vein and capillary that was filled to the maximum with embalming fluid ruptured, her entire body seeming to *pop* like a giant balloon.

The sound was so loud Neil raised his hands to his ears, but then he was unable to block the massive wave of flesh, gray meat and blubber that came his way, as well as in all the other directions. The ceiling was sprayed with fleshy goo, and every surface in the room was coated with a sticky, gray substance that was once part of a human body.

Blinking his eyes clear and wiping his face like he'd been hit with a custard pie, Neil blinked twice to see Aunt Bertha before him, though now she had received a massive weight loss.

Every bit of meat and flesh had been blown off her bones, leaving only her glistening red skeleton behind. A few tatters of gristle hung from the bones like tinsel on an old Christmas tree. The skeleton was prone on the floor, knocked to the floor when the body had exploded, but now, to Neil's amazed eyes, the skeleton began to crawl, pulling itself along as the left eye hung out of the socket on bits of ganglia, swaying back and forth like a small ball on frayed string. The other eye was still alert and this one focused on Neil. Her skull was still intact, the brain not touched by the overexposure to fluid and this drove the corpse onward, the need to feed still prevalent.

Neil began to stumble backwards, his first step causing him to slip and fall onto his ass. The floor was slick with bodily fluids and gore and he rolled onto his stomach and began to crawl also.

He yelled out when a skeletal hand wrapped around his left ankle and began to pull him backwards, his body sliding across the floor as if it was ice thanks to the gel-like fluids now coating it. He reached out for something to stop him but all he touched was blobs of fat.

Then, as the bloody teeth of the skull prepared to sink into his ankle, his hand found something hard amidst the blubber and pus coating the floor.

It was his wooden club!

Frantically pulling it to him, he reached out with his other hand, and with a two-handed grip, rolled onto his butt to gaze down on the grinning skull with its mouth wide open and one lone orb glaring at him.

With a yell that rivaled the warriors of old, he brought the club down onto the skull. The head was forced to the floor where it bounced once but the blow wasn't enough to destroy it. Neil pulled his leg free, went to his knees, and as the skull turned and the remaining eye looked up at him, he brought the club down once more with all the strength he had left. The tip of the club, the nails facing the skull, connected with bone, and wood was the stronger object this day. The top of the cranium shattered like a fresh egg, the wooden tip going deep to smash the brains to a pulp. As he pulled the club free, he quickly brought it down once more, lost in the desperation to save himself.

The club came down again and the brains were splattered in all directions, quickly lost in the detritus of body parts. Breathing heavily, he lay in a pool of liquid flesh, the viscous fluid seeping into his clothing and coating him from head to toe.

Slowly, he began to crawl to the exit, slipping more than once as he made his way there inch by slippery inch, sliding over the other bodies lying everywhere, these at least still immobile after he had destroyed them.

As he reached the door, he kept expecting to feel a cold hand on his ankle, that would then pull him back into the waiting jaws of bloody teeth connected to a monstrosity that should be dead, but each foot he traversed remained uneventful. By the time he reached the door, he was so scared he thought he would scream, and with a heave up and his left hand holding the doorknob, he pulled himself to a standing position.

Adrenalin filled his system and he let out a heavy sigh, wiping fatty tissue from his forehead. He opened the door and stepped outside, the cool air of the day wafting over him, washing the horror of the past hour away.

It was as he stood outside the funeral home, wiping his face clean now that he was safe, that he first began to hear the sirens and the faint sound of explosions. Walking to the front of the funeral home, he gazed out to the city just beyond the trees, heard the screams of frightened people floating on the wind, and spotted the first shambling figure stumbling down the middle of the street. As he took in the tableaux of horror before him, he knew deep in his heart that without a doubt, the ordeal that began inside the funeral home was far from over.

For as unbelievable as it might seem, as impossible as it was, for some unknown reason, the dead now walked, and wanted to feed on the living.

NO MORE CHRISTMAS

Mike Reynolds stared at his two daughters as they played by the fireplace. Watching the two children, and becoming lost in their imagination as they played with their old toys, he found he could pretend the dead never walked and that the world wasn't an apocalyptic cesspool, filled with rotting corpses and the animated dead.

The calendar on the wall, the one with all the blocks crossed out, said that tomorrow was December 24th.

It would be Christmas in two days and Mike had decided that no matter what, it would be a Christmas his two daughters would remember.

He had decided to leave their small cabin in the woods, about twenty miles from the closest city, and go into the nearest town and scavenge what presents he could find for his family.

Over the past year, their morale had waned and he knew this would be just the thing to raise the children's spirits. Of course, his wife, Sharon, didn't want him to go and had vehemently argued for him to stay.

"But don't you see, honey," Mike had told her the previous night. "The girls need something to remind them of what life was like before the dead walked. They need to feel like the world could be the way it was again."

"But it's too dangerous , you know that," she had said as the two whispered by the fresh-cut Christmas tree Mike had brought into the cabin three days earlier. It was decorated with whatever odds and ends they could find in the cabin, as well as small twigs that had been tied together to mimic garland. The top of the tree had a small wooden carving of an angel. It wasn't a very good likeness, but it was the best Mike could do given his skill level.

"What if you get cornered somewhere?" she asked. "What if you're trapped or hurt? We'll never know what happened to you. What kind of Christmas would it be for the girls then, for me? What if their father never came home?"

Mike had waved away her concerns with his hand. "I've made my mind up, Sharon, I'm doing this. Our girls need to have a real Christmas again, even if it's only for one day, they need to be happy."

Tears welled up in Sharon's eyes as she hugged her husband. "You just better come back to us, you hear?" she sniffed. "You better not leave us alone."

He patted her back softly, then rubbed it in small circles and began caressing her neck. After a full minute had elapsed, he disengaged himself from her and held her shoulders with his hands.

"Sharon, you should know by now that nothing would ever keep me away from you and the girls. Why, death itself wouldn't stop me."

She sniffed a little more and regained her composure, feeling slightly embarrassed by her show of emotion. She knew Mike didn't need her crying like a weak woman and have her welfare on his mind. No, if he was really going out into the world, even if it was against her wishes, she would support him with everything she had.

"I still don't like this, but I have to admit, even though I don't want you to go, it would be nice for the girls to have presents to open on Christmas morning. You just better keep your promise and get back here in one piece."

"I'll be fine," he told her with as much confidence as he could muster. "You'll see, I'll be back before you even know I'm gone."

The next morning found Mike leaving his car and walking the last half mile to the town.

It had been a hard morning for him.

After hugging his daughters and telling them goodbye, Sharon had reconsidered and had begged him to stay with them.

But his mind was made up and he had left her in tears, the girls not understanding why Mommy was crying. She had been on her knees, hugging the two girls as he drove away, glancing in the rearview mirror one last time before he turned a bend in the dirt road and the cabin was lost from sight.

The cabin had been his father's, and when the dead began to walk, Mike knew it was the only safe place to be—in the middle of nowhere, where the dead couldn't get them.

Still, every now and then a zombie would find the old dirt road leading to the cabin and Mike would have to put the thing down, using the machete to hack it to pieces like it was cordwood. There was an open pit a hundred feet from the cabin where he dumped the bodies and parts. It was already half full. Soon, he would have to cover it and make another. But he'd worry about that when the time came.

As he walked into town, he glanced one last time at the car, making sure it was well concealed.

It wasn't perfectly hidden, but it should be fine for the half day he figured he'd be gone. Then, with gifts in hand, he would return to his family and they would all celebrate a wonderful Christmas together.

He hoped to find some canned goods as well, maybe even some sweet potatoes and canned ham. That would make Christmas even better.

In his pocket he had a list of some likely presents. For the girls he was looking for dolls—any kind would do— as well as coloring books and crayons. For Sharon, perfume and any makeup he could find, as well as new pants and shirts. Out of the four of them, Sharon had the littlest amount of clothing and had to wear the same things over and over. Mike knew she would be thrilled to get a new outfit for Christmas.

For weapons, he carried his trusty machete for quiet work and had a hunting rifle slung over his shoulder by a strap. The gun was only for emergencies, as its report would alert the dead for miles that he was in the vicinity, and if that happened, it wouldn't be very good for his plan of going into town unobserved.

He walked slowly through the woods, cutting through the forest instead of following the road into town. He hoped by doing this he could sneak in quietly and unnoticed. He knew there had been rioting after the dead began to walk and frankly, he had no idea what to expect in the town.

Whether danger came from the undead or from fellow living survivors, he didn't know and he didn't want to know. If he had his wish, he would get in, search some homes for possible gifts, then get back out without a soul—living or dead—ever seeing him.

At the outskirts of the town, he paused and just stood motionless for five minutes. He strained to hear anything that would mark the presence of danger. When nothing came to pass, he continued on, stepping out of the treeline and onto the road leading into the north side of town.

It was a small town, no more than three thousand people in total, but how many were living there now was anyone's guess.

Mike assumed the entire town was evacuated when Martial Law had gone into effect, but he wouldn't know for sure until he went into some of the homes.

The first house was only a few minutes walk from the treeline and he approached it cautiously.

The front of the home was decorated with Christmas decorations. A plastic snowman was on the yellow, overgrown lawn and a sleigh with a smiling Santa waving—also made of plastic—sat on the roof, the extension cord for the electricity still dangling from where it had popped off its moorings. Large bulbs of red, yellow and blue adorned the window frames, but all were dark as the power had long failed in this part of the state.

As he crossed the street and onto the front lawn, he paused when he saw a lone figure at the end of the street. It was walking slowly and seemed to pause and look at him. But then it continued on, to be lost behind another building. Mike knew then it had to be one of the walking dead, for a living person wouldn't have continued on like that.

Unknown to Mike, the animated corpse had seen him, but from a distance, the zombie assumed Mike was just another animated corpse and had ignored him.

Mike continued on to the stone walkway and up to the porch of the home.

He barely glanced at the dry and brown wreath on the front door, now a year old.

Not knowing what to expect, he reached out and tried the doorknob.

Turning it slowly, he was only mildly surprised when the door clicked open on greased hinges. As he stepped in slowly, the machete in his right hand, he sniffed deeply for signs of the dead. Their odor was unmistakable, like rotting trash left out in the sun for too long.

Though the house smelled of stale air, he didn't detect the ripeness of the walking dead and he entered with a little more confidence. As he stepped inside, closing the door softly, he looked down to see the skeleton of a housecat. The animal must have been left behind at the evacuation and had starved to death when food had run out. Stepping over the small skeleton with bits of dry skin and fur, he headed deeper into the home, his destination the living room.

Just as he expected, the room was decorated with Christmas cheer. A once fresh tree—now brown, the needles on the floor around it like a carpet—was in the far corner and under the tree, also covered with brown needles, were faded presents, each wrapped and waiting for a recipient that would never be.

But before Mike could inspect the presents, a door at the back of the house banged open and three zombies stumbled into the living room, moaning in that dry rasping voice Mike knew so well. As they approached, their stench hit him and he fought the urge to gag as bile crept up into his throat.

His first urge was to sling his rifle off his shoulder and shoot them, but he knew it would be a mistake. Even inside the house, the report of the rifle would alert others to his location, especially when the town was as quiet as a grave. Sound carried far and the rifle shot would be like an explosion in the abandoned town.

No, this was a job for the machete, and with it still in his right hand, he raised it over his head and prepared for battle.

The first zombie to come at him was an old man, looking at least eighty, but due to the withered skin and pale complexion of death, it was hard to tell precisely. Not that it mattered. Even the geriatric dead had a new spring to their step upon reanimating. Perhaps it was that the dead felt no pain, so ailments such as arthritis and cataracts didn't bother them any more.

Mike waited for the old man to get within three feet of him and he sliced sideways with the machete. The blade was razor sharp and it took off the old man's head as if it was made of dry paper.

The head tumbled off the body's shoulders to fall before it, and the shuffling feet kicked it aside before the corpse dropped to the floor, a black ooze seeping out of the jagged neck stump.

The other two zombies barely slowed their gait, but now had to step over or around the now headless corpse. Mike used this hesitation to his advantage and swung the machete like an axe, slicing off the next zombie's hands at the wrists. The ghoul floundered as black blood seeped from the wounds, and as it reached for Mike, not understanding why it couldn't grab him, Mike finished it off with a chop to the head, slicing the dry skull in two. Like a cut melon, both sides spilled over to flop onto each shoulder, more black ooze spilling forth.

The last zombie had been a woman, and still was to Mike. Wearing a red Christmas sweater with withered mistletoe pinned to her chest, even in death Mike could see she had been a beautiful woman. Her blonde hair was plastered to her head, the roots pulled out and bloody in many spots. One of her eyes was missing, and Mike imagined the remaining one had once been a deep blue to match her blonde hair.

She opened her mouth and elicited a dry moan, rasping, like the voice of a heavy smoker. It almost seemed to him that she was trying to…talk.

He hesitated giving her the killing blow and it was almost his downfall. As he stared at her, she suddenly lunged for him, stepping onto the corpse of the old man and then seeming to jump into the air. Before Mike realized what was happening, he was being forced back into the withered Christmas tree, the dead woman on top of him.

In a crash of pine needles and dry branches, they tumbled to the floor amidst the faded presents.

Mike lost his machete in the fall and his rifle became trapped underneath him. All the while, the zombie was trying to snap at him, her once pristine teeth now cracked and yellow.

He reached out for something to use as a weapon with his left hand as his right held the zombie at bay. His fingers wrapped around a present and he tore it open, the chore harder for the lack of two hands. As he tore open the box, he grabbed what was within it and brought it up to use as a weapon. But when he saw it was a video game controller, he realized he had come up empty.

With nothing else to use, he slammed it into the dead woman's nose, the hard plastic smashing it flat. Dry air wheezed forth as yellow mucus dripped out of the open cavity. He used the controller again, slamming it into her forehead, and a soft crack came to him. Still, she renewed her attack, teeth clacking on empty air. Desperate and out of options, he jammed the controller into her mouth, breaking teeth off as the hard plastic slid into her gullet.

He jammed it in there so good it was like a large ball gag, and try as she might, she couldn't get it out.

With her teeth no longer a danger, Mike reached up with his left hand and grabbed her head, then shifted his right to the other side, and with a mighty twist, he snapped her neck, the loud *crack* filling the house like a cannon had gone off.

The zombie's arms and legs stopped moving as the connection from brain to body became severed, but still the remaining eye blinked. The brain was still active.

But Mike knew the ghoul was harmless now and he pushed it off him with a groan. He stumbled to his feet and retrieved his machete, then with one last look at the three destroyed zombies, decided he didn't want to stay in the house a moment longer.

After gathering a few presents up in his arms, he left, relishing the fresh air as he stepped outside. He checked the street and it was clear for the moment—nothing in sight—either living or dead. Sitting on the porch, he began opening the presents, hoping to find something he could use.

He ripped into the first one and frowned when he saw what it was.

An electric razor with a charger.

With no power, it was useless. He tossed it aside.

The second one was no better. A handheld video game system. But it needed batteries and he had run out of batteries six months ago. He tossed it onto the overgrown lawn where it disappeared in the weeds.

The third present was actually something he could use. It was a brand new Stanley claw hammer. He slid it through a loop on his pants for safekeeping. It worked well as a weapon and as a tool, and the one he had at the cabin was more than twenty years old with a wooden handle. The Stanley was all solid metal.

There was one last present and he opened it quickly. As the wrapping paper fell to the ground to blow away, he saw there was another, smaller box within the first one. Opening this one, he found a pair of diamond earrings.

Though items such as gold and diamonds were a thing of the past, he still pocketed them. He would give them to Sharon. He knew she would like them, even if it was frivolous.

As he watched the wrapping paper blow across the street and get stuck in some bushes, he sighed heavily.

Well, what did he expect? That he would enter the first house and come out with all he wanted? Of course not.

Standing, he brushed off the stray bits of paper and tape, and headed down the street, to try another house.

Christmas decorations adorned telephone poles, most now weathered and torn. A plastic reindeer lay in the middle of the road where it had blown out of a yard after a storm months ago. The face was pitted and the paint scratched and faded, and dried blood covered the back of it.

Mike walked around it, barely seeing it. All around him was wreckage. Abandoned cars with their doors hanging open—animals such as raccoons and skunks now using the cars as homes—were everywhere, and many homes showed signs of fire damage. Gutters on the houses were overgrown with dirt, and weeds grew out of them as if they were long window boxes, the vines hanging down.

Kudzu had returned in force, filling once manicured lawns to almost waist high, as well as growing between shrubs and bushes once trimmed and now runaway messes.

As Mike turned a corner, he spotted another lone figure standing in the middle of the road, about fifty feet away. The instant he saw the figure, the figure saw him also, and it began shambling toward him.

As it moved closer, Mike saw it was a man in a Santa Claus suit, only this suit was covered in dried blood and pus. When Santa was close enough for Mike to see the man's face, he saw it wasn't a man but yet one more zombie.

The white beard was gone and Santa's lower jaw was missing. The tongue hung down like a short necktie, the black muscle twitching back and forth. A low, gurgle of a moan escaped Santa as he began to hobble faster toward Mike.

Gritting his teeth at this display of holiday death, Mike raised his machete and prepared to put Santa down for good.

Each figure moved toward the other, and when Mike was close enough, he raised the machete high and brought it down, planning on slicing Santa's head in half. But at the last second, by accident or intent, Santa moved to the side and the machete came down on his shoulder. The blade sank six inches into dead flesh and became jammed between bone. When Mike tried to pull the blade free, he found it was stuck.

Santa barely flinched as his body was impaled by steel, and he reached out with unusually large hands and wrapped them around Mike's throat. As Mike tried to escape, he and Santa fell to the road to begin fighting.

Once more, Mike's rifle was jammed under his body and he cursed his luck.

Santa's tongue draped over his face, only an inch from Mike's nose as he struggled to keep the zombie at bay. Meanwhile, the holiday zombie was squeezing the life out of Mike's throat and he was beginning to lose focus as lack of oxygen threatened to cause him to faint.

Once more, he reached down to his side, desperate to find a weapon, and his hand found the Stanley hammer.

Pulling it free of his pants with a ripping of material, he spun it around so the claw was facing Santa. With a meaty thwack, he brought the hammer down, the claw embedding itself two inches into Santa's skull.

The zombie seemed to grunt as the hammer slammed into his head, but then he continued to try and bite Mike, despite the lack of a lower jaw. With a tearing of rotting flesh and bone, Mike pulled the hammer free and brought it down again. This time the claw went in deeper and managed to hit brain matter. Santa jerked like he was being electrocuted, and his white eyes rolled up into the back of his head as he slumped forward, limp, his hands releasing their death grip on Mike's throat.

Mike didn't move at first, just glad to be alive. Then with a heave, he rolled Santa off him. He rolled a few feet away and lay on the road, panting. His face was covered in slobber and he felt like he was going to vomit at any moment. Small pinpricks of light still danced across his vision and his throat felt raw when he tried to swallow.

Sitting up, he waited for the nausea to pass and then went to his feet. He pulled the machete from the corpse, and after wiping the blade on the back of Santa's red suit, he did the same with the claw hammer.

Now, with tools clean, he hobbled away, looking for all purposes like a zombie himself.

He walked another half block before he decided he needed to go someplace and rest for a bit. There was a house on his right that had all its doors closed and windows were intact, so with hopes of a sterile environment inside, one devoid of the dead, he limped to the front door.

It was locked but the hammer took care of that, a few whacks to the doorknob breaking it off. Then, with a good kick, the door flew in.

Mike waited for more than two full minutes, to see if anything or anyone would come out of the shadows and attack him, and when nothing did, he headed inside.

He planned on finding a couch or a bed and rest for at least an hour, then he would continue his search.

He made sure to close the door and prop a chair under it. There was a one foot tall crystal statue of an angel on a side table, and he placed it on the chair. If something tried to get in, the statue would fall and shatter, alerting him of trouble.

Barely looking at the house itself, he stumbled into the living room. The couch was there, as it was in every home he'd ever been in, and he fell onto it with a weary sigh. As he closed his eyes, he never even knew when he drifted off into an exhausted, stress-filled sleep.

Mike snapped awake with a jerk and an intake of breath. Then he winced, the breathing painful thanks to the soreness of his throat. Damn Santa zombie had almost killed him.

As he looked around the living room, he was relieved to see it was the same as when he fell asleep. The house smelled stale but not of death, and it was as empty as when he arrived.

His eyes caught a small birdcage in the corner, hanging from a metal post. Standing on weak legs, he shuffled over to it.

In the bottom of the cage was the dried husk of a canary, the date on the newspaper on the floor of the cage only three days before the world fell apart.

He could read the headline when he cocked his head a little.

IS IT A HOAX? DO THE DEAD REALLY WALK? SCIENTIST BAFFLED! In smaller font, ***Christmas shopping at an all time low due to crisis!***

Scratching his head, he felt his bladder alerting him it needed to be emptied. Wandering down the first hallway he spotted, he quickly found the bathroom. He peed in the toilet and even flushed it. But as the water went down, there was none to refill the tank. The water pressure had failed more than six months ago if not more, depending on the area.

He checked the medicine chest and found two bottles of aspirin and an open box of sleeping pills. He put them all in his pocket. A half empty tube of toothpaste sat on the end of the sink and he took that, too. Then he headed back into the living room to inspect the presents. He had already decided after this house he would head back home.

He'd already managed to burn through half a day and he knew he wanted to be home before nightfall. Being December, it was dark by four in the afternoon, and he knew he wouldn't want to be out once the sun went down.

Sitting cross-legged by the withered tree, for all purposes looking like a boy on Christmas morning, Mike reached out and picked up a present. Beside him sat his machete, rifle and hammer.

The box was heavy and for a moment it felt like something was alive inside it, but of course that would be ridiculous. The present had sat under the tree for an entire year, nothing could be alive inside.

He quickly tore off the paper, and as he pulled open the flaps of the box, he was horrified to find more than two dozen mice inside. As he stared at the little creatures, they swarmed out of the box and onto his arms, then onto his shirt. Cringing in horror, despite knowing the mice were harmless, he dropped the box and jumped up, brushing the rodents off him. They fell to the floor and scurried under the couch, chairs, and anywhere else they could find. As he regained control of himself, he looked down into the box and saw two things at the same time. The first was the wrapper of a fruitcake, now empty and chewed up from tiny teeth. The second was the hole on the back of the present, where the mice had burrowed in and fed on the sweet treat and then made the box their nest.

As the tail of the last mouse disappeared under a chair, Mike shook himself and reached for another present. This time he held it steady and gave it a gentle shake. When nothing moved within, he tore it open and peered inside. It was an iPod. Disgusted at finding another worthless present, he tossed it aside and tried another. This time he had some luck. It was a cashmere sweater. He set it aside to bring home to Sharon.

He went through the other presents and ended up with a pile of junk off to his left. A year ago, the items would have been worth a small fortune, but in the world of the walking dead, they were worth less than rocks. At least rocks could be used as throwing weapons in a pinch.

Standing up, he decided to search the rest of the house before leaving. He didn't like the idea of leaving empty handed and of returning to the cabin the same way. The girls were counting on him as he had told them he was going hunting for Christmas presents.

Leaving the living room with his machete in his hand and the rifle and hammer back on his person, he walked past the bathroom to search the rest of the house. The first bedroom he came to belonged to the adults of the home, and when he peered inside, he frowned at the sight before him. A man, woman and a child, all three bodies long desiccated, lay on the bed together. Beside them on a nightstand, was an empty bottle of sleeping pills. Mike stepped into the room and inspected the bodies a little more. As he did, he saw the large piece of meat missing from the child's left leg and the woman's right arm, as well as the back of the woman and child's head was missing, their dried brains splattered on the wall.

When he looked closer, he saw the man had what looked like dried leather in his mouth, and when Mike was right over the bed, he saw that the man's head had a large gunshot hole on the left side of his head as well. It was easy to figure out what must have happened.

The man, the father probably, had become a zombie and had attacked his wife and child. The wife had managed to shoot the man when they were attacked and then knowing she and the child were doomed, had given the child sleeping pills to kill her, then once the child died, she had put a bullet in her head so she wouldn't rise. Then with her family dead, the wife had placed the father on the bed as well and had taken her own life by eating a bullet.

Mike walked around the bed and found the revolver on the floor the woman had used, but it was empty. He searched for ammunition, and when none could be located, he left the gun. Without ammo it was useless other than as a club.

He might have pondered the fate of the family a little more, but the sunlight shining through the window was waning and he knew he needed to get a move on. Leaving the family of corpses, he stepped back into the hallway, closing the door as he left.

There were two more doors in the hallway; one was a linen closet and the other a child's room. It must have been the room of the child in the other bedroom, he mused.

It was a little girl's room and there, on the floor near the small twin bed, were a pair of dust-covered dolls. Mike was elated at the find. He scooped them up, brushed them off, and used a red sheet off the bed as a sack. He then went through the closet in the room and found dresses and other clothing that would fit his daughters perfectly.

By the time he was finished, the sack was fit to bursting and he had to use another shirt to tie it closed. He tossed it over his shoulder and headed out of the room, feeling good for the first time since his trek began. He went by the kitchen to check it and his luck held. He found a few assorted items to take with him, including a dented can of apricots, a can of beans, some stale crackers and half a bag of rice. Then, way in the back of a top shelf, he found a can of beef stew and was so happy he could cry. After the meager rations he and his family were surviving on, the stew would be a Christmas dinner to remember.

At the front door, he made sure he had everything, and with the machete in his right hand, he used his left and opened the door.

The sack was so big he almost didn't fit through the doorway, but he pulled on it and he slid through. He didn't bother closing the door behind him, as it was too difficult to turn around on the small stoop.

As he walked down the steps and onto the overgrown walkway leading to the street, he never saw the zombie that jumped out of the bushes and sank its teeth into his left wrist.

With a yell of shock and pain, he yanked his arm out of its mouth, blood spraying into the air to dance in the fading rays of sunlight.

The zombie lost its balance and fell to the stone path, right at Mike's feet.

He was so angry he dropped the sack of clothing and toys and swung the machete with both hands on the handle. The blade connected with dead tissue and the head of the ghoul went flying through the air, spinning three times before landing in the tall grass. Even as it disappeared, Mike could hear the teeth continually clacking together.

He fell to his knees and dropped the machete, trying to staunch the flow of blood squirting out of his wrist with his free hand. The wound was bad, real bad.

Like slicing your wrist with a razor blade, the zombie's teeth had torn an artery or vein and the blood was shooting between his fingers no matter how hard he squeezed.

Taking off his belt, he used it as a tourniquet, but even as the blood flow slowed, he knew it was irrelevant. He was bitten, and that could only mean one thing.

But it didn't matter, nothing did but returning home to his family, so he could give them their Christmas presents. He used one of the dresses for the girls as a bandage and wrapped it around the wound, but despite the tourniquet, the bandage was soaked with blood in a matter of minutes.

Shoving the machete into his pants, he picked up the sack and began walking back to his hidden car a half mile away.

It was a hard walk, and by the time he reached the outskirts of town, he was sweating profusely, his shirt a sodden mess of soaked material. A trail of blood drops was behind him, and if anyone was following him, Mike wouldn't be hard to find.

The sun was setting as he reached his car and he fell over the hood and sucked in air, struggling to remain conscious. He wasn't thinking straight anymore, and as fever racked his body thanks to the infectious bite, only one thing was on his mind.

Return home…for Christmas.

It took all his remaining effort to get the sack in the car and for him to follow it. With drooping eyelids and shallow breaths, as well as a complexion that made him look as white as a bed sheet, he managed to get the key into the ignition and start the engine.

Using one hand—ignoring the seeping blood as it soaked into the seat—he backed the car out of its hiding spot and began the drive home, his body going numb as the infection filled him from head to toe.

He would make it, he had to, for his wife, for his girls, he had to get home. For if he didn't, they wouldn't have a merry Christmas.

And if it was the last thing he did in this life, he wanted to give them that.

Sharon was filled with worry.

It was dark out and Mike wasn't home yet.

He'd promised he would be home before it was dark.

She jumped nearly to the ceiling when there was a dull thump at the cabin door. The girls looked up from where they were playing by the fireplace and Sharon told them to stay there after saying, "It's Daddy, he's back, and right on time!"

She dashed to the door, filled with relief that her husband had made it back safely, and with luck, he'd done what he hoped and had found presents for the girls.

Oh, what a wonderful Christmas this would be and now she regretted giving Mike a hard time about leaving.

Without a moment's hesitation, she threw open the door and then stopped cold, a scream on the tip of her tongue as her mouth opened into the shape of an 'O'.

Mike stood in the doorway, swaying back and forth, as if he heard music only for him. He held the red sack of toys and clothes like before, but that was where the picture of normalcy ended.

His clothing was stained a bright red, thanks to arterial spray when the tourniquet had come loose. As he bled out in the car and died, his life's blood had painted him red, making his attire look much like a red suit…a Santa Claus suit.

His face was ashen gray, his eyes now white, the pupil's devoid of color. His free hand reached out for Sharon, the gaping wound where the zombie had taken a chunk out of him still glistening as it reflected the firelight from within the cabin.

The girls had jumped up and ran to their mother's legs, wanting to see what Daddy had brought them, when Mike let out a loud moan. To Sharon and the girls it was unintelligible, but to Mike's dead mind, it was his last attempt at speech as he tried to say, "Merry Christmas."

Sharon broke from her stupor as she uttered, "Oh God no, not now, not like this."

Just as she finished speaking, and before she could so much as try and close the door, to keep out the abomination that was her husband, Mike dropped the sack of goodies and lunged for her.

His hands found Sharon's neck, the one he'd caressed with lips and fingers only a night previous, and now he squeezed as his mouth opened wide to sink his teeth into her tender flesh.

As she stumbled back, Mike followed, and his left foot hit the door, kicking it closed.

The girls screamed, not understanding what was happening, and as Sharon fell to the floor, Mike was on top of her. With the makeshift Christmas tree looking on from the corner, he began to feed, the blood soaking up the firelight and twinkling like lights on a real Christmas tree.

The two little girls began to cry, calling out for Mommy and begging Daddy to leave her alone.

Sharon heard none of it, suffering horribly as she died, and still Mike fed on her warm flesh.

Minutes passed, only the slurping of Mike feeding filling the cabin, and the girls sobbing relentlessly as they shook in terror.

Suddenly, Mike stopped feeding and looked up, seeing the two young morsels huddling in the corner of the cabin. Leaving his dead wife, he slowly began to shamble toward the girls as Sharon's corpse slowly began to twitch with renewed life, animating once more as movement filled her corpse.

As Mike leered over his two sobbing children, from behind him Sharon came to her knees and began crawling after him, the warm flesh of the two young girls calling out to her.

The girls, petrified to a state of absolute panic, could only sob and beg, pleading for their parents not to hurt them, but to make things right and protect them from the bad things in the world.

With blood dripping from his chin, Mike reached out for the closest girl, his mouth already open wide for the Christmas feast.

The lone cabin sat in the middle of the woods, far from civilization. Only a few crickets marred the silence, as well as a night bird or two calling out.

Suddenly, from the cabin, shrieks of the two children filled the night, causing the night birds to fly away, startled. The crickets stopped and the forest fell completely silent, with the exception of the girls' screams echoing from within the cabin.

In time, the screams faded and all was quiet once more.

NURSING HOME OF THE DEAD

"Mr. Williams, it's time for your medication," the night nurse said as she stepped into the TV room of the Greenwood Nursing Home in Belham, Mass.

Fred Williams looked up from the TV Guide in his hands to see the statuesque blonde standing at the doorway. Though he was almost eighty, he still admired the way the white nurse's uniform hugged her curves.

The night nurse, Sandy, was in her mid-forties, and compared to Fred, she was just a baby. Still, she was a baby with curves in all the right places.

"What is it tonight, Sandy? The red ones or the blue ones?" Fred asked as he eyed her with a hunger he couldn't douse. Having him staring at her in a sexual nature was like a toothless lion trying to eat a deer carcass. Though the lion could try, in the end all it would get is nothing.

"Both," she said with a grin that showed her perfect teeth. "Just like every night."

She strolled into the room, swaying her hips like a call girl. Fred knew it was natural for the woman, like breathing. She exuded sexuality without even trying.

She handed him two cups, one with the pills and the other with water so he could down them easily. He did both with practiced ease and then looked up at her with a smile.

"Ah, Sandy, my love, if I was but a few years younger."

She touched his cheek lovingly. "I would go out with you in a second, you handsome devil, but my husband might not like it much."

"Bah, the man doesn't know how good he has it, my dear. I would treat you like a queen."

She waved as she left the room and tossed her words over her shoulder. "I have no doubt of that, Fred, now don't stay up too late, you know what the doctor said."

Fred was going to reply, but she was already out the doorway and crossing the hallway to the nurse's desk, going to her tray of medication for the other residents of the home. More than ninety percent would need to be woken up, but Fred had always been a night owl.

"Don't give up, Fred, she'll crack one of these days," Roger said from across the TV room. He was one of the nurse's aids on the night shift and he and Fred would sometimes play cards together when there was nothing good on the television.

"Ah, Roger, I know when I'm beat," Fred said. "I'm just an old codger. Romance and love are a thing of the past for me." He pointed at his crotch. "The plumbing is clogged nowadays, anyways."

Roger stood up and crossed the room to leave. It was time to help Sandy with the medication. "That's nonsense, Fred. You're as young as any of us." Then he was out the door and talking with Sandy.

Fred sat quietly as he thought of his lost youth. In his eighties, he looked back on a life filled with excitement and adventure. He'd done two tours in the Navy on a nuclear submarine, and had then followed that with another fifteen years in the world of private security. He had protected very wealthy and important people at one time, those people entrusting him with their life. But now he was just an old man waiting to die.

He watched The Tonight Show, and when it was over, he decided it was time to turn in. Passing Sandy at the nurse's station, she flashed him a smile. He returned a wan one of his own as he headed for his private room at the end of the north wing.

It's a shame he hadn't waited a few more minutes in the TV room. For after The Tonight Show was the news, and the announcer was droning on about unsolicited attacks by the populace on unsuspecting victims. At the time of the news reports, nothing was confirmed, but mass hysteria and biological attack hadn't been ruled out.

Of course, Fred didn't hear any of this as he shuffled down the hallway; no one did. The television room was empty, the announcer's report falling on nonexistent ears.

Fred stirred in his bed as he dreamed of years past, back when he was young and full of life. Back then his hands weren't wracked with arthritis and his knees didn't crack like popcorn when he walked. He could barely remember a life without pain, but then he had always told himself that pain said you were still alive. Pain let you know you weren't dead, for once you were dead, you would feel nothing, let alone pain.

Suddenly, his eyes snapped open and he looked upon a darkened room. Glancing to the right, he saw the clock on his bedside table read 3:54 a.m. The red numbers of the digital clock seemed to bore into his brain so he looked away, blinking. He didn't know what had awakened him until he felt the familiar pressure on his bladder.

Of course, he thought, *I have to pee.* Since he'd hit eighty, his bladder had shrunk to the size of a walnut and he never got a full night's sleep any more.

It was as he was about to toss the blankets off his frail form that he realized there was someone standing in the doorway of his room.

The hallway was almost completely dark, only the red light bulbs on the hall ceiling now on. These lights were turned on after ten, the standard fluorescents shut off. That way the residents of the nursing home could sleep with their doors open, but yet the corridors weren't totally dark and the staff could still work when doing bed checks.

Fred rubbed the sleep from his eyes as he stared at the human shape in his doorway. At first he had no idea who it might be, but then he recognized the form of Norman.

Norman Silverstein was his neighbor, having the room next to him. He was a few years younger than Fred, but once you hit eighty, a year or two didn't matter too much anymore.

Blinking, Fred tried to see Norman better, but with the red lights behind him, all her could see was Norman's silhouette.

"Norman, is that you?"

At first Norman said nothing, but then Fred heard a low moan, like an animal that had been hurt after being rundown by a passing car after trying to cross the street.

"Norman, you okay?" Fred asked, worried for his friend. "You want me to call the nurse for you?"

Norman had a bad heart and high blood pressure. His days were numbered and he knew it, but neither spoke of it much. When you reached a certain age, death was as inevitable as the sun rising in the morning.

It was just as Norman took a step forward, another low moan issuing from his throat, that Fred reached over and turned on his bedside light.

The lamp was small, but it was more than enough to banish the darkness, and as the light chased the shadows away, Fred stared open-mouthed at Norman, not understanding what was wrong with his friend.

For Norman didn't look the same as when he had gone to bed earlier that night. Now his flesh was bone white and his lower jaw and chest were covered in blood. But it was apparent by his blood-red dentures that the blood wasn't his. It looked like Norman had been eating something...or someone, by the look of it. Fred leaned over the side of the bed to grab his slippers so he could go see to his friend who obviously needed help.

"Hang on, Norman, I'll come help you," Fred said as he struggled to get his slippers on.

But Norman wasn't waiting for Fred to come to him. As Fred leaned over the bed, Norman shambled forward, hitting the small table holding Fred's medicine, water pitcher, and television remote. All the items clattered to the floor, the medicine falling like spilled candy, the water pitcher breaking open, and the remote cracking as it slid across the floor.

But Fred saw none of this for he had Norman to deal with. As Fred looked up at the clatter of the table, Norman lunged at him, scarlet teeth flashing in the pale light of the lamp.

"Oh my God, Norman! What's wrong with you?" Fred yelled as he leaned away from Norman. Dentures snapped on empty air and Norman snarled like an animal. Fred was back on the bed now, but the hospital railing was up on the other side and he couldn't get far. Norman crawled onto the bed and then onto Fred, the two looking like young lovers attempting to figure out how to make love.

Norman snapped his dentures at Fred, the clicking sounding like a gun had gone off in the otherwise silent room.

"Jesus Christ, Norman, stop it!" Fred yelled again as he shoved his right hand under Norman's chin. The skin was sagging due to age and Fred's hand went in like he was pressing on foam. The entire time Norman tried to bite him, Fred stared into his friend's eyes and realized whatever was happening, whatever had done this to Norman, had somehow changed him to something else.

It was the eyes that made Fred think this. Those eyes were so blank, so…dead.

Dentures clacked on empty air again and Norman's right hand reached around and grabbed Fred's right cheek, Norman's nails trying to sink and literally rip Fred's face off.

That was when Fred knew he had no choice on what to do next. If he didn't stop Norman now, he knew his friend would kill him.

Fred's eyes darted back and forth and then rested on the silver, stainless steel bedpan on the small bedside table to his right. He was lucky enough not to have to use it, but it was there just in case.

Reaching out with his free hand, while Norman slavered on top of him like a wild dog, Fred grasped the bedpan tightly and brought it up and around, using all of his waning strength to force the blow.

There was a loud *clang* when the bottom of the bedpan struck the side of Norman's head, the sound similar to one cymbal crashing against cement. Despite this, Norman only grunted as his head was knocked to the side.

Now in full survival mode, Fred was committed to the cause of saving his ass, so he brought the bed pan up and down again, this time forcing more power into the blow. Another *clang* filled the room and the blow was so hard it knocked Norman's dentures out of his mouth. They shot out like they were self-propelled, arced in the air almost gracefully, then dropped down to bounce off Fred's temple, leaving a red smudge of blood there as they tumbled to the pillow and then the floor.

Fred barely noticed, as he was swinging back with the bedpan yet again. This time the *clang* was so loud and the blow so strong Fred felt the vibration crawl up his arm and into his shoulder.

Also, the clang wasn't as loud this time as the bedpan had managed to crack open Norman's skull. Fred stared up in horror as Norman's exposed brains seemed to pulse with each move the dead man made. And Fred knew this was true as there was no way Norman could be alive, not by the way he looked and the abuse he was suffering.

Norman swung out a hand, on purpose or by accident, it was unknown, but Fred saw the bedpan knocked from his grip. It clattered into the corner and the racket was unbelievable.

Surely the staff must have heard it by now. Surely they would be coming to his aid and pull this madman off of him at any second.

But brief glimpses to the doorway and the shadowed hallway beyond showed no one coming to his aid.

Fred knew he would have to save himself.

Norman leaned forward, mouth open wide, and before Fred could stop his former friend, Norman's mouth was on his nose.

Fred closed his eyes tight, expecting to feel the terrible bite of teeth as they ripped off his nose, but then he realized there was nothing there but a soft sucking sound.

He opened his eyes to look Norman straight into his dead eyes, no more than an inch separating their gazes. Norman was sucking his nose like a baby gumming a chew toy, his lack of dentures making him all but harmless. Red saliva slid to the sides of Fred's nose and slowly crawled down his cheeks, soaking into the sheet beneath.

This went on for almost twenty seconds as Fred gathered his wits.

When he was ready, he bucked his hips as hard as he could, and like a comedy show on television, Norman went flying up and to the side.

Norman landed hard, his exposed brains ejecting out of his skull where they now sagged on the side of his head like the worst ponytail in history. Fred, breathing deeply, stared at Norman, the man floundering like a landed fish. Fred rolled off the bed, his knee joints popping from arthritis. He ignored his slippers, the soles of his feet feeling the chill from the cold linoleum tiles.

Shuffling around the bed much like Norman had done, he headed for the door and the darkened hall, hoping to get some help. But as he passed Norman, the undead man swung about and grabbed Fred's ankle with his right hand.

Fred yelped in surprised and felt himself falling forward, losing his balance and teetering like an old tree in a storm. Then he felt himself going forward, the tiles coming up fast. He reached out his hands, and at the last second, stopped himself from receiving a broken nose, but his forehead smacked the cold tiles. He was dizzy for a second, stars dancing in his vision, but then he snapped out of it as he felt the tug on his leg.

Norman was trying to crawl on top of him.

Fred rolled over, kicking out with his left foot, but Norman took the blow in stride. Fred could have sworn he felt his dead friend's jaw dislocate, but other than a hunch, he wasn't sure.

With crimson drool seeping from the corner of his mouth, Norman began trying to crawl up Fred again.

Fred was helpless, not having any idea what to do. Norman was coming closer with each inch and he was trapped under the weight of his body.

Then he turned his head to the side and spotted the remote control for the television. It had shattered into three pieces, but the plastic housing had broken in the shape of a slim dagger. Desperation filling him to the core, he reached out and wrapped wrinkled fingers around the piece of plastic.

Norman was at chest level now, his mouth working as if he was already feeding on Fred's neck.

As Fred brought up the plastic dagger, Norman raised himself higher as he prepared to wrap his hands around Fred's neck. Fred howled in fear and anger and used the plastic dagger like a real one, jamming it into Norman's right eye.

The orb was no match for the dagger and it punctured instantly as Fred pushed the plastic deep into Norman's brain. A white-pink ooze slid out around the plastic piece to roll down Fred's arm, but he ignored it.

He had his hands full as Norman began to buck like he was filled with electricity. But this only went on for a few seconds as the energy that had brought him back from the dead slowly faded away.

One second Norman was like a live wire, then he was limp, sagging on top of Fred to remain absolutely still, brains seeping out of the hole in his skull. Fred didn't move for almost half a minute, just thanking his Lord his dilemma was over.

When his wits were his once more, he shoved Norman off him. The body sagged to the side, the plastic dagger so far in his eye socket only the barest of the tip could be seen. As the head dropped down, a thin, bile-like substance slid from Norman's mouth as more ooze seeped from the punctured eye.

It was as Fred lay on the floor that he suddenly realized he could hear more sounds of screaming and people in pain. It was then he knew he had been hearing it for a while but had tuned it out, as he had to concentrate on his attacker.

With moans to rival Norman's, he got to his feet, using the walker in the corner to help him stand. There was a cane in the corner and he grabbed it, feeling more confident he could now walk without falling over.

Ignoring the corpse of Norman, Fred shuffled out to the darkened hallway to go find Sandy and Roger and get some help.

But as he stepped out into the hall, he realized things weren't much better there.

It was dark of course so he couldn't see too well, but he could see the shapes of people moving about. Most were slow, very slow and he knew it had to be the other residents.

Maybe they had come out of their rooms to see what all the yelling was about? Fred thought as he watched the shapes moving from left to right and up and down.

He was relatively alone where he was; his room being at the far end of the building, as was Norman's.

Then from up by the nurse's station, someone must have found the light switch for the fluorescents, because suddenly the hallway was bathed in white light.

All the residents were now exposed for anyone to see, and as Fred took in their appearance, he came to the conclusion that Norman had been a busy boy before finding Fred's room. The reason for this assumption was the dark red stains on the bedclothes of the residents, the gaping wounds in their throats and arms, a few missing pieces of their face.

And as Fred took this all in, staring at the deathly pale appearances of his fellow residents, all their eyes turned and shifted to him, their dead gazes slicing into him like lightning.

A low moan carried from one zombie to the next as each turned to face Fred from down the hallway. And then, like another switch had been flicked, each one began shambling towards him.

Fred stared in horror, not wanting to believe what was happening.

"Oh, shit," he whispered and then he knew it was time to run.

Fred spun around, thinking he could run to the rear stairwell and then exit the building by the first floor emergency door, but no sooner did he turn, then he saw more residents coming through the open stairwell door.

What was amazing was some of the people he saw.

The first floor of the nursing home was for the very old and infirm, the ones who were basically vegetables in body suits. These were the ones who had no mind left, in other worlds, *the lights were on but no one was home.*

Out of the entire first floor population, only a handful was still in their right mind, but all were invalids, needing everything from baths to being fed by someone else. Some had suffered debilitating strokes, thus paralyzing them, while others had Alzheimers, the rot of their brains all but complete.

None of them could walk, their muscles atrophied and their limbs wilted.

So for Fred to see these people actually walking, though in a staged, monster-like way, was absolutely amazing.

A symphony of moans and wails oozed from cracked and dry lips, some not capable of speech due to their illnesses. But now, whatever had killed them and brought them back from the dead had unlocked their vocal cords.

From a casual glance they looked like they always had...which was basically zombie-like. Wrinkled skin, some loose and hanging below chins and under arms, sunken eyes, a step closer to death with each passing day, and teeth that were all but rotting inside the gums was par for the course, but now, the residents of the home had one more added description.

Each one had some form of mortal wound on their person, though many did not, making Fred wonder if they had died in their sleep or from pure, unadulterated fear.

Fred had always been a smart man, able to figure things out quickly, and if he was willing to set the unbelievable aside for just a second, it was painfully obvious the dead were walking en masse. At the moment the *how* and *why* seemed irrelevant, all that mattered was to stay alive; for it seemed to Fred he was the only one still on this side of the barrier separating the living from the dead.

Backing away from the first floor zombies, he gripped his cane tightly, realizing he did have a weapon.

And in less time than it would take to think about it, he raised the cane at the first wave of ghouls and used it like a spear.

The tip of the cane was relatively blunt, worn down from years of rubbing along the floor, but it was still stronger than the human eye.

When the first ghoul, a withered old woman with a colostomy bag and bone-white hair, came for him, he raised the cane and jammed it into her left eye. The orb didn't so much as give out, but exploded, a clear ooze shooting out of the socket like someone had stepped on a tube of toothpaste. A large spray struck Fred in the face and a little got on his lips and in his mouth. It was salty, he knew that immediately, and he choked and spit as sheer will forced the tip of the cane deep into the geriatric skull.

Then he hit brain, and like sliding into warm pudding, the cane punctured something important, the old hag slumping forward like a doll with a string on her back that had run out. As she fell, the cane went with her and Fred found himself losing his grip. But no sooner did he lose it than the dead woman was lying on her back, the cane sticking up, resembling a flag pole on the ninth hole on a golf course.

Fred grabbed the cane as the other ghouls moved in and he yanked on it. But it was stuck, the tip of the cane caught in the bone of the eye socket.

Desperate, he placed a foot on the dead woman's forehead, and pulled with all his waning strength

The cane popped out with a sucking sound and he saw bits of pink and red brain matter clinging to the end of the cane. Forcing his stomach to stay calm, he spun to face his next adversary.

It was an old man like himself, complete with sagging skin and bushy eyebrows. Fred didn't know the old man's name, but had seen him in the dining room now and then.

As the old ghoul came at him, Fred used the cane again, stabbing it into the ghoul's open mouth. The wooden tip went in with such force it scraped the roof of the old man's mouth, taking a few yellow teeth with it.

Fred stood there, the old man on the end of his cane like a landed fish, and tried to figure out what to do next. His idea came when the old man tripped on his feet and dropped to the floor. Fred was yanked along, too, and before he knew what was happening, he'd fallen onto the cane, pushing the tip into the upper palate of the old man and into the back of his spine.

From the neck down, the ghoul stopped moving, the spine now severed, but the eyes and mouth were still active. Withdrawing the cane, Fred didn't care about the man's condition. If the old man was down and had no fight left, that was good enough for him.

The others were coming closer now, and in another second they would be at him in twos and threes and there was no way he could fend them off. There was a small opening in the left side of the undead senior citizens and he knew it was his only hope.

Shoving a dead woman with a garish wig to hide her thinning hair, he charged like a linebacker, only much slower.

He was barely faster than the shuffling ghouls, his eighty-year-old plus body not able to move fast, no matter how much he wanted it to.

But he shoved by the worst of the undead crowd and made his way down the hallway, his destination the nurse's station. Sandy would be there and she would know what to do.

His mind didn't bother to consider that this wouldn't be the case, and if he had time to think, he would have reasoned that Sandy wouldn't have knowingly let a horde of walking dead residents roam the halls unattended. But he was panicking and desperate so he didn't think negatively.

Shoving past each of the ghouls, he realized they were so very slow and if he had been ten years younger he would have had an easier time of it. But he wasn't ten years younger and with his breath rasping in his throat, he dashed for the nurse's station, or more precisely, he walked as fast as he could.

Upon reaching the waist high counter surrounding the nurse's station, he saw it was devoid of life.

"Sandy? Are you here?" Fred called out, glancing over his shoulder to see he had less than half a minute before the first of the undead residents was on him.

At first there was nothing to tell him where Sandy might be, but then he heard a smacking, like when a fat man eats ribs. Cocking his ear closer to the counter, he heard it louder than before.

That was when he slowly leaned over the counter to look down at the floor behind the nurse's station.

"Oh, Jesus Christ in a hat," Fred gasped as he stared in horror at the sight greeting him.

Sandy was there, but she wasn't how he remembered her before he'd gone to bed. And Roger was there, too, both of them spread out on the floor behind the counter. Sandy was the active one and she was on top of Roger, looking at first like the two had decided to have a triple-x throw down right there on the floor.

But no sooner did Fred think this then Sandy's head snapped up, and in her teeth was a nice chunk of Roger's chest.

She shifted position at the sound of Fred's voice and that let him see Roger's condition in all his horrible glory.

Roger's chest was ripped open now, the ribs and lungs exposed to the air, the red glistening muscles seeming to reflect every bit of light cascading down on them.

His heart was exposed, but now it was hanging by a thread, or an artery. It was while Fred watched, stunned, that Sandy reached into Roger's open torso and plucked the heart from its moorings. The remaining artery stretched as she pulled, and for a brief instant, Fred was reminded of an apple on a tree before it was released into the hand plucking it. Sandy raised the heart to her mouth and sank her teeth into it, the muscle squirting blood out like she had taken a bite from the largest tomato he'd ever seen.

That was it for Fred. He leaned over and puked, a light green bile splashing to the floor between his bare feet. Sandy, deciding she was finished with Roger and now wanted something fresher, was getting to her feet as she chewed on the heart.

Fred saw her from the front now and her entire uniform was stained crimson, making her look like someone had thrown a bucket of red paint on her.

She hissed around mouthfuls of heart as she began to come around the side of the nurse's station.

Fred took a step backward and he had no more finished this then Roger popped up from behind the counter, his internal organs now sliding out of the gaping cavity that was his chest.

Roger's eyes were the same, the face glazed, but his mouth opened and he tried to issue a moan, but with collapsed lungs nothing came out.

Fred gasped in shock and then the first of the undead residents were on him.

He spun as the first hands landed on him, and he realized he had become distracted by Sandy and Roger and had forgotten the rest of the residents.

He tried to break free, but there were too many!

His cane whacked heads and he poked out eyes, but for every one he took down, another took its place.

But he wasn't going to give up, never!

He continued to fight, feeling younger than he had in years as adrenalin suffused his system. His arthritis was forgotten as he wielded the cane like a club, spear, and mace, all rolled into one.

As the undead residents moaned and wailed, Fred screamed and ranted. "You old bastards won't take me down without a fight!"

And as he swung the cane into the side of an old woman, he realized he just might win. More than a dozen geriatric ghouls were now on the floor, with some from a broken limb or wound that slowed them down.

Fred was an unstoppable killing machine, resembling an aged warrior of old, even the worn bathrobe not detracting from the tableaux.

It was as he poked out the eye of a grizzled old man in his nineties with a catheter and an IV bag hanging from an arm that he found out that though the will is strong, the flesh is weak.

As he raised the cane to bring it down over a small ancient woman with frizzled gray hair, he suddenly felt a sharp pain in his chest and then his left arm began to hurt, daggers of agony flaring up into his brain.

He stumbled and dropped the cane as he wobbled on his feet. He managed to issue only one sentence as the dead slowly surrounded him, taking advantage of the lull of his attack.

"I'm having a heart attack?" he gasped incredulously.

It was as he dropped to the cold floor and his vision began to fade that he realized the utter irony of his situation.

Just before he fell into oblivion, the first of the old ghouls reached him, but he was already gone, and he felt no pain as the first clawed and wrinkled hand touched him. Mercy had at least granted him this.

Minutes later, Fred slowly came to his feet, the residents backing away, not interested in him anymore. Only a few chunks of his flesh were missing, as he had revived before the undead seniors could do much damage to him.

His eyes were now vacant, his mouth slightly agape, like a dullard trying to figure out a complex math problem. Like the other residents, he turned and headed for the main doors and the outside world.

Though Fred's mind was empty, the zombie who was once Fred would have taken comfort in knowing his knees didn't pop as he walked and his arthritis was gone.

ONE LAST CHANCE

"There's no easy way to say this, so I'm just going to say it," Doctor Marshall said as he held the lab work in his hands.

Chad and Susan Wilcott grasped hands, the look of sadness on the doctor's face apparent.

"Go 'head, Doctor, let's hear it," Chad said with a slight stutter to his voice. His heart was beating a mile a minute and he was waiting for the other shoe to drop. The truth was, he had been waiting for more than a month, after the first signs his son had shown of being sick.

The doctor sighed heavily, perspiration coating his forehead. Looking both Chad and Susan in the eyes, he said the words no parent ever wants to hear.

"I'm afraid your son has cancer, Mr. Wilcott. And I'm afraid it's terminal."

Susan let out a muffled sob, then with her hands in front of her mouth, stood up and ran from the room, heading in the direction of the bathroom.

Chad barely knew she left, his own bafflement and shock filling him with a mind numbing feeling he'd never known before.

He shook his head, trying to disavow what he'd just heard.

"What did you say, Doctor? That can't be. He just had a sore arm, for Christ's sake, how the hell can it be cancer? And terminal? That's ridiculous."

The doctor set the lab work onto his desk and leaned forward, steepling his fingers in front of him. He'd seen this so many times, and despite knowing he was supposed to remain objective, he always felt his heart break a little.

Nodding his head, as if he knew exactly how Chad felt, he sighed yet again. "I'm afraid so, Mr. Wilcott. He has an acute case of leukemia. If we had known a little earlier, we may have been able to slow it down, but the end would still be the same. Maybe it's better this way. The chemo is hard on children. He should have a year at least, maybe more before things get really rough. At least this way Sean's quality of life will be good almost till the end."

"His quality of life?" Chad asked, his anger growing inside him. It wasn't the doctor's fault, he knew that, of course, but someone needed to be blamed. Someone needed to accept fault in this and damn it there was no one else…unless he wanted to blame God.

"His quality of life?" he said again. "You've got to be fucking kidding me." He hissed the last part, his fists now curved into balls of pure anger. "He's seven years old you son-of-a-bitch!"

The doctor remained silent, his face impassive. He'd given enough devastating news to parents in his career to know when to be silent, to stay impassive and let the parent rant.

"So what now, huh? So we're supposed to just go home and watch him die?"

The doctor remained silent and Chad's jaw grew taut. He wanted to punch something, anything, and the doctor was sitting only a few feet from him. It took every ounce of his will not to lash out, but some small part of him remained in control, though miniscule as it was.

"Look, Mr. Wilcott…Chad. Maybe you should let me put you in touch with a counselor. You're obviously having trouble dealing with this dreadful news."

"Dreadful news? Are you kidding me? Are you for fucking real? How can you sit there and even think for one damn moment you have an inkling of how I feel? You pompous bastard. If you'd caught the damn cancer earlier, maybe none of this would be happening right now!"

"No, Mr. Wilcott, that wouldn't be the case. I'm so sorry," he said and slowly raised himself from behind his desk, the subtle gesture telling Chad it was time for him to go.

Chad remained motionless, gazing with hard eyes at the doctor, his hands clenched into fists by his side. Then, slowly, his shoulders slumped slightly and the veins on his forehead receded. His adrenalin was pumping and he wanted to scream, but he was more in control now.

Standing up on weak legs, he began to move to the door and leave, knowing he needed to find Susan.

"I am truly sorry for your loss," the doctor said to his back just before he exited the office.

Chad stopped and then shifted his head slightly, so he could just catch the doctor in his peripheral vision.

"Yeah, well, your sympathy doesn't do me a damn bit of good, Doctor. My only son is dying and there's not a goddamn thing I can do about it but watch it happen."

He opened the door then, and stepped through the doorway. The secretary looked up as he exited the office, her eyes filled with alarm. She had heard him screaming of course. Her hand was on the phone and Chad wondered if she was about to call security on him.

He barely acknowledged her; simply walked out of the office and into the main floor of the hospital. With the redolence of antiseptic and ammonia tickling his nose, he went off to find his wife.

He knew she needed him, and damn it if he didn't need her, too, right now.

When he returned home tonight, he had a tough decision to make. Exactly how the hell was he supposed to tell his seven-year-old son he had less than a year to live?

But Chad did tell his son and Sean took it better than him. Chad figured it was because of the boy's age. You could look a child right in the face and tell him he would be dead tomorrow and the child would only blink at you and say you're crazy. It was the way of youth; they didn't believe they could die. But as the days turned into weeks, Sean realized what he'd been told that fateful day was true. He was now a skinny frame of bones with a coating of skin and his face looked like a bare skull. It broke his and Susan's heart but both tried to be positive, well, as positive as any parent can get as they watched their child deteriorate and die.

So it was on a warm Friday night that Chad decided it was time to get out of the house. The carnival was in town, and though Sean wasn't looking his best, the boy wanted to go.

Susan had argued, but after Chad had basically said this was probably the last time they would be able to do something as a family, she'd given in, wanting to at least feel as if things were still normal. So packing up Sean's wheelchair, they drove the few miles to the carnival.

They parked on the dirt parking area and Sean was taken out of the car and placed into his wheelchair. Chad knew he'd made the right decision. Sean's eyes were wide with excitement and he wore the biggest smile Chad had ever seen.

Pushing the wheelchair into the wide alleys of the games of chance, even Susan began to smile, the happiness of the place infective, no matter how full of despair a person felt in their heart.

The next hour and a half was filled with laughter and fun as the three of them enjoyed being together. Chad even won a stuffed giraffe for Sean;

though he had a feeling the vendor had let him win, especially after seeing his son with his white complexion and sunken eyes.

But that didn't deter them at all and they walked around, watching the people ride the carnival rides and yell and scream with fright.

It was as they were leaving that Chad met someone who would change the rest of his life.

Susan and Sean went to get some fried dough, his wife pushing the wheelchair. Sean's appetite was usually terrible and if he was hungry she wasn't going to tell him no.

Chad was standing by a tent, one colored with faded red, yellow and blue stripes, when an old woman all in black shambled out of the tent.

She stopped next to him and at first Chad didn't see her, but then she reached out with a bony hand and grabbed his wrist. Startled, Chad spun to look down on this gnarled woman, but she only stared up at him, her right eye looking the other way. It took Chad a second to realize it was made of glass.

"You," the old hag said. "I see much death around you. Someone you know is dying, yes?" She waved for him to enter the tent with her. "Come, come, I tell you your fortune. I tell you how to help dying one."

Chad made a face as she pulled his arm free. "Oh, please, are you serious? How can you be so heartless, you old bat? You saw me and my wife with our son and it's obvious by looking at him he's dying. And now you use that against me to make a buck? Shame on you." He turned to walk away when she called out to him.

"What if I told you there is a way to save him?"

Though Chad wasn't in the mood for games, he was so desperate to save his son he paused for a moment. Not much, but just the briefest of hesitations.

The old crone saw this and shuffled forward. All around them people laughed, lights flashed and music played.

"Ah, I see I have your attention. Come, come, I tell you the truth. You can save him, just come, come," she said as she took his hand and began pulling him towards the tent.

He didn't know why he went with her. This was obviously all a fraud, the way to bilk customers out of their money, but it was something about her face, her voice, that had Chad following. To say she was the stereotypical fortune teller would be an understatement. In truth, she looked a lot like a witch. Her face was wrinkled to the point her skin resembled old parchment. Her glass eye gave her the look of a madwoman and the odor coming off her was one of antiseptic and urine. But still, there was a power, a presence Chad felt that had him following her into the tent. He forgot about Susan, knowing she would be worried about where he went but he didn't care; it was as if he was in a daze.

As he was led into the tent, the music seemed to fade away and the darkness enveloped him. It was as if the carnival wasn't outside the tent, that they were now in a field somewhere, only the covering of night surrounding them.

"Sit, sit, there, you sit there," she said as she moved around a small square table. Even though he was dazed, Chad wondered where the crystal ball was. But there was no glass ball, only a deck of cards, and he had to wonder if they were tarot cards, the ones all gypsy fortune tellers used to suck money from hapless believers.

She sat down with a groan of weary bones and Chad looked at her. It was like he was in a dream. He could think, he could even leave if he wanted to, but he didn't, his desperation was that great.

She began to lay out the cards and she muttered to herself as she did this.

"I know this may sound unbelievable but there is a way for you to save your son, do you want to know it?" she asked.

He nodded. Of course he did, he would go to the moon if he thought it would help. She laid out the cards and Chad gazed down at them as she began to speak.

"You must go to Hell, my son, you must go to Hell where you must then battle your way through the seven circles to reach Lucifer himself."

"Lucifer?" he gasped.

"Yes, my boy. Lucifer. For only he can grant you your wish to save your child. But to get to him will not be easy. You must battle your way through each circle where you will be tempted and attacked. None have made it thus far, but if your will is strong, your soul true, perhaps you will be the one. Once you cross the gates of Hell and enter Lucifer's domain, he will have no choice but to grant your wish, whatever that wish may be. Most attempt this so they can be set free of Hell, not wanting to suffer for all eternity." She sighed then and she turned another card over. "Ah, but there is a catch, one you may not like."

"Go on," he said.

"To get to Hell, you must commit an act, one so vile, so heinous, that there will be no doubt about where your soul will be sent. You must commit murder." She glared at him with her one good eye. "Tell me, Chad, can you kill another to save your son's life?"

"I…I don't know." And he didn't. To kill another person would mean someone would have to die so his son would live. A life for a life. But that would be wrong, so wrong on so many levels. He knew how he felt about his son. How would another family feel to lose their husband, mother or child? No, he couldn't do that, no matter what the result would be.

"Well, then your son is lost," she said. "For you to go to Hell, to make sure there is no doubt, for if you go to purgatory your sacrifice will be in vain, you must commit murder most foul."

"I'm sorry; I don't think I can do that, even to save Sean."

"Then he is lost," she said. "Now go, I have told you the way, it is up to you to act on it or not."

He stood up as if ordered and reached into his back pocket for his wallet to pay her and she spit on the floor.

"Bah, I don't want your money, you fool. Go, go now, your family wonders where you are."

He nodded, turned and walked out of the tent, and as soon as he was back into the actual carnival, his mind cleared and he was able to think. At this time he never bothered to wonder how the old crone had known his name for he never told her it.

Susan rolled up with Sean and she looked at him like a mother to a lost child.

"Chad, where've you been? I've been looking for you for half an hour."

He checked his watch and sure enough, over thirty-five minutes had passed. He had been with the old gypsy for a half hour, but it felt like minutes. Turning, he saw the tent was still there, and wanting to tell Susan about what happened, he went to it. But when he opened the flap, all he saw inside were boxes of stuffed animals and other odds and ends the vendors used. One of the vendors saw him and yelled at him to get out of there. Thievery was always a problem and the man thought Chad was trying to steal a toy.

Chad stumbled back to Susan and Sean. His son was eating fried dough happily and Susan looked at him with an odd look.

"Chad, are you all right? You look like you've just seen a ghost."

Deciding there was no reason to tell her what he must have imagined, he nodded and smiled.

"I'm fine, honey, just tired. So, what do you say we go over to the Ferris wheel for a bit?"

She agreed as did Sean, and with one last glance at the tent, Chad walked on, putting the odd dream out of his mind, wracking it up to stress.

The next two months were hard on Susan and Chad. Sean was now beginning to have some tough days where he could barely get out of bed. Sitting up would be a chore. Other days he was better and would even have a smile for his parents. Chad couldn't imagine his son having to live this way for ten more months or longer, but there was nothing to do about it.

It was the fifth day of the second month that Chad saw something on the news that caused him to remember the gypsy fortune teller from the carnival. Since that day he'd put it out of his mind. It had to have been one of those daydreams people talk about. He was under more stress than any man should have to deal with and it was only natural he would have some kind of breakdown, even if it was a small one.

But as he watched the news that night, and the announcer went on about a missing child and then showed the hand drawn picture of who they believed was the culprit, his mouth fell open and the gypsy's words came rushing back to him.

"You can save your son, but you must commit a heinous act of murder to save him."

The announcer went on that the man in the picture was a suspected child molester and had been off the police radar for more than two years. He was arrested five years ago in Tulsa and had served three of a six year sentence, then he'd left the state and until now, the authorities didn't know where he'd been.

But as Chad stared at the screen, he realized immediately he knew who the man was.

It was Ralph from three doors down. The man was an introvert who rarely cut his lawn. The landlord was a slumlord and between the two of them, the house looked like shit. That was why Chad recognized the face from when he'd go for a walk with Sean and would stare at the man if he was outside having a cigarette, wondering why someone could live like such an animal.

And if he was right, then this man had a child in that house, and was doing God knew what to.

He never hesitated, never so much as stopped to consider what he was doing next. He got up from his chair in the living room, went to the kitchen, and gave Susan a hug and a kiss. She was clipping coupons and she barely glanced up at him.

"I'm going out for a bit, honey," he said. "Whatever happens, know that I love you and Sean and that I did it for him…and you."

"Uh-huh," she said. "Get some milk while you're out, will you? We're out."

Chad stepped back to the counter where he slid the largest knife from the wooden knife holder, palming it as he did so.

"Sure, honey, I'll see what I can do, but I might not be able to," he said as he left the kitchen.

"Whatever, dear, if you can, you can," Susan replied as she clipped a thirty-five cent coupon for grape jelly.

Chad went by Sean's room to see his son was sleeping. He didn't want to wake him so he kissed his forehead, feeling how cold it was.

"I love you, son. If this is all true then I'm going to save you. I promise."

Sean stirred in his sleep and moaned slightly, then was quiet. With tears in his eyes, wondering if he was mad for what he was about to do, Chad grabbed his jacket and stepped outside.

It was a beautiful night, and as he strode down his walkway and took a left towards Ralph's house, he gripped the hilt of the knife tighter, praying to God what he was doing was the right thing to do, and not the mindless ideas of an insane man.

Ralph's house looked abandoned as Chad made his way up the front walkway. He had to slide between overgrown hedges and tall grass. It may have looked deserted, but then it always looked this way, Chad figured as he stepped up to the front door.

There was a small, thin window made of leaded glass that was five inches wide and as high as the door. He peered through the decorative images on the glass to try and see inside the house, but all he saw was an empty hallway.

For the hell of it he checked the door, but of course it was locked.

He decided to go around to the back and was appalled by the condition of the yard. Where the front was overgrown grass and shrubs, the back was ten times as bad, with the added insult of bags of trash and other debris such as old newspapers and boxes. The yard looked like something from a third world country instead of a backyard in the United States.

Ignoring the smell of rotting trash, Chad stepped over piles of refuse until he was at the back door. The door was wooden on the bottom and glass on the upper half, not made for security, but then the neighborhood Chad and Ralph lived in was a safe one; that is until Ralph moved in.

Chad peered through the curtain on the back door and at first he saw nothing but a filthy kitchen table and three chairs, but then he caught a shadow move across the door.

Chad's adrenalin was pumping and his mouth was dry as he ducked down low so as not to be seen. He looked around at the nearby homes, but no one could see him on the back porch, what with overgrown trees in the way.

Chad risked another peek and this time there was no shadow, but as he looked, he heard a scream. It was a quick one, and it was cut short as fast as it began and only because he was standing at the back door was he allowed to hear it.

But he knew it was a scream nonetheless.

The girl was inside the house and Ralph was doing God knew what to her!

Using his right elbow, Chad broke the back door window and then reached inside to unlock the door. Without thinking about what he was doing, was *actually* doing, he opened the door and charged inside. All he was thinking about was that little girl, a child like Sean who needed his help.

As he ran into the kitchen, a half naked Ralph came around the corner to investigate the breaking glass, and he and Chad bumped into each other, the two falling to the floor in a heap. The knife went clattering away to slide down the hallway and Chad found himself now battling for his life. Ralph knew what would happen to him if he was caught with the little girl and he was prepared to kill Chad to prevent that from happening. As the two men rolled around on the ground, Chad felt hands wrap around his throat.

Like cable wires on his neck, his oxygen was cut off and he punched Ralph to make the man release him, but Ralph was a big man, most of it gone to fat, but still larger than Chad.

As Chad fought with Ralph, his foot kicked an end table and a vase and ashtray fell to the floor with a shattering of plaster and glass. Chad reached out and felt for something, anything, to make Ralph release him. His hand fell onto a glass shard from the heavy ashtray and he cut his palm as he grasped the shard, but he ignored it. Bringing it up and around, he sliced at Ralph's face, causing the man to cry out as the shard dug deep into his cheek, causing an avalanche of blood to spill forth.

Chad used this reprieve to roll away while Ralph screamed in pain as blood poured out of his gashed face. Chad crawled the few feet down the hallway and spotted his knife in the dust bunnies of the corner.

Reaching out like a drowning man to a life preserver, his hand found the hilt. Now he held the glass shard in one hand and the knife in the other.

Ralph was on his knees and he was angry. His cheek was forgotten and all he wanted to do was kill Chad.

Chad came to his knees, and as Ralph came at him, Chad put the knife between them.

By pure luck, Ralph, enraged and not looking, ran onto the blade, impaling himself. The larger man gasped in pain and glanced down at the knife hilt now protruding from the middle of his chest. Then he fell back onto his ass and stared up at Chad, not believing what just happened.

Chad, dazed himself, stepped around Ralph who was in shock, and went into the next room where he found a little girl in nothing but her underwear. She was tied to a chair and she looked unmolested. Chad had made it in time to save her.

He untied her quickly, using the glass shard as a blade to slice the ropes and then he led her to the front door. He grabbed a dusty blanket off an old couch so she could cover herself with it.

"Now you sit here, honey, and I'll be out in a bit to take you home to your mommy and daddy, okay?"

She nodded, tears in her eyes, and Chad patted her shoulder gently. "You're safe now. The bad man can't hurt you anymore."

He left her then, as he had unfinished business inside.

Walking into the hallway, Ralph was still there, staring at the knife hilt like it was magical. Chad, now full of adrenalin and disgust after seeing the little girl, not to mention imagining what this sick bastard was going to do with her, knew he could now go through with the rest of his plan.

Stepping around Ralph, he reached down and grabbed the hilt of the knife.

"You bastard, you're gonna pay for what you've been doing," Chad growled as he gripped the hilt and then yanked the knife out of Ralph's chest in a spray of crimson. The blade was serrated and it made more damage coming out than going in and Ralph screamed as blood shot out of the wound and onto the hallway walls.

Chad then walked around Ralph and grabbed him by his filthy shirt collar, then dragged him into the room the little girl had been in.

The next part was difficult as Ralph was a big man, but with a lot of perseverance and work, Chad managed to get Ralph up and hanging from the doorway. His hands were tied with rope, the same rope Ralph had used on the little girl, and he now sagged in the doorway, blocking it. His arms were spread wide as were his legs, his sagging penis hanging between his legs below his large belly, while the blood seeped from his chest wound to pool on the floor. Chad had to guess the wound wasn't immediately fatal as Ralph was still living.

But Chad aimed to fix that. He remembered what the gypsy told him. The murder had to be heinous. It had to be so bad that in the eyes of God he would go to Hell.

So simply killing Ralph wouldn't do.

It had to get messy, real messy.

"Please, mister, don't kill me. I'm sorry; I didn't know what I was doing. I have these urges and no matter how hard I try I can't stop them. I see a little girl and I have to have her, they're so young and soft, so innocent. I just want to touch them, to hold them, that's all." Ralph's voice was squeaky, like a mouse.

Chad wiped his bloody palm thanks to the glass shard, on his shirt, ignoring the blood left behind.

"You sick fuck. I felt guilty about coming here. I didn't think I could do it. I didn't think I could kill another human being in cold blood, but after seeing that little girl and what you were going to do to her, well, let's just say this just got a whole lot easier."

Chad stepped toward Ralph with the knife in his hand and the fat man tried to shrink back, but with his arms and legs trapped he was as helpless as a turkey awaiting the slaughter for Christmas dinner.

Rage roiled inside Chad. Rage at the world, for what was happening to Sean, and most of all for this sick bastard in front of him. How many lives had Ralph ruined with his twisted urges, his warped desires?

Chad stopped when he was no more than a foot from Ralph. The man was gibbering like a fool, saliva dripping out of the corner of his mouth as he bawled large tears.

Chad knew what he was going to do first before he realized it.

Leaning down, he grasped Ralph's flaccid penis with his bloody hand and placed the tip of the blade to the shaft.

"No, no, please, for the love of God! Don't do it!" Ralph screamed, but his pleadings fell on deaf ears. With one smooth swipe of the knife, Chad cut off Ralph's penis, the man's screams reaching a falsetto as his eyes rolled back into his head and he fought to suck in air to let out another shriek. Blood splattered to the floor and he looked like he was pissing blood.

Ralph was making too much noise and Chad needed to quiet him down so he decided to use what he had at his disposal to quiet the man. When Ralph opened his mouth wide to let out another ear-piercing yell, Chad shoved the severed penis into Ralph's mouth, the man gagging as the piece of meat slid down his throat. He began to choke and Chad stared at the bluing face.

"Oh, no, asshole, you're not getting off that easily. Suffocation is too good for you."

Chad raised the bloody knife and placed the tip just above Ralph's belly button. He sucked in one good breath to prepare himself, and then plunged the blade into the soft belly with all the weight of his body behind it. Ralph jerked and spasmed as the cold blade bit deep, but Chad was far from done. Spinning the blade to the left, he then began sawing at the abdomen, cutting across from the middle to the right, then back to the left. When he was done, there was a large mouth of a wound in Ralph's lower abdomen, and no sooner did Chad step away, then Ralph's intestines spilled onto the floor to splash blood and excrement in every direction.

Ralph was jerking like a mad man now, his airway still blocked by his penis and his intestines steaming on the floor. Ralph died soon after.

Chad watched this all with a stoic face, never once blinking nor a single tear being shed. His only regret was what he knew would happen next. He knew he would never be with his family again, but if the gypsy was correct, then it would all be worth it.

Ralph's head had sagged to the left now, the face a dark, midnight blue, the eyes wide and popping out of their sockets as the man now hung dead. Whatever would happen next, Chad knew that this evil bastard would never harm another child again.

He stepped around the pool of intestines and went to the phone. A quick call to the police to report Ralph's death, the address, and then the story about the lost girl, and he hung up. He walked to the front door and stepped outside. The girl was still there, wrapped in the blanket. She looked up at Chad, saw the blood covering him, and her eyes went wide with fright, but he smiled and sat down next to her.

"It's all right, honey, it's all right. You're safe now. The police are coming and they'll bring you to your parents."

She leaned into him and cried and he hugged her, caressing her hair as he thought of Sean. The two sat that way for all of five minutes, then the screaming sirens and flashing lights invaded their world.

And Chad's life, for all purposes, was over.

The next eight months went by in a blur for Chad. There was his murder trial, even though he'd pled guilty on all counts and had explained that he planned the entire thing. But the District Attorney wanted a trial; it was good for the media and public to see.

Many heralded Chad as a hero, the man who slew a child molester, but the law was the law and Chad was sentenced to death by lethal injection.

The outcry was unimaginable even though Chad told the media this was what he wanted, but still, many supporters stood behind him.

Not his wife, however. Susan never forgave him for what he did and she turned her back on him.

Sean was sicker every day and at least he never knew what happened to his father, but Chad knew about Sean and he could only pray his desperate plan would work.

Of course, as he sat in his cell, staring at the stone walls, he doubted himself constantly. What if he had imagined it all? What if there was no hope? And he'd killed a man and himself for nothing.

When the time came for him to walk the line to the death room, he could barely walk. Because he had admitted his guilt and the trial was so public, there was no wait time for him to be sentenced. Also, it was part of the deal he'd made with the DA. He would plead guilty if they waved the standard years on death row. The DA, knowing Chad was being trumpeted as a hero, bent the rules and got what Chad wanted; though once again many weren't happy.

So now, eight months after he'd slaughtered Ralph in cold blood, he was preparing to be killed by lethal injection.

While they strapped him down, he looked to the glass window to see if Susan was there, that maybe she would come to see him in his last minutes on Earth, but she wasn't. He didn't blame her, she didn't know what he was sacrificing himself for. And if he'd told her, she would think he was insane. No, it was better this way.

They pumped him full of chemicals and he felt an overwhelming sense of calmness, his last thoughts of his son. A single tear rolled down his cheek as he fell into oblivion, one he would never awaken from. Next to the gurney, the heart monitor flat lined and the doctor checked Chad's pulse.

Shaking his head, he turned and walked away. Chad Wilcott was dead.

Chad slowly opened his eyes.

He was at the bottom of a hill. Under his body was green grass and in the distance he could hear birdsong.

Sitting up, rubbing his arm where the needles had been placed, he saw his skin was clean of scars or wounds. As he looked about, he saw the sun was slowly rising and to his left was the hill. The austere landscape was devoid of all other markings except for this one hill.

Chad stood up, feeling lightheaded for a moment but then it passed. He gazed about himself, at first not understanding who or where he was. But then memory came smashing back and he remembered it all.

"I died," he said to himself. "Is this Hell? Did it work?"

Looking about the land, it sure didn't seem like any Hell he'd learned about in Sunday school. On the hill were a few trees and he could see birds flitting between them as they played.

No, if this was Hell then every man and woman on Earth had been misled.

With nowhere else to go but the hill, he set off, trudging through the tall grass. The sun was warm on his head but he was comfortable, and he didn't desire water, which he found odd.

As he reached the base of the hill, he found a path leading directly up the middle, and so with no other options, he began to climb. The path wound its way through the rocks and boulders littering the side of the hillside, and it was when he was almost to the top, where the trees seemed to beckon to him, a voice calling him, telling him this is where he wanted to go, that he found his path blocked.

In the middle of the path were three wild beasts.

A leopard, a lion and a she-wolf.

Chad stood perfectly still. He was no match for one of the beasts, let alone all three. His heart began to pound and he attempted to slowly circle around them. He didn't know why, but he had this tugging feeling he needed to reach the top of the hill.

There was something there he needed to see, or someone he needed to find.

But the beasts refused to let him pass. They did not advance but they did not retreat and eventually, Chad knew he wouldn't be going to the top. At least not if he didn't plan on battling the three beasts first.

Dejected and lost, he made his way down the slope once more, resting at the bottom. By this time the sun had moved across the sky and twilight was setting in.

Though hopelessness was filling him, and Chad was about to give up, a figure appeared out of the corner of his eye. He spun immediately, thinking one of the wild beasts had come down off the hillside to kill him, but all he saw was an average shaped man wearing a small hat. The hat was bleached white and was in the shape of a fedora, and the man wore a suit that seemed to shimmer, as if it wasn't really there and only the illusion of clothing was there for Chad's benefit.

The man walked up to Chad who merely stared at this stranger.

"Hello, Chad, welcome to Hell."

Chad blinked at the man's words. "But this can't be Hell. Where's all the fire and brimstone, all the lost souls being tortured for all eternity?"

"Ah, yes, the conventional Hell. Well, that is here, only it's in a different part. You will see it soon enough, I'm afraid. You see, for you to reach the end of your journey, you will need to traverse the seven circles of Hell."

"Seven? In Dante's Inferno there were nine, weren't there?"

The man nodded. "Yes, I suppose so, but that was just a book, this is real and there are only seven for you to deal with. If you pass all seven, if you are victorious and refuse temptation, you will have the chance to meet Lucifer himself, and if you somehow make it that far you may ask him for one wish. A wish he will grant immediately." The man leaned forward and smiled, his eyes smoldering with the very fires of Hell. "Do you think you're up to this momentous task?"

Chad swallowed the knot in his throat and nodded. "I came to Hell to save my son, damn right I am," he said with conviction.

"Good, then let us go. The doorway to the first level is far from here and it will take us many days to reach it. But fear not. Though years may pass here in Hell, mere minutes will pass on the Earth, so time is unimportant."

The man turned and headed off, not waiting to see if Chad was following. Of course Chad did, and with a brief glimpse over his shoulder at the three beasts, he headed off on his first challenge.

"Do you have a name?" Chad asked the man as they walked over and through the vast landscape.

"You may call me Virgil if you need to label me."

"Virgil, huh? Okay, so, Virgil, has anyone else ever reached the Devil and asked for a wish?"

"No, Chad, it's never been done. Each soul for one reason or another is halted on one of the levels. Whether it's avarice, greed, or lust, every man has their price." He glanced at Chad as he walked. "And I suspect you will have yours, too."

Looking insulted, Chad raised his chin. "No, I won't, I'm here to save my son, and I'll do it, I have to. There's nothing that'll stop me from doing this. I came to Hell for my son, I won't stop now."

Virgil nodded respectfully. "We shall see, Chad, we shall see."

It was the next day, and after walking the entire time, Chad was exhausted, but when he and Virgil passed through the Gates of Hell, Chad felt invigorated, seeing his mission beginning. His ears were immediately assaulted with cries of anguish as Chad sees his first true souls in torment.

Here, men and women alike are pursued by wasps and hornets as they wade through an endless sea of maggots. As they run, the wasps and other insects repeatedly stung them, causing their bodies to become pus-filled balloons that soon explode under the weight of the poison. But no sooner have they died in utter agony, then they reform into the image of a human body. Once formed, they climb to their feet and run away once again. This is their punishment. For in life, these people were selfish, they never helped another soul and now, in Hell, the hornets and wasps take on the physical form of their guilty consciences in life; now they are forever pursued till the end of time. As for the maggots, the souls wallowed in the filth of sin when they were alive and so, too, shall they wallow in death, forever wading through the muck to escape their consciences.

Chad actually recognized a few of the people running about. A former President of the United States as well as more than one celebrity. Now they were lost souls forever trying to escape their own failures.

No sooner had Chad entered the chamber, then the swarm of insects turned and attacked him. He searched for Virgil but the man was gone, and with no choice, Chad began running. He fell into the muck, maggots and worms squirming into every orifice of his body. But still he fought onward, as the insects stung his eyes, face and neck. His arms swelled to massive size, and he could feel the pus as it filled him. But he never stopped. Unlike the souls who were trapped in this chamber, Chad was a free spirit, and he was able to cross the chamber as he was stung countless times. He died hundreds of times, screaming each time and praying it would be the last, as he crossed the chamber.

A year and a half later, he reached the opposite side, a door made of bones blocking his path. As yet more wasps and bees stung him; he forced the door open and fell out of the chamber, leaving the wayward souls to their fate. As he fell, his body immediately transformed back to its normal shape and any of the insects that had escaped the chamber dissolved into smoke. He fell to his knees and gasped, not believing he didn't feel pain or agony, which had been his existence for the past year and a half. But as he looked up, he saw a pair of feet in front of him.

As he followed the feet to legs and higher, he saw it was Virgil.

"You, where have you been? One second you were with me and then you were gone," Chad demanded angrily.

Virgil shook his head. "I'm sorry, Chad, you must face each challenge on your own, I can only lead you there."

"So why are you here now?"

"Because you have reached the end of the first challenge. If you can make it past the Opportunists, then you have earned your right to battle for your son's life."

"You mean that wasn't one of the levels?"

"No, Chad, that was what you would call a warm up, now come, there is still much more for you to accomplish on your journey."

Chad, with a groan, picked himself up. He flexed his arms and found it odd how a moment ago they were the size of tree trunks, filled with wasp and bee venom. But now they were fine, better than fine. He looked up to see Virgil was already on the move, so he jogged after him. The cavern they were in was dark and brooding, bones of a thousand bodies under their feet, some crunching to dust as they stepped on them.

Virgil led Chad deeper into Hell until they came upon a river. A sign made of human flesh hung on the cavern wall, stating the river's name was **ACHERON**. This was the first of the rivers of Hell. Here is where the newly arrived souls to Hell wait for the monstrous form of Charon to ferry them across the river to their punishment. Chad looked on the shore to see hundreds upon hundreds of disheveled souls, all waiting to cross the river.

When Charon arrived, and the lost souls boarded the boat, Chad was stopped by the specter. He sees Chad isn't like the other souls and refused him passage, but Virgil is somehow able to make Charon obey him. Chad is allowed to board the boat and Charon shoves off for the far shore.

"What was that about? Why didn't he want me to come on with the rest of the souls?" Chad asked Virgil.

"It's nothing, Chad. Charon can sense there is something different about you, that's all. I merely reminded him a soul is a soul and it's not for him to judge who to take. He has been ferrying souls since the beginning of time and sometimes he forgets his place."

Chad only nodded at the explanation. The far shore was going to take time and Chad found himself sitting down amongst the souls and growing tired. Before he knew it, he drifted off to sleep.

Chad awoke to find himself across the river Acheron and on the very brink of Hell itself.

Stepping off the boat, Virgil leading the way, Chad stopped at the edge of a massive, funnel shaped cave that dropped deep into the earth. From the look of its mighty depths, the hole looked to go all the way to the center of the earth. All Chad knew was he didn't want to find out for himself.

All along the great circular pit were a series of ledges, each of which Virgil explained was one of the circles of Hell. It was here that each circle was assigned to punish one particular category of sin.

"Are you ready?" Virgil asked Chad who only nodded. "Then let us begin."

Virgil led the way once more and the two of them began their trek down the side of the massive canyon. The wind rushed up, hot as a hundred suns and Chad had to gasp and grit his teeth to suck in a breath of air. Hours later, as Chad had no true sense of time any more, they reached the first circle.

"Good luck," Virgil said simply. "If you are able, I will meet you on the other side." Then Virgil began to walk away and right before Chad's eyes, Virgil disappeared into the darkness.

Chad turned to the large door Virgil had stopped at and Chad pushed it open. At first it wouldn't budge, but soon it slowly swung inward, large hinges made of gray steel supporting the door.

Upon stepping inside, Chad glanced to the right to see another sign attached to the wall. The sign waved in the stirring of air and on it was the word, **LIMBO**.

Not knowing what to expect, Chad stepped away from the door, which slammed shut immediately, plunging the chamber into darkness.

It was then he felt a gentle caress by his cheek. As his eyes adjusted to the gloom, he began to make out shapes, and on the far wall he saw torches. His hand was on his cheek now, wondering what the caress was. It had been ghost like, as if a gossamer shroud had brushed his face. Upon reaching the torches, he picked one up and was startled when it blazed to life in his hand. He chuckled to himself, accepting the torch as fact. After all, he was in Hell, fire was as common as rain on the surface of the Earth.

The chamber went on for what seemed like miles and he began to walk, following a slim path between rocks and rubble strewn about the cavern floor. And it was here he felt another caress. As he stopped, waving the torch overhead, yet another caress came across his forehead. Then another, and another after that. But as each one passed him, it grew in strength, until the caress turned into blows with force behind them. He was knocked from his feet to fall hard on the rocks under him, crying out as a sharp one pierced his backside.

The torch fell from his fingers and rolled away, the area around him going dark again.

But he wouldn't give up, especially by what appeared to be nothing more than aggressive souls, with no true tangibility to harm him. He picked up the torch once again and held it high; and promptly gasped in shock and fear at the sight he beheld.

And then he realized where he was.

Limbo, where the souls of unbaptized babies and children resided.

Perhaps one time the souls were innocent, but now they were full of hate and anger at being left alone for all eternity in the first circle of Hell. Like banshees, the wraiths attacked Chad, ripping into him with their ethereal claws. With no defense against these non-corporeal beings, he began to run, fighting as best he could while pieces of his flesh were sliced away like a hundred daggers were having at him. As he ran, and body pieces fell off him, seconds later the wound would heal; such was the curse of Hell.

As he gritted his teeth in the absolute agony, his eyes tearing from the shock of constant evisceration, Chad fought his way across the chamber. After the first year he lost track of time, but eventually he reached the opposite end. There was a smaller door here and he waved the torch—which had an unending fire—at the wraiths to scare them away. Months ago he'd learned they disliked the unnatural fire, but there was only him and there were so many of them.

Unlocking the door, he fell out of the chamber just as a pack of wraiths took half his left shoulder and his left leg off.

As he rolled in the dirt, the door slammed closed and the wraiths were gone once more. He glanced down at his missing leg and watched it reappear. This was nothing new and it was also painful. He gritted his teeth as the thousand pins and needles of the reattached limb faded away, his shoulder healing as well.

He came to his knees, sucking in a breath that for once wasn't filled with pain, and he found himself staring at the feet of Virgil.

"So, I see you made it, Chad, congratulations," Virgil said. "I was beginning to worry you had given up after the first year passed and you hadn't reached the other side yet."

Chad stood up, sucking in another breath. "I told you, Virgil, I'll fight every damn demon down here until I can save my son."

"Hmm, we shall see," Virgil said. "Come along, the next circle isn't far."

With a weary sigh, Chad headed out after Virgil, not looking forward to what awaited him next.

Days later, Virgil led Chad to the next circle of Hell.

A blackened signpost at the entrance had the words **CARNAL** carved into it. Virgil explained to Chad this is the beginning of Hell proper and here, blocking the way, sits Minos, the semi-bestial judge of the damned. Minos' job is to assign each soul that comes to him its place in Hell according to the sins perpetuated on Earth. This is where souls have betrayed reason to their appetites, only wanting the pleasures of the flesh over all else.

Behind Minos, there is a massive precipice, a whirlwind blowing up from below. Within this whirlwind, each soul spins for all eternity, until Minos decides to set it free to then suffer a never-ending agony in one of the circles. With a whip of Minos' tail, he would deliver his verdict, thus casting out another soul with a bestial moan.

Chad stared at Minos and felt fear, for how was he to pass this giant beast?

As if Virgil could read his mind, he said simply. "You must have faith, Chad."

"Faith? In what? That creature is huge, it'll kill me with one swipe of its tail."

"Perhaps, but faith is all I can offer you." Virgil stepped back into the shadows, and as he began to fade away, he called out to Chad. "I will wait for you on the other side of the chasm, if you make it."

As Chad stood alone, he watched Minos as the beast sent soul after soul onto its final destination. As he watched, he saw there was a certain rhythm to the beast's tail. Behind Minos, the great chasm beckoned, the whirlwind like a small, captured tornado. He watched as the souls swirled within, their faces coming and going as they fought but could never break free.

And then Chad had it. He knew how to win over Minos and continue on to the next circle. He waited for the tail to wrap around the body of the beast, and when it was as fully curled, he dashed across the ground, hoping to jump into the chasm. But no sooner did he reach Minos, then the beast stood up, flicked its tail and sliced Chad in half.

His upper body slid off his lower portion and slapped the earth with a wet sound, his intestines spilling out. He screamed in torment, and as he passed out, falling into what he still called death, he then blinked his eyes and found himself lying on the dirt, back where he'd started. Minos was back to assigning souls, and had forgotten him, as Chad was barely worth the attention a horse would give to a fly buzzing around its backside.

Chad, standing up and touching his stomach, relieved to see he was intact, watched Minos' tail and tried again. This time the same result, only his head was severed from his body to roll across the dirt until it stopped. His eyes blinked as he watched his decapitated body topple over, then he died once more.

For the next two years, Chad attempted to get past Minos, each time suffering a similar fate.

Until on the last day, he tried something different. This time, when Minos struck with his tail, Chad dropped to the ground and rolled. The tail came up and slapped the earth, but Chad was still rolling.

Now that he was doing it, it seemed so easy, but each time before it had seemed foolish. He rolled as the tail rose and fell, shaking the earth like a giant hammer. Chad rolled off the precipice to drop into the chasm and just as he'd hoped, the whirlwind caught him and he began to spin in circles, while all around him, lost souls wailed in his ears.

It was as he was spinning for the thousandth time that he managed to reach the opposite side of the chasm. His outstretched hand was stretched to its fullest and he managed to latch onto an outcropping of rocks. His arm was wrenched from his socket, but he held fast and soon he was climbing onto the far side of the chasm, his face blasted red from the howling winds and his skin dry as parchment.

As he lay there, sucking in air, the moans of the souls still echoing in his head, he spotted the feet of Virgil.

"Well done, Chad, another challenge overcome. But you have a long way to go before your journey is at an end." Virgil turned and began to walk deeper into Hell, and Chad, knowing to dawdle would be foolish, crawled to his knees and then his feet.

Without saying a word, he followed Virgil to the next circle of Hell.

Chad looked on the third circle of Hell with disgust.

To his right was a stone with the words, **GLUTTON** carved into its facade.

Virgil had already disappeared and Chad was left standing alone. The massive chamber went on for miles, or so it seemed, but one thing he knew was that he couldn't see the end.

Though there were no clouds, it was snowing, but this wasn't a white snow such on Christmas day. Instead, the snow was mixed with freezing rain and was gray and black, stinking of purification which formed into a vile, messy slush underfoot.

As he stared at the slurry and the souls wallowing in it, he was reminded of a giant garbage dump. Here the souls of the dammed squirmed and moaned in the frigid, frozen paste of foulness, their bodies swollen and obscene beyond measure.

A massive beast, with two heads, similar to a wolf, guarded each soul, severing limbs from bodies, ripping and tearing them with its teeth and claws to devour them one at a time.

These souls were the Gluttons.

In their lives on Earth they made no better use of their lives other than to wallow in food and drink. They produced nothing, but merely suckled at the teat of society. All they ever produced was garbage and offal and now they will spend eternity wallowing in it while the beast mercilessly rends them asunder. They are now no better than the garbage they created, languishing in the fetid sludge while the beast consumes them the same way they once consumed food.

Knowing there was nothing to do but get moving, Chad began to descend into the mire of filth, his nose scrunching up from the smell.

He didn't know what danger lay beyond other than the beast, but he soon found out when a fat, stubby hand wrapped around his leg. Glancing down, he saw a rotund, naked man covered in bile, and as Chad tried to get free, the man leaned forward and sank his teeth into Chad's leg.

With a scream of pain, Chad wrenched his leg free, but not before the man got a piece of him. Blood oozed from the two inch wound and Chad's leg spasmed in agony. As he moved away from the man who was far too fat to chase him, another set of hands found his other leg. This woman was so fat she could barely raise her arms, but she still managed to grasp him as he passed. Her head came down and sank into his calf, eliciting another shriek from his mouth.

Pulling free with a kick to the woman's head, he continued on. But there were thousands of these sloths and all were hungry for him…for anything.

As Chad tried to race through them, he found himself dragged down and eaten alive. Pudgy hands with sharp fingernails dug into his flesh, tearing out his organs by the handfuls. He watched in horror as a balding man with three chins devoured his kidney like a mincemeat pie. Each time he succumbed to death, he would wake up in the bottom of the sludge pool, fully whole and alive. But no sooner did this happen then more hands were on him, tearing at him like a turkey feast at a homeless shelter.

Each time he woke up, he would manage to pull himself a few feet before he was set on with teeth and nails. Years passed, each death worse than the last and by the hundredth time, he felt he was as mad as any of the sloths around him. One time he actually helped them feed on his body, reaching in with his own hands to pull out a wet, slippery organ. With his eyes filled with madness, he chewed on himself and swallowed it in large chunks that were quickly pulled out of his gaping stomach by another hungry soul.

But eventually he reached the opposite side, and with half his body gone, eaten by the gluttons, he fell over the edge of the pool, leaving the last ravenous soul behind. He died of course, as he had no lower body and he quickly blacked out as his intestines dangled behind him. By this time he didn't care. Agony was a part of his existence and to not have it in his mind would seem too ridiculous to contemplate.

When he opened his eyes this time, he was gazing up at the grinning face of Virgil.

"Hello, Chad, you made it, you reached the other side of the circle."

Chad sat up, not believing the words were true, but as he glanced behind him, he saw it was the truth. The wolf beast was still feeding on the lost souls, but the pool was behind him. He'd finally reached the end.

Virgil waved to the large steel door in front of them. "Come, there are still many more to go. But you can give up at any time. Surely your punishment in Hell for murdering that man won't be a fraction of all you have endured so far. You can go to your punishment and relax as it were, leaving all this added suffering behind."

Chad shook his head. "You know my answer, let's go," he said as he stood on weak legs.

Virgil shrugged, turned and opened the door, Chad right behind him.

When Chad reached the fourth circle, he found himself intertwined with the Hoarders and the Wasters. Here, there were two raging mobs, both trying to move a massive boulder, each soul struggling on his own or with groups. Both mobs were made up of the souls who in life had lacked all moderation in regulating their expenses and spent money without care.

So in death, they now will spend eternity encumbered down by dead weights and each is so filled with rage at trying to move the impossible boulder that their souls are twisted and warped.

Chad falls into this mob and soon is struggling to push the boulder with the other ones. He does this for years, and would have done so for eternity until one day, after hundreds others before him, he turned and walked away from the boulder and out of the chamber.

Upon reaching the edge of the circle, Virgil is waiting for him. In this circle all Chad had to do was walk away, there was no way to win, and though it took him many years, eventually he came around.

Virgil waved his hand and Chad strode past him. The next circle awaited and Chad was ready for it.

Virgil brought Chad to the River Styx. On the perimeter of the river is the Marsh of Styx. Bubbles rise from the slime and when Chad moves closer, he sees the bubbles emanate from souls who lie beneath the surface in the mud. Virgil explains to Chad that below the mud, entombed forever, are the souls of the Sullen. In life they refused to let in the light of Divine Intervention into their hearts, they refused to believe, and so now they must spend eternity buried under the stinking waters of the Styx. The bubbles are the cries for help, for they are awake the entire time, their eyes seeing nothing but darkness, their bodies feeling nothing but the slime coating them.

The fifth circle of Hell confused Chad, for he didn't see what form of danger the entombed souls possessed. Virgil raised his hand and pointed to the opposite side of the river.

"There is your destination, but you must walk through the Marsh to reach it." Chad turned to the edge, and when he looked back at Virgil, he was gone, like so many times before.

With nothing to do but move forward, Chad took his first step into the Marsh to cross the River Styx and continue his journey.

But no sooner did his foot plunge into the murky water and sludge beneath, then a fetid hand wrapped around his leg. Chad stepped back, shocked to feel a clammy hand on his leg, and as he did, he pulled the soul out of the water.

He'd seen enough horror movies as a kid to know what a zombie was immediately. The body had no clothing and the flesh was a mottled blue from being submerged for years on end. The face was slack, eyes drawn, the pupils all but gone, leaving a thick layer of cataract. The mouth was open, yellow teeth poking between cracked lips, and inside the mouth a black tongue wiggled like a slug. As the ghoul stepped forward, more now rose from the Marsh to slowly surround him. Chad, having no weapons but his hands, prepared to fight the undead.

When the first one came at him, he swung a roundhouse blow to its jaw, dislocating it so that it flopped down like a door with a broken hinge. The black tongue sagged out to drape in front of the neck like a necktie.

Chad looked at his fist to see a bluefish-gray sludge now coating his knuckles. It was the flesh of the ghoul, now transferred to his hand. He ignored the revulsion he felt and prepared for the next attack. A small ghoul came at him from his left and he reached out and grabbed its outstretched hands, then yanked at them. The withered meat of the ghoul couldn't take the pressure and the two arms popped out of their sockets with the sound of a champagne cork.

He looked at the severed limbs in his hands and acted quickly, turning them on the ghoul to beat it senseless. He then spun and faced the next one. Using the severed arms, he whacked it on the head, left side then right side, the ghoul's neck giving way from the abuse. The head dropped off the zombie to plop into the marsh, quickly sinking like a rock. But there were more ghouls than Chad could ever fight and they surrounded him in vast numbers. Though he fought valiantly, they soon swarmed him and sank stained teeth into his flesh. They fed on him, tearing into his body and pulling out the moist organs within. Chad screamed as he was pulled under, and soon his screams were swallowed and only bubbles escaped his lips as he was forced down into the muck. When he died, all he saw was the murky water surrounding him.

He awoke on the shore back where he started and no sooner did he step in to the Marsh, than the first ghoul slowly rose to begin the attack anew. This happened for years, as Chad couldn't figure out how to get past the ghouls. But then he stared at the edge, his foot hovering over the Marsh. Every time he stepped into the water the ghouls rose. But what if he didn't do that?

Looking around the shore, he spotted many logs and other fauna that floated near the edge. He went to it all, gathered it into a rough, haphazard raft, and then pushed off with a long stick.

Feeling foolish for not thinking of this year's ago, he floated over the ghouls as they opened their mouths and bubbles floated to the surface. Soon he was past the Marsh and in the River Styx itself. Then he floated to the opposite shore where Virgil waited patiently.

As he glanced back at the Marsh and thought of the uncountable deaths he'd suffered there, he realized Hell had fooled him like nothing he'd ever experienced. For he'd found out in Hell that brute force wasn't always the answer and using his mind could get him through the circle unscathed.

He made up his mind then and there to think before he acted when in the final circles. For Lucifer was waiting and Chad would do what no soul had ever accomplished; he would reach Lucifer's inner sanctum and get the fallen angel to grant him his one wish.

Virgil led Chad deeper into the bowels of Hell, moving to the next level. As they entered the circle of Heretics, Chad looked out on a massive graveyard, an enormous countryside with nothing but tombstones made of all sizes and shapes.

Each tomb was lying with its lid off, the large slab now lying beside it, and each corpse within its tomb was wrapped in flames of reds and oranges. Anguished cries sounded constantly from the trapped dead, their howls filling the air like a rushing wind. These souls were trapped here forever, their punishment an eternal grave in the fiery mortuary of God's wrath.

Off in the distance, Chad could see a great pile of rocks and boulders. The rubble was the result of a great earthquake that shook Hell when Christ died. The air is so thick here it can't be breathed and any soul going near will be consumed in the fetid stench to writhe on the ground in unbelievable agony. Any soul caught in the miasma would writhe and suffer; a pain so unbearable they would beg to be returned to their rightful punishment.

Chad turned to stare at Virgil, who only pointed towards the rubble. Somehow, Chad knew that rubble was his finish line, the end of his quest. For more years than he could count he'd been in Hell, battling the minions to reach their master. And now, after decades, that goal was in sight.

But he still had to traverse the cemetery of flames.

Virgil faded away as he was wont to do and Chad turned back to the graveyard. There was no hesitation as he took his first step, for if he wanted to succeed he had no choice.

Stepping onto the main path that led deeper into the cemetery, he slowed at the first tomb. Flames licked out of the crypt and no sooner had he reached it than a flaming ghoul popped out. Its head was a burning skull, its mouth open wide as it screamed in agony. It was naked, but the blaze seemed to hug the body, the ethereal red and greens wrapping themselves around the corpse and pressing it close.

Chad, seeing he was helpless against the burning funereal pyre that was mobile, took off at a run, but no sooner did he pass the ghoul then another popped up on his left. This one came out of the tomb like a jack-in-the-box and threw itself at Chad. As the fires of Hell consumed him, his hair burning off, his flesh charring to black ash, his eyes melting in their sockets, he tried to scream, but the air was sucked out of his lungs as the heat whooshed in. He died horribly, blind and shrieking, but this was only temporary.

When he opened his eyes, he was on the path, the flaming ghoul now back in its crypt. As he stood up, he saw it rise out once again and he turned and ran. He made it three more feet before he was enveloped again. Even on fire, with his will alone, he forced his feet to keep walking. He made it another six feet before his face melted and he lost his eyes once more, then lost his sense of direction. As his body crumbled to ash, he died yet again, but he knew his quest wasn't over.

When his eyes snapped open, he tried a new tactic. His limbs tingled from the pain of burning to death, but as he stared at them they were pink and healthy. He crawled on the path, staying low, but as soon as he reached the next tomb, a ghoul lunged out, its face bathed in fire, its mouth open wide in a silent scream. Chad rolled onto his back and the ghoul consumed him, the heat so hot his lungs burned within his chest as he sucked in the blazing hot air. As he flailed on the ground, he did crawl three more feet, but soon his legs were brittle and black like fire logs too long in the fireplace, and his body collapsed in on itself, puffs of ash floating on the wind.

For years this continued, Chad burning again and again until he was insane with the pain. But for every death, he made distance, and after more than six years and countless deaths, he reached the last tomb in the cemetery. He could see the rubble of the collapse, and it was so close he felt he could reach out and touch it.

But as he reached the last tomb, once more a ghoul rose into the air. This one spread wings of flame, looking like a phoenix as it prepared to surround Chad and wrap him in its fiery embrace. But Chad, too close to give up, not wanting to suffer yet another death, sprinted away, the ghoul floating after him. As he ran, the rubble grew closer and he saw at the foot of it was a small pond, a depression that had accumulated enough water over the centuries.

Just as the ghoul landed on him, Chad reached the edge of the pond and dove off the shore, splashing into the water's cool embrace. The ghoul shrieked so loud it shook the very boulders and it turned to vapor, the water dousing its flames as Chad floated under the surface. He felt fine now, and any skin that had been touched by the ghoul was healing as he swam under the water.

When he could hold his breath no more, he popped his head up, half expecting it to be swarmed with fire. But he was fine. He was in the middle of the pond, the cemetery behind him, and with yet another circle conquered; he swam for the far shore, the rubble growing in height until the boulders were as large as three-story buildings.

Upon reaching the shore, Virgil was waiting for him.

"Chad, congratulations yet again. I have to say, that one took you a lot longer than the others. Are you sure you're not getting tired? I must say, you are the more persistent soul I've seen in centuries. Are you aware no other soul has ever reached this far? Most get as far as the cemetery but the fire ghouls finish them. To die by being consumed by fire is the most unbearable agony any soul, any human, can suffer, and I lost count how many times you died after the first hundred or so."

Chad climbed out of the water and shook himself like a wet dog. His hands and feet tingled from the last brush with fire, but he was whole and still ready.

True, he was utterly exhausted, but his resolve had never wavered. He would save his son no matter what happened to him, that was all that mattered.

Virgil pointed to the rubble. "Beyond there is a small trail. Follow it and it will bring you to the last challenge. The seventh circle will be the hardest," he grinned. "You could say we saved the best for last."

Chad ignored Virgil, but turned the way the man pointed and began his trudge to the boulders. He never bothered to turn around to see if Virgil was still there as it didn't matter to him. All that mattered to Chad was what was at the end of the trail. And he knew that would be one thing...Lucifer.

Chad headed out, but no sooner did he reach the boulders and rubble, then he fell to the ground in absolute pain. The miasma of death filling the air was so bad he couldn't breathe. But he continued on, crawling on hands and knees. As he reached the first boulder, he traversed it, and found the rubble wasn't as complete as seen from a distance. Here, a large open crater had formed from the earthquake and in this crater bodies writhed in complete turmoil.

Chad had found the origin of the foul air. As he stared out into the crater, he saw all manor of disease within. Each soul had some form of horrible symptoms, whether it was dark, black boils that popped and oozed yellow and gray pus, or others whose inflictions were beyond description.

The souls' senses were punished as well, whether by darkness, thirst, hunger or wallowing in their own filth. The shrieking din of lost souls was enough to cause Chad to wince, but he had his own problems, namely the foul air.

He realized he would have to crawl into the pit to reach the end of the circle, and so without hesitation, he crawled to the edge of the crater and let himself tumble in to join the other raving souls.

No sooner did he land at the bottom then he found he could breathe easier. It appeared the air was only foul above the crater line and down here, with the tortured souls, he was fine.

Leprous hands reached for him and he pushed them away. The offal and bile churned at his ankles, the smell still so bad his eyes watered. All around him souls spasmed and twisted in their suffering. But Chad cared not for these afflicted beings, he had his mind set on one thing, namely to reach the edge of the crater and find Lucifer.

Shoving a woman with nothing but black scabs covering her body, he headed out, wading through the prostrate souls as if he was moving through water.

Halfway there he kicked something and when he bent to see what it was, he was shocked to see it was a sword. An actual sword. This was the first time Chad had found anything on his quest he could use as a weapon. Picking it up, the sword was covered in brown and black slime, more than most of it feces, but he ignored this and strode off anew, filled with hope now that he had a weapon. He used the flat of the blade to slap the souls away from him. Though he could easily slice their heads in twain, he held back, not wanting to add to their already tumultuous existence.

Upon reaching the opposite side of the crater, Chad climbed out to see the air was clear here.

He glanced around, looking for Virgil, but the man was nowhere to be seen. Chad assumed after traversing the crater he was at the end, but perhaps he wasn't.

In front of him, no more than a mile in earth measurements, was a massive waterfall. There was nothing else of consequence, the walls carved from the cliffs and unclimbable, so he headed out toward the waterfall. His body was covered from head to toe in offal and he scrunched his nose at the smell, but after the countless deaths and sufferings he'd already persevered in Hell, a bad scent was the least of his problems.

With the sword over his shoulder, he continued on to the last leg of his journey. He never once gave it a thought he might fail, for that wasn't an option. He would save his son, no matter what.

At the base of the waterfall was a large pool. As he stared at the water cascading down, he found it odd to see this in Hell of all places. But he'd learned after the decades of being in Hell, that what he'd learned as a boy and man about Heaven and Hell was vastly distorted.

There was nowhere to go but into the pool so he dove in, the sword weighing him down. But he never considered relinquishing it. This was the first time he'd possessed a weapon and he was not going to toss it away so casually.

He swam to the base of the waterfall and found there was an opening. Going through, the water washing him clean, he stepped out into another vast cavern where the walls themselves were living fire. The heat was unbearable and his hair and eyebrows were singed to ash in less than a second but for some unknown reason his flesh remained intact. At first he didn't notice it, but the sword was cool to the touch, despite the heat surrounding him and Chad knew then it was the sword protecting him. It gave off an aura that surrounded him, keeping the heat at bay. His fragile hair still succumbed, but the rest of him was safe.

He began walking, the fire walls surrounding him as he moved deeper into the cavern. He didn't know how long he walked, time being immaterial in Hell, but eventually, after days of constant movement, he came to a smaller cavern than the one he'd been traveling in. This one was filled with stalactites on the ceiling and stalagmites on the floor. There were so many he now had to weave his way through them.

But then the protrusions stopped and he found himself in a circular arena in the middle of the cave. In this arena, the ground was void of anything but dust and Chad stood perfectly still. This arena wasn't here by coincidence, any fool would know this.

And then he heard a low growl coming from the opposite side of the arena. At first all he could hear was the animalistic growls but soon a head appeared. It was a canine's head, only four times as large as a normal size dog, but no sooner did he see this head, then another appeared, and then one more.

Each head was massive, with teeth as long as his arms. The eyes on each head swiveled to him and a loud snarl slid from each mouth. Then the paws moved forward, and as they cleared the stalagmites, Chad saw the heads all belonged to the same body.

He knew from his lessons in Sunday school that he was gazing at the mythical beast Cerberus, the three-headed dog of Hell.

"You should know, Chad," a hollow voice echoed from nowhere and everywhere at the same time. *"There is only one chance at this. You do not have an infinitesimal amount of lives. You only have the one you posses and the sword you hold in you hands. If you die by the claws of Cerberus, you will lose your quest and be thrown back with the other souls for all eternity."*

Chad stared petrified at the three-headed hound as he swallowed the large knot in his throat. He would only have one shot at this, and if he failed, Sean would die from his cancer.

Though he was scared out of his mind, his resolve was as strong as ever. Holding the sword high like he'd seen on television when he watched old Roman movies, he stepped into the middle of the arena.

Laughter filled the chamber. *"Very noble, Chad, but in the end it will still get you the same thing. There is a reason why my pet is the last challenge."*

As if on cue, Cerberus lunged, loping across the arena at Chad, all three muzzles slavering. Chad screamed and jumped aside and the first head snapped at him. He tried to swipe the sword at the left leg but he used the flat of the blade and all it did was bounce off bone. The third head came in and snapped at his arm and Chad pulled it away in the knick of time. Hot breath flowed over him, spittle now covering him, and he crawled backwards as the three-headed dog slowly moved back and forth.

He knew right then the beast was playing with him. With only one life there was no way he could kill this hellhound of legend. The dog was three times the size of him and all he had was a sword, it was more like a toothpick compared to the thick hide of the three-headed animal.

It was as he was crawling away that he glanced upward at the stalactites. They were huge, each one looking like stone icicles, the tips as sharp as daggers. But then a paw came at him and he rolled away, but not before two claws raked against his chest. His flesh was parted and he could see his ribcage within, blood pouring out of the wound. He placed his hand to the wound to try and seal it shut, but it was no use. The lipless mouth of the cut now spat blood with every beat of his heart.

The beast's heads chuffed, almost as if it was laughing.

Chad was already growing weak from blood loss and he found it ironic that after all he'd done, fighting his way through the circles of Hell, it had all been for nothing. Lucifer had known from the beginning he could never hope to beat the hellhound and perhaps this was all a part of his punishment in Hell. For what better suffering could he receive then to have false hope as he battled through Hell's minions on a desperate quest to save his son's fading life.

Cerberus came at him again and he lifted the sword with his right hand, his left holding his chest together. But the sword was too heavy. As he brought up his left hand to place it on the hilt, the left head darted in and bit his hand off at the wrist. Chad shrieked in agony as he stared at the stump where his left hand was a second ago, blood shooting from the jagged wound like a small garden hose. He knew he had less than a minute before he was dead and all was lost.

As he rolled his eyes in pain, they rested on the stalactite overhead once more. And though his vision was already growing dim, he had an idea.

Turning, he hobbled to the edge of the arena, Cerberus loping after him. The beast was playing with him, like a cat to a mouse, but Chad prayed the game would last for just a bit longer. As he reached the first stalagmite, he climbed it, his feet finding purchase easily. It was hard with only one hand

and that one holding the sword, but he used his arm with the missing hand to wrap around the cone of stone as he slithered up it. The hellhound, perhaps getting tired of the chase, swiped at his back and nearly sliced his spine in half. Chad roared with the agony and knew he had seconds before he would fall to the ground, dead for good.

As Cerberus padded a few feet below him, Chad shimmied up the stone spire, and when he was as high as he could go, he waited for the hellhound to move directly below him. With his last ounce of strength, he reached up with the sword and threw it at the closest stalactite hanging overhead.

He never saw what happened as he passed out from blood loss, falling to the ground where he lay still, his heart slowing to a stop. He had less than twenty seconds left alive before the game was over.

But a lot can happened in twenty seconds in Hell.

With the hellhound directly below the stalactite, the sword flew through the air and it struck true, right at the base of the stone icicle. The weight of the stalactite was so great the small, hairline crack in its base, thanks to the sword striking it, was enough to break it free. It plummeted to the ground and the hellhound below. The tip of the spire pierced the beast just behind its three heads, impaling it and severing the spine, then continuing into the ground, thus trapping the beast on the spike like a rare insect under a microscope. All three heads roared and snapped in pain, but it was trapped.

It didn't take long before each head began to grow weak to collapse on the dusty cavern floor, a few last chuffs of expelled air leaving each if its muzzles. Unknown to Chad, he had won.

Chad opened his eyes to see he was still in the same cavern. Standing slowly, he saw that though his clothing was torn, the skin beneath was fine and his left hand was back. He flexed his fingers in happiness. This didn't make sense; he was clearly told he had only one life.

And then he heard clapping made by only one set of hands. He looked to the forest of stalagmites to see Virgil come into the arena. His attire looked different now. Where Virgil had seemed an ordinary man; now he resembled an angel, complete with wings. His clothing was pure white and seemed to shimmer, a golden aura surrounding him.

Chad didn't move, and when he looked to his right and saw the hellhound lying dead, he jumped, expecting the heads to rear up and attack him. But after a moment he saw the beast was truly dead.

"Congratulations, Chad, that was quite ingenious using the stalactites overhead as a massive spear. Very clever indeed."

Chad said nothing, still trying to wrap his head around what was happening.

Virgil saw his dismay and nodded, smiling slightly.

"I see you're confused, yes?"

Chad nodded.

"It's really very simple, Chad. You fought through the circles of Hell, battling each level so you could finally get to see me."

"See you?" Chad asked. "Wait a second. Are you trying to tell me that…"

"Correct. My true title is Lucifer."

"But the wings, the aura, I don't understand."

Lucifer chuckled. "Chad, I am a fallen angel, remember? What you believe me to be, this mythical demon with horns and tail is all nonsense. Though fallen, I'm still an angel." He stepped to Chad and patted his shoulder. "And you have won every challenge thrust upon you. I believe you want to ask me for a favor, yes?"

Chad felt his legs go weak and Lucifer had to hold him up. It took him almost a minute to regain his composure, and with butterflies filling his stomach, he asked Lucifer what he'd wanted since killing Ralph all those years ago.

"Okay, so I can ask you one thing and if it's in your power you'll grant it, right? That's what the gypsy told me."

Lucifer nodded. "Yes, the old witch is correct. One of these days I am going to get her down here with me and she will pay for giving away my secrets. But yes, ask your request."

Swallowing deeply, Chad stood tall. "I want you to save my son's life. I want the cancer to go into remission forever and I want him to lead a long and healthy life."

Lucifer rubbed his chin. "My, that's a hell of a wish, pun intended. But though I have fallen from God's grace, I'm an honorable entity. Your wish shall be granted. Your son will live to a ripe old age, cancer free."

Chad fell to his knees and wept; tears of happiness and sadness mingling as he cried. Lucifer leaned down and picked Chad up. As Chad was raised to his feet, he heard a snarl and looked over his shoulder to see Cerberus walking around. The stalactite was gone from its body and the beast looked good as new. Lucifer saw Chad's quizzical look and he merely nodded.

"Cerberus is a part of Hell, Chad. My hellhound can never truly die." As if it heard its name, the hellhound turned to Lucifer, each head woofed once, sounding all too much like a regular dog, then it loped away into the stalagmites.

"Come, Chad, before I send you to your eternal punishment for committing murder, I want you to see that my word is good."

Chad nodded and Lucifer led him out of the cavern of the arena and stone spires, then through the cavern of fire and deeper into Hell.

When Chad walked through a dark, swirling mist and at the end of a stone hallway, he emerged in a small room. There was a puddle on the floor of this room, in more of a depression really, and Lucifer brought Chad to it and gestured for him to peer into the water. Lucifer reached down with his right hand and stirred the water, the ripples flowing and changing until Chad was shocked to see he was looking into his very own house. The picture then resolved to Sean's room, the boy on his death bed as he lay on the brink of death.

He saw Susan sitting beside Sean, while next to them both, a machine monitored Sean's heart and vitals. There was a doctor there as well as a nurse and Chad remembered the few times the doctor said he would show up would be for basic check ins and at the final day Sean would pass.

In the corner of the room a machine huffed as it breathed for his son, the boy now too weak to breathe on his own.

Chad felt more tears well up in his eyes when he saw Susan crying. His son's face was passive, his eyes closed, his breathing shallow, and Chad knew his son was ready to pass on.

Lucifer smiled at Chad and waved his hand over the pool.

Back on Earth, in Sean's room, the thin line about to flatline on the monitor began to beat faster, stronger, with each second. Immediately the doctor and nurse began checking vitals and equipment, not understanding what was happening.

And then, with Susan staring down at her only son, Sean's eyes opened. Susan began to cry, long, heaving sobs of joy as Sean looked at her with a blank expression.

"Mom, where's Dad?" Sean whispered and Susan only cried more, her hands now hugging Sean's head as she rocked him back and forth.

"It's a miracle," the doctor said. "There's no other explanation. It's an honest to God miracle." He turned to the nurse. "This is one for the textbooks. We'll have to run tests but his vitals are strong and it's as if the cancer suddenly vacated his body, as impossible as that seems."

Susan could have cared less about the hows and whys. All she knew was her son was awake, he was alive and as she hugged him, Sean asked her one question that had her laughing and collapsing with joy.

"I'm hungry."

Chad was crying, too, his journey finally complete. He'd gone to Hell itself to save his son and it had worked.

Lucifer waved his hand across the pool and the image evaporated.

"Okay, Chad, I kept up my end of the deal. Your son is alive and well. The doctors will find that the cancer is in total remission and it will stay that way until he passes on of old age. So let's go, it's time for you to join the rest of my souls."

Chad nodded, wiping his eyes clear with his sleeve. His hair was still gone, as were his eyebrows. The cavern of fire had burned it off, and though he was alive, he was hairless. He didn't care, vanity was a sin and he wouldn't miss combing it every day.

Lucifer brought him to another passageway, and as they stood in the middle, Lucifer snapped his fingers and Chad suddenly found himself in one of the circles. This one he didn't recognize, it wasn't one he'd traversed.

"Where are we?" Chad asked, not really wanting to know.

"This is the eight circle. One set aside for murders and sodomites. You committed murder, Chad; you don't get off with a warning."

Suddenly there were souls that came out of the shadows and dragged Chad to a rack, similar to a torturer's table. Chad was strapped down as the souls tittered manically.

Lucifer waved and his form dissolved and Chad was left alone on the rack. That was when he heard the screams, the anguished cries of other murderers, who were each being tortured by more souls assigned to this task.

"This is gonna hurt a lot," a female soul said as she raised a rusty knife, as did the other two, each with a blade of their own. As Chad lay struggling, each soul placed their blade to Chad's flesh, and after removing his clothing, they began to peel the skin from his body, one agonizing inch at a time.

Chad was to be flayed alive for all eternity.

Chad screamed and shrieked as his flesh was peeled from his bones, the red of muscle and tendon shining in the firelight. When the souls were through, and Chad lay panting and unconscious on the rack, he would suddenly awaken to find his flesh intact, but no sooner did he find this out, then the three souls would begin their work anew.

Chad would always scream, and would continue to scream for as long as time itself. But though the agony was unbearable and he knew he would slowly go mad with each layer of his skin removed, to him it was okay, for no matter how much pain he felt, no one could take away the satisfaction of knowing he'd won.

For as he suffered, he knew it was worth it. His son was alive and would live a long and happy life.

And Chad knew that though the skin was peeled from his face to leave a grinning, screaming skull, he would do it all over again, till the end of time, for though he was suffering in Hell, to him it was Heaven.

PARADE OF THE DEAD

John Benson, of 328 Forest Drive, peered out his bedroom window at the street below, his dark brown hair falling into his eyes so he had to brush it back.

They were still there.

The zombies.

As difficult as it was to believe, even after more than two weeks of witnessing it first hand, but it was true.

There were dead people walking around outside.

As he watched them, he recognized many of the people moving about. There was Mrs. Cullen, just shy of her sixtieth birthday. She would never reach it now; she would stay fifty-nine forever.

As John watched her shuffle about like she had amnesia, he couldn't help but stare at her withered frame. For she was as naked as the day she was born, with the exception of the shower cap on her head.

She was missing a large part of her lower right thigh and a chunk of her left arm. Coagulated blood seeped from the wounds, coating her in a sticky, red syrup that had hundreds of bloated flies feasting on her. John saw she didn't seem to notice.

It was her expression that was the most chilling, though the sagging breasts that looked like two deflated and wrinkled water balloons were a close second. Her blank gaze was chilling to behold. Her mouth sagged open and her jaw was slack, making her look like a dullard. He couldn't see her eyes from his bedroom window but he did see that she never blinked.

And why should she? She was dead after all.

Mrs. Cullen wandered past his house and then turned into a driveway a few houses down. He wasn't worried; he knew she'd be back soon enough.

Next to come by the house like an early morning walker out for a jaunt was Mr. Keelson.

He was a slovenly man with a balding pate and a large belly. Only now half that belly was missing, a cottage cheese like substance hanging out, some of it splattering to the road as he walked. It looked like someone had taken a massive drill to his abdomen and had turned it on high.

As he walked, John could see into the large hole in his torso and at the glistening organs within.

Mimicking life in death, Mr. Keelson kept reaching into the folds of flesh, rummaging around for a juicy morsel, and then he would shove it into his mouth. He was eating himself piece by bloody piece.

Bits of kidney slipped out of his mouth to land on the pavement, looking like he was leaving a trail of slugs behind him.

He walked past the house and then further down the road. Like Mrs. Cullen, John wasn't worried; he knew Mr. Keelson would be back.

As he shifted the curtain around the window for a better view of the street, John saw the next dead soul come into view.

The ghoul had been a cheerleader once, her yellow and blue uniform hugging her slim form like a second skin.

Only now she wasn't the perky young cheerleader. Now she was a creature from Hell.

She was missing her right arm, the white bone poking through the muscle and tissue, and in her other hand, the only one she had left, she still had her pom-pom. As she walked, the tinsel would swing back and forth, and it looked like she was cheering.

Yay, dead people! Go, Death!

John watched her hobble by, and though he knew he was being sick, he still admired her shapely ass when she moved off down the street, grinning at the way the material hugged her thighs.

But he wasn't worried, she'd be back in due time also.

Next came Herman, still wearing his postal uniform. John didn't know the guy's last name; to him he had always been just Herman.

Herman was missing his mail bag now, and one shoe was gone, along with a few fingers and toes. Herman looked as if he'd been through a meat grinder and lost, his uniform now hanging in rags. But still he made his rounds, even if he didn't have any more mail to deliver.

John watched the rest of them shuffle by, the other neighbors from down the street, the UPS man, still in brown khakis and shorts, and the newspaper boy who'd delivered his last paper.

They all walked by his window as if on parade.

John stepped away and turned around. He didn't want to because he knew what he'd see lying there in the bed, but he had no choice.

Tied to the bed, all fours limbs secured so she was spread-eagled, was his wife.

Marsha didn't look so hot and there was no amount of makeup that could help her complexion.

She hissed at him as he made his way around the bed, but he ignored her. It had been like this for three days after the dead first began to walk, as it had taken her that much time to succumb to the bite on her right forearm.

She had been at the market when one of the first ghouls had popped up. It made sense, too, as the Mayberry Mortuary was just down the block. The man who had attacked her had worn half a suit, the rear part open to the world, the bare-assed ghoul not at all modest about his nakedness.

When Marsha had stepped out of the store, the zombie had been there and had sunk his teeth into her arm like it was a roast duck. She pulled back instinctively and upon seeing the man's pale and haggard face, had assumed he was a bum.

Luckily a police cruiser was driving by and the two officers had witnessed the entire incident.

As the two cops jumped the dead man, Marsha took her queue and ran away, not wanting to become bogged down with questions and having to go to court later to get the man sentenced to a jail term. She was simply happy to get away from there.

For three days she'd nursed the wound until John knew something was seriously wrong with her. On the third day, she couldn't get out of bed and that night she'd slipped into a coma. Of course by now the news was rampant with reports of attacks by what appeared to be walking dead people.

But John had bigger things to worry about as his wife slipped into death. As he sat on the floor at the foot of the bed he'd cried, not knowing what to do.

His parents were dead years ago and he was an only child. The neighbors were dealing with their own grief and loss and had no time for him. So he was all alone with a dying wife and a world going to Hell in a hand basket. Or was that a coffin?

It was as he sat on the floor, his knees curled up to his chest, arms around legs, that he witnessed the dead walk for himself first hand.

He was dozing lightly, trying to rest, when he heard the sheets shifting on the bed. At first he didn't know what he'd heard but soon he was awake, the only illumination the pale light of the streetlamp coming through the main window.

He looked up to see the sheets slowly rising, like a figure from an old horror movie, perhaps Dracula rising from the tomb. It was when the sheets slid off his wife, her face now showing, that he knew there was something terribly off about her.

At first her glazed eyes saw nothing, as if she had woken from a deep sleep, but then when John shifted position, his body brushing the edge of the bed and making noise, her eyes seemed to come into partial focus.

He didn't know what he was looking at as he stared into her dead eyes. He saw something there, though vacant, but he couldn't put his finger on it.

Later, he would come to realize there was a hunger in those white orbs, a hunger he could never hope to fulfill. She hissed at him and moved to get off the bed and John, sitting on the floor, watching like a child punished for doing something bad, was frozen. She slowly got up, her arms and legs unsteady, but in a few seconds she had her balance.

Then she came for him, mouth wide, saliva dripping out of the corners to splash onto the carpet, her dead orbs piercing into his very soul.

And John knew she was gone and whatever was in the bedroom with him wasn't his wife anymore.

Though filled with fear and revulsion, he knew if he didn't stop her she would do…what…to him. The news reports said the dead were eating the living, and he could only assume she would attempt to do the same. So he did what he had to do; he defended himself.

When she was standing over him, her mouth so wide it looked like her jaw would unhinge at any moment, he kicked out with his right foot, knocking her to the floor.

She fell towards the bed, bouncing off it to roll onto the carpeting and she was now only a few inches from his left foot.

Her hand reached out like a whip and latched onto the foot as she tried to crawl up his shaking body. She managed to get halfway up, John staring into her dead eyes as she hissed and snarled.

He suddenly realized his groin was directly below her and if she figured this out, he was about to become a eunuch, so with a yell of disgust, he bucked his hips and tossed her off him.

She rolled across the room to come up against the bedroom door and John came to his feet.

His wife was only five-six, not very tall compared to his five-nine, and he pounced on her back, sitting on her so she couldn't get up.

She flailed with her arms and beat her hands onto the carpet, but she couldn't shove off his weight.

The bureau was near his reach, so he pulled each drawer open, yanking out socks, shirts and underwear, looking for something, anything that would work as bonds to secure her.

Then, in the bottom drawer, he found Marsha's scarves. They were frilly things, full of all the colors of the rainbow, and he grabbed them in hand and pulled them to him as some of them fluttered to the floor.

As fast as he could, he tied her hands and feet and then picked her up, dropping her back onto the bed.

All the while her teeth clacked as she tried to bite him.

"Honey, I don't think I'll be sleeping in the same bed with you tonight or ever," he said, his voice cracking slightly as he fought to maintain his sanity. If she heard him she gave no reaction, but merely tried to bite him again and again. Not knowing what to do, John left her then, closing the bedroom door behind him, figuring he needed a good stiff drink.

When he returned to the bedroom later that night, he found she was on the floor, wiggling around like a worm on a hook.

He decided then that just having her tied up wasn't good enough, so he transferred her back to the bed and tied her up one limb at a time until she was spread-eagled on the mattress in a perverse position, as if they were about to have kinky sex.

But that was the farthest thing from his mind. Since she'd died and returned, her skin had begun to crack, the red muscles and tendons within shining through. Her face had taken on a bluish pallor that gave her the look of a drowning victim.

Her lips were now swollen and her skin had grown tighter, making her look all the more cadaverous.

In truth, she was the embodiment of death.

But though she was dead, she was all he had left in a dying world and he found himself returning to the bedroom to be with her.

Wanting to take his mind off her, he'd taken to looking out the window, watching the walking dead as they paraded past his house.

There must have been something in their dead brains that kept them near to where they lived or worked because time and again they would return. They seemed to be walking a route, and when they reached the end of the block, they would turn and shuffle back the other way. All day, every day and night they did this.

He would watch for hours at a time, making up names for the ones he didn't know, the others, once his neighbors, he would actually smile at. They were dead and he was still alive. He was winning in the end.

It was late one night as he stared out at the dead block party, lost in the stories he'd made up for each of them, when his wife got free of one of her scarves. Whether by design or dumb luck, she was then able to free her other arm, so that her upper body was now able to reach over and grab him.

John, lost in reverie as he stared out the window, turned to check on her to see her sitting up, arms outreached to grab him. Before he could jump away, she pulled him to her and sank yellow teeth into his throat, tearing out a large portion of his neck.

Blood shot out and sprayed the wall crimson and he gagged, punching her in the face as he stumbled away. His hand reached up to his throat to staunch the blood flow but hot plasma squirted through his fingers, dripping onto the carpet to stain the shag scarlet.

His mouth opening and closing in shock and panic, he stumbled downstairs, hoping to get a bandage and save himself, but even as he stumbled towards the bathroom and the first aid kit, he knew he would never make it.

Already he was growing weak from blood loss, his vision going in and out as he bounced off the walls in the dark house. He knew then he was going to die, and he had seconds to decide how he wanted to spend eternity.

But it took only a split second for him to decide what he would do, and turning, he ignored the bathroom and half-walked, half-fell towards the front door. Opening it wide, he felt the cool air blow on his face and he then turned and walked into the living room, each step a chore as his blood seeped out of his torn throat.

Above him, on the second floor, he could hear his wife banging around as she tried to free her still secured legs. He actually grinned then, wishing her well. Maybe she would get free eventually to then join the walking dead outside in the street. John plopped down in his favorite chair and stared at the open front door, the cool night air washing the stink of the house away. He hadn't realized how bad it had become, the redolence of death filling the walls and floors, seeping into the furniture. Trapped inside with his rotting wife, he had grown accustomed to it without ever realizing it. He coughed then, spitting blood to stain his shirt a bright red and he couldn't keep his eyes open anymore, they were just too heavy. Then, closing his eyes, he slipped off into death.

Brandon Wilkinson of 456 Forest Drive peered out his living room window, watching the living dead as they shuffled past his house in the middle of the street like an undead parade was going on.

It had been more than a month and a half since the dead began to walk and Brandon had been holed up in his house, waiting for the world to return to normal. But the more he waited, the more he was coming to believe the world would never be the same again.

He was smarter than most and had stocked up well on food and water. He had enough to last him a year if he was careful, not that he believed he would need that long.

The electricity and water was out, the food in the refrigerator and freezer used up weeks ago as he didn't want to waste it and it would be instant milk for the time being until everything got back on track.

To pass the time he did one of two things. One was to read. He loved to read and had a massive library, one that would take two lives to read them all. The other thing that whiled away the hours was to sit at his living room window and watch the walking dead shuffle by his house.

They did this every day and never seemed to leave for long. They would walk a circuitous route by his house to the far end of the street to then turn back around and go the opposite away. All day, every day and night they did this.

As Brandon sat with a warm beer in his hand, he spotted a familiar face.

Mrs. Cullen was still as naked as the day she first appeared, though her withered skin was missing in more than one place as the crows got at her.

Another ghoul came around the bend and he saw it was the cheerleader. She wasn't as attractive as a month ago, but the figure was still there, as long as you didn't mind a little pus with your lovemaking.

Next came Mr. Keelson; more than half his weight gone thanks to a diet of eating himself. Almost his entire set of organs was now missing, chewed up and forced into his ever expanding stomach. Brandon figured it was going to rupture any day now. A family of rats had set up their home in his gut, enjoying the protection and comfort of the meat cave.

Then came the mailman. Brandon had dubbed him Brian, for a friend he'd known years ago. He thought the mailman looked a little like him so the name had stuck.

Oh, yes, all the residents of the neighborhood were out as always, stumbling about lazily. If they saw live prey that would be a different story, of course. There were many bloodstains on the sidewalk and street from where someone had been trying to make a break for it on foot. But once they were cornered by the larger numbers of walking dead, they were quickly brought down and eaten, usually to come back with half a face or a missing limb to join the undead ranks.

So Brandon knew he wasn't going anywhere, at least not until the dead were destroyed. And he didn't have a gun so fighting wasn't an option.

So he would wait and sooner or later the world would go back to normal; it had to.

As he peered through the wooden slats on his window, Brandon spotted a new recruit to the undead army.

The zombie stumbled like a drunkard, its head lolling to the side, the open and jagged wound in its neck filled with maggots and flies.

Brandon watched John Benson for the entire time he shuffled past his window, then he turned his attention to the UPS guy, who was having a problem with a curb on the far sidewalk.

And so the parade of the dead would continue, until either Brandon was rescued or he joined their ranks himself.

POST OFFICE OF THE DEAD

"Come on, people, listen up, there's a lot to cover and there's not much time," Fred, the supervisor for Branch 32, yelled out. He was standing at a podium in a small, stuffy room, and before him, in twenty metal chairs, were the mail carriers for the north section of the city.

Everyone was talking, their voices rising and falling in pitch as each person tried to share their stories of the night before.

It had been a hell of a yesterday, too.

For some unknown reason, the recently deceased had returned to life and were now feasting on the living.

So far the outbreak, or whatever it was, had been contained, the United States now under martial law. It had been found out early that a bite would infect someone and cause them to become one of the walking dead.

People were told to remain in their homes, barricading themselves in until the crisis passed, but despite this, despite the dead walking, the mail still needed to get through.

There were already bins of mail and packages piled in the back room, and if the post office stopped for even one week, they would become so buried in mail they would never recover, so today, though the dead were walking, so too would the postal carriers of Branch 32.

"This is crazy, Fred," Jodi called out from the side of the room. Next to her was Chris, a tall man who topped six feet. The two had been friends for years and he looked out for Jodi like a big brother.

Fred sighed from the podium as he glared back at Jodi. He saw a pretty woman in her late thirties with piercing blue eyes and dark black hair. One time, years ago he had broken protocol and had had an affair with her, but he'd ended it before his wife could find out. Jodi hadn't taken it too well, but now, years later, the two were friends again.

"Crazy? Why? We deliver in any other disaster, don't we? Thunderstorms, blizzards, wildfires, hell, we deliver in floods if the houses are still intact. The mail must go through, that's our motto, right?"

Jodi crossed her arms over her chest and frowned, Chris doing the same in the seat beside her.

"That's horseshit, Fred, there's nothin' in the manual about the mail must get delivered when the dead walk," Chris said.

"Why?" Fred defended himself. "What's the difference? It's a natural disaster, that's all. We deliver in gang neighborhoods and we deliver where murders have taken place. This is just one more obstacle to overcome."

A man with a large belly and thin legs stood up and pointed at Fred accusingly. "Then why don't you go out there and deliver the damn mail yourself!" he shouted.

Fred grinned. "Why? 'Cause I'm the supervisor. I get paid to supervise you knuckleheads and that's what I'm gonna do."

"This is nuts," Jodi said, a few others agreeing.

Fred slammed the palm of his hand on the wooden podium. "Enough, quiet down, damn it!"

The crowd settled and all eyes went to Fred. A few low murmurs were still filtering from the crowd, but Fred knew this was as good as it gets.

"Okay, so today is no different from any other day you deliver," he began. The murmur grew louder and Fred raised his voice, repeating himself. "I said, this is no different than any other day. You just need to be careful out there, that's all. And to make sure you stay safe, the higher-ups have agreed to give you some more gear to protect yourselves out there other than your keychain mace."

"Like what?" Chris asked, his curiosity peaked.

Fred pulled a two-way radio from his belt and talked into it. "Bring the stuff in, George."

All eyes turned to the one door in the room when it opened and another, lower class supervisor came in holding a large box. There were four more managers behind George.

Chris chuckled as the men walked in and set down their burdens. "Christ, when you put all the damn managers and supervisors in one place there's like one for every five of us carriers, it's crazy."

Fred frowned when he heard Chris' comment but others were talking now, the sound level going up in pitch.

"Okay, okay, quiet down so I can pass these out," Fred said as he went to George, who nodded a hello.

The other managers began taking items from the box and passing them out to each of the carriers. When Jodi received hers, her eyes went wide as she held a weapon in each hand.

"You have got to be kidding me. A gun and a machete? To deliver mail?"

"Yes, that's exactly what you need to deliver the mail. And there will be one more thing added to the list. You will all be issued plastic armor, similar to what hockey players wear. It's lightweight and is more than enough to stop a bite if one of the dead get too close."

Chris shook his head as he studied the gun in his hand. It was small, .22 pistol. "This is unbelievable. It's like a fucking horror movie."

Fred heard Chris' comment and replied, "Maybe so, but these weapons and the armor will keep you safe and that's all that matters." He walked closer to the crowd as they talked amongst themselves. "Look, people, it's a whole new world out there. No one knows how long the dead will walk. For all we know, this could go on forever. But if so, then we still have a job to do. So stay sharp, watch out for blind spots, and make sure you wear your armor." He clapped his hands loudly. "Okay, get going and be safe out there."

While a few stayed in their seats, most stood up, gathered their new equipment and headed out to gather their mail, load the vans and postal vehicles and deliver their routes.

They knew Fred was correct. Though the dead walked, they were mail carriers. They delivered in any weather, in any disaster; they were the heartbeat of a nation.

The mail had to go through, and even zombies couldn't stop it.

Jodi pulled up in her white LLV Government Issue vehicle and parked in front of a large Victorian mansion. All the homes on the street were the same size… too big. One name Jodi used for the oversized houses was McMansion, meaning far too enormous for one single family to live in.

It was the rich part of town and Jodi had been on this particular route for over three years. She knew everyone and they knew her. At Christmas time, more than half of her customers left her a Christmas tip and the extra money was a welcome extra to her salary.

There were even a few customers who would chat with her, most being senior citizens. They would wait for her each day during the hot summer months with a can of soda or a bottle of cold water.

Many had become defacto friends and she always had time to pet a dog or a cat sitting on a porch or in a front yard. She liked her job and did it well, and planned on doing it until she retired.

One more thing Jodi always did, as did other postal carriers, was to keep their eyes and ears open for trouble. Many lives had been saved by a postal carrier who had peered into a window after seeing the mail piling up on the porch or in the mailbox. There were people who had no family, and the only ones to visit them, though only technically, were the carriers leaving the mail.

So the postal carrier was the watchdog of the neighborhood, always on the lookout for trouble.

Opening the rear door to her postal vehicle, Jodi reached inside and took out the large package for the McMansion she was parked in front of. It had been too big to carry, so she planned on delivering it first, then she would drive to the next spot where she would park and continue her route.

From the street, she had to walk a good thirty feet to the front door of the home, as were most of the houses on the street. They were all set far back with large, manicured front lawns, water displays and expensive flowers.

Shifting her plastic armor to make it fit better, and making sure her new weapons were secure, Jodi picked up the package and began walking up the granite walkway. She felt ridiculous with the gear on, but she also knew it was necessary.

As she approached the front door, she paused halfway there to see it was open. Looking left and right, there was no one else on the street. It was early morning and well after morning rush hour; children were in school and now was the time for mothers and others to relax before the day truly began.

When she was ten feet from the ajar front door, she studied the opening, figuring the owner of the house had seen her pull up and had come to the door in anticipation, so she didn't give it much thought.

But as she reached the steps and began to ascend them, she stopped in her tracks when she heard a low moan, like someone was hurt.

She didn't feel threatened, assuming someone needed help. But as she reached the doorway and was about to call out, a shape popped up and blocked the entryway.

Jodi's mouth fell open at the sight greeting her. She had never seen a real zombie before, but had only heard about them from others as well as what she saw on TV. But the reality of it was far more visceral than she would have ever believed.

Before her, swaying back and forth, was the owner of the house. The old woman was in her seventies, with white hair and wrinkled and sagging skin that made her look like she had put on a dress suit that was two sizes too big.

She was naked, her hair soaked with water as well as blood.

If Jodi had to guess what had happened, she assumed the old woman had fallen in the tub while bathing, had cracked her head on the tub, which had killed her, and then had revived as one of the walking dead.

"Mrs. Carlson, it's me, Jodi," she said, not knowing what else to do. "I have a package for you, but you need to sign for it."

The old woman merely moaned louder and took a step towards her. Jodi, realizing quickly she was in danger, threw the package at the old woman, turned and ran, saying over her shoulder, "Forget it, you don't need to sign for it."

Behind her, Mrs. Carlson stumbled onto the porch and down the stairs. She wasn't very coordinated and she slipped on the third stair. She tumbled face first onto the granite of the walkway, smashing her nose and cracking her forehead. Teeth snapped from the blunt force trauma, and as the old woman tried to pick herself up, she spit bloody globules of saliva and teeth.

Jodi barely saw any of this. She ran to her postal vehicle, unlocked it, climbed in and drove off with a screech of tires.

The only thing she kept remembering was that back when she took the test to apply for the letter carrier's position, there had never been anything on it about zombies.

Jodi drove to the local donut shop ten minutes later, deciding it was time for a break. On the trip over, she had seen six zombies stumbling about the road, like drunkards late for a frat party. She'd ignored them and focused on the road ahead.

Getting out of the postal truck after parking, she walked to the entrance and stepped inside the shop. She was relieved to see Chris and Jim were there already, with steaming cups of coffee and a donut before each of them.

Chris saw her enter and waved her to join them.

"Hi, Jodi, how's your morning going?" Chris asked with a smile.

She quickly filled him in on her adventure with Mrs. Carlson and both Chris and Jim shook their heads at the end of her story.

"Wow, at least you got out of there in one piece," Chris said. "I found the mother of a family on First Street eating her two kids. They were three and four years old. I called the police and they said they'd get someone over there as fast as they could, but as you can imagine, they're pretty busy."

"How come you didn't just shoot her with the gun you got?" Jodi asked as she sipped her coffee after the waitress came over and poured her a cup.

It was a down home donut shop—not a franchise—where a waitress took your order and topped off you coffee. The three postal carriers had been going there for years.

"Why?" Chris asked. "Because if I did, there would be all kinds of paperwork to fill out. At least that's what Fred told me before I left today. Trust me on this one, Jodi, don't kill any zombies unless you have no choice. Let the cops handle it."

"Amen to that," Jim said as he took a bite of his donut.

There was a commotion outside and all three of them looked up and out the plate glass window to see that five zombies had wandered into the parking lot from the street. Two were men and the other three were women, the ages ranging from twenty to thirty. All five had gaping wounds in their necks and torso and each of them had died painfully from vicious attacks.

As the three postal workers watched through the window, their new realty hit home just a little more. People coming and going from the donut shop ran from the five zombies, more than one screaming for help.

That help arrived seconds later when two squad cars and a SWAT van rolled up and disgorged Kevlar wearing men. They formed a perimeter around the five zombies, and before any of the walking dead could so much as moan, they were shot down in a barrage of lead that blew arms off bodies and took three of their heads off in a glorious spray of blood and brain matter. A pink mist hung in the air, all that was left of the destroyed heads.

As each of the ghouls was taken down, men with body bags began stuffing each corpse into them. In minutes, the five bodies were encased in the black bags and unceremoniously tossed into the back of the SWAT van.

The two squad cars waved onlookers away, climbed back into the vehicles, then drove off, a few blips of the siren as they reentered traffic.

The SWAT van pulled out and was soon gone, and the only thing left of the scene of carnage was the pools of dark blood still spread on the pavement in the parking lot.

As the three postal employees watched the now empty scene, one of the donut shop employees appeared while dragging a garden hose. Calmly, like he was washing spilled red paint, he began spraying the blood and diluting it, until there was nothing left but a few faded spots that would also disappear when it dried.

"Well, that was interesting," Chris said as he looked at the others.

"Shit, did you see how fast the cops arrived? And now it's like nothing ever happened," Jim said.

"What do you think it all means?" Jodi asked.

Chris shrugged his broad shoulders. "If I had to guess, I'd say the cops or the establishment or whoever's running the show is trying to act like this whole dead walking thing is nothing but an inconvenience."

Jim leaned forward. "You mean like a conspiracy?"

"No, stupid," Chris joked. "I mean they don't want to admit we have a serious problem on our hands here. There trying to keep it all quiet. You know, like when a zombie pops up. They get in there, take it down, then take off, leaving things exactly like it was before."

"That's crazy," Jodi said. "Surely they realize this is serious."

Chris looked her in the face. "Oh come on, Jodi, How many times have our leaders tried to sweep something under the rug, even if it's dire to the point of being global?"

"He's got a point there," Jim added as he finished his donut.

Jodi checked her wristwatch. "Well, whatever's happening, there's nothing we can do about it now. Breaks over, I've got to get back to work." She stood up.

Chris checked his watch and nodded as well, then Jim did the same. "Shit, you're right, I gotta go too." He stood up. "Okay, you guys be careful out there."

"Same to you, Chris," Jim said and Jodi added her own well wishes.

The three carriers left the donut shot with a wave to the clerk, climbed into their postal vehicles and headed off in different directions to finish their routes.

Jodi had been delivering for about three hours when she came upon a letter that needed a signature confirmation.

Walking up to the front door, she rang the doorbell and waited. As she waited, she shifted uncomfortably in her protective gear. It was hot out and the gear only made her hotter. She desperately wanted to take it off, but knew it would be tantamount to suicide.

She had already decided tomorrow she was going to call in sick and reevaluate her future. Maybe she'd transfer to being a clerk.

No one had answered the door and she was about to ring it again when she heard a loud thump come from the other side of the door.

"Hello? Is anyone there?" she called. "I need a signature on a letter, please."

A low moan came to her ears but with the ambient noise such as the traffic on the street, it sounded more like, "*Leeeavvve iiitttt.*"

"I'm sorry, I can't leave it. You need to sign for it." She waited for a reply and when none came, said, "Hello, did you hear me?"

There was no answer and ten second later there was another thump.

Reaching for the doorknob, she found the door locked. There was a mail slot on the door and she knelt down and pushed it open with her fingers. Peering into the house, she saw the reason why the home owner wasn't answering the door.

He was dead.

In his late eighties at least, the man looked like he'd had a heart attack or some such malady that had definitely killed him. His skin was pale and his eyes sunken and one leg didn't seem to work too well. If Jodi assumed correctly, the man might have been dead for a few days before he had risen as one of the undead.

"Great, he's dead, what the hell am I supposed to do now?" she said to no one.

The old man stumbled around the foyer, bumping into walls and a small end table.

Jodi watched him for more than a minute and decided there was nothing she could do.

"Oh, the hell with it," she mumbled as she took out a pen, scribbled the man's name on the line where the signature was supposed to be, then slid the letter into the slot. "If they don't like it they can fire me," she muttered as she stepped back and returned to her vehicle.

Half an hour later, she had another package to delivery that required yet another signature. Normally, her day was filled with delivery and signature confirmations, but now, with the dead walking, they seemed to have taken on an entirely new meaning.

The house before her was a single story ranch house with a manicured lawn and yellow flowers lining the walkway.

At least, that's how she remembered it.

Now, it looked like something out of a war movie.

A ten foot, electrified chain-link fence lined the property and sandbags were scattered and piled waist high across the lawn. To the right, where there used to be a birdbath, there was now a four foot fox hole, complete with machine gun emplacement.

Jodi slowly waked up to the chained gate and tried to take in the fort before her.

There was an intercom tied to the gate with wire and she pressed the button, not knowing what else to do.

A crackled static filled the intercom and then a male voice, said, "Go away!"

She blinked in surprise at the rudeness, turned to look around the street, glad to see it was devoid of the living or undead, and pressed the button again.

More static filled the intercom and a gruff voice replied, "Fuck off, I don't want any."

She pressed the button once more and received a similar epitaph.

"Uhm, hello in there, it's the mail carrier. I need a signature for a package," she said quickly.

"Just leave it," the reply came quick and curt.

"Uhm, I can't. I need a signature. Look, if you don't come out I'll bring it back and you can go to the post office and pick it up there."

There was silence for a few seconds and then, "I can't do that. Till the zombies stop walking, I won't leave my house. It's the friggin' apocalypse, didn't you know that? Just leave it at the gate. I'll get it after you leave."

"I'm sorry, but I can't do that. Until it's signed for it's my responsibility. So either come out or I'm leaving."

"How do I know you're not one of them?"

"What? A zombie?" she asked incredulously.

"Yeah, one of them."

"Ah, well, 'cause I can talk? I don't think they can talk, at least I haven't met one that could. Have you?"

"No, not yet. They're stupid. Hell, they're dead."

"That's what I heard," she said, sounding bored.

"I heard it's from a satellite in space that's in Earth's orbit. It's giving off radiation. Either way, I'm not coming out."

"Fine, then I'm going. I'll leave the pink ticket here on the ground. It has the number of your item. So long," she said and turned to leave.

"No wait, don't go. Fine, I'll come out. I need that package. It's water purification tablets for when the water stops flowing in the tap."

"So you're coming out?"

"Yes, just give me a second to get dressed."

She sighed. "Fine, but please don't take too long. I have a schedule to keep and I'm running late as it is." She scratched her arm, the weight of the plastic armor uncomfortable, and the machete on her hip was heavy.

She waited for over five minutes and was about to leave when the front door of the home opened and a man wearing a gas mask and body armor stepped out.

As he walked down the pathway, she saw he carried a double barrel shotgun.

When he reached her, he opened the gate after looking around the street and said, "You know, miss, you really should be somewhere safe, not walking around on the street."

"Thank you for your concern. Here, sign this, please," she said as she handed the man a clipboard and pen. The brown, paper-wrapped package was on the ground at her feet. He quickly signed and handed her back the clip board. He was about to bend over and take the package when he suddenly went rigid. Jodi realized he was looking over her shoulder and she turned around to see a zombie heading right for her.

It was a middle-aged male with a large wound on the right side of its neck. The zombie had been attacked and killed and once died, had returned.

"Stand back, miss, I got this," the man said as he leveled the shotgun at the ghoul. Before Jodi could say anything, she was pushed behind the man and her ears were ringing as the man gave the zombie both barrels.

The first barrage of buckshot tore the ghoul's right arm off, and the second took the head off like it was made of wet newspaper. Blood geysered up and out of the stump as the body toppled over, the remaining arm flailing on the ground as the feet kicked up and down like a child having a tantrum. The man admired his marksmanship with a wan smile.

"Look at 'im spurt. Never understood why that is."

"What do you mean?" Jodi asked as she waited for the ringing in her ears to fade. She looked away from the headless corpse, not wanting to look at all the blood.

"The blood, miss, the blood. I never understood how those damn things can bleed if they're dead. After all, their hearts don't work any more, right? So if that's so, then why do they bleed when you shoot 'em?"

Jodi could have cared less and she told the man so. With a nod, she left him and went back to her postal vehicle, locking the doors when she was inside it.

No sooner did she do this then a pale face slapped her window. It was a woman, or had been once. Now it was a withered shell that looked like it had crawled out of the grave. Maggots squirmed about in the nose and ear canals and the eyes were bleach white orbs of nothingness. As Jodi stared at the face, the zombie slid its cheek against the glass, leaving a smudge of puss and other fluids thanks to decomposition. A few maggots stuck to the glass, wiggling free to fall to the warm pavement where they would soon die.

Jodi, trying to remain calm, knowing she was safe inside the vehicle, slid the ignition key into the ignition, turned it, and slowly began to drive.

The ghoul walked with her for a few feet and then began to fall away.

As she put some distance between herself and the zombie, she glanced in her side mirror. As she did, a boom echoed across the street and the zombie went down minus a head, decapitated at the neck. She leaned forward so she could see the far side of the street and the man in the gas mask was walking over to the zombie, admiring his latest kill. She watched as he shot the ghoul's severed head, blowing it into a hundred pieces, a pink mist floating in the air before the wind dispersed it.

Then she turned the corner and the scene was lost from sight.

She was glad it was.

Jodi parked her postal vehicle in the rear parking lot of Branch 32 and went inside. She was tired. It had been a long day.

Going to her locker, she took off her gear, placed the gun and machete in her locker—glad she hadn't had to use either one— and changed into her street clothes.

On her way out of the building, she spotted Chris and Jim near their cars, talking together. Chris was louder than usual, waving his arms in the air as he discussed something that he was emotional about.

"Hi, guys, what's going on?" Jodi asked as she got within earshot of the two men.

Chris turned at the sound of her voice and smiled. He was always glad to see her.

"Jodi, good, now I'll get someone on my side of this discussion."

"What are you talking about?" She nodded hello to Jim who gave her a nod of his own.

"You won't believe what management is going to try to do by the end of the week," Chris said, and when Jodi didn't say anything, he continued. "They're gonna start using zombies as extra help."

"What? That's crazy. Why?" she asked.

"Because we're short handed, that's why. Between all the PTFs leaving and all the people that have quit this week, there's not enough manpower to deliver all the mail," Chris said.

"But how can a zombie deliver mail?" she asked.

Jim spoke up. "That's just the thing, Jodi, they won't be delivering the real mail, so to speak. Just the circulars and flyers and junk mail, like those post cards the politicians have us deliver during voting season."

"They didn't waste any time," Chris said angrily. "Hasn't been two weeks and the guys upstairs are figuring out how to make a buck on this dead walking thing."

"Chris is upset about it," Jim told Jodi.

"Damn straight I am. They think a zombie can do our job, is that it?" he demanded.

Jim shook his head. "No, Chris, of course not, don't get upset. It makes sense though. Those circulars only have 'resident' on them. Anyone with half a brain can deliver them. It's all the rest that needs a competent person to make sure they get to the right address, forwards, stopped mail, ect."

"But what about our jobs, Jim? Next thing you know, they'll have zombies doing our jobs, too." He shook his right index finger as his face grew redder by the second. "I'll tell you both right now, I'm not sitting still for this. Tomorrow, first thing in the morning, I'll be talking to our union rep. I'll get to the bottom of this." He waved curtly, turned and head for his car. "I'll see you guys tomorrow. I'm going home to see what I can get started on. This isn't right, they can't do this and damn it I'm gonna stop it. The post office is my life. I'll die before I let them dead bastards take my job." He climbed into his car and drove off with a quick beep of his horn and screeching tires.

Jodi looked at Jim who returned her gaze.

"Looks like he's at it again," she said.

Jim nodded. "Yeah, he's like a dog with a bone, too. Were never gonna hear the end of this till it's over."

"I'm not looking forward to the next week with him, I'll tell you that right now," she said.

"Ditto for me. All we can do is nod when he talks and hope he blows himself out eventually."

She paused before speaking. "Do you really think they'll get zombies to pick up the slack for us?"

He shrugged. "Anything's possible. Shit, after some of the idiots I've worked with, maybe the zombies will be smarter. Remember that woman who was stealing cell phones? Or the guy who was dumping his undelivered mail in a storage locker every night?"

"Yeah, you do have a point there. We've had some real winners get hired, haven't we."

"Damn straight," he said. He checked his watch. "I gotta go. Susan's making veal parm tonight and I told her I wouldn't be later than six."

"Okay, have a good night," she said.

They both went to their vehicles and drove off, another day done.

Jodi drove around a few zombies in the streets but made it home without difficulty. Once inside, she locked the doors and windows and settled down for a quiet night at home. Tomorrow would be another day.

"Where's Chris?" she asked at the morning gathering.

Jim shook his head. "No one knows. He didn't call in sick and there's no answer at his house. And his cars not in his driveway."

"Oh God, you don't think…" she began, not wanting to voice her fears.

"That the dead got him on his way home last night?" Jim suggested. "Could be, we'll just have to wait and see if he turned up."

Jodi nodded, knowing Jim was right. People were disappearing every day it seemed and she prayed Chris was all right. But until then, she needed to focus on her job and staying alive.

The next two weeks went by quickly for Jodi. The dead were still walking and things were slowly growing worse. The Government was still doing its best to contain the walking dead, but each day it seemed the situation was growing worse.

Jodi was pulling into the parking lot one morning when she saw there was a commotion in the back lot.

After parking her car, she went to see what was going on. She found Jim and ten other postal workers watching two large trucks pulling into the lot. But where normally the trucks would be carrying bins of mail, there was something inside them that had never been transported before.

As the rear doors were rolled up, men wearing heavy armor and carrying cattle prods began herding zombies out of the two trucks. Jodi watched in awe as the ghouls were made to line up.

Each wore a blue postal shirt and the blue baseball caps all employees were mandated to wear.

Jim moved up next to her and she turned to look at him. "What's going on, Jim? What are they doing here?"

He sighed. "I was talking to one of the managers before you arrived. You remember a few weeks ago, back when Chris disappeared and how he was telling us about some program to get the dead to deliver circulars and junk mail?"

She nodded.

"Well, here they are, all trained and ready to go."

"But it's crazy. They can't deliver mail; they're dead for Christ's sake."

"That they are."

"Do they get paid?" she asked as she studied the pale, slack faces.

"Yeah, but trust me, you don't want to know with what."

As she watched the ghouls herded to the rear of the building by the trainers, her mouth fell open when she spotted Chris in the back of the line. His face was pale, flies buzzing around his head, and there was an eye missing as well as an ear. He had a chunk of his throat torn out, but with his shirt collar pulled high it was hard to see.

"Oh my God, that's Chris over there. Jim, look, Chris is one of them," she gasped quickly. "Chris, Chris!" she yelled to him. "It's me, Jodi. Chris!"

"I don't think he can hear you anymore, Jodi," Jim said sadly. "I guess we know where he went. He must have been attacked and ended up as one of them. Poor guy, I'm gonna miss him." He turned to walk away. "I'm going inside; it's almost time to punch in." He was shaking his head as he walked away.

Jodi wouldn't leave, not yet. As Chris came within a few feet of her, only the trainers keeping him in line, she called out to him again.

Chris slowed and then stopped, holding up the zombies behind him and he turned to face Jodi, as if he recognized her face and her voice. But then he continued on, brain dead and stupid.

"At least he's still doing his job," she said to no one. "He said he'd die before he let them make him quit."

With nothing to do to help him, she went to punch in, starting a new day in a dead world.

But there was one difference this day. Now she knew Chris was gone for good. The mystery of his disappearance had been solved.

She was really going to miss him.

REBIRTH

His name was Mark Jameson…and he was dead.

Well, maybe not dead, dead, but when your heart doesn't pump, you don't need oxygen, and your hair doesn't grow; doesn't that constitute being dead?

He stared at his face in the bathroom mirror, studying the decay slowly creeping across his worn visage.

He scratched at the wound on his arm, the one he'd received when he was attacked in the subway more than three weeks ago.

Since then he'd called in sick and stayed home.

No other living souls have seen him since he'd become a hermit, but it was easy to do this as he lived on the outskirts of town, more than a half mile off the main road. No one would come to him unless they were invited.

He held a razor in his hand, wanting to shave, but as he touched the blade to his cheek, the skin sloughed off his face like wet porridge. It dripped into the sink where the red and black gore slid down the side of the basin like small snails in a race to the drain.

His eyes were not the deep blue they once were either. A haze of milky white had coated them, making him look like a geriatric with the worst case of cataracts in history. But for some reason his vision was still good; he could see.

His brow was more prominent, but some of his hair had fallen out, making him look two decades older than his thirty-odd years.

There was a new pustule on his neck and he reached up and pushed on it with the tip of his index finger. The large pimple-like globule was punctured and a yellowish, whitish ooze dripped down his neck to the middle of his chest. His eyes followed the trail of slime to study his once muscular chest; only a few black hairs between his pectorals. But now his torso was covered with oozing masses of yellow, red and black wounds. He looked like a fungal growth gone mad and it made him sick inside.

Over the past two weeks, he'd begun to detest his body odor, too. The smell of rot seeped into his sinuses, making him want to puke.

But he would lather on deodorant or splash on some after shave, anything to cover up the redolence of oppressive death.

Deciding shaving was out of the question, he picked up a towel and dabbed his face where the blade had touched flesh. After removing the towel from his face, it was now covered with gore and he tossed it into the hamper, disgusted with himself.

What had he become? How could this be happening?

After dressing, he went into the living room to watch some television. As he turned it on, he remembered the cable had been out for weeks, about when he was attacked actually.

What was odd was the radio channels were also silent and over the past few weeks he had heard an odd assortment of explosions through the day and night.

It sounded like a war was being fought in town but of course that would be ridiculous. It must be construction, road work perhaps.

As he sat down on his favorite easy chair, he sighed, finally taking the weight off of dead muscles and tendons.

He remembered the first week as the worst. This was when his body technically died and went into rigor mortis. For a full day he couldn't move, only blink as his muscles and limbs atrophied. But eventually it went away and he was able to move again, though now there was a slight discomfort whenever his muscles were flexed.

What was strange was his appetite was all but gone. At first he had eaten fine, but then when he got a look at a vegetable it made him want to vomit. After that he went through every steak and roast in his freezer until it was all gone.

He was glad his cat hadn't returned home, now missing for more than two weeks, for he truly didn't know what he might have down if it had returned.

After the fresh and frozen meat was gone, he dove into the processed meat, beef stew, and chili-with-meat a few of the choices. He found he could barely keep it down, but it did control the hunger, if barely. He didn't understand why normal food wasn't filling him, wasn't satisfying him. He had to assume it had to do with his sickness.

He wondered if he was the only one of his kind, a man who was dead and yet not dead.

Many times he had thoughts of dressing up like the Invisible man, complete with overcoat and bandages, and take a drive into town to see if he was actually the only one suffering from this ailment. He imagined visiting his doctor to see if there was anything that could be done and the doctor's mystified face as he took his dead patient's temperature, blood pressure, ect.

But in the end Mark decided it wasn't worth the risk of being discovered. He imagined what would happen if the military found out about him. Why, they would lock him up and do tests on him till the cows came home. No, he didn't want anything like that to happen to him.

So with no television or radio, he sat down and picked up a book, deciding it would pass the time nicely.

A week later found him pacing back and forth in his small home. He was restless, more so than ever before.

He was going stir crazy.

He was a social animal and being separated from the rest of humanity was driving him nuts.

His body had deteriorated more, too. Most of it was no big deal; a fingernail here, an eyebrow or eyelid there. But when he went to the bathroom a few days ago and had taken a piss, he made the mistake of shaking his penis three times instead of two.

The third wasn't the charm, however, and the member had popped off in his hand and he was so mortified that he'd dropped it into the toilet. As he'd staggered away in utter shock, his hand accidentally pressed the plunger, and before he could cry out in loss, his penis had been flushed into the sewer system, like a dead goldfish named Goldie he'd had as a kid.

The next few days after that were a blur, as any man would attest to.

So now, days later, after becoming a eunuch, he'd had enough solitude and self isolation and decided it was time to go into town and see what was going on.

After all, something was up. He hadn't received his mail in more than three weeks and the phone lines were down as well. He figured someone had had an accident and crashed into one of the telephone poles leading to his home. It had happened before. Unless he complained about it, the phone company would ignore the downed lines, not wanting to expend the man power for only his and a few other homes connected to the line.

So with this as his motivation, he got dressed. Black sunglasses, a large fedora, black gloves and a scarf made him feel like a villain in an old horror movie.

Stepping outside, he felt himself shunning the sun, but he forced his body to keep moving. His car was only a few feet away and in seconds he was inside and out of the worst of the sun's harsh rays.

It was warm out but he noticed he didn't feel the difference in temperature. Wrapped in his coat, gloves, and scarf, he should have been sweltering like a steamed clam but he felt fine.

Turning over the engine, he backed out of the driveway and made his way into town.

As he drove down the winding road, his eyes took in the telephone poles lined up like sentries, seeing they all appeared undamaged. If so, then why were the phone lines down?

He made it to the outskirts of the main road leading into town, and from then on he had to walk. The reason was the abandoned cars and two trucks that were spread across the road like discarded trash.

A few of the vehicles had what looked like blood splatter inside them and on the insides of the windows, but it was dried to a brown color and he couldn't be sure.

Taking one plodding step after another, he made his way into the town proper.

As he reached Main Street, where the most activity would normally be, he found the street was a ghost town. Some of the storefronts had broken windows and most had closed signs hanging in the doorways, that is the ones that still had doors as most were kicked in and hanging off their hinges like drunks trying to stand up.

A few placards were hanging by one hook over doorways, the wood slapping the facades of the buildings, reminding him of one single person clapping. It was all so surreal. While he'd been holed up in his house, it seemed the town had gone to rubble.

Stepping over some bricks scattered across the sidewalk, thanks to a truck that had plowed into the corner deli, he sidestepped the truck, its front end half in the store, and continued onward, searching for some sign of life.

He walked for almost half an hour before hearing something other than silence. He immediately gave it his full attention.

At first it sounded like a howl, but then, as he listened with ears that were slowly sliding off his head, he heard the distinct scream of what was definitely female.

Crossing the street, he stepped over a strewn bag of groceries, the produce now a rotting mess, and moved to the next corner.

As he gazed out onto the deserted street, he spotted movement from the far left.

The woman's yelling was louder now, and as he watched, she slowly came into view, but the second he saw her he knew there was nothing *slow* about her movements.

She was hobbling, her right leg giving her trouble, and by the way she moved Mark had a feeling it might be a sprained ankle. The woman was crying out for help, for anyone who could hear her to help her, and a second later Mark saw what she was running from.

More than a score of what could only be called *zombies* were shambling down the street at about the gait of a casual jogger.

As Mark stared at the first ghouls in the line, he saw a resemblance to himself, and though he didn't want to admit it to himself, he looked just like them. He was a zombie, too, but for some reason he was still an individual; he could think for himself.

And as the woman came closer to him, her eyes seeing him wrapped up in hat and coat, she screamed at him and began hobbling forward with outstretched arms.

Mark stared at her, saw the panic and terror in her face, and made up his mind right then and there.

He was a man, not a monster and he would do what he could to help her.

Reaching down to the sidewalk, he picked up a stray pipe, the cast iron heavy in his grip. With his gloves on he couldn't feel the metal, but with the sun shining down he believed it would have been hot to the touch. Even with the glove on he should have felt some residual heat, but his sense of touch was less heightened than before.

Still, as the woman came to him, he hefted the pipe and stepped into the street, pointing behind him to the woman.

"Get behind me! I'll see what I can do to stop them!" he growled, his voice scratchy from lack of use.

She never hesitated, desperate for any help she could find, and as she ran by him and waited near the corner of the building, Mark waded into the charging ghouls like a Viking going to war.

He swung the pipe hard to the side like a baseball bat and a ghoul's head was caved in, the blow so strong its left eyeball popped out of the socket to roll across the road like a shiny marble. The next zombie in line had been an old woman, but Mark showed her no mercy and swung the pipe overhand, bringing it down like he was chopping wood. When the pipe connected with the top of her cranium, the blow caused her dentures to pop out of her mouth. The false teeth flew threw the air to land and bounce, shattering like dice to roll across the pavement.

The next two ghouls came at Mark at the same time and he ducked low, charging into their midriffs with his shoulder. As he knocked them off their feet, he felt something pop in his shoulder but he ignored it. Where there should have been pain there was only mild discomfort.

The next zombie had been a child, no more than ten, but Mark knew the innocence of youth was now gone, as dead as the heart inside his own chest.

With a sideways swipe, he whacked the boy on the head, sending the kid across the road with a massive dent where his right ear used to be. The child flopped around on the ground, looking like a robot with its wires crossed.

Then Mark had to focus on the here and now as more ghouls came for him.

A few got past him and he heard the woman cry out in fear behind him. She backed away and when she turned to run, she tripped over some debris scattered on the sidewalk. As she went forward, her arms were at her sides and her forehead connected with the stone curb, knocking her into unconsciousness immediately.

Mark spun then, realizing there was no way he could stop them all, so he turned and dashed back to the woman.

A zombie was bending over her, looking like it was about to take a bite out of the back of her neck when Mark kicked it in the side of the head. The ghoul fell over, its face smashing onto the pavement, flattening its nose and pulverizing its facial features.

Mark reached down and scooped the woman up in his arms, feeling how light she was. It was like she hadn't eaten in a week, and as he caught a close up glimpse of her face, he saw this was so as her cheeks were drawn and her skin was pale from lack of nourishment.

Three more ghouls came at him and he swung the pipe at two of them, the tip catching a cheek and a forehead. But the minor wounds meant nothing to the attacking dead and Mark began to backpedal.

He shoved two aside and began running, his hollow breath echoing in his chest. He ran for two blocks, each corner he turned giving him more distance from his pursuers. For whatever reason, he was lighter on his feet than they were.

Across the next street was a hotel, and Mark headed for it, kicking in the large front door and slamming it closed before the first ghoul had rounded the bend in the road to see him enter.

Hunched down low, he risked a peek over the window frame of the door, and as he watched, the hordes of undead ran past the hotel. A man who looked healthy was in the street and he was caught flatfooted by the zombies.

Mark watched helplessly as the crowd of undead swarmed over him, running him down like a pack of wolves. They dove in with teeth and nails, tearing the body into pieces.

By the time the dead had left to continue their search for their lost prey, there was nothing left of the hapless man but a large pool of blood and a chewed up shoe.

In seconds, the last zombie shambled to the end of the street, turned the corner and was gone, leaving the street deserted once more.

Mark glanced down at the woman he placed on the floor after kicking in the door and closing it, and now he reached under her and picked her up once more.

He carried her to the main desk where he picked a key for a room at random, then used the stairs to take her to the second floor.

Upon entering the room, he used his left foot to close the door and laid her gently on the bed.

As he gazed down at her, he saw she was a pretty thing. Early twenties, soft brown hair and long lashes. Her breasts were rising and falling with each breath she took and though there was an admiration in his heart for this fine looking specimen of femininity, there was no arousal.

Of course, when he remembered he had no penis, it certainly helped to douse any flames of desire that may have sparked within him.

He sat down on the bed next to her, quietly watching her sleep.

She didn't move for an hour before she finally stirred.

With a low moan she opened her eyes, and when she saw him, complete with hat, sunglasses, and over coat, she gasped and jumped up, trying to pull away from him. She went as far as the head board before there was nowhere else to go.

"Who are you?" she asked softly, her eyes wide with fear. "Are you going to hurt me?"

"I'm the guy who saved you," he replied. His voice was gravelly and he didn't recognize it as his own. He'd forgotten the last time he'd spoken aloud other than when he'd yelled at her in the street.

"Oh, I, uhm, I guess I owe you my thanks then," she said.

"Uh-huh, I guess so," Mark said.

They made small talk for a few minutes, the woman filling Mark in on what had happened and how the entire town had become zombie central. This was when he found out her name was Lisa.

Mark listened quietly, asking a few questions now and then, but for the most part just letting her talk. Finally, she pointed to his sunglasses and scarf, the latter covering the bottom portion of his face.

"So why are you wearing that scarf and glasses? Is there something the matter with you?"

He shrugged, and as he did this something popped in his shoulder. He remembered his shoulder check with the zombies.

"You could say that."

"Well, I don't care how you look. You saved my life. I'm very grateful. Please, let me see your face. I want to see the face of the man who was such a hero. The way you attacked those zombies was pretty cool."

He nodded, deciding there was really no reason for more pretenses. Either he showed her what he looked like or he should just leave now.

Slowly, he raised his hands to his face, and with each hand, he grasped sunglasses and scarf at the same time.

"Okay, don't be scared now, I won't hurt you," he said softly.

"I know that," Lisa smiled. "You're my hero."

He chuckled, the sound like crackling paper. "Now that's the corniest thing I've heard in quite a while."

She shrugged herself. "Maybe so, but it's the truth."

So with one last look at her, Lisa nodding for him to do it, he took off the facial coverings.

Lisa gasped when she saw his features, the same features the walking dead wore out on the street. As she jumped off the bed, she tripped over her feet and fell heavily to the floor, whacking her head on the bedside table.

"Lisa!" he cried out and went around to her. Her left arm had fallen over her head and the other was under her body.

Carefully, like she was made of fine China, he lifted her up and set her down on the bed again.

After covering her up, he checked her pulse and was satisfied it was strong.

He slid off his gloves so he could feel her pulse better, and as he fixed her pillow and hair, his hand came away with blood on it. She had a small cut on her scalp thanks to the side table.

As he loomed over her, he looked at the blood on his fingers, and before he could stop himself, he touched the tips of his coated fingers to his tongue, tasting the blood like a man testing a Marinara sauce.

As the plasma slid down his throat, he felt something he couldn't explain, a tingling to his extremities.

He stared at his fingers for a moment and then tried an experiment. Reaching down, he stuck his fingers into the wound on her skull and when his hand came back coated in warm blood, he licked it off his hands like a fat man at an all-you-can-eat rib joint.

As he lapped up the blood, his body began to feel energized, more alive than ever before since he was changed.

His hearing grew better, vision was sharper, and his shoulder ceased to bother him.

As he glared down at the unconscious woman, he came to an epiphany, one that the other ghouls he'd battled in the street must have already figured out.

Human blood was life to the undead.

As he leaned over her, his mouth opening wide so he could taste her, Lisa's voice floated in his head, the words she'd said upon waking the first time coming to the forefront of his mind. *"You're not going to hurt me, are you?"*

"Oh, no, my dear, I won't hurt you," he whispered as his teeth grew closer to her throbbing jugular. "But I may *eat* you a little."

REVENGE

The small house in the Midwest sat nestled within the confines of modern day suburbia, but unknown to its occupants, Death was about to collect a debt far past due.

Jacob Masters snapped awake, his tired gaze trying to penetrate the darkness. His eyes were crusty from sleep and drool coated his bottom lip. The left side of his face had wrinkles pressed into his flesh from the sheet, attesting to how deep his slumber truly was.

He sucked in a breath, the sound loud to his ears, and he could feel his heart beating quicker, as if he was a wild animal sensing something was amiss.

His left hand slowly reached out to feel for his wife beside him, but he found the bed empty.

He was about to call out to her when a voice—one he knew well—spoke up from the corner of the room.

"She's in the living room," the voice hissed. "Don't worry, you'll be seeing her soon."

"What the fuck are you doing here? How'd you find me?" Jacob asked, his heart beating faster, if it was possible. His body filled with adrenalin and he unconsciously gripped the sheets, pulling the ends from the sides of the bed.

"How'd I find you? Well, that's easy, the internet is a magical thing, isn't it? The same thing you used to hurt me is now you're undoing. And I think we both know what I'm doing here. I owe you for all the shit you did to me for the past few years."

A small flashlight snapped on and Jacob blinked, trying to see through the glare.

"Do you mind?" he said, trying to sound confident, but deep inside he was terrified. If this man was here, and had come all the way across the United States to find him, to then break into his home in the middle of the night…well, it wasn't because he wanted to have coffee and catch up.

Jacob sat up straighter, painfully aware all he had on was his underwear. He felt exposed, even in the gloom of the room. The flashlight never wavered, his eyes blinded by the glare. "You need to leave now," Jacob said in as calm a voice as he could muster. "This is breaking and entering. This is some serious shit you've done. Before, it was all talk, but now…this is serious," he said again.

The man chuckled low in his throat, the noise more feral than human. "Serious? Oh, my friend, you don't know how fucking serious this is. You think what you did to me was nothing, just a bunch of words, shit said randomly, but I'm here to tell you that's the farthest thing from the truth." He took a step forward, his breathing now heavier as anger filled him. "Some things can't be taken back, some things can cut so deep, can scar someone so much, that they never, and I mean fucking *never*, let it go!"

"So what now? Are you gonna yell at me? Tell me how mad you are?" Jacob was feeling braver now, more confident. He knew the man was a blowhard, would rant on and on about how he was unhappy, how Jacob had wronged him, but in the end it would come to nothing. Right then, Jacob knew whatever was going on, whatever twisted ideas the man had for actually breaking into his home, would be for nothing.

In the end, Jacob would call the police and the man would pay for this intrusion. And the next day, when the world found out about what the man did, his reputation would be ruined, and he would go to prison for home invasion on top of it. Just as Jacob had hoped to ruin him, this would be even sweeter.

The man walked over to the bedroom door leading to the hall and flicked on the light. White light filled the bedroom and Jacob blinked, surprised that after being exposed to the glare of the flashlight, his eyes still needed to adjust.

Jacob was about to say something when he saw two things at the same time. The first was the man's right hand held a revolver and the second was the knife on his hip, the blood dripping from the bottom of the sheathe, a hole in the leather letting it free. There had to be a lot of blood in that sheathe, on that blade, for blood to drip out of it like that.

"Get up," the man said. "I want to show you something. You want to know how far I took this? How far I was willing to go to make sure you paid for your crimes against me?" He gestured with the gun. "One wrong move, one twitch I don't like, and I promise you I will fucking kill you." The man leaned forward slightly. "Look into my eyes, Jacob, and tell me you don't believe me."

Jacob did as the man said and his heart stopped for a moment. All he saw there was hatred, and as he looked at the man's face, he saw small red spots covering it, then he saw more on his neck and shirt. His gaze went down to the man's shoes and he saw splatter there as well; dark globules still congealing, stating they were relatively fresh.

"Get up and go into the living room. Move!"

Jacob did as he was told, the chill air caressing his exposed skin. As goosebumps appeared on his arms, he began to walk through his house. The man followed behind, his footsteps silent. Jacob let his eyes play over the photos on the wall of the hallway. There was one with his wife and their two children. They had been lucky, having a boy and a girl, so had stopped at two. Now their children were three and five years old, perfect ages for his perfect family.

As he walked into the living room, he saw the lights were on. All seemed as it should be until he walked around the couch and looked down. The instant his eyes saw her, he knew she was dead. There was no way she could be alive. He gasped and spun to face his intruder, at the same time knowing he was going to turn and run to his fallen wife.

"I wouldn't, asshole. I can squeeze this trigger long before you can reach me." The man gestured to the body on the floor. "Go, see to her."

"Bastard, you fucking bastard!" Jacob yelled as he turned and went to his wife. "She did nothing to you!"

She was dead, her throat slashed from ear to ear. Her eyes were still open, glazed over in death, her tongue protruding from her mouth. It had been bitten in half when she died. Her hands were curled into fists, each an inch deep in the blood-soaked carpet.

The once tan shag was now almost black with spilled blood. Jacob cradled his wife in his arms and cried, the loss, anger and fear welling up inside him. He wanted to kill the man, wanted to shove his gun down his throat and pull the trigger. He knew he would, too, if given the chance.

The feud between the two of them had been going on for years, a back and forth that seemed to never end. Though Jacob had never thought it would become physical, perhaps that was why he'd instigated it for so long, feeling safe with only words. But now, with his slain wife in his arms, he realized that what was said could have a deadly impact on his reality.

The man stood silent in the corner of the room, making sure he was far enough away from Jacob in case he tried anything. Jacob wanted to jump up and run at the man, but knew it would be futile, and besides, he had his children to think about, sleeping in their rooms, not knowing their mother was now dead, slain by a madman out for revenge.

The man waited a full ten minutes as he watched Jacob suffering on the floor, crying over his dead wife.

"Just so you know, I raped her before I killed her."

Jacob's eyes went wide at that. She was in her nightgown still, the lace see-thru, and underneath she wore nothing.

"I fucked her in the ass, and you know what? I think she liked it."

Jacob couldn't stand it any more and he jumped up, ignoring his wife's head falling from his lap. "You motherfucker, I'll kill you!" He began crossing the room.

The gun clicked in the man's hand as it was cocked. "One more step and you're dead." The voice was calm, in control. Something in its tone caused Jacob to stop walking, something said if he *did* take another step, he would be killed.

He stopped, trembling with rage.

"Good, that's very good. I wouldn't want the fun to end so quickly. I want you to suffer, like you made me suffer. It's payback time, pally boy and I'm gonna make sure you get everything you have comin' to you."

Jacob was still shaking in anger, the rage, loss, grief, all fighting for dominance of his soul. If only he could reach the man and kill him.

The man gestured to the hallway again. "Go check on your kids, after all, shouldn't they had woken up with all this yelling going on?"

A light went off over Jacob's head upon realizing the man was correct.

He'd been screaming at the top of his lungs, surely his children should have been woken by the noise. With panic filling his chest, he turned and ran to the children's bedroom, the man following close behind.

All thoughts of dashing into one of the adjacent rooms and slamming the door closed went out the window as Jacob thought of his offspring. His safety was forgotten, his dead wife was forgotten, only his children mattered.

The door was partially ajar and he pushed it open, turning on the light as he entered the bedroom. The room was large with a bed on each side. The children were young and for now were sharing a room.

When he stepped inside, he slipped on something and fell heavily, the light coming on at the exact same moment. As he fell to the floor, his eyes took in the Rorschach splashed walls, crimson still dripping in dark rivulets.

He landed hard, the breath leaving his chest as he grunted. He was up an instant later, rolling onto his side as he crawled to his little girl's bed.

He screamed.

She was dead, there was no question about it. Her arms and legs had been cut off, as if she'd been drawn and quartered. Her tiny organs had been scattered across the bed as if for inventory, and her face and hair—all covered in blood—was propped in the middle, set up like a dime store statue.

"Oh God, oh my God!" Jacob screamed, as he called out his child's name.

"Don't forget the boy," the man said from the doorway.

Jacob spun and gasped again, feeling as if he was going to faint. His son's bed was awash in dark plasma as well, his small frame gutted from groin to neck. The ribcage had been cracked and the heart was cut out, where it had been shoved into the boy's mouth. The small blue eyes were glazed over in death and Jacob fell to the floor, the unbearable loss simply too much to handle.

How does a man handle his entire family being slaughtered like so much cattle? How does a man handle retribution being delivered to his family, when deep down, he knew it was all on him? His crimes were the result of this, his actions, and though he hated the man before him for all he was worth, deep down, where no man wants to delve, he knew this was all his fault, he'd pushed the man too far.

"Why?" Jacob cried? "Why would you do this? How could you do this? You're a fucking monster, you hear me, a fucking monster!"

The man chuckled, as if Jacob's pain was nothing, as if instead of standing in the middle of a charnel house, he was leaning against an oak tree in the public park.

"A monster you say? Perhaps, but you made me this way, Jacob. You couldn't let things go, could you? You had to keep on going, adding fuel to the fire. And the funny part was there was no way to stop you. All you had to do was keep talking, to keep creating lies, and as far as you were concerned, it could go on forever. Well, guess what, pally boy. What you do and say matters in the real world, and I've decided not to take any more of your shit." He gestured to the mangled little girl and licked his lips. "By the way, your wife was sweet, but I have to say, your daughter was even sweeter. She died a woman, you know."

There was a small wooden baseball bat near his son's bed and Jacob didn't let on that he'd spotted it. He remembered clearly when he'd bought it for his son. His boy was only two at the time but the bat was on sale, and he knew his son would be a ballplayer one day.

He'd taken it home after paying with his credit card and his wife had shaken her head, wondering what her husband's obsession with baseball really was all about.

As the man talked, Jacob saw the gun being waved around. The man liked to talk with his hands and the gun barrel waved up and down, side to side, as if it was an extension of his arm.

At the right moment, Jacob went into action, reaching for the wooden bat, jumping up, and preparing to charge the man, to get revenge for his family, to kill the man who had taken everything he held dear, leaving him with nothing to live for.

Jacob barely made it to his feet when the gun went off, the bullet crossing the distance between him and the man in less than a second. As the bullet struck Jacob's heart and pulverized it, the man shook his head, mumbling about how he had wanted Jacob to suffer more before killing him.

The man was already unbuckling his belt and unzipping his pants before the report of the gun faded. Dead or alive, he would have his final revenge.

There were no last thoughts for Jacob, there was no life flashing before his eyes, only darkness.

SURVIVAL OF THE FITTEST

The city was nothing but a blasted out ruin of its former glory.

For more than six months the dead walked and the world would never be the same again.

Rodney was one of the few remaining survivors of the human race. This city had been his home and he'd be damned if he would let the walking dead chase him away from it.

So like others hiding here and there, he rummaged through the remnants of a dead city in search of food and supplies, all the while on guard for the dead which now roamed the streets like rats.

Moving from the burned out wreckage of a mini-van to the shattered hulk of an SUV, Rodney slowly made his way down 22nd Street.

Earlier in the week he'd ran into a few fellow survivors. While the two men and one woman wouldn't let him join their group, they did share some information with him and that info was that there was a relatively untouched convenience store on 22nd Street, filled with bottles of soda, cigarettes and canned and boxed food.

The large front glass window was still intact and only the lock on the door had been jimmied. The small group had been there and had then left with as much food as they could carry. For though the store was a find, it was in a heavily populated area of walking dead, and to stay there would have been tantamount to suicide.

Once the dead knew where you were it wasn't long before there were dozens, then hundreds, then thousands trying to reach you.

Picking his way through the rubble, Rodney soon arrived at the convenience store.

His rifle was ready in case there was trouble and a machete hung at his hip for more silent work, but for the most part the street was quiet and he was alone and relatively safe.

But he knew that could change at a second's notice.

At the end of the street, he could see a few shambling corpses meandering about like homeless people once did, but they hadn't spotted him yet. He planned on disappearing before they did.

As he opened the door and stepped into the convenience store, a tinkling of a bell chimed his arrival.

He almost expected to see some Indian fellow pop up from behind the counter and welcome him into the store. But there was no one there of course, nothing but a thin layer of dust.

As he moved through the aisles, gathering food, he couldn't help but smile slightly.

Though there was no reason to be happy in the world he now existed in, he'd learned fast to appreciate the little things in life, such as having food and drink at hand.

It was amazing what the human mind could adapt to if it wanted to survive. There was a plastic basket on the floor and he used this to drop supplies into as he ate a few candy bars and drank greedily from a can of Coke at the same time. He was still hungry but it took the edge off for now.

Once done, he headed for the front of the store. He planned on returning after he'd stashed his supplies, and as he passed the counter he almost felt like he should toss a few bucks onto the counter top so he wouldn't be accused of stealing.

But of course that was silly. The morals of right and wrong weren't the same as a few months back. Rodney had already done things to survive he would never have imagined possible a year ago.

With one last glance at the empty place, he exited the store, making sure to close the door behind him. With luck, when he returned the next day the store would still be untouched. And with so few remaining Homo sapiens left in the city, he was confident this would be the way of it.

But where the street had been empty when he had entered the store, now there were five zombies coming straight for him. These were the ones he'd seen at the end of the street. Cursing his carelessness for being observed, he made a mental note to be more observant and stealthy in the future.

Though he wanted to just run away from the five ghouls, he knew once they had his scent they would follow him for blocks, so he decided to let off a little aggression and take them down.

His rifle wasn't his first choice to use, as it was too noisy, so instead he set it down with the basket of food and reached for his machete.

Hefting the blade, enjoying the feel of it, he moved towards the zombies.

The first wasn't much of a threat by herself as she was only twelve. The dead girl wore a dirty pink sweater and a dress that went to her knees. She'd been pretty once and Rodney had no doubt all the young boys would have had a crush on her.

But now she was only death walking, and as he moved up to her, the girl opening her mouth wide and hissing, he brought the machete down in an overhand chop that had it splitting her head almost in twain.

The blade was halted in the middle of her face, just above her nose. Her arms were flailing as Rodney tried to pull the machete out of its bone prison with little success. Looking over his shoulder, he saw the remaining four ghouls heading right towards him and he knew only speed would see him through this without harm.

Deciding the machete was in there good, he pushed the dead girl to the street, then stepped on her chest. With leverage now, he yanked up, the machete coming free with a crunch and gobbets of gore and ichor were tossed across the rubble.

The girl was down for good now and he turned to face his next opponent, a geriatric Chinese man with wisps of white hair fluttering in the breeze. He was so ancient at first Rodney wondered if the man wasn't a zombie, but was perhaps pretending, but when the old man looked at him, Rodney could see the same milky white eyes he had come to hate.

With a yell of revulsion, Rodney slashed at the old man's face then spun the machete around and jabbed it into the ghoul's left eye. The milky white orb was pierced and the blade slid deeper as the ghoul danced like a puppet.

Using his foot again, he kicked the old zombie to the street, the machete sliding out of the eye socket. Metal grated on bone and he cringed, the sound filling him with something like when a teacher scrapes her fingernails against a chalkboard.

With the old man now down, he ran a few feet away to give himself some clearance and then turned to face the last three zombies,

The third was a middle aged man wearing a t-shirt with a picture of a clenched fist and the words. **Want an Irish Kiss?** printed in bold letters. He had a beer belly and a balding pate and his face was almost entirely gone, only the red and black of the underlying rotting tissue prevalent. Insects and flies crawled about the ghastly wound, feeding on the walking corpse.

Disgusted, Rodney ran at the zombie and slashed with his machete, taking off the ghoul's right hand at the wrist. No sooner did he do this then he was slashing at the remaining hand, both dropping to the street to lay forgotten.

Ichor seeped from the jagged stumps but the ghoul wasn't deterred in the slightest.

Rodney took a step backwards as the other two zombies moved on him and he scrambled over a pile of rubble.

When he was in a clear area again, he picked up a three foot piece of rebar out of a pile of shattered reinforced cement, and with a grin, waited for the bald zombie to climb over the rubble.

When the zombie was halfway to him, it slipped and tumbled down the incline to sprawl at Rodney's feet. Pleased with his good fortune, Rodney raised the rebar and brought it down hard, the tip of the metal piercing the forehead and into the brain within. Twisting the rebar, he made sure the zombie was out of action, then turned to face the last two ghouls who had simply walked around the pile of rubble instead of trying to climb over it like their unfortunate brother.

The next zombie was a young woman in her twenties, or had been. She was naked as the day she was born. Even in death, with wounds and bite marks across her body, he could see she was an attractive woman. Her pendulous breasts, now pale, with veins prominent in them, swayed as she walked, and her dark mound of pubic hair had small insects crawling around between the follicles. Her hips were curved and her abdomen was flat, muscles hard and tight. Her blonde hair, once perfectly groomed, was now a matted and tangled mess of gore where flies and other flying creatures swarmed and lived.

But despite this she was still beautiful.

Her cheekbones were high and her eyes were wide, though the deep blue had long faded to white. She had a perky nose and manicured eyebrows and Rodney imagined her on a runway somewhere, strutting around wearing today's latest fashions.

Or was that yesterday's latest fashions?

She was the first of the duo of the two zombies arriving, and behind her, the dead frame of what had once been a male soldier, complete with bloody fatigues.

He couldn't help but wonder if she wasn't a mindless corpse, if she was still capable of reasoning power, just what she would think of her present predicament, walking around the city naked for all to see her goodies.

He could only hope if he ever ended up as one of the walking dead that he would at least have a little more dignity.

To walk around to the end of the time with your ass hanging out, now there's a sobering thought.

Well, whoever she had been in life and no matter how she looked, now she was the enemy who would rip him apart and feed on him if given half the chance.

Raising the machete, Rodney moved to meet her and took her head off with one powerful swing. It was something he was wont to try, but today he felt over confident.

The blade sliced through the dry skin and sinew like a hot knife through butter and her head bounced away like a run away soccer ball to land on its side in a pile of rocks. A geyser of black blood shot up and out of the jagged neck stump catching the light of the day.

Idly, he was always amazed at this result whenever he took off a limb. If the zombies were truly dead, then how could blood still pump through arteries and veins now immobile? For blood to pump a heart needed to be beat and if so, would that mean the dead weren't truly dead?

These and other ruminations were cut short when the dead soldier came at him. If the soldier was bothered that Rodney had destroyed his woman sidekick, he gave no sign, his face filled with the same blank stare.

Rodney knew he needed to finish this fast. He'd been in the area too long already. With the commotion they were making, it was just a matter of time until more of the dead things made their way to his location.

The soldier growled low in his throat and lunged for him, but Rodney stepped nimbly aside and swung the machete. The blade took the dead man's left hand off at the wrist, more black blood shooting out like a garden hose set to high.

Laughing a little with the ease of the battle, Rodney grew overconfident, and when the soldier turned to attack again- unfazed at the loss of the limb- Rodney swung the machete again.

The blade sank into the zombie's upper arm, but instead of slicing clean through, Rodney's blow wasn't powerful enough and the blade became lodged in bone.

A look of panic came across his face, and as he tried to decide what he should do, the solider reached out and wrapped pale fingers around Rodney's throat with his one remaining hand.

The dead man was bigger than him and the hand squeezed around Rodney's neck like a vice as the fingers sunk deep into his throat, causing him to see spots of yellow and white.

And then, to Rodney's shock, the zombie began to lift him into the air, his feet now dangling a few inches off the rubble strewn ground.

Rodney let go of the handle of the machete and both his hands went to the arm now holding him in thrall as the other, handless arm, seemed to be punching his abdomen. With each blow a black stain was left behind and

Rodney could smell the foul stink of the viscous fluid that was considered blood for the zombie.

Rodney became filled with panic as he tried to suck in one more mouthful of air, but the grip on his throat was too strong and he felt himself blacking out.

In that brief flash of an instance between losing consciousness, he heard the report of a powerful gun and watched the zombie's head explode, like a stick of dynamite had been shoved into its ear and then lit.

He felt his face and arms sprayed with bone fragments and gray matter, the wet slapping sound filling his ears and a feeling of disgust as the gore caressed his skin, but then he slid into the dark void of oblivion and knew no more.

"Hey, buddy, you all right? Come on, man, get the hell up. We have to get outta here."

Rodney heard the words as if he was in a long tunnel and the speaker was at the opposite end from his location. The voice was also muffled, like the owner was under a blanket or pillow.

Rodney's eyes fluttered and he parted them a bit, still groggy from losing consciousness, and at first he didn't understand where he was or what had happened. But then his eyes took in the shape of a man standing over him and his eyes went wide, fearing a zombie had snuck up on him.

Rolling to the side and reaching out with his hands to get to his feet, his right hand sank up to the wrist in the remains of the soldier zombie. The cool brains felt like cold spaghetti under his palm and he yanked his hand back with revulsion, the taste of bile already touching the back of his tongue.

The man standing over him knelt down and placed a comforting hand on his shoulder.

"Easy there, partner, just slow down, you're safe for the moment."

"You, you can talk?" Rodney said as he shook his hand clear of brown and black goop.

"Sure can, why, that something new ta ya?"

"No, I…uhm, what I mean, I thought you were one of them, you know, dead. It's just, I haven't seen another living person in a while and…" Rodney drifted off then stopped, realizing he was rambling.

"Same goes for me, too. You're the first live human I've seen in quite a spell." He held out his hand to Rodney who was still sprawled on the ground. "Names, Jed, Jed Manners."

Rodney reached out to take the proffered hand and realized he was going to use the one covered in brain bits, so he quickly switched and shook the hand with his clean one.

"Rodney."

Jed motioned if Rodney wanted help getting up, and with a nod from Rodney, Jed yanked him to his feet. Jed was a large man with wide shoulders and a beer belly. He had a hard face with a few days worth of stubble and a scar on his chin, looking so old he may have received it when he was a child. Rodney had never been a good judge of age, but Jed appeared to be in his late sixties or early seventies.

A low moan carried on the wind and Jed glanced over his shoulder to see the shapes of zombies as they worked their way through the rubble.

"Damn, there's more of 'em. Look, buddy, it's time to vamoose from here. I got a place a few blocks over, it ain't pretty but it's served me well for a while now. If you want, you can come with me, stay for dinner. I've got plenty of food, meat, too. After that we can take it a second at a time."

Rodney could see the shapes as well and knew it was time to leave. With nowhere else to go and glad to see another living being, he agreed.

"Oh, wait, I got some food, too," Rodney said as he went to retrieve his basket from the convenience store.

Jed slapped Rodney's back jovially, turned, and headed off, Rodney following right behind after he picked up his rifle, the food and machete. As they moved through the wreckage, Rodney saw a few more fresh corpses scattered about the street that weren't there before. Evidently while he was out cold, Jed had done some cleaning up. The man had protected him, had watched over him, a perfect stranger. That wasn't at all what he would have expected. Since the dead began to walk, most people had become even more selfish, especially as food supplies and the power had dissolved.

Rodney's stomach was growling even more now in anticipation of eating meat.

He assumed it would be rat or cat, as most of the dogs were long gone or had been eaten by man or the dead.

Still, it had been days since he'd eaten anything he could call a *true* meal. Which of course had him imagining what Jed had waiting for them back at his hideout. Rodney imagined cans of fruit, beef stew and chili as well.

Boxes of juice and maybe even bottles of beer. He would kill for a bottle of beer, Hell, he'd drink it warm, wouldn't matter at all.

Jed led him deeper into the city, the man not talking, his eyes alert for danger.

Every now and then a zombie would pop up from an alleyway or from behind a car or truck, but either Jed would shoot it down or they would simply outrun it.

In no time Jed slowed at a destroyed building with a crumbling façade. A few destroyed cars and a bread truck lay scattered on the street like giant Matchbox cars left by a bored child at the end of playtime.

Jed pushed a large piece of plywood aside and gestured for Rodney to enter first. There had been a small piece of red brick on the top of the plywood, wedged between the building and the edge. Jed had studied this before moving the wood.

Rodney hesitated, looking at Jed. The gaping hole in the building the plywood had hidden was so black it resembled a massive pool of ink and his mind raced with what might be waiting for him on the other side.

"Go on, there's nothin' in there that's gonna bite ya. This piece of wood and the brick was right where I left it."

Rodney nodded, understanding immediately. If the brick had been moved or wasn't in the exact same spot as before, Jed would've known someone had been inside his sanctuary.

Rodney, now more confident, nodded and entered the hole, Jed directly behind him. As Rodney shuffled a few feet away from the hole, his eyes adjusted to the gloom and he realized he could see what little there was to see. But then Jed entered and pulled the plywood back over the hole, thus blocking out what light had been seeping in.

Rodney felt his heart flutter in panic, the darkness not his friend, but then Jed flicked a match and the darkness was banished once more. The man grabbed a makeshift torch from a barrel set to the side of the hole and lit it, the flame like a miniature sun as it filled the area around Rodney with yellow light.

With the darkness banished, Rodney saw he was in an underground parking garage, complete with vehicles still parked where their owners had left them. The only difference now was the inch layer of dust coating each car and truck like a blanket.

"This way, right this way," Jed said and moved off, walking comfortable, a man who knew he was safe in his own home.

Rodney followed, the rifle slung over his back and the machete still in his hand, but now forgotten. If anything came out and tried to jump him, both he and Jed could deal with it easily.

Jed weaved through the maze of cars until he came to a small camper parked in the middle of the deserted lower level. The top of the camper was inches from the ceiling of the garage and Rodney mused at how the owner must have been biting his nails in worry as he'd driven through the entrance to the garage.

"Here we are, home sweet home," Jed grinned and opened the side door to the camper. "After you."

Rodney nodded, not worried in the least as he moved to enter the camper. And why would he be? Jed had saved his life after all. If the man had meant him harm, there'd been a hundred places where he could have attempted it, not the least of which was when Rodney was sprawled on the ground unconscious.

So when the blow to the back of his skull filled his vision with white light and he went head first onto the top stair of the camper, his mind's only thought was why this was happening, because every reason why made no sense. Jed conking him on the head was irrational.

And that was the thought he took into the darkness as his mind tumbled back into the void.

Rodney didn't know how much time had passed, but it felt like more than an hour and less than a day, as he slowly came back to consciousness for the second time in what was a matter of hours.

When he tried to sit up, he realized his arms and legs were tied to something. Turning his head from side to side, he found himself to be on a makeshift platform.

No, not a platform, a door, a wooden door propped up on two saw horses.

A torch burned silently a few feet away, casting a small circle of light around him.

Struggling for a few minutes, he found he wasn't going anywhere, he was stuck.

Looking through his feet, he could see the camper sitting quietly.

So he was still in the parking garage.

Then he remembered being hit and it all came back to him.

Jed.

Jed had knocked him out. But why?

"Hello! Hello, anyone there? Jed? Why am I tied up?"

At first there was no answer, no sound other than his echoing voice. He felt so helpless strapped to the table. A zombie could come out of the shadows and there would be nothing he could do.

And then he saw the camper's weight shifting on its shock absorbers, as if someone was walking inside it, and a muffled voice could be heard.

After another few seconds, he heard the distinct sound of the camper door opening and then footsteps as someone approached him.

No, wait, there were two people approaching him, though the second one seemed to be a wisp of a thing, half the size and shape that was Jed.

Jed seemed to be leading the second shape along, and when the two people reached the edge of the small perimeter of light, Rodney let out a gasp of shock.

Jed was there, of course, but it was what he was leading by a leash that was so startling.

It was one of the dead, a shriveled old thing that even in life would have resembled a zombie.

Jed slowed when he reached Rodney who was even now struggling in vain to get free.

"Momma, this is Rodney, he's come over for dinner tonight," Jed said, his eyes filled with more than a touch of madness.

Rodney could feel a tightness in his bowels and his heart skipped a beat.

"Jed, what's going on here? Let me up, untie me, man, please. And what the hell are you doing with that *thing*?"

Jed's face grew cloudy with anger and he reached over and slapped Rodney on the face.

"That's my mother, damn you, not *thing*, and you best watch your mouth."

Rodney realized Jed wasn't all there and his best chance of getting out of his present predicament was to try and sweet talk the man; gain his trust so he would let him go.

All the while the old woman was straining at the leash, but she was so small and frail she was like a feather in the wind. Rodney also saw she wore a gag so she couldn't bite anyone.

"Okay, sorry, she's your mom. So, what's she doing here?"

Jed smiled then, a manic smile that had Rodney pissing his pants in fear. As Jed spoke, he was removing the gag from his mother's mouth. Then he reached into his pocket, pulled out a pair of dentures and popped them into her mouth with practiced ease.

"Like I just said before, Rodney, you're here for dinner. But I think you misunderstood me. You're not here for your dinner; you're here for Momma's."

And with that he dropped the leash attached to his mother and let her move forward, directly at Rodney who was as helpless as a human could be.

"But if you just wanted to feed me to her then why didn't you just knock me out in the city? Why did you wait till we got back here?"

Jed shrugged. "That's simple, I didn't want to drag you all the way here and I couldn't carry you seems my back is shot. It was easier to just get you to come on your own and then sack you when your back was turned. Now shut up and let Momma eat. She likes peace and quiet, says it's better for the digestion."

Rodney had time for one good scream as he felt the sharp dentures of the old woman tear into his throat. He could feel his blood pumping through his carotid artery and into the old woman's mouth with each beat of his pile-driving heart.

Slowly the pain began to fade as his senses became dulled and he managed to hear Jed one last time as he spoke a few last words to him.

"Sorry, buddy, but it's dog eat dog out there now. Survival of the fittest and all that. I loves my momma somethin' fierce and she's gotta eat. So I gotta…"

Rodney didn't hear the rest of Jed's words, and he never would.

All the while Jed talked, his mother feasted on his now cooling corpse.

And why wouldn't she?

Rodney was a meal fit for a king.

THE AIR ITSELF

"Well that's it, the filters are clogged with ash again," Dr. Frank Mathis said, as he climbed down from inside the ventilation shaft that led to the surface.

"Great, so what do we do now?" Bill Johnson asked as he helped Dr. Mathis off the ladder.

"It's simple, really. We have to do what we've done before. Someone needs to go outside and clean them," Dr. Mathis said.

"But that's a death sentence," another man added.

There were a total of six men gathered around Dr. Mathis and Bill, each with concern clearly written on their faces.

"Yes, I know, but we don't really have a choice now, do we. If we don't get those filters clean, we're all dead anyway. Better one dies than all of us."

"Easy for you to say, Doc," one of the men said. "We all know it won't be you that has to die."

"What do you mean by that? I have as much chance as going as the next man," Dr. Mathis replied.

Bill shook his head. "That's not true, Frank. We can't afford to lose you, and you know it. No matter what, it can't be you who goes up there."

Dr. Mathis frowned as he made eye contact with each of the other men, but he knew Bill was correct. Though he wasn't afraid to do his part, he was the only one of them that knew how the vent and filtration system worked, and if he wasn't around to fix it when it became clogged or needed to be calibrated, then they were all dead.

"Well, that may be true, but if there was anyone else that could do my job, I'd be there like the rest of you," Dr. Mathis said sadly.

"Sure you would," one of the men said under his breath, the sarcasm obvious.

Bill turned and glared at the men, hearing the remark but not who said it. "Shut it, all of you. I want to know who said that." No one answered. "Dr. Mathis is the only reason we've survived for as long as we have. If not for him, the filters would have clogged more than a year ago, and with no way of knowing how to flush and clean the system, we all would've suffocated a long time ago."

"That's easy for you to say, Bill. You're the only one with a woman," one of the men said and Bill saw it was Brad, a twenty-two year old college drop out. Not that it mattered anymore what Brad had done before they all became trapped inside the bunker. Now they were just human beings, no one man better than another.

Bill knew what Brad was talking about instantly. There had been a total of five women in the bunker with them when they had sealed themselves inside it, but through fate or bad luck, four of the women had died. Two had died from pneumonia, one had suffered an accident while preparing a meal and had bled out after severing a major artery, and the last had killed herself, not able to handle the pressure of perhaps spending the rest of her life underground. That left his wife, Sheila, as the last woman in the bunker and for all he knew, the last woman left alive on Earth.

And Bill knew the other men coveted her badly, each one wanting to be with her. After months of being celibate, the men had needs and Sheila was the only one who could fulfill those needs. A few of them had become gay out of necessity, such as in a prison, but most saw Sheila and wanted her for themselves.

So far no one had tried to take her, though Bill saw the way the other men looked at her during meal time. There was a hunger there that no food could fill and it scared him, not for himself, but for the woman he loved.

"That's beside the point at the moment, gentleman," Dr. Mathis said, trying to change the subject. "Nothing else matters but getting those filters clear of ash. As of now, we only have what recycled air is inside the bunker with us and given the amount of people down here, I'd say we have about two days worth of air and by the second day it will be thin at that."

"So someone has to sacrifice themselves again, is that it?" a man asked.

Dr. Mathis nodded. "I'm afraid so. Look, we've been through this before. We don't have a choice in the matter. Either one of us sacrifices himself or we all die. It's as simple as that."

Arguing and angry voices filled the passageway and Bill raised his hands over his head and bellowed loudly, "Enough! That's enough! Christ, what the hell are you yelling about? Look, you can argue all you want but the end result is still going to be the same. One of us dies so the rest can live, end of story. Now, listen, we don't have to decide right now so everyone, please, go back to your quarters and we'll meet in the rec room tomorrow morning. Then we'll decide who is gonna do it."

More grumbling filled the passageway.

Bill lowered his right hand to the .45 pistol on his hip. He was the only one with a gun, the rest of the weapons locked up in the armory and he with the only key, and though he hated it, sometimes it was the threat of the handgun that kept the others in line.

"I said that's enough. Let's not make this any more difficult than it has to be."

A few of the closer men saw where Bill's hand was and could read the hard look in his eyes.

More than a year ago, before they had agreed that Bill would be the leader, there had been an altercation by a small group that wanted to leave the bunker, despite it being suicide. They believed it was safe outside, that the air had cleared, and they wanted to leave.

It got out of control and three hostages had been taken, one of them Dr. Mathis. When the men refused to listen to reason, Bill had shot the leader at point blank range in the face, killing him instantly.

The fight had left the others then and Bill's dominance had been established in blood, and though he had always felt guilty for killing the man, he knew it was the right thing to do.

So when he placed his hand on his .45 now, the men knew what the gesture meant and their voices faltered and they began to disperse. When only Bill and Dr. Mathis remained, the doctor leaned against the wall and rubbed his face with his hands.

"It's getting harder to keep them in line, Bill, you see that don't you?"

"Yeah, I do. Ever since Carol took her life it's been like this."

"Do you ever worry about Sheila? I mean, really worry," Dr. Mathis asked.

"All the time. I see the way they look at her and it fills me with dread, but what can I do?"

"There's nothing you can do," Dr. Mathis said as he turned to walk away. "But I'd be more on guard than ever before. Remember, one of those men is going to be committing suicide tomorrow and I doubt he'll go with a smile. That man will have nothing to lose before he goes."

"What are you saying?" Bill asked.

"I'm saying until those filters are clean, I'd keep an even closer watch on Sheila."

With a nod and a wan smile, Dr. Mathis headed off, his destination the filtration room. The system needed constant monitoring and now with the intake clogged, he needed to shut it down. Now was the perfect time to run a diagnostic check although he would have preferred not to do one. Because the system was down meant another man would have to give up his life and that was always hard to deal with.

Bill watched Dr. Mathis walk away and he sighed heavily as he waited for the man to round the bend in the corridor. He looked up at the hatch leading to the surface and the intake vents, wondering what it was like up there.

He decided it probably wasn't very good, not if the intake filters were choked with ash yet again.

He supposed he shouldn't complain. It had been over seven months since the last time they had been clogged, the longest so far. Seven months ago another of their little group had sacrificed himself and he and every one inside the bunker owed the man a debt that could never be repaid.

Feeling survivor's guilt, but still glad to be alive, he moved off to his quarters, the burden of command weighing heavily on his shoulders.

He knocked twice on the door to his quarters, and a second later, it was opened. Sheila stepped back so he could enter.

"How'd it go?" she asked. She was wearing a bathrobe, her long brown hair covered by a towel wrapped around her head. There were a few drops of water still on her neck and the room smelled of steam. She had taken a shower, one of the few luxuries they had in the bunker thanks to the recycled water.

"Not good," he said as he kissed her cheek. She smelled of soap, clean and natural. The shampoo had run out months ago but there was still a good supply of bar soap. "The filters are clogged again."

She raised her right hand to her mouth and stifled a gasp. "Oh, no, does that mean..."

"Yeah, it does."

"Who is it this time?"

He shook his head. "Don't know yet. We'll draw lots tomorrow morning."

"Will you be there, too?"

"Yes," he said as he took her into his arms. She placed her head on his shoulder. "I have to. I'm no better than anyone else. If they're willing to do it, I have to be, too."

"I know that, of course, it's just..."

He pushed her back a bit so he could look into her eyes. "I know, Sheila, believe me I know. But we don't have a choice. Either one of us goes up there or we all suffocate."

Tears had formed in her eyes and she was doing her best not to cry. Though he was a hard man, he had to admit deep down, he wished he could join her. A good cry would help to relieve the tension he felt. But he had to stay strong; for her and everyone else.

"Look, tomorrow isn't here yet. And we still have the rest of the night."

She wiped her eyes with the back of her hand. "The rest of the night? What do you have planned?"

He smiled mischievously as he slowly opened her robe. It fell to her ankles and she stood before him, her naked body soft and supple.

"For this," he said as he took her into his arms again, their lips meeting, tongues exploring one another's mouths.

Sheila sighed as he kissed her, a slight sniffle all that remained of her tears. Though the next morning would arrive before they knew it, for now they were timeless, lost in the other's embrace, their love making them one soul.

Bill walked into the rec room early the next morning to find he was the last to arrive instead of the first. Apparently, with the fate of one of them on the hook once more, no one could sleep.

All of them were there, sitting around the three tables as they talked and watched news footage taped just before they had gone underground and sealed themselves inside the bunker.

On the television screen, a frazzled news anchor was talking about the global catastrophe that had befallen Earth while behind him, the scenes of devastation were being shown.

Bill leaned against the wall and watched the screen for a few minutes as he remembered what had happened.

No one could have imagined that the Earth would shift slightly on its axis and because of it, volcanoes across the planet erupted, spewing ash into the air to choke the skies.

The ash became so thick that airplanes and motor vehicles wouldn't run, their engines choked by the ash, and to breathe for more than a minute without an oxygen mask was death. Rebreathers were useless as the filters clogged in seconds, and before anyone realized how serious it was, people began suffocating on the streets and in their homes as the ash seeped into any structure that wasn't vacuum sealed to be air tight.

Many self-contained buildings were air tight but once their filters clogged, the air stopped circulating and soon the people died. What was amazing was how the ash got into absolutely everything. Even something such as a refrigerator in a home would be opened to find it was filled with ash.

In no time, the entire planet was consumed and with the ash in the atmosphere, it blocked the sunlight and soon all plant life withered and died.

As far as Bill knew, his small enclave was all that remained, but he was confident there had to be more survivors scattered across the globe, for to imagine there wasn't was to bring on hopelessness.

The bunker he was in had a self-cleaning filter system for the air, but even that wasn't enough to keep it clean forever, for the ash was too heavy and persistent. And every so many months, due to no fault of theirs, the filters had to be cleaned manually.

But there were no hazmat suits to be worn if someone needed to leave the bunker, just one of many oversights when it had been stocked quickly as the ash filled the sky.

So someone would have to go outside without one, and by the time they finished cleaning the filters, they would be gasping for air, their lungs coated with soot, a death sentence if there ever was one.

Bill walked over, turned off the television, then turned to look at everyone and said, "All right, that's enough of that. Let's get this done. No use putting it off."

"How are we going to do it this time?" a man asked.

Dr. Mathis stood up. "We'll draw lots, just like before. I've already taken the liberty of preparing straws. The short straw is the one that goes."

"Here," Bill said to Dr. Mathis. "Give them to me, I'll hold them."

Dr. Mathis handed them to Bill and he placed them in his hand, closing it. He looked at them sticking out of his hand and cringed, knowing one straw in there would doom one of them to death, but save the others.

"Okay, line up and each man pick one," Bill said.

Each man did as instructed and soon, one at a time, each man pulled a straw from Bill's tightly squeezed hand.

Bill looked each man in the eye and nodded, knowing that each one picked could be the fatal straw.

It went quickly and by the third to last man, the fatal straw was found.

Bill opened his hand to see that the remaining straws were all long. Ernie, a middle-aged, balding man, had picked the short straw.

Ernie stared at the straw, his eyes wide at the revelation that it was him who was going to give his life so the others would live. The other men all walked up to him, shaking his hand and patting his back, thanking him for his sacrifice, the mood solemn. But when Bill walked up to Ernie to give him his thanks, Ernie snapped, tripped Bill and pulled Bill's gun from its holster. Bill was dazed, his head striking the floor as he went down hard.

Cries of worry filled the room, each man not understanding what Ernie was doing.

"What the hell, Ernie, give that back!" a man yelled as he took a step towards him.

"Stay back, Mike, don't come any closer or so help me I'll shoot you," Ernie warned the man.

"What? Why?" Mike asked.

"Because I'm not going out there, I won't do it!"

Another man spoke up. "But, Ernie, you picked a straw like the rest of us and you lost."

Ernie shook his head as sweat beaded on his forehead. "I know that but I didn't think I would actually get the short one."

Bill was coming awake now and was slowly realizing what was happening.

Mike took another step towards Ernie and said, "Just give me the gun, Ernie. No one has to get hurt here."

Another man was sneaking up on Ernie from behind, his mouth open slightly as he concentrated on remaining silent.

"I'm warning you, stay back. I'll shoot, I swear," Ernie warned Mike once more.

Ernie realized there was someone behind him and he spun, saw the man reaching for him and in his panic, he fired. The bullet went right into the open mouth of the man, blowing out the back of his head. Brains and skull fragments painted the wall red as bits of brain slid down the surface like dead snails. As the man toppled to the floor, dead, the rec room erupted into chaos.

Some of the men jumped at Ernie after seeing what he'd done while a few others tried to run away.

Bill, seeing what was happening and knowing Ernie had lost it, turned and ran for the armory, knowing the only way to stop the unstable man was to put him down with a bullet.

Three men came at Ernie but none of them reached him. One at a time, Ernie shot each one in the face or torso. Blood now covered the floor, making standing or running treacherous, and the moans of the dying filled the air.

Ernie was now in full killing mode, his eyes so wide they looked about ready to pop out of his head. He was yelling manically as he shot anyone still standing.

A man had almost reached the doorway to the outer hallway when a round struck him between the shoulder blades. A large hole appeared in his chest as if a fist had been punched through him. With his mouth opening and closing like a landed fish, he slumped to the floor, not understanding why he was dying.

Ernie laughed devilishly and searched for another target. All around him were dead bodies.

Mike moaned loudly on the floor, his right shoulder a mass of blood and bone. Seeing Mike, Ernie walked over to him, placed the muzzle of the gun on Mike's forehead, and squeezed the trigger, blowing out the back of his head.

"Who's next, huh? Who wants to die next?" Ernie screamed as he waved the gun in the air. He caught movement to his right and spotted Dr. Mathis standing stock still, shocked by the violence before him. With a roar, Ernie raised the gun and fired but missed when Dr. Mathis dodged to the right, making a run for the door. A fist-sized piece of plaster was missing thanks to where the bullet hit the wall.

Ernie gave chase, the two men dashing through the curving hallways until Dr. Mathis reached his sanctuary, which was the air filtration room, complete with computer displays, monitors and printouts. This room was where the system was kept functioning, the heart, soul, and brains of the system.

Dr. Mathis dashed into the room and tried to close the door behind him, but a bullet ricocheting off the doorframe caused him to jump back. Ernie kicked the partially open door in and charged into the room.

Dr. Mathis tried to run but he tripped on his own feet. He fell against one of the computers that controlled airflow, his head striking a display of blinking lights.

Ernie laughed at his trapped prey, and with a guttural yell of glee, shot Dr. Mathis in the throat.

The bullet sliced through Dr. Mathis' carotid artery, severing his spine, then continued onward into the computer behind him. In a spray of sparks, the lights blinked faster and went out as blood shot into the bullet hole, saturating the wiring and making sure the machine would be ruined and beyond fixing. Not that there would be anyone with the knowledge to fix it. Dr. Mathis was the only technician and he was now sputtering his last bloody breath on the floor. His eyes glazed over as his right hand reached for Ernie, as if his killer could now somehow save him.

Ernie laughed and leveled the gun, prepared to finish the job.

A loud report filled the room and Ernie's chest disintegrated into a bloody spray of gore. His ribcage erupted outward, the bones fragmenting into razor sharp shards. Heart, lungs and kidneys were blasted into bloody pieces, the visceral mess spraying Dr. Mathis and the nearby computers.

Ernie's face took on one of confusion, and before he could get so much as a scream out in pain, his destroyed lungs robbed him of this and he fell face forward onto the floor, the gun clattering away to end up under a steel table covered in printouts.

Bill stepped into the room, the barrel of the shotgun in his hands still smoking.

Barely acknowledging the twitching body of Ernie, he went to Dr. Mathis to see if he could help him.

It was as he looked into the doctor's eyes that he saw he was too late. The eyes were glazed in death, the blood not pumping out of the gaping neck wound.

His friend was dead, gone, and worse, with him dead, there would be no one to fix the filtration system. Even if Bill went topside to clean the filters, the system wouldn't work.

As he thought this, he looked up at the vent grating on the wall and the small blue ribbon hanging from it. The ribbon hung slack, impotent, thanks to no air flowing through the air shafts.

With his left hand, Bill placed his fingers on Dr. Mathis' eyelids and closed them gently. Then he turned and walked out of the room, stepping over Ernie as he exited.

Upon returning to the rec room, all he found was more death. No man had survived Ernie's wrath—his madness—each one gunned down and murdered.

With nothing else to do, Bill turned and left, closing the door behind him.

Sheila would be worried, probably petrified from hearing all the gunshots.

He needed to tell her he was fine, but also to break the bad news to her. With everyone but him and her left alive and the filtration system destroyed, there could be only one outcome for them.

He didn't know how much time they had left, how much oxygen remained within the bunker, but however much time they had would be spent together, until the last breath was made.

And that's what they did. Bill and Sheila spent the next three days together, never leaving each other's side. They talked and made love and ate whatever they wanted, for food reserves were the least of the troubles. They dined till their stomachs were about to burst and then slept in each other's arms.

Bill woke on the fourth day to find the air was staler than ever. He had to breathe harder as his lungs struggled to pull in what meager oxygen remained in the bunker, and he had a headache to end all headaches.

As he sat up, he felt lightheaded and he knew this would be their last day together. When they went to sleep that night, he had a feeling he and Sheila would never wake up again, deprived of the oxygen they needed to survive.

It was as he looked down on her sleeping form that he decided that wasn't how he wanted to go out. He didn't want to think about him and her lying dead in their bed, the bodies forever sealed in the bunker, a giant tombstone no one would ever know about.

"Sheila, wake up," he said softly, shaking her shoulder. She stirred slightly and it took him four more times before she finally woke up.

"Huh, what? What do you want? Let me sleep, God I'm so tired," she said groggily.

"That's just the lack of oxygen," he said. "It makes you want to sleep."

"Then let me. Bill, there's nothing we can do, you know that. All we can do is accept our fate. The ones who were shot by Ernie were the lucky ones. At least they went quickly."

"No, don't say that. I wouldn't trade this last week with you for anything. At least we got to say goodbye and make our peace."

"Huh, some peace."

"Listen, I've been thinking about something and I want you to join me."

"Go on," she said, her voice slightly stronger in curiosity.

"I want to go topside." He held his hand up to stop her protest. "Wait, hear me out. There's no more oxygen left, it's almost gone. I can barely breathe as it is and I'm lightheaded. This is it, our last day, and I don't want to die down here. Let's go up there one last time. If we're gonna die, then let's do it together on the surface, not down here in this giant coffin."

"But the ash, we'll choke to death when it fills our lungs, it's suicide," she said while sitting up, her adrenalin now flowing.

"It's suicide to stay down here, Sheila and if we're gonna die, if we have no say in it, then let's go for a walk one last time together, like we used to do in the old days."

"I…" she began, but when she looked into his eyes, seeing his resolve, she stopped, nodded, and closed her eyes and said, "Okay, fine, like you said, we don't have a choice." She smiled. "I would like to go for one more walk with you, Bill…outside."

He took her hand. "Well then, there's no time like the present. Let's get dressed."

He helped her stand, and after the dizziness passed, she dressed as did he. They wore their best clothing, as if they were preparing to go to a funeral, and though they didn't discuss it, they both knew they actually were…theirs.

When they had dressed, combed their hair and brushed their teeth, both looking wonderful with the exception of their pale skin from lack of sunlight and their sunken eyes, they headed for the ladder leading to the surface.

"I'll go first," he said to her when they reached the ladder. She nodded and he slowly began to climb. He had to stop more than once and gather his strength from the exertion, the oxygen in the bunker fading fast.

When he reached the underside of the hatch, it took all his might to spin the wheel to release the locking mechanism, and he wasn't able to push it open with his shoulder, plus white spots filled his vision and he thought he was going to faint.

"Are you all right?" Sheila asked from below, holding onto the ladder with her arms wrapped around the iron rungs.

"Yeah, just give me a second to catch my breath for the hundredth time." He looked down at her. "You ready? Once I open the hatch, it won't take long for the ash to clog our lungs."

"Just do it. We've already said our goodbyes."

He nodded and winked at her, she grinning back.

"I love you," he said.

"I love you, too," she replied.

When he felt he was as strong as he possibly could get under the circumstances, he pushed one final time as more white spots filled his vision and he knew in a second he was definitely going to pass out. The hatch cracked and ash flowed inside, the vacuum of the bunker pulling it down like a depressurized airplane in reverse.

He spit the ash from his lips as he pushed the hatch open some more, then began to climb out.

Blinking black soot from his eyes, he wiped his face clean with the back of his hand, and as his eyes cleared, he gasped in shock.

With tears in his eyes he said, "Sheila, come up here, oh my God, you have to see this!" he cried in amazement.

"What is it? What's wrong?" she called, too terrified to climb up and step out of the hatch and be suffocated by the black and gray ash.

"Just come up here, hurry, oh my God! I don't believe it, it can't be true but it is!"

Sheila paused and considered his words. He didn't sound like he was choking, in fact, his voice sounded stronger. With shaking arms and her heart pounding in her chest, she climbed higher, and when her head poked out of the hatch, her mouth fell open and her lightheadedness faded as oxygen flooded her system.

"What? How, it's impossible," she gasped as clean air filled her lungs.

"It's over, Sheila, it's finally over," Bill said and spun in a circle, the ash at his feet stirring slightly but then falling back to the ground. All around him was a sea of ash, but in that ash were small seedlings, the fertile ash now giving forth lush greenery. Overhead, the clear azure sky bathed them in sunshine.

Bill took her hand and smiled as she joined him. There had been ash covering the hatch and that was what had fallen onto his face and hair when he opened it. "Since the last time we had to clean the filters, the volcanoes must have finally ceased spewing ash into the atmosphere. It all finally settled and the sun's back."

"You mean…" she began.

He nodded. "Yes, if we had stayed inside we would have died and all for nothing. Ernie, Dr. Mathis, Mike, and everyone else died for nothing. We could have left the bunker at anytime."

Sheila had tears in her eyes as she looked up at the shining sun, feeling its warmth on her face. "I still can't believe it. So, what do we do now?"

He hugged her tightly and kissed her gently on the lips. "That's simple, we start over."

THE BITCH GETS IT IN THE END

Corporal Greg Saunders and Private Bob Satchel sat down with their trays in the cafeteria as Greg let out a low groan.

"What's the matter?" Bob asked as he placed his silverware next to his tray.

"Look over at the next table and you'll see," Greg said as he did the same thing with his silverware.

Bob looked where Greg was gesturing and let out a groan of his own. "Oh, shit, not her again," he said. "Why the hell did we do to deserve her here?"

Greg nodded as both men watched the woman sitting at the next table eating.

"God, she really looks like a pig when she's eating, doesn't she?" Greg asked.

Bob nodded. "More so than usual. Christ, she's such a cunt, I tell ya. All the people that have died and that fucking bitch is still walking around pushing paper."

Across from them, the obese woman continued to eat from the mound of food she had taken from the serving line. Waffles, pancakes and canned fruit was piled high as the woman shoved mouthful after mouthful into her gaping maw. Bits of food fell out and dropped onto the table and Bob shook his head in disgust. "Christ, it's like she's a giant squirrel and she's trying to store away food for the winter."

As the woman ate, her arms jiggled from side to side. She had to weigh three hundred pounds easy—all of it flab—and her face looked like someone had molded jell-o into the image of a female.

"Shit, I lost my fucking appetite," Bob said.

"Tell me about it," Greg replied. "My God, I swear if I had a choice between fucking Mrs. Tillman and fucking you, I think I'd pick you. And that ain't saying much."

As if she'd heard the two men talking, the woman belched loudly, pushed her tray to the side, and stood up, heaving her enormous bulk from out of her chair. Bob could have sworn the seat sighed with relief as the woman stood up.

She waddled towards the two men, a manila folder under her fleshy arm. When she reached the men, she pulled the folder out and dropped it before them.

Bob forced a smile and said, "Hi, Felicia, how are you today?"

"Yeah, you look pretty today," Greg added, the words tasting like bile in his mouth.

"Cut the shit, both of you," Felicia said as she wavered in front of the men. She could never stand for too long without getting tired. Already, sweat was beading on her neck and back and she was feeling winded. She knew once she returned to her small office, a Twinkie would help her feel better. Or better yet, maybe a Ho-Ho. "And it's Mrs. Tillman to you two assholes."

"Sure, okay. So, Mrs. Tillman…what can we do for you today?"

She pulled out two pieces of paper from the folder. On it was a big red stamp that said **REJECTED.** "It's about this report you filed yesterday, Bob."

"What about it?" he asked.

"What about it? My God, it was terrible. I had to edit it as I read it. Did you know before everything happened I used to be an editor for a small publishing house? Manuscripts used to come by me and if I saw too many mistakes or didn't like them, I got to shitcan them. I had people's dreams in the palm of my hand and I crushed them whenever possible."

"Sounds like a wonderful job," Greg added with a forced smile.

"Quiet, I wasn't speaking to you," Felicia snapped, her jowls shaking like pudding as her head turned. She pointed to the folder. "This report needs to be edited better, Bob. If you can't do it then find someone who will. Maybe you can barter with someone or ask them to do it, or you can pay them later."

"What? Are you serious? Jesus Christ, Felicia, these damn reports are ridiculous as it is. It's a fucking zombie apocalypse out there and you want to bust my balls over some unedited reports?"

"Yes, that's right, I do. We need to keep reports and they need to be properly edited. Now I'll let you off with a warning this time but the next time I'll be informing your supervisor. And I will be leaving a full review stating how terrible your editing skills are."

Without waiting for a reply, she scooped up the folder and waddled away.

"Jesus, will you look at that?" Greg asked as he watched Felicia walking away, his eyes staring at her giant ass. "It's like two baby elephants are wrestling for a peanut in her pants."

Bob frowned as he let his eyes slide to Felicia's ass. Though he was upset, he had to admit Greg was right. Her ass did look like two elephants fighting, the large cheeks shaking and rolling like the earth in the middle of an earthquake. He couldn't help but wonder how she wiped her ass. I mean, how *did* she get her hand all the way back there? She probably didn't and her ass must always have shit on it. He couldn't help but wonder if there was shit in there from a year ago, you know, way up there in the top of the crack where she could never possibly reach. Well, maybe she could get at it with a sponge or a stick. Imagining Felicia in the shower with a sponge tied to a stick was totally hilarious and he began to chuckle.

Greg glanced at his friend in curiosity and his left eyebrow rose slightly as he asked a silent question.

"Nothing, man, its nothing, just had an ugly thought," Bob said as he tried to control himself. Still, now no matter what he did, he couldn't get the image of Felicia in the shower with a sponge on a stick as she tried to reach over her shoulder and wash the crack of her ass. He knew he was going to pay for it in his nightmares but there it was, and he dreaded going to bed that night. Hell, just thinking about her naked was enough to make him want to jump into D Block with the zombies and let them have at him till he was nothing but a pile of bone and rags of shredded clothing.

The sergeant walked up to them and slapped the table with a large hand with hairy knuckles.

"You two fuckheads done eating or what?"

"Hey, Sarge, almost, why what's up?" Greg asked.

"We need you to go get three more deadheads from Cell Block D and bring them to the professor."

"Already?" Bob asked. "Shit, Sarge, we just brought him two the other day."

"Maybe so, but he's carving them up like they're turkeys on Thanksgiving with his experiments, so go get him some more."

Greg shoved a few mouthfuls of food into his mouth and pushed off from the table. "Okay, no problem, we got it," he said as Bob did the same.

"Good men, and be careful, the fuckers are biting more so than usual today."

"Will do, Sarge," Greg said with a wave.

The two men made their way through the prison until they reached Cell Block D. This part of the prison had been converted into a storage area for the captured zombies. The rest of the prison was now living quarters for the military and civilian personnel. When the outbreak had grown out of control, the military had fallen back to the prison and had made it their base of operations. Now they were trapped inside with a thousand zombies at the walls and gates of the prison. But they were safe enough. The prison was built to keep people in, and dead or not, it also kept them out.

At the door to Cell Block D, Greg and Bob opened it and stepped inside. Here, in each cell, where there were once murderers and killers housed, now there were animated corpses. Two per cell, they filled the block from one end to the other.

"Shit, seems like there's more of 'em every day, don't it?" Bob asked as he eyed the cells with the zombies. Arms were reaching through the bars to grab them, the moans filling the cell block and echoing off the stone walls.

"Yeah, I guess so. Well, let's do this and get it over with," Greg said. "Let's get two now and then we'll come back for the last one."

"Fine," Bob said.

They went to the closest cell and when both men had their poles with nooses on the ends ready, they opened the cell door. As the two zombies stumbled out, each man was ready and they snapped the collars on the corpses' necks, much like what a dog catcher would do to a stray dog being captured.

"Okay, you got yours?" Greg asked.

"Yeah, you go first," Bob said as he slammed his ghoul against the wall. Its head bounced off the stone, leaving a dark smear, but otherwise it was fine.

Greg led the way, and as the two men reached the door to the cell block, Greg was caught off guard when Felicia seemed to jump from the side and come for him. He saw another folder in her hand and her beady eyes, peering out from under the folds of flab, were alight with condemnation.

"Felecia, what the fuck? Get outta here before you…" Greg began but he was too late as exactly what he was going to warn her against happened.

Felecia, acting like usual, as if she owned the place and could do no wrong, came forward at Greg, about to badger him over editing of improper paperwork when the zombie at the end of Greg's noose lunged for her. Before Felecia could heave her bulk aside, the zombie's teeth were sinking into the ample flesh of her cheek, tearing the flab away to leave the bright red of muscle tissue.

Felicia screamed and tossed her folders into the air, for once forgetting about her precious editing and focusing on something real, something that mattered, such as her life.

"Jesus fucking Christ!" Bob screamed from behind Greg as he watched the fat slob get attacked.

As for Felecia, she raised her meaty arms and thrust the zombie away from her, then turned and ran off into the hallway, her yells echoing back to the two frazzled soldiers. As for the zombie, it chewed happily on the large portion of flesh, its eyes rolling back into its head happily as if it was a human eating the finest steak money could buy.

Disgusted with what had happened, Greg pulled his revolver and shot the ghoul in the head. Brains splattered the wall as the ghoul slumped to the floor, the remnants of chewed cheek sliding out of its mouth to splash onto the floor.

"Dumb cunt, I've warned her a thousand fucking times to stay away from the deadheads when we're moving them," Greg hissed.

"Shit, Greg, what the hell do we do now?" Bob asked, his eyes open wide as he fought to control his zombie.

Greg turned and went back to retrieve another specimen. "One thing at a time. First we bring these two dead fucks to the professor, then we go find Felecia." He smiled widely. "You get to fulfill a wish today Bob, you know that?"

"What do you mean" he asked.

Greg pointed at the dead ghoul with half its head missing. "That fucker bit Felicia, she's gonna change now. You get to blow her fuckin' head off."

Bob's smile slowly widened as he realized what Greg meant and he chided himself for not figuring it out sooner himself.

"Shit, yeah. Oh, yeah, I don't believe it. Finally, I can put a bullet in that fat cunt's head. It's a dream come true."

Greg now had another ghoul in his possession from another cell and he led the way, Bob following. Another soldier ran up after hearing the gunshot and yells, his gun drawn, and Greg pointed to the very dead zombie sprawled on the floor. "Clean that up, Private."

The soldier nodded and Greg and Bob moved away, leading their charges before them.

Twenty minutes later, both men had deposited their zombies and were free to find Felicia. They were in luck and the professor had changed his mind and had told them that two ghouls were enough for the time being.

With weapons drawn, the two men went on a hunt, one they were looking forward to the end result of.

"Where do think she went?" Bob asked.

"Let's try her office, I bet she's in there. Shit, it's like a fucking church in there to her."

The two men moved through the prison and it was Greg who slowed as they approached the administration wing. When they had almost reached Felicia's office, he pointed to the floor and said, "Look, blood. She definitely came this way."

"You wanna go first?" Bob asked.

"Sure, but I won't shoot unless I have no choice," Greg said. "She's all yours, buddy."

Bob nodded and gestured for Greg to keep going.

The two men moved forward and when Greg was standing directly outside Felicia's office, he stopped, listening to the area for signs of movement.

There were offices on both sides of the hallway and on the glass of the door they stood before were the words, **Felicia Tillman, Editor and Manager**. They had been written in black marker, the original office owner's name crossed out messily.

"Will you look at this shit? Who needs a fucking editor in a zombie apocalypse?" Greg said. He reached out for the doorknob and with a nod to Bob, he turned it and pushed the door open. The glass rattled in its frame as the door smacked the wall and both men charged inside, Greg leading the way. Though both men had their guns drawn and ready, neither man fired, and the reason sat before them.

At her desk, Felicia was working, though her eyes were now glazed over in death and a pool of blood now coated her desk from end to end where she'd bled out.

It was terribly obvious she had died and returned but that wasn't the oddest thing. The oddest part was that she was sitting behind her desk and in her left hand she held her stamp with the word **REJECTED** on it. With her right hand she was taking a crumpled paper from the pile on the corner of her desk, sliding it to her, then using the stamp to press a **REJECTED** stamp on it. Only now, the red stamp was covered in her blood and each time she stamped a piece of paper, her sticky blood left its mark.

She was oblivious to the two men in her office and Greg and Bob were both stumped.

"Shit, I've heard of this happening but I've never seen it before," Greg said as he holstered his revolver. Bob didn't know what Greg was talking about so he kept his gun trained on her. His finger was itching to squeeze the trigger so he could blow the fat cunt to Hell where she belonged.

"Heard of what happening? What are you talking about?" Bob asked. "Can I blow her away or what?"

Greg reached out and made Bob lower his gun. "No, don't shoot her yet, I have a better idea. Trust me on this, buddy. You want to make the cunt suffer, right?"

He nodded. "Fuck, yeah. Every time she busted my balls over some fucking editing issue in my reports. I wanted to blow her goddamn head clean off. So yeah, I want her to suffer."

"Okay then, listen to me and wait and see what I have planned. Believe me, man, it's way better than shooting her. That'll only give you pleasure for a second. What I got panned will last a lifetime."

Bob shrugged. "Fine, but if I don't like it, I reserve my right to blow her fat head off, deal?"

"Deal," Greg said. "But I know you'll like it."

Later that day, back in Cell Block D, Greg and Bob stood before one of the cells. Before it had been empty but now it was full.

Only one zombie occupied the cell, but its girth was enough for two standard ghouls.

Inside, sat Felicia in all her undead glory. Her desk was there as well and on it was a pile of unedited papers, more boxes stacked on the floor. In her hand, she held her rejection stamp, the wooden handle now connected to her palm by screws driven into the bones of her hand so she wouldn't drop it.

Just like before, she went through the motions, stamping paper after paper as **REJECTED**, her dead mind the same as her living one. In her reality, it was never good enough and so would always receive a rejection.

There was no ink for the stamp, only her own pus and blood, an unending supply of bodily fluids that seeped from the open wound on her cheek as well as bloody saliva that drooled from her open, slack-jawed mouth.

"So, what do you think?" Greg asked as he crossed his arms.

"I don't know, you tell me?" Bob said, still anxious to shoot her and be done with it.

"Look at her. She's one of the few that still remembers her former life. She's such a fucking bitch that even in death she can't help stepping on people. That's why she used that damn stamp. Only now she can do it forever. Every day, for as long as her body holds out, she can use that fucking stamp and pretend she's somehow important, as if what she's doing actually still matters in a dead world."

Bob glared at the fat, pus-filled zombie, at the half-eaten face that stared into the abyss, and shook his head.

Before Greg could do or say a thing, Bob raised his revolver and shot Felicia from less than four feet away. The round hit her right between the eyes and her head snapped back as her brains shot out along with bone matter and bits of her scalp.

No sooner did the head snap back then it snapped forward again, the body slumping to the desk as if she was tired and had decided to take a nap.

"What the fuck, Bob? What'd you do that for? After all the time I took setting her up in here, and you go 'head and shoot her anyway?"

Bob holstered his gun as all around the two men, the dead moaned and wailed from their prison cells.

"Sorry, Greg, but you said I still reserved the right to shoot her, and frankly, dead or not, I just couldn't resist putting a bullet between those two beady eyes." He glanced one last time at the heaving bulk of dead flesh in the cell and said, "Burn in Hell, you fucking cunt. You can edit the Devil's papers now." He began walking away and called over his shoulder, "See you at dinner?"

Greg didn't reply, only stared at the massive corpse in the cell. After more than a minute, he scratched his head and said, "Great, now how the hell am I gonna get that fat fuck outta there?"

THE DAY'S END

The massive yellow fireball that was the sun was at its peak, the worst time of the day for the once blue planet called Earth.

For more than five years, the Earth had been slowly orbiting closer to the sun to the point that now the oceans were practically gone and the once wet planet was as arid as the deserts that dotted the sphere.

Maggie Canton knew all this but just barely. She was ten now, and ever since her fifth birthday she had known she would die of dehydration. Not if, but when.

She turned to gaze around her apartment, at the blankets draped like makeshift curtains across the windows, and the two floor fans her father had managed to salvage from a trash heap.

The temperature of Earth was now a cool hundred degrees in the shade and a hundred and thirty in the sun, sometimes more depending on what part of the world you lived in.

The deserts were three times that, the sand having melted to glass in most places, a molten sea that no man dared set foot on. At night, though still unbearably hot, the sea of glass would cool enough to harden, but if a traveler wasn't able to make it across before morning, they would find themselves swallowed alive to be trapped in a glass prison forever, the molten crystal their tomb for all of eternity.

Volcanoes had erupted across the globe, too, spewing molten ash into the atmosphere. Many scientists thought this might help reflect the sun's rays away from the beleaguered planet, but the ash was quickly burned off as if it had never been.

Maggie went to one of the windows and peeked outside, looking up at the unforgiving blue sky. Clouds had been gone for more than year, burnt off by the harsh rays, and some scientists believed they would never hang in the Earth's sky again.

Water was more valuable than gold, with the exception of a gun, which was only more valuable because with a gun you could take more water for yourself.

Society as a whole was gone, and now it was every human for his or herself, as each human being struggled to squeeze one more ounce of water from the dry sponge that was the dead planet.

Manufacturing water from the air was a lost cause as there was no moisture to suck out of the air, so as the population slowly began to die out, the remaining water supply nourished the dwindling survivors.

Maggie didn't entirely understand what was happening, though she was no fool either. But to her young mind, she couldn't fathom how she was possibly going to die in a month, or a year, or two years.

As she peered past the blanket on the window, the last desperate attempt to try and keep some of the burning rays out, she watched a gang of men walking down the street. Then her eyes went to the opposite end to see a man and woman walking, the man holding a paper bag with what, if she had to guess, was the couple's ration of water for the week.

She saw this every Friday when the government brought the large trucks that once held milk or apple juice, but now carried water, to the populace. The truck would park near city hall, and military men with large guns with banana clips would line up to keep the crowd under control. A few Humvees were there, too, with large rifles mounted on the backs of the vehicles that her Daddy called M-60s.

It didn't happen often anymore as the crowd had learned their lesson, but back a few years ago, the military men had had to fight to control the crowd, often shooting men and women who only wanted water to live.

That was how she had lost her mommy.

Her mother and father had gone to get their water rations when a riot had broken out. Daddy had lost Mommy in the crowds and when the soldiers had shot into the crowd, Mommy had been there. The bullets had torn into her chest and face; mangling her visage to the point she could barely be recognized. Daddy had known it was her from her bloody clothes and the wedding ring still on her finger. No one cared about diamonds anymore, they were worthless.

You can't drink a diamond.

Maggie had cried all night, after Daddy had come home and told her about Mommy. She had shed tears of loss and thought how those tears were so precious, lost fluids she needed to survive.

When Daddy had handed her a cup of water, the water he had received in exchange for Mommy's life, she had swatted it from his hand to splash on the floor.

He'd slapped her then, hard across the face, and had dropped to the floor to suck the fluid from the shag like a dog. He understood that every drop was precious and later had apologized for striking her.

She hadn't replied, so lost in her grief and Daddy had left her alone then. That night, she heard him in his room, crying for hours, the pain of losing Mommy too much for him to bear.

But the next morning Daddy had smiled to her, keeping a strong front up for her if nothing else.

And now it was Friday again, but Daddy hadn't come back from getting the water rations.

Maggie was pulled from her reverie from the activity on the street below. The couple carrying the paper bag had reached the gang and Maggie could see what happened all the time on the streets of the city was about to happen yet again.

But though she thought all she was going to see was the couple getting beat up and their water taken, this time something very, very new happened.

As the couple reached the gang, the man pulled a gun, but before he could use it to defend himself, one of the gang members pulled a knife and threw it across the seven feet separating one group from the other.

Maggie watched the blade fly through the air, the sun's rays reflecting off it as if it was made of polished glass.

And then the knife sank into the man's throat, causing him to drop the bag as the gun fell from a limp hand.

The woman screamed as the men attacked, but where normally the gang would have merely stolen the water and gun and ran off to enjoy their ill gotten gains, this time there was a spin on the end to this encounter.

As the men reached the prone man and screaming woman, two of them dropped to the ground over the knifed man, while the others grabbed the woman, forcing her to the sidewalk as well.

Another knife appeared, and as the woman screamed in fear, her neck was slashed, just where the carotid artery was.

Arterial blood shot out, but instead of leaving the woman to bleed out, the men fell on her and began drinking the blood like dogs lapping at a shallow puddle.

All the while the man was getting the same treatment, the men like vampires as they sucked the couple dry.

This went on for almost five minutes before the screaming siren of a police car could be heard.

The gang of men looked up, their faces covered in blood, droplets dripping from their chins to splatter onto the sidewalk, their eyes twitching like some kind of pack of wild animals.

One of the men gathered the fallen paper bag, ripping it to shreds to expose the water jug within, and like a pack of wolves chased from a feeding; they galloped away into a nearby alleyway as the squad car pulled up.

Two officers got out of the car, their bodies coated in white. The blue uniforms of old were long gone, white was easier to wear with the unforgiving sun's rays always beating down on them.

The first officer knelt down and inspected the corpses and then the first man called to the other cop to call it in. Then as Maggie watched in horror, she saw the policeman lean over and begin to drink from the woman's neck, lapping up the crimson dribble that still seeped from the wound. He was careful not to get any on his white uniform as he drank like a hound dog.

The officer wiped his mouth and chin on the dead woman's blouse where it was still clean, looked around once to make sure no one had seen him, and then stood up as if nothing had happened. He asked the other cop if he wanted some, but the man declined.

Then both officers picked up the bodies, carried them to the rear of the squad car, and set them into the trunk. Maggie knew why they did this. With things the way they were, there were no more people to pick up the dead bodies. It was just easier for the police to do it and drive them back to wherever they brought people when they died.

But the squad car didn't go far. It only drove to the end of the street where the two bodies were unceremoniously dumped in an alleyway. When the cops were finished, they climbed back into the vehicle and continued on their patrol of the city.

Maggie watched the squad car drive away and then she stared at the dark spot where the blood was already dried. It didn't take long, usually less than a minute, sometimes less.

She knew why the police did this. An hour from now the two bodies would be gone, either the gang would return for them to finish the job of draining the blood or someone else would take the corpses. In a dying world, many did what they could to survive, ignoring old taboos.

Closing the curtain, she went to a side table and picked up the small bottle of water there. She poured herself a half cup and then took one of the pills Mommy and Daddy made her take for as long as she'd been alive. She didn't know what they were for but Daddy said they were to keep her healthy, that they were vitamins.

She figured they must be vitamins, too, though she always wished they came in better shapes, like dinosaurs or maybe letters. But her pill was just round and it was nothing special.

She popped it into her mouth and drank it down with the water.

Checking the battery-powered clock on the wall, she felt a twinge of concern. Daddy should have been home over an hour ago. Where was he?

She heard a voice in the hallway and she ran to the door. Getting down on her knees, she peeked through the keyhole with her left eye. From the angle of the door, she was able to see down to the metal fire door for the stairs and the now broken elevator. For more than a year now everyone on the fourth floor had to take the stairs.

As sweat ran down her back, she watched a large man with a bushy beard walking down the hall. He was talking into a cell phone, yelling about wanting his payment or there would be hell to pay. Then he was past her door and was turning the corner. A second later a door opened and slammed closed and the man's voice was gone.

Maggie turned and slumped against the door, worry and fear eating at her. Daddy should have been home by now and she was really beginning to get worried.

The heat in the apartment was well over a hundred and she knew it was no better outside. Daddy had sold their last air conditioner months ago for extra water rations. Many had done the same, and though at the time it seemed to be the right thing to do, now most showed regret.

Crawling back to the fan, she lay down beside it and closed her eyes. Though the warm air touching her was barely better than the rest of the room's temperature, she closed her eyes and tried to sleep, praying the entire time there wouldn't be another rolling blackout which would plunge her into darkness and no fan.

Dreams of cool days and rainfall filled her mind as she drifted off into a heat-induced, restless slumber.

Two days later and she was out of water.

An hour ago she had swallowed one of her vitamins and had finished off the last two tablespoons of water with it.

And worst of all, Daddy still wasn't home.

She heard gunshots from outside and she ran to the window, pushing back the blanket to see outside. It was daytime and she first spotted the place where the couple had been killed. Now all that remained were a few dried spots of blood on the cement, now a dark brown. She glanced to the end of the street where the bodies had been dumped in the alley, but she couldn't see if they were there or not.

A black, four door sedan sped by with another following, the gunshots echoing off the buildings. The first car had men sticking out the windows as they fired at the trailing car. At the same time, two men in the second vehicle shot at the first one. It reminded her of old movies about gangsters her Daddy would watch late at night. The grainy, black and white films seemed the perfect analogy for what she was witnessing.

Suddenly, the window she was peering out of cracked a foot above her head and she looked up to see a hole in the glass, the bullet hole also in the blanket. She ducked down as the two cars shot past her building and only looked up again when the two vehicles turned the far corner to be lost from sight, retorts of the gunshots continuing until, they too, faded away.

Scared out of her mind, Maggie began to cry. She knew it was wrong to cry, wasting water with her tears, but she couldn't help it. She was all alone, out of water, and her Daddy was gone. What ten year old girl wouldn't cry? Hell, what human being, regardless of age, wouldn't cry?

She sat against the wall, tears sliding down her cheeks, as she watched the thin line of sunlight cut through the room, thanks to the bullet hole in the blanket.

Maggie watched that line crawl across the room, moving an inch an hour, as the sun slid across the sky, for hours. And though eventually darkness fell and the light faded, the heat remained.

Maggie went to the refrigerator, her stomach rumbling, but there was nothing to eat, only a few morsels barely fit for a mouse. But she ate them anyway, her stomach happy for the sustenance, and she knew she had to take her vitamins with food.

For the next two days she wandered around the apartment, and with still no Daddy, she realized she would have no choice but to go outside and find help.

She was weak from lack of food and water and knew she would die if she didn't find something to drink soon.

Daddy had taught her that water was needed to live; it wasn't just something she just drank for the fun of it. It was life.

She figured she could go to one of her neighbors. There weren't many left in the building, but she knew of at least two.

There was the old woman who lived at the end of the hallway and the big man she'd seen talking on his cell phone who lived at the other end. She decided to go to the old woman first, and with one last look at her apartment, she opened the front door and stepped into the hallway.

The heat in the hallway was worse than inside her apartment and she wiped the sweat from her brow and headed for the old woman's door.

Upon reaching it, she stared up at the number 10 in the middle of the faded brown door and the hanging two ears of corn that signified the coming Fall. She wanted to reach up, take the corn down and eat it, but she knew it was covered with polyurethane so it was inedible. Still, staring at the corn made her stomach growl.

She knocked on the door, hoping the woman was home, and was surprised when the door was pushed inward by her wrapping knuckles. Maggie stood perfectly still, her right hand in the air from where she had tapped the door.

Desperation spurred her on and she pushed the door open some more, poking her head inside.

"Hello? Is anyone home? It's me, Maggie. I live down the hall with my dad."

She waited for a reply, but none was forthcoming.

Swallowing the knot in her throat, she stepped into the apartment, her eyes darting back and forth like a trapped animal.

She knew if Daddy was here he would be mad at her. She knew she was never supposed to go into someone else's apartment without their permission, but a small inner voice inside her head said that Daddy wasn't here right now and she was hungry and thirsty.

Taking another faltering step into the room, the door swung closed, but remained ajar behind her.

It was then that she detected a sour smell; like someone had left meat out in the sun for too long and the maggots and flies had gotten to it. Covering her nose with her shirt, she continued deeper into the apartment to investigate, her thirst driving her on.

The apartment was set up in the same design as hers and she turned and headed for the kitchen, knowing that would be where to go for food and water.

As she moved through the place, the heat in the room and the smell of rancid meat began to grow, until it was so strong the miasma of death was like a fluid wall she had to push through.

Her nose and mouth were now buried under her shirt and she pushed hard on the material with her hand to try and keep the stink out, but her eyes began to tear up and she was beginning to have second thoughts about this.

Gritting her teeth, and wanting to be strong, she pushed forward until she was at the threshold to the kitchen.

And then she saw and heard what had made that awful smell.

Seeing was the worst, as her eyes took in the corpse of the old woman. The body was slumped down near the sink and refrigerator, the housedress she wore hiked up to her thighs.

The sound Maggie heard were the hundreds upon hundreds of flies feeding on the corpse, crawling in and out of the nose, ears and open mouth like they were tourists at an attraction for underground caves. Maggots squirmed in every crevice of the body, but the worst sight to behold was the eyes.

The old woman's eye were still open, but now the orbs were all but gone, to be replaced with dozens of squirming maggots which writhed inside the sockets as they struggled to mature.

Maggie was frozen in shock as she stared at the corpse of the old woman. She had never seen a dead person before, not like this, not up close.

Sure, she had seen people get killed on the street outside the apartment as she watched through the blanket, but they had been so far away, but this…this was something different altogether.

Maggie stood perfectly still, wondering if the old woman was going to somehow get back up like a zombie and stumble toward her. She imagined the legs cracking as bones fought to move and then the hands reaching out for something to support her. The maggots in the eyes would fall out of the eyes as the body rose, and the flies would all begin to buzz around the head, angry their meal was moving.

But after two long minutes and the body remained immobile, Maggie realized she was letting her imagination run away with her.

There was a table cloth covering the kitchen table and she went to it, pulled it off, ignoring the salt and pepper shakers that fell to the floor, and tossed the tablecloth over the old woman's face.

Immediately more buzzing began to fill the kitchen and the trapped flies under the cloth became agitated. But after another minute, they settled down, accepting their fate.

Feeling better now that she didn't have to stare at that dead face, Maggie worked her way around the old woman's legs, careful not to step in the puddle of urine and feces that had splashed on the linoleum when the old woman died; voiding her bowels.

The refrigerator was a two door type and she opened the freezer first as it was closest, but when there was nothing in it, not even ice, she closed it.

With her heart in her throat, she opened the refrigerator side, and though it was basically barren, in the middle of the top shelf was a can of apple juice, the big red apples emblazoned on the side and the words,**100% Not From Concentrate**, below them.

Ignoring the redolence of death in the kitchen, her heart leapt at the sight of the can of juice, and she reached in and grabbed it.

But as she pulled it to her and raised it to her mouth, she found there was barely a table spoon of liquid remaining.

Still, she drank it greedily, the cold liquid flowing down her throat like the sweetest ambrosia. She held the can tipped over her mouth for almost a minute, wanting to get every drop, and when she was through, she set the can back in the fridge and closed the door.

Feeling slightly refreshed, the body on the floor didn't seem like such a big deal now, not when the prospect of getting food and drink was so close.

Still terribly thirsty, she moved to the cabinets to see what she could find.

One cabinet had Saltines inside it and she felt like laughing. She knew to eat those without something to drink would be like eating sand in the desert. But she set them aside anyway. After all, food was food.

She searched the rest of the cupboards and found nothing, that is until the last one produced an actual can of peaches.

The can was a pull top and she greedily opened it, sucking down the sweet syrup and peaches within. She made sure not to waste a drop, even to the point of using her tongue to clean out any residue; though she was careful not to cut her tongue on the edges of the can. Now that would be a laugh; to slice her tongue.

Still starving, but with the edge now taken off, she finished searching the kitchen, and when she was confident there was nothing else to eat or drink—the tap as dry here as her place—she headed for the front door. She glanced one last time at the covered corpse, but then moved on as there was nothing she could do and no one to tell.

As she passed another room just off the kitchen, she glanced inside and saw the desiccated carcass of a housecat on the floor. It lay on its side, its tongue protruding, its eyes open, and next to the small form was an empty food and water dish. The fur of the cat rippled and rolled, the decomposing gases within making the carcass appear as if there were creatures inside it, just under the skin, trying to break out.

For some reason the dead animal with the undulating fur unsettled her more than the corpse of the old woman, and she turned and fled, not wanting to remain a moment longer in this apartment of death.

Upon stepping back into the hallway, she closed the door behind her and relished the relatively clean smell of the building compared to the fetid odor of the apartment. The hallway smelled of old carpeting and sweat but it was like flowers to her sinuses.

She still needed to get food and water so she did the only thing left to do, and that was to go to the opposite end of the hall where the bearded man with the cell phone lived.

For the hundredth time, she wished her daddy was here with her, but at the moment, she knew her wish wouldn't come true, so she had to stay strong.

Daddy would want her to be strong.

With hesitant steps, she slowly moved down the hallway, passed her own apartment door, and continued until she was standing in front of the man's door. The odor of old and new cigarette smoke wafted through the sides and bottom of the door and she could hear someone either yelling or arguing from inside the apartment.

Swallowing the lump in her throat, she knocked on the door.

At first no one answered, and though her heart was beating fast in terror, she knocked again.

Abruptly, the voice inside the apartment ceased and then there was no sound. Maggie strained her ears to hear the man, but when more than a minute passed and still no voice, she placed her left ear against the door, closing her eyes as she tried to hear what was going on in there.

Suddenly, the door swung inward and Maggie opened her eyes to look up into the wide muzzle of a large handgun.

Though she didn't understand what was happening, the man's finger began to squeeze the trigger to send a bullet through her skull.

"Well, well, what do we have here?" the gruff voice asked as Maggie slowly blinked in fear. "Hey, wait a minute, I know you. You're that kid who lives down the hall."

Maggie didn't move, didn't say a word, her gaze locked on the round hole of the muzzle. She knew what a gun was and knew what would happen to her if the man decided to squeeze the trigger.

"What's the matter, kid, cat got your tongue?" He was holding a bottle of Grey Goose in his free hand and he took a long pull, wiping his mouth with his sleeve. Maggie felt her nose scrunch up at the acrid odor of the booze.

"Well, say somethin', you stupid or what?"

Maggie blinked again, swallowed the knot in her throat and quickly told the man her tale. When she was finished, the gun had been lowered and more of the bottle was empty.

"Shit, kid, that sucks. Okay, come on in, I think we can work somethin' out."

Though filled with fear, she did as he said, stepping into the confines of the apartment. The door slammed shut behind her and she jumped; it was like a prison door had slammed closed.

"Come on, kid, I got somthin' for ya ta drink," the man said. Maggie wondered what his name was, but was too scared to ask. If he cared what her name was he didn't show it.

He went to the small kitchen and rummaged around for a few seconds, then came back with a beer. Setting it on the table, he cracked the lid and pointed to Maggie.

"Go 'head, it's good for ya," he grinned, then took another sip of his bottle. Now that she was closer to him, Maggie could see there were bits of food and grime in his beard.

Made sense, she thought. No one was wasting water on bathing anymore, it was too precious.

Maggie took a few hesitant steps towards the table and the beer and then she reached out her right hand and picked it up. The can was warm, she noticed, as she slowly raised it to her lips.

When the liquid flowed into her mouth, she swallowed some, but then she began to choke. She'd never tasted beer before and found she didn't like the taste very much.

He began to laugh. "Easy there, sweet'ums, don't waste any of it."

"It doesn't taste good. Do you have any water?" Maggie asked.

He shook his head. "Nah, ran out a while ago, but I got a shitload of beer in the back, cases of it. Should do me for a good long time." He tapped his forehead with his index finger. "See, when everyone was runnin' around buying up all the water and it was ten bucks a gallon, I went and got all the beer I could find." He nodded, proud of himself.

He pushed the beer can to her lips again. "Go on, drink up, it'll make you feel good." She did as she was told, her thirst overriding her taste for the beer, and as she did; her head began to feel fuzzy. With an empty stomach and only being ten, the alcohol went right to her head.

As she drank, her vision getting fuzzy, the man leered down at her, his eyes creasing with expectation. She was a cute little thing, and though she wasn't as young as he usually liked them, he would make an exception in this case as pickings had been slim lately.

Maggie finished the beer and a wave of dizziness came over her. All she wanted to do was sleep. The can almost fell from her hand, but he grabbed it, but instead of placing it on the table, he casually tossed it into a corner, adding to the trash already there.

"Here ya go, darlin', come and lay down for a bit. My bed's right back here."

His breath was coming in gasps as he prepared for some fun. Though the Earth was turning into a charred cinder, and everyone on it would die sooner or later, at least he could go out by having some fun.

Maggie took three steps before her legs gave out, but the man scooped her up and carried her the rest of the way.

Maggie had the feeling of floating for a second, but then she fell into an alcohol induced slumber.

Maggie awoke that night, her head hurting and her mouth as dry as a piece of cotton.

The heat in the small room was stifling and only the alcohol in her system had allowed her to sleep. Looking up at the ceiling, a ceiling fan spun ineffectually. Much like her apartment, the room's windows were covered with blankets and sheets to keep the harsh glare of the sun out and she could barely see because of this.

Then she looked to her right and saw what had to be the bathroom, the door partially open and the dim light that was on inside seeping through the cracked door. That was why she was able to see anything.

It was then she looked down at herself to see she was naked, her body covered in a sheen of sweat, and as her hands explored her skin, she gasped when her right hand touched her inner thighs.

Her fingers came back partially wet, and as she stared at it in the wan light, she realized it was partially congealed blood.

She was bleeding between her legs!

Or had been.

Frightened for what this might mean, she rolled to a sitting position on the bed, careful not to wake the bearded man up. His snores filled the small room like a locomotive engine.

As she sat up, she felt a discomfort in her groin and realized something had happened to her down there, like something large had been inside her. It was a weird feeling and hard to put into words, but it felt like there was a pressure where there should be none.

And then she got a better look at the walls of the bedroom and how they were decorated. Instead of pictures of family members or maybe one of flowers or a beach shore, the walls were covered in photographs of young girls, the average age around five. All were posed either naked or in their underwear and all had smiles that didn't seem to be genuine. The exotic poses showed private parts, places Daddy said were personal and should never be seen by strangers other than a doctor or Mommy at bath time.

Maggie knew right then this was a bad place and she needed to leave immediately. That there were things worse than death in this world, and if she stayed here with this man, who as she glanced at his sleeping form, she saw he was also naked, she would wish she had died again and again.

Sliding off the bed, she turned slightly, and when her eyes fell on the door that she believed would bring her to the front of the apartment, her left foot caught the electrical cord for the bedside lamp.

As she raised her foot to take her first step, her foot pulled on the cord and sent the lamp plummeting to the hardwood floor where it shattered with a crash.

The bearded man snapped awake with a groan and sat up as if he was on a spring, his eyes darting back and forth as his left hand reached out to where Maggie had been sleeping. Like a sniper zooming in on his target, he zeroed in on her. And with a roar of rage at seeing her sneaking towards the bedroom door, he jumped out of bed and charged after her.

His new plaything wouldn't escape him that easily.

Maggie ran, ignoring her nakedness in her desperation to be free.

He came off the bed in a crouch and began to chase her to the door, but his balance was off thanks to the alcohol he'd consumed the previous night and his legs became tangled in a pile of dirty laundry that would for all purposes never be washed.

Like a fallen oak tree in the woods after a hurricane, he toppled over, his arms waving in front of him as he fell heavily to the floor.

Even while Maggie ran, she felt the heavy *thump* when his body landed, but by then she was in the living room and making her way to the front door.

Upon reaching the door, she began to fiddle with the lock and for a heart-wrenching moment she didn't think she could get it unlocked in time. Behind her, in the bedroom, the bearded man was getting to his feet, and with another bellow of anger, he practically ripped the bedroom door off its hinges as he came for her.

Then the lock on the front door unlatched and she opened it, running out into the hallway, sweat pouring off her like a river. The heat was as unbearable as ever, and even though she was naked, it did nothing to ease her suffering.

She dashed down the hallway and sprinted to her apartment door.

Under the mat, there was a tear in the carpeting where her daddy had hidden a spare key. She grabbed it, opening the door and slamming it closed, just as the bearded man came around the corner. He saw her go into the apartment, but by the time he reached the door, Maggie was safely ensconced, all the locks now thrown and a chair under the doorknob for good measure like she'd seen people do on television.

The man pounded on the door.

"Go away! I have a gun! My Daddy taught me how to use it. I'll shoot you through the door if you don't leave me alone!"

"Bullshit, sweet'ums, you don't have a gun. Now come on out and come back to my place and we'll forget this ever happened. You forget, I got beer, you need to drink, don'tcha?"

"No, I'm fine, now go away or I'll start shooting!"

The man punched the door two more times, but in the end decided it wasn't worth taking the chance she had a gun, besides, she would come to him sooner or later. She had to drink and what he offered was better than death, at least that's what he thought.

"Fine, have it your way, but you know where I am when you get thirsty enough," he grinned lecherously. "And then we'll have us some more fun." He left and Maggie put her ear to the door. She could hear him stomping away. A few seconds later she heard his door slam closed.

She fell to the floor and cried as she tried to figure out what to do next. She cried for over an hour before finally running out of tears.

She went to the table in the living room and took her vitamins, swallowing them down without anything to drink. It was hard, but her daddy had told her they were important, and though she felt a little silly bothering, she wanted to do what he told her, even if he wasn't around.

That made her wonder where he could be. Was he dead? He must be or he would have returned for her by now. An abhorrent thought crept into her mind. Would her daddy have left her? Maybe gone somewhere else? No, he wouldn't do that, he loved her.

Tears began to well up at the corners of her eyes at the thought of her daddy being dead, but she forced it down.

As time passed and her adrenalin drained away, she felt groggy and drifted off into a restless slumber.

Unknowingly the night before, she had sat down across from the window with the bullet hole. The next morning, the thin streak of light hit her in the face and caused her to wake up. Groggy, she went to the bathroom and tried to figure out how to clean herself up without the use of water.

Finally an idea struck her and she cleaned herself up with some hand lotion and an old towel, tossing both to the floor when she was finished. She wished she had water, but she knew if she did she would have drank it, not wasted it on washing up.

When she was cleaned up as good as she could with her limited resources, she dressed in a tank top and shorts. It didn't take her long to realize she needed to leave her apartment, and the building too, as the bearded man and her were the only people left on this floor, perhaps in the entire building, and sooner or later her bluff of a gun would fall woefully short. Then he would break in the door and take her as his plaything.

She put on a pair of old sneakers and gathered what she could into another backpack. There wasn't much to take. A photo of her dad, herself and her mother, some spare underwear and t-shirts, a few pairs of shorts.

Her vitamins she tucked into the front pocket of her shorts and then prepared to leave. She took one last look at her home, wondering if she would ever return. She did write a note and left it on the counter, just in case her daddy came back to find her gone.

This time she used the back door, wanting to make sure the bearded man didn't see her. The back door led into an old service hallway that connected to the rear stairwell and the freight elevator. The latter didn't work of course and the former smelled like pee, as many of the tenants would piss in it when they were too drunk to make it to their floor after a night of drinking.

The stale aroma of urine assaulted her senses as she opened the stairwell door. The echo was monstrous and the creaking hinges bounced off the stone walls and reverberated up and down the stairwell. Swallowing her fear, she stepped in and began the descent to the street.

She didn't know what would come next, but she knew it had to be better than dying like the old woman did in the other apartment.

She was too young to die like that.

No, there had to be something better out there in the world. Even if the world was slowly melting like a neglected ice cream cone.

The sun had just risen for another scorcher of a day when Maggie stepped out into the back alley of her apartment building. The alley was still partly in the shade thanks to the towering walls of the neighboring building, but the sun would be roasting the interior soon enough.

She had a baseball cap on to keep the sun off her face and she headed for the street, the one the front windows of her apartment overlooked. As she stepped onto the street, she looked around to see no one else was about.

She was alone.

Picking a direction, she moved out and a minute later found herself standing on the spot where the couple had been killed, their bodies drained of blood. She wondered how the blood had tasted, and as she was so thirsty herself, she wondered if she ever had the opportunity, would she drink some herself.

Maggie knew hunger and thirst made people do things they would never have done in a normal world and she was feeling the desperation with each passing hour. Back when she had been cleaning herself up with the hand lotion, it was all she could do not to squirt it into her mouth. After all, it was wet, and though toxic, would have felt wonderful sliding down her throat.

The blood on the sidewalk was all but faded away, burned off, the flakes blowing away. What had stained the cement was now faded, like an old oil stain in a driveway.

The sun was at her back and she could feel it cooking her exposed skin so she began walking again, the warm wind blowing on her face reminding her of standing in front of an open over door.

In school she had learned about global warming and how the Earth would slowly become warmer as the temperature rose and the ice caps melted.

Now, all that talk was worthless. Yes, the Earth was heating up, but it had nothing to do with pollution and what man spewed into the atmosphere. It was God, or fate, or the Universe, that had decided the final chapter for humanity.

And by the way things looked, there wouldn't be an epilogue.

A few cars drove past Maggie as she made her way down the street in search of water and food. Every car had the windows rolled up, the occupants enjoying the air conditioned interior. Maggie watched a few cars drive by with longing; wishing she was inside the cars where it must be cool. A few drivers cast her curious looks, wondering why a ten year old girl was out by herself, but no one stopped.

Everyone was worried about themselves now, and though there were still good Samaritans, they were few and far between.

She made it to the third block, her apartment building now behind her, when she turned a corner and walked right into a tall man wearing a bandanna, a white t-shirt, and faded jeans. Behind him, five more men wearing similar apparel waited.

Maggie looked up into the man's deep green eyes and she saw no mercy there. This wasn't someone who would help her, and as she stared into the cold visage, she realized she'd just walked into more danger than she could ever dream possible.

She tried to take a step backwards, to run away, but the man's right arm whipped out and grabbed her left wrist, causing her to cry out in fear and a little bit of pain. His grip was strong and immediately the flesh on flesh connection caused his palm to sweat, making her wrist twist back and forth in his grip like her arm was lathered with butter.

"Goddamn, this is got to be our lucky day," the man said as he pulled Maggie to him, holding her other arm with his free hand.

"Ow, let me go!" Maggie screamed, but a slap to the face silenced her immediately.

"Shut up, kid, you're ours now and you don't speak unless we tell you to; hear me?"

Whimpering softly, her face red where he'd slapped it, she held her tongue, not wanting to be hit again.

Maggie looked at the faces of the other men glaring down at her and this was when recognition flooded her mind. These were the same gang of men who had attacked the couple on the street to then drink their blood like modern day vampires.

She began to shake, wondering if she was going to suffer the same fate.

A police cruiser turned the far corner and the man pushed Maggie behind him, where the other men took her and hid her from view. The police cruiser pulled up to the men and through their arms, Maggie could see the squad car had two policemen inside, both cool with their air conditioning cranked up to high.

She knew what she was going to do when the chance came; she would yell out when the policeman opened their windows to speak to the men.

As the squad car pulled up within a few feet of the gang, the passenger side window rolled down.

"Gentlemen," one of the cops said. "You staying out of trouble?"

"Yes, officer, we're just out for a walk," the leader of the gang replied.

Maggie saw her chance and sucked in a breath to scream for help, but as her mouth opened, a hand clamped over her lips, silencing her. Another arm wrapped around her arms and she found she was trapped.

She grew hotter and hotter, the larger body, sweaty and slick, covering her like a wool blanket. The hand over her mouth stank of garlic and cheese and she felt like she was going to vomit. But she knew what would happen if she did. She'd seen enough shows on TV. If she threw up she would choke on her bile and suffocate…or worse.

The two policemen chatted for a few more seconds, warning the gang leader to stay out of trouble, then the window was rolled up, to the policemen's relief, and they drove off, leaving Maggie to watch the taillights flash in the bright sun before the vehicle turned the next corner.

The gang leader spun and looked down at Maggie, a leer on his face.

"Damn it that was close. Come on, guys, let's get her back home where we can enjoy her to the max."

With a few whoops and hollers, Maggie was picked up like she was a life-size doll and carried along with the men. She was so screwed she felt like she was about to wet her pants any second and it was all she could do not to. Her body shivered in panic and thoughts of the bearded man back at her apartment building came to mind.

What had she done? Had she left that man only to be captured by a half dozen more who were going to do the same to her?

These and other thoughts swirled through her mind, as the leader of the gang led them back to their home.

Home was an abandoned pool supply store at the opposite end of town. As Maggie was carried into the store, her eyes took in the pool supplies that were now about as needed as an anvil was to a drowning man.

Skimmers, chlorine tablets and inflatable blowups were scattered amongst bags of 'Shock It' and algae control. Pamphlets lined the walls, telling customers how having a pool was the most wonderful thing to have in the world.

Though scared out of her mind, Maggie still stared longingly at the pictures of families playing in the water, floating on small rafts and splashing one another. To her, it was like a dream and she wished she had been born earlier so she could have appreciated even once what it was like to go swimming in a pool or the ocean.

The atmosphere of the pool store was oppressive, the heat a tangible thing.

The gang headed through the store and into the back, knowing exactly where they were going. The front windows were made of thick glass and were now covered with heavy tarps to keep the worst of the sun's rays from heating the inside up too much. There was power, but no air conditioning.

As Maggie was carried into the rear of the store, her senses were assaulted with the smell of fresh blood and decay.

It was like a pile of road kill had been tossed into the corner to rot, but before being left alone, had been doused with fresh blood.

She was brought to a small worktable stained with blood where she was dropped down hard, her arms and legs strapped down like she was a going to be a sacrifice to some unknown god, and the table was the altar.

She began to scream then, long and loud, and before she had managed to get out five screams for help, a piece of duct tape was secured over her mouth. Her eyes were wild with fright as she stared up at the faces of the men who had captured her like she was a small animal caught in a trap.

Her eyes went to the far corner of the room, and when they settled on the pile of corpses there, she shrieked so loud even the duct tape could barely contain it.

There were four corpses, the oldest perhaps three days old. Each one was pale white, looking as if it had been drained of blood. Two of the bodies were of the couple she'd seen on the street days ago, the ones the gang had killed and fed on. They must have brought the bodies back to finish the job after the police had dumped them in the alley.

The third body was a young woman, maybe fifteen or sixteen. Her frozen eyes were wide and her mouth was hanging open, but she was dead as a person could be. But that wasn't what made her shriek in terror and sadness, though it could have.

It was the face of the last corpse, the one on the bottom of the pile.

It was her Daddy.

His eyes were closed and his lips were tight, as if he had gritted his jaw as he'd died. He, too, was drained of blood, the skin so white it was almost chalky. His neck and wrists had large slashes, showing where he'd been bled out.

Maggie felt her world falling in on her and she began to grow dizzy. The heat in the room was like a weight on her chest, and with the sight of her dead father, and herself being trussed up like a pig ready for the slaughter, it all became too much for her and she passed out.

As she slipped into oblivion, she could hear the gang leader talking about her and she didn't like what he was saying.

She awoke with a start, feeling a pain on her left wrist. No sooner did she come to from the pain, then another sharp twinge of agony went up her right wrist.

Opening her eyes, she moved her head to see her wrists had been slashed, her blood now seeping out of the open wounds to drip into bowls.

The bastards were draining her for her blood!

One of the men was holding a picture, and she recognized the wallet in his other hand as that of her Daddy's.

"I'm tellin' ya, this one looks just like the girl in this guy's wallet."

The gang leader took the photo and stared at it, then down at Maggie.

"Holy shit, you're right, it does. Look, she's even got the same barrette in her hair as the one in the picture. Hey, you remember before we bled that guy he pleaded for his life, that he said he had a daughter waiting for him? Well, shit, this must be her."

The other man grinned as he agreed with his leader. "Yeah, man, that's great. If she's half as sweet as her dad we got us some good drinks here."

"Fuck, yeah," the leader replied and then flicked the photo at his buddy. The picture hit his chest and fell to the filthy floor, where the other man stepped on it. He tossed the wallet into the corner like it was trash and moved back to Maggie, who was beginning to feel faint from blood loss.

To the side, her backpack was being rummaged through as the man digging through it looked for anything worth taking. Eventually he gave up and threw the bag away.

"Nothin', just clothes," he spit, annoyed. "Hey, man, is she done yet? I'm dyin' of thirst over here."

"Yeah, me, too," another member said.

"Hell, yeah, let's have us a party, better than beer nowadays," another member said.

Maggie slammed her head back and forth, wanting to break free of her restraints, but her arms were strapped down too well.

They were draining her blood and were going to have a party with it.

"How could this have happened?"

Thinking back, maybe the bearded man in her apartment building wasn't so bad after all. At least he hadn't wanted to kill her and drink her blood in place of water.

"Okay, there's enough to get started," the gang leader said. Switch out the bowls and when she runs dry slice her throat, there's usually a little more that way.

One of the men did as he was told and quickly switched out the half full bowls with empty ones, careful not to waste a drop.

As for Maggie, she was in a fog, her mind ready to fall into a deep pit she would never climb free of. Her vision was dim and she blinked up at the men who were killing her like she was a nothing more than a rabbit found in a warren.

The two bowls were passed around as each man sipped of her blood, like she was the modern day Jesus Christ. They smacked their lips and got red mustaches which they used their tongues to lick clean.

In no time the two bowls were empty, only a congealing residue on the bottom of each. But the other two bowls were filling up, and a few seconds later, they had been switched out and they were soon drinking like dying men who had stumbled out of the desert to find an oasis.

It was a party atmosphere as the men smoked and drank her blood, her plasma a substitute for beer and hard liquor.

She felt her mind going numb and she found that the pain she'd been feeling had faded. She felt herself floating above her body, looking down on her wide spread arms and placid, though pale, face.

Even at ten, she accepted death for it had been with her for more than five years. The world was dying; burning up to a cinder, and even these men would eventually die when the last drop of liquid on the once lush world was gone forever.

They were just delaying the inevitable.

As the men cheered and partied, one man inspected Maggie's clothes, wondering if there was anything in her pockets worth taking.

As he touched her hips, his hand fell on the bump that was her vitamins.

Reaching in, he pulled them out, then paused to take a drink of the bowl of blood being passed around. But now all the members had drunk their fill and Maggie was all but drained of her life's fluid.

After passing the bowl to another man, he brought up the orange plastic vial to his eye level so he could read the label. He was hoping it was some form of amphetamine but even aspirin would be good. He got headaches all the time and could use a few aspirins to help ease his sore head.

But as he read the label on the 'vitamins' his mouth slowly fell open and he began to panic. His mouth began to open and close as if he knew something that terrified him. It was an odd sight, Maggie's blood on his chin from where he'd messily partaken from the bowl, his eyes darting back and forth, first to his fellow gang members, then to the plastic orange bottle in his hands.

His skin became bone white, which was a sharp contrast to the plasma on his chin and lips.

The leader of the gang noticed this and he stepped closer to him.

"What's wrong, Ernie? You look like you've just seen a ghost. Lighten up, man, things are good. Now that we figured out how to deal with the water shortage, we'll be livin' like kings forever."

"No, we won't," Ernie said as he held up the vitamins to the leader.

The man looked at the bottle, not understanding what was going on. It was like he'd just walked into the middle of a conversation.

"So, then, what the fuck is your problem?"

"It's these pills, I recognize the name of these damn pills, man. Oh, shit, we are so fucked, oh, shit."

The gang leader was growing impatient. Someone handed him the bowl of blood and he sipped it, the warm liquid sluicing down his throat. It tasted sweet, much better than the father or the couple. He realized maybe it had to do with Maggie's age. Maybe it was something in the age of the blood that reflected the flavor of it. He was already thinking they needed to find some more kids. Not to mention that children were easier to subdue due to their size.

The gang leader grabbed Ernie by the scruff of his shirt and shook him like a rag doll.

"You better spit it the fuck out or you're gonna be next on the table, ya hear me?"

Ernie's eyes were wide, already knowing his fate and he nodded, the gang leader letting him go. He let out a heavy breath, a large sigh really, and then he showed the leader the plastic pill vial one last time.

"It's these fucking pills, man. I know the name of these pills from my brother. He had to take them, too."

"Yeah, so, what are they for?" the gang leader asked, annoyed it was taking so long to get the information out. Behind him, his men were whooping it up, the bowls of blood all empty, the men getting their fill.

"They're for Aids man, my brother had Aids. He had to take one of these everyday. And it's not HIV either man, these pills are for full-blown-fucking-Aids. The girl here has it man, and we all just drank her blood. That means..."

The gang leader pushed Ernie away from him.

"Fuck off, I know what it means, goddamn it!"

The gang leader turned and stared at his men, his infected men. Each had drunk their fill of the girl's blood and now they were all as good as dead.

As he stared down at the placid, pale face of the little girl, he realized by killing her he'd just signed their death sentences, and though the girl was just about dead, she had handed down a small form of justice for herself and her daddy.

He screamed his rage to the ceiling, his men all becoming silent as they stared at him, not understanding. And he had to wonder what they would do to him when he told them what he'd let happen.

Somehow he doubted they would be very forgiving.

On the table, Maggie was slipping into death, but not before hearing what Ernie said.

She had never known this about herself. But after hearing the word, *Aids*, it all made sense; her life made sense.

That's why she was home schooled before the world began to boil. And that was why she couldn't play with other children at the park, that is before the park became too hot to visit, the slide so hot you could fry an egg on it in seconds.

She remembered her Mommy and Daddy talking about how Mommy had been in a car accident when Maggie was still in her uterus. How she had received tainted blood at the hospital when in need of a transfusion.

But Maggie had been so young and had never understood what they were talking about.

But now it all made sense.

As Maggie slid into the oblivion of death, her lips actually creased into a smile.

Her suffering, and that of her daddy, was over.

But for the bad men who had killed her and her daddy, theirs was only just beginning.

THE END OF CHRISTMAS

Santa Claus closed the computer laptop and shook his head while taking off his thin, wire-rimmed reading glasses. He walked over to the television and stared at the screen filled with white snow.

"Still nothing, I just don't understand what's happening," he muttered under his breath.

Mrs. Claus entered the room, carrying a silver tray of milk and cookies—Santa's favorite snack.

"It's probably nothing, dear," Martha said as she placed the tray on a table beside Santa. "A solar flare or some such thing."

Santa picked up a cookie and took a bite. As crumbs fell into his white beard, he sighed. "For over a month, Martha? I highly doubt it. No, there's something wrong in the world. No phones, cable television or internet service for almost four weeks. I fear the worst."

"You said it was everywhere, right?" she asked.

He nodded. "As far as I can tell. Well, everywhere but here, and as you know, we're hidden from plain view."

"Well, dear, tomorrow night is Christmas Eve. When you head out to deliver presents to all the good little children, I guess you'll find out then what's been happening to the world."

He merely grunted in response, as he took another bite of his cookie.

Half an hour later, Santa left his small home to cross the town of Santa's Village. His destination was the main toy workshop, a warehouse located at the west side of town. This was where almost all the toys were designed and made.

The village was alive with activity as everyone rushed to finish the last toys so Santa could head out tomorrow night. Everywhere Santa looked he saw smiling faces. He nodded to a few elves as he walked, but most were so flustered with their chores they barely noticed him.

He didn't mind. While in the outside world Santa was a celebrity, loved by millions, here at Santa's Village—his home—he was just another worker—even if he was the boss.

Crossing the street, he waved to a few more elves and soon was at the warehouse.

From the outside, the building was rather plain, with snow piled five feet on all sides. Like all buildings in the village, this one was painted white.

Despite the invisibility spell that kept Santa's Village hidden from the outside world, camouflage was still necessary in case the spell ever failed.

Santa stepped through the front door and into a cacophony of busy elves. Tables were lined up throughout the warehouse, each one for an elf. Here, they fabricated toys the old fashioned way, though many of the items were flown in from outside sources by using dummy accounts and false businesses.

Loud holiday music was being blasted through hidden speakers, adding to the merriment and chaos.

The instant Santa entered the warehouse, an elf with thick black glasses appeared, standing right behind Santa.

"Hi, Santa!" the elf yelled and Santa jumped a foot into the air.

"What the…? Who?" Santa yelled as he turned and saw the elf where a moment ago there was no one. "Rufio, what have I told you about sneaking up on me?" Santa asked as he frowned at the elf who had almost given him a heart attack.

"You said not to do it," the elf replied. "But I have big news to tell you."

"Oh, and what might that be?" Santa asked.

"I just got the latest statistic report and it looks like not only are we on time, but we're ahead of schedule in manufacturing all the toys you requisitioned, Santa."

"Wonderful, that's wonderful news, Rufio. Well done. I'll have to make sure to thank everyone personally at the party when I return from my deliveries on Christmas morning."

Santa was talking about the party they had in the village every year to celebrate another successful Christmas. The entire village would relax and have fun, with food and games and joviality. But the next day they would get right back to work, for there would only be a year before the next Christmas and there was always so much to do.

"Excellent, I'll make sure to pen you in for that speech," Rufio said as he pulled a small, computer notebook out from behind his back and began typing. "Oh, Santa, any word from the outside world?" Rufio asked. "I still can't get internet service and all the lines seem to be down. I've called Tokyo to Africa, and then Ireland, but it's like the entire network is malfunctioning."

"Yes, I'm well aware of it, and have been for quite some time. At least when I leave tomorrow night, I can see first hand what's going on with communications across the globe."

"Do you think its anything serious?" Rufio asked.

Santa frowned, the gesture seemingly out of place on his usually happy, jolly visage. "I don't know, Rufio, we'll just have to wait and see when I get to the United States."

A chorus of yells filled the warehouse and Santa and Rufio looked up to see a five foot, plush teddy bear walking down the center aisle. It had an adorable face, with big button eyes and a smiling mouth. But despite this, the bear looked mad, and as the elves tried to stop it, the stuffed animal would push them away.

One elf tore off his shirt to expose a muscled upper chest, and he pulled a small knife from a hidden pocket. He placed the knife in his mouth and growled like a warrior going into battle. He climbed onto a table and jumped onto the back of the teddy bear, to then hack and slash at the fake fur.

Stuffing went everywhere as the teddy bear tried to yank the elf off, but the tiny warrior was in the center of the bear's back, and the arms wouldn't go that far. Slash after slash, the elf cut and hacked and soon the air was filled with stuffing.

The teddy bear took a few more faltering steps and then fell forward, its fluffy limbs twitching before finally remaining still.

Another elf came running up to Santa. This elf was breathing hard from the exertion of the battle and he had a small cut on his forehead. The bells on his pointed green shoes were missing, having been torn off, and his green tunic was ripped.

"I'm so sorry about that, Santa," the elf said. "Herman sprinkled too much pixie dust into the stuffing and well, you saw the result."

"Is anyone hurt?" Santa asked with a look of concern.

"No, Santa, a few bumps and bruises, but everyone's fine."

"Good, that's good. Well, tell Herman to be more careful, will you? Little Suzie doesn't want to wake up Christmas morning with a killer bear under her tree."

"Yes, Santa, right away, Santa, it won't happen again, Santa," the elf said quickly, and jogged away to help with the cleanup. Santa watched for a few seconds as the elves picked up the corpse of the teddy bear and dragged it away. A trail of stuffing was left behind, an aftermath of the toy carnage.

He turned and looked down at Rufio. "Things seem to be under control here, I think I'll go check on the reindeer."

Rufio saluted like a soldier. "Will do, Santa, just let me know if you need anything else."

Santa left the warehouse, relishing the modicum of silence as the door closed behind him.

With a heavy sigh, he let out a plume of air that coalesced into fog before him, and walked to the stables, where his cherished flying reindeer were housed.

Once more, the instant he stepped inside, an elf popped up between two bales of hay.

"Hi, Santa, what's up?"

"Oh, hello there, Marvin. I just wanted to drop by and check on the reindeer."

Marvin smiled proudly. "They're all set for tomorrow night, Santa. I've fed them and brushed them and made sure they have enough water. They'll be fed tomorrow afternoon, that way they won't be too full to fly." He chuckled at that, finding it amusing.

"Good, good, excellent. I want to see them."

"Of course, right this way." Marvin led Santa deeper into the stable until he stopped at a wide barn door. Opening it, he gestured for Santa to go first. As he did, he entered a large room the size of a three car garage. Here, the reindeer were basically lounging around, a few sitting while others stood. When they saw Santa, they all stood up and came to him. Santa reached into his pocket and pulled out a handful of oats, which he fed each of them in kind. He counted them, making sure they were all there.

"Ah, Dasher, Dancer, Prancer, Vixen, Comet, Cupid, Donner and..." He paused. "Where's Blitzen?" Santa asked.

"Huh? I don't know, he should be here," Marvin said as he counted the reindeer.

Then, from behind a small wall of hay, Blitzen appeared. He trotted over to the rest of the group and Santa patted his head. "Ah, there you are, old friend, I was worried there for a second."

Blitzen snorted like a horse and ducked his head. Santa smiled widely, letting out a loud bellow of laughter. "Ho-ho-ho! Well done, Marvin, they look fit and ready for their long journey ahead. I don't know what I'd do without them, you know."

"Take a plane?" Marvin inquired.

Santa laughed again and patted the short elf on the head, much like the reindeer. "Very funny, I highly doubt that would work as well as my reindeer do. Well, I'll be going now, I will see you boys tomorrow," he said to the reindeer as he left the stable.

All was well, or as well as it could be given his lack of communication with the outside world. At least whatever was happening hadn't affected his village.

Now that it was getting so close to departure, he had to admit he had a bad feeling deep down inside. Of course, it was possible something silly had happened. But for the entire world to go dark and cease communications, well, that couldn't bode well.

Either way, he would find out tomorrow night when he went on his yearly trek to deliver presents to good little boys and girls. Until then, he would have to wait and do what he did every year, which was to eat. He had lost some weight over the summer and had been doing his best to bulk up. After all, no one liked a skinny Santa.

Hoping Martha had baked those chocolate chip cookies she had promised earlier that morning, he headed back home to check.

"Now you be safe, dear," Martha told Santa as he finished checking his sleigh. The bright red sled was sitting outside the stable, the reindeers harnessed and ready to go. More than ten elves were all rushing about; making sure Santa was as ready to go as he possibly could. There was only one large sack in the back of the sleigh; it was all that was needed.

Using Christmas magic, the one toy sack had an infinite bottom. All Santa had to do was reach inside it and pluck out the toy he needed. After all, how else could he deliver all those toys all over the world in only one trip?

"That's a funny thing to say, Martha," Santa replied as he stepped up into the sleigh. "What makes you say that?"

"Oh, I don't know, it's just…well, we still don't know why there's a blackout across the world, and for all we know there could have been some calamity or natural disaster."

"That's silly, Martha, you're being overdramatic. If it was something like that, then we would have felt the effects here in the village, too."

"Not if it was something viral. Maybe one of those Middle Eastern countries let loose a biological agent or some awful thing."

He chuckled, his ho-ho-ho, barely a whisper. "Martha, I swear, you've been watching too many horror movies. I'm sure there is a perfectly rational explanation to whatever has happened. Now, my love, it's time for me to leave. Boys and girls everywhere are waiting for me."

She stepped close to him and kissed his cheek. "I know that, and that's why you're Santa Claus. Just promise me you'll come back in the morning, no matter what."

He sighed and with a nod, decided to humor his wife. "I promise, I'll be back, no matter what." He picked up the reins and gave them a gentle tug.

Blitzen was in the lead and when Santa gently nudged him, he snorted and began to move, causing the other reindeer to do the same. Santa circled around the stable until he was in an open clearing used for take-offs and landings, and with another tug on the reins, he let Blitzen know it was time to go.

All the reindeer began to jog, then run, and soon they were galloping across the snow-covered ice. And then, when Blitzen jumped, the others followed suit and the sleigh lifted into the air, floating on a cloud of Christmas magic.

Santa banked around the roof of the stable and with a, "Ho-ho-ho! Merry Christmas!" he flew over the village and into the clouds, soon lost from sight, the tinkling of sleigh bells wrapped around the necks of the reindeer also fading.

Martha hugged herself as she stared up into the night sky, her mouth set in a slim line. Rufio walked over to her and tugged on her apron. Looking down, she saw the elf frowning.

"You look like I feel, Mrs. Claus," he said. "Care to share why you look so worried."

She nodded slightly. "Oh, Rufio, I don't know why I feel this way. I should be happy. After all, it's Christmas Eve. But for some reason, I have this feeling of dread that I just can't shake."

"Yes, I feel it, too. It has to do with us losing communication with the outside world. Whatever the reason, it can't be good."

"I agree," she said. "I just hope he comes back to us safe and sound."

Rufio plastered a wide smile on his face, only half of it forced. "Hey, of course he will, after all, he's Santa Claus."

After crossing the ocean, Santa came in for landing in a small town in Maine. He noticed that the town was dark, which seemed odd to him. As he flew over the town square, he saw the Christmas tree was dark, where it was normally lit up, a beacon he would normally use to find the town.

This was his first stop. From here he would continue across America and then head out to other countries.

There was a small park near the first house he planned to visit and he landed in the white fluff of the light snowfall. In the wan light of the moon, the snow glistened like glass, reflecting the light as if a thousand stars had fallen to earth.

Climbing off the sleigh, he patted each reindeer in turn, the animals sniffing and growling playfully. Each reindeer was covered in a thin sheen of perspiration from the long flight from the North Pole and their breath blew out in great clouds as they exhaled.

No sooner did Santa turn and walk away, then the reindeer began to root under the light snow, searching for tender grass. Santa looked all around him, making sure it was clear. A spell of invisibility covered the reindeer, but only from sight. If a passerby stumbled into the sleigh or the animals, they would be in for quite a surprise. Thus was the reason why he landed in the park and from there would make his rounds in a large section of the town. Then he would fly to the other side and do the same there. He rarely landed on rooftops such as the stories told as there was no room. Much like an airplane, he needed room to take off and land.

With his magic sack of toys over his shoulder, he began walking to the dark house fifty feet away.

As he exited the park to cross the road, he did see one lone figure in the shadows at the end of the street. He stopped to see what the figure would do but as he watched, the figure turned and shambled away, as if he or she was drunk. What was odd was the figure didn't seem to be wearing a coat, but looked as if he or she was wearing only pajamas. Shrugging his shoulders, deciding someone was out for a late night walk and must like the cold weather, Santa crossed the street to the house.

He scurried up the side of the home like a squirrel, using his Christmas magic to make himself lighter than air. Once on the roof, he made himself thinner and down the chimney he went.

Like a ghost, he shimmied down and came out into the living room, solidifying back into himself. He smiled as he shook his arms, the feeling always leaving his entire body tingling, much like when a person's leg falls asleep to then come back to circulation with pins and needles, only minus the pain.

The room was dark as well, the lights on the tree dead. He saw presents under the tree but they looked like they had been opened already. Or perhaps an animal had gotten into them. Ribbons and wrapping paper was scattered across the floor and he had to be careful not to step in it, or the crunch would awaken the residents.

Santa reached into a pocket and pulled out his magic notebook. Whatever house he was at, the notebook would show the names, ages and what the children wanted.

He saw there were three children in this particular home. Little Maggie, who was five, little Timmy, who was eight, and Baby Suzy, who was only a few months old. He read that Maggie wanted a dolly that sang songs and Timmy wanted a new video game system—the Z BOX.

He also read that both children had been good, or had been until a month ago. Since communications had gone down, he wasn't able to update his notebook.

Santa reached into his magic toy sack and pulled out each present, placing them under the defunct tree.

He was about to leave when he heard the sound of small footsteps coming toward him. Turning around, he saw two small figures come running out of a side hallway and charge into the room. Before he could do anything, the two children were upon him, each lunging for him.

Little Timmy jumped high and latched onto Santa's right sleeve, trying to bite him. Only Santa's heavy red suit protected him from a wound. Little Maggie stayed on the floor and jumped for Santa's right boot. Her small teeth began gnawing on Santa's black boot like it was prime rib, while her tiny arms wrapped around his ankle.

"What in the name of Christmas?" Santa yelled at the two wild children who seemed to be trying to eat him, of all things. Though he would never hurt a child, he acted on instinct, too startled to think about what he was doing. Before either child could do him any damage, he plucked each one off him and tossed them to the couch a few feet away. The small bodies bounced off the cushions and rolled onto the floor. In a split second, both were on their feet again, each crouched low and growling. Timmy had material in his mouth and Santa realized it was a piece of his red suit.

Pulling a flashlight from his pocket, Santa turned it on and aimed the beam at the two tykes. He let out a gasp when he saw their faces.

Instead of two sweet visages of innocent youth, he saw two little monsters. Their eyes were sunken into their heads and their lips were pulled back on their faces, as if the skin had dried and pulled taut. Their teeth flashed in the beam of the light and their growling increased.

Santa saw both children's pajamas were covered in what looked like dried blood, and their eyes were a milky white, for all purposes void of emotion.

With a snarl and a moan, they came for him again, and he kicked out and sent them both rolling across the floor.

Not knowing what to do, fearful for the two children's well being, he broke his rule about being seen and ran deeper into the house, in search of the parent's bedroom. He found it easily enough, and with his flashlight bobbing up and down, he entered the room.

As the beam of light landed on the bed, he let out another gasp at the sight greeting him. The mother and father were there in their bed, but they weren't *all there* exactly.

As Santa's eyes took in the scene before him, he saw that Mom was missing her arms and Dad only had one leg. All three of his other limbs were long gone and where they had been detached looked raw and torn, as if small teeth had worried away at the meat.

Both parents had large holes in their heads, as if something had been burrowing in their skulls, searching for the tender brains within. The bed was soaked in blood, and the once white sheets were nothing but a dark brown now. Flies buzzed about and the smell knocked Santa nearly on his butt, the charnel house odor potent beyond belief.

As he stumbled away from the murder scene, and back into the hallway, he looked back down the hallway to see the two children coming for him. Looking to his left, he saw another room and he dashed into it. He realized it was the baby's room. There was a crib in the corner and he stumbled over to it. But when he pointed the beam into the crib, all he saw were raw baby parts. A tiny arm, a piece of leg, half of a foot, and something that might have been an ear, was all that lay in the crib. The sheets of the crib was also stained a dark brown, thanks to the blood drying weeks ago.

He turned when the door was forced in and the two children dashed into the room, both attacking Santa again. He used the flashlight and hit Timmy over the head, dazing the boy. When Maggie came for his leg, he kicked her away, then pushed Timmy with his free hand. Both little monsters fell into the corner. Acting fast, Santa pocketed the flashlight, and in the gloom of the room, he spun, picked up the crib and flipped it over, then used it like a cage to trap the two children. Baby parts spilled out to fall onto the floor as the two little monsters became trapped. They reached through the wooden bars of the crib, trying to reach him, but the bars were close together and they could only get their hands part way through.

Needing to catch his breath and try to make some sense to what was happening, Santa sat on the crib, thus trapping the two tykes.

Timmy and Maggie hissed and snarled as they fought like wild animals to get free.

Santa didn't get more than a few seconds respite before a shrill scream rent the night, followed by another and another after that. Though the screams sounded almost human, he knew immediately it was his reindeer.

Jumping up, he dashed out of the bedroom and into the living room. No sooner did he leave the two children, then they pushed the crib off them and ran after Santa.

But Santa was already gone, up the chimney and onto the roof.

As he climbed down the side of the house, he stopped and cast a glance over his shoulder.

In the dark house, at a window facing the street, were the two children, clawing at the glass. One managed to smash a pane but neither could climb out, as the single pane was too small. They snarled and hissed as Santa ran across the street and back to the park.

Upon entering the park, Santa stopped short, his mouth hanging open at the sight before him.

Where his eight reindeer had been waiting for him, there was now nothing but bloody carnage from end to end. As for his reindeer, they were all dead, torn apart by what seemed to be *people*. There had to be more than fifty people huddled around his dead reindeer, each tearing at the carcasses, chewing on the meat. Some had their heads so far inside the stomachs of the reindeer that they couldn't be seen, while others had organs hanging from mouths as they chewed and swallowed, chewed and swallowed. Many of the people had stomachs so bloated with raw meat they looked ready to burst, and Santa took a step back in horror.

"Donner, Cupid, Comet, oh God no!" he yelled, too shocked to realize that calling attention to himself probably wasn't a very good idea.

As he yelled out, every person feeding on the carcasses stopped eating and poked their heads up, much like a wild animal would do upon spotting prey.

All eyes went to Santa Claus, who with his bright red suit, stood out like a white spot on a black piece of paper.

"Uh-oh," Santa said softly as he stared at the crowd of zombies with blood covering their faces and soaking into their clothes. In the moonlight,

Santa could see their eyes, and he saw the same dead look that had been in the two children's.

Crunching snow caused him to spin around, and when he did, he found another dozen or more zombies surrounding him. As he watched them come for him, he put all the pieces together and realized the reason there had been no contact with the outside world from his village was that there had been a zombie apocalypse.

Santa found he had nowhere to go, all avenues of escape cut off. His mind raced with ideas of what he should do.

He knew about zombies from when he delivered toys to Haiti, and he knew to remove the head or destroy the brain would take them down for good. But he had no weapons, only the toys in his magic sack.

A zombie lunged for him, the first in the group, and Santa jumped out of the way, the body falling to the snow. Santa kicked the ghoul in the face, sending bloody teeth to splatter the snow like red hail. He spun when another zombie came for him and he used his belly, butting the ghoul in the chest as it tried to wrap its arms around him. Like a trampoline, the ghoul snapped back and fell into the others.

Desperate for a weapon, Santa reached into his magic sack and pulled out the first thing that came to mind.

One half of a pair of women's ice skates.

The skate was black with white trim, and the blade was honed to perfection. It was suppose to be for a girl named Cindy, who lived in the next town. She wanted to be a figure skater.

Spinning the skate so that the blade pointed out, Santa used it when the next zombie came for him. This zombie was female with a red Christmas sweater on with a green Xmas tree on the front. As she lunged for Santa, he raised the skate and brought it down on her head. The skate slid into her skull like butter and he sawed it back and forth, cutting deep into the scalp and the brain within, nearly slicing her head in two. The woman dropped to the snow, all her Christmas cheer leaking out of her to soak into the snow.

Santa spun and used the skate on another ghoul, but when he whacked it in the head, the skate became stuck! Letting it go, he pushed the body away and reached into the magic sack for something else.

He came up with a handful of music CDs. Cracking the cases, he used them like mini throwing stars, adding a little Christmas magic to see them find their targets. The silver circles flew threw the air to become embedded in faces and chests. But this did nothing to stop the undead crowd and Santa went back in the sack for something else.

He came up with a hockey stick and he swung it like a madman. The blade connected with heads, and those that had muscle and tissue missing from their necks, found the hockey stick was more than a match for their weakened throats. Heads went flying and blood sprayed into the night air as Santa went to town on the undead horde.

Head after head went flying into the night until the hockey stick cracked and the tip broke off. Using it like a spear one last time, Santa jammed it into the chest of an attacking ghoul. It didn't stop the dead man but it did allow Santa a moment to reach into his magic sack and pull out another toy.

It was a toy train, the age level under three. It was made of soft plastic and had wheels that made noise when you squeezed them. Santa stared at it, wondering what he could do with it. Then he saw the pull string on the front. It was made so a child could pull it around the house, hearing the sounds it made as he did it.

Grabbing the pull string, Santa used it on the closest zombie. He wrapped it around the ghoul's neck like a garrote, then pulled it taut. String sank into dead flesh and as he used his bulk, he pushed on the zombie's back with his knee, causing the head to snap backwards and the back to arc. As the string severed the spine from the brain, the body collapsed to the snow.

More zombies surrounded him, and seen from above, he looked like one red dot surrounded by a sea of bodies.

His magic sack was pulled from his shoulder and he tried to get it back but was too slow.

As the ghouls came for him, he reached into his pockets and pulled out candy canes. Using them like small daggers, he jammed them into the eyes of the zombies. Sometimes the candy canes would go so deep that the brains would be punctured and the body would fall to the ground, but most of the time only blindness was the result.

From between the legs of the attacking horde, two smaller monsters crawled.

Little Timmy and Maggie had managed to wiggle through the broken window of their home and they were still hungry for Santa's flesh.

While Santa fought off the ghouls from on high, the two ghouls attacked from below, and Santa let out a cry as they wrapped their small arms around his legs. As he reached down to pull them off, his left sleeve rode up on his arm, exposing the pink skin of his wrist.

A geriatric zombie with a balding pate and a Christmas shirt that said, **KISS ME, I'M OLD, MERRY CHRISTMAS**, saw the opening in Santa's armor and took advantage of it. Yellow teeth sank into Santa's wrist, but not very deep and Santa barely felt the bite. When he spun to throw the kids away, the old man was knocked away also. Santa kept on fighting, oblivious to his wound.

He pushed through the undead crowd to try and break free, but there were too many! His eyes went to the zombie standing before him, one that was holding his magic toy sack!

Before the zombie knew what was happening, Santa reached out and pulled the sack back to him. Thinking of a toy he needed, he reached in and pulled out a high-powered BB gun.

It was fully loaded, and as fast as he could pump it, he shot each ghoul in the face, aiming for the eyes. It took more than one BB to put a zombie down, but when enough BBs penetrated into the brain through the eye sockets, down they went.

He exhausted his ammunition and then reached into the sack for more toys.

This time he was creative and he pulled out a large handful of firecrackers, M80's being a few of the more powerful ones.

As the zombies came for him, trying to bite, he lit the fuses and jammed the fireworks into their gaping maws.

There were muffled pops each time the firecrackers went off and a few heads exploded like a watermelon hit with a sledgehammer as the powerful firecrackers ignited.

But though he fought the good fight, Santa knew he was losing fast. Surrounded on all sides, he knew he couldn't keep up the battle indefinitely.

He came to a section of the park that the snow was crushed flat and he reached into his magic sack and pulled out two big handfuls of glass marbles. Tossing them onto the ground, the zombies began to slip and slide as they stepped on them, some falling so hard they cracked their heads open on the ice, staining it red.

Santa tried to see over the undead crowd to find a way to escape, but there was none.

He was about to give up hope and accept his reality, when a shadow flew over him, causing him to look up.

It was Blitzen!

Santa quickly realized he was mistaken when he had seen all his reindeer killed and being eaten. With so much blood and animal parts strewn about, trying to count all the carcasses had been impossible and it was now clear that Blitzen had escaped, flying out of harm's reach.

And now he had come back for Santa.

Acting fast, Santa reached into his toy sack and pulled out two cans of silly string—yellow and pink. He sprayed these into the faces of the zombies, causing the ghouls to sputter and spit out the foul tasting foam.

Some were blinded momentarily and Santa used this as his chance to break free of the horde. Running as fast as his chubby legs would allow, he reached a small clearing in the center of the park.

Overhead, Blitzen floated down, and before the first zombie could reach them, Santa jumped onto the reindeer's back, Blitzen taking to the air once more.

As they flew high into the night sky, Santa looked below. Now, the dark town came into focus and he fully understood what it meant. As he looked on the horizon, where there should have been the lights of other towns, there was nothing but pitch darkness.

Breathing hard, Santa repositioned himself on Blitzen and said, "Let's go home, boy, there's no reason for us to stay here any longer."

With a snuff, the reindeer turned north, flew into the clouds and continued toward home.

Hours later, Santa and Blitzen arrived back at the North Pole.

Everyone gathered around, not understanding why Santa had returned so soon and why he was riding only one lone reindeer and was minus his sleigh.

Martha walked up to him and Santa kissed her on the cheek.

"It's as you feared," he told her. "It looks like there was a zombie uprising and that's the reason why the world has gone silent." He quickly filled them in on his night and what had happened to the other reindeer.

"Oh my lord, no," she said. "Those poor reindeer. Are you all right?"

He nodded, patting her arm. "Yes, yes, I'm fine. As I said, I ran into a town full of them but I managed to fend them off. But I have to be honest. If Blitzen hadn't arrived when he did, well…" he trailed off and she knew exactly what he was trying to say. She hugged him and muffled her sobs of happiness that he had returned to her.

Rufio pulled on Santa's jacket. "Santa, what are we going to do now?"

Santa shrugged. "There's nothing we can do, Rufio. The world as we know it is gone. There's no use for toys in a land of the walking dead. I guess we're out of business."

Other elves standing around them began to talk and murmur amongst themselves.

Santa raised his hands in the air to calm them. "Now, now, it's not so bad. At least we're safe here at the North Pole from whatever caused this terrible thing. We'll be fine and someday, when this is all over, we can go back to what we know and love. There's sure to be survivors."

More murmurs began and Santa quelled it once more. "That's enough for now. Tomorrow afternoon, there will be a village meeting in the main toy workshop. That's where we'll discuss what to do next. Now everyone, go back to your homes, I know for me it's been a long night and I need to rest."

Everyone began to shuffle away and Rufio pulled on Santa's jacket yet again. "Are you sure you're all right, Santa? Is there anything I can get for you? Do you need the village doctor?"

"No, Rufio, I'm fine, really, I'm just tired. I just need to sleep." Santa patted the elf on the head with a wan smile. Santa and Martha walked to their home, Martha asking question after question.

When they finally arrived home, Santa took off his blood-covered, torn red suit and went right to bed. He was so tired, which he didn't fully understand. He was immortal after all and normal ailments didn't affect him.

Martha made him a cup of hot cocoa and after he drank it he quickly he fell asleep.

He slept so heavily, some would say he slept like the dead.

As he tossed and turned, mumbling to himself about zombies and his slaughtered reindeer, the small bite on his wrist pulsed slightly as thin blue lines of infection crawled up his arm.

The next day would indeed be a memorable one for the North Pole, for in the morning, Santa would be a brand new man.

Or is that *dead* man?

THE HOLE

"You wanna see something really gross?"

When Timmy heard those words, two things went through his mind. One, Josh was fucking with him again or two, he was in one of his rare moods when he considered Timmy a friend.

Those six words could either bode extremely well, or could end up with Timmy's sneakers hanging on the telephone line by their laces; the clean white-only two week old- sneakers swinging back and forth lazily, never to be returned to the earth again.

Timmy weighed his reply to Josh, knowing the simple words he could say would result in the former event.

Then with a sigh and a breath, both similar to how a cliff diver looks before taking that leap, he said, "Sure, I guess."

Three simple words spoken quickly and succinctly; three words weighed carefully and then phrased with a slight shrug to the shoulders.

Josh grinned. It wasn't an evil grin, like the one he flashed Timmy before he yanked his shorts down last month in gym class. There, Timmy had stood in his tighty-whities, for the entire fifth grade class to see. He just thanked God he had been *wearing* underwear at all.

Timmy looked at that grin, the not so evil grin that was more *malicious*—no, wait—malevolent was the better word to describe the visage of Josh the Bully, Josh the Torturer and Josh the Punisher. But despite being all these things, Timmy still idolized Josh.

See, Josh was in the seventh grade. He had stayed back twice, so he was the oldest kid in his class. He had wavy brown hair that all the girls loved and he wore a wallet—black leather—with a chain on it.

Timmy thought that was the coolest thing ever. An actual chain hung from the back of Josh's pocket and trailed up to his belt loop on his hip. Add that to his all black wardrobe, a t-shirt with some heavy metal rock band on the front, and Josh was the poster child for an American bad boy.

"Good," Josh grinned so wide his teeth peered through his lips. "I knew you weren't that big of a pussy. Come on, follow me." He turned and began walking, Timmy following like an obedient lap dog.

The two boys walked down the street of their neighborhood, past the gas station, a 7-11, and a Laundromat until Josh reached the end of the street. The dead end sign with its dents from rocks, leered over them like a cross adult. Josh entered the woods lining the road.

He glanced over his shoulder just once to make sure Timmy was still behind him. Timmy was, though the deeper they penetrated the thick forest, Timmy began to have second thoughts. Was Josh going to do something to him once they were so deep in the woods no one would hear him scream?

To make matters worse, Josh glanced over his shoulder as he climbed over a fallen tree and the look in the older boy's eyes gave Timmy the chills.

"Come on, it's not much further," Josh said and continued on.

Timmy scurried over the fallen tree and picked up his pace to keep up. Glancing over his shoulder, he found he was so deep in the woods he could no longer see the dead end sign. All around him the trees leaned inward, their branches stretching outward to pull him close, holding him tightly so he could never escape.

It's a trap! his inner voice screamed. *Get out of here!*

He was about to do that—turn and run—when Josh crested a slight incline and stopped walking.

"We're here," he said, huffing and puffing from the exertion. Timmy wondered if his shortness of breath was due to all the cigarettes he smoked. If Timmy was correct, Josh sucked in a pack a day at least.

"Come here, take a look at this shit," Josh said.

Hesitantly, he ascended the slight incline and stood next to Josh. Timmy looked down where Josh was pointing, the bully's legs spread wide to prevent him from falling. Timmy's mouth fell open and he let out a silent gasp of shock and surprise.

There was a large hole at the bottom of the incline. It reminded Timmy of a bear trap. He could see the branches and leaves on the sides of the hole, residue from when *something* had fallen through and into the camouflaged trap beneath.

Timmy thought the word *something* was the best description to describe the occupant of the hole. It had once been a woman—he was sure of it—but that was only because of the tattered, muck encrusted skirt the occupant of the hole wore. Her lips were gone, leaving her visage a rictus grin that would never fade. The meat on her left cheek was missing, maggots squirming about the jagged wound, some losing purchase to fall to the ground. Her left eye was punctured, looking for all purposes like a deflated condom, the milky white pus dripping from the socket nothing more than expelled semen.

As Timmy stepped up to the hole, the zombie howled, the dead woman's moan filled with—what Timmy believed—was sorrow, loss and pain.

"Who is she?" Timmy asked as he stared at the walking corpse.

"Don't know," Josh replied. "But she's the first zombie I've seen since all the shit began to happen."

Timmy nodded, understanding completely.

The dead recently had begun to walk a little more than a week ago. Morgues, hospitals and nursing homes were the major hot spots for this bizarre phenomenon. No one knew why and so far the walking corpses had been easy to contain. But Timmy's dad said things were going to get worse real soon. As the news reports kept filtering in. It was clear to most people that whatever was happening was growing each day.

"What are you gonna do with her?" Timmy asked as he stared at the grisly face. Even though the face was filled with rot, Timmy could still see that when the woman was alive, she had been pretty.

"It's not what I'm going to do with her," Josh said, his voice cold and cruel. "It's what you're gonna do with her."

And with the words barely out of his mouth, Josh leaned forward until he was right behind Timmy and he pushed him into the hole.

Timmy let out a cry of surprise to find himself tumbling forward. He went head first, tucking his head in at the last second, and landing more on his shoulders and back. With the breath whooshing from his lungs like a spent balloon, he fell to his side, laying still, his vision flashing white from the impact.

"Let's see if she's hungry!" Josh laughed as he knelt down to look into the hole.

Slowly, Timmy came back to his senses. The first thing he saw were the dirt walls of the hole. Earthworms were squirming out of the walls, and twigs and rocks dotted the surface. The smell of garbage that had been left out in the sun for too long assaulted his olfactory senses, the aroma hanging on his tongue, causing him to gag.

The zombie had soiled herself at some point, the dry rivulets of shit, looking like streaks of mud, ran down her legs. Timmy could see small holes in her legs, and tiny white maggots crawling out. The zombie's skin undulated as the maggots wiggled beneath the surface, as if they were miniscule prisoners trying to break free.

He craned his neck back to look at her—this dead woman, this *abomination*—and his mouth fell open in terror. He'd heard the stories of what his dad had said.

"The dead were eating the living…"

He knew she was dead, that there was no way to escape. The hole was six feet deep, the walls of soft dirt and clay. There was no way he could climb out. And even if there was, as he struggled to break free, the zombie would be on him, tearing at his flesh, consuming him.

But despite this, Timmy still tried to climb out. His hands dug into the soft earth, the soil falling to the bottom of the hole, some spraying into his face. He spit out what went in his mouth and blinked to clear his vision.

Frantic and panicking, his breath came in short gasps and his hair stood up on the back of his neck as he anticipated feeling the cold hands grasping him, followed by the feel of teeth sinking into his tender flesh.

Minutes passed, and as he scraped at the wall like a dog digging up a bone, he slowed his actions, realizing if he was going to be attacked and eaten, it should have happened by now.

Finally, he stopped trying to climb out. The dirt was piled at his feet, covering them, and he slowly turned around. The zombie was still there, but the dead woman was immobile. She was just standing there, looking at him. No more than a foot away, she could kill him instantly if she wanted to.

Timmy waited for the end, closing his eyes so he didn't have to see it coming.

Seconds passed then…

"Come on, you stupid fuck! Kill him already!"

Timmy opened his eyes and looked up to see Josh standing right at the edge of the hole. The tips of his sneakers were an inch over the edge and he was leaning over with a five foot stick in his hands.

As he poked the zombie, he yelled at it.

"What the fuck are you waiting for? Eat him!"

Josh poked the dead woman in the right shoulder, the tip of the stick penetrating the soft, rancid flesh. Black, congealed blood oozed out. A few maggots were set free and they fell to the churned earth to wiggle and squirm.

Timmy said nothing as he watched Josh beat the zombie. He was still too scared to move, but though frightened, deep down inside, he realized Josh was doing something far worse to him than the other times.

This time Josh was trying to kill him.

Josh whacked the zombie in the head, causing one of her ears to fall off. She moaned loudly and Josh raised the stick again.

"Come on. What the hell are you doing?" Josh yelled, the stick raised above his head, ready to plop the dead woman on the top of her mop of a hairdo.

Before Josh could bring the stick down—all the way down—the zombie did something both Josh and Timmy never expected.

The dead woman raised her left arm and with her hand open wide, she caught the stick as it careened toward her head. The bones in her hand snapped and cracked as the weight and force of the stick destroyed brittle bones.

"What the fuck?" Josh grunted as the stick struck dry flesh.

But the dead woman wasn't finished, and she walked across the few feet to reach Josh rather quickly and stretched out her right hand and wrapped her fingers around Josh's right ankle. She was missing her pinky finger above the knuckle, but it didn't seem to matter.

"Hey!" Josh screamed as the cold hand contacted the warm skin of his ankle.

With a jerk of her arm, the zombie yanked Josh's leg out from under him and he found himself in the air. He landed on the ground hard, knocking the air from his lungs, and as he tried to focus and clear his head, he found himself being dragged into the hole.

He landed heavily, dirt cascading over his face and chest, and as he tried to blink the dirt clear of his eyes, he waved his hands in the air.

As his vision cleared, he spit dirt, and the first thing he saw was the zombie as she leaned over and sank her teeth into his neck, just below his chin. His jugular was severed in an instant and he felt warm blood splashing onto his chest—his blood! The zombie began to slurp and chew and Josh found himself trapped beneath her.

Timmy stared in horror, feeling a trickle of urine seep down his leg, he was so scared.

And as Josh's arms waved and he yelled for help, his screams quickly becoming a gurgle, Timmy snapped out of his fear and saw his chance to escape.

With a yell of his own to gather his courage, he ran at the zombie and Josh, then jumped up. Using Josh's left shoulder as a step, he was now able to reach the edge of the hole, and he leaped up, catching the edge and then kicking his legs to push himself out. There was a moment when he didn't think he was going to make it, but then his right sneaker found purchase and he was scooting over the edge.

He spun around and peered down into the hole. Josh wasn't moving anymore, the zombie feeding on his neck, chewing and tearing, the skin stretching like elastic before it would snap off in a spray of blood.

Timmy stared down with an impassive face as he looked into Josh's glazed-over eyes. He'd never seen a dead kid before and he didn't know exactly how to feel about it.

Not knowing what to do, and realizing he was now safe, Timmy sat down at the edge of the hole. The zombie continued feeding for the next three minutes and then stopped.

Timmy leaned forward, expecting something to happen. If the news had been correct, he knew exactly what would happen next and he was curious to see if it was true.

Timmy didn't move, didn't breathe, as he watched Josh's corpse. The dead woman, still chewing on a piece of flesh, seemed not to care about Josh anymore, as if as soon as he was dead, he wasn't appetizing.

And then it happened, just like the news said.

The fingers on Josh's right hand began to twitch and soon the entire arm was moving. Timmy watched Josh as he moved his head, trying to turn it left and right. But with half his neck missing, this wasn't at all possible.

With a gurgle-like moan, Josh tried to stand up. At first he couldn't do it but after a few more tries he managed it.

"Whoa," Timmy said, his voice cracked and dry.

Josh heard him and his body turned to face Timmy who stood up and backed away from the edge. He felt his stomach turning upside down in fear once more. If Josh was bad before, as a zombie he would be ten times worse.

Josh's eyes locked on Timmy and the newly revived ghoul tried to get at him. But as Timmy had done before, Josh couldn't escape the hole. As he tried to climb, all he did was pull dirt onto him.

As Timmy watched, he realized he was safe and he scooted closer.

The dead woman did nothing, just stood in the corner and stared at the bottom of the hole, while chewing on the last remnant of flesh in her mouth.

Timmy moved as close as he dared and gazed down at Josh. Then he looked at the woman zombie and said, "Thank you."

The dead woman looked up at him but didn't respond. How could she? She was dead.

Timmy watched Josh as he tried to escape the hole, the same one he'd thrown Timmy in only minutes before, and Timmy's face grew hard, his eyes taking on a coldness never seen before.

His mouth went up into a slight smile and he spit into the hole, the wad of saliva landing on Josh's upturned face. Timmy kicked at the edge, splattering dirt into Josh's face. Particles went into Josh's eyes but the dead bully didn't care.

He opened his mouth and groaned and Timmy kicked dirt into it.

Timmy stopped kicking and merely stood there, watching the dead boy, understanding Josh had wanted the same fate to happen to him.

But it hadn't.

For some reason, the woman zombie hadn't wanted him, she had wanted Josh. Could it be that there had been some small memory inside her dead brain? Maybe she wanted the person who had thrown her into the hole, some sort of revenge?

Timmy didn't care. It was over.

Turning, he walked away from the hole, leaving the two zombies there forever as far as he was concerned.

He was going home.

He needed a shower.

THE ILLUSION OF BIGFOOT

"Shhh, keep quiet," Carson whispered as he pried open the window to the one-story home after disabling the alarm to the window. The window was six feet off the ground and he had to stretch up to reach it.

"I didn't say a thing," his partner replied.

"You sure, Max? I thought you told me to hurry up."

"I did say that but I wasn't talking to you."

"Then who the fuck were you talking to?"

"Myself," Max said.

"Well, next time, keep it to yourself," Carson whispered. He returned to the window lock, sliding the thin piece of metal between frame and lock. After a full minute passed, he smiled, which was followed by the soft sound of the lock unlatching. "Gotcha, you little bastard."

Slowly as he could, he opened the window. When it was halfway open, it squeaked a little and both Carson and Max cringed, but then whatever was rubbing let go and the window slid up into its frame.

"You go in and I'll wait here," Carson ordered.

"Me? Why do I have to do it?"

"Because I fucking said so, damn it," he hissed, his voice a loud whisper. "Now get in there and get that kid before we're seen."

Max opened his mouth to protest but Carson pointed a finger at him. Max closed his mouth and reached up and began climbing through the opening.

"Give me a hand, will ya?" Max asked as his feet scraped against the siding, trying to find purchase.

Carson rolled his eyes and pushed Max by the butt, practically sending the man flying through the window.

There was a soft thud, and a second later Max's head was sticking out of the window. "I'm in."

"No shit," Carson hissed. "Go get the kid."

Max's head popped back inside and Carson checked his watch. It was ten past three in the morning. They were in the backyard, which was surrounded by a six foot wooden fence. Other than a porch light on the house behind him, the night was nice and dark.

It was the perfect night for a kidnapping.

Little Timmy Sheldon was eight years old. His father was the CEO to some conglomerate in the city. Carson had been hired to take the kid and bring him to a cabin in the woods, then wait for the call to release him. If everything went as planned, he and Max would have to spend a day or two tops at the cabin. Then after the ransom was paid, they would bring the kid to within shouting distance of the nearest ranger station. The kid would be set free, and by the time he reached the station and explained what had happened to him, Carson and Max would be long gone.

Then they would pick up the rest of their fee—half the fee having been paid up front—and fly off to some tropical beach for a few years. They would then spend their days sipping drinks with umbrellas in them and banging a different island girl every night.

A delivery truck drove by the front of the house, the entire vehicle shaking when it hit a bump, and Carson jumped slightly. He wondered what was taking Max so long.

He began biting his nails, something he did when he was nervous, and hummed a song he'd heard on the radio on the way over.

His car was parked one house down, the doors unlocked so they could slide inside and take off before anyone might see them. The car was stolen of course, the plates taken from another vehicle. He'd done this in case someone spotted the car and took the license plate down to report to the police. He'd made sure to cover all the angles. Getting caught wouldn't happen if he was smart, and Carson thought he was damn smart.

Damn it, what's taking Max so long? He should have been back by now, he thought. He was about to see if he could find something to step on so he could climb into the window, such as a planter or a large rock, when Max's head appeared.

"I got him," Max whispered.

"About damn time," Carson hissed back. "Hand him to me."

Max's head pulled back and then a small wrapped object appeared, Max holding it up from underneath. He lowered the wrapped figure into Carson's waiting arms.

"Did you give him the ether like I told you?" Carson asked as he took the small figure and stepped away from the window so Max could climb out.

"Sure did. Just like you said." Max slid one leg through the window, but didn't compensate when the second one came through, and he lost his grip on the frame. He tumbled ass-up to the ground, landing in a heap.

"Be careful, damn it. You okay?"

"I'll live," Max said, his voice muffled.

Holding the small bundle with one hand, Carson helped Max stand up.

"Let's go. The sooner we're at the cabin the better," Carson said and began making his way to the front yard and the street beyond.

Max, now hobbling slightly, was right behind him.

Using a burner phone, Carson reported in that the job was done. His employer was pleased, and an hour after the call, would make the ransom demands, no doubt waking up the boy's parents in the process.

This was the plan, to wake the parents from a deep sleep, and when they found out their son was missing, would be too terrified, disoriented and full of panic to alert the authorities. Of course the warning that to do so would kill their son helped as well.

The next morning when the banks opened, the father could get the ransom, pay it, and the boy would be freed.

The only problem would be if they didn't pay. Carson hoped it wouldn't come to that. Though he'd done it in the past, he never enjoyed killing children. But it had to be done, for if a bluff was called and the kidnapper was squeamish, then the entire plan would fall apart.

Sometimes sending a severed finger would do the job before an actual killing had to take place, though.

The streets were relatively quiet, traffic light due to the lateness of the evening, and two hours later Carson rolled up to the cabin and turned off the headlights. The cabin was a dilapidated-looking structure with moss growing on all but one side; part of the roof needed to be replaced—badly. A thick bed of pine needles littered the ground, attesting to the rundown look—one of abandonment.

"Get the kid inside," Carson ordered. "I wanna check around the perimeter and make sure it's clear."

"Why wouldn't it be?" Max asked.

Carson sighed. "Just do what I say, will you?" He walked away as Max entered the cabin. His eyes scanned the ground for signs of disturbance but nothing popped out at him. Not that it would. Carson had lived in the city his entire life. He knew nothing about being a woodsman. Unless a bulldozer had scraped a furrow in the earth that he came upon, he wouldn't be able to tell if anything was amiss.

After doing a full circle of the perimeter of the cabin, Carson entered it, closing the door behind him.

Max had laid the kid down on the dusty bed in the corner of the one-room dwelling, and was seeing if he could start a fire in the fireplace. Carson walked over to the boy and checked on him. The child was sleeping soundly, the drug-induced slumber making his breathing slow and steady.

Carson nodded, figuring the boy would be out for at least another two hours before the ether wore off. He wasn't looking forward to when it did. He knew what would happen. Timmy would wake up, either screaming or crying, and Carson would have to do his best to shut him up, to explain that if he was quiet, nothing would happen to him.

"Max, go get the food we brought out of the trunk," Carson said and sat down at the small wooden table in the center of the room. Three wooden chairs surrounded it.

"Sure. I'll be right back."

Carson leaned back in the chair, his eyes playing over the small room. Over the mantle was a moose head, the glass eyes reflecting the wan light in the cabin.

He looked up when Max entered, carrying bags of food and a case of beer taken from the trunk of the car. He placed it all on the table.

"Okay," Carson said and stood up, to begin unpacking the food. "Let's get comfortable, we're gonna be here for a few days."

Carson didn't know how it was happening, but he was a boy of ten again, swimming at the local reservoir in Connecticut, where he'd grown up.

The sun was high in the sky, the sand pristine. There was a tire swing that hung over the water. He remembered how hard it had been for himself and three of his friends to hang it there on the overhanging tree limb. Each of them had fallen off the limb at least once, and Carson had scraped himself up something awful before finally managing to tie the rope and secure the tire permanently.

As he swam through the warm, clear water, his friends, Jason and Sean, played with him.

He laughed with them, and played games till the sun began to set. Then they all climbed out and lay in the cooling sand, staring up at the sky as the stars came out one by one, each one blinking to the rhythm of the cosmos.

Sleeping in one of the kitchen chairs, Carson smiled to himself as he relived the event from his past.

Back then, before he had turned to a life of crime and was always looking over his shoulder, life was good. He knew that when he left the lake that day he would go home and spend the night watching television with his mother and finally go to sleep feeling happy.

Then, like a movie being slowed down and rewound, he watched as the entire day began to go backwards, before blinking out.

His eyes snapped open and he found himself in the cabin once more.

The fire was still burning but it was a fraction of what it had been hours ago. The wan light it gave off was barely enough to see the interior of the cabin with.

He looked over at the bed to see the boy was awake and sitting up. Timmy was staring at him.

"Did you have a dream?" Timmy asked, his voice high, a smile on his lips.

"Yeah, how'd you know?"

"I put it there for you." Timmy cocked his head to the side, as if he was curious about something.

"What are you talking about, kid?"

"Your dream. You were at a lake. It looked fun. I love to swim."

Carson blinked in amazement. "How…how could you know what I dreamed?"

Timmy shrugged. "Like I said. I put that dream in there for you. You looked sad when you were sleeping so I made you remember something when you were a kid, like me."

"That's impossible."

Timmy smiled. "That's what my mommy and daddy used to say but not anymore. I can make you remember something or even put new thoughts in your head, make you see stuff you never saw before."

Carson sat up straighter. "Okay, kid, I'll humor you a little." He was glad the boy wasn't crying or screaming. "Can you do it again?"

Timmy shrugged again. "Sure." He set his jaw and creased his eyes, staring at Carson intently.

Suddenly, the cabin faded out and Carson was at his high school prom, dancing with his best gal. He'd thought he would marry her but it hadn't worked out in the end. If he had, he always wondered how his life would have turned out.

Carson had stood up from the chair and was slowly dancing in the center of the cabin, his arms held out to hold someone who was only in his head. He swayed back and forth until the image dissolved, leaving him standing in the cabin. Timmy was looking at him, a smile on his face.

"How the hell did you do that, kid?"

Timmy shifted slightly on the bed and wiped his eyes from sleep. He was still groggy from the ether. "My daddy says it's a form of hypnoti… hypnotis… hypnoti…"

"Hypnotism?" Carson broke in.

Timmy's eyes lit up and he smiled as wide as he could. "That's it. Hypnotism. That's what my daddy says. He says there's some telepathy in there, too. I know that word easy."

Carson's mind was racing with ideas. If he hadn't experienced it for himself he would never have believed it but he knew it was true. This kid was some kind of freak, but in away that could make Carson a lot of money, a hell of a lot more than from the kidnapping. All he would have to do is get the kid a new look, say some light plastic surgery, make his hair a different color, and then they could go on the circuit. He'd be rich? Las Vegas would be perfect for the kid's tricks.

But he had to make sure.

"Okay, kid, do it again, only this time make it something I've never seen before."

"Sure, I can do that," Timmy said and creased his eyes.

Carson glanced over at Max, who was sleeping on an old stuffed chair in the corner of the room, then Max faded away and Carson found himself outside the cabin. He was about to ask Timmy what was so special about this when he heard a crashing through the underbrush, small trees seemingly being knocked aside by something huge.

Carson reached into his jacket and pulled out his gun, but didn't use it. After all, this was a dream, right? He waited as the crashing grew louder and then something large and hairy came bursting into the clearing the cabin was in the middle of.

The creature was huge, over eight feet tall and was covered from head to toe in dark brown fur. The face was similar to a human's though there seemed to be a hint of gorilla or monkey mixed in there, too. The arms were longer in proportion to the body than they would be on a human and the feet were long and wide, five digits on each one.

Carson leveled his gun, his eyes wide in fright. He knew what he was seeing though he didn't believe it.

It was a Bigfoot.

But…but they weren't real, they were a myth, his mind told him.

The creature roared and came at him, its feet crushing the plant life beneath it, flattening it into the earth.

Carson raised his gun and prepared to fire, but then he found himself back in the cabin. His gun was in his hand and he was facing Max, who was standing in the corner with his hands up.

"Cut it out, Carson. Put the fucking gun away. What's wrong with you?"

Carson shook his head and the fuzziness drifted away and he realized where he was. He lowered the gun and looked at Timmy. "You, what did you do?"

"I didn't do anything. You said to show you something you never saw before. I did."

"What's goin' on, Carson? What the hell's wrong with you?" Max asked, slightly relieved that the gun was lowered, though he was afraid it would be raised again at any moment.

Carson tucked the gun in his belt and Max sighed heavily. Safe at last.

"Nothing's wrong, I was just playing with you, that's all. A bad joke. Sorry, Max, my bad."

"Well. It ain't funny, Carson, Don't do that again."

"I won't, like I said, I'm sorry."

Max went to the door. "I'm goin' to get some more firewood. Okay?"

"Sure, Max, that sounds fine. Tell you what, while you're gone I'll whip us up something eat."

Max grunted and nodded his head and walked outside, closing the door harder than he normally would.

"What was that thing?" Carson asked Timmy, walking over and looking down at the boy. "It was so real."

"He's my friend," Timmy said.

"Well, he's not mine. Don't do that again, all right?"

Timmy nodded.

Carson walked to the table and began digging in the bags of food.

"So, kid, tell me something," Carson said while Timmy sat at the table and ate a sandwich. Max was outside having a smoke.

"What?" Timmy asked.

"How come you're so calm about this kidnapping thing? I mean, you do understand what's happening here, right?"

"Sure, but I'm not worried."

"You're not? Why?"

Before Timmy could answer, Max came back in. "Man, it's getting cold out there," he said and walked over to the table and grabbed a warm beer.

He cracked the top and downed half in one gulp. "Heard anything?" He was referring to the ransom.

"No, Max, nothing yet. Relax, we have at least another day before we'll hear anything."

Max nodded and crossed the room. He dropped down in a chair by the fire and closed his eyes. Max could sleep anywhere and usually did.

"Can I ask you something?" Timmy said as he chomped on his sandwich. It was only peanut butter but that was okay. He liked peanut butter.

"Sure, kid, go 'head."

"How come you haven't told Max about what I can do?"

Carson gave it a moment's thought and said, "No reason. Let's just keep it between us for now, all right?"

"Sure, it's up to you. My daddy says I'm not to tell anyone anyway."

"Then why did you tell me? Why did you show me that dream and the monster?"

Timmy gave one of his patented shrugs. "I just felt like it." He took the last bite of his sandwich and washed it down with warm soda from a can. The rest of the six pack was in the corner, on the floor in a paper grocery bag.

"Would you like to see some more?" Timmy asked after wiping his mouth on the sleeve of his pajama shirt.

Carson glanced over at Max to check on him but the man was already out cold, snoring softly. "Sure. How 'bout showing me New York City. I haven't been there in a while. I love it there."

"Sure," Timmy said and creased his eyes slightly in concentration.

Suddenly, the cabin faded away to be replaced by tall buildings and neon signs flashing. A cool wind blew through the streets as people rushed to and fro on the packed sidewalks. In Central Park, trees sprouted leaves and grew tall and majestic. Yellow and black taxis glided back and forth in the night. Further away, bridges rose over the water and tugs chanted their siren call in the harbors, and on star-spangled musicals, curtains rose and fell on Broadway.

In the center of it all, Carson stood transfixed. He was so shocked he couldn't so much as utter a sound. The lights, noise and people were overwhelming, overriding his senses after being in the cabin an instant ago.

It went on for what seemed like hours and then, through all the noise, Carson heard snoring and a second later found himself back in the cabin. He saw Timmy sitting at the table with a smile and Max snoring even louder.

"Sorry, Max startled me and I lost my concentration. He sure is a loud snorer," Timmy said.

"It's…its fine, kid," Carson said, trying to regain his composure. It was all so surreal. All his senses told him a second ago he was standing in the middle of New York, yet now he was in the cabin. This kid was amazing! He'd already decided that no matter what happened tomorrow with the ransom; Timmy was leaving the cabin with him. As for Max, well, it was time they split up anyway. He would simply pull into a rest stop and tell Max to get him a burger. When the man went into whatever restaurant was there, Carson would drive away, never to be seen again, the kid and him heading out to Vegas, just like he'd first thought.

"What do you say we take a break for a while? That stuff sure does take it out of a guy," Carson said and sat down. He took a warm beer and drank more than half in one breath.

"Sure," Timmy agreed. "Hey, do you have any games I can play? I'm bored."

Carson thought about it and realized he didn't. Then he remembered his cell phone. After locking the keys so Timmy couldn't make any calls, he handed him the phone. "Here, I think this has a few games on it."

"Cool, thanks," Timmy said and took the phone over to the bed, lying down and playing.

Carson leaned back in the chair, finished his beer, and began counting the money he'd soon be making in his head.

The rest of the day was uneventful. Timmy played games on the cell phone and Carson and Max watched him. Carson reminded Timmy not to do his trick with Max around and the boy consented.

Carson was itching to leave the cabin and was now hoping the ransom went bad. He would then say he killed the boy but instead would take him with him. No one would look for him then, thinking he was dead.

Carson was fast asleep in the same chair as before, the fire crackling softly, when something woke him from his slumber.

He opened his eyes in time to see the door of the cabin burst in, and in the doorway, having to hunch down to enter, was Bigfoot again. Carson got over his initial surprise and then slumped back in his chair. He'd told Timmy not to do this illusion anymore and he was slightly angry at the boy for doing it anyway.

He was more than a little surprised when he saw Max jump up and begin screaming, pulling his gun and aiming it at the creature. "What the fuck is that thing? Carson, get up! Shoot it! Shoot it!"

"Relax, Max, it's not real. It's an illusion. The kid makes them up," Carson said from his chair, his voice calm.

"Not real? What's wrong with you, Carson? It looks pretty fucking real to me!" Max prepared to shoot the creature, his finger tensing on the trigger.

But the creature was faster. It roared, its arms rising over its head to scrape the low ceiling and knock down pieces of wood. With its long stride, it crossed the cabin in the blink of an eye, far too fast for Max to handle. He let off one shot but it went wide, the bullet sinking harmlessly into the wall of the cabin behind the creature.

Bigfoot reached Max and with one mighty swing, knocked the gun from his hand. Max stood in shock, his neck craned so his head was almost looking straight up. Then he snapped out of it and pulled a knife. His arm went back to slam it into the creature's gut, but before he could, Bigfoot reached out and grabbed Max by his head, one large hand on each side, the palms so large Max's head and face were all but swallowed up within them.

With a twist of its arms, Bigfoot tore Max's head clean off his shoulders, blood spurting up to splash the ceiling in dark red, and the rest raining down on the floor in thick droplets. Max's headless body went falling backwards to land on a pile of logs for the fireplace. The body dropped, the feet resting on the logs like they were propped up. The feet still twitched slightly as the nerve centers shut down, thanks to the command module—namely his head—being torn off and tossed into the corner as if it was a beach ball.

"Max! Jesus Christ!" Carson screamed, not understanding what was going on. The creature wasn't real, so how the hell could it have killed Max? At his scream, the Bigfoot turned and glared at Carson, snarling as it lowered its head slightly so it didn't brush the ceiling.

Carson pulled his gun, not understanding how this was real, but knowing he had to defend himself. The creature came at him and Carson raised the gun, but once more was far too slow. The gun was knocked from his hand by the swipe of a hairy arm, the weapon clattering across the floor to end up under the bed.

Reaching out with both hands, the creature picked Carson up and held him a foot in the air. Carson could feel his ribs cracking and he tried to breathe in as he stared at the sniffing face. The creature was smelling him!

Then it tossed Carson across the room. He was airborne for a few seconds, then his back crashed against the cabin wall and he tumbled to the floor in a heap, the moose head falling off the wall to land upside down on the floor. The wind was knocked out of him and Carson saw stars. He briefly wondered where Timmy was, but then the creature was coming for him and he had more important matters to worry about, namely his own life!

Carson reached over and grabbed a fireplace poker to use as a weapon, holding it tightly with two hands, waving it before him like a sword.

Out of the corner of his eye, he saw Timmy in the bed, sitting silently, a wide smile on his lips.

"Kid, stop this vision! I don't like it!" Carson yelled. "Do it or so help me you'll regret it!"

Timmy did nothing, but only sat smiling, watching events play out.

Bigfoot roared loud enough to shake the rafters and charged Carson, who swung with the poker as hard as he could. He felt it hit solid flesh and bone, and once more didn't understand. Bigfoot roared in either pain or anger and swatted at him, sending Carson flying backwards again, just like the last time he was thrown through the air.

Carson landed near Timmy this time. From the floor, he looked up at Timmy's smiling face. "This isn't funny, kid. Cut this shit out right now or so help me God I'll..."

Timmy only smiled in reply. Bigfoot ran across the cabin, shaking the pictures on the walls with each step. The creature bent over and grabbed Carson, then carried him outside. Carson fought the entire time, kicking, screaming, and punching, but it was all for nothing. He was like a newborn baby in its mother's arms—helpless. The sky was dark, only a few stars visible to witness the spectacle of a giant creature of myth carrying a screaming man.

When they were outside, Carson felt himself being repositioned, and a second later found himself dangling by his arms two feet in the air. Then there was sudden pain as Bigfoot pulled, tearing Carson's arms out of their sockets so that he fell to the ground, blood pumping out of the exposed holes on either side of his torso. There was blinding pain and he let out such an agony-filled howl that the treetops shook as startled nesting birds took flight in fear.

Through the pain-induced fugue, he heard his inner voice yelling, "This is fucking real! Bigfoot is real!"

Reaching down after tossing the severed arms away, where they landed in the forest, Bigfoot picked up Carson and spun him around so he was upside down.

Holding Carson by the legs, the creature spread its arms wide, then pulled like the creature was making a wish with a chicken bone, separating Carson's legs from his body, muscle and bone cracking and filling the night with sounds of carnage.

Though not believing his threshold of pain could go up, Carson soon found this to be a falsehood as blood shot out of all four holes in rhythm to his heartbeat, which was in overdrive due to fear and pain.

His vision was growing dim as he lost more blood. But before he passed out, Bigfoot grabbed his head in one meaty hand, the other hand holding onto his torso to get a good grip, then the creature pulled yet again, taking Carson's head off. It tossed the head into the forest. The creature didn't eat human meat, finding it distasteful.

Timmy appeared at the doorway to the cabin. He walked outside, careful not to step in any blood soaking into the dirt and only stopped when he was before Bigfoot. Looking small and frail, he gazed up at the large creature, his smile never faltering. "Thank you for helping me."

Bigfoot wiped its blood-covered hands on its chest and knelt down by the boy. It patted Timmy on the head like a pet, then turned and loped off into the forest. Timmy watched it go, and then walked back inside the cabin and to Max's corpse.

He began searching the body's pockets. When he found Max's cell phone, he dialed his home number and got his father on the first ring. After doing his best to explain where he was and being told to leave the phone on so the police could track its location, he went back to the bed and sat down. Crossing his hands on his knees, he waited patiently to be picked up.

As Timmy sat on the bed, the smile on his face never wavered.

THE LAST CHRISTMAS

Thomas Jurgensen wandered the cold lonely street, wrapped in nothing but rags. The snow on the ground was two feet deep and he could feel the ice crystals inside his worn boots.

All around him were the signs of a dead neighborhood, the same as every other one he'd passed through in the twelve months since the dead began to walk and swarmed across the world like locusts.

Stopping in the middle of the street, he stared at the house to his right. It was a standard two-story house with a two car garage and a large picture window in front. In that window, Christmas decorations still hung, the scotch tape holding the cardboard cutouts of Santa and his reindeer firm.

After a full year of hanging in the window, the sun beating on the facades, the colors were now washed out and only the dark lines of the shapes could be seen.

On the front lawn, buried under two feet of snow, three unlit plastic reindeer frolicked. Their white skeletal frames were once lit up, but now they truly looked like skeletons.

Hanging askew on the roof, a life-size sleigh clung to its moorings. Exposed to the winds and weather, it wouldn't be long before the sleigh was forced off the roof to crash to the ground below.

Thomas shook his head in sadness, wondering how it could have come to this.

It wasn't a long story how the dead came to walk, it was quite simple actually.

A cure to the common cold, it was heralded as. Finally, no more runny noses and chests full of phlegm. But the cure hadn't been tested as well as it should be, the drug companies in a rush to get it on the market. To make up for the loss of cough syrup and allergy medicines, the price of the cure was incredible, but nine out of ten people were happy to pay it.

So when the first fatality was admitted into a local hospital, no one gave the woman much thought. At least until the patient died and returned as a living corpse, sinking her teeth into the nurse administering over her.

From there it was a domino effect, and in the blink of an eye, a year later, Thomas was standing on a holiday festive street in the middle of Nowhere, USA, shivering in the cold. The wind blowing in from the north felt like it would freeze him to the bone, and he turned and headed for the ranch house.

All around him were the frozen corpses of zombies, each as stiff as the day it had frozen months ago. But Thomas knew when spring came they would thaw out and be free to roam once more.

There was a time when he would have tried to destroy them, to chop off their heads and break their legs as they lay helpless in the snow. But months ago he had finally given up. There were just too damn many to destroy.

So now he used the winter time to stock up on whatever he could find, and when spring arrived, he would hole up somewhere until winter returned.

The front door of the house was locked, so he went around to the back. This door was locked too and it was a heavy wooden fabrication. But there were more ways to enter the house and he found it by using a basement window. After kicking out the glass with the heel of his worn boot, he scurried in like a worm sliding into its hole.

The basement was dark and dingy, but was slightly warmer than outside.

That made Thomas nervous. Anywhere the temperature wasn't below freezing, a zombie could be lying in wait.

He remembered the last time he found a zombie in a house.

It was three weeks ago to the day. He had climbed in through an open window to find the bedroom door leading to the rest of the house empty. Upon opening the door, he found himself standing face to face with a dead man in a Santa Claus suit. With the door closed. The rest of the house had managed to stay above freezing.

But Santa wasn't as jolly as days past. This Santa had a massive hole in his throat, a missing arm and intestines hanging like dangling rope from his abdomen.

As the dead Santa raised its one remaining hand, Thomas heard the tinkle of jingle bells, the three red bells sewed to the sleeve of the red suit. As the zombie moaned, the bells jangled, and Thomas slammed the door in the festive ghoul's face.

As the holiday zombie pounded on the bedroom door, Thomas had climbed out of the house to find another hiding place.

So now here he was again, inside a house searching for anything useful. Empty cardboard boxes sat on his left, the words **XMAS** written on them in black marker. He chuckled slightly at the sight. Of course they were empty. All the decorations were set up around the home. It was like this in every house he went to. When the outbreak began, it had been three days to Christmas, and though the world died, at least it left a festive corpse.

The basement was relatively empty, though he found an old claw hammer on a dented and rusted metal shelf. The hammer was better than nothing, so he tossed away the cracked bat he'd been using, knowing the bat's days were numbered. Swinging the hammer once or twice to get a feel for it, he turned and began climbing the steps to the first floor.

The door was locked, but his new acquisition saw him through. With the door lock now splintered and lying on the top step, he pushed the door in and waited for signs of trouble. He was confident that any zombies would have been attracted to the noise he made breaking the lock. He waited for a full minute, and when still nothing arrived to attack him, he stepped inside the kitchen.

It was a kitchen like any other he'd seen over the past year. A snowman cookie jar sat on its side on the counter, even the crumbs now gone. Christmas potholders hung from the cabinets and small statues, five inches in height, sat on the edge of the stove, while salt and pepper shakers of elves lay on their side in the middle of the kitchen table.

That was the only sense of normalcy in the kitchen, however, as the rest was a maelstrom of tossed aside empty boxes and brown, dirty dishes. When he reached the kitchen sink, he turned up his nose as the sight greeting him. A large, dried turd, human by the size and shape, lay in the bottom of the sink, and Thomas had to wonder what kind of human would feel the need to climb up onto the counter to defecate like that. But he'd seen worse in his travels and he moved on.

As Thomas searched the cupboards, they were as bare as the preverbal old woman in a shoe. When he was through searching, not finding so much as a crumb, thanks to the looters before him, he went into the living room.

He had his fingers crossed about what he might find there, and sure enough, he was correct.

In the center of the large living room, stood a brown Christmas tree, all the needles now on the floor. Ornaments still hung from it, but as the once fresh tree was now long dead, the branches looking unappealing and ugly in their bareness.

The tree was like the world now. A few pretty baubles on its surface, but underneath, it was dead and rotting.

But that wasn't what Thomas was looking for. It was what was below the tree that had him coming to the living room in the first place.

Below the dried and brown tree, a fire hazard in the waiting, sat the presents of this home's family, every one still wrapped with care a year ago.

For some reason, looters didn't think to check the presents, only going to the obvious places, such as the kitchen, pantry and medicine cabinets in the bathrooms.

But Thomas had figured out long ago that there were hidden treasures to be found sitting under desiccated Christmas trees. Setting the hammer down, he dropped to his knees and bean ripping open the presents.

To: Timmy, Love, Mom and Dad, the first one had written on the wrapping paper, and when Thomas opened it, he saw it was a video game. He tossed it aside and went for the next one.

To: Sally, Love, Mom and Dad, the next card said and this one had a pink ribbon on the corner.

Thomas ripped the ribbon off and tore into the present, to an outsider looking like a kid on Christmas morning. All he got for his trouble was a new cell phone.

Beyond worthless, he thought, as he tossed the box aside.

But this had happened before which was why looters didn't bother.

Thomas picked up the next one. ***To: Daddy, From: Timmy***, was on a homemade card. There was a drawing there, too. Timmy had used crayons to draw Santa and his reindeer as they flew across a happy town. Thomas ripped the card off and threw it behind him, then he ripped open the present like a hungry dog and cried out in relief to see what was inside.

It was a summer sausage gift set, complete with two blocks of cheese, mustard, and crackers. The perfect present to give a man who needs nothing but you have to give him something.

Ravenous beyond imagining, Thomas tore into the package and feasted on the sausage. Though it was processed meat that he would have shunned a year earlier, now it tasted like the finest New York sirloin. He ate half the sausage and then a quarter of the cheese, devouring half the crackers with it. Then, his stomach feeling better, he continued opening presents.

He went through four more, one was a new IPod for the little girl, the other was an action figure from some Japanese cartoon for the boy. The second to last was a sweater for the mother, cashmere if he was right. Not worried about fashion sense, he set it aside to take with him. Warm was warm and there was no one to impress anymore. And besides, the dead didn't judge you, they only wanted to eat you.

The last present was addressed to the father, and when Thomas opened it up, he gasped in happiness to see a brand new Browning Hi-power, complete with a box of ammunition. This was the find of a lifetime. And to think, it had been sitting here for all this time, ignored by others!

After loading the gun, he felt so much better, knowing he wouldn't have to get close to an attacker to defend himself.

Going to the front door, he stepped outside and grabbed some snow from the front porch, eating it. It melted in his mouth and he sighed, washing the salty taste of the sausage and crackers from his palate. At least with the snow he had all the water he could ever want, but he still needed food. At least now, for a day or so, he had both.

When he had his fill, he closed the door and went back into the living room. This time he noticed the rest of the holiday decorations spread out across the room.

Near the front window were two animatronic statues of Santa and Mrs. Claus. Both were covered in a layer of dust and hadn't been on in more than a year. Off to the right was a fireplace, the family stockings hanging in front like a classic Christmas card. Two large ones had Mom and Dad on them, while the other two had the names Timmy and Sally.

Made sense to Thomas, especially after ripping open the presents and reading the cards.

On the walls were holiday cardboard cutouts similar to the faded ones on the front window. Rudolph, Santa, and Frosty all smiled down onto the living room, where once a happy family had laughed, loved and played together.

That had Thomas wondering where the family might be. Had they evacuated like so many families had in the beginning? He felt for them if they did. The rescue stations had quickly become concentration camps, where death and sickness ruled with an iron fist.

Luckily Thomas had been alone when it all started. He was already a widower and he and his wife had never had kids. All his family was either dead or estranged when the world crumbled. Which was why it had been easy for him to adapt, as he had no one to worry about but himself.

With a full stomach and the inside of the house much warmer than outside, he felt his exhaustion sneaking up on him, and he decided it was time to get some rest. He did a few things before he slept, however. The first was to use the bathroom, not caring about his waste being left behind in the empty bowl. The second was to use one of the kitchen chairs to block the basement door from opening. If he thought to enter the house that way, so could another. He hadn't seen many other people in this part of the town, but one could never be too careful. At least if one wanted to stay alive, that is.

When the house was as secure as it could be, he went back to the living room and dropped down on the dusty couch. There was a dust-covered throw blanket on the back cushion and he pulled it down onto him.

Then, snug and comfortable, he drifted off into sleep, into a world where Christmas didn't equal death, and if you saw Santa Claus on the street, he wasn't going to try and rip your throat out.

Thomas came awake with a startled groan. He'd heard something, the question was: What was it?

Always on the run, he had learned to sleep lightly, and no matter how tired he was, he always managed to do this.

So he knew something had woken him from his troubled rest.

He sat up and could barely see, darkness having descended almost completely. Checking his wristwatch, he saw he had been asleep for almost four hours.

His bladder required attention and he silently padded to the bathroom, took care of business, and then proceeded to go back to the living room.

That was when he heard the noise again. It was a scratching sound, like a dog wanting out and its claws brushing the door.

It was coming from the second floor. He hadn't checked the second floor, not feeling the need. The gun was in his waistband, but he went back to retrieve the hammer, then, as well armed as one could be in this day and age, he began to climb the stairs leading to the second floor.

Halfway up, he paused to study the family photos hanging on the wall. There was a small fixed window that allowed light in and the wan illumination was enough for Thomas to see the smiling faces in the pictures. A man, woman and two children, a boy and a girl, looked out at him, with cheerful eyes and wide smiles. This must be the family that lived here, the two children named Timmy and Sally.

They looked so happy and Thomas couldn't help but feel his heartstrings tugged just a little.

But then the scratching could be heard again and he was brought back to the here and now. He reached the top landing, and he walked down the small hallway, peering into each room as he went. There was the parents' bedroom, the dust thick with disuse, the floor void of fresh footprints; the bathroom was empty and the first child's bedroom was empty also.

That left the last room at the end of the hall.

The door was closed and the name **TIMMY** was on a small sign tacked to the middle of the door.

Thomas stepped closer and placed his ear to the door.

There it was again, that scratching noise.

While there was absolutely no reason for him to open the door, he felt his curiosity get the better of him. It didn't hurt that he now had a gun and if there was any true danger he could shoot the problem and then leave.

For once he felt in control and he was damned if he would run away.

He wanted to know what was in the room, and had been inside for a year or so.

So with treacle-like slowness, he reached out to the doorknob with his free hand.

Turning it careful, he pushed the door open and took a step back, lest a hidden ghoul attack him.

But there was no attack, nothing happened. But the scratching began to grow louder.

When he was sure it was safe, he raised the gun and stepped into the room.

Immediately he was blasted by the rank odor of stale death and the reason for this aroma was apparent the instant he entered the room.

There were two zombie children, a boy and girl, only the clothing allowing Thomas to know this for sure. Both were tied by the necks like dogs, their small bodies far too weak to ever hope to break their leashes.

Below them, on the floor, were the remains of two adult bodies. There was no meat left and the skeletons pieces that were till intact looked chewed on, like someone had been gnawing on them for some time.

The heads were tossed to the side, the skulls empty, as if a small hand had plunged into the neck cavity of each to scoop out the juicy brains within.

Thomas took the room in at a glance. There were pieces of rotted, dried meat off to the side, and a few of the pieces looked as if they may have been human.

It wasn't too hard for Thomas to piece together what must have happened.

Somehow, the two children had been infected and had turned into the walking dead. The parents hadn't the heart to destroy their offspring and so had penned them up, tying them up like wild animals. Then the kids had been fed a diet of raw meat and human when possible. But something had gone wrong, perhaps the kids getting the drop on their parents. And then the parents had become a meal for their children.

The two little zombies snarled and hissed at him, their drawn visages basically nothing more than human skulls wrapped in dried skin. The small zombies hadn't eaten for a very long time and were ravenous for human flesh.

They were an odd sight, the two wearing festive holiday clothing, though now it was covered in brown and crusting blood from meals long past. The boy wore a yellow sweater with Santa Claus on the front, while the girl wore a blue sweatshirt with a snowman with a black top hat.

Frosty, had to be, Thomas figured.

Thomas stared at the kids and then at the gun in his hand. In the end, he decided he didn't need to waste two bullets on them. They were trapped and small and he had the hammer.

Shoving the gun in into his waistband, he raised the hammer and stepped closer to the boy. He was less than a foot away, but the leash was short and the boy couldn't reach him. He raised the hammer high and then brought it down hard; the skull cracking like it was made of plaster. The boy dropped to the floor, gray brains seeping out the hole in his head.

Thomas barely felt anything as he turned to face the girl. She hissed and snapped; her hands out in front of her. The leash was taut as she stretched to reach him.

He laughed, feeling powerful, knowing it was petty, but still relishing his power. After a year of being on the run by these *things*, it was nice to be in the driver's seat for a change.

Almost casually, he raised the hammer again, his attention barely on the task at hand. He was already thinking about eating the rest of the summer sausage with mustard.

His carelessness was his undoing, as he had learned a long time ago any zombie was a danger, no matter how helpless it might seem.

As he raised the hammer and looked away for the briefest of seconds, the leash holding the zombie girl snapped, and she came at him with mouth open wide.

He brought the hammer down, but only grazed her head, the blow breaking her clavicle instead of her skull. But the little girl could have cared less. Before Thomas could stop her or jump away, she sank her brown teeth into his right leg, just above his knee joint.

He screamed in pain and anger and raised the hammer again, this time his attention fully on the killing. The hammer cracked her skull like a melon and the point of the hammer sank halfway into the small skull, the girl twitching on the end of the hammer like she was being electrocuted.

Her teeth clamped down in her death throes and tore a two inch size chunk of flesh from his leg. Howling in pain, he kicked the corpse away from him and dropped the hammer.

The girl was very dead now, the small body dropping onto the two skeletons of her parents.

Moaning in pain, Thomas left the bedroom, slamming the door behind him. He wasn't cursing himself as he wasn't thinking that far ahead. Instead, he rushed to the bathroom and ripped open the vanity.

He found what he needed, but it was in short supply after looters had taken what they wanted, but he ripped open his pant leg and cleaned the wound. Then he bandaged it.

With nothing left to do, he went downstairs and sat on the couch, his leg throbbing with each beat of his heart.

He still didn't want to admit it, but he knew what that little zombie girl had given him for Christmas.

A death sentence.

Though he was hurting and upset, eventually he fell back to sleep, though now his dreams were plagued with even more zombies, and by the end he found he was one of them.

When he woke up his leg was numb, and when he checked under the bandage, he saw the wound had festered. It had already started and there would be no stopping it.

He finished off the sausage and cheese, sucking every last ounce of mustard from the packet. He wasn't worried about eating it all. He didn't need to save it anymore and at least this way he would die with a relatively full stomach.

Then he sat and waited, only getting up to use the bathroom and eat some snow.

By the second day, he didn't bother to do that, and the last time he needed to pee, he'd said the hell with it and had simply leaned over the edge of the couch and urinated on the floor. Hell, it wasn't his house and in another day he wouldn't be alive to care.

That night he was holding on to life by his willpower alone. He knew if he passed out that would be it.

And he knew for a fact he didn't want to become one of *them*.

He picked up the Browning and held it in his grip. He remembered just a day or so ago when he'd found it, and how lucky he'd felt.

In fact, he had been so happy it had been just like Christmas to him, what with finding the gun and the summer sausage. He wasn't sure, but he was pretty sure December 25th was close, the anniversary of the outbreak the same week.

So it was Christmas again, albeit a rather lonely one for him.

As he placed the gun to his temple and closed his eyes, he mumbled one last sentence.

"Some Merry Christmas."

He held the gun there for almost ten minutes, not having the courage to go through with it. But then he felt a sharp pain in his chest, one that filled him with agony.

That pain gave him the courage to do what had to be done.

He squeezed the trigger.

THE LAST ONE

Marvin Greenburg never thought he was a lucky man.

In his lifetime, nothing had ever gone his way.

But as he walked down the middle of Nowhere, USA, amid the blasted out ruins of the apocalypse, he had to admit his luck was getting better.

To this day, almost seven months after the world dropped dead, he still didn't know why he was the only one left alive.

For some unknown reason, whatever virus, bacteria or plague that had killed every man, woman and child on the face of the Earth, had somehow spared him.

He stepped over the small corpse of a newborn baby, the overturned baby carriage just beyond. The mother was lying on her side, one arm stretched out, as if she was trying to pull her baby back into her arms. The corpse was nothing but a dry husk, the skin pulled taut to the skull like dried parchment.

As for the baby, it was shriveled into beef jerky, the pacifier still stuck in its small mouth at time of death.

There was a time when something so horrible, so visceral, would have broken Marvin's heart, but no longer.

After months of seeing nothing but corpses, the sight had hardened his heart and soul into cast iron, not even so much as a crack in its facade. In his right hand he carried a double barrel shotgun, but he had never had to use it since venturing forth into a dead world. Even the animals were dead, and if it wasn't for canned and processed food, Marvin knew he would have been dead long ago, too.

He did have one weakness, however, and that was for Hostess cupcakes.

That chocolaty brown pastry with the fudge icing and exactly eight little swirls on top made his mouth water whenever he consumed one. His backpack was stuffed to the brim with them, and with the exception of drinking water, that was all he carried with him.

He slowed outside a small diner; the neon lights forever dimmed and peered through the dirty glass plate window. Inside, bodies were slumped over tables, some face first into their clam chowder or chili—with or without meat.

Others were sprawled on the floor, their cash or credit cards still in their hand as they waited to pay for their meal.

Marvin shook his head, a small spark of sadness welling up in his chest before he pushed it back down.

He was so alone.

Surely there had to be someone else in the world who had avoided the virus or whatever. As he turned and walked away from the diner, he thought back to when it had happened and still wondered what was the true reason behind it.

When a tragedy happens, the news would normally cover it until no one cared anymore, but the plague that swept the world happened so fast there was no time to speculate, let alone discuss it.

As cameras ran, news anchors dropped dead, taking solace in knowing their makeup was perfect as their heads slapped the news desk.

So now Marvin traveled from town to town, city to city, state to state, searching for someone else. So far he'd found nothing but death and despair.

His life as an accountant had never prepared him for such as this.

Feeling tired, he plopped down on a bus bench and swung his pack around. Opening it, he took out a package of cakes and quickly ate them. Closing his eyes, he relished the chocolaty taste, the sugar rush making him feel giddy.

After washing the last bite down with some water, he felt better and began his trek once more.

When he had walked no more than twenty feet, he came across a ten speed bicycle. Deciding riding would be better than walking; he picked up the bike, climbed on it, and went on his way, leaving the town behind.

The next town was no different than the last.

The bike had worked well for him, allowing him to make better time. There had been a time when he had tried to drive but clogged highways and roads made it a moot point. His feet had been the best way to travel, and besides, it wasn't like he was in a rush to go anywhere.

It was spring and the weather was close to perfect, most days hovering around the seventy degree mark.

And he liked to walk, so he cared less when he left a car idling in the road so he could climb over the pile-up and continue onward. That is until the next pile-up.

People had dropped dead while driving and had created quite a mess for the traffic department. Well, that is if there had been anyone left alive to clean it up.

He slowed at the sign on the side of the road that signified the town's limits.

On the sign, the painted number was 2579. But Marvin knew that wasn't very truthful so he stopped at the sign, took out a big black magic marker—indelible of course—and drew a big fat zero over the 2579, changing it to **0**.

Then he put on the cap to the marker so it wouldn't dry out and he entered the town.

Night was coming, so he picked a small hotel at random and entered the building. The corpse behind the desk was slumped over the sign-in book. Using the butt of the shotgun, he shoved the corpse to the floor, and as he waited for the dust to settle, he grabbed a pen from a small cup and signed in.

Hey, the world may be over, but he still knew his etiquette.

He grabbed a key off the wall behind the desk and headed up to his room.

His footfalls echoed against the walls and he felt yet another pang of loneliness fill him. But he pushed it down. After so many months, he knew he had to come to grips with his new world. He was alone, that was it. The human race ended with him.

When he died, so too did mankind. It sucked but that was life.

Entering his room, he went right to the small mini-bar. Raiding it, he chowed down on peanuts, candy bars, and for the hell of it he drank a couple of the liquor bottles, deciding it would be kind of fun to get drunk.

Three bottles became four, and soon he had consumed every bottle in the cabinet. Then, feeling exhausted, drunk and sleepy, he dropped onto the bed and passed out.

Like most nights, he dreamed of how things were before he became the last human alive. He remembered the bustle of cars and crowds on the busy city streets and how it used to drive him crazy.

Now, he longed to hear the cacophony of civilization.

And of course, he missed the touch of a woman. He had been married once but it had fallen apart at lightning speed. It was neither of their faults. He married her fresh out of high school, the two sweethearts thinking marriage was the way to go. But no sooner had they tied the knot, then their perspectives began to change. He wanted to settle down and have children, while she wanted to have some fun and enjoy adulthood while they were still young and free of responsibilities. In the end it drove them apart.

So she got her wish, and on their two year anniversary, they signed the divorce papers.

He missed her now and wondered where she was. He had no doubt she was dead and that made him sad. The thought of her dried-up corpse lying in the road somewhere back home filled him with remorse and loss.

Usually she would pop up in his dreams and he would pretend they were together once more, but sometimes she would turn into Death incarnate, her eyes filled with sunken shadows, her mouth a gaping hole where maggots squirmed and festered.

This was one of those nights.

Like a wraith in a horror movie, she came to him. He tossed and turned in his bed as she attempted to pull him down into Hell, where she assured him he would be happy.

"You won't be alone anymore, Marvin, just give in and come with me," her words taunted and teased.

But even in his dream, he knew what she offered was Death, an end to everything. And though he was the last one left, he still wanted to live.

He awoke in a cold sweat, the sun slowly rising in the distance, painting the darkened sky with golden light as the shadows were chased away for another night.

Going to the window, he stared out at the ruined worlds he'd inherited. Across the street was a dry cleaners. The sign above the shattered glass facade was now hanging by one side, slowly swaying with the gentle breeze.

Trees lined the sidewalk and the wind sloughed through their branches, the limbs swaying and dancing, immune to whether mankind existed or not.

Newspapers blew across the street like tumbleweeds and Styrofoam cups rolled and bounced until they became jammed under a car or in a bush-lined walkway.

Limp, desiccated forms were strewn about like discarded trash, and to Marvin, they stopped being human remains and had simply become part of the landscape.

There was no noise, nothing but silence, only the leaves rustling in the trees to break the solitude, the prison he now lived in.

Turning away from the window, he dressed, used the facilities, ignoring his waste in the dry and empty toilet bowl, and then headed out back to the road, to see what he might find in the next town, the next place.

He made sure to raid a few more rooms for the mini-bars, wanting to take a few liquor bottles and peanuts for the road. Food was never a problem for him, for the entire world was waiting for him to take what he wanted.

Still, if only he had someone to share it all with. He knew his predicament would be infinitely more tolerable if he had someone by his side. Man or woman, it wouldn't matter, though female would be preferable.

Stepping onto the sidewalk, he closed the door to the hotel out of habit. Then he set off, his boots slapping the pavement one step at a time. The bicycle had gotten a flat and so was in his back trail now.

Near the end of town, he passed through a large auto wreck. Ten cars by the look of it, a tractor trailer the cause of it all. Body parts and dried, flaking blood were everywhere, coating every surface. A severed head lay to the side where it had flown out a window after the owner had been decapitated.

If he had to guess, it looked like the cars and one pickup truck were waiting at the stoplight to the left of the intersection. The driver of the semi had died suddenly when whatever plague or virus killed him, and the semi had plowed into the idling vehicles. Marvin couldn't help but wonder what it must have been like in those last seconds on Earth. To glance at your rearview mirror as you waited at the stoplight. To be thinking about work or dinner or getting a movie at the video store; all the little things we all think about every day that truly add up to nothing in the end. All of it rendered irrelevant when the semi began to grow larger in the mirror. What it must have felt like when the semi's front bumper connected with the first car, sending it into the next one, each one getting crushed like an accordion.

Metal creaked in the wind somewhere in the mish-mash pile of bones and metal, but he couldn't see what was making the noise. Not that it mattered.

He picked his way through the pile-up, and once clear, continued onward.

It was as he was approaching a white van, the front windshield facing him, the name of some obscured electrical company scribbled on the side, this vehicle not actually in the wreck, but sitting on the side of the road, that he kicked a soda can with his foot, sending it bouncing across the road.

The can bounced off the side of a car and it sounded loud in the stillness.

Marvin paid it no mind.

As he passed the van, and it was no more than ten feet behind him, the rear doors to the van were thrown open, each door smacking the sides of the rear bumper.

"Oh my God, I don't believe it! You're alive!" a voice screamed loud and relieved, elated to have discovered someone living other than themselves.

But Marvin didn't have the same reaction.

At the sound of the voice and the crashing van doors, he raised his shotgun and spun around, the fight or flight instinct kicking in, and he had chosen to fight.

As he turned to stare at the face of a beautiful, curvaceous, red-headed woman in her early thirties climbing out of the back of the van, the shotgun was already going off as he squeezed the trigger.

The barrage of death was aimed directly at the woman's head, and she had just enough time to open her eyes wide, her mouth taking on the shape of an O, before her head was obliterated in a magnificent spray of blood and bone.

The decapitated body stood on its feet for almost ten full seconds, as blood shot straight up like a fountain. But then the body bent at the knees and slumped forward, the torso slapping the cement with a meaty *thwack*. Blood still spurted out of the neck stump, but now it slowed to a trickle.

Marvin stood transfixed at the carnage he'd wrought, not believing what just happened.

He didn't want to shoot, it had been instinct. Why did the woman yell at him like that?

He stared at the woman's corpse of what was probably the last woman left alive on Earth, and he shook his head, sadly.

Then, when he decided what was done was done and no matter how much he wanted to change it, he couldn't, he turned and began walking out of town, hoping in the next town or city there might be someone, anyone, still living other than himself.

And this time, if he was lucky enough to find someone else, he would make damn sure to ask questions first and shoot later.

THE LAST SUPERHERO

He looked out over the devastated city, his heart breaking once more.

No matter how many times he saw it, he knew he would never stop caring. It had been more than five years since he'd seen another living human being, and though he still found it hard to believe, he knew it was true.

He was the last one.

As he gazed out across the rooftops of the skyscrapers, he let out a weary sigh of loneliness.

The sun was just beginning to rise and with it, the creatures that had inherited the Earth would be seeking cover. He didn't know why they feared the day, and only came out at night in force, but he surmised it had something to do with the rays of the sun. Which was amusing for the fact that what the creatures feared, gave him his power.

Rising gently off the rooftop, he flew slowly over the buildings. He rose higher to get a better vantage and curved to the north to investigate the devastation.

To him, flying was the same as walking, and he hadn't given it a second thought since he was a small boy.

Back then, when he had discovered he was superhuman and that he was impervious to harm, he had been ecstatic. His parents had raised him well and had instilled in him a strong value of right and wrong.

He had taken to become a superhero, battling crime wherever it raised its evil head. He believed in the betterment of mankind, for truth and justice, and yes, though it sounded clichéd, for the American way of life.

Only all of that was gone now.

Eight years ago, the first corpse rose from a mortician's table and began to walk. Soon there were others and sooner after that, an army of the dead began to sweep through every city across the world.

Back then he hadn't been alone. There had been others like him, some superhuman, some only human but with courage far beyond normal men and women.

There had been his best friend, who had dressed in black and had called himself The Bat. A rich man, he had been able to fund his crime stopping activities with ease.

As for him, he had merely worked as a reporter, hoping that by being in the midst of the information channels, he might find out about calamities faster, and by doing so, stop them before they grew worse.

As he soared through the clouds, he let his mind drift back to how it had been, how he had lived a normal life when not fighting crime, how he had been happy.

If he had known then what he knew now, he wondered if it would have made a difference.

Probably not.

For no matter how powerful, how invulnerable he was, he couldn't stop the dead from rising. He was superhuman, not omnipotent.

He began to descend into the city, his cape flapping behind him. It was filthy now and covered in blood splatter, as was the rest of his mostly blue uniform. The dried blood wasn't his, nor was it from any living being. It was from *them*, from the ones he'd destroyed since he'd decided there was no hope…only vengeance.

What he once stood for was gone, leaving only a bitter hatred for the walking dead.

As far as he knew, he was the last living person alive on the planet. Being invulnerable, he was immune to the infectious bites of the dead, and so as every man, woman, and child succumbed over time, either by starvation, sickness or attack, he remained.

It was hard at first, and he refused to accept he was alone. Back then, he spent each day traversing the world, searching city after city, country after country.

He had hopes that maybe there would be some people in the mountains, far away from civilization, but as each year passed, the ones he'd known about had disappeared, until finally, after a long winter, there was no one left but the animated dead.

When he had come upon the last settlement he knew about, to find it overrun by the undead, he had made sure to burn the entire place to the ground. With his heat vision set on full blast, he had seared every zombie within his range. His red beams of death had pierced brain after brain, had blasted bodies into mush. A few, he had spent longer on, setting his heat vision to a lower setting, then letting the rays slowly cook the ghouls' brains in their heads. When the pressure was too much, the heads had literally exploded from the expansion of heat, sending skull fragments and brains flying in all directions. Others he had taken a more hands on approach.

He was as strong as a thousand men, stronger actually, and he had used anything within his grasp as a bludgeon. Picking up abandoned cars, he had slammed them down on the zombies, the bodies popping like water balloons. As the undercarriages pulverized the corpses, red and brown slurry seeped from beneath the vehicles.

That was when he had changed, had become something he never dreamed possible.

Now, he was only a force of destruction, a force of violence.

Alone on a dead world, he had nothing but his hate to keep him sane.

If he was even that.

Though powerful beyond measure, inside his mind, he was still a man, with the same frailties every man had. He still loved, still felt jealousy and now, was filled with hate. He flew deeper into the bowels of the city, where the sun's rays still hadn't penetrated. Here he would find what he was searching for this morning, as he did every morning before this one.

Curving around an office building, his eyes barely looking at the blasted out windows and fire scorched facades, he dropped lower as his target came into view. A zombie horde was below him, more than three dozen of the walking dead, all gathered together as they walked along the street. They were like sheep in many ways, one leading for no apparent reason while the others merely followed out of blind instinct.

He pulled up and floated above them, the ghouls spotting him instantly. As one, they raised their hands into the air, as if they could pull him out of the sky, and began to moan, long and loud.

His square jaw grew taut as he listened to the wails of the dead, the song of death carrying on the wind. He had heard it before and it still filled him with horror, despite knowing they couldn't hurt him.

This morning he was tired. It had been a long night, and with the sun rising fast, he knew this would be the last horde he would find until sunset.

He decided to end them quickly.

Swooping to the right, he plowed directly into an office building on its north side, taking out half the foundation in one blow. With concrete and metal raining down, he flew out and then came back to the building, but this time on the west side. The sound of him striking the building was like a bomb had gone off and the echoes reverberated off the tall edifices surrounding the one he was demolishing.

As he flew out the other side, the building began to teeter. With a large portion now missing, it resembled a tree after a lumberjack had chopped away enough to make it fall in the direction he wanted it to.

With the rumbling of thousands upon thousands of steel and stone collapsing, the building began to fall, the massive structure coming down directly over the horde of zombies. The ghouls never moved, never so much as turned away, not understanding that their pitiful existence was about to come to an end. As for him, he flew high over head, out of the rising cloud of dust and grit, and watched the building pummel and flatten the animated corpses to paste.

He floated, and waited as the dust cloud spread out and began to dissipate. When the cloud had settled enough for him to see his handiwork, he nodded to himself at what he'd wrought.

The horde had been destroyed, leaving nothing but a few stragglers at the perimeter of the debris.

Swooping in, he used his heat vision to pick them off one by one. When he was down to the last few, he picked up a massive piece of debris and lifted it into the air. The debris had been a wall, with bent rebar jutting out at all angles. It was a wicked looking piece of wreckage and that was why he picked it. As the last remaining zombies moaned and wailed at him, he came down out of the sky, and when he was over them, he threw the wall as hard as he could. It didn't so much as hit the street as it went through it, sending the wall and the zombies beneath it into the sewers below, the street collapsing in on itself from the weight of the stone missile.

The zombies disappeared, almost as if they had evaporated from the impact of the wall, their bodies no match for the speed and weight of the massive bludgeon. He knew it was overkill but still he did it. He wanted to see them killed up close, to see the bodies destroyed like so much garbage.

His job finished for the night, he soared back into the sky and this time headed west.

Tonight, when the sun went down he would come out again. Tonight he would find another city where the dead walked unhampered, thinking in their feeble minds—if they did think—that they owned the streets.

But for now it was time to rest, to regroup and prepare for the next mission. It was time to go home.

He had a name once, two names actually.

One was the name his parents had given him. That name he used to identify with fellow humans, friends, loved ones and lovers.

Then he had the second name, the one he used as a superhero.

It was a name that inspired people to be better than they were, and made criminals shake in fear.

Neither name mattered now.

For what was a name when there was no one to speak it? What was the point of a title when there would never be another individual other than himself to acknowledge it?

No, names were irrelevant now.

He soared across the heavens and slowed as he approached the Midwest.

With his super vision, it didn't take him long to find the farm he wanted. He banked to the west and sped up, breaking the sound barrier easily.

He streaked in like lightning and landed on the roof, then slipped in through the open sunroof.

There had been a time he would have never done this during the day, for risk of exposing his parents to who their son truly was, but now like everything else, it didn't matter.

Dropping down from the sunroof, he found himself in the attic, the familiar all around him. Christmas decorations in the corner, old photographs of him and his parents in another, and in the far corner his old clothes. His mother never had the heart to give them away, even when she knew there was no purpose to keeping them.

Walking to the stairs leading to the second floor, he crept like a cat.

As he descended, he slipped off his cape, letting it drape over the banister.

When he reached the bottom step, he turned left, knowing the way well and walked the few feet to his bedroom from when he was a boy. It had been his room until he left for the big city at the age of nineteen.

But when you could fly, you were never far away from home, and he would visit often, sometimes more than he should have, though both his parents said he wasn't. They enjoyed having their son come by, always interested in his adventures in the big city.

Before reaching his room, he stopped to look at the pictures on the wall. There was one with his parents and another with all three of them. They were smiling, and he wondered what the picture would have looked like if they had known the future at the time of taking it. He doubted there would have been smiles.

Pulling himself away, he walked the few steps to his bedroom, trying his best not to let his sorrow get the best of him. He knew coming back here again and again was only opening the wounds of loss, but he couldn't help himself.

The cities were filled with the dead, the odor alone enough to cause him to want to gag. Though invulnerable, he still had ordinary taste and smell, and anything that would disgust a normal human would do the same to him.

So he came out to the Midwest, where people were few and far between. He'd decided if he had to go somewhere, then it might as well be to a place he was familiar with, a place he called home.

And then there was what he kept in the basement.

After stripping off his uniform he took a shower, the pipes fed by an underground well. As the cold spray cascaded over his hard, muscled body, despite his not wanting to remember, he found himself drifting back to the first month of the outbreak and the first tragedy he'd suffered.

"I have to get you out of the city," he told his wife as they stood on the rooftop of the newspaper office. They had worked together for years at the newspaper, until finally he had come clean to who he truly was two years ago. At first she hadn't believed him, but after he picked her up and soared into the sky, she knew he was telling the truth. That the man she knew as a reporter and friend, was also the superhero she had come to love.

She was embarrassed that she had never put the two men together, but when one can stop bullets, bend steel in his bare hands, and hurtle tall buildings easily, even a few small cosmetic changes to his face and changing the tone of his voice was enough to fool her and the rest of the world.

"But I can't leave now," she said. "Someone has to cover this catastrophe. Someone needs to report it."

"Well, it can be someone else because I'm getting you out of here right now." It was as he reached for her that his super hearing picked up screams for help.

She saw his face, the way he cocked his head, and knew immediately what was happening. "Someone needs help," she said, the sentence a statement.

"Yes, I… they can wait, first I need to get you to safety," he said, as he looked out over the rooftop to the cityscape before him. Smoke drifted from dozens of buildings, many burning uncontrollably. A downed helicopter was jutting out of the twentieth floor of an insurance building a block away and sirens and gunshots echoed through the stone and steel canyons.

The city was in dire straits, the thousands upon thousands of people all packed within its perimeter now fighting to escape, to stay alive, as the walking dead slowly gained ground.

"No, that's not the man I fell in love with," she said. "We both know you can't let those people suffer. It's not in you." She reached under her windbreaker and pulled out a small pistol. "Go, I'll be fine here till you return. This roof is safe, I'll be here waiting for you. Then we can leave together, with you knowing you've done all you can to save the people of this city."

"I…" he began, but another scream pierced the air and he knew he needed to leave now or whoever was in peril was doomed. "Okay, but I won't be long. You stay here, make sure the rooftop door is secured, and I'll return as soon as I can."

She leaned up on her toes and kissed him. "I'll be waiting, now get out of here. Your city needs saving."

He kissed her once, the passion brief but sensual, then he stepped away and soared into the air.

He glanced down one time before shooting off to the far west corner of the city. As he did, he saw his love standing there, looking up at him, a slight smile on her lips. She knew the man she fell in love with, and she accepted him for who he was.

A hero.

Then he was miles away and she was lost to the rising smoke filling the sky.

He didn't mean to stay away for so long, but there were so many people in need of his help.

An apartment complex had been surrounded by the dead, and if it wasn't for him, no one would have escaped alive. Back then he didn't kill the zombies, thinking of them as people, humans that were sick and needed medical help.

He had made short work of the undead horde by carving a moat around the building, cracking a water pipe to fill it, then letting the zombies mill about, the few falling in not able to scale the dirt walls.

He flew away without waiting for a thank you. For that wasn't why he did what he did.

The next emergency was an out of control fire. A tanker truck filled with gas had overturned on the outskirts of the city. He had used his super breath to snuff out the flames, then moved the wreckage out of the way. Any zombies he saw he merely picked up and dropped in a quarry outside the city limits.

He gathered them up in loads of half a dozen, wrapping them in his arms. As he flew with them, their teeth snapped and they tried to bite him, only their teeth would shatter on his hard skin.

He did this countless times until he realized it was hopeless. There were simply too many animated corpses to deal with, and though superhuman, he was still only one man.

Hours passed and he went from emergency to emergency.

A squad of police and firemen were pinned down by more than a hundred zombies. He had swooped in, knocking the bodies aside like tenpins, sending them sprawling to the street. Before he had struck the last one, his head was already cocked and listening for the next situation that required him.

As the police and firemen waved to his fleeting form as he rose into the sky, he soared over the buildings to come to the aid of citizen after citizen.

It was night when he finally came to the realization that no matter how much he did, there was simply too much chaos for him to contain.

He remembered his wife, and swinging around, he soared across the horizon to return to her. He needed to get her out of the city. At least then he would know she was safe and he could concentrate on the undead menace.

He arrived at the rooftop of the newspaper building in seconds, but as he hovered above it, his heart jumped in his chest when he saw it was filled with zombies. More than a score were milling about on the roof, the service door hanging open, the lock pushed out from where the weight of many bodies had forced it open.

His wife was nowhere to be found.

He landed on the roof, punching ghouls out of his way. Some tried to attack him and he pushed them away, his strength sending them over the roof to splatter on the ground below.

He wouldn't have done this normally, not wanting to take a life, but his concern for his wife was that great to block off all rational thought.

His eyes studied each zombie, praying against everything he cared about that her face wouldn't be in the crowd. After minutes of searching, he let out a sigh when she wasn't there.

There was also no blood or body parts on the roof, which meant she hadn't been killed and eaten.

Then where did she go?

His eyes went to the edge of the roof, and he wondered if she could have taken her life, stepped off the roof to fall to her death rather than be eaten alive.

No, he knew she would never do that. She would have fought to the very end. She was that strong, and it was one of the things he loved about her.

His x-ray vision searched every crevice of the rooftop but there was nothing of her remaining.

With trepidation in his heart, he even checked the streets around the building, in case she had fallen accidentally, but there were no remains there either.

She was gone, vanished. It was like she had simply flown off like he always did to disappear.

With nothing else to be done, he rose into the air, leaving the zombies on the roof alone; killing them would serve no point.

The rest of the city was forgotten, only his desire to find his wife remaining. He would search every single building, underground garage, and structure until he found her. He flew off into the night as the city he loved so much burned around him.

He searched for days, checking each building with his x-ray vision, but he never found her.

She had just disappeared. There was nowhere for her to go, so though it broke his heart, he knew he had to accept that she was dead, she had to be.

Like a person going to a cemetery where a loved one is buried, a month after losing her, he returned to the roof. A few zombies were still there and he killed them easily, taking heads within his hands and crushing them to a red and brown pulp. After more than a month of fighting the dead, he was desensitized to their plight. They were no longer sick citizens to him. Now they were the worst evil imaginable, and he killed all who he came upon.

When the last zombie was put down, nothing left of the undead but body parts that twitched and steamed in the hot sun, he began to walk around the roof, searching once more, but knowing there was nothing to find.

It was when he reached the far side of the rooftop that he heard a small mewling sound, then scratching and a soft banging.

It was so subtle that even his super hearing would have been hard pressed to pick it up when all the zombies were on the roof, each one moaning and howling.

Following the sounds, he found himself standing before an air conditioning vent, one of dozens of ductwork strewn across the roof.

He used his x-ray vision to peer into the duct but found that he couldn't see into it. It was lined with lead, he assumed, it had to be. The one metal he couldn't see through.

Grabbing the edges of the duct with his hands, he tore it open, shredding the metal like it was nothing but paper.

When it was open and he peered into the black hole, he once more saw nothing but darkness.

But the noise was louder now.

He didn't know why he bothered, but for some reason, he wanted to know what the odd sounds emanated from.

Not worried about property damage, he began pummeling the roof, digging through the cement and steel and into the floor below. Dropping down, he used his x-ray vision to find the duct in the closest wall. Though he couldn't see inside the duct, he could see its outline clearly.

When he found it, he began punching the wall, tearing at the plaster like it was nothing but paper mache. Plaster dust began to fill the room and he clapped his hands hard, blowing it away to funnel up the hole in the roof.

When the duct was exposed, he grabbed it and yanked it out of the wall.

Foot after foot came free until the entire room was filled.

When he was finished, he stopped and listened once more. His eyes played over the ductwork as he listened intently. There was the sound again, it was over there in the far corner.

Hovering a few feet off the floor, he flew over the ductwork, then landed right on top of the noise. Reaching down, he tore the duct open.

And gasped in horror at what he found.

Though he was invulnerable, he felt his knees go weak and his entire world came crashing down on him.

For all these months, deep down and buried, there was a spark of hope that his wife was still alive.

After all, there had been no sign of her body, no sign that she had been killed. So though he knew it was improbable, he had held onto that small spark, praying one day he would find her alive.

All that was gone now, as he gazed down at the zombie before him.

It was his wife.

Within half a second he pieced together what must have happened. She had been trapped on the roof and he was nowhere to be found. She may have called out to him, her thinking that he would hear her no matter how far away he was. But he hadn't heard her and she had done the only thing she could think of to survive.

She had raced to the duct, crawled inside, and had waited for him to return to her.

She must have crawled in too far and become stuck.

With the zombies on the roof, and the echo inside the duct, it was possible she had been calling out and he hadn't heard her.

Or worse, she had died in there and had turned. The entire time he had been on the roof searching for her, his wife's body had only been a few feet from him. So close and yet still so far.

Truth was, how she died was irrelevant.

He fell to his knees and cried as the zombie crawled out of the torn-open vent and tried to bite him. Her hair fell across her face and he reached up and brushed it aside, like he used to do when they would cuddle on the couch in their apartment. She bit his finger but it was like biting down on a piece of stone, her teeth doing no harm. She did chip a front tooth, however.

With his cape wrapped around him, he placed his head on the floor and sobbed, the entire time his wife crawling on his back, repeatedly trying to bite his neck. All she got for her trouble was an empty belly.

After a full half hour had come and gone, he finally pulled himself together enough to think about what he might do now.

He took in all his options, finding there were none.

How it had it all gone so wrong? How was it that no matter how powerful he was, in the end, he wasn't strong enough to save the people he loved? To save her?

The guilt rocked him to his very core. By saving the city, or trying to, he had lost the one thing that meant the most to him.

His wife was dead, and worse, had reanimated. He may have loved his country, his world, but he loved her more. Without her it was all for nothing. Without the light at the end of the tunnel that was his prayers she was still alive, he had only emptiness in his heart.

Picking her up, he flew out of the building and into the coming night.

He knew where he would bring her immediately.

He would bring her home, to the farmhouse, the only place he truly felt like any other human.

With the moon rising on a dying world, he soared off into the horizon.

He landed on the rooftop of a skyscraper as thoughts of the past were pushed deep down yet again.

Down on the street, a massive crowd of undead had gathered for some reason.

When he cocked his head and listened, he heard the distinct sound of a dog barking.

So that was what the creatures had found and were gathering to kill.

As he gazed down to the street, he saw more than a thousand zombies were packed tightly together. He knew they had no real intelligence, but surely, even one zombie in the crowd knew how foolish it was for a thousand ghouls to try and kill one lone dog.

The memories of the loss of his wife were quickly being replaced by the hatred, the unending anger he felt almost every second of each day. The living dead were a curse, a blight on the planet that might very well never be eradicated.

Stepping off the roof, he floated to the ground. Off to the left was a gas station, the lanes for the pumps packed with cars and trucks, all with dried blood splattering the windows and the doors hanging open.

He gauged the distance of the gas station and the closest of the massive undead horde, then used his heat vision on one of the cars near the gas pumps. His vision sliced into the gas tank like a laser beam, cutting the car in two before the fuel in the vehicle's tank ignited, sending a rolling fireball in all directions. It was still a small blast but he wasn't finished yet. His heat vision was still moving, and he sliced into car after car, truck after truck, igniting all their fuel tanks.

When he finally hit the first of the gas pumps, it was like a small sun had gone supernova right there in the street.

The shock of the blast was strong, and it knocked hundreds of ghouls over, their arms and legs becoming tangled as they tried to get up, not understanding what had happened.

He had learned over the years that one thing the zombies feared was fire. He had found it an effective weapon in the destruction of the undead, and used it as often as he could.

Flying to the burning gas station, he swooped under a large Ford pickup and picked it up. The flaming wreckage dripped fire and fuel all around him but he felt nothing, his invulnerably allowing him to feel the stifling heat as if he was simply out in the sun on a warm day.

Holding the truck, he flew back to the middle of the undead crowd and dropped the flaming debris on top of them. The truck landed like an anvil, smashing the ones unfortunate enough to be directly underneath, the flaming pieces breaking off to take out dozens more. One hapless zombie was decapitated when a particularly nasty and sharp piece of metal flew at it. The head slid off its shoulders to roll on the ground before it was kicked away by another ghoul's foot.

The decapitated zombie toppled over, black ichor spurting out its neck hole.

The man who had once been considered *super* went back for more wreckage, and this time he simply picked it up and threw it at the crowd. The burning cars looked like comets as they flew through the air, to then land and crush the bodies beneath them.

The odor of burned flesh filled the street in all directions as the horde continued to moan and wail, a requiem of the damned that filled the air with their call of death.

He ignored it all, only wanting to destroy the foul monsters. He had long ago stopped seeing the zombies as human beings, now they were nothing more than cockroaches.

Wanting to get more 'hands on', he flew into the crowd, only a few feet off the ground. He struck them like a missile, the bodies exploding on contact from his dense frame. He landed and began crushing heads as if they were rotten fruit, taking his hands and clapping them together while a zombie's head was in between them.

The eyes would pop out and fly through the air, the ganglia trailing behind like streamers. Teeth would pop forth to litter the ground like hail, and the headless ghoul would fall over. The zombies attacked him each time he landed among them, for to them he was food.

He punched and kicked, his fists caving in chests, his blows so hard they went into the chest cavities themselves. He would then pick them up and throw the bodies at others, each corpse exploding on contact from the human projectiles.

There were times when he killed zombies for hours, one after another, one body at a time. Though he could have frozen them all with his super breath and simply smashed them to pieces, there was a certain satisfaction in getting 'down and dirty.'

Arms and legs were torn off bodies as if the ghouls were nothing more than paper dolls, and soon the street ran dark with viscera and rotting organs. Flies hovered above the horde like a giant black smoke cloud, the buzzing so loud it nearly droned out the moans of the dead.

Taking two zombies and holding one in each hand, he brought his arms together, the heads and torsos smashing as one until the bodies had nearly molded together. As he dropped the mutilated corpses to the ground, he stopped fighting and looked up at the sky through the cloud of flies.

"Why? Why did this happen?" he screamed "Why am I the only one left? Why can't I die?"

What's the point in going on like this forever? he wondered. It's been five years since the dead began to walk and still, he hadn't seen another living soul since a few months after the outbreak, no matter where he searched. Every bunker, every mountain retreat, everywhere, all the humans he'd found were either dead or zombies. Whatever the ailment was, if you died you came back, so no matter where a person was, when they finally died, they returned, to then kill the rest of their group.

How do you escape death itself?

Simple…you can't.

Then, through a hole in the crowd, he spotted something that held his attention. While the zombies tried to bite him and he shoved them away, the ghouls now nothing than an annoyance, he saw something that rocked his world to its very core, its very foundation.

Suddenly, all the killing, the destruction, the carnage, it all seemed for nothing, for it was at that moment, as he watched a family of zombies stumble on the sidewalk at the edge of the crowd, that he realized it is he who was the intruder, it is he who didn't belong in this new world of the dead.

Mom was carrying an infant, now zombified, and Dad was holding the hands of two undead children, a boy and a girl, both around eight when they had died. The family looked like they were going for a walk, the group staying close together.

He heard that inner voice inside him telling to go kill them, to destroy the mockery of the family unit, but something held him back.

He watched the family reach the corner and disappear onto the next street, and he fell to his knees, an epiphany rushing over him as he realized it was truly over.

It's done, he's done. No more killing, no more searching. He's had enough, he can't go on any longer.

It's all been for naught, a waste of time and energy.

He came to the realization that everything he was doing, all the killing, it had all been about him not wanting to accept that he wasn't needed anymore, that he *was irrelevant.*

He was a relic from a distant time, a time when human beings ruled the planet.

That time was gone, now was a time for the dead.

He burst free of the zombies climbing over him as they tried to kill him, sending their bodies in all directions. One held onto his leg as he flew into the air.

When he was three hundred feet up, the zombie let go and tumbled to the ground, limbs flailing. The body exploded on impact with the ground, nothing more than a human rotten tomato.

Moans of a thousand voices floated up, the song of the dead filling his heart and mind with a resolve he had never known till now.

He knew what he had to do.

Turning to the west, he streaked off into the night, heading to the only place he truly ever called home, and to the one thing waiting for him that he had never been able to let go of…till now.

He slowed and came in for a soft landing in the front yard of the farmhouse. He didn't go inside, but instead walked around to the back.

Here, there were compost heaps and old tractor parts scattered across a large field. His youth came to his mind and he smiled at the pleasant memories.

His father had saved every piece of machinery he could find, almost never using the old parts, but pleased to know they were there.

On the far side of the field was another tractor. It had no wheels and was rusted to the point of being useless to even the most dedicated craftsman. He went to it and picked it up, tossing it aside as if it was nothing more than a tin can. The tractor soared through the air and landed in a cloud of dust a quarter mile away, the impact shaking the ground slightly.

He barely noticed.

Using his x-ray vision, he searched the ground where the tractor had been, and without preamble, began to dig.

Like a machine set on high, he scraped mounds of dirt from the ground until a large hole was created. At the bottom of the hole was what he wanted. A safe, lined with lead.

Picking up the safe, he flew out of the hole and landed at the back door to the farmhouse. He stepped inside.

Walking to the basement door, he opened it and descended the stairs, the wood creaking slightly from his weight.

The odor hit him immediately, but he ignored it.

It was the smell of death, a charnel house redolence of decay.

Putting on the one light, a small naked light bulb, he walked over to the metal cage in the corner, putting the safe down as he crossed the basement floor.

His wife snarled and reached through the bars at him, wanting to eat him. Even after all this time she still tried, no matter how many times she failed.

He opened the door, which was locked with a simple steel pipe that had been wrapped around the metal bars. After untwisting the pipe, he tossed it to the cellar floor, knowing there would be no more need of it.

"Hi, honey, I'm back for good this time," he said to the zombie. She snarled and came at him, but he put out a hand and stopped her. She snapped her teeth—many which were missing from trying to eat him, his hard skin no match—and drooled onto the floor.

When she wouldn't stop fighting him, he merely pressed on her shoulder, making her sit. At first she wouldn't cooperate, but after a few minutes, she stayed put. She reached out and picked up a hunk of animal hide and began to chew on it, trying to scrape any residual meat from the dry skin.

The entire cellar was littered with animal parts, from where he had caught and brought them to feed her.

He had always wondered what he would do if he couldn't find any more animals and there were still people to take, but luckily he had never had to deal with that question head on. The people had vanished long before the animals.

With her occupied, he went to the safe and brought it closer, then sat down beside her. Whether she was used to him or not was unknown, but she didn't attack him, instead concentrating on her animal hide.

With one hand, he snapped the handle off the safe, ripping open the door.

As soon as he did this, he felt a wave of weakness wash over him.

Inside was a glowing rock, a piece of a meteorite that had fallen from the sky back when he was a child.

For some reason, the rock had an effect on his constitution, and when exposed to it, it sapped his strength to the point he became human. All his powers would vanish as long as he was exposed to the glowing rock.

Reaching inside the safe, he picked up the rock, his skin rippling from touching it.

He held it in his hands for almost five minutes, and before he felt all his strength fade away, he stood up and threw the rock at the ceiling.

It went through like a missile, then through the wall of the farmhouse and into the sky. Where it would land was anyone's guess, but it would be miles away.

He slumped back to the cellar floor and sucked in a breath of air. He felt terrible, nauseous, and it had taken all he had to throw the rock away.

Slowly, he turned to his wife and held out his arm, rolling up his sleeve as he did so.

"It's time, honey. I'm ready to join you," he whispered. "I don't want to be alone anymore."

She looked at his arm, and without giving it any thought that every other time she had tried to bite him had failed, she leaned forward and sank her teeth deep into his flesh.

Blood squirted from between her lips and he gritted his teeth from the pain. Physical pain wasn't something he was used to, having never felt it before.

She began to slurp at the blood, taking out small chunks of meat. As she began feeding, he felt his strength returning now that the rock was gone. By the fifth bite, she could no longer tear at his flesh and it began to heal, mending itself on its own accord.

But that was all right. He could feel the virus, the infection within him, feeding off him, changing him into one of the walking dead.

His powers were returning, but with it something else was happening. Due to his accelerated chemistry, he was succumbing a hundred times faster than an infected human would. Picking up his wife, he flew up the stairs and outside.

He put her down and she looked around, blinking up at the sun. She hadn't seen the sun in years, since he had found her and brought her to the farm.

She shielded her eyes from the glare and went over to a tall oak to stand under its canopy for shade.

The sun would be going down in a few hours, then she would venture forth. But till then she would remain in the shade.

He joined her a minute later and sat down so his back was leaning against the tree.

Looking down at his hands, he saw the pigment was now paler, and when he touched his face, he found his brow more pronounced, his eyes sunken in.

It wouldn't be long now.

He reached out to his wife and she didn't flinch. She sniffed his hand once and then ignored it, recognizing one of her own kind.

When he pulled her close and had her sit beside him, she didn't resist.

With his arm around her, the married couple sat silently, waiting for the sun to go down, and for the moon to rise on an undead world.

THE LAST WAR

Mark's Journal: entry 503

We never saw it coming.

One year ago, while the people of Earth slept in their beds, or on the opposite end of the planet where they were working and playing, the aliens came out of the sky.

There was no warning, nothing. Our radar defenses were useless, their technology far beyond anything we had at our disposal.

And so too were our weapons.

We threw everything we had at them. Rockets, missiles, jet planes with smart bombs, nothing so much as put a dent in any of the fifty mother ships that hovered above the major cities of the world. The U.S. military was about to try nuclear arms but were destroyed before any could be deployed.

The most terrifying thing was why they came to our world.

They came because they were hungry.

The term *monster* had been used in science fiction for thousands of years, but the aliens that visited our world were the very essence of what a monster should be.

The smallest one was well over seven feet tall. They had three eyes, and four arms. Other than that they were frightening similar to humans. The third eye was directly in the center of their oversized foreheads and their arms were in the same place humans were. The one main difference was their skin tone. Where Caucasian human beings were flesh-colored, say 'pink' for an easier reference, the aliens were as white as clean sheets of the same hue.

Which was how the slang name for them was created.

We called them *sheeters.*

To anyone reading this who never saw one in person, the name might sound odd, but trust me, when you have a *sheeter* standing over you, ready to rip your head off so it can suck you like a silly straw, the name is very apt.

When they first arrived, we had hopes they were friendly.

There was even a large assembly on the front lawn of the White House, where the President of the United States and the alien commander gathered to discuss why they came to our planet.

But no sooner did the alien commander and its delegation arrive and stand before the President, then the commander reached out, took the

President's head in two of its large hands, while the other two hands held the man by the waist for leverage, and pulled upward, tearing the President's head off like his neck was made of paper mache.

As you can imagine, pandemonium ensued, as Secret Service agents started shooting. The second the chaos began, the alien delegation pulled out some strange kind of guns. They were short, stubby even, no more than four inches long, and they didn't shoot conventional bullets. They shot out a beam of light. Not a laser, but an actual beam of pure energy.

Wherever the beam touched human flesh, said flesh began to sizzle and melt. Within a minute of the initial killing of the President, the entire crowd surrounding the podium had been turned into a pink ooze that soaked into the grass.

A few escaped and spread the word as well as what the cameras got before the operators were killed, melted like ice cream in the hot sun.

It was chilling to say the least.

From that moment on we were at war, and from the looks of the planet, this may very well be the last war ever fought here.

I suppose it's a small consolation that we as a world, as in mankind, didn't end up destroying ourselves; it was an outside enemy that was doing it. Small consolation, I know.

"Hey, Mark, it's time to leave, get a move on," Peter snapped out to me from across the room.

I looked up and gave him a wave, letting him know I'd heard him. Closing my journal, I came back to reality and where I was. I was in the underground vault and basement of a bank on West 54th with twenty other survivors.

As far as we knew, we were the only ones left in the city. The sheeters had been hunting humans more than normal lately and were taking out our camps by the droves. Some of us had decided to leave the city, to head to the mountains where there was a better chance of surviving. But most of us—the ones who still wanted to fight—who hadn't given up entirely, we stayed; no one was gonna make us leave our city, our home. This was our planet, and by God we would take it back or die trying.

Unfortunately, the latter was what was probably going to happen as we were overmatched, outgunned and low on supplies.

As a rebel unit we were pathetic and where we once would venture out to attack guerilla warfare style, now all we did was search the remains of the destroyed city for food and other essential supplies.

As I put my journal away, I let my eyes scan over the people who had become more than just friends to me; they had become my family.

Peter was our leader. He was a little over six feet tall with long blonde hair and a pale complexion. Before the sheeters arrived, he would have been considered to be a surfer boy. He had that look.

Next was Mary. She was short and stubby, with black hair cropped tight to her head. She wasn't very pretty, I'm sorry to say, and she was covered from head to toe in tattoos. She looked like a midget biker chick. But they say it's inner beauty that matters, and Mary had it in droves. She could make you laugh in a second and always had a smile for you, no matter how hard things had become.

The next of our ragtag group was Marty. In his late fifties with gray hair and a beer belly, he would be the last guy you'd think would be a rebel. He'd been in the Iraq war and he knew how to survive. He'd been a handyman in his former life and he was the one in the group who would keep things running, such as the generator we had. Truthfully, I don't know what we would have done without him.

The next in the group was Rose. She was in her late twenties but had a soul much older. She was like our mother. She would always be there when we lost someone on a raid or out searching for food, or just needed a shoulder to cry on in general. She was beautiful, and even with her face and clothes covered in dirt from lack of water from washing, she always seemed to look better than the rest of us. It was just her way.

There were others, too, but they weren't in my immediate circle of friends so I won't go into details on who they were or what they looked like. The ones I described were the only ones that *really* mattered to me. They were my family now.

I looked up to find Peter was standing over me, talking.

"Huh, what?" I asked.

"I said, snap the hell out of it and get your gear, we're leaving in five," he said and walked away.

Mary came over to me and I looked down on her. She was a foot shorter than me easy, though she wore boots with heels that added a few inches to her height. She handed me a pistol.

"It's all cleaned, Mark," she said. "It has a new coat of oil, too."

"Thanks, Mary," I smiled. "All I know how to do is point and shoot it."

"And you can't even do that too well," Peter called from over his shoulder. A few other guys within earshot chuckled but I ignored them.

"Hey," I said casually. "We all can't be action heroes."

"That's for sure," Peter replied, getting more laughs from anyone close enough to hear.

"Peter, that's enough. Mark does what he can, we all do," Rose said like a stern mother. "Now say you're sorry."

Peter looked down, like he was a child caught with a cookie before dinner. "Sorry, Mark."

"No problem," I replied.

Peter cleared his throat and clapped his hands. "Okay, let's get moving. Bruno and Garibaldi, you're coming, too."

Two disheveled men in their thirties looked up from where they sat playing poker in the corner.

"Seriously?" Bruno asked, annoyed.

Peter nodded. "Yeah, we need two more sets of hands. The last search party thinks they found the rubble of what was a supermarket. If it's true, we'll need more men to carry what we can find back here."

"But we just got back this morning from a run," Garibaldi said.

Peter walked over to the man and pulled the cards from his hand, dropping them on the table.

"Hey, what the hell?" Garibaldi yelled.

Peter leaned over and went nose to nose with the man. "Listen up and listen good; in case you hadn't noticed, we're in a fucking war and we're losing badly. I don't care that you were out this morning, we need the manpower and you and Bruno are who I want. Now stop complaining, grab your gear, and let's go."

Garibaldi looked like he was going to say more, but when he looked past Peter's face to see Bruno looking at him, Bruno shook his head slowly, the gesture clear: 'shut up and do what you're told.'

Garibaldi merely nodded his head and Peter's face calmed. "Good, I'm glad we're on the same page." He turned and walked back to Mary, who was chuckling, a big smile on her face.

"For a second, boss, I thought he was gonna give you shit," she said.

"Well, he didn't, so let's forget it and focus on the mission," Peter told her. Mary nodded and went back to packing her gear.

Rose came over to me and rubbed my shoulder. "You okay?" she asked, her white teeth peeking out of her mouth. I never understood how she was able to keep them so clean. We'd run out of toothpaste more than a month ago and most of us had given up on dental hygiene altogether. Hell, on any kind of hygiene.

"Yeah, I'm fine, just another day in fantasy land, right?"

She smiled, the gesture going right to her eyes, making me feel safe and secure, even when I wasn't. "That's the spirit, it's not over till it's over. We'll beat them, we just have to find out how."

I nodded slightly, not commenting on her morale speech. Sure, we were going to find a way to kick the aliens off our planet, because the entire might of the Army, Navy, Air Force, Marines and every other military machine across the planet just didn't have what it took to get the job done. But our little band of rebels did.

With everyone getting ready to leave, I did the same, as Rose walked away to spread her high spirits to the rest of the group.

Two hours later found us picking our way through the rubble of what was once a U.S. city. On both sides of us was nothing but steel and concrete wreckage, the buildings destroyed by flames and sometimes artillery fire.

Bruno was on point, then came Peter, myself, Mary, and Garibaldi brought up the rear. Garibaldi carried one of our most prized weapons, a grenade launcher which was connected to his rifle. If we were attacked, hopefully that would do the job of taking down our enemy.

The sun was high in the sky as we made our way to the location Peter had marked on a map. If the last search party was correct, there could be canned food that our group sorely needed.

My palms were sweaty and I had to keep switching hands with my gun to wipe them clean on my pants. I wasn't a warrior, and never claimed to be one, but through simple circumstance I now found myself playing soldier, only this game was far deadlier than anything I might have played as a boy with my friends.

The enemy I was up against was ruthless. The enemy didn't want to just kill me, but if possible, wanted to capture me so I could be made into a meal.

We had all heard the stories of humans becoming nothing more than cattle and there were rumors of breeding camps near Australia.

Stolen pictures by spies who somehow managed to escape, showed aliens sitting at tables while human torsos were served up, much like humans cooked pigs whole. From what I'd heard, it was our eyeballs that were the cherished prize, a delicacy to the aliens. But though the eyes were popular, believe it or not it was male testicles that were the caviar to the enemy. I tried not to think about some alien sheeter munching on my balls as if they were fine chocolate, but the images I'd seen back when the internet was still up would stay with me forever.

Like most of the old life, the internet was long gone thanks to the aliens blowing up all of our satellites.

"I got movement at three o' clock," Bruno said and held his hand up to stop us.

I snapped back to reality and felt my heart beat faster in my chest. Man, I swear I wanted to piss myself right then and there and only force of will stopped me. Next to me, Mary gripped her M-16 tighter and grinned slightly. She was fearless and I had to say I was envious. Being scared all the time wasn't a good thing, though some said it was why I'd stayed alive for so long.

"Firing line, now," Peter snapped, and we all lined up beside one another so there would be no chance we would shoot a friend instead of the enemy by accident. If there had been more time we would have spread out so not to be such a close target, but no sooner did Peter give the order to line up, then we heard the rubble shift some more as something approached from around a large pile fifty feet ahead of us.

The soft click-clack of safeties coming off and weapons being cocked filled the air around me as I waited for what would come next.

Bruno was the first to speak as the origin of the noise was discovered. A dog appeared and walked closer, its hackles raised upon seeing us, while growling softly. "Oh shit, it's just a dog."

We all let out the breath we were holding as the mangy, half-starved dog stopped walking and stared at us, as if it was trying to understand just what the hell we thought were doing in its territory.

Bruno was about to say something else when there was a beam of light and the dog exploded into a hundred bloody chunks, gore and viscera splashing all of us, despite being more than twenty feet away.

"Jesus Christ!" Peter yelled as he wiped blood from his face.

Before any of us could do anything, no matter how small, an alien patrol appeared around the same pile of rubble, their white complexions standing out like an ink spot on a clean piece of paper. We were caught out in the open, there was nowhere to run to, and though we were sorely outmatched, all we could do was fight and hope for the best.

With a warrior's yell, Peter leveled his AK-47 and began spraying the alien patrol with bullets—there were six in all. Beside me, Mary did the same. I saw her bullets crawl across the ground then jump up and begin peppering a sheeter. The alien took the barrage stoically, barely moving. Other than taking a step back from the force of the rounds, it remained unhurt.

See, sheeters have body armor that our weapons can't penetrate. Only head shots will do the job. For some reason, sheeters don't wear helmets. I've never seen one with head gear, which is odd. Someone once said it was some kind of weird honor thing with them, as if they weren't afraid of the humans enough to wear helmets. But if that was true, then why wear body armor?

As soon as the patrol saw us, they began firing at us, too. But instead of the sound of gunfire, there was only the hiss of their beam weapons.

Falling to the ground, I began to shoot, though I don't know if even one of my bullets hit anything. I heard a thumping sound and looked over my shoulder to see Garibaldi fire off a grenade. I saw his face light up as he fired and then I saw that same face vaporized as a beam weapon hit him above the neck.

Like hot wax sliding off a mold, his face melted, the skin sloughing off to puddle at his feet. He didn't even have time to yell, the air in his chest sucked out of him from the heat of the blast.

The beam weapon began to go down his body, cooking him from the inside out. His clothes blended with his flesh and his internal organs popped before the man became nothing but a pile of ooze. Even his bones were melted.

The grenade soared through the air, the man who fired it dead before the grenade landed amidst the alien patrol. When it went off, four of the sheeters were caught in the blast, and their exposed heads received shrapnel, which shredded eyes and sliced their pale flesh.

Peter whooped in victory, thinking we had the upper hand, but no sooner did the whoop leave his mouth, then one of the remaining two aliens shot him. The beam weapon was set to a finer scope, and before Peter knew what had happened, he glanced down to his abdomen to find there was nothing there but a gaping hole about six inches in circumference. He felt no pain yet and there was no blood, the beam cauterizing the wound as it happened.

Peter reached down and put his hand through the hole in his body, and as I was standing behind him and to the side, I saw the fingers of that hand wiggling back and forth, almost as if the man was waving to me.

He turned to look at me, his eyes wide with shock, then he spit blood and crumpled to the ground, very dead.

"Come on, Mark, shoot the bastards!" Mary yelled from my side. I had stopped shooting, stunned at seeing Peter disemboweled without the weapon leaving a trace behind other than a hole in his body.

Mary got in another good shot, hitting an alien in its third eye. Its head snapped back and it dropped to the ground. There was one left and I began to shoot it, squeezing the trigger again and again until the clip ran dry. I was yelling, too, or at least I think it was me yelling. Looking back, I don't even know if it was actually me or if it was Mary.

All I know was that when I opened my eyes, I saw there were no more sheeters to shoot.

"Nice shot, Mark, I guess you're gettin' better," Mary said and walked over to the aliens to make sure they were all dead. "Check on Peter," she told me sadly.

I watched her shoot a couple in the head for good measure. They may have been alive or were truly dead, but I know Mary felt good shooting them again anyway.

"Uh, thanks," was all I could think to say to her compliment. I must have gotten lucky and one of my bullets hit where it was supposed to. I went to Peter. The instant I saw his eyes I knew he was dead. I knelt down and closed them, it was all I could do for him. There was no time to bury him, as the sheeters would have called in that they'd found us. We had to move and fast or we would be in yet another firefight.

I glanced at Bruno and Garibaldi, or what was left of them. I felt my bladder want to let go again as I thought how that could have been me. I was lucky today, that's all.

"Peter's gone," I said and stood up. Mary came over to me carrying a small suitcase. "That sucks," was all she said about Peter. "We lost three good men today, Mark, but I think it might not have been in vain."

My eyebrows went up, as I asked her a silent question.

She held up the suitcase. "I'm not sure exactly what this is, but I think we just scored big-time."

"Where'd you get it?"

Mary pointed to the dead sheeters. "It was with them. One of them was carrying it." She began to walk back to the bank, casting a sideways glance at Peter as she passed him. "Get Peter's and Bruno's weapons, they're still good."

I did as instructed and asked, "Where are you going? Are we gonna check out the supermarket still?"

She stopped walking and looked back at me. "No, that's irrelevant now. We need to get this back to the bank, and pronto. What I found may give us an upper hand in this war. Or at least do some damage."

Before I could ask her more questions, she turned and began jogging away.

Not wanting to be left all alone, I took one last look at my dead teammates, and quickly walked, then ran, to catch up to Mary.

I had to admit my curiosity was piqued. What could be in an old suitcase that was so powerful it could do real damage to the sheeters?

We arrived back at the bank more than three hours later.

Mary made us take a roundabout route back; she was worried we might be followed. As we approached the entrance to our base, a voice called out, "Halt, state your name!"

"It's Mary and Mark," she called out. "Returning from the field."

I watched a man appear as if from nowhere. He was camouflaged with bits of debris to look exactly like the wall and debris he was standing in front of.

"You're overdue. Where's Peter, Bruno and Garibaldi?" the guard asked.

Mary shook her head. "Dead," she replied flatly.

The guard didn't ask anymore questions. We had all lost friends and loved ones and it had become par for the course. Sure, we mourned their loss, but when people died constantly, a long grief period wasn't a luxury. There wasn't time. Sometimes, all the consolation the death of a friend would elicit would be a quick nod, a handshake, or a pat on the back.

"Go 'head, we're good here," the guard said and Mary and I walked by him to the hidden opening to the bank vault.

The opening was a three foot hole that we had to slide down. The top five floors of the bank were gone, sheared off as if a giant sword had sliced it. The lower half was intact, but the windows were all blasted out and the frame of the building was severely compromised. Truth be told, we didn't know if one day the entire thing would come crashing down on us.

Mary went first, sliding into the darkness, and then it was my turn. Feet first, I went down it like I was a boy playing on a slide in the school yard. The only thing I had to remember was that I needed to keep my back pressed to the slide or I might end up without a head by the time I reached the bottom.

As I went downward, the wind whipping the sweat dry on my face, I felt the air grow cooler. Then white light blasted me and I closed my eyes, knowing I had reached the bottom. Mary wasn't there, she had already headed off to the command base, or what we called the command base, which was the vault, which I stated earlier. It was funny in a sad way each time I entered the vault. I had seen all the jewelry, money and bonds that filled the safety deposit boxes, and now, most of it littered the floors of the vault. They had been searched in hopes of finding guns or ammunition. But the contents of the boxes were pretty much worthless to us. If you couldn't shoot it, eat it, or drink it, it was all a waste of space.

I arrived in time to see Mary had placed the suitcase on a bench. With tools already in hand, Marty was looking at it, while Rose and Mary talked.

When I entered, Rose looked up at me and smiled, "Good to see you in one piece, Mark, we lost too many good people out there today."

"Yeah, I'll miss Peter, he was a good guy," was all I could think to say.

Rose nodded, turned to Marty, and asked, "Well, what is it?"

Marty was concentrating on the contents of the suitcase and he whispered to himself as he touched this and fiddled with that. I noticed a small red light start to blink on and off near the bottom, but it meant nothing to me. I watched Marty connecting a few wires and then more lights lit up. He had fixed something, I knew that. Man, he was some handyman.

Finally, Mark looked up and with a deep frown and said, "It's a backpack nuke. A dirty bomb."

"I fucking knew it," Mary said, proud of what she'd found.

"A bomb?" I said, amazed. " You're kidding. What would the sheeters be doing with that?"

Marty shrugged. "They probably raided another camp somewhere and found it. Before the communication lines went down, we were gonna use our nuclear arsenal, my guess is whoever made this was planning to do just that."

"Okay, so what can we do with it to help us fight them?" Rose asked.

Marty rubbed his chin as he considered it. "That's a tough one. See, when this thing goes off, nothing for miles in every direction, including straight up, is gonna be able to live for a long time. The radiation spreads fast. That's why it's called a dirty bomb. It's fucking nasty. Some have timers so the guy who sets it can get away but this one doesn't. It has a 'dead man's' switch." He pointed to a black button in the center of the dials and gears. "Press this button and 'boom,' no more whatever you want to kill."

"So, what? We have to kill ourselves if we want to use it? That's crazy," Mary said.

Marty nodded in agreement. "It might be to us, but to someone else, it was the only thing that made sense. The only way to make absolutely sure this baby will go off is to activate it manually. Timers and radio signals can fail. Someone went to a lot of trouble to make this. Hell, where ever they found the radioactive waste probably killed the people who got it. Probably at one of the destroyed reactors near the shore, I'd guess."

"So whatever we do with this bomb will be a suicide mission for the team that uses it," Rose said, frowning deeply.

I was about to raise a question when an alarm bell began to sound.

"They've found us!" someone yelled. "They're right above us!"

"Shit," Marty spat. "The bastard's found us." He turned and his eyes shot daggers of accusation at Mary. "They followed you back here, you dumb bitch, it's the only explanation."

"I didn't do anything of the kind!" Mary yelled back as an explosion rocked the very foundation of the bank and the ceiling shuddered.

Rose spoke up. "It doesn't matter how they found us, they're here and we have to fight them off and escape. Pass the word, anyone who can get away, fall back to Base C on East 23rd Street." She waved her gun in the air and turned to me. "Mark, you're with me and Mary. Marty, get everyone you can and form a defensive line. They may be bigger than us, but down here that should be a disadvantage to them."

I knew what she meant. There was so much stuff stacked everywhere that the larger sheeters would have a hell of a time maneuvering around, while we could squeeze between piles of supplies.

"Now go!" she yelled and we moved out. Marty took the dirty bomb with him and disappeared down a side corridor.

Rose led, Mary followed, and I had took up the rear. As we moved through the corridors, I could hear gunshots and people screaming, and even over their shrieks I could hear the hissing of beam weapons.

I didn't want to, but I felt my bladder let go and I peed my pants. Embarrassing I know, but everyone was a little busy to notice, and for all I knew, the rest of the camp was pissing themselves as well.

We came out in a small lobby that led to a set of stairs that would bring us to the first floor. We had blocked it off with rubble and debris, but I could see there was now a large section missing, having been blown apart by the sheeters.

They were pouring in by the dozen. I counted over twenty before the onslaught slowed.

My God, we were so fucked.

More than a dozen of my people were firing at the sheeters, the sound of gunfire deafening. Rose and Mary each went to a marble support pylon and I did the same, coming up on Rose's right side.

As Rose and Mary began to fire, I found I was frozen. All I could do was watch the battle, too scared to contribute.

I watched a man jump up from behind a stack of flour cans we'd liberated from a food warehouse and begin spraying the sheeters. The man held a riot shotgun, a Remington 870. The weapon had a short barrel and no butt stock so he could easily carry it around. It was coated black so it wouldn't catch the light and on human beings the #1 buckshot would have been deadly.

But against the sheeters it was as if the man was shooting ping pong balls.

As the man ran out of ammunition, a sheeter fired its beam weapon at him. The beam caught the man straight on, and with one yell of fear or pain, the man began to melt, becoming a puddle of goop in less than three seconds.

The shotgun dropped to the floor, the severed hands that hadn't been in the beam still attached to the weapon. The gun clattered on the floor once and remained still.

All around me was a nightmare, one I prayed I'd never be thrown into. People were screaming, some partially melted from being hit, and they dragged severed bodies across the floor. A woman I only knew as Tina had been sheared in half. She was crawling slowly away from the battle, her intestines dragging out behind her like tied cans on a wedding car. A sheeter walked up to her and stepped on her intestines, but instead of stopping her, her entrails began to spool out, reminding me of a garden hose being unwound. The sheeter raised and lowered its shoulders and I wondered if that was how they laughed. Then it grew bored and shot her in the back of the head, the face and skull disintegrating, leaving only a torso with arms.

"Come on, you fucking coward, fight!" Mary yelled when she saw I wasn't shooting. But still, I was frozen. Anger flared in her eyes because I wasn't helping, and I saw Mary swing around with her rifle to shoot me.

She would have killed me then, but a sheeter popped up behind her and grabbed her by the head. She was lifted up as if she was a doll in a child's arms, and as I stared in horror, the sheeter popped her head off her shoulders. As blood geysered out, the sheeter began lapping at it, an ambrosia of the most horrific kind.

I began to back way, too frightened to think straight, not realizing that I was walking out into the open. My eyes went to the pylon where Rose was supposed to be, but she wasn't there. I cast my eyes to the left and right and then I found her, or what was left of her.

"There's a fucking mother ship over us!" someone yelled, who had a two-way radio. "We are so screwed!"

Before I could do anything, I felt searing heat on my right side and I casually looked down, like when a fly is on your arm, and my mouth fell open in absolute horror.

Where my arm was supposed to be, right up to my shoulder, there was now nothing.

A beam weapon had caught me and my arm was gone, the wound cauterized at the shoulder. There was no pain as it had happened so fast, but as each second ticked by, my body came to the realization that there was definitely something wrong with it.

As the first bout of pain filled me, I screamed. Then, out of my mind in pain, I turned and ran. Disintegrating rays sizzled past me, the smell of the air being superheated coming to my nose. But I could smell something else, too. I could smell the odor of my own dissolved flesh.

I ran, the sheeters right behind me, their heavy boots clopping on the floor.

The entire bank rumbled as the mother ship settled into a holding pattern and I knew I was going to die. Off a side corridor, the ceiling collapsed, the foundation finally giving up, dust and grit filling the air, making me cough.

I rounded a bend in the corridor and tripped, falling face first to the floor. My nose was smashed and I began to taste blood. It dripped down my chin and I rolled over to see what had tripped me.

Marty was on the floor, his chest a raw mass of meat and bones. He'd been shot and the hole was similar to the one that killed Peter, only this one was more primitive, as if the beam had been set to a lower setting and the wound wasn't cauterized as well.

I reached out with my one hand to get up and my palm came down on something hard. Grabbing it, I pulled it close and saw it was the dirty bomb.

The sound of running boots came to me again and I knew I had seconds before I was caught. I was blinded by pain now, my body not happy about losing a limb. In front of me, where I had been running, the ceiling collapsed, blocking my escape route. I coughed as concrete dust filled my lungs.

I did the only thing open to me, an option I would have never thought I could possibly do.

I opened the case and pressed the button to activate it.

The instant I did, it began to hum, as if something was cycling up or perhaps counting down. The sheeters appeared at the end of the corridor and I heard them saying something in their native language. They didn't shoot me, knowing I was helpless.

You know, I'd like to say I was being brave. That in the end I was the most heroic person in the base, but I'll be honest as I have seconds left to live and there's really no reason to lie now, not to me or anyone else.

It's easy to be brave when you're gonna die anyway. When there's nothing left to lose, thinking of the greater picture is simple.

As the humming grew louder and the sheeters walked closer, I glanced down at the bomb once more and realized that the small red blinking light must have been a tracking chip.

It had all been a setup so we would take the bomb back to the base. The only thing is, the sheeters didn't figure on Marty getting it to work. They didn't think a simple handyman might have the knowledge to fix the bomb, nor that a coward would have the fortitude to do what was right, despite the consequences.

That's the funny thing about wars. Many times, the side with the superior technology thinks that because they have cooler toys, they're stronger and smarter.

But sometimes, they're wrong.

The humming came to a stop and there was a blinding white light that seared my eyes from my skull.

What happened next?

Sorry, I can't tell you that.

THE LIGHT OF THE FULL MOON

"What have we got here?" the doctor asked as he flashed his penlight into the eyes of the man on the wheeled stretcher.

"Man in his early thirties, has been bitten multiple times by what we believe to be a dog. He's suffered blood loss and lacerations to the upper right clavicle and right arm," the paramedic said as he wheeled the unconscious man into the Emergency Room of Boston City Hospital in Dorchester, Ma.

Two nurses ran up to the stretcher and the doctor hovered over the prone man as he checked vital signs.

The doctor looked at the first nurse to arrive. "Get an IV drip going and prep O.R. 2," he said as he peeled back the pressure bandage to inspect the wound. "Jesus Christ, it looks like this guy went three rounds with a Doberman and lost."

"I know, right?" the paramedic said. "That's what I thought."

"Where did this happen? We're in downtown Boston, for Christ's sake," the doctor asked as he probed the wound. "Wild dogs don't usually roam the city streets."

"Near Boylston Street. He was barely conscious when we found him. He was babbling something about a wolf jumping out of an alleyway and attacking him, but he was delirious. It had to be a dog and a big one at that."

"Shit, every friggin' full moon all the crazies come out to play. All right, let's get him to the O.R. before he bleeds out," the doctor said.

The paramedic stepped back and let the nurses take over, pushing the stretcher through the doors labeled **Authorized Personnel Only** printed in bright yellow letters.

His partner came up behind him, carrying a clipboard with all the relevant information on the wounded man. "They take him?"

"Yeah, he's going up to the O.R. now."

"Then he's not our problem anymore. I'm gonna drop off the paperwork at the nurse's desk and I'll meet you back at the rig," he said. "The sooner we get back out there the better."

"Yeah, I know what you mean. Like the Doc just said to me, all the crazies come out at the full moon."

His name is Vincent Miller, but at the moment, he didn't know his name or how he came to be in a hospital room.

As he lay supine in his hospital bed in recovery, he slowly began to change into something not human, as the light of the full moon filtered through the window.

It had been three hours since he'd been attacked by what to him looked like a wolf, only this wolf stood on its hind legs and had shoulders as broad as a wrestler, with large claws and teeth that gleamed in the gloom.

The creature had appeared from the shadows of the alley and had pulled Vincent off the sidewalk, where he then found himself battling for his life.

He didn't remember much about what happened after the creature grabbed him, only brief visions, flashing images of teeth, claws, and blinding pain as he was attacked.

Luckily, from the far end of the alley, a passerby heard the attack and had yelled out, scaring the creature. It was gone in seconds, climbing up a fire escape to disappear over the edge of the roof of the closest building.

Filled with blinding pain, Vincent had crawled out of the alley where he had collapsed onto the sidewalk, his blood seeping around him to mimic a halo.

Soon, there were flashing lights as a police car pulled up, and the last thing he remembered was a paramedic leaning over him trying to get him to state his name as more passersby gathered around him, eager to see blood and carnage firsthand. He had babbled something but then the darkness had enveloped him and he slipped blissfully into unconsciousness.

Now, all he felt was more pain as the Lycan virus suffused his system, morphing his body into that of an animal.

He shook his head back and forth as his mouth and nose began to elongate, bone growing where none should exist. His teeth began to grow, becoming pointed, the razor-sharp incisors gleaming in the overhead florescent lights.

Every pore on his flesh began to open and thick, matted hair burst free, a dark carpet that covered him from head to toe. His ears recessed, becoming more pointed and his eyes shifted from the brown they originally were to a yellow the color of gold.

His arms and legs began to twist and reshape as the man took on the form of a werewolf, and as he shifted and changed—he screamed, as if his very insides were on fire, or better yet, being torn out—which wasn't far from the truth.

His screams filled the hospital, and no sooner did they begin, then three nurses came running into the room, while a fourth paged the on call doctor.

When the women darted into the room, each stopped in horror and amazement to watch the man twist and jump on the bed, his body spasming as if he was being electrocuted.

One of the nurses, braver than the others, burst forward to aid the suffering man, and when she was close enough to touch him, the newly transformed werewolf lashed out with a large paw-like hand filled with razor-sharp claws.

The woman was eviscerated in the blink of an eye, her intestines spilling forth to splash over her white nurse's shoes. The redolence of offal filled the room as the woman's bowels let go in death. Before she could crumple to the floor, the werewolf reached its clawed hand into her gaping cavity and lifted her off her feet as if she weighed nothing.

As the other nurses screamed, the beast threw the dead nurse at them, the body flying through the air to strike the other two nurses in the chests, all three falling to the floor. The two struggling nurses attempted to free themselves from their very dead coworker, one shrieking uncontrollably as she was covered in gore.

The nurse who had the lower half of the corpse on her was almost free when a shadow fell over her. Looking up, she gazed into the yellow eyes of the beast as it reached down and snapped at her with its open hand.

She screamed, long and loud, but it was cut short by one slash of the already bloody claws. Half her throat was torn out, the blood spurting across the room like a water fountain with its top broken off, her legs kicking as she thrashed in her death throes.

The remaining nurse was now shrieking as she was splattered in warm blood. Her eyes were closed and she shook her head back and forth, her tongue sticking out as she let loose a voice filled with terror.

The beast swiveled on its clawed toes, and with one meaty swipe, sheared her head from her shoulders. As the head rolled across the floor, more blood shot upward, the scream continuing for another second.

The decapitated head's eyes blinked once or twice, the woman seeing her own headless body slump to the floor. But the oxygen in her brain was fleeting, and she had just enough time to witness her demise before the eyes glazed over in death.

The werewolf saw none of this as it burst through the door and into the hallway. The nurse at the desk that had been paging the on call doctor dropped the phone and stared in astonishment at the mythical creature before her.

She had time for one quick bleat of fear before the werewolf attacked, covering the distance between them in less than a second. The nurse, though panicked, turned and tried to run, but let out a gasp of shock as the werewolf split her back in two, the long vertical slice exposing her spine.

As she dropped face first to the floor, her spine glistened amongst the seeping blood as she struggled to pull herself along. The beast watched her as she dragged herself across the floor, her legs now useless. It cocked its head in curiosity, much like a cat would to a mouse it was playing with.

Then the beast pounced, and using both its clawed hands, wrapped them around the woman's head before twisting. The neck began to show stress marks as the head was turned like a corkscrew, and when the head had almost reached a full revolution, weak flesh gave in to tension and split, spurting more blood out in front of the beast to bathe the floor in red.

The werewolf let the body slump to the floor and turned and roared to the ceiling, the very walls shaking from the vibration. The heavy tread of running men filled the hallway, and a moment later, three security guards rounded the bend, each with weapons drawn.

"What the fuck is that?" the first man yelled as he stopped in his tracks.

"Who cares, just fucking shoot it!" the second guard yelled as he pulled his sidearm and fired three times into the beast's chest.

The werewolf staggered back from the impact of each blast but still remained upright. It lowered its head, and before another round could be fired, it dove into the mist of the three guards.

The first man let out a high-pitched scream as he was disemboweled with one quick blow. As his insides splashed to the floor, his scream faded to be lost in a sea of gurgles as he drowned in his own blood.

Before the body had struck the floor, the second guard was feeling the wrath of the beast. With one clawed hand on the right side of the guard's torso, the left did the same on the other side, and with one squeeze of muscular arms, the hands closed together, severing the man in twain.

The upper half splattered to the floor and the guard's arms went out before him, as if he was falling after slipping on a wet floor. It was as he fell that he realized his legs weren't coming with him and he looked back to see his intestines were splayed out in front of him.

As he watched, the last security guard took a faltering step and placed his boots onto the intestines, causing them to erupt like uncooked blood sausage. The bifurcated guard was screaming, which quickly changed to shrieks, and when the first guard looked down and realized he was stepping in his coworker's organs, he too, joined the cacophony of yelling, his face now pale as a ghost.

But he didn't have long to voice his terror before the werewolf reached out and lopped off his head, severing his voice box and jugular in one massive swipe. The head rolled away like an errant kickball as the body toppled to the floor to join the other two corpses, more blood geysering in all directions to paint the walls crimson.

Once more, the werewolf growled to the ceiling, the end result a low howl. Seeing nothing left to kill, it loped down the hall, until coming to a window.

With no way of knowing what lay beneath the window, it smashed through the glass and landed ten feet below. By luck or fate, the beast had been on the first floor.

Landing amid a spray of glass, it howled once more to the moon and galloped into the street.

As soon as the beast reached the street, a racing ambulance, complete with flashing lights and siren, struck the werewolf head on and sent it soaring twenty feet into the air.

The fur-covered body flew gracelessly, its arms and legs seeming to flap on their own accord until the body landed in a pile of trash next to a battered dumpster.

The body was quickly lost amidst the trash as the ambulance came to a halt with screeching tires, and two paramedics jumped out, the driver's face one of terror at hitting a pedestrian.

The patient in the back of the rig was stable and they had enough time to see to yet another wounded soul before leaving to deliver their charge safely to the Emergency Room.

Both men ran towards the pile of trash where they'd seen the figure end up as the driver continued to say, "Oh, man, it wasn't my fault, the guy ran right out in front of me. It wasn't my fault."

The second paramedic didn't know what to say. He had been in the back of the rig with the patient when the accident had occurred. As the two paramedics approached, they each paused at the sight of the one leg protruding from the trash.

The driver then moved forward, shoved the trash bags away, and checked for a pulse at the prone body of the naked man with bloody hands and torso before him.

"Well?" the second paramedic asked.

The first man shook his head. "He's dead." He pointed to the man's chest which had multiple lacerations, most looking like old scar tissue, but in the middle of all the scars was one, bright red hole an inch in diameter. "This guy looks like he's been in a war. If I'm right, these look like old bullet wounds."

The second man turned and looked back at the ambulance and his eyes went to the silver plated grille, which was now smashed and broken.

A few of the mesh bars that made up the grate were now bent and twisted, and one of them that protruded had blood on its tip.

"Looks like the guy got stabbed by the grille when you plowed into him, Mike."

"I didn't plow into anyone, he ran out in front of me."

"Okay, okay, I believe you." He shook his head. "To bad for him huh? He never had a chance."

Mike nodded. "Yeah, you know, it's the weirdest thing. When I hit him, I couldn't see him very well, I could've sworn he was wearing a fur coat or a heavy jacket."

"I doubt that, Mike, the guy's naked." He shook his head once more and slapped his partner on the back. "Come on, we got a patient to get to the E.R. We can call this in on the way. Poor bastard ain't goin' anywhere."

Mike stood up, and with one last look at the naked, bloody man, he turned and headed back to the ambulance. "What do you think he was doing out here naked like that?"

The second man shrugged. "Who the hell knows? Shit, man, it's a god-damn full moon. All the crazies come out tonight."

THE OTHER FOOT

The water splashed against the hull of the small fishing boat as Martin hauled in the last catch of the day.

There weren't many fish in the net and he frowned deeply.

Swinging the net onto the weathered deck, he began pulling the fish out and tossing them into a bin near the aft end. Next to the bin was a wooden table, its top scarred from years of blades being used on it. The table stank of fish guts and seawater, the latter used to clean the former.

When all the fish were pulled from the net and tossed into the bin, Martin pulled the first one out and slapped it down on the table. Pulling his favorite carving knife, he jammed it into the stomach of the fish and began sawing from top to bottom.

The eyes of the fish grew three sizes bigger as it was gutted while still alive. Sometimes Martin could swear he heard them scream, a high-pitched one, so high only a dog could hear it.

He liked to think that was true anyway; he liked to cause pain.

When Martin was a boy, he used to sit for hours on end in his backyard, using a magnifying glass to burn ants. He loved the way they sizzled under the thin ray of burning fire, like a tiny laser beam. As the smoke curled up from the small carapaces, he always felt a rush fill him, like when a skydiver jumped out of a plane for the first time.

Soon he graduated from ants to larger bugs, such as grasshoppers and beetles. He would use pins and tack them to a piece of corkboard, then one at a time, he would pull off their legs, watching as they squirmed in what he dreamed was unimaginable agony.

But soon that became boring so he moved on to small rodents, such as mice and rats. Field mice were prevalent in the large field near his house and he had more than enough specimens to torture.

Frogs were another fun creature to play with and he loved pinning them down and slicing them open, then slowly taking out their organs, thrilling at the sight of the small heart in his hands. Then he would squeeze the tiny heart between his fingers, loving the feel of the blood and fluid coating his skin.

Years later, Martin graduated to small dogs and cats. What he did to those animals would make the most hardened serial killer wince and grow nauseous.

It was very possible that Martin would have graduated to serial killer status very soon if not for his father taking him on as one of the crew on the fishing boat he worked on.

On the boat, Martin excelled as an expert gutter. Shark, tuna or squid, Martin sliced and diced them with skill that made the most experienced crewman jealous.

As for Martin, he was able to keep his bloodlust in check, slaughtering the sea life day after day, reveling in the fish guts that became so much a part of him it was all he smelled no matter how many times he bathed.

Now he was middle-aged and was the captain of his own fishing boat. He didn't work with anyone, wanting to do it all himself and thus earning the greatest reward.

Besides, he didn't want to share the killing with anyone, either, enjoying being alone as he worked.

He pulled the next fish out of the bin and began carving it. The mouth opened and closed, as if the fish were screaming, and Martin felt himself grow hard as he reached inside it and pulled out the guts. Then, with the fish dead, he cut off its head and tossed the leftovers into the water. He never chopped the head off first for that would be too quick a death for the fish. Instead, he gutted them first, loving every second of the pain he believed he was dishing out.

Hours went by and he gutted fish after fish, his mind lost in the carnage. This was the best of both worlds. He needed to clean the fish and he got to feed his lust for blood and death. No one would ever criticize a fisherman for cleaning his catch—no one.

Hell, most people never even bothered to consider where their food came from, how it had once been a living creature until it was slaughtered, sometimes without mercy. All the customer saw was the nice clean, sterile packages in the frozen or fresh meat section of their local grocery store—that piece of fish or meat wrapped in cellophane and ready to be breaded and fried.

Martin reached into the bin and pulled out one of the last fish. It was a big one, twice as large as the rest, and its scales gleamed silver, looking like precious metal.

As he slapped it down on the table and prepared to slice into its stomach, anxiously looking forward to when the innards would squirt out and splash onto the table, the fish did something that none before had ever done.

It talked.

"Wait, please don't kill me," its garbled voice said.

Martin blinked and held the blade an inch from the fish's gullet.

Surely he had imagined the voice he just heard. It was hot out, the sun bright, baking anything not protected from its harmful rays, and surly he must be suffering from heatstroke.

The fish looked up at him with wide eyes and Martin stared at it for another five seconds before he prepared to slice it open.

His arm flexed.

"No, please, I beg you. Don't kill me."

Martin looked around the boat, as if he expected to see someone standing near him—perhaps a ventriloquist throwing his voice. Ha, ha, a big joke, and all at his expense.

Of course there was no one there. And there would never be as Martin was a loner.

"Please, I beg you, show me mercy," the fish pleaded.

Martin looked down at the fish and this time he saw the fish's mouth move in rhythm to the words spoken.

"You can talk," he said. A statement, not a question.

"Of course I can talk, I'm a fish," the fish said matter-of-factly.

"Well, either I'm crazy or you can really talk, which is it? I have no idea."

"No, Martin, it's true, I can talk. Many of us can, we just choose not to."

"Uh-huh. Well, good for you." He raised the blade to slice into the fish and continue filleting it when the fish cried out once more.

"No! Please, Martin, don't kill me, show me mercy."

"You know my name. How is that possible?"

The fish seemed to nod as it lay on the table. "Most of us know of you. You are the Great Killer. You slaughter our kind and after vivisecting us, you toss our insides into the ocean."

"Yup, that sounds like me. I'm a fisherman, it's my job."

"Perhaps, Martin, but the way you kill my kind is so barbaric. You don't cut off the heads first like other fishermen do. You gut us alive. *Alive*, Martin."

"So, what's it to ya?"

"Martin, we are living creatures. And most like me, are sentient. I have feelings, I think, I dream. Don't you have any empathy for me?"

Martin paused as he stared at the fish. He looked at the knife in his hand, considering the fish's sage words. Then he shrugged and said, "Nope,

I gotta eat," and he plunged the knife into the fish's belly, slicing it up and then down, its insides squirting out to slide across the table.

The fish's mouth went wide and its eyes practically bulged from its head as it looked up at Martin. With its dying breath it said, "Martin, you are evil and you will get what you deserve. You will know how it feels to be a fish on your carving table."

"Uh-huh, sure I will," Martin said and he raised the blade and hacked off the fish's head, then scraped the offal into the ocean.

As he carved the fish into strips and scraped the silver scales off its sides, he shook his head as he thought about what the fish said and the reality that it had actually talked.

"Huh, so fish talk. Imagine that. You learn something new everyday."

He reached in to pull out another fish but as he placed it on the table, this one didn't talk. It just glared up at him with its eye, the other facing the table.

"So, go 'head and talk. Beg me to spare you," he said to the fish.

The fish did nothing but open and close its mouth as it struggled to breathe.

"That's what I thought," he said and he gutted it, pulling out its insides like he had done a hundred, no, a thousand times before.

By the time he was finished with his entire catch, and had put away a six pack of hard ale and was working on the second pack, he had totally forgotten about the talking fish.

Now, as he thought about it, he decided it was nothing but a weird day-dream, brought on by the hot sun.

"Fish don't talk," he slurred as he cracked open another beer. He was good and drunk and on his way to being completely plastered. He wasn't the only one who liked to get good and drunk after a hard day at sea. He knew many fishermen that drank till they puked, most of them lonely men without families.

He steered the boat back to shore, but halfway home the motor began to sputter and then died completely. Cursing his foul luck, he went to the aft end to inspect the motor, which was in the lower deck under a hatch.

As Martin pulled on the hatch to open it, he cursed repeatedly. The hatch swelled from the moistness of the sea air and he always had to tug on it until it finally popped free.

But as drunk as he was, he wasn't standing correctly, and when he yanked on the hatch, it popped open, sending him falling backwards and over the railing.

He went under, turned in the water and swam back to the surface. He found he was immediately covered in seaweed and kelp.

Spitting water, he saw red leave his mouth.

A sudden pain in his mouth told him he had bitten off the tip of his tongue. He yelled out and his voice was garbled, the entire tip now gone, causing him to mumble unintelligibly. He splashed in the water and tried to swim to his boat, but as he turned around, he saw that the boat was a hundred yards away and still moving. Caught in the current, it was already too far away to catch by swimming alone.

He treaded water, not knowing what to do. He stayed calm, knowing that was the only way to survive. He was in the main shipping lane. Cargo and other fishing ships used this route all the time. If he could hold out long enough, he might get lucky and be saved.

And so the day moved on as Martin floated in the water. The seaweed was wrapped around him tight and he couldn't pull it off or risk sinking in the process. He floated on his back, blending in with the ocean, looking like a small manatee to the casual eye.

Two hours after he had fallen in, he found himself surrounded by a school of fish. They did nothing but jump around, some over him and some swam under him.

He ignored them, though a few times he yelled at them out of anger but his words were nothing but guttural grunts. The blood in his mouth had slowed but his tongue was still bleeding. He would need stitches and he imagined his stomach must be full of blood by now.

Hours later, his lips cracked, his face beet red from exposure, another fishing vessel came upon him and the school of fish surrounding him.

He called out but his voice was lost in the engine noise and the churning of the water, as the boat cut through the waves. There was a man on the port deck and as Martin watched, the man dropped a net right over him, catching the school of fish and Martin, too.

Oh what luck. He thought as the net was hauled in and he was dropped onto the deck amidst the jumping fish and pounds and pounds of seaweed. Martin looked like a sea monster, wrapped in so much dark green.

The man stumbled over to the net and began opening it. Martin tried to say something but all that came out were weird noises. He tried to lift his arms, to wave to the man, but they were lead weights from all the hours of treading water. He could barely move his limbs, and when he tried, all he did was roll around on the deck a little, in more than one way mimicking the fish flopping around him.

The fisherman wobbled on his feet and Martin could see the man was stone cold drunk. The fisherman's eyes were glazed over and his mouth hung slack, the look of a man who liked his liquor hard, such as vodka or scotch.

The man was old, well in his seventies, with a balding pate, liver spots covering his arms and head, and thin lips. An aquiline nose rounded out the picture, giving the man a hawk-like appearance. The man wore rubber boots and overalls, his chest bare and dark from the sun. He sang a tune to himself as he drank from a clear bottle of liquor.

Martin called out again but all that came forth were more garbles. He heard his voice and thought he sounded like a walrus.

The old man began picking up the fish and tossing them into a bin, one very similar to the one on Martin's lost boat.

As the man worked, he downed more than half the bottle, and by the time all the fish were in the bin, he was so drunk he couldn't see straight.

Martin called out again, but once more his voice was nothing but grunts and groans.

The fisherman dropped the bottle, burped loudly, and walked over to a small cabinet, where he opened it and pulled out a long serrated knife.

The old man looked down at the seaweed-covered body of Martin and licked his lips greedily.

"My, you're a big one. I'll have to gut you right here on the deck. These old bones can't pick you up, as big as you are." He began walking towards Martin whose eyes were now wide with fright.

"Damn if you ain't the biggest tuna I ever caught. Your meat's gonna fry up good tonight on my grill, yessiree, you just wait and see," the old man said as he knelt down next to Martin and prepared to get to work.

Martin tried to raise his arms and push the man away, but the seaweed and the net were constricting his movements so all he could do was flap his hands a little.

To a stinking drunk of a fisherman, Martin looked just like a big tuna flapping its fins.

"This is gonna be fun," the old man said. "I like to have some sport before I kills ya," he said as he slid the carving knife into Martin's abdomen and began sawing upwards.

Entrails spilled onto the deck, offal sliding into the seaweed to mix with it. As the old fisherman sawed away, Martin screamed in absolute agony. His eyes popped out of his head and his tongue, missing the tip, splashed blood everywhere.

The old man never stopped carving, and soon was slicing into Martin's throat, severing his jugular and then cutting back down.

As Martin twitched in his own gore, the man began pulling out Martin's insides, tossing the offal to the side to be used as chum later.

Martin's screams went higher in pitch as each of his organs was pulled out, much in the same manner as he had done to countless fish. As of yet, the old fisherman hadn't touched Martin's heart and thus, he was still alive, though in abject pain.

As Martin let out yet another blood-piercing cry that reverberated out over the water, the old man cackled and said, "Well, I'll be, fishy, you almost sounded like a real man there for a second."

Then he went back to work, gutting his catch and preparing it for the grill waiting for him back on shore.

Later, as the old man washed the deck clean, and bits of Martin's now-cooled organs sluiced off the boat and into the water, the waiting fish began dining, knowing in this one particular moment, revenge really was best served cold.

THE SANCTUARY

The snow blasted the man's face like tiny daggers, freezing his expression of suffering as he made his way through the desolate forest. The trees hung heavy with ice, more than one having collapsed under the weight of the snow.

The wind howled like a living thing, so loud he couldn't think.

With nothing to do but continue, he wrapped his thin coat around himself tighter and marched onward.

He didn't know how long he'd been walking in the solid white forest; more than a day, less than a week. He remembered times when he found a place to rest, huddling under an overhang of tree limbs or inside a small outcropping of boulders. With no fire, he would curl up into a ball and shiver uncontrollably until sleep finally took him into its cold embrace.

But he never slept for long, and would venture forth once more when the chill was too unbearable to ignore.

Images flashed through his mind as he walked; visions of a collapsing world.

Oil and gasoline had become scarce to the point the average man couldn't afford it any longer. When this happened, riots began in the streets, and once tall, ivory towers were soon torn down by angry, jealous hands. Where only the rich could afford to have electricity, as they purchased the fuel to run their generators on the black market, so too, did the desperate masses gather their weapons, their bombs, and their anger.

In time, the wealthy were in ruins and society was a distant memory.

Those bombs were sometimes nuclear, evil factions attacking the nuclear power plants, and after every meltdown, and multiple explosions that shook the earth to its core, the planet was thrust into a modern day ice age, the soot and dust clogging the atmosphere to the point the sun's rays couldn't penetrate to the land below. Plants began to wither and livestock died, the human race soon finding out it wasn't as invincible as it once thought.

The man lost his footing and fell face first into the snow, his mouth filling with ice and muffling his cry of surprise. He rolled onto his side, knowing he needed to get up, for to lie down now would mean certain death. But he was already at the end of his rope, and as exhaustion set in and he tried to raise himself to a sitting position, his arms wavered and he fell back to the frozen ground.

His will to survive was still strong, though his body was weak, so he began to crawl, one agonizing inch at a time. His feet were numb, as were his fingertips, and both had ceased feeling hours go, as did the end of his nose. But still he crawled, though the next hill would only play out as the other hundred had done so before it.

As he reached the top of the final hill he would be traversing before death took him, his eyes, now red and blurry, spotted something through the trees. It looked like it was made of glass and metal, the glossy finish reflecting what ambient light filtered through the clouds.

Filled with renewed hope, he gathered what strength he had left and forced himself onward; knowing whatever he'd spotted would be his final destination one way or another.

An hour passed and his head was growing foggy, but as he reached the edge of the property line to what was a large house, he dropped to the ground and passed out.

In seconds, the falling snow began to cover him.

He would have died then, buried under the snow, if not for the simple motion sensor that had picked up his body as he crawled over the property line.

Ten minutes after collapsing in the snow, three figures emerged from the house, each bundled up to the point their features were hidden. Scarves, ski masks and large parkas adorned each figure, their genders unknown.

They reached the fallen man and one each picked him up under the arms and began to drag him towards the house, while the third of the party walked beside them. He seemed to be the leader of the group, and when they reached the house, it was he who opened the door to let the others carry the man inside.

Quickly rushing into the house, the door was slammed closed, none of them wanting to let more of the precious heat within the home from escaping than necessary. As the door clicked closed, locks could be heard being latched over the howling maelstrom. The snow storm continued unabated, as it had done so for the past fourteen months.

Ever so slowly, he opened his eyes and looked around him. He was in a queen size bed, the blanket was up to his neck, and he felt warm for the first time in he didn't know how long.

The room was clean, with a desk in the far corner, and a small daybed near one of the insulated windows. Outside, the wind howled, and he felt himself shiver despite the warmth of the bed.

The bedroom door opened and a man in his late sixties walked in. He had a receding hairline, white hair, unkempt, and bushy eyebrows that almost made him look as if he had a unibrow. He wore a gray turtle neck and a pair of black cotton slacks, his feet in a pair of thousand dollar shoes. On his wrist was a Rolex and diamond rings flashed on three fingers of his left hand, while the right one was bare. As he stepped into the room, he smiled at his guest, and after taking the chair at the desk, he dragged it across the plush rug and sat down, crossing his legs. "So I see you're finally awake. The first thing to ask I suppose is your name," he asked.

"Brett…Brett Butler. Where am I? And who are you?"

"Ah, right to the point, good for you. My name is Arthur McMillan, perhaps you've heard of me."

Brett blinked. "I've heard of *a* Arthur McMillan. He was on that apprentice reality show, and made all that money in textiles and oil. Is that you?"

"One and the same. So tell me, Mr. Butler, how did you find this place?"

Brett shook his head as he sat up some more in the bed. He tried to remember but it was all a haze, but now that he was warm and rested, he began to remember bits and pieces. He recalled being in a enclave that was struggling to survive. Raiders had attacked, killing almost everyone and he had managed to escape into the mountains. After that it all became a blur. He told McMillan as much, the older man nodding as he listened.

"I see. I've heard the same story countless times on the shortwave radio I have here. That's why I built this place in the middle of nowhere when the first hint of global strife began. I guess you could say I'm a bit of a survivalist nut." He chuckled slightly. "I guess the last laugh was on me though, huh?"

"You built this place?" Brett asked.

"That's right. I made sure to use the money I had while it was still good for something. Took more than six months but this sanctuary will see me and my few guests through until the world can get back on its feet." He looked down at his shoes. "That is if that is even possible, of course."

"Of course," Brett said.

"You are aware I can't let you leave here, I suppose. This sanctuary is a secret. If you left and told others what's here, well, you know what would happen." He grinned widely. "But I suspect you wouldn't want to leave anyway. There's nothing around for miles in every direction. I made sure of that when I picked this location. We're on the top of a mountain, you see, one I bought before society collapsed. Before the first bombs fell, I was already set up here, well stocked with food, water, and an armory to make any gun nut proud."

Brett said nothing, only nodded.

McMillan stood up and Brett saw the large revolver on the man's hip. "Well, I'll leave you to rest. Someone will come by later and escort you down to dinner. That is, if you think you'll be up to it."

"I'm sure I will," Brett said.

"That's good, because we have a strict regime here and all who stay under my roof agree to follow it in exchange for my protection. Now that you're here, I expect you to do the same."

Brett could hear the warning in the older man's voice and he nodded, flashing a weak smile. "You'll get no trouble from me, sir. And I thank you for letting me stay."

"And well you should. I could have easily allowed you to freeze to death outside. But I chose to retrieve you."

"Then why did you? Not that I'm not grateful," Brett said.

"Why? Simple really. After more than a year, it will be good to have some new blood around here." He walked to the door and paused before leaving. "You get some rest now. Dinner is at eight sharp." He exited and closed the door, leaving Brett with more questions and no answers.

But he supposed he would get them at dinner. Sliding deeper into the covers, he closed his eyes, and before he knew it, had fallen back into an exhausted sleep.

A knock on the door woke Brett from a light sleep.

"Come in," he said and the door opened, revealing a man in his forties who had similar facial features to McMillan.

"Hi, I'm Jeff, I'm here to bring you down to dinner." He crossed the room and placed a set of clothes on the foot of the bed. "These are mine but you can have them."

"Thank you, that's very kind of you," Brett said as he pushed off the blankets and began dressing.

"I suppose, but it's not like I really had a choice in the matter," Jeff said as he walked to one of the windows to gaze out into the blizzard.

"How so?"

"Huh? Oh, never mind. You'll find out how things are run around here soon enough."

Brett nodded, though out of politeness more than any understanding. "Is Mr. McMillan your father? If not, you sure look a lot like him," Brett commented as he slipped into the brown loafers Jeff provided. He now wore a white long sleeve shirt, and a pair of tan slacks along with clean underwear and socks.

"No, you're right, I'm his son. Lucky me."

Brett was about to ask what he meant by that when Jeff walked by him and then paused at the door. "Good, the clothes fit you almost to a T. I thought as much when I carried you up here last night. Well, come along, we don't want to keep the master of the house waiting." He frowned and his eyes went cold, and Brett was sure he saw a touch of fear there as well. "It wouldn't be a very good idea."

"Ah, at last, our new arrival is here and we can get on with dinner," Arthur McMillan said grandly. He wore a black sport coat with a gray vest, matching slacks and casual shoes. "Come, Mr. Butler, sit over here next to me."

Brett did as he was told, eyeing the other new faces as he sat down.

"Let me introduce you to the rest of your small team of survivors of this Ice Age," McMillan said with a wave of his left hand, his other on the butt of his gun. "The lovely woman across from me is Wendy. She's my..."

"I'm his mistress," Wendy said blandly to Brett.

"Wendy, really," McMillan said, as if he was insulted.

"What's wrong, Arthur? It's the truth, so I might as well just get it out in the open. He's going to find out soon enough anyway." She looked away from McMillan and back to Brett. "That's right, I sleep with him and in exchange he lets me stay here, protects me."

"Ah, okay," Brett said, not understanding what was going on. But it was obvious the conversation he was now in had begun a long time ago and was just continuing with him in it

McMillan slapped his hand on the table, the dishes and glasses jumping. "Enough, that's enough, Wendy. If you don't stop, so help me I'll..."

"You'll what? Arthur? Kick me out like you're always threatening to do? Maybe you'd be doing me a favor," Wendy scowled deeply.

McMillan raised a hand and jabbed his finger at her. "Just one more word, Wendy, and so help me, you'll find out."

Wendy opened her mouth but held her tongue. Brett sat perfectly still, staring at the tableaux before him. He saw Jeff was picking at one of his fingernails, oblivious to what was transpiring, as if he'd heard it a thousand times before. The other man at the table was slightly more interested and he smiled widely as he watched.

When McMillan was confident Wendy was through, he cleared his throat and then gestured to the other man. "And this is Andy, he's Jeff's best friend from college. His parents were lost when L.A. was bombed and I invited him to join us."

"Hi," was all Andy said.

"Hi, yourself," Brett replied.

McMillan stood up and crossed the room, pausing at the door leading to the kitchen. So, if the introductions are finished, then come along and you can get your dinner.

Brett watched as Andy, Jeff and Wendy each stood up and crossed the room to line up behind McMillan. It reminded him of schoolchildren waiting in line for lunch at the cafeteria. McMillan looked over at Brett and waved him to follow as well. "Come along, Mr. Butler, if you want to eat this is how it's done here," he called.

His stomach rumbling at the mention of food, Brett did as he was asked and followed the others. Soon he found himself in the kitchen and McMillan was standing in front of a large pantry door with a heavy duty combination lock on it. As everyone waited, he turned the dial and opened the door. Then, one at a time, he handed each of them a can of food.

Brett was last, and as the others went back to the dining room, he stared at the can of chili in his hands. "What's this?"

"It's your dinner," McMillan said.

"I don't understand. Why is the food under lock and key?"

McMillan touched his gun in his waistband as he closed the pantry and locked it. "Because that's how we do things around here. I'm in charge of the food and I say what we do and don't do."

"But what if I'm still hungry?"

"That's not my problem, Mr. Butler. Now, be grateful like the others and go back into the dining room where you'll find a can opener and silverware." McMillan had a can for himself under his arm and carried a one gallon bottle of water in his free hand, his other hand always on the gun. Brett was beginning to realize McMillan ruled his little sanctuary by fear, namely by using the gun as his instrument of control. But without a way to defend himself, and not wanting to risk trying to take the gun away from the older man, Brett nodded and returned to the dining room.

The others were already seated, each eating from their can. Brett sat as well and picked up the can opener in the middle of the table. Once he had his can opened, he dug in, taking a fork from a small pile in the center of the table.

McMillan came in and sat down at the head of the table, and after opening his food, dug in. His gun was on the table to his right, in easy reach if need be.

No one spoke, each concentrating on eating, and Brett found his gaze constantly drifting to Wendy. Though any man would be attracted to her, especially as she was the only woman in the house, he still couldn't fight the instant attraction he felt for her upon meeting her.

Once or twice, he spotted her looking at him and she would smile slightly, then stop, not wanting the others to see.

But McMillan did see and he frowned deeply, but said nothing.

When everyone was finished eating and the meal was about over, McMillan cleared his throat and gestured to Wendy.

"Come here, my dear, and get under the table, I need you and I don't want to wait."

"No, Arthur, please, not now, can't we go upstairs?"

"Are you arguing with me?" The tone of his voice was clear to Brett. It reminded him of the tone his father would use with him when he was told to do something and he was hesitant.

"No, of course not," she said as she lowered her eyes in compliance.

"Then get over here and get to work, woman," he said.

Wendy wiped her mouth and pushed off from the table, her chair sliding lightly on the hardwood floor. Brett watched her, not understanding what was going on. What was it she needed to do that couldn't wait?

She walked around the table and stopped in front of McMillan, and when he gestured with his chin for her to get down on the floor, she went to her knees and slid under the table.

McMillan's eyes creased in pleasure as he leaned back in his chair and relaxed.

It took Brett all of three seconds to figure out what was going on and he stood up, dropping his fork to the table. "What the fuck is this shit?"

McMillan's eyes opened and he touched the gun as he glared at Brett. "I would sit down if I were you, Mr. Butler. I didn't say dinner was over yet."

Brett remained standing as he stared at McMillan. He could hear the slurping sounds coming from under the table and he squeezed his hands into fists.

"I won't tell you again, boy. Do what I say or pay the price, that's the exchange for living under my roof."

Brett hesitated for a moment longer but in the end decided defiance was useless at this time and sat down, crossing his arms over his chest.

The slurping grew louder and McMillan began to buck his hips, a serene look coming over him. Then he grunted and placed his free hand on the top of Wendy's head, thrusting as hard as he could and letting out a low growl of joy.

His body went rigid and then relaxed as he sighed. Wendy crawled out from under the table while wiping her mouth. Brett looked at her but she wouldn't return his gaze, her eyes only for the polished hardwood floor.

"Very nice, dear, very nice," McMillan said as he buttoned his pants. "All right then, dinner is over. Toss your cans into the trash and go to your rooms. At ten I want everyone to meet in the main room for a nightcap. Then we can all get to know Mr. Butler a little better." He looked at Brett and stroked the gun. "Isn't that so, Mr. Butler?"

"Yeah, I guess so," Brett replied.

"Good, then I will bid you all a farewell for now. I'm tired and want to take a quick nap."

He stood up and walked deeper into the rear of the house, leaving the others alone to stare at one another. Then, as if a starting pistol had been fired, Jeff and Andy turned and quickly walked away to dispose of the empty cans and leave. Wendy was hugging herself with her arms, her hair draped over her face, her eyes hidden.

"Wendy, I…" Brett began, but she held her hand up to stop him.

"No, don't say anything, please. This has happened before when he wants to show his dominance over me, over all of us."

"He's a pig, I can see that already. Why do you let him treat you like that? Why do any of you? He's only one man."

"Yes, one man with a gun, and others locked up in his safe as well as all the food."

Jeff walked back into the room as Andy headed off to his own room.

"I heard you, Brett, and you're right but also wrong," Jeff said softly as he looked where McMillan had disappeared, making sure his father wasn't returning to overhear him. "My brother was here with us, too, that was six months ago. Back then my father wasn't as bad, though he was always a little bit of a megalomaniac. Makes sense, though doesn't it? To be a success in big business, to take over companies and send thousands of people on the streets with no jobs, well, it takes a heartless son-of-a-bitch to do that anyway, doesn't it? The corporate world is as cutthroat as any jungle, only it's more *civilized*. But make no mistake, there has to be a piece of a man missing to achieve the power my father has in the real world, well, before the collapse and the bombs."

"What does that have to do with anything?" Brett asked.

Jeff continued. "When we first arrived, my brother Doug was part of our group. He was my older brother and he was so much like Father it was amazing, they looked like each other, too. I took after our mother more. Doug and my father always butted heads, about everything you could imagine, so when my father began slipping slightly into madness, it was Doug who called him on it. In the beginning, when my father tried to control us, Doug always stopped him. But then, one night, something changed in my father. That was the first day he arrived to dinner with his gun. Doug told him to put it away, that it wasn't needed inside the house, but my father told him he was in charge and could do what he wanted. Doug tried to take the gun away from him and my father…" His voice cracked slightly at the remembrance. "My father shot him at point black range. Shot his son and killed him. Doug fell to the floor, bleeding out and dead in seconds and do you know what my father did?"

Brett shook his head.

"He poured himself a glass of wine and smiled. Like it was no big thing, as if he hadn't just shot dead his first born son."

"What happened then?" Brett asked. Wendy was hugging herself tighter as the images of that night were recalled, tears streaming down her cheeks.

"We finished eating if you would believe it. My father made us. Then he had Andy and I drag my brother outside and the next day the body was gone. Wolves I suppose." He touched Wendy's arm. "Wendy and Doug were engaged to be married, that's why she was able to come here, too."

"Oh, Jesus, I don't know what to say…" Brett began.

"There's nothing to say. We're trapped in here with a man who is sick. There's no place to go so we have to endure."

"That's not true, you could leave. There has to be someplace else where we could go. We could leave in the morning," Brett reasoned.

"No, there is no place to go," Jeff said. "The cities are blasted land-scapes and there can't be more than a few thousand human beings left on the entire planet. Look at you, you left where you were, and for what? No, we're in Hell, and it has finally frozen over. All we can do is wait to die. Then the suffering will end."

Brett took a step closer to Jeff. "Look, I can see you've given up and I can't blame you. To live like this for so long, and after seeing your brother killed. But I won't stand by and let him boss me around. No one's going to control me, not like he wants to."

Jeff waved a hand and turned to leave. "Then I wish you luck, but be warned, my father is an expert shot. You cross the line and you will join my brother in feeding the wolves." He took Wendy by the arm. "Come on, Wendy, let's get you to your room so you can lie down for a bit." She went without hesitation, looking to Brett like a scared little girl. He wanted to go to her, to hold her and tell her it would be fine, but he didn't, knowing he had just met her and his compassion wouldn't be welcome…not yet anyway.

They left, leaving Brett alone with his thoughts. He picked up the fork he'd used as he looked around the room. His eyes went to a dark stain on the floor, as if wine had been spilled and then had soaked in before being cleaned up. The stain looked a lot like blood. As he stared at the stain, he bent the fork in two, never aware he'd done it until it was folded in half.

Tossing it to the table, he left the dining room.

At ten sharp everyone gathered in the main room. A warm fire crackled and brandy was poured for each of them, Wendy acting as server.

"So, Mr. Butler, how goes the world outside these walls," McMillan asked.

"About what you'd expect," Brett said, knowing the man was asking for the others' benefit.

"Ah, then I was correct in setting up my little sanctuary, wasn't I?" McMillan looked at Jeff. "See, son? I knew it was the right thing to do. Without me, you would be dead now, just ash back in Los Angeles." He gestured to the window, the snow falling in heavy flakes. "It's hard to believe it's August when you look outside. We could be here for years, hell, we may die in here."

"Then what's the point?" Andy asked. "What the point in going on?"

"The point, my boy," McMillan said. "Is to survive, by any means necessary, and goddamn it that's what I plan to do."

They talked for another fifteen minutes, Brett telling what little he knew of the world, how he had left his enclave and how life had been there when finally McMillan clapped his hands and sat up straight in his chair.

"I'm bored. I want to try something new tonight." He pointed at Andy. "You, go over there and give my son a blowjob."

Andy blinked, not believing what he'd just heard. "Excuse me?"

"You heard me. Go over there and do to my son what Wendy did to me at dinner. And do a good job, I want to see him cum hard."

Andy shook his head in defiance, but when McMillan touched the gun and scowled, Andy knew he had little choice, not if he wanted to live.

Slowly, he crawled over and knelt between Jeff's knees.

"Father, please don't do this, it's sick. Neither of us is like that, you know that. Please," Jeff whispered.

"Shut up. I say what goes on in this house and you'll do as I order, now take off your pants and let's have a show."

Brett stood to the side, his mouth hanging open, appalled and disgusted as Andy did what he was ordered to do. He took Jeff into his mouth and began working, similar to what Wendy had done only hours ago. Brett watched as McMillan reached his free hand into his pants and began massaging himself as his eyes grew wide with excitement. Wendy was in the corner, looking at her feet, shaking her head as she whispered to herself.

"Good God, this is a fucking freak show. McMillan, what the fuck is wrong with you?"

McMillan pulled his hand from his pants and swung the gun onto Brett, cocking it. "You have something to say to me, boy? Best pick your words carefully, they might just be your last."

Brett could feel the rage building within him but he knew he was helpless. He calmed himself and said. "No, sir, I don't have anything to say. You're in charge here."

"Damn straight. Now shut up and enjoy the show."

Despite Jeff's best intentions, he orgasmed and Andy spit as he wiped his mouth. His eyes glared hatred at McMillan, who seemed to soak it up, his grin so wide it threatened to split his face in half.

Andy went to the bottle of brandy and poured himself a drink, then another, and then another. No one spoke, each lost in their private thoughts. Jeff pulled up his pants and pressed his open palms to his forehead, wondering how things had become so out of control. Brett watched Andy, seeing the man taking drink after drink. If he didn't stop soon, he would become drunk, and once his inhibitions were down, there might be trouble.

Brett stood up and crossed the room, his plan to take the bottle away from Andy.

"Leave me alone, fuck off!" Andy spit to Brett.

"Give me the bottle, Andy, you've had enough," Brett said. Out of all the others, Brett seemed to be the only one not lost in a fit of despair

"Screw you, get away from me!" Andy shouted and pushed Brett backwards.

McMillan laughed and pointed to Brett. "Best do as he says. Never a good thing to get between a man and his liquor."

Brett could see Andy had downed a third of the bottle and his eyes were already glazed, his words now becoming slurred.

"Fine, but let me take him back to his room. You've had your fun for the night," Brett said.

"Uh-huh. I say when it's time for this shindig to end and it's not yet. Now sit your ass down or else." McMillan's eyes were hard and Brett knew if he pushed his luck any further he might end up like Doug. "Fine, but this is sick."

Wendy was silent, glad McMillan was leaving her alone for a change and Jeff had his face covered with his hands. Andy continued to drink until he was very drunk. Brett could see the glares Andy was throwing at McMillan and he hoped Andy wouldn't do something or say anything rash.

It was as if Andy had read his thoughts as he stood up, the brandy bottle falling to the floor to roll until landing at the hearth of the fireplace. It was so empty only a few drops spilled out of the open top.

"You," Andy hissed as he came to his feet, swaying back and forth. "You no good prick. Think you're so fucking tough 'cause you've got that damn gun. Well, fuck you. I'm not scared of you anymore."

"You should be," McMillan said softly with a slight grin.

"Andy," Brett whispered loudly. "Sit down, that's the booze talking."

"Stay out of it, new guy, this is none of your business," Andy snapped then turned back to McMillan. "So, did you like watching me suck on your son's dick? Huh? Bet you wished I was doing it to you, huh? Admit it, you're a fag and you want me to suck your dick!"

"Careful there, Andy," McMillan said. "I'll allow you some leeway because you're drunk but you will still talk to me with respect."

"Respect? You? Bah! You're just a loser who had to trap us here so you would have a captive audience. You're nothing, you're as extinct as this damn planet we're on!"

"This is your last warning, Andy, sit down and we'll forget this happened," McMillan warned.

Brett felt his body going stiff as he watched Andy stumble over to the fireplace and pick up the black metal poker. He swung it back and forth a few times as if he was testing its heft.

"Fuck your warnings, asshole, I'm through listening to you! Tonight was the last straw!" And as Brett watched, Andy began a drunken charge at McMillan, the poker raised high to crack open the man's skull.

The only sound was Andy's footsteps as he crossed the room, but he was halted as McMillan raised his gun and fired. The report was loud in the confines of the room and multiple things happened at the same time. In the far corner, Wendy covered her ears and slid to the floor, cowering as she squeezed her eyes shut. Brett stared in horror as the gun went off, the bullet striking Andy directly in the chest. Jeff pulled his hands away from his face to become splattered with Andy's blood, the drunk man standing almost directly in front of Jeff.

As for Andy, he stopped running and his body jerked back and forth as the bullet blew out a fist-sized hole in his back. As Jeff yelled in shock, smudging the warm blood on his face, Andy fell back to sprawl across the floor, blood spurting from his mouth as he died.

The metal poker slid across the floor to land at Jeff's feet. At first, the man looked down at it as if it was a dead snake, or something that had materialized out of thin air. But then, his eyes cleared, and before Brett could stop him, Jeff picked up the poker and charged at his father, mimicking Andy.

McMillan wasn't ready for this and he actually hesitated for a fraction of a second, as if he realized he was about to kill his last remaining family member. But then instinct took over and he shot the attacking man coming for him, no longer caring that it was his son.

Jeff was hit in the neck, a massive amount of flesh and muscle blown away in an instant. Blood geysered from the open wound to spray the entire room in crimson. Brett saw half of Jeff's neck was now missing, his head slumping to the side at a macabre angle. With blood sputtering from the jagged wound, he dropped to the floor, twitching and spasming in his death throes.

No one spoke, no one said anything for a full five minutes. By the time the silence was broken, Jeff's kicking feet has ceased for more than four minutes.

McMillan stood up on weak legs and looked down at a cowering Wendy, who when she saw McMillan look at her, cringed, squeaking like a mouse. She expected him to shoot her, too, but the bullet never came.

McMillan turned and settled his gaze on Brett, who was staring silently at the two dead bodies. He raised the gun and pointed it at Brett's head. "Are you going to be a problem, too?" he asked Brett softly.

"No, no problem here, sir" Brett replied as he swallowed the large knot that had appeared in his throat.

"Good, then clean this mess up and feed the bodies to the wolves," he said to Brett. "Have Wendy help you." He glanced at the body of his son cooling on the floor. "Pity, really, but then he was always a disappointment to me." Without waiting for a reply, he turned and walked out of the room, the gun hanging by his side in an arm that seemed limp. "And have Wendy join me in my room when she's finished cleaning up."

Brett watched the man go but didn't move. Other than Wendy's frightened sobs, all was silent.

In the fireplace, the burning logs crackled with an intensity of heat only rivaled by the fire raging within Brett's heart for vengeance.

Wendy didn't talk as she and Brett dragged the two bodies into the snow. He tried a few times to get her to speak, but each time was met with only silence.

Once the bodies were outside, already an inch of snow covering them in less than a minute, Wendy went to a small closet, took out a few cotton towels and began wiping down the furniture and soaking up the blood in the main room. Brett helped, and an hour later there was almost no sign of what had happened. It was as if the two murders had never occurred and everything was as it was before.

When they finished and Wendy had carried the towels into the back of the house where laundry was kept, she walked back into the main room. She barely looked at Brett as she turned to follow that same route McMillan had used an hour previously. She was going to his bedroom, as the man had dictated.

Brett crossed the distance separating them and grabbed her arm. "Wendy, wait, you don't have to go to him."

"Yes I do," she said softly, gently trying to pull her arm from his grip.

"No, you don't. Look, we can still fight him. He's only one man. Andy was drunk and Jeff acted rashly. Neither had a chance against an alert man with a gun. But together we can stop him."

She yanked her arm free as she looked into his eyes. "No, we can't! Don't you see! Only he knows the combination to the pantry. Without him, there's no food."

"Then we can leave here," Brett reasoned. "Why do we have to stay? We can take what we can salvage and just go. There must be someplace else."

"No," she said. "Arthur told us there's nowhere else to go. This is it."

"He's lying. There has to be someplace else, this can't be it. Christ, Wendy, he killed your fiancée and now Andy and Jeff. Who knows who'll be next?"

"No," she said. "You're wrong; he wouldn't hurt me, not like that. Now leave me alone. I don't want to die like Andy and Jeff, just let me be!" She turned and ran from him, her sneakers slapping the hardwood.

"Wendy, wait!" he called, but she was already around the corner and gone.

He stared at the empty hallway for more than minute as his mind raced with all he'd experienced in such a short time. To be saved from the frigid cold only to find himself in a worst predicament; ruled by a madman with a god complex. Slapping the wall with the palm of his hand in frustration, he headed to his room. He was too wired to sleep, but he didn't know what else to do.

Brett had thought once he was in his bedroom he wouldn't sleep, not after everything that had transpired that night, but once he'd lain down, he soon drifted off to sleep, his body still weak from his time in the freezing cold.

He didn't know how long he slept but he was snapped awake by Wendy's voice as she whispered into his ear and shook him frantically.

"Come on, Brett, you need to get up," she whispered, her voice full of haste.

Brett slowly came back to the waking world and he blinked up at her face. He could barely see her, the room wreathed in darkness. It felt late, but the exact time was unknown.

"What? What's wrong, what's going on?" he asked as he tried to focus on her voice.

"Shhh, don't talk so loud," she whispered. "I thought about what you said and you're right. We need to leave here before he kills us both."

"Is there a light? I can't see a damn thing," he said.

There was a soft sound of a cigarette lighter being flicked, and a moment later, a small orange glow was near his bedside. Wendy leaned over and lit a candle.

"There, better?" she asked as she sat on the bed.

"Yeah, I guess." As he sat up, he could see Wendy was wearing a thin nightgown. Her nipples pushed up on the thin material and he felt himself growing aroused, though he knew this wasn't the time. He also saw that her neck had a bright red ring around it; a few places tinged a dark blue.

"Your neck," he said.

She raised her right hand to her neck, touching it. "A souvenir from Arthur. He...he choked me tonight while having sex with me. I...I thought he was going to kill me. But he didn't. Then I realized next time I might not be so lucky so after...after he was finished, he fell asleep like he always did. I was going to try for his gun and kill him right there, but when I tried to reach for it, he woke up. I told him I was going to the bathroom and he let me be. I...I should have tried again but I was too scared." She looked down, ashamed of herself.

"No, you were right," Brett said. "If he'd woken up he would have killed you for sure. Whatever piece of sanity he's been holding onto went away earlier tonight when he killed Andy and Jeff." He slid out of bed and began getting dressed. "Go get dressed. Make sure you dress in layers, as many as you can. I'll meet you in the dining room. We'll see what food there is around and take all we can, then we'll get the hell out of this madhouse."

She nodded and slid out the door, her gossamer nightgown seeming to flow about her.

Brett continued dressing, his mind racing on what they were going to do next. He wasn't looking forward to going back out into the snow, but he knew there was little choice. Better to take their chances out in the storm than wait to be slaughtered by a crazy old fool.

He searched the room, checking the closet and then under the bed. He found a backpack under the bed, the name **Doug** stenciled on the front flap. He didn't give it much thought as he quickly took what was useable in the room, such as the blankets and the pillowcase. He blew out the candle and stuffed it into the pack as well; then, with a few other odds and ends, he left the room and crept down the hallway.

Wendy wasn't there yet and he went to the kitchen. He found a half open box of this and a quarter full of that, not much but better than nothing. He put it all into a wool bag found under the kitchen sink, and when he was done he carried it to the front door where he set it down. He looked up at the sound of footsteps and saw it was Wendy. She was fully dressed, wearing a heavy parka, gloves, scarf and hat. She had a parka for him, too. As he slid into it, she said, "It was Doug's."

He nodded and zipped it up, then took the proffered hat and gloves from her. When he was ready, he looked her straight in the eyes. "You ready for this? We need to keep moving when we leave here or we'll freeze to death. In the morning, we can find a place to rest and maybe make camp. Then we'll have to head out until we find someplace safe."

"I'm ready, it's not like we have a choice, right?"

He smiled at her. "Right, we don't."

Taking her hand, they walked to the front door. Brett fixed the backpack on his shoulder to get it more comfortable; Wendy with one as well. After that he shouldered the bag of food, and with one more glance at Wendy, he opened the front door.

Hand in hand, the two stepped into the frigid night and left the sanctuary behind.

The first night was the worst, as they both had to become acclimated to the harsh environment. They walked for hours, and when they couldn't go anymore, the dim sun finally rising, casting the land in a pallid gloom barely better than dusk, they found shelter in an old camping station, barely bigger than a large, walk-in closet.

They rested and ate snow, saving their meager rations for when they would need it most, and after catching a few hours of sleep—curled up together for warmth—they headed back out into the frozen wasteland.

They didn't talk, each covering their faces so that only their eyes were visible, and they walked, day after day.

By the end of the first week, they crested a large hill, and as they reached the top, Brett, who was in the lead, stopped walking and fell to his knees as if he'd seen something devastating.

Wendy came up behind him, not understanding what was wrong. Was he sick? Tired? Why had he fallen to the snow-covered ground?

And then, as she joined Brett and laid her eyes on what he'd seen, she too, fell to the frozen ground and wept.

Miles away, lost in the swirling maelstrom of snow, they saw the remnants of a grand city. Now it was a burnt out wreck of battered debris, more than ninety percent of the city unrecognizable and covered in snow.

But as their eyes played over the devastation, here and there large signs could be seen from where the wind had blown the snow clean.

Massive fiberglass and steel signs with The Palms, The Rio and Terrible's Casino, dotted the landscape between the rubble and debris.

The Las Vegas Hilton was nothing but smashed concrete and metal, looking as if a giant hand had flattened it in a fit of rage. In the distance, where The Stratosphere once stood tall, the area was empty, the structure having collapsed.

Small dots that were once cars and trucks were scattered about, most flipped onto their roofs, a few lodged in the debris, as if a giant wind had picked them up to deposit them higher up.

From where Brett stood, he couldn't see smaller details, such as the remains of human bodies, but he had no doubt they would be there, buried in the snow, if a more detailed search was made.

"Oh my God, no," Wendy said as she began to weep.

Brett said nothing, only stared in horror. The heart of Clark County, Nevada was nothing but blasted, snow-covered wreckage, and for as far as he could see the same vista greeted him.

They stared at the destroyed city for a full half hour until the cold became too much and they knew they needed to get moving to build up their body heat.

"What do we do now?" she asked Brett as they turned away from the dead city, cocooned forever in a coffin of white snow and ice.

"We go back to the sanctuary."

"But what about Arthur?"

"We'll deal with that when we get there. We'll just have to hope he'll let us back in. But he doesn't strike me as the forgiving type."

"And if he doesn't let us in?" she asked, her lower lip trembling from more than just the cold.

"Then we're dead."

The return journey was harder now, the knowledge that there was nowhere else to go almost too much to take.

They sought shelter in the same camping station as before, and made it to the small shelter only an hour before a massive storm struck the area, the snow falling so hard and fast their footprints were buried in seconds after making them.

Huddled together in the middle of the small hut, they wrapped themselves in the blankets Brett had carried with him, and waited for the storm to break.

In that time, they talked for hours, slept a lot, wrapped in each others arms, and on the third day, made love for the first time. At first it was awkward, the two shy and cold, but as their passion grew, so too did their confidence.

The last two days trapped in the hut were one of bliss, as they grew closer, falling in love. If it wasn't for the want of food, which had run out two days ago, they would have been blissfully happy, despite the cold.

When the storm finally broke, they pushed out a window, and crawled onto the three feet of newly fallen snow, and began their trek back to the sanctuary.

Though closer now, they mostly stayed silent, each filled with the dread of their return. Once back, even if McMillan allowed them inside, the couple would be torn apart by McMillan, who claimed Wendy as his property.

But Brett figured one problem at a time, the first being to make it back safely and alive.

Days passed and eventually the sanctuary came into view with Brett leading the way. They were both tired and on the edge of total exhaustion as the weary couple stepped up to the front door of the sanctuary and looked at each other.

"You sure about this?" he asked her, his cheeks bright red from exposure.

She nodded, only her eyes visible from behind her scarf and hat. "We don't have any choice."

"Okay, cross your fingers that he's in a forgiving mood," he said and then banged on the door.

More than a minute passed and the door remained unopened. As the next minute ticked by, Brett tried to tell himself that it would take time for McMillan to get to the door.

That was if he planned on opening it at all.

Another two minutes went by and Brett was beginning to become nervous. His mind began to work frantically as he tried to figure out what he and Wendy would do next if they were ignored.

The truth was, he didn't know what to do.

It was below freezing and there was nothing even remotely close to the sanctuary where they could hole up. And then there was the matter of food, which they had none.

He knew if they didn't get back inside the house, they were both as good as dead and he let his eyes play over the reinforced windows, wondering if he could break in when the lock to the door clicked and it slowly opened.

McMillan was in a bathrobe, his revolver in his right hand, as he glared at Brett and Wendy. "Well, well, well. Back from your walk?" he quipped, his eyes cold, the gun aimed at Brett's chest. "Well, come on, get in here, you're letting all the heat out."

Brett stepped inside with Wendy behind him, Wendy closing the door behind her. Once inside, they slipped out of their backpacks and parkas, setting them on the floor where they dripped water from the melting snow covering them.

"When I woke up and you two were gone at first I was upset," McMillan said. "But then I figured if you were stupid enough to leave then you deserved each other out there in the cold. I can't believe you have the balls to come back. So, why did you?"

Brett pulled off his gloves and hat, holding them, as he stared at the revolver in McMillan's hand. His one hope was that if the man was going to shoot him, he would have already.

"There's nothing out there," Brett said. "We walked for almost a week and found nothing but rubble. There was nowhere else to go but here."

"Uh-huh. That's what I figured. The whole damn world is gone, but I still remain. And I will remain for a long time to come." He raised the revolver a little higher. "But I can't have you around here, not after stealing Wendy from me. I'd be looking over my shoulder every second of every day."

"Then why did you let us back inside?" Brett asked. He shifted slightly, moving closer to McMillan who caught the movement.

"Stand still. Don't move a muscle or I'll shoot you." McMillan looked at Wendy with what almost would pass for compassion. "I let you in because I had to if I wanted her back. But she's the only one I want." He looked her in the eyes. "As far as your betrayal, we'll talk about that later when it's just you and me."

Wendy looked down at her feet as she took off her gloves and hat, holding them in her hands. She knew when they talked it would involve pain for her.

McMillan turned back to Brett and said, "Goodbye, Mr. Butler, I can't say it's been a pleasure knowing you." He prepared to squeeze the trigger and Wendy yelled, "No, Arthur, don't do it!"

Brett saw McMillan's arm tense as he prepared to fire and he acted quickly, using the hat and gloves in his hands as a distraction by throwing them at McMillan.

The old man was caught off guard, for a split second jerking his head back, not realizing it was only the hat and gloves, and in that space of a heartbeat, Brett lunged at him, the two falling to the floor as they wrestled for the revolver.

Wendy moved closer, trying to decide what to do, but she was helpless as the two men rolled across the hardwood floor, grunting and gasping to gain the upper hand over the other. Brett managed to send a punch into McMillan's side, causing the older man to grunt, who then in turn sent a knee into Brett's groin, causing him to see stars. Despite their difference in age, both were evenly matched and neither could gain the upper hand on the other.

The revolver was lowered until the muzzle was an inch from Brett's forehead but at the last instant he bent it back and down. As the two men came to their knees, each facing one another, the gun was pointed down at the floor, both holding onto it. Then, the gun slowly was raised until it was jammed between the two men, their chests touching, and neither knowing who had a finger on the trigger.

Wendy jumped when the gun went off, sounding muffled, the two bodies pressed together stifling the report.

Both men toppled to the floor, McMillan on top of Brett. For a moment, neither man moved, as Wendy stared in fear, tears flowing down her face. If McMillan was the winner, her life would be ten times worse than it had been.

And then to her horror, McMillan pushed off of Brett's still form and stumbled to his feet. Wendy could see both he and Brett had dark blood stains on their chests and it was obvious Brett had been shot.

McMillan took two steps towards her, his right hand out in a fist, and Wendy shook her head, knowing it was all over.

But when he took another faltering step, he halted and stared at her. But she realized he wasn't really seeing her, his eyes now holding a haunted look. And then he coughed, blood spurting from his mouth to drip down his chin and spatter the floor. His legs bean to shake and he fell to his knees, then hands, looking like a toddler who had fallen down. He wheezed twice and then looked up at her, his left arm coming up and his hand reaching for her, begging for help. She did nothing of the kind, but stared at him, not understanding what was happening.

And then, his arm supporting him let go and he fell heavily to the floor, his breath coming in a few strangled gasps before he went still. His eyes remained open, gazing on something Wendy hoped not to see for a very long time.

She fell to her knees and sobbed, all alone now, and at first she didn't hear the low moan through her tears, but when it grew louder, she looked up and to her astonishment saw that Brett was slowly moving his head back and forth.

She jumped up and ran to him, falling by his side, and as she touched his chest, the dark blood staining her hand crimson, she saw there was no bullet hole, only transfer from where McMillan had been shot.

As he rolled over and coughed heavily, she saw the large bruise on the back of his head where he'd struck it upon falling. While she had thought him dead, he had only been dazed and was now returning to consciousness.

As he coughed and sucked in a breath of air, he opened his eyes and looked up into Wendy's tear-filled eyes.

"What happened? Are we okay? McMillan, is he…"

"Yes, he's dead, we're safe."

"Good, that's good," he said, still dazed and not fully with it yet.

"But Arthur had the combination for the pantry. How will we eat?" she asked.

"We'll be fine," he said. "The pantry's in a room with plaster walls. I can make a hole in the wall and get at the food, it's okay."

As the young couple sat on the floor, holding each other, Wendy wiped her eyes and asked, "So what do we do now?"

He reached up and touched her cheek, wiping away a tear as the wind howled outside. "Now, we live."

TIME TO MOVE ON

The bat came down hard, connecting with the side of the zombie's head. Wood impacted into flesh and bone and the latter lost, the bat sinking in more than halfway into the skull.

Brains shot out the sides like spent jello from a plastic bag and the zombie stumbled and fell. But there were more behind that one and Kurt Sandberg raised the bat yet again. The second ghoul in line stumbled forward, its mouth hanging slack as it moaned like an old man.

The bat ceased the moan a second later and shattered every tooth left in the undead mouth. Spitting teeth, gums cracked and pulped, the ghoul fell away, but the rest moved closer.

Kurt took a step backward, raising the bat like he was a batter at home plate, awaiting the next pitch.

He was looking head height at the next zombie, so he almost missed the zombie child that sprinted between the legs of the oncoming ghouls.

It was a little girl, no more than five, with pigtails and a Carebears yellow shirt and matching jeans. She had freckles and small kitty-cat earrings in her ears and even dead she was still cute. But Kurt's heart was immune to such sights, and as the little girl came at him, he swung for the pitch, the girl's head becoming the substitute for a baseball.

The bat cracked like a homerun had been hit and the girl's head sailed over the crowd, bounced off another zombie's head and fell into a trash can. The small body fell to the side as the hands and legs twitched, not fully getting that there was no head there.

Kurt grinned malevolently. He knew it was wrong to enjoy killing the zombies, but hey, everyone needed a hobby.

"Come on, you undead bastards, I'm ready for ya," Kurt snarled as he shifted his stance. He was wearing a black jumpsuit and his bright red hair was uncut. Carrot top and other names had once been thrown his way, but when he had learned to fight, those names had abruptly ceased. Those same skills that had served him so well in the school yard, now worked equally well in the streets of Davon County, where the dead walked and wanted to eat the living.

Kurt hadn't planned on staying in the town when his car had broken down, but it was painfully clear the town needed a hero.

And that was him.

The police force of the town consisted of one old sheriff in his seventies and two deputies in their twenties. All together the three men that consisted of the security force barely equaled one good cop out of New York or D.C.

But that wasn't the only reason Kurt had stayed and he knew the reason though he hated to admit it.

It was because of Sally.

Sally was a tall blonde with legs that went up to here. Mimic holding a hand up to your chin. She was statuesque, smart and beautiful and she had loved Kurt and he had loved her, from the day they had met. She had been cornered by a couple of the town's bullies and Kurt had kicked their asses and sent them on their way.

She rewarded him with a kiss, and like every red-blooded man in the world, that kiss had been enough to have him stick around for a few more days. They had dated and then, on the third date, she had taken him home and rocked his world. And that, as they say, sealed the deal. Like many men who only thought with their little head, Kurt was hooked and had stayed in the town for more than a month. So when the dead began to walk, it wasn't a big surprise when he began patrolling the town's streets, searching for the undead menace.

Sometimes he thought he should wear a cape and tights, like a superhero, but of course that would be ridiculous, though like most men, the kid in him wouldn't have minded giving it a try.

Another ghoul came at him from his right and he shoved it away, whacking its left knee and sending it to the ground, the knee now nothing but crushed flesh and bone. He followed through from the first blow with an uppercut with the bat. The tip of the weapon caught the zombie under the chin and sent the head rocketing back like it was on a spring. When the head snapped back at the end of its tether, the jaw was a pulped mush of teeth and facial muscles.

Kurt grinned, proud of his handiwork as he shifted and went for another target.

A dead mother, who had eaten way too many pies in her life, came at him. She was almost twice his size and was butt naked, her heaving breasts swaying back and forth as she walked. Her abdomen was a garish mess of torn flesh and insides, her intestines spilling out like summer sausage hung out to dry. Droplets of blood splattered the pavement as she walked and her greasy hair was wrapped around her face to the point Kurt couldn't see her features clearly.

Kurt frowned.

She was a big one and the bat might not work on her. But he was willing to give it a try anyway.

Shoving and tripping the surrounding ghouls out of the way, he yelled a war cry and ran at the mother zombie. He smacked her right between her breasts, but all that happened was the bat sank in three inches, like he'd tried to hit clay.

She roared in anger and swiped at him like a Grizzly bear, and though he ducked, a piece of her fist connected, stunning him as he fell back and to the ground.

His hand landed in the open cavity of a dead body and he pulled it free, a gel-like mucus stretching, looking a lot like red and black snot.

Flicking the foul gel off his hand, he rolled to the side as the mother came at him, her mouth opening and closing in anticipation of a Sloppy Kurt sandwich.

She was tall, almost six foot one, and was almost twice his width.

Kurt came up in a crouch and realized he needed a different tactic.

When she came at him this time, he whacked her right knee, shattering the kneecap.

Like a tree ready to fall after being cut, she wavered, her mouth opening and closing as congealed blood dripped from the corner, then her knee gave out.

"Timber!" Kurt couldn't help but yell as the mother zombie dropped to the ground, her face hitting so hard her features were flattened in an instant.

Kurt was ready when flesh touched pavement and he raised the bat over his head like he was chopping wood, bringing it down on the back of her head, caving in the skull and exposing the moist brains within.

Breathing with the exertion, he spun, and with another yell, took out the rest of the zombies. By the time he was finished, he was covered in gore, blood and viscera, his new wardrobe, and without a glance to the corpse, he strolled out of the alley and down the street.

As he walked back to his apartment where Sally would be waiting for him, his eyes took in the once quaint town.

Bullet holes pockmarked the facades on vintage-looking buildings and dead bodies were sprawled across the road and sidewalk, remnants of another day's kills.

He shook his head at the sight. The cleanup crew wasn't doing their job if the bodies were piling up. He slowed as he passed the rotting corpse of a woman. She had one arm draped over her face, as if she was trying to take a nap and block out the sun. Her exposed rib cage glistened in the sun, showing off the punctured lungs within. By the look of it she had taken a blast right to the chest, the force of it ripping her open like a ripe honeydew melon. One pale, shriveled breast lay to the side of her chest where her blouse had been opened, the buttons breaking free. It had a floral pattern on it and it reminded Kurt of something his mother would have worn.

As he passed by the corpse, the heavy aroma of blood and excrement touched his olfactory senses and he began breathing through his mouth. Flies buzzed about the corpses, feeding on the remains as maggots squirmed in every crevice of the dead flesh.

He turned his gaze away from the death and carnage, wanting to focus his eyes forward, to the future, where he and Sally were making love.

So with one eye open in every direction for signs of danger, he headed home.

Sally was waiting for him as he walked inside their apartment. But she didn't run into his embrace. Instead, she pointed for him to go directly to the bathroom and strip and shower.

He did as he was told, a wan smile on his lips. The routine was always the same. He would come home covered in blood and gore and go directly to the shower. While he was in there, she would take his clothes and the baseball bat and get the clothes washed and the bat cleaned.

Stepping into the shower, the warm spray hit his skin, the needlepoints of water not only washing away the dirt and grime, but the day's events, all of it swirling down the drain.

He grunted as he thought that. If only all of life's troubles could be disposed of so easily.

Finishing up, he stepped out of the shower and wiped away the condensation on the mirror. He stared at the face looking back at him, seeing something familiar and yet different. He looked aged, as if doing what he was doing was taking a toll on him.

And why wouldn't it? Though the undead weren't technically people any longer, the shell still was and Kurt had to go out day after day and kill his own kind.

No, they weren't his kind any longer. They were flesh-hungry enemies that wanted to eat him and anyone he loved.

Toweling off, he padded into the bedroom where Sally was waiting for him. This, too, was part of the routine.

She was spread out on the bed, nothing but a light sheet covering her. Her right leg was partially exposed to the air and Kurt felt himself growing aroused at the shapely limb.

She beckoned to him and he smiled again, dropped the towel he was using to the floor, and climbed into bed with her.

They wrapped arms around one another as lips met in a gentle kiss. Tongues explored one another and soon Kurt was kissing her neck, then shoulder and soon he was moving down to places made of secret desires.

Sally moaned loudly, her eyes closed, her head pushed back into the pillow as her brown hair cascaded around her like a halo. His tongue knew what to do, the familiarity of their lovemaking so complete that two bodies meshed into one.

When he entered her, she let out a low moan that had Kurt thinking of the walking corpses outside. Though he tried to put the images out of his mind, they refused to leave entirely.

"Whats wrong, baby?" Sally asked when she noticed he wasn't into it like he usually was.

"Huh? Oh, nothing, honey, I…I think I'm just wasted, it's been a long day." He slid off her and dropped to the bed, one arm going to his forehead.

She turned to her side, her glorious body exposed for him to admire, a thin film of sweat coating her curves.

"Fine, baby, maybe we can just cuddle for now," she said.

He wrapped his arms around her and she moved in close, her warm body touching his, causing tingles wherever the connection was made. He didn't reply to her, there was no need.

As he lay there, listening to her breathing, he found himself drifting off to sleep, feeling safe with Sally by his side.

Later that night, in the wee hours, Kurt woke up. Sally was still by his side and he gently rolled on top of her and began nuzzling her neck. She moaned softly in her sleep and this time the images of dead people stayed away.

He made love to her then, gentle and caring, the two coming to a simultaneous orgasm that had both of them shaking in pleasure.

He drifted off to sleep again, though he hadn't planned on it, and when he awoke the next morning he was thankful for a dreamless night.

The next day was the same as the last; Kurt was out on the streets taking out the walking dead.

He found himself surrounded by a pack of ten, but they were slow, decrepit ghouls and he made short work of them in minutes. The last one had been a scarecrow-like boy in his teens. He was so skinny his ribs poked through his flesh. Kurt had used the baseball bat to flatten those ribs, cracking them until they seemed to float under the skin in pieces. A few whacks at the head and the zombie was down, one more corpse amongst the wrecked and shattered bodies.

Kurt looked up at the sound of a car. It was the sheriff, his pale visage resembling one or more of a dozen zombies. He was over the hill, there was no doubt about it, but every single man was needed in the town as more and more of the undead flooded in from the nearby city. With hundreds of thousands of people living there, there would be no end in sight to the influx of living dead.

That was fine with Kurt. He was here in this town for Sally, and as long as she wanted to stay, he would too, fighting to defend the town she loved so much, as it was her hometown.

"Kurt, I see you got another group of 'em," the sheriff said as he slowed the squad car to a halt a few feet from Kurt.

Kurt walked over to him, his bat dripping brown and black sludge, the congealed blood sticky like syrup.

"Yeah, they thought they had me surrounded till I turned the tables on 'em."

The sheriff nodded and then his face went solemn.

"What's wrong, Sheriff, I know that look," Kurt said.

"I...I don't know how to tell you this, Kurt, but there's been an outbreak at an apartment building a few streets over." His eyes bore into Kurt's. "It's your apartment building, son."

Kurt's eyes went wide with the realization of what the sheriff had said. "Oh, Christ, Sally? I gotta get over there, now," he took off at a run.

"Wait, Kurt, it's too late! The entire damn building is infected!"

But Kurt wasn't listening, only the wind in his ears and his breathing filling his hearing, a void of doom slowly creeping up from deep inside him.

Sally...she couldn't be dead, he wouldn't let it happen.

That's why he was in this damn hick of a town in the first place, for her, to protect her. As he ran faster, the bat swinging by his side spraying bloody droplets, he knew she had to be okay, that she was waiting for him in their apartment, and when he got home she would come out of the closet and smile, falling into his arms.

Yes, that's what would happen; it had to be, because the alternative was too much to contemplate.

Running through the last intersection, he came face to face with his apartment building. Just like the sheriff said, the entire building was in chaos. The few police and the inadequate fire services had the building cordoned off, and every now and then a survivor would run out of the front doors.

When this happened, all guns were aimed at the individual, but when the survivor acted like a real person and not a zombie, they were let through. Of course, they were inspected for bites before being allowed to go free.

Kurt ran up to the edge of the cordoned-off area and stepped inside the police line. Immediately, one of the deputies walked over to him. He looked like he'd started shaving last week, his face resembling a teenager in a poster for abstinence.

"Kurt, oh, man, I'm so sorry," the deputy said.

"Sorry for what? Do you know something about Sally?"

The deputy shook his head. "No, I haven't heard, I just assumed…"

"Well, don't assume shit, all right? She could be fine; a lot of people could be fine." He frowned deeply as he set his jaw into a tight grimace. "I'm going inside. I'll find Sally and clear out any that have turned."

"You can't, it's too dangerous, the entire building is full of them," the deputy said.

Kurt shoved him aside. "Watch me, kid; now get the hell out of my way."

The deputy held up his hands in surrender and let Kurt pass. The other deputy saw Kurt and moved to stop him, but when the first deputy waved Kurt through, the second young man merely nodded and stepped out of the way.

Kurt moved past the deputy with barely an acknowledgement, racing to the front doors.

Stepping inside, the lights were flickering, signifying the power was fluctuating.

Stepping into the shadows, a shape jumped out from the far hallway. The second Kurt saw the figure, the way it stood and moved; he knew it was a zombie. And as the figure moved under one of the flickering lights, his assumption was proven correct.

Kurt never hesitated; he stepped forward and flattened the ghoul's head with his bat, the body slumping to the carpeted floor.

He took the stairs to his apartment, having to take out five more zombies on the way. A trail of bodies now lay behind him, a visceral tableaux of breadcrumbs for anyone to follow.

Once he was on his floor, he spotted three shadows in the darkness. The lights were out with the exception of one bulb over his position, and though the gloom was all pervasive elsewhere in the hallway, he could still see the silhouettes of the approaching figures.

"If you're human, call out, or you're gonna get a bat to the head," Kurt stated as he hefted his bat.

Low moans were his reply and he nodded, having his answer.

"All right, then, come and get it."

The zombies stumbled forward and he raised the bat. The first ghoul to come into the light was his neighbor, Ruth. She was in her late fifties, divorced and had three cats. But from the tufts of bloody fur on her shirt and sticking out of the corners of her mouth, he had a feeling the number of felines she owned had been drastically reduced.

Ruth growled from deep in her throat and Kurt saw the gaping wound on her neck, seeping blood. When she was close enough, he cracked her over the head. Her eyes seemed to contract as the bat sank deep into the top of her skull, and when she fell over, there was a large piece of scalp still stuck to the end of the bat. Kurt didn't have time to admire his scalp job however, as another ghoul was following Ruth. This was his neighbor from across the hall. His name was George, but everyone called him Skippy. No one knew why this was as Skippy wouldn't tell, but Kurt had assumed it was a nickname from when he was a child. George/Skippy was a transplant from Los Angeles, and though Kurt liked to be friends with everyone, he had to admit that Skippy was an asshole. The man was so full of himself that horseshit seeped from his ears. So as Skippy came at him, Kurt had to admit he was relishing what was to come next.

The bat came at Skippy in a sideways swing, connecting with Skippy's right ear. The ear was destroyed, or more accurately, it was forced inside of Skippy's head, the bat continuing into the brain. With his skull now concave, Skippy stumbled back and forth, looking like a drunk at last call. That looked about right as Skippy was a raging alcoholic, a remnant of his past in L.A.

Kurt finished off Skippy with another swing of the bat, this one shattering the skull and sending brain matter to splatter across the carpeting.

George, or Skippy, to his friends, dropped like a sack of potatoes, dead. Kurt barely gave the dead man a glance; he wasn't worth his attention in life and death rated even lower on his scale of who was worth it.

No sooner did Skippy go down, then the last ghoul came at him. This was his neighbor from down the hall and his name was Jacob. Kurt didn't know Jacob very well, but he knew he was a flaming gay man. Now not that there was anything wrong with being gay, but this man was down and out flaming. He talked like a woman and wore loud, obnoxious clothing that the average gay man wouldn't be caught dead in…well, at least the ones with style.

And that was the ensemble Jacob was wearing now. A pink shirt tied up so that his midriff was bare and a pair of low-cut jeans that had large holes in the back to show off his ass. His hair was cut tight to the scalp and an earring sparkled in his right ear. All of this was par for the course for Jacob, but not the massive wound on his face. The gay man was missing his left cheek and the flesh had been torn down to his throat, leaving a massive, gaping wound that still seeped blood. To round off this horror show, Jacob was missing an eye, only a dark hole where the blue orb once was. The eye socket seeped a clear ooze, pieces of ganglia still swinging back and forth from where the eye had been attached.

Kurt swung the bat over his head and flattened Jacob's skull. The blow was so hard and so complete that Jacob's other eye popped out of its socket.

The orb arced through the air and Kurt had to lean back as the orb shot past his face. He could have sworn the eye looked at him as it flew past, but that was probably just his imagination.

Jacob was dropping to the floor, his head now resembling a flattened balloon.

Breathing hard, Kurt spun around; searching for more attackers, but the hallway was empty.

Satisfied he had taken out any potential threats; he went to his door and reached for the knob. But as his hand went out, he saw the door was ajar. Using the bat to push it open, it silently parted for him.

Light from inside the apartment spilled out into the hallway and Kurt saw the door had blood on it in the shape of one perfect handprint.

He wanted to call out to Sally, but held off; not knowing what would greet him if he did.

Stepping inside the apartment, he slowly closed the door behind him, not wanting to worry about what might sneak up on him. The apartment was quiet and he strained to hear the slightest sound, something that would tell him if Sally was home.

Finally, after minutes had passed, he spoke.

"Sally, are you here? Honey, it's me, Kurt."

At first there was no sound, no response to his query, but then he heard a door creak open from the direction of the bedroom. Kurt's heart soared with happiness. It had to be Sally. She must have been hiding in the closet, just like he'd thought.

Obviously a zombie had banged on the door and Sally, not knowing what was happening, had opened it to see what was going on. The zombie had come in and Sally had run to the bedroom, locking herself into the closet. The zombie had slapped the front door with its bloody hand, but then had moved on when it couldn't find her.

And now she was coming out of her refuge at the sound of his voice.

Footsteps could be heard coming closer and he lowered the bat, ready to take her in his arms.

And then she was at the bedroom doorway and moving toward him.

Kurt's heart broke the instant he saw her. Where his true love once stood there was now only the former shell.

It was Sally, but only in name only. He saw her throat had been torn out, and as she moved her head, the wound flexed, congealing blood seeping down her nightgown to strike the carpeted floor. Her complexion was pale and her eyes were vacant and Kurt knew there was absolutely no doubt his love, his Sally, was gone forever.

She growled deep in her throat, the sound like a wild animal. Then the growl shifted into a low moan. It reminded him of the sound she made in bed when they made love and it only made him want to weep more. But he held it together, he had to.

She began to stumble towards him, her arms raised, her hands ready to grasp him, her teeth preparing to sink into his warm flesh.

With tears in his eyes, Kurt raised the blood-soaked bat.

It looked like in the morning he'd be moving on.

UNCLE JOE

The Fourth of July party was in full swing in Topsfield, Mass, in the yard of one Mary Simon. She held the party every year, figuring it was one of the few times her and her friends could get together. With people always so busy, it was rare for everyone to set aside some time to get together, but at least one time a year (excluding Christmas) they did just that.

Mary's husband Dave was on the grill, flipping hamburgers too early as usual. They broke up and left bits of themselves on the grill bars, the scorch marks barely visible. He was one of those cooks that couldn't leave the food alone, but had to roll the hotdogs, flick the sausages and of course, flip the hamburgers five times before even one side was cooked.

A few feet from the grill were three coolers filed with ice, each one holding something for the appropriate audience. The first carried beer and wine coolers, the second soda and ice tea, and a few lemonades if you wanted to dig around a little. The third held bottled water, for those too finicky to drink from the tap.

The party had been going on for hours, everyone eating and having a wonderful time. There had to be over fifty people easy, all laughing and catching up.

A dozen children ran about, playing ping pong on the set-up table or basketball near the end of the driveway. It was a warm day but not so warm it was uncomfortable in the shade, though most of the older men with balding pates would have been better off if they'd stayed out of the sun altogether.

Some of the guests had brought friends of their own so everyone didn't know each face they saw, but that was okay. It was a party, a time to meet new people, to eat, drink and be happy.

While everyone was going about the serious business of having fun, a tall figure hovered near the edge of the yard. See, Mary's yard was in the middle of the forest, with only a few other homes surrounding her.

In times past, she'd seen deer and rabbits, owls and raccoons and one time could have sworn she'd seen a bear. But Dave had told her she was mistaken, for bears didn't live in this part of the state. Overdevelopment had chased them away to easier hunting grounds.

On the edge of the treeline, the tall figure went from tree to tree, slowly making his way closer to the party. On closer inspection, the figure was clothed in an odd assortment of attire.

The shirt he wore had a Red Sox logo on the front, but the arms and shoulders barely fit, the girth of the figure too wide. The figure wore a pair of pajama pants with small trains on them, too baggy even for his ample frame. No shoes were on the large hairy feet and a Yankees baseball cap and dark sunglasses rounded out the attire.

When the figure was right at the edge of the yard, he stood tall and strode out of the woods and into the party as if he belonged there. No one noticed him, all having fun, and from a quick glance, he was just another guest, albeit taller and with more hair than the rest.

The figure towered over the tallest person by almost a foot so he hunched over so as not to call attention to himself.

The figure went to the buffet table where Dave had just put out the plate of cooked meat. As stated before, the burgers were overcooked, because after playing with them continuously, Dave then left them on the grill for too long.

It wasn't his fault really; he had gotten into a conversation about the new Hybrid cars and became distracted. The hotdogs were charred on the edges but that was all right—some people liked them that way.

The figure picked up a paper plate and began heaping meat onto it, taking more than half of what was on the serving tray. Next came the macaroni salad, fruit salad and finally, hamburger and hotdog rolls—a bag of each. He even went to the cooler with the beers and grabbed two.

He was a Coors man by what he grabbed, totally ignoring the Budweisers and Coronas. Then, going over to the side and a little away from the main group of partiers, he sat down in a wooden chair—which groaned, and if it could have talked would have begged for mercy—and began to eat.

Dave's brother-in-law Bob was making his rounds and he finally came upon the eating, hairy figure.

"Hey there, I'm Bob. I haven't seen you around here before," he said as he looked down at the Yankees cap, the figure hunched over, his face hidden. Bob could see a thin beard and a thick mustache covering almost the entire face by his quick glance.

He wasn't a big sports fan so to him the cap and Red Sox shirt was just fine, though he knew many of his friends who would have exploded at the sacrilege. Then recognition came to him. He knew Dave's uncle liked to wear his hair long and was such a hairy bastard that he looked more like a bear than a human being. He said, "Wait. You're Joe, aren't you? You're Dave's uncle? I remember you now. Wow, I haven't seen you in what, three years?"

The figure didn't reply, but continued eating in silence, enjoying the hamburgers, not at all unhappy with Dave's cooking. He was a sloppy eater, bits of meat and crumbs from the bread rolls falling onto his lap.

Bob sat down next to the figure and pointed to a woman across the yard. She had bright red hair, a frumpy looking blouse on, and her makeup was simply garish. "See that woman over there?" Bob asked. "That's my wife of over thirty-five years. Man, I tell ya, I could use a change of pace; know what I mean, pal?"

The figure simply grunted.

"She's always nagging me and complaining, as if she's so much better. I swear, one day I'm gonna simply run off with another woman." Then he regretted what he'd said and he glanced at the eating figure. "Nah, I'm not gonna do that, sorry for even sayin' it. I'm just blowin' off some steam." He patted Uncle Joe on the shoulder, a little surprised when he felt the taut muscles rippling beneath the shirt. "Thanks for letting me vent, Joe, I appreciate it." He leaned a little closer. "I hope we can keep this conversation between us."

The figure merely grunted again, but whether it was because of the food or what Bob had said was unknown. Either way, Bob took it as a sign that his secret was safe. He stood up and began to walk away. "I want another beer." He was soon lost in the crowd of revelers.

The figure didn't look up as Bob left. He'd just finished devouring everything on his plate and was still hungry. Then he looked at the paper plate covered in juices and ate that, too. He'd already finished one of his beers off and he popped the second one, guzzling it down in one quick breath, after which he let out a loud burp that had a few guests chuckling at the sight of the hairy man with the beer making a scene.

When he was finished, he stood up, wiped his mouth with the back of his hand, turned, and loped off into the forest, his arms swaying back and forth by his sides.

Bob returned from getting a beer and looked for Uncle Joe, wanting to talk a little more. After all, if Joe was willing to listen, he had a lot more stuff he'd love to get off his chest.

But Uncle Joe was nowhere to be seen, the figure having disappeared from whence it came.

Dave walked up to Bob and patted him on the shoulder to get his attention. "Hey. Bob, what's up? You look like you lost someone."

"Well, yeah, I kind of did. I was talking with your Uncle Joe but he seems to have disappeared."

"My Uncle Joe? Here? That's impossible. He died two years ago," Dave said, wondering if Bob was drunk.

Bob's face went blank and he shook his head. "But if that wasn't your uncle, then who was I talking to?"

Dave shrugged. "Who knows? We get party crashers all the time around here. Campers hear the party and come in from the woods, then they leave after they've gotten fed and drank all my beer. Sometimes I kick them out, other times I let them stay. Hell, one time a guy had a guitar with him. He entertained us for a free meal."

Bob nodded slowly, understanding. "Oh, okay, that makes sense. I guess it must have been one of them. He was a nice guy though. Not much of a talker but a great listener."

"Sure, that must have been who it was, one of them freeloaders coming by for some free food," Dave said. He was going to say more but Mary called out to him.

She wanted him to put on more burgers and hotdogs. It seemed they had gone through much more than usual for this time of day, the data taken from past parties how she gauged how much was gone. Dave patted Bob on the arm and walked away, leaving Bob alone.

Bob's forehead creased in thought as he sipped his beer, gazing off into the forest. "Huh, campers, that must have been it. Still, that guy sure was hairy for a camper. And he needed a shave real bad."

UNDEAD DELIVERY

Harold Mitchell reached over and turned off the alarm clock before it sounded. His internal body clock had woken him before the radio alarm as it usually did.

Beside him in the full size bed, his wife snored loudly. As he glanced over his shoulder at her, all he could see was a large lump twice as big as the one he made in the bed. Sliding out of bed as quietly as possible, he reached down for his slippers and began to walk out of the bedroom, to the bathroom. When he was halfway there, a floorboard shifted beneath his pressing weight and a soft *creeeaaaak* filled the room.

"Quiet down, Harold! God, you have no respect for others," Helen hissed between clenched teeth.

"Sorry, dear," he simply replied.

Other than snorting in an annoyed grunt, Helen went back to snoring, as if she hadn't spoken. Harold padded the rest of the way out of the bedroom and into the hallway, relieved when he didn't step on any more loose floorboards. His clothes were already laid out on a small table and he quickly got dressed, then went into the bathroom to do what everyone does every morning. When he was finished, he went down to the first floor of their small one bedroom house and prepared to do his chores before going off to work.

First he had to make Helen's breakfast and lunch so she didn't have to stop watching her 'stories' during the day. He would prepare dinner when he returned home from work, so he at least didn't have to deal with that meal at the moment. When he was finished with the meals, he did a quick load of laundry and made sure Helen's clothes were set out for her on a small bedside table upstairs.

When he was through with that, he checked his wristwatch to see it was ten minutes to six. He had risen at five in the morning, as he always did, and now that his chores were done, he grabbed his sandwich from the refrigerator—one he'd made the previous night—and headed off to work, using his beat-up and worn down Honda Civic. It was rusting from the outside in and he tried not to look at Helen's brand new Cadillac in the driveway as he climbed into his old car. The door squeaked and shifted when he opened it and he saw that the upper pin holding the door to the frame was about to snap off. He could buy a pin at the auto store on his way home, that is if there was enough time. Helen didn't like it if he worked late and she had to wait for her dinner. He pulled out of the driveway, and with one last look at his home, aimed the broken grille of the Honda to the freeway.

As Harold drove, he hummed softly. He was a cheerful man, despite all he had to put up with. He never gave it much thought to how he'd ended up in an abusive relationship with a hulking sow of a wife, and even if he did, he probably wouldn't want to dwell on it.

Harold was a postman for the city, and though the job was demanding, he enjoyed being outside and meeting people on a daily basis.

Though meek at home, he was very outgoing in the world and everyone who met him liked him.

He was just a likable fellow.

Twenty minuets later, he pulled into the parking lot and climbed out if his car. As he walked away from the Honda, he remembered he'd forgotten to grab his lunch so he went back, opened the door, and reached in. He didn't lock the car, for there was nothing even the most desperate car thief would want, including the car as a whole.

With a bounce to his step, he headed off to the building to begin work.

It was as he was *throwing mail*, which is what he did to get ready for his route, by organizing the packages and letters so he would have a bundle for each section, that his cell phone rang. Looking at the screen, he saw that the number was for his house—it was Helen.

"Hello, dear, I can't really talk now. I'm at work. You know they frown on cell phone calls unless it's an emergency."

"This is an emergency, Harold!" she screamed into the phone.

Harold's heart began to beat faster as different scenarios flooded his mind. Was she sick, a heart attack maybe? Were his or her parents sick? Oh God, did one of them die? Her tone, she sounded so upset, it must be terrible. He quickly asked her what was wrong, his mouth suddenly dry.

"I can't find the remote control for the television!" she yelled into the phone in reply.

Harold sighed heavily, a small crack in his normally pleasant veneer showing through. "Did you check under the couch cushions?"

"Yes, and it's not there."

"Harold," the office manager called from the other side of the room. "No personal calls unless it's an emergency. That's going on your personal record if you don't hang up right now. I just gave a speech about that two days ago."

"Yes, Mr. Swanson," Harold replied. Then into the phone he said, "Helen, I just got in trouble with my manager, I really have to go."

"But what about the damn remote!" she yelled.

He sighed again. "Did you check under the couch itself? Maybe it fell off the table and was kicked under there last night when you were getting ready to go to bed."

There was a brief pause, some scuffling, and then Helen said, "You're right, it is under there. I can see it, but I'll need to get a broom to reach it."

"Harold, get off the damn phone!" Mr. Swanson snapped, his tone heavy with impatience.

"Yes, dear, well I have to go, see you tonight," Harold said, and as he was closing the phone, he could hear Helen calling out, "No, wait, what about dinner toni…"

Harold tucked the phone into his pants and was about to get back to work when Mr. Swanson stepped up to him. "Can I see you in my office, Harold, we need to have a talk."

Harold rolled his eyes inwardly and did as he was asked, knowing he was about to get a verbal warning.

It was two hours later and Harold was out delivering his route.

His mood had soured since arriving that morning.

He now had a verbal warning on his permanent record and worse still, he was being audited today.

As Harold walked his route, delivering to the homes and apartments, he had another man following him with a clipboard. The man's job was to evaluate Harold's efficiency. What aggravated him the most was that every now and then the man would write something in his notebook, and would then smile wanly to Harold.

He hated that smile.

And of course, because he was being audited, the mail was suspiciously 'light' today. It was always like that during audits. Where normally, he would have twenty to thirty bins of flat mail and another ten to twenty packages, today he had less than half that amount. He always wondered where the mail was being hidden and he knew it was, because tomorrow, when the auditor was gone, he would end up with double the mail for the day.

Through some light chit-chat, Harold found out that the auditor had been a letter carrier himself for just under a week a year ago, and had then transferred into the managerial section of the post office.

Harold knew what that really meant.

The guy couldn't hack it as a letter carrier and so had gone into management. And like so many other jobs out there, the ones who can't do the job, manage the ones who can.

Harold walked along the sidewalk, and then after delivering to a small, one family home, he walked back to the street, down the sidewalk, then up the pathway leading to the front door of the next house.

He glanced over his shoulder to see the auditor was scribbling away again.

Though he knew it wasn't a good idea, he couldn't help himself and said, "Would you please tell me what I just did that made you write something down?"

"It's nothing," the man said curtly.

"Come on, don't give me that, just tell me already."

"After I submit my evaluation, your supervisor will talk with you; it's not for me to say out here."

Disgusted, Harold turned and walked over to the auditor, and before the man could stop him, he pulled the clipboard from his hands and took a step back.

"Hey, give that back!" the man yelled like a child on the playground who'd had his ball taken away by a bully.

Harold wasn't listening, he was scanning the last sentence the man had written.

"Didn't walk on the grass. Went the long way around," Harold said as he read. He looked up at the man. "Seriously?"

The auditor nodded. "Yes, that's correct. On that last house you walked up the pathway to the sidewalk then around and used the next walkway. All you had to do is cut across the grass and you would have saved 8.9 seconds."

"I don't like to cut across people's grass, I find it disrespectful," Harold rebutted.

"Well, Harold, maybe so, but we need you to be as efficient as possible and cutting across people's grass and driveways is one way. Every extra step you take is one more than is needed to do the job correctly."

Harold frowned. "I've been doing this job for over ten years and I do it well. Where in the hell do you get off…" He stopped, realizing he was going to blow up. "Look, I'm sorry, I shouldn't have said anything." He handed the auditor back the clipboard. "I'm sorry I took this."

The auditor merely frowned and began scribbling again as soon as he got his clipboard back. Harold rolled his eyes and resumed his route.

It was near the end of the day, an hour to go when the auditor stopped walking and called out to Harold. "Okay, I have everything I need. I'm leaving now."

"Good," Harold muttered under his breath, but he merely smiled at the man. As the auditor turned to leave, he stopped, and in his eyes there was a little bit of mischievousness. He knew he wasn't supposed to tell Harold any of his findings, but after what Harold did to him earlier, he couldn't help himself. 'Payback was a bitch' as the saying went.

"I just thought I'd let you know, Harold, that I believe you could easily have another ten streets added to your route if you simply did the job better. I'm recommending your route be extended. As you know, the post office is cutting manpower and some routes need to be absorbed into others. If you take the north side of Route C into your own, that would mean the other carriers could take the others sides and...wallah…one less route to worry about."

Harold said nothing, knowing it would be fruitless, but deep inside he wanted to scream.

This man knew nothing. The mail was light today and to top it off it was a beautiful sunny day. Try doing the route in the rain, or in the snow, when half the pathways weren't shoveled and there was no place to park. Harold had more than fifteen hills on his route and each one was a nightmare to climb when it snowed.

"Well, anyway, take care, Harold, it was nice meeting you today, best of luck in the future," the auditor said and turned and walked away, whistling a tune as he went.

Harold stood still for more than five minutes as the auditor walked away and disappeared around a corner. He was so angry he wanted to explode. The saying, *going postal* came to mind.

But Harold was a kind man, and as soon as the anger rose, it went back down, buried deep within his psyche.

With a weary sigh he turned around to get back to work, knowing when he got home that night, he had dinner and cleaning to do for Helen. If he didn't, she would yell and scream at him and basically make his life more miserable than normal.

As he spun around, he idly wondered how his life had become so difficult, but then any further thoughts were shattered from his mind when he saw what was now standing before him. The only word to describe what was standing in front of him was a *zombie*.

Yes, that's right, an honest to God living dead person.

Harold could see where the zombie had walked out of the backyard of the house on his right, the shrubs were broken and damaged, leaves on the grass and walkways from where the zombie had pushed its way through.

It was tall, nearly a foot taller than Harold and had wide shoulders and thick muscles beneath its weathered and dirty shirt.

Its hair was sparse and seemed wet against its skull…or was that slime or pus?

Its head seemed oversized, or perhaps the skin had just shrunk against the skull, but none of that mattered at the moment.

The zombie was standing still, looking at Harold as if it was a cat and he was a mouse…a small mouse…a tasty mouse.

Slowly, the zombie leaned over and opened its mouth, a load roar ensuing. Harold had mail in his hands, and as the zombie roared, he found the mail was flying into the air as he freaked out.

A fucking zombie! he thought. And if it was like the ones in the movies, then it wanted only one thing…to fucking eat him!

Harold turned and ran, the mail flying out of his sack as he dashed down the street and into a front yard three houses down. Breathing heavily, he looked back to see the zombie was still standing in the same spot…it wasn't following him.

He waited for a full minute, his heart pounding in his chest, and though he knew it was crazy, he began to walk back to the zombie.

When he was a few feet away, he stopped and looked at the animated corpse, one foot ready to slap concrete if he needed to escape.

The zombie didn't move.

"Uh, hi there, big fella. What's your name?" he asked like he was talking to a stray dog.

The zombie merely growled, saliva dripping from the corner of its mouth. Harold's nose wrinkled from the scent of rot and decay. The odor was sickly sweet and each time the wind shifted, he had to fight down the urge to retch. Still, bile crept up into the back of his throat.

"Uh, I'm Harold. Are you going to try and eat me, Mr. Zombie?"

No reply…obviously.

Harold scratched his head, wondering what was going to happen next. Though intimidating as hell, the zombie didn't seem to be threatening him. He looked around the street, not knowing what to do. He guessed he could go to the house the zombie came out of the yard from, and knock on the door. He could say, "Hi, did you lose a zombie? I found him wandering around." Hell, he might even get a reward, a tip.

Then the zombie raised its right hand and opened its mouth a little, the hand cupped so the fingers were pressed together. It moved the hand back and forth to its mouth. It only took Harold a second to figure out what the zombie was trying to tell him.

"You're hungry? Oh my, Uhm gees, if you eat what I think you're supposed to eat, I don't know what to tell you," he said with a frown.

His cell phone buzzed and he reached for it on instinct. "Hello?" he said absently.

"Harold? What are you doing for dinner tonight? I'm starving. The second you get in tonight I want you to make dinner. And I spilled coffee all over my favorite muumuu, I need you to do another load of laundry. Oh, and the toilet is filthy. I had one of my 'episodes' and it splattered under the seat. It needs to be cleaned. It must have been that four bowls of Raisin Bran I ate last night before bed. Harold, are you there? Do you hear what I'm saying to you? Harold?"

"Uh, yes dear," he said idly and hung up on her. He wasn't listening. An idea had popped into his mind like a freight train crashing through a brick wall. It was evil, devious and downright mean, but the more he thought about it, the more it made sense. At that exact moment in time, as Harold stood before the zombie, he decided it was time for a life change.

It was just after six when Harold entered his kitchen through the back door by way of the garage. As he stepped into his house and took off his jacket, he could hear the television on in the living room.

"Harold? Is that you?" Helen yelled through the house.

"Yes, dear, I'm home," he called back.

"Good, I'm starving, get to work making dinner!"

"I have a surprise for you, dear, do you want to see what it is?" he called.

"Yes, but bring it in here. I'm watching Oprah and I don't want to get up."

Harold grinned malevolently, the look seeming right at home on his once kind face. "Not a problem, dear, I can do that."

He walked back to the garage and then returned to the kitchen a few seconds later. In his right hand was a rope and connected to the rope was the zombie he'd come across on his mail route. The zombie's hands were tied and there was duct tape on its mouth.

On the way home, the zombie had tried to take a bite out of Harold so he'd quickly taken precautions. It had been evident after being with the zombie for a while that it had been trained like a dog to eat only when told to, though like a hungry dog, if it went without food for too long, it might snap at a hand holding a sandwich.

Harold untied the zombie's hands and slowly peeled the duct tape off, not wanting to be rough, though he was pretty sure the zombie didn't care. Bits of flesh came off with the tape and there was a slight layer of pus and blood connected to the adhesive side.

Harold pointed to the living room, and then mocked that he was eating by placing his hand—with fingers pointed and closed—to his mouth and moving it back and forth to mime eating. The zombie looked at him and cocked its head, then seemed to understand what he was telling it.

Harold got behind the zombie and gave it a gentle push to the living room, while calling out, "Are you ready for your surprise, Helen?"

"For the last time, yes. Now where the hell is it? Bring it in here right now. I can't wait to see it," she replied.

"Oh, I have a feeling you're gonna love it," he said under his breath with a sly grin on his lips.

Harold watched the zombie cross the kitchen floor, stumble down the small hallway, and disappear as it turned into the living room.

At first there was no sound other than the television, but then an ear-piercing scream rent the air, followed by the sound of tearing meat, as if a butcher was separating the bones of a large rack of ribs by tearing each one apart with his bare hands.

As the screams began in full force, and Helen cried out for help, Harold went to the refrigerator and grabbed a beer. Then, after making sure the back door was wide open as well as the garage door, and after tossing some mud on the floor near the entryway, he called the police to report a zombie attack.

VALENTINE'S DAY CANDY

Gene Watterson opened the main door to the Hallmark store on the corner of 8th and Main and nodded to an old woman with a walker. But the old woman barely looked at him, her face filled with fear and concern as she hurried to exit the building.

Not understanding what might be wrong with the woman, he merely shrugged and entered the store, figuring she was just acting senile like most old birds he'd met in his twenty-two years of living on the Earth.

It was Valentine's Day and he was in the store to get candy and flowers for his best girl, Sandy. They had been going out for almost three months and he was head over heels in love with her. They'd had sex a total of six times so far and each time was better than the last.

He was confident when he gave her the flowers and candy; he would be in line for number seven, too. As he entered the store, he heard some muffled screams and yells, the voices all male.

Stepping with trepidation down the center aisle, ignoring the cards on display for the moment, he slid up to the counter at the back of the store.

As he moved to the edge of the aisle, he saw what looked like a scuffle between a homeless man and two policemen. It was just as Gene poked his head around the corner to see what was going on, that one of the cops pulled out a stun gun and zap the shit out of what had to be a bum—a homeless man.

The bum danced a jig as he was filled with electricity, his nerves freezing up, and Gene could swear he saw smoke come out of the bum's ears. Then the man dropped to the floor, and no sooner did this happen, then the cops were on top of him, handcuffing his arms behind his back. In the scuffle there was a soft crack, like a neck snapping, but no one heard it, or if they did, they didn't give it much thought.

"Get 'im cuffed, hurry the fuck up," the first cop snapped at his partner.

"I am, hold on a sec," the second cop yelled back. As he leaned down to use the cuffs, the bum's eyes snapped open and he took a small chunk of flesh from the cop's arm.

"Son of a..." the cop screamed as he punched the bum in the head and pulled his arm back. "The piece of shit just bit me, Carl, what the fuck!" the cop screamed.

But Carl the cop wasn't listening, instead he was finishing the job his partner began, and he handcuffed the bum. With blood-red lips, the bum snarled like a wild animal as Carl pulled the raving lunatic to his feet. No one seemed to notice the bum's neck was broken, after all, the bum was still moving so he was alive…right?

"You okay?" Carl asked his partner who was cradling his arm against his chest with a handkerchief.

"Yeah, I'll live. It looks worse than it is," he said as he checked the wound. It was already slowing, the blood clotting.

"Come on, you asshole," Carl said to the growling bum. "We got a room with your name on it down at the precinct." He turned to the store clerk who was watching in shock. "Sorry about the mess, pal, but we had no choice."

The clerk, a pimply kid in his late teens, only nodded. "Sure, Officer, you did your job. Thanks for coming so fast." The voice was high and nasally.

Carl nodded and yanked the bum towards the front door, his partner right behind.

"Sure, pal, protect and serve, that's our motto."

Then the two cops and the bum were moving and soon were out the front door as pedestrians paused to watch them drag the bum to their squad car.

Gene watched them go with his mouth hanging open. He had never seen such violence. Well, not in real life, anyway. Sure the television was full of that stuff but not right in his face. He walked over to the clerk who had begun picking up the items knocked to the floor by the scuffle.

"What was that all about?" Gene asked.

The clerk shrugged, as if what happened was no big deal.

"Not much. Another bum wandered into the store so I had to call the cops. I tell ya, though, this guy was on somthin'. Did you see the way he got zapped and he was still kickin'? Shit, my uncle got tasered once and he was out for almost the entire night. That bum must have some constitution."

Gene only nodded, not knowing what else to do.

The clerk stopped cleaning to look over at Gene, where before he had been concentrating on working. "So, mister, can I help you with something?"

Gene blinked and nodded once more. "Huh? Oh, shit, yeah, I need a box of heart-shaped candy and flowers."

The clerk pointed to the west side of the store. "Sure, whatever's left is over there. Man, you sure waited for the last second, huh?"

Gene scratched his head. "Yeah, I guess I did. I work a lot and well, you know…"

The clerk stopped cleaning and stared at Gene, crossing his arms. "No, not really, I don't. I sure wish I did, though," he said.

That was when Gene realized from a female point of view, the clerk was pretty nerdy looking, not the first pick for a boyfriend.

"Oh, sorry, man, yeah, I get it. Maybe next year," Gene said ruefully. "So, I'm gonna go see what's left."

The clerk watched him go for another few seconds, made an annoyed face behind Gene's back, and got back to work cleaning the store. Greeting cards and other miscellaneous items were strewn about, knocked from the shelves from the fight. Gene was forgotten from the clerk's mind as soon as he walked away.

Gene made his way to the section where the Valentine's Day items were stored. The shelves were all but empty, only a few stray and open candy boxes strewn about like wreckage from a plane crash. With no choice but to try and find something, he began pushing items aside. He searched for almost ten minutes, and was about to give up, when he found an unopened heart-shaped, bright red box of candies on the bottom shelf. By the looks of things, it had gone unattended by pure luck.

Taking the box off the shelf and holding it up like he had found the Holy Grail, he beamed with delight.

"Now for flowers and I'm good," he said to himself, feeling like a kid finding the last Easter egg at the hunt.

There was a refrigerated glass case in the next aisle and this section was more trashed than the Valentine aisle. Metal shelves with serrated racks stared back at him like a Communist peasant's refrigerator, the entire scene bathed in a pale white light from the two anemic bulbs mounted to the ceiling of the glass case.

More metaphors of deserted cupboard and shelving units came to mind but he refrained from using them, as he didn't want to become redundant.

Opening the glass case, he felt the rush of cool air and began picking up a flower here, a stem there. By the time he was finished, he had a haphazard bouquet, filled with carnations, baby's breath and three roses, two red and one white. A couple of pedals were missing but in the arrangement it wasn't immediately noticeable.

Carrying his finds to the counter, the nerdy clerk glared at him.

"Wow, you found somethin', huh?"

Gene nodded. "Yeah, this is it, though. The next guy is shit outta luck."

He handed the clerk the flowers who began to roll them with paper decorated with little hearts. When he was through, Gene had to admit the bouquet didn't look half bad. The clerk rang up the box of candy and then the flowers.

"I'm gonna give you fifty off on the flowers considering what you did to get them. How does that sound?"

Gene smiled as he reached for his wallet. "Yeah, that sounds good, thanks."

The clerk shrugged. "Hey, it's only fair."

The transaction was completed and Gene picked up his candy and flowers. As he turned to leave, the clerk called out, "Hey, I hope she's worth it."

Gene paused and glanced back to the clerk. "Oh, yeah. She sure is, see ya."

The clerk waved and then Gene was forgotten as another customer came up to the counter to buy a pack of cigarettes.

Gene left the store and began walking down the sidewalk, a skip to his step and a smile in his heart. He couldn't wait to see Sandy's face when he gave her the Valentine's gifts. Yes, sir, this was going to be the best Valentine's Day ever.

There was a news stand on the corner, and a crusty old man hiding behind a pile of newspapers and magazines like a W.W.2 solider taking cover behind sandbags. Five people were gathered around the small shack and Gene strolled up to see what was so interesting.

A small man with a balding pate, a pale complexion, and square glasses glanced at Gene as he came up. The man gestured to a small black and white television the owner of the newsstand had on and everyone was watching attentively.

"The whole damn world's goin' ta Hell," he said as he turned and walked away. Gene saw the briefcase in his right hand and figured the guy was one of those Wall Street types or maybe a lawyer.

Turning back to the television, a report was droning on about unsolicited attacks on unwary pedestrians. Gene watched for almost a minute and then turned and moved on, not caring about what was happening.

After all, if it didn't affect him personally then in the end it didn't really matter. He had learned a few years ago that he couldn't save the world. At such a young age, he was proud of knowing that, as many others his same age would take another decade to figure it out.

As he walked down the sidewalk, he grinned widely, thinking what Sandy would say when he gave her the flowers and candy. He imagined she would gush with happiness and give him a big kiss. Then they would eat dinner, the special one she was making just for him and her. Then later, if he was lucky, they would spend the night together. Just thinking about touching her curvaceous form caused his pants to grow tighter.

He turned the corner and headed down 5th Street, knowing he only had three more blocks to go. All around him the city was full of life, cabs honking, people yelling and a few sirens in the distance.

If he had paused for a second, he may have realized there were more sirens than normal, but it would have been a fleeting thought.

As he passed by a line of cabs, the second one in line had the radio blasting, the windows open, despite the fact it was February. The radio announcer was yelling about some kind of tragedy on the west side, some kind of massacre. Police were called in and every person involved had been put down, killed with shots to the head. They were on so much speed or LSD that nothing but a head shot would work.

Then Gene was past the cab and whatever else was being said was lost in the cacophony of the city. With a renewed hop to his step, he reached the next corner and made his way to Sandy's apartment.

But on the next corner, there was something going on. Three squad cars were surrounding a car crash. From the looks of it, a cab had plowed into a Lincoln Town Car. But that wasn't the real problem. The true problem was the fact that the people in the wreck, covered in blood and one with an arm hanging by tatters of flesh, seemed to be up and attacking nearby gawkers. The cops were screaming at them to stop and of course they weren't listening. Gene stood stock still as he watched a policeman put three rounds into the cab driver's chest. The man, Pakistani or from the same region by the looks of his dark complexion and head wrappings, staggered backwards from the blasts, but no sooner did he stumble, then he was moving forward once more. Only now there was a gaping hole in his chest where the rounds had blown through and out his back. Blood and viscera dripped like slime from the edges of the wound and Gene was amazed the guy was still mobile.

A veteran cop by the look of his hard, chiseled face, stepped forward and shot the cabbie from almost point blank range in the left ear. Brain matter shot out of the right ear, blowing half the cabby's head off. Like a sack of potatoes, the guy dropped to the street, stone dead.

More shots echoed in the street and the other victims of the crash were riddled with bullets, their bloody frames twitching as each shot took out a chunk of their bodies. A middle-aged woman with bright red hair, who had been riding in the back seat of the cab before she was ejected through the windshield, came at the police like a banshee, snarling and growling. She absorbed five shots to the chest and lower torso before one cop shot her in the face. Her mascara, already running, was ruined forever when her faced dissolved into a mini-implosion. The back of her red hair flew out like it had been caught in a wind tunnel as her brains splashed the pavement and she fell to the road. Gene could see that no amount of lipstick and blush was going to save that train wreck of a missing face.

He stared in shock and quickly decided this wasn't where he wanted to be, so turning, he got the hell out of there, while the sounds of screams and gunshots followed him.

By the time he reached Sandy's building, he was feeling a little better. The carnage of the accident was a few blocks behind him and he knew in the city what he had witnessed, though visceral, was nothing new.

The doorman nodded politely at him, knowing him from past visits, and in no time he was riding the elevator up to the fifth floor.

Inside the elevator, the flowers smelled even more fragrant. He fiddled with the bouquet a little, fixing any of the flowers that weren't as perfect as the others. He patted himself on the back once more for managing to actually make the bouquet at all. He wouldn't have wanted to try to search another store if he had struck out at the Hallmark store. He checked three other stores before that one and each of them had been cleaned out, picked so clean it looked like a Valentine's Day apocalypse had occurred and people had hoarded every item they could find with a red heart on it.

The elevator pinged and he stepped out onto the fifth floor. As soon as the elevator doors closed, he began to hear a lot more noise than usual. Thanks to the sound deafening doors and walls, it was all muffled, but as he walked to Sandy's apartment, he could hear muffled yells and what appeared to be screams coming from the other apartments.

But once again, he barely gave it much thought. If people wanted to fight and argue, that was their business. All he cared about was himself and his best gal.

At the end of the hallway was apartment 3D. That was Sandy's place.

Looking down to the mat outside her door, he saw a pair of worn loafers sitting like an old incontinent dog forced to stay outside for risk of peeing on the carpet. He recognized the loafers immediately.

They belonged to Sandy's mother, Agnes.

Made sense, he figured, Agnes probably came over to help with the dinner Sandy was making. That bode well for Gene's stomach. Agnes and him got along all right, though Sandy's father was another matter altogether. If he had been visiting, as well, his old black work boots would have been sitting shotgun next to the loafers. He liked Agnes. Despite her name making her sound old and ugly, she was very attractive, and it was obvious where Sandy got her good looks from. There had been times when Gene had admired Agnes when no one was watching him, staring at her curves and shapely butt.

He reached up to knock on the door, careful not to drop the flowers, and as he tapped the wood with his knuckles, the door creaked inward.

It was open.

That was odd. But maybe she knew he was here and had unlocked the door for him.

No, that didn't make sense. As he pushed the door open, his eyes immediately went to the doorjamb and what was splattered on it.

Ketchup?

It had to be. It looked like someone had been trying to open a bottle and had accidentally sprayed some on the jamb. Stepping inside, he saw the jamb had a handprint on it, the palm pressed into the ketchup.

Oh, what a mess, Sandy must be so upset. She must be going to get a cloth to clean it up, he thought as he closed the door with his foot. Both hands were still holding the flowers and candy.

"Sandy? It's me, Gene," he called out. He could smell the delicious aroma of a roast in the oven and his mouth began to water. He walked deeper into the apartment, his eyes playing over the furniture. On the end of the couch was Agnes' coat, the one with the imitation fur on the collar.

"Sandy? Where are you?" he called again. He was anxious to see her, he couldn't wait to see her face when he handed her the candy and flowers.

With both still in his hands, he went to the kitchen, but just as he got to the entrance, Sandy poked her head out.

He expected her to be in an apron, so she wouldn't ruin her clothes while she cooked, but his actual image of her was far different.

Sandy was covered in ketchup, her white teeth peeking out of the scarlet syrup, and her hair was hanging limply over her shoulders, because there was more ketchup in her hair. To Gene, it looked like she had squirted an entire bottle over herself and rubbed it all in.

"Sandy, what the hell is going on? Why are you covered in ketchup?"

Sandy lowered her head and bared her teeth like a wild dog, a growl emanating from deep in her throat.

That was when Gene took a step closer, wanting to go to her. His eyes caught movement behind her, on the kitchen floor, and he spotted two stocking feet twitching like the body they belonged to was being electrocuted. The heels of the feet were beating a steady staccato on the linoleum and Gene figured out almost immediately it was Agnes.

He stepped closer and the legs became the lower half of the woman and he gasped in shock when he saw that Agnes had no abdomen, only a jagged hole where what looked like wild dogs had attacked her, tearing and rending her flesh from her body.

"Holy shit, Sandy. You're mother; what happened?"

Sandy's reply was to lunge at him like a sprinter at the sound of the starting gun. Gene was caught off guard and he was thrown backwards with Sandy on top of him. At first he tried to fend her off, not understanding what was happening, but then some of the ketchup on her chin dripped into his open mouth. Instead of tasting the tangy spices of the confection, he tasted copper, realization flashing through his mind instantly.

It wasn't ketchup on the door jamb or on her body, and he was positive what she was covered in was blood—Agnes' blood.

Then he had no time for thought as Sandy tried to sink her teeth into his throat. He used the flowers like a bat, slapping her on the side of the face, but all that happened was the stems broke, the flower pedals evaporating, loose pedals drifting to the floor like feathers.

As he swiped at her again, one of the thorns on a rose stem caught her open right eye and tore it sideways; opening the orb up like it had been sliced by a tiny knife. Clear ooze dripped out and Sandy roared in either anger or pain.

Gene was still slapping her with the flowers, the pedals falling around him like snow, and when they were nothing but small nubs, he dropped them, the stems falling around him.

Sandy was still trying to eat him, as unbelievable as that seemed, and her teeth clacked on empty air as he fought to keep her at bay. He hit her with the box of chocolates, but the box was weak and it broke open, chocolates falling onto his chest and around his head. All the while Sandy hopped on top of him, desperately trying to sink her bloody teeth into his flesh.

He managed to get his left hand under her chin and try to push her off, but her weight on him was at such a point that he couldn't get any leverage. She was about the same size as him, though was curvaceous like a woman should be, and he was evenly matched as long as he was trapped on the floor.

Her teeth clicked shut an inch from his ear and he winced, expecting to feel pain, then he shoved her away again. His free hand reached out; all that was close was the scattered chocolates, so he grabbed some with his hand and brought them up. When she came at him, he shoved the chocolates into her mouth, her teeth clamping down on a pink nougat and apricot swirl.

Now she couldn't bite him; her mouth full of chocolate.

That gave him an idea and he quickly reached out for more stray candies. Finding three, he brought them up and forced them into her mouth. Her cheeks plumped up like she was a squirrel carrying nuts and she groaned and mewled like a wounded animal. It was obvious she didn't want sweets, she wanted meat…his meat to be exact, and not in a good way.

He forced the candy deep into her mouth, a peanut brittle and a chocolate nougat becoming squished, her cheeks stretched so thin it looked like they were going to blow out.

As she fought him, she shifted her body, and he took the opportunity to throw her off. She rolled to the side and he got on top of her, now having the upper hand. Not knowing what to do next, he continued doing what he'd been doing, and that was force-feeding her candies.

With his legs on both sides of her chest, and his butt on her breasts, he reached out with both hands and grabbed more candy. Then, with a rueful look, he shoved them into her mouth and down her throat. Peach nougat, dark chocolate and the dreaded lemon crèmes, were squished and pressed into her mouth. Some of the chocolaty clump began to work its way down her throat and it looked like there was an apple in there.

The entire time he shoved candy into her mouth, tears fell down his cheeks. He knew she was suffocating, her airway clogged with chocolate and nougat. As he shoved more and more candy into her mouth, he didn't hear the soft footsteps coming up behind him.

But he did feel the strong white teeth of Agnes when she sank them an inch deep into the back of his neck.

He cried out in pain and surprise and punched back with his free hand. He caught Agnes in the nose and it fractured, now looking like she had run into a glass door and smashed her face like putty. But she barely felt the blow and an instant later was jumping on Gene's back, her teeth tearing off his right ear and woofing it down like taffy.

Gene roared with pain and terror as he tried to get her off him, but she was like a gymnast, her wiry body moving about. As he fell off Sandy, she got up, soon coming for him, too.

As the two women began to tear into him, sharp, manicured fingernails like small razor blades, he thought back to a wet dream he'd had a few months ago.

Back then he had dreamt of a mother-daughter tag-team, with him in the middle, but this wasn't what he had dreamed about.

Agnes came around to face him, and Gene got a good look at her torn-out torso, her insides dripping and sagging like a rotting pumpkin. Her lungs glistened in the light of the living room, her rib cage cracked open like a spent turkey carcass on Thanksgiving.

Gene managed one last look as both mother and daughter growled at him, then Agnes sank her fingers into his eyes as Sandy brought her mouth down over his in a perverse French kiss.

As she sank her teeth onto his lips, melted chocolate seeped from her mouth, soon to mix with his blood. When she lifted her head and sat up, his lips stretched like taffy, until like an elastic at its limit, the flesh parted, leaving him forever grinning with no lips. He screamed in pain as blood mixed with chocolate flooded into his mouth, the world forever dark thanks to Agnes plucking out his eyes.

Agnes shoved both morsels into her mouth, the orbs popping like grapes. She chewed merrily as viscous ooze dribbled down her chin. Agnes had once been a polite eater, but now she was just shameless.

Gene screamed again, his tongue protruding from his mouth and flapping past his lipless mouth, and was rewarded with Sandy leaning down and clamping her chocolate-covered teeth on his tongue.

Bleached enamel sliced the tongue in half, and she wolfed it down, the lump in her throat growing ever larger. It appeared the candy hadn't made it through her esophagus and now all the flesh she consumed was becoming impacted, like rush hour gridlock in Boston.

Of course, Gene didn't know any of this.

His torn throat was still pumping blood, and as each squirt bathed the carpeting, a little more of his life's fluid seeped out.

Agnes and Sandy went in for more, again and again, teeth and fingers finding flesh. It was Agnes who bit off his dick, chewing on it like it was the best summer sausage she'd ever had. By then, thankfully, Gene was past feeling anything.

His heels were tapping a steady drum roll on the floor and his blood had ceased to pour from him.

Agnes leaned over and pulled Gene's right hand to her mouth, biting off the first three digits. Finger food at its truest form, the mature woman chewed happily, crunching on bones like they were pretzels dipped in blood.

The mother-daughter team ate heartily for the next hour, and when Gene was all but consumed, they stood up. Agnes' belly was distended from all the human meat she'd consumed and Sandy's throat had indeed blown out, chocolate and partially eaten flesh now dripping out of the open wound.

No matter how much she tried to eat, it would only fall out of her neck hole, and there was no way for the mindless woman to realize her dilemma. But still she would try, until the end of time if she was allowed.

Mother and daughter moved to the front door of the apartment, which was still partially open from Gene entering, and both stepped out into the hallway.

Other doors were opening now as tenants, once dead and then revived, joined Sandy and Agnes in the hallway.

As one crowd, similar to a high school band, all the people turned to their right and marched towards the stairwell door.

Upon reaching it, one pushed it open, by luck or design, and each of them filed down the staircase to the street below.

By the time they reached the street and the light of day, more screams of chaos filled the air. Sirens wailed, people screamed, and humans dying was the status quo, and with barely a nod to one another, the tenants joined the fray, feeding, killing, and eating.

For this would be a Valentine's Day to remember, where the tagline should be, *You always hurt the one you love….*or was that *eat* them?

WHAT COMES AROUND. . .

The rotting head exploded like a ripe melon, spraying blood and brains across the alley wall behind it. Gobbets of flesh and brain matter dripped down the brick wall, leaving slimy snail trail patterns.

The body swayed on its feet before tumbling hard to the ground, blood now seeping out to stain the cobblestones lining the alley a dark brown.

"Take that, you dead bastard!" Miles Carson yelled as he lowered his M-16 and flicked it from semi auto back to full auto. It had been a tricky shot from where he stood, but he'd managed it. He was just under six feet, with broad shoulders and dark hair. A deep scar was on the left side of his face, running from his temple to his upper lip, a memento of a past battle he barely survived.

"Lucky, is what it was," Jones said from his side. He was a tall, black man with a perpetual scowl.

"Real lucky," Tammy added for the hell of it. She had ivory skin, brown, shoulder-length hair and a slim figure that made most men drool.

"Bullshit, it was skill," Miles said in his defense.

"Maybe," Scott said, not too sure himself. He shook his head, his blonde hair waving in the wind, crystal blue eyes twinkling in a way that made women melt.

The group of four hunters continued across the street as the herd of a dozen ghouls turned upon seeing them. The rest of the street was empty of pedestrians.

It usually was when a zombie sighting was announced.

Though the dead walked, it wasn't like they were everywhere. Sure, they were around, but as each year went by their numbers were shrinking.

'Course, back in the beginning it wasn't like that. Then they were everywhere, eating people and just making a nuisance of themselves. Not to mention when they bit someone and the victim got away. That was the worst. No one had known at the beginning to be bit was a death sentence, but now it was well documented.

If you got bit, you got a bullet in the head, immediately if possible.

No one wanted to take a chance you would turn when no one was around and you would end up biting more people. If that happened, the outbreak could start all over again. And no one wanted that.

And that was why hunters were created. Mercenaries hired by the cities and states across the country for the sole purpose of eradicating the walking dead. Sure, the police would help, but they had their hands full with the day to day crap, such as domestic violence and robberies. They didn't have enough manpower to fight the ghouls, too.

With no one but the four hunters on the street, the zombies turned together and began moving in slow, lurching motions towards them. Miles chuckled as he watched the rotting piles of shit stumbling across the road. One tripped, its face going splat onto the pavement. Pus and something that was once blood shot out of the shattered nose to splash onto the street. But the zombie felt no pain, and its brethren moved on by, ignoring it. Slowly, it ponderously climbed to its feet again, only now a slime trail dripped down the front of its torso like someone had turned on a spicket just a fraction.

Tammy raised her pump-action shotgun, prepared to take out the first body in line when Miles held up his hand.

"No, wait, give 'em some more time to get closer. Let's not screw around here. Let's take 'em down all at once and then we're outta here," Miles said.

Miles was the team leader, and had become one because of his skill with killing the undead. No one could take out a group of ghouls like him; no one. He was quick on his feet and a damn good shot, plus he felt absolutely no compassion for the pieces of shit. They may have been human once, but all they were now were just rotting piles of pus wrapped in what looked like human skin, though now with flesh peeling off their bones like rotting fruit.

"Fine with me," Scott said with a grin. "I got a date with the waitress from the diner we were at this morning."

"You mean the red head with the big…" Miles held his hands in front of his chest to Tammy's annoyance.

Scott nodded. "The one and the same."

"So how did you manage to hook this one?" Jones asked. He had always been slightly jealous of Scott's pretty boy looks, what with the deep blue eyes, strong physique and hair that any man would kill to have, let alone a woman.

Scott chuckled. "That's the funny thing, she picked me up. Go figure; guess I'm gettin' so good at it I don't even have to talk to 'em."

"Oh, please, the only thing she did was sense how desperate you are," Tammy commented as she hefted her shotgun. The ghouls were still twenty feet away and making time like old men out for a morning constitutional.

Scott checked his Browning high-power to make sure it was loaded, though he'd checked it no more than ten minutes ago. It was a nervous tick and it was tantamount to OCD. The others didn't mind though. If the man needed to check his ammo, then who were they to judge?

A moan carried on the wind and the hunters glanced to the zombies. They were still a good fifteen feet away, taking their sweet time like they were union workers going to work, and they'd get there when they got there.

Jones raised his .38 Smith and Wesson, getting ready for the slaughter to come. With four well armed hunters against even a dozen unarmed zombies, the outcome was pretty much assured, still, to get careless could get you dead.

Not that Jones wasn't careful. He wore a heavy leather jacket with reinforcement on the arms in case teeth tried to get at his tender flesh beneath the material. The knees of his pants had small metal plates sewn into them, just perfect for using when he slammed his knee into a ghoul's nose after a kick to the gut to get one to bend forward. Yup, he wasn't gonna take chances with his beautiful body.

Unlike Scott who stood next to him in a t-shirt and jeans. The man was a maverick and wouldn't listen to reason, despite protocol making him wear protective clothing. Miles had written him up more than once and finally decided, fuck it. If the guy wanted to run around unprotected, that was his problem.

"Are they close enough yet?" Tammy asked as she racked a shell into the chamber, then ejected it, then slid it back into the breech. That was her nervous tick; she liked knowing she had a fresh shell in the chamber.

"Just about," Miles replied as he flicked the selector from single and auto shot. He had a tick too, though it wasn't as pronounced. He shifted his stance as he braced the stock of the M-16 against his shoulder.

"Let them come to you," his former team leader had told him. "They're too stupid to understand they're walking to their own demise, just be patient and it all comes together."

Miles had nodded at his mentor's words, and so far his instructor had been correct. It was a damn shame when the man had been bit and put down like a mangy dog.

That was the downside to being a hunter. If you got bit, you got a bullet in the head, no wasting away, no tearful goodbyes.

No one wanted to take a chance you might revive and escape. It had happened in the past before protocol had been changed. A hunter had been bit and taken to the hospital. He'd been treated, but when he died and returned, he'd run amuck in the hospital, attacking the patients like they were lambs to the wolf. A child had been infected as well and the news had covered it for weeks.

Something about a child dying always got people worked up.

The ghouls were almost upon them and weapons were raised, but then the sound of a motorcycle filled the street and Miles turned to his right, his mouth opening in shock to see a helmet-less rider coming down the street.

The rider was a man, and he had on headphones, his head nodding to music only he could hear. His eyes were staring straight ahead and Miles realized the idiot wasn't paying attention. The rider must have seen the ghouls and just assumed they were people, not walking corpses.

Miles raised his hands into the air, yelling out to the rider, but the man was oblivious, unaware of his surroundings.

But his surroundings were aware of him, and as he drove up and was planning to drive past the ghouls, two animated corpses at the rear of the pack suddenly spun around and reached out their hands, grabbing the rider by his left arm and yanking him from the motorcycle.

The bike continued onward, now without a rider, and it veered to the left and crashed into a parked car, the driver's side window imploding from the impact. The bike toppled to the street, the rear tire spinning impotently as the engine died.

And so too did the rider, dying that is, as the ghouls swarmed over him and began tearing him apart, ripping his arms and legs off with what seemed like super human strength, but was in fact just basic physics of tactile pressure. Once the man's skin and muscle had been chewed into, taking some of the flesh away, it wasn't hard to worry away the limb from its socket. It was much like when a fresh tree branch has been cut halfway and you now have to twist it around and around to get it to separate, while usually the bark, still supple, is hanging on till the last moment.

That was what was happening to the motorcycle rider, and then some, as each of his limbs were ripped out in bloody sprays of scarlet. The man screamed of course, they all do, long and loud, but soon it was replaced by bloody garbles as the dead hands began ripping into his torso, cracking his rib cage and diving into the warm innards that had kept this man functioning his entire life. But now the parts of the living machine were being dismantled and the man was finding that without certain parts, he couldn't remain functioning. Spitting a gout of blood from his mouth, he gasped loudly and succumbed to death, all within the breadth of less than a minute.

The zombies wasted no time, they were hungry, and when they had meat, they dove in with a ferocity that belayed their slow, lumbering gate.

"Holy shit, did you see that?" Jones gasped as he watched the man being torn apart in the span of a minute.

"Yeah, I did, I'm fucking standing right here," Miles shot back. He raised his M-16. "Take the fuckers out!"

As a well drilled team, each of the group raised their weapons, and began firing, sending a barrage of lead into the undead bodies. One ghoul received ten shots to the torso, then the bullets climbed higher until one found its face. The lead slug impacted just above the bridge of the nose and the head exploded, like internal pressure had been too much. Brains and bone fragments went in all directions, splattering the other ghouls like dark rain.

The next ghoul in line had both its arms blown off, the shattered bone now peering through the rotting meat like a baby bird from its nest. But the shooter wasn't finished and five more rounds found the body, taking off the ghoul's knees and then finishing with a shot to the head. The rest of the ghouls received similar punishment, their bodies becoming nothing but rotting hamburger as round after round found the soft, putrid flesh.

When the targets were taken down, Miles held up an arm, yelling to the others. "Hold your fire; hold your fire, that's enough!"

Scott was still firing, lost in a world of death, so Miles turned and moved so close to the man he could smell his aftershave. "I said enough, goddamn it! Cease fucking fire!"

Scott stopped, blinking as he came back to reality. The air was filled with cordite mixed with decay, a smoke cloud drifting over the hunters until a gentle breeze began washing it away.

The bodies were still settling; a slurping sound coming from them as the built up gases inside the rotting corpses began to escape. The miasma of rotting meat was almost overwhelming, but the hunters had seen and smelled it all before and took it in stride.

"If you got so much damn energy, Scott," Miles shouted. "Then you can go see if that guy is still alive, though I doubt it." He gestured to the motorcycle rider.

"Not a prob'," Scott said with a grin and jogged away from the others. He flashed Tammy a grin. "Now don't shoot me in the back, honey."

She rolled her eyes. "Don't tempt me," she muttered.

Scott crossed the short distance in a few seconds and then slowly stepped over the prone corpses, his Browning pointed at each head as he did so. He was ready if one of the ghouls decided it wasn't quite dead yet.

When he reached the motorcycle rider, he bent over to inspect the man. His torso was torn open and his limbs had been dragged away before the ghouls were taken down. The man's eyes were closed, as if he'd realized he was dead and wanted to save anyone the trouble of having to do it for him.

Scott was standing over the corpse while shaking his head. "Poor bastard," he muttered. Turning, he called out to the others. "He's dead, shit, beyond dead," Scott quipped with a smirk.

But Scott had been lazy this time out, a tad too cocky, and he wasn't paying attention when the eyelids of the rider snapped open and glazed eyes of death began to look around. Before Scott knew what was happening behind him, the torso shifted and Scott felt a sharp pain in his calf, just above his ankle.

Spinning, he stared in shock at the reanimated biker now with a chunk of his pants and skin in its mouth, and with a muffled curse as he fell backwards, he lowered the Browning and shot the biker from less than two feet. The round entered the top of the open mouth and blew off the ghoul's jaw, teeth and pieces of tongue splattering the road, along with a generous helping of pink brains.

Scott was off balance, and he fell heavily to the pavement as the rest of his team, upon seeing what had happened, charged to his aid.

Sitting on his butt, Scott stared down with wide eyes at his bleeding leg, knowing what it would mean to his future, or lack of one.

Tammy, Miles and Jones reached him and all three gazed down at his leg.

"Oh, Scott, oh no," Tammy gasped when she saw the seeping wound.

"Shit, Scott…" Jones said, but he couldn't say another word, knowing what the bite meant.

Miles moved closer, pushing the other two back a little. As Scott looked up with tears of fear, he found himself staring down the barrel of Miles' M-16.

"Miles, what the hell are you doing?" Jones asked askance of him, not understanding. Miles ignored the question, his jaw hard; his eyes cold.

"Sorry, Scott, you know what happens next," Miles said softly, his voice strong and sure. There was no hesitation as his finger squeezed the trigger.

"No, Miles, wait, don't...!" Scott yelled as he raised his left hand in front of his face to stop the slug. But it did nothing, like trying to protect himself with a piece of paper. The slug went through the palm of his hand and entered his skull just to the left of his right eye. There was a loud retort and then a splat as the back of his skull was sent across the pavement to mix with the gobbets of rotten meat already there. The man's head, what was left of it, rocked to the side and the body slumped forward, a geyser of blood shooting from the jagged hole, spewing into the air as it slowly receded like a spent fire hose.

The others stood in shock, seeing their leader take down one of their own and it was Jones who spun on his heels and shoved Miles away, knocking the rifle to the side.

"What the fuck, Miles? Why in God's name did you do that?" Jones screamed.

"He's right!" Tammy yelled. "You just shot Scott down in cold blood. Why would you do that, Miles? Why?"

Miles looked to his two remaining team members and frowned, his eyes creasing with anger.

"Why? Are you two blind? He was bit. You hear me? Bit! We all know what happens when someone gets bit. I did what had to be done!"

Jones shook his head as he waved Miles reply away. "That's horseshit, man. Yeah he was bit, but he wasn't gonna turn in a minute. There was time. Time for him to say some goodbyes, to get his shit in order, maybe send a few letters to his family or something before he had to be put down."

Miles shook his head. "That's bullshit, Jones, and you know it. Every one of us should have all our shit in order each time we go out on a hunt, simple as that. We all know the risks and we all agreed to take them. So did Scott. The arrogant bastard got lazy and now he's dead, end of story. Now that's enough, from both of you. You can think whatever you want but at the end of the day this is my team and I call the shots. You hear me?" He was looking at both Tammy and Jones, his eyes flicking from one to the other. "That's the job, deal with it or get the fuck out."

Jones held Miles' gaze and it seemed he wasn't going to back down, but eventually he looked down, nodding slowly. Tammy did the same and Miles nodded. "Good, now that that's settled, let's call this in. We need a cleanup crew down here ASAP," he snapped, his patience gone for the moment.

Tammy pulled her two-way radio from her hip and called it in while Jones stood silently, staring down at Scott.

This time Miles said nothing. In his heart he knew where Jones was coming from, but sometimes it was better to do it quick, before the victim knows its coming. Scott would have wasted away, and in a few days would have been put down like a dog, and the entire time he would have known it was coming, like a massive sword hanging over his head just waiting to be dropped at some unknown time. Deep down in his gut, Miles knew he'd done Scott a favor, though at the moment it didn't feel that way.

"They say they'll be here in ten," Tammy told Miles as she hung the radio back on her hip.

"Hmmph, we'll see if they get here on time for a change," Miles replied as he walked away to check the corpses one last time.

Jones watched Miles walk away, Tammy by his side.

"Miles is an asshole, Tammy. He didn't have to do that. He didn't have to take Scott out like he was no better than one of them," he gestured to one of the prone corpses.

Tammy didn't reply, she just turned and walked away, leaving Jones alone to stare at the destroyed head of Scott, who had been one of his best friends. He decided right then and there that if there was a God in Heaven then Miles would get what's coming to him one of these days, but he knew that probably wouldn't happen.

Unlike in the movies, this was real life. And in real life the asshole rarely got what was coming to him.

The three remaining team members waited for twenty minutes for the cleanup crew to arrive, the flies gathering on the corpses by the hundreds. Now that the excitement was over, the civilians in the nearby buildings began to filter out, wanting to see the carnage for themselves.

Miles knew the cleanup crew would have to set up police tape to keep the gawkers away while they wrapped the bodies in black plastic and tossed them into the back of black vans. Then they would be taken to an undisclosed location where they would be incinerated and the ashes stored in metal drums. The reason the dead walked was still unknown and all authority figures had agreed scattering the ashes would be a mistake, as would burying them. So treating the remains like hazardous waste seemed the best way to go.

Scott's body would be given a proper funeral, but it wouldn't be buried. After the funeral, the body would be taken away and destroyed like the others, but he would receive a grand send off. He had died in the line of duty and in the end that was what any hunter could hope for.

The ride back to the base was quiet, neither Jones or Tammy speaking, and Miles wasn't trying to strike up a conversation with either of them.

Miles weaved the black SUV through traffic, sometimes cutting another vehicle off. He wasn't worried. No one would bother him, he was a hunter after all.

The police were given strict orders not to bother official hunter vehicles. Other than a small decal on the license plate, no one knew who was inside the dark SUV.

And Miles should know the rules of the police force; he'd been a cop for more than ten years, until he abandoned the force to become a hunter.

The SUV pulled into a gravel driveway that led around a large factory. In the back, hidden from the street, was a nondescript one-story warehouse. Where it had once been used for storage, now it was the base for the hunters of this city.

Miles pulled into a spot near the main doors and turned off the engine. Next to him was Tammy, and as he turned to look at her, she was already opening her door and stepping out onto the driveway. Jones made a disgusted sound from behind him and did the same, slamming his door closed and leaving Miles alone in the SUV. Miles watched his two teammates walk to the door and enter the building, neither sparing him a glance.

He let out a heavy sigh.

What happened to Scott sucked but it happened, there was no way to ignore it. He knew his teammates would accept it in time, but until then he had a feeling he was going to be the scapegoat.

Opening his door, he nodded to himself, accepting the blame if that was what it took to keep his team together. He would just have to be patient until both Jones and Tammy came to realize he'd done what was necessary.

Opening the door to the warehouse, he stepped inside the large building. Sections were partitioned off for office space, a gym, showers, and storage, as well as the armory and garage. They were entirely self contained, even down to a generator in the back, in case power went out for some reason. And it had in the past. Back when the outbreak first began, the city had been in chaos and it was all the police could do to maintain order. He remembered those times with a pang of loss, but for another reason he didn't want to think about. So he forced the images back down from whence they came and focused on the here and now.

Stepping up to a desk just off the entrance, a seated man in his sixties with large muscular arms and a thinning pate greeted him.

"Hey, Miles, sorry about Scott, that sucks," Pat Collins said in a soft voice. "He was good guy."

Miles smiled wanly. He and Pat went way back. Pat had been a detective on the force and Miles had worked a few cases now and then with the grizzled vet when he'd been first on the scene. But of course uniforms wouldn't stay for long. Once the scene was cleared they would move on, letting the detectives get to work. Now Pat was his superior and they had a good working relationship.

"Thanks, Pat, yeah, he was. He'll be missed," Miles said, remembering the look in Scott's eyes before he'd blown his head off.

Pat smiled wanly and Miles moved on. He was tired and wanted a shower.

Tammy and Jones were somewhere in the building, and unless an alert came in, there would be no reason for him to find them. As team leader it was his job to fill out the reports about what happened today.

Detouring to the armory, he dropped off his M-16, then headed for the locker room. Once there, he stripped and entered the shower, a large tiled room with multiple shower heads on both sides. His M-16 would now remain locked up in the armory and would stay there until needed. They had a weaponsmith who would clean it, oil it, and make sure it was ready when he needed it again.

Letting the warm spray cascade over his body, he pressed both hands against the tiles and closed his eyes. As the water pummeled his head, he attempted to block the images of Scott's pleading face before it was shattered into a hundred bloody chunks.

With his eyes closed, thoughts of his family came to him. And though he tried to force them back down, they bubbled forth to the top, like oil mixed with water.

It had been a year ago that he'd lost his family to the ghouls.

He had been at work, trying to quell a riot, when the undead bastards had managed to get onto his street. His wife was careless and left the back door open to let in some fresh air, and though he'd yelled at her constantly about keeping the house secure, she had a mind of her own, and said she refused to live in fear.

What actually happened to his wife and son that day was unknown, as he only had the remains of their bodies to use to piece together what had occurred. As far as he, and the forensics team that had done the investigation could tell, the zombies had entered through the rear door, had found his wife in the kitchen and had ripped her apart, leaving only bloody bones and rags of material in their wake. With the death of his wife, her screams filling the house, his one-year-old son had woken from his nap. He began to cry in his bedroom, and like a dinner bell, the ghouls had followed the sound until reaching the crib.

There had been nothing left for the CSI crew to use for identification but a few baby teeth and one tiny fingernail.

Miles had quit the force that day, too distraught with grief to work another hour. He'd moved from the blood soaked house to a low rent apartment and wallowed in misery for the next six months.

That is until he had heard about a new squad being assembled to hunt the ghouls. With only anger now driving him, he'd signed up and in less than a month had become the leader of his squad.

Shaking his head to clear away the painful thoughts, the water washed away any tears that seeped from saddened eyes. He gritted his teeth and stood tall, the water sluicing off his hard body.

Deciding he'd had enough of walking down the horror that was his personal memory lane, he left the shower and toweled off, then dressed in a clean black jumpsuit; the same outfit all hunters wore when they were off duty.

Inside the building, he didn't carry his M-16, instead preferring to simply wear a sidearm.

So after strapping on a flat-black finished S&W .38 with a chrome grip securely in a shoulder holster, he went to his office to do the paperwork which followed every engagement with the walking dead.

As he walked through the building, he passed the familiar faces of other hunters who were off duty. He nodded politely, a few muttering greetings as he made his way. It was when he passed the gym that he slowed, hearing something different from the odd grunts and groans of exertion he would normally hear. Poking his head through the doorway, his eyes went wide when he saw a ghoul chained to the wall, another hunter standing only a few feet away. With a deep scowl, Miles entered the room, his eyes watching the ghoul warily.

"What the fuck is going on here, Buchanan?" Miles snapped at the younger man.

Buchanan was in his twenties with light blonde hair that was so fine it looked like it was spun from gold. His complexion was so pale he looked like he had lived his entire life indoors, and the freckles on his cheeks were the only color therein.

"Oh, hey, Miles, what's up?"

Miles blinked in blatant surprise. "What's up? That's all you have to say to me?" He pointed to the ghoul. "What the fuck is that doing in here?"

"Who, him?" He gestured to the ghoul that was obviously male. The strong shoulders and broad chest were a dead giveaway. And if that wasn't enough to identify gender, then the open zipper on its pants and the sagging penis would have settled the discussion. The smell of rot filled the air, only Miles' hardened sinuses able to ignore it.

Buchanan continued. "Me and a few of the guys thought it would be great if the newbies could practice with a real one. You know, so when they're in the field they won't be so surprised."

Miles stared at the man, then turned his attention to the ghoul. It was chained to the wall like a dog, the leash straining on its rings. The moaning and wailing was filled with anger, like a hungry guard dog who just wanted to take a piece out of your ass.

Miles never hesitated. Drawing his .38, he took five steps towards the ghoul, raised the muzzle to its forehead and squeezed the trigger.

Brains shot out the back of the rotting skull to splash on the wall like stewed tomatoes. Bits of faded white mixed in with the browns and reds to make a kaleidoscope of gore. Maggots crawled around in the brain matter, still feeding on the putrid meat.

"Holy shit!" Buchanan screamed. "What the fuck did you do that for?"

"'Cause there's only one way I want to see those things, and that's in pieces. Don't ever bring one of them in here without my say so, you hear me?" His eyes were hard.

Any more protest fled Buchanan when he saw the visage of anger in Miles' face, not to mention the .38, which was suspiciously hovering in his direction.

"Yeah, man, I hear you. This isn't over though. Collins is gonna hear about this."

Miles barely twitched an eye. "See that he does. He knows how I feel. As far as I'm concerned this shit is over, Buchanan. Do us both a favor and leave it that way." Without waiting for a reply, he spun on his heels and exited the room, while behind him, brains slid down the wall like spilt porridge.

Miles dropped down behind his metal desk and sighed wearily.

His mind was racing with what had just happened. Imagine, Buchanan actually bringing one of the dead bastards into the building with them. The man had never been that bright, but this was a new low for him.

Letting out another sigh, he reached over and opened a drawer to get the correct form for his report of the day's events. He always found it odd that though he now lived in a world where the dead walked, he still had to fill out paperwork on a daily basis. As he began writing, his eyes caught the one picture of his wife and son on his desk. Though he tried to ignore it, for some reason today the images of the past were particularly strong.

Setting down the pen, he reached out and picked up the photo, staring into the small eyes of his wife. Even tiny, they were still the clearest blue he had ever seen. He reached out and touched the photo, his fingertip caressing her cheek, then it slid to his son in her arms, touching the pouting chin and chubby face.

Realizing what he was doing to himself, he set the picture down, this time laying it flat. Sometimes he didn't know why he kept the photo on his desk, as it only brought back bad memories. But then, if he didn't remember them, who would?

He looked up at the sounds of some kind of commotion coming from down the hallway, roughly where the main doors to the building were. At first he ignored it, knowing Pat could handle it, but as the voices grew more heated he decided to check it out. Maybe he could help.

Reaching up with his right hand to touch his .38, he strode out of his office to the front of the building, where Pat and Jones were standing together with a woman. Pat appeared to be trying to calm the woman down. Miles couldn't see who the woman was just yet, as Pat was blocking his view of her, but then she shifted on her feet and Miles realized it was Claire, Scott's younger sister.

Walking up behind Pat, Claire's eyes went wide when she spotted Miles.

"You, you bastard, you killed him!" she screamed as she pushed away from Pat and dashed up to Miles. "You killed my brother, you piece of shit!" Tears rolled down her cheeks and her eyes were red as she began slapping his chest.

Miles turned to Pat who only shrugged, then he let his eyes wander to Jones who stood to the side with arms crossed over his chest, his jaw tight. Miles picked up the gesture immediately. Jones told Claire that he had put Scott down.

"I'm sorry, Claire, I had no choice, he'd been bit," Miles said, his voice cold.

"Bullshit, that's bullshit and you know it!" she screamed as she slumped to her knees, leaning against him as she cried, her shoulders trembling from loss.

Pat moved up behind her and took her into his arms. "Come with me, darlin', let's get you a glass of water, there, there," Pat whispered as he half-dragged, half-carried her down the hall to a small room used for conferences and sometimes a place for off duty hunters to hangout.

Miles watched Claire go, and when she disappeared through the doorway, he spun on his heels and charged Jones, slamming the man up against the wall.

"You prick, why the fuck would you tell her I killed her brother?"

Jones sneered widely. "What's wrong, you ashamed 'bout what you did?"

"Hell no, he was bit, he had to be killed, you know that. Shit, if it happened to me I'd want you to do the same thing," Miles reasoned.

Jones reached under Miles' arms and pushed the man off him.

"Hmm, we'll see," he muttered.

Miles stared at him hard. "What the fuck does that mean?"

"Nothing, Miles, it doesn't mean a goddamn thing. Look, I don't care what you said after killing Scott, you could have waited. Scott was just bit. He still had time. He could have said his goodbyes, is all. You took that away from him. In my eyes you murdered him in cold blood, plain and simple."

"I murdered him?" Miles gasped. "You're joking."

Now it was Jones' turn to go on the offensive. He stepped into Miles, making the man move backwards and Jones shoved his index finger into Miles' chest.

"I don't joke about a member of our team getting killed, Miles, and don't you forget it." Without waiting for a reply, he turned and strode away, leaving Miles standing alone, still wanting to finish their argument.

"This isn't over!" Miles called to Jones' back.

"No, it isn't," Jones replied, but never slowed his pace.

Miles stood perfectly still, his breathing still coming hard as adrenalin pumped through his system. After more than a minute and he was still alone, he decided there was no point in staying where he was, so he headed back to his office. As he walked, he could still hear Claire's sobs as if they were following him. He ignored them.

Miles had barely managed to get comfortable in his office when an alarm began to sound.

He knew that siren well. It was a call for the on duty hunter team to suit up, it was go time.

Jumping up from his desk, he dashed out of the room and towards the armory, wanting to retrieve his M-16 after suiting up in his tactical gear. Upon arriving, Jones and Tammy were waiting. Tammy was taking her shotgun from the man in the armory, a short, stocky fellow Miles only knew as Tom. If the man was married or had a family, Miles didn't know or care.

Tammy flashed Miles a cold stare when he stepped up to get his weapon. Tom knew Miles well and was already reaching for the M-16.

"Here ya go, sir, all cleaned and greased," Tom said with a smile.

"Thanks, appreciate it," Miles replied, though his eyes were cold.

Miles turned to Jones and Tammy, both waiting in the hallway.

"You two ready to do this? We need to be a team. What happened to Scott sucks, but whatever shit you two feel about it needs to stay here. You read me?"

Jones seemed like he was going to protest, but then he nodded. "Yeah, Miles, I'm cool."

"Me too, what's done is done," Tammy said.

"Good, then let's head out," Miles said and spun on his heels as he headed for the garage and their SUV. Since arriving back at the base, the SUV had been taken into the garage, cleaned and the fuel topped off.

When they reached the garage, Pat was waiting, another man standing by his side. The man was closer to a boy, really, no more than nineteen or twenty.

"Who's this?" Miles asked, impatient to get moving. There was an outbreak somewhere in the city and every second they took to get there could mean someone's death. People could die, people like his wife and child.

No, he wouldn't go there, not now.

Now he needed to get hard, to focus on the mission.

"This is Joseph," Pat said. "He's Scott's replacement."

"Jesus, Pat, that's fast, isn't it? The guy just died a few hours ago," Miles said as he gestured for Pat to walk a few feet away from the others so they could talk privately. Miles stared at the new recruit the entire time.

"Maybe so," Pat said. "But you know hunters are four man teams. You're down one man so he's here to fill the open slot. Make him feel welcome, no one wants to join a team under these circumstances."

Miles didn't reply, but just glared at Pat.

"He looks green, he got any experience?"

Pat shook his head. "Nah, he's fresh from training."

All hunters went through an intensive one month training course with firearms and hand-to-hand combat. The fact the man had passed said he wasn't a total loser, but still, only real action hardened a man and made him so you could entrust your life in his hands.

"Christ, Pat, I don't have time for this. I don't need to nursemaid some damn kid," Miles spat.

Pat handed Miles a piece of paper with the location and relevant information about the outbreak. "Take this and get going, and the kid comes with you. I don't want to hear anymore shit about this, Miles. Last time I checked, you still take orders from me. After what happened with Scott, you shouldn't be on active duty, you know that. But we don't have time for an evaluation right now. We're low on manpower as it is." He slapped Miles on the shoulder, like a father would a son. "Listen, just keep the kid out of harms way. Surely you, Tammy and Jones can handle whatever comes around."

Jones, hearing his name perked up. "Hey," Jones called. "You two ladies done cackling or what? We gotta go."

Miles decided there was really no getting out of this. If Pat had his mind made up then that was that.

"Fine, Pat, I'll take him along," Miles said. "But he stays out of the fight unless there's no choice. I won't have him screwing up and either getting himself or another of my team killed."

"Fair enough," Pat grinned. "Now get going, there's a hell of an outbreak going on, you're needed out there. If it's worse than you think, make sure to call for backup, no Wild West crap."

Miles grinned as he turned away, heading to the SUV. He waved for the others to jump into the vehicle. "Hey, Pat, when do I ever not follow the manual?"

"Every damn time you go out," Pat replied. If you'd made Scott wear protective clothing he wouldn't have been bit in the first place.

Miles pace faltered but he forced himself to keep moving. He knew Pat was right, but he wouldn't admit it to the man. Jones was in the driver's seat, tapping the steering wheel impatiently.

Climbing into the passenger seat, Miles slammed the door.

Before the door latched, Jones was flooring the gas pedal, the SUV surging out of the garage with tires squealing. Miles looked over his left shoulder at the new recruit. He was sitting next to Tammy like they were a couple on their first date.

"So, kid, what was your name again?" Miles asked.

"Joseph, sir, Joseph Malone."

"Well, Joseph Malone, you ever see a real zombie?"

Joseph nodded. "Yes, sir, they had a few in training. They were in cages so we could see them up close, why?"

Miles chuckled as he glanced to Jones and Tammy, who shared a grin of their own. Both remembered their training like it was yesterday.

"'Cause seeing one in a cage isn't the same as when they're on the street tryin' to bite your ass off. When we get there, you do exactly what I say or so help me I'll shoot you myself, you hear me?"

"Yes, sir," Joseph said, swallowing a knot in his throat.

Miles glanced to Tammy who returned his gaze.

"You watch him, Tammy, he's your new puppy."

"Oh, Miles, come on, I…"

"Don't argue with me, goddamn it. I say he's your puppy, he's your puppy!" His tone was hard and Tammy cowed under the intensity.

"Yes, sir," she said softly, her jaw set.

Jones was weaving through the city streets, the siren on, lights flashing as they rushed to the center of the outbreak. While he drove at breakneck speed, Miles sat back, as relaxed as if he was on a slow country drive to the mountains.

Joseph leaned over so only Tammy could hear him. "What's a puppy mean?"

"It means you shadow me like you're a damn dog, that's what. When I move, you move, and when I stop, you do the same. Got me, puppy?"

He nodded. "Yes, ma'am, got it."

Miles found himself grinning in the front seat, having heard Joseph's words.

As the SUV rushed through the city, he studied the paper Pat had given him to get the full info on what they were heading into. As he began reading, the statistics, numbers sighted, and potential chances of casualties scrawled in Pat's neat script, he shook his head.

This looked to be one of the largest outbreaks in more than a year and he was going into it with two senior vets who were still upset with him and an untested rookie. Though he didn't know why, he had a bad feeling about this one, but then again, with everything that was going on against him, an upset gut seemed to be par for the course.

The outbreak was on the north side of town, near the water front.

By the time the SUV rolled up to the quarantined border, Miles had informed his team of what to expect.

The zombies had chosen a different path to access the city this day. Coming from the other side of the bay, more than seventy ghouls had walked out of the water to enter the exposed city.

This had never happened before and all of Miles' superiors, according to what he'd read, assumed this was just dumb luck. Evidently a ghoul had fallen into the water on the opposite shore and more had followed; the herd mentality. Not needing to breathe, the undead simply walked along the bottom of the bay until stepping out onto the far shore.

Now that the city was vulnerable from this side, it would be dealt with, but all of that was in the future. Miles was living in the present, and now it was his job to wipe out the dead bastards before they could cause more harm than they already had.

Police had set a perimeter around the infected area, four blocks from east to west, and so far the infestation had been contained. But the screams of its citizens inside the area being attacked and killed proved the situation had only begun.

With lights flashing on every squad car, Miles and his team climbed out of their SUV with weapons drawn, then approached the yellow tape cordoning off the area. All along the tape, cops with weapons ready waited for a ghoul to appear.

Miles found the officer in charge and showed him his credentials, not that they were needed. The captain knew of Miles, even if the knowledge wasn't reciprocated.

"Captain, what've you got?" Miles asked as his team moved up behind him. Jones was loaded for war this time, wearing a bandolier with ammo and five grenades hanging from a web belt. Tammy had two wicked looking blades hanging on both of her hips and her web belt was full with shotgun shells, set higher up on her waist for easy access. The new kid, Joseph, had a black plated .45 with a rubberized grip so sweaty hands could maintain control. On top of this he had a backup pistol strapped to his ankle and a long hunting knife on his hip. All four hunters were garbed in black, looking more like Navy Seals prepared to be inserted into a war zone...which wasn't far from the truth.

"Carson, good to see you again," the captain said as he held out his right hand for Miles to shake. Miles did and the men shared a reassuring grip.

"Same here, but what's going on, I need to know now," Miles said, all business.

The police captain frowned deeply as he took his hat off and wiped sweat from a furrowed brow.

"It's bad, Carson. The worst yet," the captain said. "There's got to be three score and then some skulking around in there." He gestured to the empty streets, only stray trash from overturned garbage cans blowing around when a particularly strong gust of wind came through. "We've got reports of more than two dozen casualties with probably double that not reported yet. The dead bastards came out of the bay. Now I ask you, how the hell did that happen?"

Miles shook his head and flashed Jones a hard look. The tall, dark man didn't return it, his gaze only for the streets on the other side of the yellow tape.

"Doesn't matter how it happened, Captain, all that matters is it has and now we need to deal with it. You got a map of the city on you?"

"Yeah, I do, follow me," the captain said and Miles and the others were led to a nearby squad car. Other officers watched with bland faces. Some were envious of the hunters, wanting to go inside the perimeter and kick some undead ass, but others had no problem with staying on the safe side of the tape.

Let the hunters risk their lives. That's what they got paid for; though to most cops the extra cash for hazardous pay wasn't enough to make it worthwhile.

The captain spread out a paper map on the hood of a squad car and pointed to a large red circle made with a colored pen.

"This is the area infected at the moment, but that could change if you don't stop this shit now," he said, glancing to Miles.

"Don't worry, Captain, when we're through in there all you're gonna need is a dozen meat wagons to clean up the mess." As he spoke, Miles studied the map, trying to get the lay of the land, so to speak. He tried to memorize where the backyards to homes were, where streets met with others; the four way intersections being the hardest to defend.

"Hey, kid, come over here," he said to Joseph. "Take a look at this map and learn it all, 'cause if you get separated from us this might just save your life."

"Yes, sir," Joseph said and moved closer. As for Tammy and Jones, both had seen all they needed. Jones had his .38 Smith and Wesson in his right hand, his knuckles tight as he squeezed the grip. He was anxious to get moving, his adrenal gland pumping like an out of control engine.

Five minutes later Jones had his wish, the four hunters crossing the police tape to enter the infected zone.

Miles was in the lead, with Tammy on his right. Jones was slightly on his left with Joseph in the rear.

There were more than a dozen bodies sprawled on the road, bullet-riddled corpses of ghouls that had tried to breach the perimeter and lost. The cops had taken them down with ease.

They hadn't walked thirty feet before the first walking corpse appeared, shambling out of an alley between two homes while holding a severed limb in its hands. Like a leg of beef, the ghoul was tearing into the flesh of the lower thigh, the sneaker of the leg's owner still attached. Bloody drool slid down the pale chin and Miles raised his M-16, sighted, and shot the dead bastard in the head. The round connected with the ghoul's forehead and the rear of the skull blew out like it was attached to a string yanked by a child playing tug of war. The body toppled to the ground, gobbets of chewed flesh seeping out of its open mouth.

"One down, a shitload to go," Miles said to the others.

Neither Miles nor Tammy replied and Joseph stared in amazement.

They continued moving deeper into the area, and wondering where all the zombies were, when a low moan came to their ears, drifting on the light breeze.

Each hunter looked to the other and then forward once more.

They were now a block into the infected zone. A wail added to the moan, followed by the sounds of dozens of feet slapping asphalt. There was another sound as well, similar to rubbing parchment. The flesh of the ghouls brushing against more flesh caused an odd sound, like rubbing sandpaper on wood. Though three of the hunters were hardened warriors, the rustling of the walking cadavers was unsettling.

"Keep an eye out, guys, they're coming," Miles said to the others.

And then they appeared; more than sixty ghouls, all shambling out from yards, side streets, and alleyways, where two homes were built with only a few feet separating one from the other.

They were a mottled parade of death and decay.

Some had faces covered in sloughing skin, their skulls peering through decayed flesh like wallpaper through ripped curtains in a dilapidated home. All the while, brown and yellow teeth stained red with fresh blood clacked like two dozen baby rattles. Many had arms missing, a few legs, though they dragged themselves along like worms, only their raw palms to propel them forward.

The hunters weren't worried, they were trained for this, but when the sounds of more bodies caused each of them to spin around to see more than thirty ghouls coming at them from behind, Miles realized they might have a problem.

Tammy hefted her shotgun, prepared to begin firing. "Should we call for backup, Miles?" she asked as she stared at the approaching dead.

"No, we can handle this, that's our job. Any one of you think we can't?" He glared at each of them, one at a time, but even Joseph held his ground, though his face was awash with concern.

"No, Miles, we got this, we got this by the ass," Jones said as he pulled a grenade from his bandolier. "So, are we gonna get this show started or what?"

His question was valid as the ghouls were only fifty feet away and closing.

"Okay, let's do this," Miles said. "Jones and Tammy, you take the front, Joseph, you're with me taking out the ones on our rear."

"Yes, sir," the recruit said.

Jones smiled widely, pulled the pin on the grenade and tossed it into the approaching horde. The grenade landed in the middle of the crowd, bounced once before hitting the leg of a zombie. It rebounded off the leg and came to rest, rocking slightly like a fallen hardboiled egg. The ghouls, oblivious to the small orb, walked past it, at least until the grenade went off, sending shrapnel into the closest bodies, obliterating the ones in the immediate blast radius and tearing off arms and legs like they were made of paper. As ten ghouls went down with missing limbs or were destroyed all together, Miles yelled for them to open fire.

Standing back to back, the four hunters began spraying lead into the approaching corpses, round after round finding a home.

Miles' vision was cloudy and he saw red, shooting ghoul after ghoul, wanting to destroy as many as he could. He remembered his wife and son, remembered how the dead had taken everything he'd ever loved. Now all he loved was death and revenge, and he was going to get his fill of both today.

The M-16 in his hands shifted back and forth, spraying 5.56 mm slugs of death and destruction into the rotting husks of the ghouls. Heads were blown off slumped shoulders, and ribcages were pulverized as bullet after bullet found its target.

Next to him, Joseph fired again and again, taking more care to only shoot the zombies in the head. He was falling back on his training and it was serving him well.

Tammy used her shotgun to take down multiple targets at once. Raising the barrel of the weapon to head height, she would take out two and three ghouls with a single shot, either destroying their heads or blinding them. Once blind, they were usually helpless, now only a danger if a human was foolish enough to stumble into their attack radius.

The odor of cordite mixed with the redolence of decay, rot and spent brass littered the streets around the four hunters.

While the zombies seemed endless, they were being kept at bay, and Miles saw some of the undead weren't originals. Many were the citizens who lived in the nearby homes, now returned from the dead to join their killers. If there was animosity to one another the dead didn't show it, and killer and victim alike attacked the four warriors.

Holding the M-16 at waist level, the rifle grew hot in Miles' hand as he sprayed the bodies with lead. He ignored the heat, riddling the corpses with steel death. And then a ghoul came at him from the left, and when he turned to blow its head off, instead of hearing the satisfying report of the rifle, there was only an ominous click.

In the heat of the battle he'd shot off the last rounds in the magazine. The ghoul was too close to ignore, and he knew there was no time to reach for his .38, so he swung the barrel of the rifle around in a horizontal swipe.

The large front sight on the barrel ripped open the ghoul's cheek from eye to jawline, but the zombie paid the wound no mind. Gritting his teeth in anger and frustration, Miles spun the weapon around and slammed the butt into the ghoul's jaw, the blow so hard it shattered the mandible, the slack jaw now hanging by pulverized joints.

Now with a moment to draw his .38, he whipped it up and shoved the muzzle under the hanging jaw, squeezing the trigger and sending the top of the ghoul's skull spinning through the air while droplets of red and black ichor flew off to spray other dead faces. The corpse fell backwards, but there were three more to take its place. Setting his jaw tight, Miles slapped in a new magazine for the M-16 and continued firing as the massive crowd of undead walkers came at him.

Jones screamed a war cry, reveling in the moment, shooting his .38 as fast as he could squeeze the trigger, destroying the dead like a scythe to wheat. This was why he became a hunter, to kill the undead.

Next to him, Tammy fired blast after blast with her shotgun, blowing heads apart and destroying human forms like they were made of fetid pudding, the foul smelling, maggot-infested meat slapping the pavement like road kill sitting in the hot sun.

When she ran out of shells, she jumped behind Jones who covered her, the tall man's weapon firing death with each shot.

A group of ghouls were getting too close for his liking, so Jones pulled another grenade from his bandolier, pulled the pin, and prepared to toss it across the ten feet separating him from the zombies while yelling "Grenade!" in a throaty warning to the others.

The hunters scattered out of the blast radius as Jones threw the grenade.

"Here, catch this, ugly!" Jones called out to the first ghoul in line as the grenade spun in the air like a child's small ball. The ghoul, hearing the command, something deep inside its dead brain comprehending, actually opened its hands as the grenade plopped into them. It was more luck than skill on the ghoul's part for catching the grenade, but Jones wasn't complaining.

The zombie stared at the small orb in its hands for two more seconds, wondering if it could eat the grenade, and then the body disappeared in a blinding flash of light and exploding body parts, entrails and organs flying off in all directions. One ghoul got a rotting human liver in the face like a pie, the pinkish brown organ sliding off the face like a massive snail. Hungry and not fussy, the zombie picked up the liver and began chomping down as brown juice seeped from the organ like a blood-soaked washcloth.

Seven zombies were destroyed in the grenade blast and Jones whooped in pleasure as body parts rained down on the area.

Miles frowned at Jones' recklessness, ducking as an arm fell out of the sky like a tiny meteor. But there was no time for chastising him now and he spun and fired at a trio of ghouls coming for him.

This was getting bad, he thought. It seemed like for every one he shot there were four more waiting to replace it.

And then he caught movement in his peripheral vision, and when he spun to take out the threat, he didn't see the danger at his feet.

Two things happened simultaneously.

The first was Miles shot the ghoul coming for him in the face, blowing its visage into gobbets of dripping flesh, but while he did this, a legless ghoul had managed to crawl up to him unnoticed. It opened its fetid mouth and the head darted forward like a starving cobra.

Before Miles knew what was happening, he felt a sharp pain in his left calf and looked down to see a pale, bloody face with a chuck of his leg and a two-inch piece of cloth from his pant leg hanging from its mouth.

Snarling in anger, he aimed the rifle down and blew off the ghoul's head.

The bullet entered at the top of the skull, then exited out the chin, taking brains, teeth and tongue in its wake. The piece of his leg fell out of the zombie's mouth to hit the pavement, but Miles wasn't watching, as he had ten more attackers to deal with.

Blood seeped from the wound on his leg and he could already feel it soaking into his sock. At the rate he was bleeding, he knew his boot would be filled with his life's blood in less than a minute. But he ignored, it, as there were still ghouls to destroy.

The battle raged hard and fast for ten more minutes, the hunters now at the point where they were beginning to worry they would run out of ammunition, when the last ghoul was finally taken down with half its skull missing, gray brains splattering onto the road to sizzle on the hot pavement.

All four hunters sucked in air, exhausted, each covered in the gore of their kills, their weapons dripping dark, congealed blood.

"Damn, I can't believe we did that," Tammy said as she ejected a spent shell and quickly reloaded. Her web belt, once full of fresh shells was now empty and she could only pray there were no more ghouls.

"Goddamn if that wasn't intense," Jones said. "I just wish Scott could've been here for this. He would've loved every second of it." His dark visage was awash with gobbets of rotting meat, and as he surveyed the carnage before him, the flies began to descend on the slaughtered ghouls en mass, feeding on the dark ichor.

Breathing heavily, his boot soaked in blood, Miles turned to Joseph. His face was a mask of pain from his leg wound. "You did good, real good. You kept your head and did what had to be done. You'll make a good hunter someday."

"Thanks, sir," Joseph replied and his eyes went wide when Miles stumbled and fell clumsily to the road.

"Sir, are you all right?" Joseph asked while turning to Tammy and Jones for help, both hunters looking the opposite way. "Hey, guys, I think Miles is hurt?"

Jones spun at the man's words. "What? Oh, shit, not another one," he said as he turned and strode the few feet separating him from Miles now seated form. Tammy came up beside him, her eyes still searching for more targets, but it looked like the ghouls had been destroyed.

There were probably a good amount still inside the houses, feeding on their kills, but they could be found later. At least the worst of it was over; the main horde had been destroyed.

Miles reached down and ripped open his pant leg to expose the ugly wound. His lower leg was stained a dark red, blood pooling over the lip of his boot to spill onto the street. There had to be at least a pint of plasma in his boot as it was.

Lowering his left hand, Miles tried to staunch the blood flow, but it appeared the ghoul had nicked an artery. Pressing his fingers into the jagged hole, he managed to apply pressure and the spurting blood ceased.

Breathing a sigh of relief, he knew he would be okay. Once Tammy called in that the area was secure, they could send for a medic to patch him up. Sure, he'd been bit, but he still had time before he turned. It usually took up to three days before a bitten human was too weak to function and had to be quarantined.

He still had time to kill more ghouls before it was his turn to die.

All these thoughts flooded through his mind as he kept pressure on the wound, so when he heard the soft click of Jones' .38 a foot from his head, his head turned suddenly, eyes going wide as he stared down the barrel of the gun. Behind the barrel, the hard visage of Jones glared back at Miles with open contempt.

Miles saw those eyes held no mercy, and in fact there looked to be a hint of revenge swimming in the dark orbs.

Miles let go of his bloody wound and raised both hands in front of him, as if that could stop a .38 slug from penetrating his skull.

"No, Jones, don't! Please! I still have time left!" he screamed, but Jones wasn't hearing him.

"Sorry, Miles, but you're no different than Scott. What comes around…" he trailed off and pulled the trigger.

Then there was darkness.

WHAT DWELLS BENEATH

"No way, I'm not going in there," Brett Masters said as he stared at the abandoned ice-skating rink.

"What's the matter? Scared?" Mark Addison asked with a devious grin.

"No, that's not it," Brett replied.

"Then what?"

Brett scrunched his forehead into multiple creases as he tried to come up with an excuse not to follow Mark into the dilapidated building. The truth was that he *was* scared to go in there. As he stared at the broken windows and cracked concrete he felt an unsettling feeling in his stomach, like a hundred butterflies had just woken up and were now all fluttering around within him.

Brett studied the two story structure, its peeling paint, its trash and debris strewn parking lot. Remnants from homeless people to teenagers who drank beer on the weekends, to regular citizens that had snuck in at night and dumped yard waste, couches, refrigerators and ovens. Even a few microwaves and television sets, their screens shattered, looking like eye sockets without the eyes, adorned the outside of the building.

There was so much trash the area around the ice skating rink resembled a junkyard. There were plans to tear it down and build apartments or condominiums, but something with the back taxes had put the development on hold. That's what Brett had heard his father and mother talking about one day when he had asked about the old rink. They had warned him never to go in there, not to even play around it.

The area was dangerous. Some of the flooring had become rotten from the leaky roof, and if he got hurt, there would be no one around to help him.

Of course, he hadn't heeded their advice and had hung out around the outside with Mark. The two boys searching through the trash to find some true treasures.

They had found a large piece of plywood and on one side someone had painted a large black and white skull. Mark had taken it home and had cut the skull out of the wood. After the two boys had built a go cart out of shopping carriage wheels and scrap wood, Mark had nailed the skull to the back of the go cart.

They had taken turns pushing each other around, a simple string used to steer the cart. Pull to the right and the wheel would be turned, the one bolt in the center of the two-by-four allowing for easy control.

But eventually they grew bored and had returned to the skating rink. This time Mark wanted to go inside.

They had never gone inside before, and though they knew deep down it was dangerous, the draw of mystery and adventure only a few blocks from home seemed exciting and safe at the same time.

"Then, what is it? *If* you're not scared?" Mark asked again, breaking Brett from his reverie.

Brett weighed his options and realized he had no choice. If he chickened out and didn't go inside with Mark, he knew his friend would never let him live it down. Every time the two would be at odds, Brett knew Mark would use the time he didn't go into the rink against him.

Though Brett knew with all his heart it was a mistake to go inside, he still turned to Mark, crossed his arms and said, "Never mind. I'll go with you."

Mark's face lit up with excitement and he slapped Brett on the shoulder. "All right, that's awesome. Come on, let's go. I can't wait to see what's in there."

Brett watched his friend walk away, and when Mark stopped, seeing Brett wasn't moving, his eyes went up and his hands went out before him as if to say, *well, come on then.*

Brett began walking as Mark turned and continued onward. Brett looked up at the daunting building as he moved closer, seeing the cracked shell and wrecked walls as something more than just a structure. The closer he got to it, now that he knew he was going inside, the more it seemed like a giant monster waiting to devour him.

He felt a tingle go down his spine and he hoped it was just nerves and not some kind of omen of what was to come.

As the two boys entered the skating rink from the west side, both of them let their mouths go slack as they stared at the inside of the decrepit structure.

The building was more than thirty years old, six of those years being abandoned, and there was refuse everywhere.

There was a second floor on one side of the building and the boys went to the stairs, slowly walking up the creaking steps. When they entered the first hallway, they found office space, still with cabinets and desks. Old files and manila envelops were scattered across the floor in each office, as if someone had been searching for something. With the windows broken, water had seeped in each time it rained and many places near the windows were water damaged; the floor uneven and in a few places the planks had begun to rise and crack.

Remains of animals were here and there, small bird skeletons as well as rat droppings. The air had an *off* smell to it, as if something old had combined with something dead, and that had joined with something wet. The aroma caused each boy to cover their noses and not talk.

Moving from office to office, kicking items out of the way with the tips of their sneakers, they soon began to grow bored.

Mark, the leader of the expedition, led Brett back down to the main floor, where the rink was.

Trash was piled in every curved corner. Dented, rusted shopping carts and blown leaves the predominant items. Beer bottles were second, as well as small liquor bottles. Many were broken and shattered, the small glass shards twinkled in the faint light, as if giving homage to the ice that once covered the forgotten surface.

The two boys walked around the rink, kicking anything that seemed interesting.

Brett was growing increasingly unsettled and was about to tell Mark he'd had enough and was going to leave, when Mark led them to the far end of the skating rink.

There was a small staircase there, made of poured cement, no more than four stairs high. As Mark looked down the stairs, he saw it led into a dark service tunnel that seemed to lead under the building.

"Cool, I wonder where this goes," Mark said as he and Brett peered into the Stygian darkness. Other than the few feet of light that penetrated the opening, the tunnel was an absolute mystery.

"No idea. Look, Mark, I think we've seen enough. I want to leave," Brett said hesitantly.

"What? Why? Not now. I just found this cool tunnel! This is so awesome! It must go all the way into the ground. Imagine what's under there."

Brett didn't want to think what was in the dark tunnel. Though he knew monsters weren't real, staring into the inky blackness, he had to admit, if they were real, then that's where one or more would want to live.

"Just think about it, Brett," Mark began. "No one's probably been in this tunnel for years. We can be like those explorers in Africa, who knows what we might find in there!"

"Yeah, that's what I'm afraid of," Brett said under his breath.

"What was that?"

"Nothing, I didn't say anything," Brett said. "Look, Mark, even if we wanted to go in there, we don't have a flashlight or anything."

"I have my lighter."

"A lighter won't do it and you know it. It'll get too hot after a few minutes and then where will we be?" Brett reasoned.

Mark gave that some thought and he let his eyes play over the floor. After a few seconds of looking, he went and picked up a two foot pipe, one of a half dozen littering the ground. He kicked a few items with the tip of his left sneaker before picking up a shirt. It had been blue once, but now it was faded to the point the color was almost gone. Bits of leaves, dried bugs, and dirt clung to all parts of it. Mark wrapped it around the top of the pipe, and when he was finished, he used his lighter and lit a stray piece of fabric jutting out to the side. It took a few seconds before the shirt began to burn, and as the makeshift torch flared to life, Mark beamed at Brett proudly. "There, now we can see. Come on, let's go check it out and when we're through, we can leave."

Though Brett knew he should say no, the truth was, as he looked at Mark standing there with a torch, the flames crackling, his friend looked like an adventurer from a movie. Brett couldn't help but feel some of that excitement as well, and being a normal boy, the call of mystery was too much to ignore. Against his better judgment Brett nodded and walked over to Mark. Both boys stood at the top of the small stairwell, looking down into the dark depths they prepared to take the plunge.

"Okay, let's go in a bit. But when I say I want to leave, we leave," Brett said.

"Fair enough. We'll go as far as we think it's safe, then we'll come back," Mark agreed.

Holding the torch before him, Mark began to descend the stairs, Brett right behind him.

The acrid stench of the burning shirt caused Brett to cover his nose with his shirtsleeve.

They had gone far enough into the service tunnel that the light at the opening was gone. This was due to the fact that the tunnel had been slowly curving downward for more than five minutes.

The floor was covered in more trash. Soda and beer cans, newspapers from ten years ago, and more rat droppings. Each step the two boys took sent debris rattling out of the way.

"Okay, Mark, we've gone far enough. I want to go back now," Brett said nervously.

"No way, this is so cool. I wonder how deep it goes." Mark asked as he stepped over a pile of refuse.

"I don't want to know. I want to leave," Brett said. "Come on, Mark, you said we'd go in and when I wanted to leave, we would."

Mark stopped walking, the torch illuminating his face in flickering shadows. The oily smoke roiled over their heads and floated down the tunnel, following the slight breeze. "I know what I said, but I changed my mind. I want to keep going." He smiled then, an evil smile, a knowing smile. "You can go if you want. I won't stop you."

"But I don't have a light. I won't be able to see."

"Exactly," Mark said.

"Fine, then give me your lighter," Brett demanded.

Mark shook his head. "No way. That's mine and I'm not giving it up."

"You're being a jerk you know."

Mark shrugged. "Maybe. So, what's it gonna be? You staying or going?"

"Like you don't know," Brett said angrily.

Mark turned and began walking and Brett stared at the back of his friend's head, his jaw tight with anger. Mark was being such a jerk. He began walking, following Mark again.

The two boys continued for another five minutes and the torch began to grow dim, flickering badly as it prepared to go out.

"Uh-oh, need some more fuel," Mark said. He lowered the torch to the floor and began searching for something to burn. It only took a few seconds before he found a dirty red and yellow scarf. Picking it up, he slowly wrapped it around the torch. At first it looked like the flame might go out, snuffed by the new material, but a second later it was burning brighter than before.

"There we go. Good as new," Mark said with a smile.

Brett said nothing, feeling like a prisoner, trapped deep inside the tunnel. With no light, there was no way he was going to try and leave the tunnel alone. It was a long walk back and though he could hold onto the wall, the imagery of being in complete darkness was too much to consider.

As they walked, the trash began to thin. Conduits that ran along the wall near the ceiling began to dwindle until they were gone completely.

"Gees, how far down does this thing go?" Mark asked, his voice echoing off the walls.

Brett looked at the ceiling, and another shiver filled him. He felt as if he was a thousand miles underground, the weight of the world over his head. He had a vision of an earthquake, of the ceiling cracking and tons of concrete and dirt falling in on him, crushing him, burying him. He realized his mom and dad would never know where he was. He would be buried alive, then he would die and no one would know he was down here. Served him right, he thought. He never should have come down here. What was he thinking?

Suddenly he wanted his mom more than anything, to feel her arms around him, her soft voice telling him it would be all right. But she wasn't here. He was alone with Mark. He had to be strong. He had to stay calm and sooner or later Mark would get bored and they would leave. He knew once he was free of the tunnel he would never come within ten feet of the skating rink again.

He had learned his lesson well.

Mark stopped walking and kicked something with his sneaker.

"Hey, look at this," he said to Brett as he knelt down to inspect the item.

Brett looked despite himself. The sooner he pleased Mark, the sooner he would want to leave. Brett looked at what Mark had found and he blinked into the flickering light, not believing what he saw.

"No way," Brett whispered. "It can't be."

Mark reached down with his free hand and picked up the item he'd found. "Sure looks like it to me. I had to get a physical last month and there was a skeleton in the doctor's office. I was bored so I was messing with it. This looks like the arm of that skeleton."

Brett made a raspberry. "That's crazy. It must be a mistake."

"I don't know, looks pretty real to me."

Brett began to get scared. "Gees, Mark, if it's true then we need to get out of here right now. We need to tell someone, the police, my parents."

"Whoa there, Sport. Look at this thing. It's old, real old. Probably been down here for years. There's no rush. I say we leave it here and we can take it back with us when we leave."

"Why don't we leave now?" Brett asked.

"Because this is getting good, that's why." Mark began walking further down the tunnel, dropping the ulna bone on the ground.

Brett looked at it for a second before he hurried to keep up with Mark. Like it or not, Mark was his lifeline.

They found more human bones as they went deeper into the tunnel, and the floor began to grow steeper, continuing into the earth. Some of the bones they now found didn't look so old. More than one looked like they had teeth marks on them, like they had been chewed on by an animal that was trying to get at the marrow within.

And then the cement walls were gone, to be replaced by hard-packed dirt.

"Okay, Mark, this is as far as I go. There's no more tunnel left."

"What are you talking about? There's still a tunnel and I want to see where it goes. This is so awesome! We're probably the first people down here in like ten years!"

"But, Mark, what about the bones? They had to get here somehow. Please, for me, can we go back now?" Brett pleaded.

Mark shook his head. "No way. I want to see what's at the end of this tunnel. Maybe it's some secret society, like cannibals or something. Maybe there's like people from a hundred years ago. You know, like mole people. They have white eyes and they can't see 'cause they live in the dark. Wow, can you imagine that? We'd be heroes, finding this new species of people right in our own backyard."

"But, Mark..." Brett protested.

"But nothing," Mark said, his voice firm. "We keep going. When we get to the end, we'll go back, not before." He pushed past Brett and made his way down the tunnel.

Brett bit his lip, wishing he had the courage to just leave, to go back even though it was pitch black. But he couldn't, not yet anyway.

Turning, Brett followed the flickering torch ahead of him.

More minutes past and the air grew cool and the sound of dripping water came to their ears.

The tunnel was still going downward, and as it curved to the left, the two boys found it had come to a junction.

Before them was a wide open space, about the size of an average living room. Like the tunnel, it was carved from the earth, the sides made of hard-packed dirt and clay. To support the ceiling, odd sized, leftover pieces of wood were propped as rafters. In the far corner, lost in the shadows, the dripping was slightly louder.

"Whoa, will you look at this?" Mark said, his eyes wide with amazement. He moved the torch back and forth, illuminating the cave. When he reached the far right, he stopped moving, his mouth falling open in awe. Brett saw what the torch's feeble light had brought into view and he was speechless, the terror itching at his back again, making his legs shake.

On the floor of the cave, scattered about like trash, were piles of human bones. Many were cracked in half, as if a giant animal had fed on the marrow within. All had scrapes and gouges on their smooth surfaces, and not one had so much as a scrap of flesh remaining. In the pile, a few grinning, bleached skulls glared back at the two boys, as if accusing them of invading their inner sanctum.

Something lived here, something that ate people!

"Oh my God, Mark, those are bones! We need to leave, right now."

"Why? There's no one here. This place looks abandoned. For all we know these old bones have been here for decades. We're fine," Mark said, though his eyes were moving around faster as he peered into the shadows just out of reach of the torch's perimeter.

"I don't care. I want to go... right now." Brett was adamant and was considering just turning and running, not caring about the darkness any more, his desperation to escape stronger than his fear.

Mark ignored Brett's pleadings. He felt immune to the threat of potential danger. After all, he was a kid. What could happen to him?

Brett was about to reply, to try and plead his case yet again for leaving, when a scuffing sound came from somewhere in the cave.

"What was that?" Brett asked, his voice shaking.

Mark didn't reply. He stood stock still. Brett was about to speak again when the scuffing echoed to them once more. Mark raised the torch higher and took a few steps into the center of the cave.

As the light pushed back the darkness it exposed another tunnel on the far side of the cave. It was smaller than the one they had used to enter and it went even deeper into the earth.

As the two boys stared in silence, fear eating at their insides, a scraping sound could be hard...and it was coming from the other tunnel.

Swallowing the knot in his throat, Mark turned to look at Brett. "I think we can leave now," he said nervously.

Brett only nodded and began backing away from the other tunnel, Mark right behind him.

Meanwhile, the scraping, scuffing grew in pitch, and as the two boys were about to turn and run, a misshapen form appeared at the opening to the tunnel at the opposite end of the cave. Mark and Brett could only see the creature in dull outlines. Brett blinked repeatedly as he stared, not believing what he saw.

The creature was hunched over, like it had a bad back, and it was bald with the exception of a few scraggly wisps of white hair. It was human, or humanoid, though its arms and legs seemed shorter, squatter than a standard human being.

Its exposed flesh was devoid of hair, only a pair of shorts, covered in dirt and grime, adorning its pale body.

Pale was an understatement. The skin was so white it seemed to glow in the dark, the skin color the same as the eyes. Both orbs were bone white, and if it could see, Brett wondered how.

As the two boys took a step backwards, the head of the creature turned sharply, telling Brett it may not be able to see at all, but hunted by sound alone, which made sense in the darkness of the tunnels.

As it homed in on the two boys like a bat, it opened its mouth wide to expose pointed yellow and brown teeth, the incisors flashing in the dim light of the torch.

Without warning the creature lunged for them.

"Go, go, it's coming!" Mark yelled as Brett turned and began to run into the tunnel they had used to enter the cave, his hands out before him as he plunged into the darkness.

Behind him, Mark followed, the torch jumping up and down in his hand, causing the light to barely penetrate in front of Brett.

But there was no time for Brett to stop and let Mark get ahead of him nor did Brett want to do so. As he ran, he could hear Mark's footsteps behind him and beyond that, the hissing and scraping as the creature followed them.

Everything became a blur for Brett as he stumbled up the tunnel. As he now ascended, his legs began to hurt, but he ignored the pain, only wanting to be free of the tunnel and its cannibalistic dweller.

"Hurry up, Brett! It's right behind me!" Mark yelled as he pushed at Brett, who stumbled forward.

Righting himself, Brett tried to run faster, his hands sliding along the dirt walls as he tried not to hyperventilate. He was so scared. He had never, ever been this scared in his life.

His heart was beating so fast it was like a jungle drum in his head and his stomach was filled with more than a million butterflies. He felt like he had to go to the bathroom but he ignored it, only wanting to break free of the tomb he now found himself in.

Behind him, Brett could hear Mark's heavy breathing and every now and then low sobs. Mark was crying, his facade of bravery now gone. Brett didn't hold it against him, in fact he wanted to cry too.

The two boys were more than halfway through the tunnel, and had just past the area where the walls had been made of dirt and had once more become concrete, when Mark let out a piercing yell and fell heavily to the tunnel floor.

The torch fell from his hand and rolled a few feet to lie in the dirt. Luckily, it didn't go out, though its brightness went down by more than half. In the half light the tunnel was nothing but gloom and shadows.

Brett turned around to try and help his friend, but when he spun about, he was able to look deeper into the tunnel and over Mark's prone body. His breath lodged in his chest at what he saw.

The creature was there, the ghoul, as Brett called it in his mind, for what else could it be but a ghoul? It lived underground and ate humans. And as no one had been reported missing, the remains had to be of dead people.

There was a cemetery not more than a mile away and Brett wondered if the other tunnel went all the way to the graveyard. After traversing what seemed like hundreds of feet of tunnel the idea didn't seem so farfetched.

The ghoul stopped right behind Mark, seeming to stare at Brett in accusation. It cocked its head to the side, its mouth opening slightly and Brett could imagine what it wanted to say. *"How dare you come into my home uninvited?"*

Mark was crying now, and as he tried to get up, he fell back down. His ankle was sprained; he was wounded, like an old zebra at the end of the herd, the lion waiting for it to straggle to the end of the line so it could pounce.

Mark's face was a rictus of pain and he didn't realize the ghoul was behind him. With tears rolling down his cheeks Mark reached up with his left hand, "Help me up, Brett. My ankle...I can't walk."

Brett couldn't move as he stared at the ghoul behind Mark, and slowly Mark realized Brett wasn't looking at him. Finally, Mark rolled onto his side and looked behind him. He peered up at the ghoul and let out a loud scream that bounced off the walls of the tunnel.

As Brett watched in horror the ghoul bent over and grabbed Mark by his ankles, causing Mark to scream yet again. It began dragging Mark deeper into the tunnel, back to its lair of bones and dirt.

"No, don't let it take me! Help me Brett! I don't want to go! I want my mommy! Help meeee!"

With arms and hands outstretched like a drowning man, Mark was dragged into the darkness until he vanished from sight, the light of the torch only penetrating a few feet in either direction. Brett was still too scared to move and he knew if the ghoul wanted him as well, it could easily take him. The sounds of Mark's body being dragged on the tunnel floor continued, as did his screams.

His pleadings for help and mercy never stopped. His sobs for his mom and dad never ceasing until finally a chilling sound came to Brett's ears that he would never forget, no matter how long he lived.

Mark was in mid-yell, his wails so loud they filled the tunnel like a living thing and then, as if a light switch had been flicked, they ceased. But that wasn't the sound that haunted Brett.

Just before the cries of his friend stopped, there was a dull cracking sound, similar to the sound a finger thick tree branch would make when it was broken over a knee. Like the breaking of a neck.

Then there was silence, followed by the sound of more dragging which soon faded away. Soon, Brett could only hear his breathing and his heartbeat pounding as adrenalin filled him to the point he was going to explode, but still he couldn't move.

Finally, shaking himself free of terror, he reached down, picked up the torch, and began running as fast as he could. At a half-jog, half-run he proceeded through the tunnel, towards the surface.

It seemed to take forever, but eventually he reached the exit. As he came out of the tunnel and into the skating rink, he dropped the torch into the accumulated dirt where it was extinguished, and ran all the way home.

When he was asked by his mother why he looked so scared, he said he was almost hit by a car. It was accepted as true and he went to his room, where he hid in his closet for the rest of the night, too scared to come out.

The next day the word went out at school that Mark was missing. No one knew what had happened to him and foul play was suspected, perhaps a kidnapping though the boy running away from home wasn't ruled out.

Apparently Mark had an argument with his father the night before.

Brett never told another soul what had happened under the skating rink, for who would believe him?

He knew anyone he told would merely say it was the rantings of an overactive imagination.

Six months later, the ice skating rink was torn down and condominiums were built. If any of the demolition crew found an underground cave, human bones, or Mark, Brett never heard about it.

As the years went by, Brett even made himself believe it was all a dream, that it had never happened.

But late at night, when the moon was full and the darkness enveloped the land, he would look out his window and sometimes, if he looked just right, he believed he saw a humanoid shape in the shadows at the edge of his yard, watching him, waiting.

Waiting for the one that got away.

YES, VIRGINIA, THERE REALLY IS A ZOMBIE SANTA CLAUS

It was well past midnight on Christmas Eve, and was now officially Christmas day.

A bright red sleigh filled with presents floated across the sky, a jolly man in a red suit its sole passenger.

Chris Kringle, or Santa Claus, to the world, leaned back in his seat as the reindeer cut through the clouds, their small bells jingling on their collars.

It had been a busy night so far but the southern hemisphere was finally finished.

Below, Haiti waited for its share of Christmas joy.

Pulling on the reins, he angled the sled downward, the drop enough to make his stomach jump. He laughed, long and loud. Even after all these years, he still didn't like to fly.

Moments later he was on his first roof top, a shanty-like home with a patched roof. He was in the poor part of town, but to him it all looked the same.

Rich or poor, he had a present for every child across the world.

Turning around, he reached into his magic sack; the voluminous red bag looking like it only had a few toys in it. But when he took a toy out of the bag, another would appear almost immediately.

And this made perfect sense to Santa, as how else would he be able to carry an entire supply of presents to the world's population of children in simply one night?

The chimney was a dilapidated mess, as was the rest of the home, but he ignored it. There was a child inside and that was all that mattered to him.

Sliding down the chimney, he came up in a small living room. There was a small Christmas tree in the far corner and he waddled over to it, all the time humming a holiday tune. He didn't see the talismans to the voodoo religion, nor see the dead chicken or dried crows feet dangling from a nearby alter.

No, Santa only had eyes for the Christmas tree.

So when he set the present down under the tree, he was shocked when a shadow lunged out from the darkness and attacked him.

What was this? No one ever attacked Santa Claus; he was welcomed with open arms wherever he went.

But this dark man, with face drained of color and drawn visage, didn't seem to care who he was. Before Santa could do anything to protect himself, he felt the sharp pain of teeth on his left hand, right above the fingers.

Though he was always jolly, Santa roared with anger and punched the man square in the head. The attacker fell away and Santa kicked him once in the stomach for good measure. But the attacker was only down for a moment and was soon crawling toward Santa again.

Deciding there was no time for this, and if he wasn't wanted he'd just leave, Santa retreated to the chimney and scooted up it like a worm.

On the roof, the reindeer snorted impatiently, and in seconds Santa was flying off to the next house.

His hand was bleeding profusely and he wrapped it in a bright red handkerchief. After bandaging it, he tried to flex it and he winced in pain. The guy had gotten him good, that was for sure.

He went to the next house and the house after that, still having to do his duty as jolly old St. Nick. But as the hours passed, Santa began to feel feverish, something that had never happened before.

As Santa Claus, he was immortal, and age and sickness didn't affect him. But for some unexplainable reason, he felt ill.

So with sweat beading on his forehead, and his breath coming in gasps, it became harder to deliver the presents to children all over the world. But he was Santa Claus and he would continue, he had to; children everywhere were counting on him.

It happened somewhere over the Midwest of the United States.

Santa was steering the sleigh to the next city when he felt woozy, and before he knew what was happening, he passed out. The reindeer, old pros at their jobs, took the sleigh in for a landing on a nearby roof.

The roof the sleigh set down on was part of a massive, Victorian affair with ornate moldings and large picture windows. It was obvious the family living here was one of wealth.

The reindeer snuffed and snorted on the roof as Santa lay sprawled in the sleigh. This became the scene for almost ten minutes after touchdown, Santa never moving. But then Santa's right hand began to twitch and a moment later his eyes opened.

Looking around, he had no idea where he was or how he'd arrived here. And he felt weird, sort of hollow inside. There was a strange feeling in his stomach now, similar to hunger, but that didn't make any sense as he hadn't been hungry before passing out. He had been eating all night, cookies and milk mostly, but that was part of the job.

But then he realized he didn't feel sick any more, that he wasn't sweating, and that was a bonus. There was so much to do in so little time, and to get sick tonight of all nights was unthinkable.

He flexed his hand, the one with the bite, and found it didn't hurt any longer. That was also an added bonus.

Stepping out of the sleigh, he breathed in the night air, both fresh and crisp. There was a light dusting of snow across the city and he could see the blinking lights of Christmas decorations as they hung from doors and gutters of nearby homes.

Ignoring the odd feeling welling inside him, one he now felt deep in his gut, one of hunger but for what he had no idea, he reached into his magic sack and pulled out two toys. One was a train and one was a doll; then he dropped into the chimney to continue his work.

He never gave any thought to why he passed out, nor why there was no more pain in his hand, nor the odd craving in his gullet for something he couldn't put his finger on.

All that mattered was to deliver the toys to the children.

He dropped down the chimney and into the living room of the home. To his left was a large, eight foot Christmas tree, filled with red, yellow and blue blinking lights. A small angel was perched on top, its angelic face watching over the room.

Santa paused at a small table set up near the tree.

Milk and cookies were laid out for him like always, the cookies on an expensive China platter.

"Oooh, chocolate chip," he whispered as he reached out and took one. The hunger was growing inside him and the cookies should do the job nicely. But instead of enjoying the first bite, he spit it out, the chewed-up mush falling to the expensive carpet. It tasted terrible. He had to wonder if this was some sort of prank, perhaps the cookies were tainted?

Deciding that was crazy, he set the half-eaten cookie down and reached for the glass of milk.

This should settle my stomach, he thought as he began to drink. But it was like he took a sip from a bucket of sewer waste. He spit out the foul tasting liquid, wiping his mouth with his sleeve. Perplexed, but not giving it too much thought, he decided this was just an anomaly. He would have a snack at the next house, but for now he had gifts to leave under the tree.

Setting the glass down, he went to the tree, admiring his reflection in the glass ornaments. As he stared at himself, he didn't like what he saw. His face was now very pale and he had dark circles under his eyes, his forehead also looking more pronounced. Gone were the rosy cheeks, to be replaced by a bluish tint.

Once again he brushed it off as the simple distorted reflection in the ornaments. Leaning down, he set the two toys under the tree. But his left arm brushed the tree and one of the ornaments was knocked off the branch to roll across the floor. Santa turned to retrieve it, and when he bent over to pick it up, he realized he wasn't alone.

A little girl, no more than four, was standing in the doorway leading to the rear of the house. She was in red and green pajamas and wore a pretty bow around her neck. She was holding a small brown bear, the bear too, having a bow around its neck. Her hair was done up with barrettes and she was the cutest thing he'd ever seen.

"Santa?" she asked in a small, tiny voice, her big blue eyes gazing up at a holiday legend.

Santa Claus didn't know what to do; he just stared down at her.

Normally he would have hypnotized the girl then sent her off to bed. In the morning, she would have believed she'd dreamt the whole thing, but instead of doing this, he found himself looking at her like a lion to a gazelle.

She gazed up at him with those wide orbs, so young and innocent, and Santa found his mouth watering with anticipation. She looked so sweet and tender, like Grade-A veal fresh out of the slaughter house.

Before he knew what he was doing, he leaned down and picked her up, and before the girl knew what was happening, he bit into her throat, just below her chin.

The girl tried to scream of course, frightened beyond belief, but Santa Claus ripped out her larynx and began to suck at the wound like he was a dying man just out of the desert. The small feet clad in pajamas kicked back and forth, but soon they stopped moving and only hung limp.

Santa Claus fed then, tearing off large chunks of the soft, pink meat. He fed until he thought he would burst, but even then he found he was still hungry.

Dropping the carcass of the girl to the floor, he went to the back of the house where the bedrooms were located. Halfway down the hallway, there was a door with the name **Johnny** on it and he entered, another shadow amongst shadows.

Before the little boy knew what was happening, Santa Claus feasted on the little girl's brother, tearing the small form apart and feeding on the warm, juicy innards.

When he was finished he went to the parents' bedroom, killing both with teeth and fingernails. But when he began to feed, he found the taste of adult meat unappetizing and he spit it out.

No, the flesh of the children, of the innocent, was what he craved.

With his belly stuffed to the limit, he flew up the chimney and onto his sleigh. The reindeer snuffed a few times but didn't seem to pay him attention.

With a jerk of the reins, the sleigh took off to his next destination and then to every other house with children in the world.

But first he was going to the Smithfield Orphanage.

And he knew when he was finished there; Mrs. Claus was going to have to let his red suit out once more.

The father closed the book he was reading from and looked down into his daughter's eyes as she stared at him with trepidation from his lap.

Little Virginia Montrose blinked back a tear and touched the book her daddy had been reading from. "Is that really how it happened, Daddy? Is that why we board up all the windows and doors and block the chimney every Christmas Eve?"

The father nodded. "Yes, honey, that's exactly right. You see, Virginia, there really is a zombie Santa Claus, and every Christmas Eve he leaves the North Pole in search of the fresh meat of innocent children."

"So I have to hide and hope he doesn't find me?" she asked.

"That's correct, honey. It's so he can't get in and eat you. I wouldn't want to lose you to zombie Santa."

Virginia nodded, understanding. She knew there was once upon a time when Santa was a friend to children all over the world, and he would bring presents to them on Christmas Eve if they had been good. But now he was a flesh-eating zombie who fed on the innards of little children.

Father and daughter sat quietly for a time, both staring at the blinking Christmas tree in the corner of the living room. No pictures of Santa were to be found in the house, for he was all that was wrong with Christmas.

Finally, the father set his daughter down and stood up, crossing the room to unplug the lights of the Christmas tree.

Then he turned off the lighted decorations outside and every light in the house, bathing the home in darkness.

From outside, the house looked as cold and dark as the rest of the houses on the street, nay, the entire state, or better yet, the entire country.

"Now you go to bed and tomorrow it will be all over and you'll be safe for another year," he told Virginia when the house was darkened and all the barriers were checked once, then rechecked twice.

"Okay, Daddy, I love you. Merry Christmas," Virginia said and then ran off to bed. Her father sighed as he watched her leave, wishing things could be like they once were, when Christmas was a time of joy and cheer, not fear for ones children from an undead demon in a red suit and white beard.

He walked over to the chair he'd sat in with Virginia and plopped back down, only one small night light in the corner of the room to keep the darkness at bay.

On the small coffee table next to him sat a half bottle of Jack Daniels and one small shot glass. He poured himself a shot and then took a small sip. He planned on nursing the bottle, for it would be a long night of watching over his family.

His wife was already asleep, but she would be up in the morning to take over for him, just in case Santa was running behind this night and tried for one more child before the sun came up.

It had happened before, some unwary parent thinking it was over when it wasn't.

After sipping the liquor, he reached around to the back of the chair and pulled out a semi-automatic rifle. Now that Virginia was in bed, he could get ready. Flicking the selector switch to full-auto, he stared at the fireplace across the room. Though it had a sheet metal barrier across it, Santa had been known to slip past the barriers in other homes.

Curse him and his damn Christmas magic, he thought.

"Come on, Santa, I'm ready for you, you fat, dead bastard," he mumbled as he glanced at the now dark Christmas tree.

It was then that he heard, ever so softly, the ringing of sleigh bells. It was coming from outside the house, sounding like it was coming from far away, but he knew as time went by it would grow louder.

But there were many other homes to pick this night and he hoped the odds were with him that zombie Santa Claus would pass his house by.

Feeling a shiver go down his spine, he gripped the rifle more tightly.

YOU ARE WHAT YOU EAT

"Wow, it's really coming down out there," Stella Ryan said as she peered past the yellow curtains of the living room and out into the storm. "I guess this is just another excuse for you to sit on your ass and do nothing, Walter."

New England was being pounded with a snow storm the likes of which it hadn't seen since 1978.

The roads were buried under three feet of snow and it would be days before cities would be able to dig themselves out, if not longer.

For the time being, people were trapped in their homes and at work, wherever they had been when the storm hit.

Walter sat in his living room chair, the material worn and stained from years of use, and he stared at his wife's wide back, his eyes drilling into her. He hated her with every fiber of his being but he never told her this. He never said one word to contradict her, for Walter was a beaten man.

Stella turned to look at him, her lips turned down into a deep frown. "You know, Walter, there are plenty of things you can do around the house while we're trapped in here. There's that broken chair, the loose step, and that fixture in the second floor bathroom needs to be tightened down."

"Yes, dear," he said as he drank half his beer to try and dull her voice as it penetrated into his very soul.

"Why I ever married you I'll never know," she said. "Mother told me not to, you know. She said you were worthless. But did I listen? No, of course not." She turned her heaving bulk and waddled over to his chair. She was a good three hundred pounds and the exertion of crossing the room had her huffing and puffing. She reached into a candy dish next to Walter and scooped up a handful of M&M's, then proceeded to shove them into her mouth. A few made it to safety, falling to the rug but the rest went to their chocolately doom, sliding down her gullet as she continued to complain. Walter could almost imagine their tiny screams.

"Mother told me to marry that nice Will Thompson from down the block, but did I listen? Oh no, I had to marry you."

"Yes dear," he said.

She continued, not paying him a bit of attention. "And now we're trapped in the house for days. I hope we have enough food. I told you to go shopping yesterday on your way home from work but you didn't listen, did you."

"But I had to work for fourteen straight hours," he protested meekly. "I had to cover another shift. And you had me up the night before thanks to..."

"Thanks to what?" she asked.

"Nothing," was his reply. He knew better to say the reason he was kept up was the fact she had had gas that would have put a longshoreman to shame. Though he knew what would happen, the previous night she had eaten three bowls of baked beans. That night, the music had begun and the aroma had been overwhelmingly atrocious. Even with the sheets jammed over his nose, as he buried his face in the bedclothes, the smell of her farts permeated his sinuses, making him think he was sleeping in the middle of a trash dump.

And thanks to her body fat, the farts had to work their way out of the crack of her ass, seeping, the sound like a bird was slowly dying in the folds of her flesh.

Walter had curled up into a tiny ball, squeezed his eyes shut, and had wept softly.

He was a small man, just a little over five feet, and she was almost six feet in her slippers. With her added girth, she was a behemoth, the Goliath to his David, and she had succeeded in making him a meek little coward.

After ten years of it, Walter's spirit was firmly broken, the man a former shell of what he'd once been before marrying her.

As she finished off the M&M's—what had been an entire two pound bag—the phone rang and Stella waddled over to it, her arm fat swaying back and forth in a fluid motion. Walter watched her go, thinking the folds of fat moved like a Lava lamp, almost hypnotic in its evolution.

Stella answered the phone and smiled. "Hi, mother, no, he's sitting on his ass as usual. Uh-huh, yes, we're totally trapped here. The TV said it will be days before they can get the roads clear. No, Walter isn't helping, he never does. Yes, mother, I love you, too. Okay, I'll call you later, bye."

She hung up and shifted her bulk to glare at Walter.

"That was my mother; she wanted to make sure we were okay."

"And are we?" he asked softly.

"I guess so, for now. Now, be productive and make me something to eat? I'm starving," she said as she went into the kitchen, sitting down on the heavy duty chair Walter had bought just for her. In the past, he had found a normal wooden kitchen chair just couldn't handle her girth and so he had searched high and low for a heavy duty one. The one she rested on was made of solid oak, with reinforced wooden slats. The legs were three inches thick and thick dowels held the legs together. For added support, metal straps were weaved into the chair, so that a woman twice Stella's size could use it comfortably.

At least that was what the brochure said, but Walter had noticed in the past few months whenever Stella sat in it, the chair groaned softly, as if it was letting out a heavy sigh. Perhaps it was his imagination, but either way, he knew better than to mention it to Stella.

In the past, if angered, she wasn't afraid to hit him if she deemed it necessary. With so much weight behind her, even a light slap would send him across the room, and he would have to make up something at work to explain where the bruises came from.

He began tinkering in the kitchen, getting out a loaf of bread, a stick of butter, and a pound of cheese so he could make her half a dozen sandwiches for her *snack*.

While he worked, she continued her tirade.

"Mother said you would always be a loser, you know. She said I would never get the things I deserved if I married you."

"Yes, dear," he said as he placed the heavy skillet on the stove and dropped the stick of butter into the pan.

"She told me, 'Stella, he's a loser and will always be a loser.' But did I listen? Oh, no, I had to feel sorry for you. Pity, Walter, that's what it is, just pity." She glanced over her bulbous shoulder at him, her eyes squinting so her face looked like Playdoh with two marbles stuck in the center where her eyes should be. "You're nothing but a waste of space, Walter, a joke. In fact, Mother and I laugh about how pathetic you are all the time."

Walter's hand gripped the handle to the skillet harder as his internal rage began to build. As he stared at himself in the stainless steel backsplash behind the stove, he saw his jaw set and his eyes go hard.

Maybe it was the fact that he knew he was trapped with her inside the house—snowed in—for days, but something snapped inside him, and before he realized what he was doing, he let out a scream that shook the plates in the dish strainer and had Stella trying to turn around, wondering if Walter had burned himself.

He felt like he was at a movie, as he watched himself pick up the skillet and turn to face Stella.

It was like everything went to slow motion, and as she slowly turned to see him, her mouth opening slowly, a banana jammed in there from the bowl on the table as she couldn't wait that long to eat, Walter used the skillet like a bludgeon and brought it down onto the top of her head like a hammer to a nail.

The half-eaten banana in her mouth was catapulted outward like a rocket, the gooey white and yellow mush splashing the cabinet a few feet away to drip down in a snail trail. Meanwhile, the heavy skillet was doing what gravity had intended, nay demanded, and as the bottom of the hot pan struck Stella's head, her skull cracked like an eggshell and flattened her cranium like a giant stepping on an empty soda can. Hot butter from the skillet splashed the kitchen walls as brain matter soon joined it, the mish-mash of fluids becoming a Rorschach painting worthy of any museum.

Stella made no sound as her head imploded and the frying pan stayed on top of her neck stump, the hot metal sizzling as the odor of burned bacon filled the kitchen and brains oozed out of the sides.

Walter stood immobile; his hand still on the handle, his breathing coming in gasps, and that was when Stella teetered on her chair.

As Walter watched, the body toppled to the floor, sliding out from under the skillet, which now had Walter holding it out at arm's length.

As the body landed heavily, resembling an enormous bag of pudding, he dropped the skillet and went to his knees.

He had no feelings inside, neither happiness nor horror, just total numbness.

With the clang of the skillet still reverberating in his ears, he stared at his very dead wife, while the wind howled outside in an accusing tone, the snow drifts growing higher.

Walter stared at his dead wife as blood pooled across the kitchen floor for hours, and may have continued to do so for hours more if not for the ringing of the telephone. Pulled from his fugue state, he crawled to the kitchen wall and pulled the phone off the hook.

"Hello, Stella, is that you? Hello?" a voice asked.

Walter didn't speak at first, only cradled the phone to his ear.

"Hello? Who is that? I can hear someone breathing. Walter? Is that you? Put my daughter on, now!"

Walter swallowed hard, then spoke, his voice weak and faltering. "Uhm, hi, Mona. Uhm, Stella can't come to the phone right now, she's uhm, sleeping."

"Sleeping? Really? It's five in the afternoon," Mona declared. Walter could hear her wheezing on the other end of the phone. Mona was bigger than her daughter and was confined to a bed.

Walter had wondered if Stella would ever get like that but he guessed now that wouldn't be a problem. In fact, Stella had just lost some weight. She had no head and that had to be good for a couple of pounds. How much did a brain weigh?

He began to giggle as he thought about it; the madness of what he'd done sinking in, but Mona brought him back to reality.

"Walter, you tell my daughter to call me when she gets up, you hear me?"

"Uh-huh," he said simply. He opened his mouth to say more but the phone was rudely disconnected from the other end.

Breathing a sigh of relief, he hung up the phone. Then he turned and stared at his dead wife, at a loss for what he should do next.

At six sharp, Mona called again, and Walter said she was in the shower and would be in there for a while. Mona, not deterred in the least, said she would call back at seven.

At seven sharp Mona called again. Walter stared at the ringing phone, wondering if he should ignore it, but in the end he decided to answer it.

"Hello?" he said dully, knowing who it was.

"Put my daughter on the phone, Walter."

"Uh, I would, Mona but she went back to bed again, this time for the night. I guess she's not feeling so hot."

"I don't care, damn you. Now you put my daughter on this instant."

"Uh, okay, Mona, I'll tell her. Look, I have some water boiling on the stove, as I'm making Stella some tea if she wakes up. I'll tell her you called, bye." He then hung up the phone, cutting off Mona's angry protests.

At five past eight Mona called again, and before Walter could speak, she began her tirade.

"Now, you listen to me, Walter. If you don't put my daughter on right now, so help me..."

He hung up the phone, not knowing what else to do. As he stared at the phone, he began to smell something disgusting, and when he turned to look down at Stella's headless corpse, he saw his wife had released her bowels and bladder in death.

Knowing he had no choice but to clean it up, he went to get some towels, already dreading the loathsome task.

Mona called back three more times that night but he ignored the phone and slept restlessly on the living room couch. All the while the storm continued to blow and once or twice the lights flickered, but they never quite went out and the next morning he was thankful for small favors when he turned on the kitchen light to see there was still power.

Stella was where he had left her, only now she had a sheet placed over her—he'd put it there the previous night—the large piece of linen looking like it was covering a massive pile of dirt. He thought he was supposed to feel guilty over what he'd done, maybe after letting it sink in overnight, but the truth was that he felt fine, better than fine actually. It was like a giant weight had been lifted from his shoulders. He was finally free of the fat shrew, free to live his life how he saw fit.

The phone rang, and without thinking, he let reflex do what it was trained to do and he picked it up. No sooner did he place the receiver to his ear then he regretted his action.

"Walter, you better put my daughter on this phone right damn now?"

"And good morning to you, too, Mona," he said almost cheerily. "Sorry, but she's still in bed. Seems to have caught the flu."

He could hear Mona growling, the noise coming from deep in her throat.

"You listen to me, Walter. That snowstorm may have that city locked down but as soon as the streets are clear, I'm going to send the police over there. Do you hear me? I know something has happened to my baby and I'll see you pay for whatever you've done. So help me if you've hurt my precious angel!"

Walter pulled the phone from his ear and stared at it. Did she know? How could she? Did the mother somehow *sense* the daughter had suffered a tragic end? He'd heard it was possible, but would never have believed it was true.

"Mona, Stella's fine, she's just sleeping, now if you'll excuse me, I have things to do, goodbye." He hung up the phone but, as he did, and glared at the large corpse in the middle of the kitchen, he knew he needed to dispose of the body. For Mona was a lot of things, but a blowhard she wasn't. If she said she was going to call the police then Walter knew she would.

He went to the second floor bedroom window to peer outside and he frowned deeply at what he saw. The drifts were higher than the first floor windows of the neighboring homes, his included. The doors were buried, too, and it would take a lot of shoveling to free people from their trapped residences.

He went back downstairs and stared at the corpse, tapping his finger against his chin. So he couldn't drag her outside and hide her in the snow, there was just no way to get out there. Besides, even if he wanted to she was so big and there was no way he could move her. He thought about rolling her and decided he should give it a try.

Bending over, he tried to push her like she was a large log, but all that he got for his trouble was an expelling of gas, the farts of the corpse a hundred times worse than when she was alive.

Now, as he breathed heavily from exertion, he knew he wouldn't be moving the body anytime soon.

But he needed to get rid of it, and if he couldn't bury it, then what? How do you hide the meat and bones of a three hundred pound woman in plain sight?

How do you get rid of all that dead flesh?

The phone rang and he frowned, assuming it was Mona. Deciding it was time to tell his mother-in-law to go to hell, he picked it up and said, "What the fuck do you want, Mona?"

A man's voice was taken aback for a moment but quickly recovered. "Uhm, is this the Ryan residence? Stella and Walter to be exact?"

"Uh, yeah, it is, who's this?"

"I take it this is Mr. Ryan?"

"Yeah, I asked who you are, pal," Walter said angrily. He hated when people called and didn't identify themselves immediately.

"This is Officer Mac Calhoun of the Baltimore Police Department. We received a call from a Mona Williams stating that she feared there might be something wrong at your home."

Walter felt his heart skip a beat. "Oh, uhm, nothing's wrong here, Officer, you need to ignore my mother-in-law. We're having an argument and she can be quite vindictive."

"Oh, really. She said there might be something wrong with your wife…a Stella Ryan?"

"That's right, yes, but my wife is fine, she's in bed with the flu, and Mona won't take no for an answer when she asked to talk to her."

"I see, well, considering the fact that even if I wanted to I couldn't come by your house right now, I guess I'll have to take your word for it."

"Huh, I guess so," Walter said.

"But as soon as possible, when the more important calls are addressed, I or one of my associates on the force will be swinging by for a visit. It's protocol…I'm sure once we drop by and see that you and your wife have weathered the storm safely, we can leave. Won't take more than a minute." He paused. "You could save us a trip by putting your wife on the phone right now, though."

Walter held in the scream beginning in his throat. With an act of incredible will, he kept his voice calm and in fact added some indignity to the tone as he said, "Look, Officer Calhoun, I'm happy to cooperate, but not if it will jeopardize the welfare of my wife. Now I told you she's sleeping and I won't play the games my mother-in-law seeks to drag me into. If I do then she's already won."

"I see, Mr. Ryan. Well, I have to say I have a mother-in-law, too, but we get along fine, I know that isn't always the case, mind you. Fine, then, we'll check on you when the storm breaks."

"Oh, uhm, that will be fine, Officer, we'll be here when you get here. Hey, it's not like we could go anywhere if we wanted to, right?"

"Yes, right, very true, Mr. Ryan. Okay, well, you stay safe, and take care of that sick wife and we'll be *seeing you real soon.*

The phone went dead and Walter stared at it, his heart beating like a triphammer in his chest.

The way the officer said the last part—as if he was making a solemn promise. Hanging up the phone, Walter turned to Stella's corpse with a determined look on his face.

As panic seized him at the realization he would be caught and sent away for murder, or worse, the gas chamber, he knew he had to get rid of the body and he needed to do it before the roads were cleared of snow.

The only trick was how?

As he stared at the body, his eyes began to drift over the kitchen. First he stared at the sink, the dirty dishes still there from last night, then he looked to the stove, at the burner missing the skillet he'd used to kill Stella, and on the rear burner the tea kettle. Stella always kept water in it, even though she wasn't using it. She said if the burner ever got turned on, then the water would keep the tea kettle from burning on the bottom. Humoring her, he had always made sure to keep water in it.

His eyes continued across the stove to the counter, and the one pound package of hamburger resting on it. Last night the meat had been frozen and he had set it there to thaw out overnight before killing his wife. He had planned on making Stella half a dozen hamburgers for supper but now he figured he wouldn't need it.

That made him chuckle a little and he held it in, knowing if he began to laugh, to let out the panic inside him, he would end up on the kitchen floor a raving lunatic. No, he needed to stay calm and focused, to let loose control would only lead to madness.

The hamburger had him thinking about things he would never have so much as considered a day ago, but now, well, things had most definitely changed. At first he dismissed the horrible idea as ridiculous, but as he continued to wrack his mind for what to do, he found he could come up with nothing else.

He reviewed his dilemma once more.

His wife of over three hundred pounds was now dead on his kitchen floor and the police would be coming in a few days as soon the snow storm was over and the roads were clear. He needed to dispose of the body but in a way that no one would ever be able to find it.

Four days, maybe five, if he was lucky and then he would be caught, sent to jail or perhaps death row.

As he stared at the body, he made up his mind–desperate times called for desperate measures and all that.

Casually, he walked around the corpse and went to the kitchen drawer next to the sink. Opening it, he slowly pulled out a large carving knife. It was his favorite knife, one he used on Thanksgiving to carve the turkey. It had a nice weight and feel to it and he kept it perfectly honed.

With his jaw set tight and his eyes cold, he crossed the kitchen and leaned down over Stella. As he slowly began to cut away her dress, he couldn't help but grin and say, "This is gonna hurt you more than it will me, dear."

The first cut was the hardest, but after taking off a large slice of meat from her left thigh, Walter found it became easier with each consecutive piece. It was a lot like carving a deer, he soon found out.

When he had a pile of meat on a dish taken from the cupboard, he went to the stove and fired up a large saucepan after adding some oil. Olive oil, he figured, as vegetable oil was fattening and high in cholesterol.

As the oil began to heat, he took out a meat grinder from under the sink, attached it to the counter, and began to go to work. One piece at a time, he ground up the flesh carved from his wife into what looked like ground pork.

When it was all ground up to the proper consistency, he dropped it into the oil and began to stir.

As he cooked it, the aroma of cooked meat wafted up to him, and despite the heinous situation, he found his stomach grumbling. Deciding in for a penny, in for pound, he took some spices from the cabinet and began seasoning the meat. An onion and some crushed garlic added to the dish until it was a rich, dark brown.

He scraped it into a bowl and then went back for more meat, now casually carving the corpse up like it was a dead carcass.

He quickly learned to cut different sizes, some to look like pork cutlets, some to look like tenderloin. When he got down to the bone, he used a different knife to scrape away the muscle from the bone.

There was a lot of meat and Walter spent the entire day and most of the night just cooking his dead wife into different dishes, picking at each one as he worked. He made chicken fried steak out of the flesh from her arms and took the meat from her ass to make a hearty stew.

There was leftover tomato sauce in the refrigerator from a pasta meal two nights ago and he took that out, fried up some more of her ground flesh, and added it to the sauce, letting it simmer and boil until the aroma wafted through the house.

Taking a spoon, Walter dipped it into the sauce and scooped up a hearty spoonful. Careful not to burn himself, he slid it into his mouth, letting the tanginess of the meat roll on his tongue. He found his wife tasted a lot like pork, but if he cooked the meat just so, the flavor of veal wasn't out of the question.

Taking the fat from under her thighs, he seasoned it and rolled it into a tight ball, then used thread to keep it closed. He dropped this into the tomato gravy and let it cook until it was a golden tan. Why not, he thought. Italians ate pig skin, what was wrong with him eating *Stella skin*?

By the time he was finished, he was exhausted and there was nothing left of Stella but bones. Every organ had been cooked, most used in meat pies after Walter had taken a recipe off the internet. Kidneys, spleen, even her intestines, once cleaned and then stuffed with her ground meat, to make a luscious sausage–he had a ball. He'd always loved to cook and now was his most important meal ever.

By the time he was finished, he took a step back and admired his culinary skills.

On the counter and the kitchen table were piles of cooked meat, dish after dish of every meal imaginable. Sloppy Joe, pasta sauce, chili, what looked like fried beef tips slathered in Worchester sauce, ribs smothered in barbeque sauce—his personal favorite —as well as what looked like breaded pork chops and fillets.

If it could be made with beef, chicken or pork, Walter made it with *Stella meat.*

Once finished, he took the denuded skeleton up to the bathtub and began cleaning it in the tub, letting it soak in bleach.

As the bones were soaking, he went back downstairs. He was starving and he already knew what he was going to start with first.

The storm finally ceased five days later and it took another four days before the police could find the time to visit Walter.

As Walter sat in his living room, eating a bowl of *Stella chili*, three policemen searched his house from top to bottom for his missing wife.

When the officers were done, Officer Calhoun scratched his head as he stared at Walter, who after letting the three cops in, had gone back and sat down.

"All right, Mr. Ryan, where is she?" Officer Calhoun asked.

Walter shrugged as he shoveled another heaping spoonful of chili into his mouth. He had put on over thirty pounds since the day he killed Stella, his all meat diet doing a number on his system.

"I told you, Officer, she left. As soon as she could, she said she couldn't stand me any more and went to see her mother. If she didn't make it there, I don't know what to tell you."

One of the other officers walked into the room, his nose sniffing the air. "Damn, that smells good, what is it?"

Walter never stopped eating as he muttered, "Chili, it was my wife's recipe. She used to say she put a little of herself in every batch."

"Well, it smells damn good, sir," the cop said and then turned to Calhoun and shook his head. "Not here, Mac. And we checked everywhere." He had a picture of Stella in his hand, one taken from her driver's license. In the picture, the bloated face of a woman squinting at the camera and her large shoulders could be seen. He whispered so only Calhoun could hear him. "There's no way that woman's body is in this house, no way. All I found was enough food to feed an army in the freezer downstairs. Man, his wife liked to eat meat."

"Yeah, I saw her picture, too," Calhoun whispered so Walter couldn't hear him. Calhoun nodded and then scratched his head. He had been sure he was going to find something. He turned and walked through the house one more time and paused when he came to a small den/office in the back of the house.

In a corner, covered with a sheet, was a human skeleton minus its head. He turned to see Walter standing behind him, still shoveling chili into his mouth like he would die if he stopped. "Man, you sure like that chili."

Walter nodded. "Yeah, you could say that. I got hooked on this meat I'm using a while back and since then I can't get enough."

"Oh, yeah? What kind?"

"Pork, I guess, why, do you expect me to feed you now, too?"

"No, sir, of course not." Calhoun pointed to the skeleton. "What this?"

Walter shrugged as he slurped a particularly fatty piece of meat into his mouth. "A leftover prop from Halloween, I got lazy and didn't bother putting it into the attic. Lost the head years ago." He sighed and burped at the same time. "Look, Officer, you had your look around, and like I said, she isn't here, now I think it's time you left. And tell my pain-in-the-ass of a mother-in-law to call me when Stella shows up. She must have gotten detoured by a fast food joint or something."

Officer Calhoun glanced at the headless skeleton for a moment and then sighed, knowing whatever he'd hope to find wasn't here. "Very well, Mr. Ryan, but if your wife comes home you need to contact us, as of now she's officially a missing person, one of more than a dozen reported so far since the storm hit."

"I will. Now if you don't mind, I'd like to finish my lunch in peace," Walter said, slurping another spoonful.

Calhoun turned and walked to the front door where the other two cops were waiting. One at a time, they filed out of the house, and Walter, with a semi-polite smile, closed the front door on them.

He did take a moment to go upstairs to the bedroom window and watch as the squad car pulled away, then he went back downstairs, went to the stove and the large kettle full of chili on the front burner, and ladled another heaping serving into his bowl.

Grabbing a beer from the refrigerator, he turned on the television and dropped down into his favorite chair.

As he shoved another spoonful of *Stella Chili* into his mouth, he grinned, red sauce coating his lips like lipstick. Man, he couldn't get enough of this meat, and he wondered what he was going to do when he finally ran out.

Until then, he had already decided he would have the *Stella Beef Tips* for supper, and after that, well, it was a big world out there. He was pretty sure when he finally ran out of *Stella Meat*; he would be able to rustle up some more.

He casually thought of his next door neighbor, Mary.

"Mmmm, *Mary Meat*," he said to himself. "Has a nice ring to it."

YOU ALWAYS EAT THE ONES YOU LOVE

I sit in a pool of blood and gore, small piles of offal in the corners.

I'm in my basement, the gobbets of flesh that surround me are what is left of my family.

They say you always hurt the ones you love and until now I never really knew what that statement meant.

You see, more than three weeks ago the dead began to walk. No one knew how this happened, it just did. Those who refused to believe were the first to go.

I believed and as fast as was humanly able, I began to barricade the house and inventory our food supplies.

But just like in the movies, the amount of dead is truly overwhelming. In less than three days after the first outbreak or whatever it was, there were hundreds, then thousands of walking corpses shambling down my street.

Me and my family—my wife, Emily, my two children, Tommy and Sherry—were all holed up in the living room as the world outside slowly collapsed.

At first we were able to watch the television, the small picture screen at least making us feel like we weren't alone in the world, but soon the power went out and like a house of cards in a hurricane, civilization fell the rest of the way back to barbarism.

And then they came, as I had a feeling they would.

Though we had tried to be as silent as possible in the days the dead rose and filled the streets with their putrefying masses, eventually our hiding place was given away.

It was Tommy who did it, and though I loved him with all my heart, is it wrong to hate him just a little for bringing them down on us?

It was near the end of the first week. Tommy was playing in the corner, quietly of course, and Sherry was reading a book by candlelight. Now Sherry is a year younger than Tommy but she's more mature in so many ways, as little girls are wont to do.

But this day she was feeling childish and for what to be was no apparent reason, but to a sibling seemed perfectly natural, she put down her book and reached out and took the two matchbox cars Tommy had been playing with, a mischievous grin on her face.

Tommy was so upset he screamed at her to give them back and as he uttered that scream, my heart jumped in my throat, praying what would happen wouldn't.

But as I ran to the boarded up living room window and peered through the slats of wood, I knew my wish to God was going unanswered.

It seemed a lot of prayers to God were being ignored since the dead began to walk.

I stared out onto the street and watched as the dead turned enmass and began moving towards my house. I watched as my wife's prize rose bushes were trampled to the ground by stomping feet without feeling.

And then the first pale fist struck the house, a dull thump causing me to jump like a cannon had gone off.

No sooner did one thump begin then it was followed by another, and another until the staccato beat on my home made it resemble a massive drum.

My wife called out and my two children screamed, running into their mothers' arms.

"Just stay calm," I said. "Maybe the barricade will hold, I did a good job of securing the doors and windows," I told them with less confidence than I felt.

I did what I could, but there had only been so much time and I only had so much wood and nails for the entire house. But it should hold.

Still at the front window, I stared through a crack in the wood at a dead face. It was truly horrific and at the same time something absolutely amazing.

Up till now I hadn't actually seen a dead person walking up close. The television had shown them, but as you know, the TV isn't real, even if what they show you is live. No, you need to see it up close, to smell it to believe it's actually real.

And as I stared at the ghoul on the other side of the window, I knew that what had happened to us was real. The face of the zombie was pretty much gone, only a jagged hollow where its features once resided. One eye swung back and forth on residual ganglia and the tongue flopped around the open jaw like a landed fish.

The face reminded me of that poor soul on one of those Ripley series, about the man who had half his face eaten away, but still he managed to survive, though blind and with no nasal cavity.

This ghoul resembled that man but the difference was the one remaining eye that swayed back and forth like a pendulum and actually shifted and looked at me through the cracks in the wood.

It was at that exact moment that the entire house seemed to shudder and windows imploded on the first floor as hundreds of hands shattered the glass like it was made of spun candy.

Only the wood on the front window protected me from being sprayed with dozens of crystal shards but despite this a few still managed to fly through the cracks of wood, their little crystal shards like splinters.

With the glass gone, undead hands and fists now had access to the wood covering the frames and it wasn't long before the weight of bodies managed to worry the wood free of its moorings.

I staggered backward; too shocked in this surreal vision to realize I needed to act fast.

Behind me my wife called out and my children screamed in terror.

"Get to the basement! It's our only chance!" I screamed as I turned and dashed back to my family.

But in my haste I tripped over the ottoman set to the side by the couch and I went head first to the carpet.

"Don't wait for me, go, Emily, save the children!" I screamed as I struggled to get back to my feet. All around me the house was filled with crashing wood, wailing moans and shattering furniture as my house was invaded by dead creatures one only found in nightmares.

Emily did as she was told, and gathered the children and dashed across the house. By then the ghouls were inside and I heard Emily scream when one came for her and the children.

Whether she was lucky or fighting for her babies, Emily swung out a fist and punched the ghoul in the face. Though the blow did almost nothing to stop it, the zombie did pause for a half second, thus giving her time to push the children in front of her and then follow behind. She reached the basement door, a heavy wood structure and a second later was in the cellar, safe for the moment.

But I still needed to follow them and I was finding my predicament had gone from bad to worse.

As I came to my feet I realized there were more than a dozen zombies in my house with more pouring through the open windows with every passing second. Even now there were five or six bodies blocking my access to the basement.

But I knew my family needed me, hell, I needed them more, and I felt my love to be with them give me the courage I needed to carry on in the face of utter depravity.

Reaching out, I picked up a lamp my mother had given me last Christmas, and used it as a club, charging forward with a throaty yell to psych myself up.

The lamp connected with the first zombie's nose and I felt the cartilage crunch as metal met bone. As that body stumbled away I swung the lamp yet again, connecting with a forehead. Brittle skull caved in and a large dent appeared where the lamp had been an instant ago. The lamp had done its job well and as the ghoul stumbled away, pink and gray brain matter seeped from the wound. I swung the lamp without abandon then, barely seeing what I was doing. I was in a panic as I struck blow after blow at once was living breathing people but now were nothing but hollow shells.

Thoughts of morality never came into play. Did these ghouls have souls? Did they think? Was any part of their former personalities still in there with their rotting hearts and minds?

None of this mattered as I fought like a demon to reach my family.

Eventually I made it and with one last blow that caved in a skull like it was putty, I opened the cellar door, lunged in to the waiting darkness within, and slammed the door closed, locking it.

A rotting hand managed to become lodged in the jamb and when I forced the door closed the three digits remaining were cut off to fall to the top stair. They wiggled for a few seconds in the shadows and for some reason I found that even more unsettling than an entire house filled with walking corpses.

My breath came fast and I began to wonder if I was going to hyperventilate. As I stood on the top stair leading to the cellar, the door in front of me began to shake as undead hands pounded on it. But I knew they would not be getting through there, not today, not ever.

My wife called to me and I told her I was fine, to just stay silent. Then I gathered my thoughts, wanting to be strong for my family, and I went down to the basement to join them.

As I went down the stairs, I absently scratched the small wound I now had on the back of my right arm. Even up till this day, I don't know how it happened, but somehow, one of those dead bastards had snuck in and taken a nip out of me while I was fighting to reach the cellar.

If I had known what I was going to do next I probably wouldn't have entered the cellar. If I had known I'd been bit…but come on, who would have ever believed by being bitten or scratched you would become infected and then turn into one of the walking dead? I mean sure, its okay in the movies, but this is real life. No, even if I had known I probably wouldn't have done anything different. I still would have come downstairs and joined my family.

So here it is three weeks later and my family is gone.

Well, maybe not entirely gone, after all they're inside me now, we're together forever.

The infection didn't take long to invade me you see and days after I had been bit I turned. Emily didn't understand what was happening either of course, none of us did but when I opened my eyes and reached for her, taking a bite out of her neck, I believe we both realized what had happened.

She didn't fight me of course, but with her jugular torn out she couldn't.

With my two children huddled in the corner, their eyes wide by the one flickering candle, I devoured their mommy like a turkey buffet.

After I fed on her again and again over the next two days I felt satiated. Days went by and still I wasn't hungry.

Eventually even Tommy and Sherry calmed down. I still was able to talk then and I tried to explain what had happened to me, talking in a rational tone. Though they were frightened out of their wits, they were young and eventually they believed me. In a way they had to. If they didn't, they would have to accept they were trapped in the cellar with me while hundreds of zombies rampaged above their heads.

So as I still munched on their mother, my two children learned not to fear me and for almost a week we still remained a family, minus one of course.

Emily's body kept me fed each time the hunger grew inside me, but eventually I had devoured her to the bone, literally. Her bones, my teeth marks indented on them, were now in a corner of the cellar, as was her bloody clothing she had once worn, though the blood had been sucked out of it like it was a sponge.

And as my children sat in front of me, staring out into nothing, I can feel my hunger growing again.

I ignored it for more than a day but the urge was just too much to fight.

As I had always been partial to Sherry, as she was my little girl, I picked her first. Tommy had screamed when I reached out and grabbed his sister's arm in a vise like grip and he had scurried to the corner of the cellar with tears of fear dripping down his cheeks.

Sherry fought me for barely a minute, her small frame no match for me. What I found most odd was the taste. Where my wife had been rather tough, my daughter was like the freshest young veal, almost as if I could taste her youth.

It was only when my hunger had been satiated yet again that the guilt of what I had done filled me with horror. I cried then, while off in the corner, in the shadows, Tommy cried too.

But though I was saddened and riddled with guilt, I still dove back into my precious daughter's insides and scooped out her small heart, eating the bloody organ like it was the utmost delicacy. Her now cooled blood slid down my chin and I couldn't imagine how I must have looked to my son as I fed on his sister. I imagined the boy knew he would be next once his sister was nothing but a hollow carcass.

But as before when I had been satiated, I calmed down and in time, the innocence of youth, Tommy came to me, and let me wrap my arms around him, rocking him back and forth as I told him things would be all right.

He fell asleep in my arms that night and with the redolence of death all around us, and the steady thrumming of hundreds of feet overhead; we sat in the darkness, father and son.

But on the second day the hunger returned and though I tried to fight it once more, I was a slave to this that was so much more than me and with Tommy sleeping fitfully in my arms, I reached down with my already bloody teeth and tore out his carotid, the tender young flesh seeming to split like parchment. His eyes shot open and he gasped, his small orbs seeming to plead why I would do that to him, but only a bloody froth seeped out of his small mouth and as his eyes dulled, I began feeding. I cried as I ate my only son, but still I fed, like a fat man filled with gluttony to the point of bursting. So now its days later and my son is nothing but scraps of flesh, tidbits of youth now spread across the cellar floor.

And now I am hungry once more, but there's nothing left to eat. The hunger had been growing for two days now and it's so bad I can't stand it.

They say you always *eat* the ones you love, or is it the word *hurt* that should go in the saying somewhere?

Anyway, it doesn't really matter. It seems the longer you're a zombie; the more of your mind slips away. Now that my family is gone I'm finding it hard to remember their names anymore.

So anyway, if you always eat the ones you love, then I guess I might as well get started, because I'm so hungry, and like most people in the world, I love myself most of all.

WAKE THE DEAD

The dead man slept the slumber of oblivion.

Interred in his grave more than twenty years ago, he was lost to the ages, forgotten in the passage of time.

No one visited his grave as he lay rotting in the earth. His tombstone was covered with moss and lichen, the grass so high it nearly hid the crumbling marker.

The entire graveyard was a shambles, a dilapidated junkyard of discarded humans. More than five years ago, the owner of the cemetery had gone under due to financial concerns and once the bank retained ownership, the land quickly fell into disrepair.

One year ago, a small housing development purchased the adjoining acres, and within six months new houses had sprouted up around the graveyard. There had been talk in the back hallways of City Hall of disinterring the bodies of the old cemetery so that even more homes could be built.

The bank wasn't complaining, for they wanted the money the land would provide and this was a world for the living after all, the dead were merely in the way of what many called 'progress.'

As the machinations of the living conducted themselves above ground, below in the cool soil, the dead man slept, cradled in Death's embrace.

His casket had given way to the animals and insects that thrived around him many years before. Worms crawled across his legs, some burrowing into his withered flesh. Rats clawed their way through the soft wood to then feed on bits of skin, nibblets of muscle and tendons.

Maggots were no more, as the flesh was now dry, but beetles still clung to the desiccated skin. The eyes were withered and dry, two dull orbs that for some miraculous reason had never been touched by the vermin seeking sustenance. The tongue also remained, shriveled and small but still lying within two layers of yellow teeth.

As the dead man lay rotting, a vibration began to seep into his casket. Similar to the drums of Africa, the cadence began to infect the cadaver, filling it with energy. Slowly, as the hours passed, the body began to become stronger. Flesh began to mend itself and muscles filled with strength.

The music never stopped, the steady cadence hitting the perfect frequency, as if some voodoo master was aspiring to some unholy ritual.

Slowly, ever so slowly, the zombie's eyes opened, the dry orbs now filled with dead-life. The irises were pure white, and almost seemed to glow in the darkness of his small tomb.

With what seemed like Herculean effort, the zombie raised his hands and began to explore his prison. Fingernails, now long from recessed skin, began to scratch at the moldy wood of the coffin, weakened from years of water damage. As time passed yet again, progress was made. An inch at a time, but slowly, the zombie began to free himself.

Sometimes the savage drums would stop. When that happened, the zombie would fall still, just another corpse in a graveyard of putrid remains, but soon the music would begin anew and the newly wakened zombie would once more begin his quest for freedom.

As the coffin was torn apart, wet soil cascaded into it, covering the zombie's chest, stifling it. But the dead don't need to breathe and once more the zombie would scratch and claw, making the hole wider, then digging a tunnel in the soft earth.

When enough of a hole was created, the ghoul began his upward climb. Halfway there, an infinite time having passed, the music stopped yet again.

With no drums to further the zombie's animation, the corpse stopped in mid-climb, sagging into the casket where it ended up half-in and half-out of his tomb. The dead man didn't know how much time passed, but eventually the drums began again, and it was woken from his oblivion dream to start his journey to the surface once more.

How long it truly took was unknown. Weeks, months, perhaps years, but finally, like an earthworm waking in the early morning before even the bird is up, a withered, pale and cracked hand of dried flesh broke through the surface of the soil and into the air.

The hand slowly flexed and then slapped the hard-packed dirt. As it snaked along the ground, an arm began to appear, then the top of the head.

Blinking dirt from eyes that could barely see, the head popped free of the cold earth and then a shoulder. With both arms now free, the lower torso and legs were easy to pull loose of the sucking dirt that seemed to fight to hold onto its charge.

The dead man lay prone on the ground, staring up at the dark sky. Stars twinkled here and there, tiny jewels in the darkness. It was possible the zombie would have stayed there forever, content to gaze up at the stars, but the drums called him, forcing him to rise, to seek out their origin.

Standing was awkward, his legs unused for more than two decades, his feet bare. When the dead man had been interred, shoes weren't placed on his feet.

And why should they?

He was dead and the viewers at his wake were not able to see his footwear, and what dead man would need to go for a walk in the afterlife? Even socks were spared this dead man, for they were not needed either.

His toes curled back and forth, the soil squeezing between the digits. But it was reflex, for the dead man felt nothing such as pleasure…or pain.

But there was something deep inside him that filled him to the core. Hunger? Anguish? Perhaps even annoyance?

Deep within his fugue-filled mind, the drums beat, calling him ever onward.

His glazed eyes looked around him. The graveyard was silent, the moonlight casting it in a pallid glow. Only he had risen, the others all still slept the never-ending sleep.

A beetle crawled out of the animated corpse's nose and fell to the dirt to scurry off, while nightcrawlers slid from cracks in his skin.

Taking a halting step forward, the zombie began to walk. The first few steps were trepidatious, like a toddler taking those first hesitant steps into a new world of motion, but with each step, the dead man grew more confident.

He began to walk across the graveyard, passing tombstones much older than his own. A few pieces of dried flesh fell off his body to fall in his backtrail, but the zombie paid it no mind.

It took over an hour for the ghoul to reach the perimeter of the cemetery and stop at the gate to peer out at the outside world.

Only one house surrounding the graveyard was lit up, the moon high in the sky, denoting how late it was by human standards of time.

Grabbing the rusty wrought-iron gate, the bars cold within his even colder flesh, the zombie pushed the gate open.

There was no lock for it had disappeared years ago. There was no reason to lock the gate anyway, for many places in the wrought-iron fence surrounding the grounds had missing bars, so an adventurous spirit could easily gain access if they so choose.

This had happened on many occasions, evident by the cigarette butts, fast food wrappers and beer bottles littering the graveyard like fallen leaves. There was no caretaker either, for there was no money to pay for one.

The gates opened on equally rusty hinges, the creaking lost in the night.

The zombie took his first step out of his home and entered the world of living man, leaving the death and despair behind.

Moving faster now, the dead man headed straight for the house with the lights. Shadows could be seen moving past the windows, and as the living corpse grew closer, the drums never ceasing, the sounds of people laughing and talking came to his ears.

Upon crossing the street, headlights lit up the night as the dead man turned to face an oncoming car. The driver leaned on the horn and drove around the figure standing in the road, yelling as he passed the lone zombie.

Passing so fast, the driver never got a good look at the living dead man and was soon gone, brake lights fading into the night.

The dead man continued on his short journey until he reached the front door of the house. He could feel the bass of the drums right through his bare feet and it filled him with anger and rage.

The steady staccato was an abomination to music, and with rage filling his desiccated muscles, he reached out and pushed on the door.

With the strength of the grave, the door was pushed in, torn from its hinges, as if made of paper.

The dead man stood in the doorway, his glazed eyes taking in the party before him and registering that not one of the revelers had noticed him yet. None had seen or heard the door fall in, for all were drunk, high and the music too loud, thus masking the crash of wood connecting with the floor.

Pot smoke hung heavy in the air and one side of the room had a table filled with an assortment of alcohol. On another table, a large glass dish was filled to the brim with narcotics and barbiturates. On a table off to the side, three men and a woman did lines of cocaine on a mirror using a rolled-up hundred dollar bill.

The dead man entered the dwelling and gazed about.

A young white girl with half a shaved head, covered in tattoos, as well as wearing more earrings on one ear than any woman had a right to, walked by the dead man, a drink in her hand, her midriff showing thanks to the shirt she wore cut raggedly with scissors. Her bellybutton ring and the tramp stamp above her ass were in clear view also.

The dead man reached out and grabbed her head between his hands.

With one mighty yank, he tore her head off her shoulders, the rip of flesh and muscle slicing through the cacophony of bass and heavy music.

Holding the head in his hands, the body slumped over to land heavily, the jagged stump spitting blood that slathered the floor in crimson.

A partygoer, not yet knowing mayhem had happened behind him, stepped back and slipped on the blood. He went falling on his ass, the world turning upside down.

Then he looked up and saw the dead man and the severed head in his hands. He screamed.

But only for a moment, for as he opened his mouth and yelled, a skeletal hand thrust itself into the open orifice, grasped his flailing yet pierced tongue, and tore it out. As the man began to choke on his own blood, his eyes went wide, nearly popping out of his head.

All revelry stopped then and each partygoer turned to face the walking dead man. Only the steady bass of the music continued to pound and fill the air with its annoyance.

The dead man hissed angrily, and before anyone could move, he dropped the severed head and reached for another reveler. A black man with a thick cornrow and gold teeth, his arms heavily tattooed, found himself the next victim. Grasping the cornrow in one hand, the zombie pulled as hard as he could, tearing the scalp and half the black man's face off in one mighty heave. A rictus of a smile was the man's new appearance, thanks to half his face being torn off. As he reached up and felt his missing skin, he ran off screaming.

Pandemonium ensued as everyone began screaming and tried to escape. But the zombie stood before the door, and as each one attempted to run by him, he took them down, one at a time.

Eyes were pulled from sockets and abdomens were sliced open with long fingernails that appeared to have grown after death.

Eviscerated bodies with viscera strewn about and limbs torn clean off screaming victims, became the theme of the party as one by one the guests were slaughtered. Limbs were used as bludgeons and intestines as garrotes.

By the time the zombie was through, not one person remained alive. Internal organs covered the floor, making a soggy, splashing sound as it settled.

The aroma of offal, blood and bile filled the air with its heady scent as the zombie stood and surveyed the carnage it had wrought.

A charnel house of corpses was now the decorations for this home, blood an inch deep from wall to wall.

The zombie hissed angrily as it turned to face the stereo lining the far wall. It was a massive machine with speakers towering to the ceiling.

The bass still filled the home and surrounding night with its insistence, and as the zombie went to it, his feet splashed in the still warm gore.

Three times the zombie slipped and fell on the slippery floor, and by the time the dead man reached the stereo, he was crawling on his hands and knees.

Coming to his feet once more, he reached out and grasped the stereo in his blood-covered hands. Picking up the main housing, he raised it over his head and smashed it to the floor, wanting to silence the infernal racket for good. But the dead man wasn't done yet. He tore down the speakers, the wooden shells cracking and breaking as they hit the hardwood floor.

He tore out the speaker wires, tossing them away where they landed to be lost in the gore and blood covering the floor like a carpet.

When the last speaker was smashed, the drumbeat finally ceasing forever, all became silent once more. Without so much as a backward glanced at the carnage, the dead man walked out the front door and back to the graveyard. Bloody footprints followed him for more than halfway before the blood simply ran out and the trail stopped completely.

The dead man even took a moment to close the wrought-iron gate behind him as he entered his home of more than twenty years.

Crossing the cemetery, the moon waxing down on his blood-covered form, he finally reached his final resting place and carefully climbed back into his hole. He slid down inside, and began to cover up the hole with as much dirt as possible, wanting to reclaim what he'd lost.

As the last handful of dirt was dragged across the hole by the skeletal hand, the dead man opened his mouth to speak.

With withered vocal cords and a tongue that was nothing more than a dry muscle, the words were difficult to make out and were more than a hiss than true words. "*Damn rap music, loud enough to wake the dead.*"

If any ever came to visit the grave of this man, they would still be able to make out the inscription on the marker.

JOHN STILLMAN
1954-1991
FATHER
HUSBAND
COUNTRY MUSIC SINGER
HE MAY BE DEAD BUT HIS MUSIC LIVES ON

The hand was withdrawn into the earth. With the hole refilled, the dead man returned to the sleep of oblivion, the silence of the grave restored once more.

ABOUT THE AUTHOR

Anthony Giangregorio is the author of 38 novels, almost all of them about zombies, and has edited over 40 anthologies and books.

His work has appeared in Dead Science by Coscomentertainment, Dead Worlds: Undead Stories Volumes 1-7, and Wolves of War by Library of the Living Dead Press. He also has stories in End of Days: An Apocalyptic Anthology Vol. 1-5, the Book of the Dead series Vol. 1-6 by LDP, Zombie Zoology by Severed Press, and two anthologies with Pill Hill Press. He is also the creator of the popular action/zombie series titled Deadwater and his action/ horror novel Dead Rage is being optioned for a movie.

Check out his website at www.undeadpress.com and on Facebook.

ALSO FROM OPEN CASKET PRESS
BY ANTHONY GIANGREGORIO

RATS

Killer black rats the size of dogs are roaming the streets and no one is aware of their existence.

Wild dogs, the authorities warn. Stay indoors and all will be fine.

Domenic Salvatore soon finds himself in the middle of a cover-up of epic proportions; where no one will believe the truth.

And why would they? After all, he's just a kid.

What no one knows is that the rats have taken on a taste for human meat, a particular kind of meat actually…young flesh…the flesh of children.

As the kids are hunted one by one, killed and dragged off into the night to be devoured, Domenic realizes that it's only a matter of time before he's next.

Something evil stalks the town of Wakefield, Mass…and it's hungry.

ANTHONY GIANGREGORIO

www.ingramcontent.com/pod-product-compliance
Lightning Source LLC
Chambersburg PA
CBHW020259030826
48979CB00026B/1497/J
9781611990393